THE CHRIST-KILLERS

A Fictionalized Historical Analysis of How the Jews Got Blamed for the Crucifixion

by

Russ Weinstein

The Listening Post of Melbourne, Inc.

(est.1983)

Melbourne, Florida U.S.A.

International Standard Book Number 0-9639402-0-1

Library of Congress Catalog Card Number: 93-93728

First Edition, July 1994
Current Edition:
8 7 6 5 4 3 2 1

Printed in the United States of America.
Book Design: Christina Pechstein

Published in North America by The Listening Post of Melbourne, Inc., P.O. Box 361035, Melbourne, Florida 32936-1035

Additional copies may be ordered from the publisher.

DEDICATION

To Rev. Jamie Buckingham,
who encouraged me to seek the truth.

THE CHRIST-KILLERS

FORWARD

It is not often that an academic historian can professionally endorse a work of fiction, even a work of so-called historical fiction. In my own field the list is short — Gore Vidal's Julian, Marguerite Yourcenar's, Memoirs of Hadrian, perhaps Robert Graves' I Claudius. They all have their weaknesses and problems. It seems that the exacting ideal of the historian is inevitably breached by the imagination given such a medium. When it comes to works dealing with early Christianity, examples are few to none. Perhaps, Gerd Theissen's little book, Shadow of the Galilean, stands out, largely because he is a trained historian himself and overlays his work with only the lightest fictional plot. Emotions and personal agendas seem to play too strong a role in this particular area. For most such writers too much is personally at stake.

This narrative, The Christ-Killers, I can endorse even with a degree of academically-tempered enthusiasm. I am impressed with the ease of style and grace with which Weinstein has been able to weave fairly hard core historical materials into his work. The notes alone are worth the price of the book. Every area that is touched upon has been meticulously documented from the ancient sources or from the work of academic historians. The results are impressive. The reader has the pleasure of dipping deeply into the story, while all the time having the sources cited to run down this or that point of interest.

Dr. Weinstein's essential interpretation of the rise of early Christianity is a provocative one. It will surely stir controversy. But it is not an irresponsible one. He has actually resurrected in living fictional color the perspective of the early Jewish followers of Jesus of Nazareth. Their voice and cause have long been muted by the New Testament in final edited form and the development of Catholic Christian orthodoxy. Yet their names are familiar to us all: James the brother of Jesus; Cephas, better known as Peter; Barnabas, the companion of Paul. The book centers on the central question we historians in this field constantly face: how did an obscure Jewish apocalyptic movement in Roman Palestine become transformed into the triumphant world religion of

Christianity? And further, what accounts for the hostility Christianity eventually exhibited toward the Jewish people? Weinstein, like all of us who work in this field, does nothing less than tinker with the foundations of our western Christian European civilization.

We historians constantly look to the past to understand the present and think for the future. It is rare that our insights can be so readily shared with the public. Both Jews and Christians will find this book thoroughly fascinating at every turn. I heartily recommend it on every level. This is truly a book for our ecumenical times, a book for the turn of the millennium.

James D. Tabor
Associate Professor of Ancient Judaism and Early Christianity
University of North Carolina at Charlotte
May, 1992

PREFACE

When S.G.F. Brandon's book, Jesus and the Zealots, first appeared, Time Magazine reviewed it. Brandon was Professor of Comparative Religion at the University of Manchester and was considered one of the leading historical scholars of the early Christian period. The theme of his book was that the early writers of the New Testament seriously misrepresented the relationship of the Jewish people to Jesus. This was a bold assertion, considering the venerable immunity accorded these ancient texts by so many people. The reviewer expressed regret that historical information such as this seldom finds its way into the pulpits of Christian churches. It seemed to me at the time that the reason for this was that the promulgation of such information would be an admission that some parts of the New Testament were unreliable, which might then open the door for other parts to be so analyzed. Yet a critical analysis of the early Christian movement, misrepresentations about Jews notwithstanding, need not be construed as a threat to the entire Christian belief.

The need for truth about these ancient events is not merely an academic indulgence. Belief in these reports has influenced people's conduct for thousands of years, and the claims are popularized and revitalized annually through passion plays at Oberammergau, Germany, and Lake Wales, Florida. No such popularization of Brandon's work exists. From the Christian viewpoint, we must ask if it should. Lloyd Gaston, in his essay, Paul and the Torah, implies that it should when he asks whether a Christian Church with an anti-Semitic New Testament ought to survive.

Why is it that the correction of historical misinformation in the New Testament should imply the invalidity of that entire body of work? Christian belief can still stand strong and may well be rendered stronger by its ability to correct an ancient wrong. Indeed, this work, while it presents conflicting religious viewpoints that existed in the First Century A.D. or C.E., does not refute any of the presently held central Christian

v

beliefs about Jesus of Nazareth: messiahship, resurrection, saviorship and divinity. It does, however, present cogent reasons for accepting a different view of the relationship between the Jewish people and Jesus than that presently held by most Christians. It is my sincere belief, based on historical information, that Vatican II was remiss in its total responsibility when it exonerated only present-day Jews from culpability for Jesus' death, even that not having been achieved without strong protests against it. The Jews of Jesus' time deserve that same recognition so that this ancient injustice can be corrected.

This work attempts to bring, in the form of a fictionalized narrative, a history of the people and events involved in First Century Mediterranean politics and religion. These events are documented in the Gospels, the Book of Acts, Josephus' Jewish War, Josephus' Antiquities of the Jews, as well as in the writings of the Ebionites and other ancient accounts. In this story, the reporting and interpretation of these events are, conjecturally, those of Barnabas, who accompanied Paul of Tarsus in his missionary work and later separated from him. Barnabas sees and describes events through the eyes of an early Nazarene. He knows the old and the new and must respond to them both. Where the report of an ancient writer is inconsistent with other events of the time, Barnabas reports it as I believe an early Nazarene would have but mentions the conflicting report sooner or later in the story. Conversations are taken either from historical accounts or, if fictionalized, are kept in harmony with reported events.

For those concerned with the historical bases for the claims made in this story, the notes at the back will be important. These contain not only references but also challenges to traditional interpretations. A look at these after reading each chapter, especially where discussions exist, will help establish the authenticity of the claims. But, also, they may be read independently, like a continuous story in themselves, since every event and point in the text is contained in them.

Just as important as the chronology of the events is the chronology of their writing. Paul wrote his letters between 50 and 60 A.D. or C.E.; the Jewish revolt against Rome ended in 70 and 73 A.D. or C.E.; the Gospels and the Book of Acts were written by Pauline-oriented followers of Jesus (not by the Apostles) about 75 to 95 A.D. or C.E. Hence, while the events described in the Gospels preceded Paul's letters, the writing of them came years after those letters were written. The writers of the Gospels were concerned not only to avoid any contradiction with Paul but, moreover, to give support to his views. If an earlier tradition did contradict him, it was either suppressed or minimized into insignificance.

Truth, like the elusive pimpernel, is hard to find. Sincerity in the pursuit of it should never defer to obligatory loyalties or inviolate beliefs. Barnabas struggles, as we all do, to find a meaning to life and a pathway to God. Freedom to look, to examine, to consider, is our one inherent right. That much, at least, we should allow ourselves.

Russ Weinstein 1991

THE CHRIST-KILLERS

If a man believes things only because his pastor says so,
or the assembly so determines, without having other reason,
though his belief be true, yet the very truth he holds
becomes his heresy.

Milton

THE CHRIST-KILLERS

CHAPTER I

Saul of Tarsus, at the end of his first three months in Jerusalem, received a message to come to the house of his teacher, the Pharisee sage, Gamaliel. He hurried through the streets excitedly, hoping the news would be good. Three months was the usual trial period for all Gamaliel's new students, and, at the end of that time, they were always told whether or not they could continue to study with the master. Saul felt confident that he would be accepted. After all, he had been studying the Torah for years.

On a narrow, uneven dirt street along his usual route, a crowd blocked his path. He knew that he could choose an alternate way, but curiosity made him determined to see what was going on. The people's backs were turned to him. They were looking at something farther down the street. He squeezed his way through the compacted melange of men and women and craned his neck to see. A barefoot man was lurching, staggering, under a heavy wooden cross, carrying it, dragging it, as he moved along. Its bottom plowed a direful furrow, like an epitaph in the ground. The back of the man's white robe was stained with blood. Saul thought: the Romans are at it again. Four leather-sandeled Roman guards, each wearing a sleeveless coat of iron mail over a knee-length brown woolen tunic, two of them with drawn swords and two with uncoiled whips, prodded the man along and reviled him as they did. "You stinking Jew! Your mother was a whore! Your father was a pig!" rose in mingled cacophonies as the soldiers spewed their curses. Like a pilotless boat, Saul felt himself being pushed along with the crowd, at a close but safe distance from the guards. Occasionally, a guard swung his whip sadistically across the legs and side of the man. The man himself, black-bearded and swarthy-skinned, sweated under a baking sun. A lithe, barefooted girl in a knee-length dress rushed out of a house with a bowl and gave the man water to drink. A guard with a sword rushed at the girl, raising his weapon to strike. But the girl was too swift; she darted away, and the guard did not give her chase. The people cheered the girl and even laughed at the guards.

"Who's the man?" Saul asked a heavy, perspiring woman, who was pushed against him by the crowd.

1

"Some Nazarene fellow," the woman replied. "He was preaching against the Romans. They're going to crucify him."

Then, as if the incident with the girl had been a mere prelude to the next event, a group of men — maybe fifteen in all — rushed at the guards from doorways on both sides of the street. The guards raised their swords to kill their attackers, but they were completely overwhelmed.

A shout of approval rose from the crowd.

"It's Stephen!" the trickling woman said.

"Give it to them, Stephen! Give it to them!" a man shouted from the crowd.

The attacking Jews pinioned the Romans' arms and confiscated their swords, as parents take weapons from children. They pushed the Romans onto the ground and held them there. Two of the attackers relieved the victim of his cross and whisked him away from the scene. Then the others, as quickly as they had appeared, disappeared into the doorways and side alleys of the street and left the Romans weaponless and shamefaced on the ground.

The crowd laughed and jeered at the soldiers, who picked themselves up and wiped the dust from their faces and clothes. They were wise enough not to answer the crowd. Without weapons they had no defense, and the Jews outnumbered them considerably.

When the crowd dispersed and the Romans were gone, Saul continued on his way through the narrow back streets of the city. The squeals of running children merged with the hoarse cries of their parents for their return, and the stench of discarded offal deposited by unsavory persons the night before competed with the fragrance of roses and lilies displayed at the upstairs windows of some of the houses. This was Jerusalem, teeming with life, whose sounds, sights and smells rose like a perfumed miasma from the floor of the city below it. But Saul was half oblivious to this, for he was busy reflecting on the meaning of the incident he had just seen. He had heard of Stephen, a Nazarene leader, very militant and prone to fight; a follower of Jesus, that dead Messiah who had briefly come back to life and whose followers were claiming that he would soon return to establish the kingdom of God. It was interesting to him that the Nazarenes had not killed the Romans as the Zealots would have done but had simply disarmed them in order to get their condemned compatriot away. It seemed to Saul that the Nazarenes had shown a degree of restraint in this affair.

Saul arrived at Gamaliel's house. He was taken inside by Jephthah, one of Gamaliel's disciples. He waited on a bench in the sparsely furnished vestibule while Jephthah went to tell Gamaliel he was there. Though Saul felt confident, he was nervous. This interview was important to him. He had come to Jerusalem to study with Gamaliel, the leader of the Pharisees. All his life, for as long as he could remember, he had wanted to become a Pharisee sage, and Gamaliel could ease that path for him as no one else in the world could do. But he kept secret the fact that he was not a Jew — though he intended to become one soon. For all his yearning to become a religious philosopher, a leader and teacher of men, for all his attraction to the Jewish religion, he had not taken that final step that would have made him irrevocably a Jew. He had not gotten circumcised. He had taken Jewish vows, recited Jewish prayers and eaten Jewish food, but he had not submitted himself to the one commandment that would have made him a part of Israel. Only his sister, with whom he lived, knew about that. To the rest of the world, he was a Jew.

His parents had died in Tarsus. They had been God-fearers like himself. They had come to believe in the one true god and had allied themselves with the Jews in that city. Like God-fearers everywhere, they had gone regularly to the Jewish synagogues and had prayed alongside the Jews. They had entered into religious discussions with them and had learned from the Pharisee sages. Like God-fearers everywhere, they had contributed money to the Temple in Jerusalem. And they had followed the minimum essental laws of morality that God had given to Noah.

And here was Saul of Tarsus, a God-fearer who was almost a Jew, studying the books of Mosaic law as if he already was one. And studying them not just from some ordinary sage but from the leader of the Pharisees himself. This was an honor he had never expected. He considered it a gift from God.

Jephthah returned and entered the room with a doleful look on his face. He walked sluggishly towards Saul.

"The master will see you now," he said, and he dropped his eyes.

Saul knew from the look on Jephthah's face that something definitely was wrong. Ordinarily, Jephthah was a cheerful fellow, a young man who laughed at every opportunity. Now, for some reason, he was despondent, and Saul could only attribute it to himself.

"Thank you, Jephthah," he replied, and he walked into Gamaliel's study.

The leader of the Pharisees sat in a spare wooden chair with his elbows on his writing table. His black beard was tinctured with incult threads of white, like a seamstresses clippings. His grandfather had been the great sage, Hillel, whose words were quoted with the same reverence as the words of Moses. And Gamaliel himself had been groomed from childhood to follow in his grandfather's footsteps. For any serious student of the Torah (the books of Mosaic law), to study with Gamaliel was considered an honor and an achievement in itself. Gamaliel indicated a chair for Saul, and Saul sat down.

"It's been three months since you came to us from Tarsus," Gamaliel said.

"Yes," Saul acknowledged, "it's been three months."

"When you came to me, I was led to understand that you had studied with the sage, Macaiah, in one of the synagogues in Tarsus and that you were ready to progress beyond that."

"That is so," Saul confirmed. "I did study with him, and then I was ready to study with you."

"Did he tell you that you were ready?"

"He didn't have to," Saul said. "I knew that I was."

Gamaliel tapped his finger lightly on the writing table, his eyes looking down while he thought. Then he looked at Saul.

"You know, Saul, a man like myself has many people who want to study with him." Saul nodded. "Because of that, I must choose only the most advanced." Saul nodded again. "I cannot take children, and I cannot take beginners, and I cannot take those who might progress with other teachers before they come to me." Saul felt the impendency of a fall. "During the time we have spent together, I have found you willing and eager, both admirable traits in a man. But I also have found you unknowlegeable in many of the basic concepts on which greater knowledge must stand. With regret I must tell you that you are not yet ready for me. You need to study with someone else for a while and then come back to me when *he* thinks you are ready."

Saul felt his stomach sink. It was as if the sun had plunged into the sea. He was crushed, mortified — even ashamed.

"I understand," he said, maintaining his composure. He did not know what else to say. He at least wanted to make his departure in a dignified way. All that work, all that work! And to have it come to this: that the foremost teacher in the world was telling him that it was all for nothing.

He resented that. An anger began to stir within him. He knotted his fist and inwardly railed against the injustice that was being done to him. If there were things he really didn't know, they were surely things he could learn. If there were things he didn't understand, then surely Gamaliel could make him understand them. This total rejection, this turning him out, was not what should be done. Gamaliel should at least give him a little more time. He could learn what he had to learn. What

4

was being done to him now was an act of utter cruelty. Only a person who was insensitive could be doing such a thing.

"You worked in leather before you came to us. Do I remember that correctly?" Gamaliel asked.

"Yes," Saul said, "that was my trade. I learned that trade in Tarsus."

"Couldn't you do that work again? There's a market for that sort of skill."

"My ambition was to leave it and become a sage," Saul said. "To do that work again would be going backwards."

"But you still could study while you do that work," Gamaliel said. "Many of my students work at something else. Even the sages themselves do not earn their livelihoods by charging for their their teaching. Most of them do some other work and then teach without getting paid for it. I myself do a little work in writing and copying books. It's part of our tradition to work at other things and then to teach without getting paid."

But it was not really the line of work that bothered Saul; it was the fact that he was being denied the chance to study with the best teacher in the world. His goal, his lofty ambition in life, was being destroyed. What a credential he would have if he could tell people he had studied with Gamaliel! What a set-back he was being given by the inconsiderateness of the man! Gamaliel, who preached compassion and brotherly love to his students, was privately shattering him. He swore that he would not forget this hurt. He would not forget this insult from a powerful man.

"I will do as you say," Saul said, quite calmly, hiding his inner pain.

"Good," Gamaliel said, smiling with satisfaction. "Take your time. You'll find yourself progressing with time. Then, when you've advanced enough and your teacher thinks you're ready, feel free to come back to me."

Saul left him. He wandered aimlessly through the convoluted streets. The sultry air was oppressive and thick, and breathing seemed arduous, as if the atmosphere were a paste, difficult to inhale. Gone were the laughter of children and the clatter of merchants selling their wares; gone was the chatter of women busily doing their wash; he no longer saw the lecturing pedagogues walking the streets with their disciples. All the sights and sounds and smells that ordinarily assailed the senses of the pedestrian were unable to penetrate him. He walked like one who was dead. Even a squad of grimfaced Romans, marching menacingly toward some ominous mission, failed to elicit the normal response of a citizen stepping aside, and he vaguely felt himself being pushed out of the way, as if he were feeble-minded and incapable of reason.

It was nightfall by the time he realized that he had been drifting through unfamiliar streets and that he was hungry and thirsty from walking. He saw a hooded woman standing outside her house, and he asked her for a drink of water. She went in and returned with a cupful.

"God be with you," she said, as she handed it to him.

"And with you, good woman," Saul answered.

There was this law, you see, this Mosaic law, that when a stranger comes among you, you must treat him as one of your own. That was why the woman responded as she did.

"Have you heard about Stephen?" the woman asked, not attempting to conceal her excitement.

Saul remembered that that was the name of the militant Nazarene who had led the attack on the Romans that morning.

"The one who attacked the Romans?" he asked.

"Yes," she said. "Then you've heard."

Paul drank the water slowly, savoring its convalescent effect. He handed her the cup and thanked her for the drink.

"Wait till Jesus returns," she said. "Then we'll be free again."

Saul listened to the woman and looked at her. She was radiant with what she believed. He realized then that he had not been affected by the passion of the time — the desire to drive out the Romans — but this woman's desire for that very thing gave his mind a needed diversion until he could get back home. He thought about the woman's excitement, this latest mania, this popular madness for freedom from Rome, but he found himself unconcerned about it and preoccupied with his personal loss.

He made his way to his sister's house and poured out his disappointment to her. He poured out his resentment, too, over what Gamaliel had done.

"People who rise too high," he said to his sister, "deserve to be brought down. They forget what it feels like not to have power and influence."

But the power and influence that Gamaliel had was far less than what Saul attributed to him — especially in this time of the Romans. Who among us had any power with the Romans ruling Judaea as they did? Was it the Pharisees or Sadducees or Essenes, all of whom were subjects of Rome? Was it the mass of our weaponless people who could fight only with words or bare hands? I will answer that for you. I will tell you how our people were divided at that time and where the small

6

amount of Jewish power that did exist lay. The real power, wherever it existed, did not exist with Gamaliel.

The Pharisees and Sadducees were the two most influential groups in our religion. There were the Essenes, too, who strove for spiritual perfection but who, because of their clannishness and the strict demands of their customs, did not have so many people joining them. This is not to say that they were not respected, however. They were always looked up to for their religious purity. And though many of them lived in the cities, many others lived in the desert, away from the population centers. One of these desert communities was near the Dead Sea, and I will have more to say of this later.

As for this power that Saul was referring to — whether it was political or religious, whichever he meant — the Essenes had none of the former and, officially, none of the latter. But they did exert their influence in religious affairs by making it known that purity such as theirs existed and by setting a standard for others to follow.

For influence on a practical and daily basis, the Pharisees and Sadducees were the most common. They differed, however, on both politics and religion and, therefore, did not like each other very much. The Sadducees consisted of the chief priests and wealthy landowners. Through successive occupations by conquerors, the chief priests had ruled. Ptolemaic Greeks of Egypt, Seleucid Greeks of Syria — it was all the same to them. They worked with the conquerors, made it easier for them to dominate and were rewarded for their work. They lived well. Even when the Jewish kings, the Hasmoneans, took over, the chief priests thrived, for even the Hasmoneans gave them power. And when the Romans arrived, they did the same.

From among the chief priests, the Romans selected one to command. He would be the high priest, and he would have the authority to execute people for religious transgressions. *There* was the power to control people's lives! *There* was the power of life and death. Gamaliel did not have that.

But even that authority of the high priest was tempered by controls, one of which was the Sanhedrin. This was the council of seventy-one elders who ruled on religious affairs. It consisted of Pharisees and Sadducees alike. When the crime was great enough, they could vote for death by stoning. But they could also thwart the high priest's desire to execute someone if they found that person innocent. The majority of the members of the Sanhedrin were Pharisees, and they were more lenient than the Sadducees in the punishments they imposed. They frequently acted to thwart the Sadducees, who tended to be more severe. Because of that restraint, the high priest sometimes called only *some* of the members to sit in judgement and, in that way, stacked the votes in his favor. The other restraint was the Romans. No Jewish execution could take place without the approval of the governor, and, in fact, the Sanhedrin could not even be convened without his approval. Then, too, the Romans could appoint and depose high priests as they wished, and frequently they did just that. In former years, a Pharisee might preside over the Sanhedrin — Gamaliel's grandfather, Hillel, had done it for forty years — but later it was always the high priest.

So the power that Saul was attributing to Gamaliel was not at all political. In religion, whatever power he did possess was due to his ability to sway people and influence them by speaking. He had no power to force people to do his bidding. He was not a king or an emperor, nor was he a high priest who could command the Temple police. With Saul, of course, Gamaliel did have the power to refuse to teach, which was what he was doing now. But that kind of power was as much Saul's as Gamaliel's, for a student could refuse to learn.

So Saul, resentfully bearing his disappointment, gathered his tools from storage. He had thought he was finished with them and would never need them again. He took his measuring rod, his knives and his cache of leather and put them into a bag. He got the wooden poles and coverings that he had used in the past for a stall to sell his wares and took them without enthusiasm to the bazaar. From leather worker to scholar to leather worker. The cycle was now complete. He had not taken a step upward on the ladder of success but a step around a circle that led him to where he had begun. So much for being a Pharisee sage! So much for being a Pharisee!

CHAPTER II

This was a time of turmoil, a time when people felt helpless to change things, so that in their desperation, they looked to God. And what they wanted from God was to be saved, rescued, from the hopeless condition of their lives. I was one of them. I am a Jew.

We were a godly people ruled by an ungodly conqueror. So it was not just a matter of political power that concerned us but one of religious sacrilege too. And when we looked to God to save us, we looked for it through a Messiah, an anointed one, a great and fearless leader who would drive out the Romans and establish God's kingdom in our land. This had been promised by our prophets. Philo of Alexandria recorded an apt description of him. He said, "For there shall come forth a man, leading his host to war, he will subdue great and populous nations... dauntless courage of soul and all-powerful strength of body, either of which strikes fear into the heart of the enemy." That was the Messiah for whom we hoped, the man for which we prayed.

Such a one we thought was Ezekias, who arose in Galilee and called our people to arms. But Herod, King Antipater's son, captured him and executed him, and the nation silently mourned. Yet we did not lose our faith, for we knew that God would save us. We had a prophecy — the prophecy of Shiloh in the book of Moses — and it told us that from Judah would arise a world leader. We would wait, and he would come.

Some forty years later, the son of Ezekias, the physician and scholar named Judas of Galilee, came forth and called us to arms, and everyone thought that *he* was the one, the chosen Messiah of God. Coponius was procurator then and Quirinius was legate of Syria. And the man whom Quirinius appointed high priest was Ananus, the son of Seth, whom we usually called just by the name, Annas. Herod, the man who had killed Ezekias and earned his people's hatred for it, succeeded his father to the throne and then passed away himself. His son, Herod Antipas, now became king to rule as his father had done. But the Romans had other ideas. They took from this young king his dominion over that part of our nation called Judaea and placed it under their own direct control, with the procurator as governor and the legate of Syria above him. Judaeans would now know a harsher and more repressive existence than their northern brothers, the Galileans.

9

Judas of Galilee protested that, but that was not all he protested. The question of tribute was before us, the paying of money to a conqueror. Judas said that to pay such men for not killing us or for not imprisoning us was to accept them as our masters and that that was disloyal to God. It was a sin to pay tribute, he said.

And then there was the question of the census. Judas claimed that that was a virtual insult to God. With the census the Romans would know where each and every Jew lived and be able to exact their taxes more easily. That also was to be resisted. To do otherwise was to act like a coward.

These were the things that Judas of Galilee said when he rose up and called us to arms, when he called upon Jews to attack where they could and establish God's kingdom in Israel again. But Judas was not just a man of words; he was a man of action too. First, he took over Herod's palace at Sepphoris and declared himself king of all the Jews. Then he joined forces with Zaddok, the Pharisee, and declared that God's kingdom was at hand. Together they marched with their army to the walls of Jerusalem and were on the verge of taking the city from the Romans when two legions sent by Varus, the new legate of Syria, along with cavalry and infantry, sent by Aretus, king of Nabataea, and others, came down to stop them and overwhelmed them by sheer force of numbers. Judas and two-thousand of his men were crucified, their bodies nailed to wooden crosses, left hanging to writhe and thirst and starve and suffocate, for all would-be rebels to see and for the children of God to mourn.

So he too was not the one, not the Messiah who would lead us to freedom, not the redeemer who would save our honor, not the king who would rule under God. But something of Judas lived on. He was a martyr, a hero, an inspiration to our people. And from his effort, from the spirit of his endeavor, came the group that were called the Zealots, the soldiers of God, the torchbearers of Judas and Zaddok. They rebelled where they could, harassed as opportunity allowed and resisted when resistance seemed futile. They taught their children and their children's children to accept only God as their master and to work for the day when they could drive out the Romans. No torture, no threat of death, could sway them. That was the way of the Zealots.

The Pharisees and Sadducees, as I have mentioned before, differed on both politics and religion. The Pharisees had started as a rebellion movement against foreign rule after the oppression of Antiochus Epiphanes. When they did that, they opposed the agents of that rule — the chief priests — and they had to be suppressed into compliance. But through successive generations of co-existence with the Sadducees, they carried their desire for freedom.

On religious matters, as I have said, they differed as well. The Pharisees believed in the resurrection of the dead, as did most of our people. The Sadducees did not. The Sadducees said that they obeyed our religious laws correctly while the Pharisees did not, that the Pharisees deviated from our religious laws, bending them to the circumstances, instead of adhering strictly to them. They said that the Pharisees could not even agree among themselves about it and that they thought such disagreements were actually desirable. That much was true. The Pharisees did discuss religious laws and attempt to interpret and apply them in ways that seemed appropriate for our time. They even created an oral law out of their discussions, so that to them the written law was not immutable. The Sadducees, on the other hand, claimed to obey the written law quite literally and did not bend it to suit a particular situation. For example, since the Bible says that one must rest on the Sabbath, the Sadducees would not treat a sick person on that day. The Pharisees, on the other hand, said that you *could* treat someone on that day, especially if a human life was at stake. And since the Bible says, "An eye for an eye," the Sadducees took that literally, but the Pharisees said that while the injured person must be compensated for his doctor bills and loss of income, he must not take out the eye of the other person. That was the oral law, and the Sadducees rejected it; to them the written law was all that counted.

The leaders of the Pharisees were called sages. They came from every level of society, including the poor. That irked the Sadducees, because *their* leaders, were the chief priests, who were descended, they said, from the brother of Moses, Aaron, to whom the priesthood had been given. The Pharisee leaders had no such purported pedigrees; they attained their positions strictly through their knowledge of the Torah, our book of Jewish law. They led the prayers and discussions in the synagogues, the communal meeting places where people prayed when they were not performing some obligatory function in the Temple. And, unlike the chief priests and the lower priests, the sages were not paid for their work. They earned their livelihoods elsewhere. The Pharisees revered them as men of the highest learning. In contrast, the Pharisees did not consider the high priest a scholar but only an administrator of the Temple. They considered him ignorant in matters of religion. "A learned bastard," they would say, "is better than an ignorant high priest."

Even the lower priests, who earned their livelihoods from the moneys in the Temple, recognized the sages as their spiritual mentors. And that also irked the chief priests: that their own subordinates were disloyal to them.

After Coponius as procurator came Ambivius and then Rufus. And during each of their reigns, Annas retained his post as high priest. I can say without question that he was the most influential Jew in Jerusalem at that time. He was wealthy, he was haughty, even arrogant. And he was also blessed with children. He was a patriarch in the old biblical way, and he wielded his power like a king. When his daughter married the son of another chief priest, shortly before Tiberius became emperor, the party he threw was lavish, worthy of a Roman patrician, with music and dancing and food and wine. As I have said, the chief priests lived well. Of the three sons of Herod the Great, who ruled different parts of our land, the two who were still in power (Philip and Herod Antipas) sent gifts to the bridal couple. The bridegroom's name was Caiaphas, and the name of the bride was Naomi. The first child born of their union was a girl, whose name was Rabath.

But Naomi was not the only child who came from the seed of Annas: he had sons to carry on the family work — the business of being high priest. So when the emperor, Tiberius, took Rufus away and sent Valerius Gratus to be procurator, and when Gratus decided that Annas was either too old or too influential to be allowed to stay in office, he appointed, successively, one year apart, Ishmael and Eleazar, both sons of Annas, and then Simon, the son of Camithus, to be high priests. But all of them were swayed by the old man's will. So then Gratus appointed a man whom he thought might be more independent of the wily old patriarch. This new appointee was Caiaphas, who had married Annas' daughter. But Caiaphas, seeing the nature of things, knew how to play his part well. While he kept his unruly countrymen in line and superficially did what Gratus said, he still, behind the scenes as it were, got Annas to approve of every move.

When Pontius Pilate became procurator, some eight years after that, he established himself in Caesarea. But soon, under the emperor's orders, he moved his army to Jerusalem for the purpose of establishing winter quarters there. There was another purpose behind it though: he wanted to flout Jewish law by displaying in the city the busts of the emperor attached to the military standards of his soldiers. He knew that Jewish law forbade the presence of sculpted images. Cleverly, Pilate did this thing at night while the populace was asleep and then left before dawn for Caesarea. In the morning, when our people discovered what had been done, a large delegation went to Caesarea to petition Pilate to remove the standards. He refused at first, saying that that would be an insult to the emperor. But the delegation persisted for a full six days, and maybe because he was new to the office and did not know how far to wield his power as an effective administrator, he finally granted the request. After that, however, as if he wanted to compensate for what he later felt was a weakness he had shown in this matter, he became a virtual tyrant. He began to insult us at every opportunity, he stole property whenever he wished and, finally, he began to kill completely innocent people for what sometimes seemed nothing more than his desire to test the limitlessness of his power over us.

One day, on his own volition, not that of the emperor, he set up some gilded shields in Herod's former palace in Jerusalem. These shields referred to the emperor as divine, and that, of course, was against our religious law. To us, to call any man divine was an insult to God. To pagans, of course, it was not. As before, we sent a delegation, this one led by four of Herod Antipas' sons. We emphasized that our objections were only on religious grounds, not political, and we reminded him that other kings and emperors had respected our feelings on this subject. But Pilate, unlike his former accommodating self, which, as I have said, may now have seemed like weakness to him, remained obstinate in this affair. The shields, he said, would have to stay. We told him he was forcing us into a conflict between loyalty to our religion on the one hand and loyalty to the emperor on the other. We asked for proof that the emperor had ordered this and said that if he didn't produce it, we would appeal to our master, the emperor, himself. Yet, in spite of the fact that an imperial investigation might reveal even more wrongdoing than just this matter of the shields, he refused. So we did what we had threatened and wrote to the emperor, Tiberius. Our king, Herod Antipas, joined us in that, and Pilate never forgave him for it. The emperor then sided with us and rebuked Pilate and made him move the shields to the Temple of Augustus in Caesarea. Pilate obeyed, but he resented us for having embarrassed him in front of the emperor, and his animosity towards us grew even worse after that.

Tiberius' decision to side with us in this foolish affair of the shields was, I think, prompted more by a desire to avoid civil unrest than because he particularly liked us. I say this because, some years earlier, when Jews in Rome were found to be converting many of the people to Judaism, Tiberius had all the Jews expelled from that city. The approbation of Judaism had been pervasive in Rome and especially in the Roman Senate. Then Fulvia, the wife of a leading Roman senator, had made the conversion, and that had been the final affront. Our religion was popular among many of the pagans, and the pagan establishment did not like that. Tiberius' anti-Jewish advisor, Sejanus, was particularly hostile to us. So, under his prodding, we Jews were banned from Rome, and this lasted for twelve years until Sejanus was removed from office.

Pilate's insensitivity — perhaps I should say hostility — towards our religion showed itself when he wanted funds for an aqueduct he wanted to build in Jerusalem. He found the funds by raiding the Temple treasury, taking the money intended for God. That money, you see, was contributed by Jews and God-fearers throughout the world and was used for the needs of the Temple: the daily offerings; the shew-bread display; the incense preparation; the high priest's garments; the red heifer; the scapegoat; the wages of the chief and lower priests; the wages of the women who wove the Temple curtains and the men who corrected the holy books. And after all these expenses were paid, there were still large sums that remained. And that was the money that Pilate would use in order to build his aqueduct. The taxes we paid to the Romans, of course, would never be used for that.

A great multitude went to Pilate to protest this outrage. When he came back to Jerusalem, a virtual mob of people cursed him in the streets. Yet he remained cool, seemingly unmoved by the violent emotional outbursts of the populace. But not so unmoved, we later learned, as not to do something to get back at the people who had reviled him. The crowd of protesters gathered each day, and one day Pilate had his soldiers disguise themselves as Jews and mingle with the crowd but with clubs and knives hidden beneath their robes. At a pre-arranged signal, the soldiers attacked the protesters and killed them or wounded them, and Pilate had his revenge. And also the protests ended. But also the aqueduct did not get built just then and had to wait for the future to be continued.

When Jesus came onto the scene, Pilate was the same tyrant he had been all along. He looked upon Jesus as another troublemaker to be dealt with like all the others.

Jesus came out of Galilee preaching Pharisaic philosophy, calling on people to repent their sins and proclaiming that the Kingdom of God was at hand. His cousin, John the Baptizer, a holy prophet who had been sent by God, had predicted that a great spiritual leader would come to lead us. When Jesus came to him at the Jordan River and asked to be baptized, which is the symbolic washing away of sin by immersing the body in water, John identified Jesus as the one he had been referring to and called him master. But there were followers of John — they exist to this day — who believed that John had made a mistake in thinking that Jesus was the Messiah (or that he never really recognized him as such) and that John himself was the true Messiah and Jesus a false one. But they, of course, were wrong. Their own leader knew who the true Messiah was: It was Jesus of Nazareth, the anointed of God. Although Jesus himself never baptized anyone, his disciples began to baptize after that, and they did it in the manner of John.

Shortly after that, John was executed by Herod Antipas because he was publicly denouncing Antipas' marriage to Herodias. She was the wife of Antipas' half-brother, Philip, and she also was related to Antipas himself. In marrying her, Antipas had cast away his own wife, the daughter of our neighbor, the Arabian king, Aretus of Petra. This scorned lady went back to her father in tears, and Aretus, outraged over this insult to his daughter, prepared for war. Antipas was not going to buckle under Aretus' threat; he prepared as well. Antipas set up his battle headquarters at the fortress of Machaerus in Perea, east of the Dead Sea. He prepared for battle and sought more soldiers from among his people. And just as he started to do that, John began to denounce him publicly. This was the last thing that Antipas needed: someone turning his people against him when he needed them to fight for him. And if his people did not help him, worse still, if they rebelled against him because of the lunatic ravings of this wild man, who went around the country garbed in an animal skin like an old prophet, what then? A total defeat because he couldn't raise an army? A stern rebuke from the emperor? He couldn't risk that. He couldn't risk his own political annihilation because he had allowed a public defamer to go unchecked.

So he had John arrested and imprisoned in the fortress at Machaerus. Beyond that, he chose to do nothing.

John's disciples visited him in prison. They told him that Jesus was preaching and healing and that many Jews were calling him the Messiah. They knew that John had recognized Jesus as such, but still they asked John to reconsider. John himself was the Messiah, they said, and he should recognize that about himself and openly make it known. They prodded him enough to make him doubt his original decision. Could it be true, he wondered, that Jesus was not the one for whom they had been waiting, that he (John) was actually the one, the true anointed of God? Jesus would give him an honest answer if he asked him. John was sure of that. So he sent his disciples to ask Jesus that question: "Are you the one we've been waiting for, the one foretold by our prophets? Or should we look for someone else for that?" Jesus told them to report to John the things they were about to see: sight restored to Jews who had been blind and hearing restored to the deaf; Jewish cripples enabled to walk again; lepers cleansed of their sores. He had brought some dead Jews back to life, he said, and was preaching hope to those who were poor. So they went back to John and told him about these things, and John believed in his original impression again.

Herodias, meanwhile, did not know what Jesus was doing. She felt that as long as John was alive, he could be construed by the Jewish people to be the Messiah — the new king, the spearhead of a rebellion, the usurper of the Romans. At the very least, he could still threaten the legitimacy of her marriage. Only his death could ensure Antipas' position — and her own as well. So she asked Antipas to kill him. But he feared God's wrath if the man *should* turn out to be a prophet or, even worse, the actual Messiah. He refused to do it.

Herodias, however, knew her husband. She saw his lustful eye gaze on her daughter, Salome, whom she had instructed to dance naked and lascivious before him one evening. And when she heard the king offer Salome any gift that she wanted, she told her daughter to ask for the severed head of John brought to her on a platter. Antipas was shocked. He asked Salome to choose something else: jewels, gold, silver, land. But, no, she wanted the head of John; she insisted he keep his word. Antipas, she said, had offered her anything in his kingdom that he the power to give, and this was what she desired.

He dropped his shoulders; he could not refuse. There were witnesses to what he had said. He might be better off anyway, he thought, getting rid of the troublesome preacher. He was trying to raise an army to fight King Aretus, and this wild man preacher was making it difficult. So he gave the order to kill the prophet, and Salome, dutiful daughter that she was, brought the bloody head of John the Baptizer to her mother, offering it to her on a platter, as food is served at a feast.

In the end, though, in spite of the elimination of this diverter of his people, Antipas lost the battle with Aretus. Many Jews thought that this was God's way of punishing Antipas for having killed a holy man; but Antipas did not see it that way, and he appealed to the emperor, Tiberius, for help.

In the meantime, John's death did not stop Jesus. In spite of the danger it conveyed, he went on preaching wherever he could and attracting large crowds of Jewish people at each place. And his message, like John's, was about the kingdom of God that was soon to come to Israel. Some, as I have said, started calling him Messiah. When Herod Antipas heard about this, he thought that John had come back from the dead. Or that if Jesus wasn't John resurrected, that he still was a threat to the monarchy. So he set about to kill him. But some Pharisees found

16

out about this and came to Jesus to warn him to get away. Jesus was teaching what they were teaching, and they considered him one of their own. For he taught the lessons of Hillel and the other venerated sages of the Pharisees; he taught their lessons and expanded upon them and often presented them in colorful parables, and the Pharisees respected him for it. The parables, I should mention, were sometimes ways of saying things that might otherwise be interpreted as seditious. And since spies were always about, it was better to speak only of moral issues, while those who knew the true meaning of things would understand the hidden political messages intended.

As a true moral teacher, however, Jesus stood with the best. Where Hillel had said, "Do not do to others what you would not have others do to you," Jesus said, "Do to others what you would have others do to you." Like a true Pharisee and like an Essene as well, he opposed the corruption of the chief priests. He told us to love each other and to love even our enemies, just as Moses in his time and Philo in his had taught us to do, and that if someone slaps your cheek, you should give him the other to slap as well. But that last thing was to be done only under certain circumstances. When resistance was appropriate, as he considered it was shortly before his arrest in the garden at Gethsemane, he advocated resistance.

Besides preaching, he *did* things. He healed sick people, some with afflictions previously thought to be incurable. One time, he increased tremendously the small amount of bread he had available to him, in order to feed the multitude of Jews who had come to hear him, and he changed water into wine for them to drink. Once, he actually walked on water to join his disciples on a boat. And once, as he had told John's disciples, he restored a dead child back to life. And he did the same for a young man in Nain and the same for a man named Lazarus.

So strong was his influence in Galilee, so irresistible his personality when he was there, that the Jewish people organized themselves to take him by force, if necessary, and to set him up as king without any further delay. But Jesus was not prepared for that. His time to be king had not yet come. He actually had to flee from all his Jewish admirers and find safety in the hills.

When he decided to go to Jerusalem to carry his message of the kingdom of God into the south, he knew that he would have to pass through the land of the Samaritans and that there was danger there, for the Samaritans looked upon the Jerusalem temple as a false sanctuary, the real one to them being on Mount Girizim. That and other differences made the Samaritans hostile to any northern Jews passing through their territory en route to Jerusalem for a religious festival, and they sometimes attacked the travelers. But Jesus chose that danger over the greater one of going by the alternate route through Perea, east of the Jordan River, where he might encounter Herod Antipas' soldiers. He knew that in Jerusalem, things were not all that safe either. Word of Pilate's slaughter of Galileans and others who had protested the confiscation of Temple money for an aqueduct was still fresh in his mind, and to enter Jerusalem as the Messiah was to court the same response from Pilate again. But he went because he *was* the Messiah, and it was his destiny to go to God's city.

When he came into Jerusalem, he came riding on a donkey, fulfilling Zachariah's prophecy, and the Jews of that city hailed him with hosannas and laid their clothes and the branches of trees on the road in front of him to do him honor. He entered through the Valley Gate, near the Pool of Siloam, and took the street that led to the Temple. The high priest Caiaphas got news of this and wondered if he had another troublemaking rebel on his hands. He soon found out. Jesus went to the Temple and told the moneychangers who worked there that they were doing evil by turning God's house into a commercial establishment. Then he overturned their work tables and scattered their coins and accounting books all over the floor. He stationed his men at the gates of the Temple and did not allow anything to be carried in or out from that afternoon to the evening. Thus, he further fulfilled Zachariah's prophecy that there would be no merchants in the House of the Lord on the day the Messiah arrived. He was a man who did things; he didn't just talk. Some Sadducees, years later, talked to me about that event. The moneychangers, they said, were performing a useful function: pilgrims who came from distant lands had to buy doves and other things to offer as sacrifices in the Temple, and they couldn't buy them without local currency; the moneychangers were simply exchanging the pilgrims' foreign coins for local ones and charging a fee for their service. I told those Sadducees that Jesus had never objected to such exchanges; he had only objected to them being done in the Temple. But I knew that there was something else to it too: he had despised all the chief priests; he had hated the corruption, the avariciousness, the ungodly indulgences of those sinful men, who used the offices they were supposed to use in the service of God to support the pagan defilers of our land.

Caiaphas heard about Jesus' activities. He heard about the miraculous cures: a blind man having his sight restored, a crippled man made capable of walking again. And he heard about what Jesus was teaching, the most significant thing being that he would destroy and rebuild the Temple in three days and that a new kingdom of God was at hand. And he heard that Jesus was also telling people not to pay tribute to the Romans. Those things, along with the fact that a lot of people were calling him the Messiah, caused Caiaphas concern. Then, when he learned that one of Jesus' closest associates was a Zealot, he decided to act. He was not going to allow a rebellion to get started by this Jesus and then have the Romans depose him from his position as high priest just because he couldn't keep order.

He and some of the other chief priests came to Jesus when he was teaching and challenged him by asking the source of his authority. When Jesus cleverly answered with a question about John the Baptizer, one that would entrap them whichever way they answered (for if they answered one way, it would show their disobedience to God, and if they answered the other way, it might arouse the people, for whom John had been a popular prophet), they decided not to answer at all, which led Jesus to do the same.

Caiaphas decided to place Jesus under arrest. But he dared not do it during the Passover celebration that was taking place at that time, because the pilgrims and the city's residents had welcomed Jesus into the city with such jubilation that they might rise up and rebel if they saw the arrest of such a popular figure. Better to wait until the holiday was over and the pilgrims had gone home. So he waited, and meanwhile he bought off one of Jesus' followers, a man named Judas Iscariot, and found out where Jesus would be at a certain time. Yes, Judas betrayed Jesus, but just as the chief priests feared a rebellion of the Jewish people if they arrested Jesus openly, so did Judas fear an attack against himself if the people saw what he was doing. He knew how popular Jesus was, and he didn't want the people turning against him and maybe threatening his life when they found out what he had done. So he did what he did clandestinely and collected his money in the same way — secretly, as if to hide from God the evil that he was doing.

Jesus suspected the danger and made sure his followers were armed when they went out that night. He also gave orders that his brother, James, was to take over as leader in case of his absence. At the olive garden at Gethsemane, the encounter took place. Caiaphas sent some of his Temple guards, and in the fray that ensued, Peter, Jesus' first disciple, sliced off the ear of one of the guards, a man named Malchus. But in the end, they took Jesus prisoner and took him to the house of Caiaphas' father-in-law, Annas, and they questioned him there. The reason they went to Annas first was because, as I have said, Caiaphas did not make a move without Annas' approval. Then they sent messages to some of the Sanhedrin members to come to the Temple to sit in judgment of Jesus. But they did not call *all* the members, because they had heard that the Pharisees in Galilee had saved Jesus' life, and because they knew that Joseph of Arimathea, one of the Pharisee members of the Sanhedrin, was one of Jesus' supporters and that Joseph had been campaigning among the Pharisees for a full recognition of Jesus as the Messiah. They knew that a Pharisee majority in the Sanhedrin would vote to release him. They had to get around that. So they summoned just enough Pharisees to make a show of fairness, while they kept the Sadducees in the majority. Then, also, they did not conduct the trial in the usual manner. As a rule, the Sanhedrin was not convened without the governor's permission. But Caiaphas did not seek the governor's permission. He called the meeting himself. And since it was not an actual Sanhedrin Council that he was convoking, he could always say that such permission was not required. What he needed was just a few answers from Jesus given in front of witnesses that would enable him to present Pilate with a charge of sedition. He produced two witnesses to testify that Jesus had threatened to destroy the Temple and build it up again in three days. Such an act would surely have been disruptive to the peace and tranquillity of the nation. Caiaphas asked Jesus to respond to that, but Jesus just kept silent. Then Caiaphas commanded him in the name of God to say once and for all if he considered himself the Messiah, the anointed one, the chosen one of God. An affirmative answer would have meant that he had pretensions to be king, just as Judas of Galilee had had at Sepphoris when he had declared himself king of the Jews. Now Jesus answered and said, "You have said it," which Caiaphas knew meant yes. Caiaphas exploded with anger. In his rage, he tore his robe as one does at the death of a family member, and he cried out, "Blasphemy! He has uttered blasphemy!" Then he turned to the others and shouted, "What is your judgment?"

"Death!" some of the Sadducees shouted. Then one of the Sadducee elders came forward and spit in Jesus' face, and another came forward and struck him. Then another came forward and slapped him and said, "Prophesy to us if you are the Messiah!"

The Pharisees who were there tried to stop it, but they were outnumbered. Caiaphas declared that Jesus would start a rebellion if he were set free and that the Romans would then be down on us all. A vote was taken, and the majority followed the Sadducee line and recommended a death penalty. The Pharisees, as I have said, were powerless to stop it. They could not help him here as they had in Galilee when they had helped him escape from Herod Antipas.

But this was one execution Caiaphas was not going to perform himself. First, he could not perform it — not legally at any rate — because he did not have the full Sanhedrin with a majority vote for death by stoning. And even if he had had such a vote, he could never have carried out the execution legally because the Sanhedrin would have been convened without the procurator's permission. But also, he reasoned that if the Jewish people might rise up in rebellion over just an arrest (which was why he hadn't arrested Jesus during Passover), how much more might they rise up in rebellion over Jesus' death? High priests who were not popular with the people were deposed by the Romans, as he remembered had happened in the days when Quirinius had been legate of Syria and Joazar had been the high priest and that, in spite of Joazar having gotten the people to cooperate with the census, which had made tax-collecting that much easier, Quirinius had deposed Joazar because of his unpopularity. And he remembered that Valerius Gratus had appointed and deposed three high priests before appointing Caiaphas himself to that post, and that, although the reason in those instances had not been because of the people but rather because of Annas, the lesson of Roman fickleness had impressed itself on his mind. Caiaphas was not going to get himself deposed because of the people, and he was not going to be the cause of a rebellion. He would let the Romans handle Jesus, and, considering Pilate's appetite for crucifying, he had no doubt about what would be done. Then, if the people wanted to blame anyone, they would blame Pilate and not him.

So he took Jesus to Pilate. Along the way, he learned more about the things that Jesus was teaching, one of which was a confirmation of something that he had heard before: that we should not pay Roman taxes. He conveyed all this to Pilate, but Pilate asked Jesus the only question that really concerned him: "Are you the king of the Jews?" And Jesus answered, "You have said so," which meant yes.

The memory of Judas of Galilee, who also had declared himself king of the Jews, was still fresh in Roman minds. And Pilate was aware that the Jewish people were stirred up and were hailing this Jesus as a king and that Jesus and his men had seized the Temple and had controlled what went in or out for most of the day. A king of the Jews to Pilate meant the usurpation of Roman authority, and for that and that alone, he condemned Jesus to death. His soldiers took Jesus into the courtyard. They stripped him and put a robe on him and stuck a reed in his hand, as if it were a scepter, and mocked him and tortured him and put a thorned wreath on his head, which caused him constant pain. They spit on him and bowed before him and mockingly called him King of the Jews. Then they put his clothes back on and made him carry one of those heavy wooden crosses that they nail people to when they crucify them and had a passer-by help Jesus when he couldn't go any farther. I cannot describe to you the throng, the multitude of Jewish people, who followed him, crying, wailing, lamenting his demise. The Romans made him go to a hill outside the city, and there they crucified him. On his cross they nailed a sign. It said his name and then said, "King of the Jews." It was their way of making fun of him — and of us. And the multitudes of our people, who had come to show their support for him and to pray for him, now returned to their homes, beating their breasts in despair and bemoaning with unabashed tears this unwanted death of the Messiah.

He was not on the cross as long as most crucified people were. The Roman idea of killing that way was to make the death slow, not fast. Romans wanted their victims to suffer before they died. That was why they tortured Jesus in the courtyard and made him carry the heavy cross as far as he could. And once the person is nailed to a cross, he must not be allowed to bleed; he must be made to suffer for as long as possible. But Jesus died after only a few hours, with a Roman soldier piercing his side with a spear, and that much at least was a blessing. Joseph of Arimathea, who had not been summoned by Caiaphas to the council meeting, got Pilate's permission to bury the body, and he wrapped it and placed it into a tomb.

But this was not the end, because after Jesus' corpse was entombed, it came back to life. The stone was rolled back from the entrance to the tomb so that Jesus could leave. In his wounded body, he visited some of his followers and told them that he was going away for now — some of them even saw him ascend to heaven — but that he would return very soon to lead them again. And from that promise and the hope that it inspired came the Nazarenes.

Saul, when all these events occurred, was studying in Tarsus with the sage, Machaiah. He had grown up hearing about the revolutionary, Ezekias, and his warrior son, Judas of Galilee. He had grown up hearing about a Messiah who would come to establish a kingdom of God. This Jesus of Nazareth, so admired by the Jews of Galilee, that they tried to make him king and so adored by the Jews of Jerusalem that they laid their clothes in his path, was still someone to be reckoned with in spite of his crucifixion. God had raised him from the dead, and Jesus had promised to return. Machaiah, Saul's teacher, being a Pharisee, had accepted this, for not only did Pharisees accept resurrection as a natural phenomenon, but they also accepted that Jesus was, or could be, the chosen Messiah of God. That was why so many of them had joined the Nazarene movement and why so many others were considering doing it. Machaiah had taught this to Saul, and Saul had accepted it as true. It had not been difficult for him to do that. He had been raised among pagans as well as Jews all his life, and pagans, like the Pharisees, believed in resurrection. Attis in Phrygia, Baal-bel-Marduk in Babylonia, Adonis in Phoenicia and Osiris in Egypt — all had been resurrected from death and attained the status of gods. So when the Pharisees spoke of Jesus' resurrection, Saul, already accustomed to hearing about the phenomenon from other sources, considered it possible.

And I, whose name is Barnabas and who writes this account for you now, was in Cyprus during this time. My parents had died and had left me an inheritance of land. I heard about Jesus and the Nazarenes from travelers. I heard about them, and I believed. I believed in the resurrection and the kingdom to come, and I believe it still to this day. I told my uncle I wanted to join these people. He thought it unwise. He had taken the place of my father as a source of worldly advice, and it was his considered and protective opinion that I should stay where I was.

"You have a comfortable life here in Cyprus," he said, accepting a cup of wine from an elderly manservant. "You'd be leaving that for a life of danger."

"Or glory," I countered. "It might be a life of glory too, uncle. Did you ever think of that?"

"Glory," my uncle muttered with a low, contemptuous grunt. "There are many glorious things done in this world, dear nephew, but most of them go unrecognized. You're young," he sighed. "You're young and idealistic, and that's why you think as you do."

But even as he said it, I could sense a certain nostalgia in his voice, a certain longing for the days when his beard was not so gray and thoughts of excitement and travel and adventure leaped through his mind like a mercurial nymph, a time of longing for the uncertainties of life rather than the boring security of knowing what tomorrow would bring.

"Where will you stay?" he inquired, apparently resigning himself to the inevitability of my decision.

"With Mary," I said, referring to my sister, who was living now with her husband in Jerusalem. "I'll stay with her at first, and then I'll find a place of my own."

23

"And what will you do for money?" he asked, concerned to instill a measure of practicality into my decision.

"Uncle, I'm going to sell my land," I said. "I'm going to join the Nazarenes and give the money to them. God will provide for me after that, I'm sure."

My uncle's sun-darkened face seemed to pale. "That's everything you own," he said. "Your parents worked all their lives for that land. Your father was a Levite. He worked hard for his money. You're going to give it all away? If you sell the land and give away the money, you'll be giving away a lifetime of your father's labor. And if things don't go right out there in Jerusalem and you have to come back here, you'll have nothing of your own to support you."

I know that, uncle," I answered appreciatively. "I know that you're thinking about what's best for me. But I believe in my heart that what I'm doing is right. I have to build a life of my own, just as you did. And I'll stand or fall by what I decide. But whatever happens, it will be my decision and my life. It'll be my success or failure and not someone else's."

"Very well," my uncle said. "Let it be so. But let your father look down on us and bear witness from heaven that this is not what I advise."

"So be it," I said," and I sold the land and took the money to Jerusalem.

CHAPTER III

When I lived in Cyprus, my name was Joses, but when I joined the Nazarenes in Jerusalem, the disciples gave me the name Barnabas, which means The Son of Consolation. I joined the Nazarenes, as I have said, because I believed in the promise of Jesus; I believed that he had been resurrected and that he would return to restore the kingdom of God.

I have told you that the Pharisees believed that a dead person could come back to life. Jesus, while he was among us, proved that they were right in that by restoring a child and then a young man from Nain and then Lazarus to life after each of them had died. And then God restored Jesus to life after he had been crucified. The Sadducees, of course, did not believe that; they did not believe that any of those things had occurred; to them, the whole idea of resurrection was absurd. They challenged us Nazarenes by asking us *when* Jesus of Nazareth would return. We told them that while his return would be soon — certainly within our own lifetimes — we were not privileged to know the exact date of that event. Jesus himself had told us that. To which the Sadducees replied that that was too convenient an excuse and that maybe Jesus was not going to return at all.

One of our Nazarene leaders was Peter, although he had been known as Cephas and Simon at different times. He had been Jesus' foremost disciple. He announced that God had ordained that a descendant of King David would mount the throne of Israel and that Jesus, being descended from David, was the one that God had intended. The Romans took notice of that. New kingdoms were not part of their plans. And Caiaphas, or any other high priest in power, in order to show the Romans that he could keep order, had to suppress such movements when they arose. For that reason, he pursued Nazarenes, just as the Romans pursued Zealots.

You should not think that Nazarenes and Zealots and Pharisees formed distinctly separate groups. That was not true, for there was overlapping among them all. The Pharisaic religious philosophy, whether the more conservative type of Shammai or the more liberal type of Hillel, was intrinsic to all three. When Judas, the founder of the Zealots, joined forces with Zaddok, the Pharisee, it was because they shared the same religious philosophy as well as the same political aspirations. When Jesus taught his great lessons of morality, he was teaching Pharisaic philosophy, and, indeed, we Nazarenes, while we resembled Essenes in our religious practices, were like Pharisees in our religious beliefs, except that we believed that Jesus was the Messiah while the other Pharisees — those who had not joined us yet — adopted a wait-and-see attitude. Pharisees had saved the life of Jesus when Herod Antipas was out to kill him. They did this because they considered Jesus one of their own. And James, Jesus' brother, was esteemed by all the Pharisees — and by the Essenes too, I might add. And many of the lower priests, who already had swarmed to the Pharisee sages as their spiritual mentors, now joined the Nazarenes to await the coming of Jesus. John, who was sometimes called the Beloved Disciple, was himself a lower priest. As for the Zealots, one of them, a man named Simon, joined Jesus as one of his first disciples, and Jesus saw no reason to reject him because of his willingness to fight for freedom and the liberation of Israel. Indeed, he saw reason to do the opposite, and he accepted Simon because of that.

It was during this time, when Tiberius was emperor and Pilate was procurator of Judaea, that Peter faced the man who controlled the high priesthood even though he was no longer the high priest himself. This, of course, was Annas, the father-in-law of Caiaphas — Caiaphas who held the title but not the power at the time. Annas heard that Peter and John, the son of Zebedee, and two of our other Nazarene brothers were teaching in the streets about Jesus' resurrection and the kingdom that was to come, and he became concerned. He was determined that his son-in-law should show the Romans that he could keep order. So he and Caiaphas and some of the others in his family, along with some Temple police, went into the street to see these preachers for themselves. They heard that Peter had cured a crippled man miraculously and that he was now quite popular with the Jewish people because of that. It was estimated that five-thousand Jews had joined the Nazarenes because of that one event alone. They found Peter and John and the others in the evening, and they took them into custody in order to question them the next day. The next day, they asked them by what authority they did their preaching. Peter pointed to the former crippled man, who was with them now, and said that he preached by the same power that had cured the man. That power, he said, came from Jesus of Nazareth, whom the chief priests had been responsible for getting executed. Annas and Caiaphas checked with the police officers, who told them that the people in the neighborhood corroborated that the man had been lame and that Peter had cured him. Annas did not want those people stirred up by an imprisonment of Peter, so he simply warned Peter not to preach about Jesus anymore. But Peter refused, saying that he had to obey God's command to tell about the things he had seen and heard and that God's command took precedence over Annas' command. Annas warned him again but then let him and the others go, because he was concerned about how the Jewish people would respond if he didn't. Peter, you see, was popular not just among Nazarenes but among all Jews — except for the Sadducees, of course. As a matter of fact, with the exception of just Sadducees, I believe I can say without hesitation that all our people, from Judaea to Galilee, favored us Nazarenes, held us in esteem and treated us with respect.

But Peter did not heed Annas' warning. He and the others continued to preach about Jesus and the kingdom that was to come, and many people believed them. Many of our Jewish people brought their sick into the streets, laying them on beds and couches so that Peter could heal them by touching them or even by having his shadow pass over them as he walked by. As word spread, Jews came from outside Jerusalem too, and Peter cured many of them through the power that God had given him.

Annas was displeased when he heard about this. He told Caiaphas to have the guards arrest Peter and the others and this time to put them into prison. Then, with the procurator's permission, Caiaphas summoned the Sanhedrin. Annas felt certain that the Pharisees would see eye-to-eye with him that these men were preaching rebellion and posing a threat to the peace of the nation. They came, Sadducees and Pharisees alike, and among them was Gamaliel, Saul's former teacher, the revered sage who was the leader of the Pharisees and, to many, the wisest man alive.

But even before the first of them arrived, the captain of the prison guards came to Caiaphas to tell him that the prisoners had escaped. Someone, he said, had let them out. Caiaphas was about to order a search for them when another policeman arrived to tell them that the prisoners were preaching in the Temple. And not only were they preaching about Jesus, he said, but they were telling people that an angel had opened their prison doors to let them out. Caiaphas turned to Annas, as if to ask what he should do. Annas told him to have the guards arrest Peter and the others again. But Caiaphas still feared the Jewish people and how they might react to the violent seizure of such popular figures, so he told his officers to arrest them courteously and to refrain from any show of force in front of the people. As it turned out, that was accomplished easily. The policemen simply asked Peter and the others to come with them, and they did so without protest.

The members of the Sanhedrin sat in the Council Hall, in the Chamber of Hewn Stone, in the western area of the Temple grounds. The chief priests and the other Sadducees took the center front rows simply out of past habit, and the Pharisees took the rest.

Before bringing in the prisoners, Annas primed his audience with warnings and dire predictions about the consequences of allowing rebellious preaching to continue unchecked, and then he had the prisoners brought in.

"Did we not warn you to stop preaching about this Jesus of yours?" he asked them.

Peter lifted his rugged, black-bearded face and said, yes, but that God had commanded him to do otherwise. To which Annas replied that Peter was a liar and that it was not God but Peter's own mind that had given him that command. Then he appealed to the Sanhedrin, Pharisees as well as Sadducees, to recognize the danger that these people were incurring for the entire nation if a rebellion and a Roman response to it should take place. He pointed out that the Romans had attacked other rebellious movements, and he mentioned some of them for effect. He mentioned the one led by Ezekias, which had come to naught, and the one led by Judas and Zaddok, which had failed, and he mentioned others whose names were now obscured by the smallness and brevity of their movements and the growing number of their competitors on the scene. He asked the Sanhedrin for the penalty of death. If the leaders of the Nazarenes were killed, he said, that might stop the movement once and for all. Better that a few should die and the Romans be reassured than to have thousands slaughtered by an aroused Roman army. There was another motive behind this request, however, and that had to do with the loyalties of the lower priests. Most of them secretly were Nazarenes by now, and that took away their loyalties to the chief priests. The elimination of the Nazarene movement would bring the lower priests back again, he thought.

It was at this point that Gamaliel, wearing an ash gray robe, stood up. The venerable leader of the Pharisees, the grandson of the great Hillel, was not to be ignored by anyone. All eyes turned to him, and all voices were stilled.

"Will our high priest permit an older member to speak?" he asked.

Caiaphas, the official presiding officer, answered with unctious respect. "The leader of the Pharisees knows that his voice is always welcome among us."

"Thank you, Caiaphas," Gamaliel said. "May I first request that these men be removed for a few moments so that we may speak in private?"

Caiaphas gave the order, and the guards took Peter and the others away.

Gamaliel went on. "For some time, I have observed the Nazarenes without comment. I have wondered whether their movement is or is not a manifestation of God's will. Their religious beliefs are the same as we Pharisees have. Their religious practices are such as to make even the most demanding Sadducee proud. James, the brother of Jesus and the leader of their movement, prays in the Temple every day and is a strong follower of the Torah. He has taken the Rechabite and Nazarite vows and is one of the few who is worthy of entering the inner sanctuary of the Temple. These men who have been brought before us today, I have heard, are also pious Jews, obedient to God and respectful of the Torah. These are good things, and we must not ignore them."

Annas interrupted: "But, Gamaliel, what if the things they teach endanger the welfare of our people?"

Gamaliel answered, "Annas, neither you nor I know for certain that their work endangers the welfare of our people. Indeed, it may be that their work will benefit us all. If a true Messiah rises up among us, surely you will agree that that will benefit us all. And if that Messiah establishes a kingdom in which God is the supreme authority, should we not welcome that? The comforts and privileges you now enjoy under Roman rule are surely not more attractive to you than a free Israel under God's rule. The emperor is not to be preferred over God."

Annas answered, "God forbid that such a thought should enter my mind. It is not the end but the method I object to. Isn't it better to bide our time and be safe for the present until we can gradually convince the Romans that the occupation of our country is no longer necessary, that they can collect their tribute and have our loyalty as allies without that? Isn't it better than making them think that we're trying to overthrow them?"

"Do you think the collection of tribute is something we should accept without protest?" Gamaliel asked.

"Of course," Annas answered. "What else can we do?"

"You do realize, Annas, that many of us feel that to give tribute to Caesar is to show disloyalty to God."

"But we have no choice. If we don't pay it, we invite disaster from the Romans."

"And if we do pay it, are we not inviting disaster from God?"

"But we *have* been paying it, and we've had no disaster from God."

"Yes, we have been paying it but never willingly, and we've been paying it with less and less regularity, so that now we're behind in our payments."

"And if we should stop paying it altogether, the Romans will start a campaign of destruction against us."

"Then we would have to fight."

"With what? We have no army."

"We have had leaders arise in the past, men who have called us to arms."

"And look what happened to them," Annas sneered. "All of them said that they were the Messiah, and all of them were destroyed. And if these Nazarenes ever get the idea that their dead leader has returned and then try to set up a new kingdom because of it and mislead the people while they're doing it, the Romans will send an army against us, and thousands of our people will get killed. That's why we have to stop these Nazarenes now."

Gamaliel looked around the room at the faces of his listeners. He spoke slowly, measuring his words. "Men of Israel, honorable Annas and Caiaphas, I remember with sadness Eleazar and Judas of Galilee, each of whom we thought was the Messiah but whom we saw were not the ones who could deliver us. And I remember Jesus, who raised our people's hopes for freedom but whose death at the hands of our Roman oppressors shattered those hopes for the present. All these men, and the others whom Annas has mentioned without naming them, were courageous people, who wanted freedom for our nation and a government led by God. They died, but though they died, their influences are still with us. From Judas of Galilee have come the Zealots, who still defy the Romans and fight as they can for freedom. They are brave people. If they are captured, they are contemptuous of the pain the Romans inflict on them. In their resolve to acknowledge no master but God, they remain indifferent to the tortures even of their parents and friends. Will Judas return to lead them, to lead all of us, to drive out these Roman idolaters? That, I believe, is highly unlikely, since so many years have passed. But with Jesus, I cannot say that. From his inspiration have come the Nazarenes, and they say that Jesus will return. Time will tell us if this is true.

"In regard to the men who have been brought before us today, time will tell us if the movement they represent does or does not come from God. If it does and you harm these men, you will be going against the will of God; you will be at war with God. Therefore, I adjure you to let these men go in peace and do them no harm."

He sat down, and the audience remained silent, the faces of the Pharisees not stirring as each soberly considered the words of their leader.

Caiaphas broke the uncomfortable silence. "We all have heard the words of the learned Gamaliel, but I believe it is incumbent on me to make a comment. With no disrespect intended to the learned leader of the Pharisees, I wish to say that you Pharisees have an unhealthy bias towards these Nazarenes. I think it's clouding your judgment about what's best for our nation."

A Pharisee at the back of the room stood up and protested. "That's not true, Caiaphas. Our nation comes first; it always will."

"Nevertheless," Caiaphas persisted, "you Pharisees protected this Jesus person when Herod Antipas tried to arrest him, didn't you?"

"Because he was one of us," the Pharisee said. "We were protecting one of our own."

"Then you're saying that you Pharisees *are* in sympathy with these Nazarenes?"

"We are," the Pharisee said, "because they share our religious philosophy. The only significant difference between us is that while some of us believe that Jesus is the Messiah and that he'll return, the rest of us are just not sure, as Gamaliel has said."

"Well, since you choose to put it that way," Caiaphas said, "I will simply say that these Nazarenes are a political threat to the present government, just as the Zealots are, and that we ought to eradicate them in order to protect our people against the catastrophic fate these Nazarenes will lead them to."

"Is that what you really want to protect us against," the Pharisee asked, apparently determined to get in the last word, "or is it your own privileged position? Your fancy house, your clothes, your food and wine, your authority over other people? Isn't the truth that you don't want the Romans to leave, that you're afraid that if they do leave, our own people will depose you?" Without waiting for an answer, the Pharisee sat down.

Caiaphas did not answer him. He may have thought it better not to do so, perhaps because the Pharisee was too close to an embarrassing truth. He remained silent, acting as if the question was unworthy of an answer. Then he said, "Does anyone else wish to speak?"

No one responded, so he asked for a vote. "All those in favor of execution?" And only the Sadducees raised their hands. "All those in favor of freeing the prisoners?" And the Pharisees raised their hands. The Pharisees were in the majority, and so Peter and John and the others were to be freed.

The assembly disbanded then, and only Annas, Caiaphas, Ananias and two other chief priests remained. Annas ordered the guards to bring back the prisoners, and while the priests were alone, they bemoaned the injustice of allowing such criminals to go free.

"We ought to do *something*," Caiaphas said, "something to teach them a lesson. A good beating might get through to them."

"Yes, you're right," Annas said. "We can't let them go just like that. You're right. A good beating might teach them a lesson they won't forget."

When Peter and the others were brought in, Annas spoke to them. "Listen to me, and pay attention to what I tell you. You were lucky today. Gamaliel spoke in your behalf, and you're getting off with your lives. If it had been up to me, I would have had all of you stoned immediately. You don't deserve to live after all the trouble you've been stirring up. But the Sanhedrin voted to let you go, so I'm abiding by its decision. Not willingly, but I'm abiding by it. But that doesn't mean that we're going to tolerate what you've been doing. You got off with your lives today, but next time you won't be so lucky. You're not to go around talking about this Jesus person anymore. And you're not to go around talking about a new kingdom in Israel. Do I make myself clear?"

They did not answer, and Annas became infuriated. To him, the intransigence of these Nazarenes was like the intransigence of the Zealots.

"Beat them!" he shouted to the guards, the corners of his mouth pulled downward in an open display of rage. "Beat them, and send them on their way!" He turned to the other chief priests. "Come, let's leave these oxen. I won't waste another breath on them."

The priests then left, and the guards pulled whips out of their belts.

"You dogs," the first guard said, "get down on your knees. We'll teach you what happens when you disobey the high priest."

The prisoners knelt, and the guards began to wield their whips. But no one spoke, and no one cried out. A Nazarene was no less brave than a Zealot, and suffering pain was a way of proving one's devotion to God. The guards stopped only when their arms became tired. Then they rebuked the prisoners and ordered them to leave.

While the other three Nazarenes stood up, Peter remained kneeling. "God," he said, "I rejoice that you have permitted us to suffer for our

Messiah." The others, hearing this, fell to their knees in prayer as well, while the guards walked off in disgust.

That evening Peter had dinner with his wife. She smeared ointment onto the welts on his back and served him the bread and fish she had prepared. He recited the Nazarene prayer that is said before meals, in which thanks are given not only for bread but for God having sent his servant, Jesus, to us. Then, while they ate, she complained to him about the dangers of his involvement as a Nazarene leader.

"It hurts me to see this happening to you," she said. "You risk your life when you go about preaching like this."

"Not just preaching, Rachel. I heal people too. Many people have been healed by what I do."

"I know that," she answered. "I've seen what you do. I've seen them throw away their crutches because of you. But you're talking openly about a new kingdom. Caiaphas could take you to Pilate for that, just as he did with Jesus."

"It would be worth it," Peter said, undismayed by her warning. "It would be worth it. I was a coward about him once in my life. I denied I knew him after he was arrested. I was afraid they'd arrest me too. I won't let that happen again, Rachel. I would die for him now if I had to."

"And how would your dying help your family?" she asked. "You have a wife to support and a son to raise. Doesn't that mean anything to you? We need you alive, not dead. Why can't one of the younger men take these risks? You've done enough, haven't you? What about that new fellow, Barnabas, and some of the others who aren't married? Why can't they take the risks? Why does it have to be you?"

"Rachel," he said compassionately, "they can't heal the way I can, and they didn't know and speak to Jesus as I did. I was his first disciple. I was with him longer than anyone else. I defended him with my own hands. He said he would change me from a fisher of fish into a fisher of men, and he did. I can't stop walking on the path he started me on, no matter what the risk to my life. If I'm a leader, it's because he made me a leader. If I'm a leader, it's because the others look to me as one. I can't turn my back on my destiny, Rachel. I've got to live my life."

"Does James take the risks that you do?" she asked, a resentful tone in her voice. "Does he go into the streets and into other cities the way you do?"

"Rachel, Rachel," Peter said entreatingly, "he's Jesus' brother. He's our bishop. Jesus himself appointed him. We've got to keep him alive.

He's the closest thing we have to Jesus himself. He's a symbol of Jesus until he comes back. We can't let him go into the streets. We can't let him risk his life. We can't give the authorities, Roman or Jewish, any excuse to arrest him. He lives like an Essene, a pure spiritual man, and he doesn't speak in public. That way they can't accuse him of anything political."

"Even though he's head of a movement that wants political change," she muttered sarcastically.

"Yes," Peter answered, "in spite of that. Stephen and his militant followers; John and James, the sons of Zebedee, with all their public declamations and denunciations; Simon and his Zealot friends who join us and who would sooner kill Romans than eat — all of them, and myself too, are prepared to risk our lives. But James has to be protected. My task is to work in the field, to spread the word to as many Jews as possible — and even to some of the Gentiles if they want to become Jews and join us. But James' task is to stay alive, so that a blood relation of Jesus will always be there to lead us."

She said nothing more but only looked at him, this big husband of hers who could hold his own with a wrestler because of his sheer size and physical strength. She walked to him and leaned down to kiss his forehead.

"I love you," she said, the tears welling in her eyes. "I don't want to lose you."

He kissed her hand. "I promise you, Rachel, I'll be careful."

CHAPTER IV

Caiaphas returned home that evening and was met by his daughter, Rabath. She was a ravishing brunette who could turn the head of any man, and she was her father's greatest pride. Her most attractive feature on a first encounter was the strange felinity of her eyes. They were green and slitted like a cat's. Her eyebrows formed twin arches over them, and her long eyelashes canopied them like the large, slow, languid fans that Roman slaves wave vertically to cool their masters on torrid days. Her lips were full and pouted, as if always ready to kiss. Her cheekbones were high and her profile straight — so straight that a Greek geometrician could have plumbed a line from her forehead to her chin with impressive Euclidean precision. But not only was she beautiful, she was intelligent, clever, perceptive and knowledgeable about the world. She was also self-indulgent and willful, a woman not to be coerced into anything. She had a mind of her own. She was religious, yes, but not intimidated by religion. Because of her beauty and her father's position, she did not practice the cultivated humility of other Jewish women, and if she sometimes feigned submission to her father's will, she did it fully confident that she would ultimately have her way.

Caiaphas slumped wearily into a chair. "Well, what did my beautiful daughter do today?" he said.

Rabath answered, "Oh, I helped mother select the dinner, and then I spent time with Eleazar."

"Ananias' son?"

"Yes, father. We're still good friends, you know."

"Should I be arranging a wedding soon?" he asked.

"No, father, he's younger than I am. And besides, we're just friends."

Caiaphas gave her a half-hearted smile and knit his brows. It was obvious he was thinking about something else.

"Father, what's wrong?" Rabath asked with a tone of genuine concern.

"It's those Nazarenes. They're agitating again," he complained.

"The followers of that man you took to Pilate?"

"Yes."

"But their leader is gone. What are they trying to do now?"

35

"They're going around telling people that he's coming back, that he's going to set up a new kingdom here."

"Coming back from the dead?"

"Oh no, he's already done that. Now he's coming back from heaven."

"Well, can't you stop them?"

"There are too many people who believe them. Our people are joining them in droves. They perform these miracle healings — Who knows if they're true? — and then our people believe anything they say. They supposedly cured a crippled man recently, and five-thousand people joined them after that. Can you believe it? Because one man gets healed, five-thousand Jewish people suddenly believe what's being said about this Jesus! And most of the five-thousand weren't even there to see the healing!"

Rabath knelt down and removed her father's shoes. She began to rub his feet. "People don't appreciate you," she said. "I know how difficult it is for you: trying to appease the Romans and keep our people orderly at the same time. You have the hardest job in Jerusalem."

"And trying to please your grandfather too, Rabath. Don't forget that. Every time I want to make a decision on my own, I have to get his approval for it."

Rabath stopped massaging her father's feet. She sat on the floor and looked up at him. "I'm curious, father. If grandfather hadn't pushed you into bringing that Nazarene to Pilate, would you have done it?"

Caiaphas thought for a moment. "Probably. What choice did I have? The people were demonstrating for him in the streets, and he and his men had taken over the Temple. Who knows what he would have done next? The Romans aren't blind, you know."

"He couldn't have taken over Jerusalem, could he?"

"No, but I think the people expected him to. I think they did. I think they thought God was going to intervene somehow and help the man drive out the Romans. And us too. He was saying some very nasty things about us, you know."

"He was jealous," Rabath said.

"Probably," Caiaphas answered. "But a lot of people talk against us now because of him. I don't mind when those Essenes out in the desert do it, but when they start doing it around Jerusalem, I get worried."

"Well, then you had no choice but to take him to Pilate. It sounds as if the Romans would have arrested him themselves if you hadn't."

"Absolutely," Caiaphas agreed. "They weren't going to let a man stir the people into a state of rebellion without doing something about it.

And if they *had* arrested him without me, then Pilate might have deposed me for not having acted sooner. I'm supposed to keep public order, you know."

"Did you know Pilate would kill him?" she asked.

"I wasn't sure," Caiaphas answered, "but I thought there was a good chance of it. You know how easily our dear procurator crucifies people. But whether he would have or not, I had to take him. I had no choice."

"You and grandfather couldn't have handled him yourselves?"

"And do what? Condemn him to death by stoning? We couldn't do that without a majority vote of the full Sanhedrin. And we hadn't convened the full Sanhedrin. We would have to have gotten Pilate's permission to convene it first, and then what would we have condemned him for? We can only condemn someone for religious transgressions. We have no jurisdiction over political offenses. We have to turn those kinds of people over to the Romans. It was sedition, pure and simple, and the Romans demand *that* jurisdiction for themselves. Besides, even if we *could* have found something to condemn him for, once the full Sanhedrin was there, the stupid Pharisees would have voted to free him. They'd already helped him escape from Herod Antipas up in Galilee. Joseph of Arimethea, one of our own Sanhedrin members, was actually campaigning for the man. Can you believe it? And then, even if we could have found a way to execute him ourselves, the people would have demonstrated in the streets against me — or they would have rebelled. Then Pilate would have deposed me because I was an unpopular high priest. That's what they did to Joazar, you know, even after he had helped them with the census. No, I did what I had to do."

"I just thought maybe prison would have been enough to get him out of the way."

"Prison, my dear daughter," Caiaphas opined, "is the palace and throne of rebel leaders. No, I had no choice. He was preaching sedition, and the Romans would have killed him sooner or later. This way, I could at least show them that I wasn't passive about keeping order.

"And now, today, the same thing. One of his followers, a man named Peter, and some of his agitating friends are there before the Sanhedrin, and the Pharisees vote to free them. I can't accomplish anything when the Pharisees are always against me."

"Then act without them," Rabath said. "You're the high priest. Use your authority."

"I can only do that up to a point," he said. "I have to at least give the appearance of including them."

37

Rabath stood up. She stood straight and proud, as she always did. Even through the respectable concealment of her purple caftan, it was obvious that she had the finely developed figure of an active young woman, not one softened by indolence and overindulgence in food. "All right, enough of this dreary business," she said. "Mother and I have arranged a delightful dinner for you this evening. Come on, put a smile on your face, and let's go in."

Caiaphas looked at his daughter and felt the load on his shoulders lighten. He got up and accompanied her to the dinner.

CHAPTER V

Jacob, Caiphas' secretary, was a bright-faced young man with wide, brown eyes and an air of ingenuous philanthropy. He stopped at a shopping stall in a downtown bazaar, seeking to buy a leather pouch. He thought he might find one in this particular stall, since it contained only leather goods. He had come from Alexandria the year before to further his study of the Torah. His family connections had led him to Caiaphas, who had offered him a job as secretary. It had seemed an unexpected piece of good fortune, and he had accepted the offer eagerly.

The leather worker who greeted him was a young man from Tarsus, who introduced himself as Saul. As they eased comfortably into conversation, Saul revealed that he had come to Jerusalem to stay with his sister and her family. As Saul spoke, Jacob observed that Saul was short in stature but with strong, broad shoulders. He saw Saul's eyebrows, thick and luxuriant, covering his eyes in an unbroken line. Saul revealed that he had come to Jerusalem to study under Gamaliel. His heart's desire was to become a Pharisee sage. But Gamaliel, he said, had rejected him after a brief period of study, because Saul's knowledge of the Torah had not been advanced enough to warrant his studying at Gamaliel's level. Jacob empathized with him and said that his own knowledge of the Torah would also probably be considered deficient by Gamaliel but that Saul should not feel bad about that, since Gamaliel's interpretation of the Torah, being a Pharisee one, was erroneous anyway.

Somewhere in this conversation, Jacob got the idea that a young man of Saul's intelligence and physical strength might find better employment with the high priest than in a shopping stall selling wares. Caiaphas was in need of policemen to carry out his campaign against dissidents, and Saul might do very well as one of the high priest's officers.

Jacob arranged an interview for him, and two days later, Saul ascended the Temple stairs to meet his new friend again. They went into an inner room where they waited for Caiaphas. The waiting made Saul nervous, and he began to pace the room like a captured lion.

"Relax," Jacob said to him. "He'll like you. I know he will."

"I'm anxious to make a good impression. Do I look all right?" Saul asked.

"You look fine," Jacob said reassuringly. "Look, Saul, try to calm down. You want to give him the impression that you're self-assured, that you're fearless, that nothing can faze you. That's the kind of person you should show him. If Caiaphas sees that in you..."

"If I see what, Jacob?" came a voice from the doorway, and Caiaphas, the high priest of Israel, entered the room. If the salient feature of his daughter's face was the arcane shape of her eyes, then the salent feature of Caiaphas' was the sharp angularity of his nose. And, as a matter of balance, his nose was too large for his face. He wore a white robe and the headdress of a chief priest.

Jacob said, "Oh, your eminence, I didn't see you. This is the young man I told you about."

Caiaphas looked Saul over quickly with an ascending sweep of his eyes, as Romans do when they examine new slaves.

Saul, anxious to impress him, said, "Your eminence, I am honored, deeply honored."

Caiaphas smiled and said to Jacob, "Well, he's polite at any rate, isn't he?" Then to Saul, "So you want to work for us, do you?"

"Yes, very much," Saul answered.

"Do you have any idea what kind of work you'll be doing as a member of the Temple police force?"

"Yes, your eminence, I do. Jacob has told me. It means keeping order, arresting people, quelling riots and, sometimes, assisting in executions."

"And you don't have any hesitation about doing that kind of work?"

"Oh no, your eminence, not at all. I'd be pleased to serve in that capacity."

"A lot of people won't like you for the work you do. You know that, don't you?"

"That doesn't matter, your eminence. It's what God thinks of me that counts."

"That's true," Caiaphas said, feeling embarrassed by Saul's unexpected reference to the Almighty. "Jacob tells me you come from Tarsus."

"I do, your eminence. I come from Tarsus in the province of Cilicia."

"Yes, I know where it is. There are many Greeks in Tarsus, aren't there?"

"Yes, your eminence, there are."

"Many of whom have converted to Judaism. Isn't that so?"

"Yes, your eminence, that is so," Saul answered again.

"And you," Caiaphas asked, "were you born a Greek or a Jew?"

It was a question that Saul had hoped Caiaphas would not ask. "If a man embraces Judaism, is he not a Jew?" Saul replied.

"Yes, of course he is," Caiaphas answered, "but I was wondering — just out of curiosity, you understand — if you were born of Jewish parents."

"My parents were God-fearers," Saul confessed, and he wondered if he had lost the job.

"But you yourself are a Jew?" Caiaphas asked.

"I am, your eminence," he said, and he silently asked God to forgive him for not revealing the truth. He was afraid that if he told Caiaphas he was not a complete Jew, he might not get the job.

He saw a young woman with long black hair appear in the doorway. He almost gasped at the sight of her, so beautiful did she seem to him. She entered the room with what Saul thought were light, panther-like steps and walked up to Caiaphas.

"Ah, Rabath," Caiaphas said and then, turning to Saul, he said, "This is my daughter, Rabath."

Saul bowed his head and said, "I am honored, my lady."

Rabath gave the slightest nod of her head in response.

"Saul wants to join our Temple police force," Caiaphas said to her. "He comes from Tarsus, and he's living here with his sister."

Rabath listened perfunctorily and then said, "I hope you will find Jerusalem to your liking, Saul."

"I already have, my lady," he answered.

Then, with no more attention to him than that, she said to Caiaphas, "I'll see you later, father." And she left the room with that same animal-like grace with which she had entered it.

Saul realized that she had come in just to find out who the stranger was, and, having determined that, had left with no further interest. But for Saul, it was a moment not to be forgotten. Rabath had aroused his interest as no woman had for years. He remembered fleetingly the brief marriage he had had in the past and his lovely young wife who had died in her youth and his inability to become interested in another woman after that. But now, this daughter of the high priest had awakened something in him and had made him remember that he was a man and that it was natural for him to find a woman attractive.

Then, as if from a distance, he heard Caiaphas saying, "The job is yours," and he turned and saw the face of Jacob, smiling.

CHAPTER VI

Among the more militant of us Nazarenes was Stephen. Unlike Jesus' brother, James, who could wait for Jesus' return without agitating against the high priest and the Romans, Stephen was aggressive. He spoke forcefully about the new order of government that would exist when Jesus returned. And he preached not only to Jews but to Gentiles, that being something that James could not understand, since Jesus had ordered his disciples to limit their preaching to Jews.

We had a diversity of people among us, but two main divisions actually existed. On the one hand, there were those who were Judaean and Galilean in their thinking, and on the other, there were those who were more Greek. The Greek thinkers were more oriented towards Gentile ways: they dressed more like Greeks and even spoke the Greek language. Stephen was one of their advocates, and when a complaint once was lodged about the widows of the Greek-oriented people not receiving their fair share of the food that was distributed to the widows of our group, Stephen and six others were chosen to correct and oversee the problem, and they did so to the satisfaction of all.

As I have said, he was more aggressive than most, and for that reason, Caiaphas wanted him silenced. Of course, Caiaphas would have eliminated all Nazarenes if he could have, but even a high priest needs an ostensible reason for doing things. For example, while Caiaphas disliked James, especially since so many of the lower priests had flocked to him, he could not bring any charges of sedition against him and certainly none of blasphemy, since James was so punctilious in his attention to his religious duties as a Jew. But Stephen was another matter: Stephen spoke against the chief priests and said that they would be destroyed by Jesus. Stephen's activities were more militant and could be considered seditious, and Caiaphas could legally do things against him that he could not do against James.

So he had his police pursue Stephen. And when they caught him, Caiaphas and an ad hoc group of Sadducees ordered his execution. They did this on religious grounds, although the real reason was to protect themselves, and they did it without the formal legal procedure that such an order required. They brought false witnesses against him, whom they themselves had instigated and who claimed that he was against the Temple and the Torah, both of which he would destroy or change. All that was false, of course. How could it have been otherwise? James, under whose leadership Stephen pursued his activities, was said to be "strong for the Torah." Nazarenes, the people of whom Stephen was a part, were said to be "the Zealots of the Torah." And Stephen himself, before he was finished with what he had to say, would rebuke his executioners for not following the Torah, which the angels had delivered to them. So these statements against Stephen were entirely false and were based on the statements of liars. Stephen, like James and Peter and all the Nazarenes, was a man who was strong for the Torah.

Years later, when Saul would speak of this, he would say that he himself had consented to Stephen's death, which implied that either there had been a vote that included policemen or else that the policemen had been acting under Saul's orders and that they had needed his consent to perform the execution. If there had been a vote — I was never sure about this one way or the other — then I should point out that the Sanhedrin could not have been involved, because Saul was not a member of that body and would not have been permitted to vote in it. (It was only if the Sanhedrin had *not* been involved that Saul could have cast a vote.) And if the situation was that there had been no vote at all and that this was an execution that needed Saul's consent (it went beyond mere approval, you see, for he actually gave his consent), then again the Sanhedrin could not have been the means by which Stephen's death occurred, for Saul's consent was not necessary in order to implement the decisions of the Sanhedrin. I mention this because of what was later said about how this affair took place.

Stephen defied his executioners in spite of his helplessness and spoke out bravely against them. As I have said, he adhered to the Torah and, in spite of the threat of death that hung over him, he excoriated his captors for breaking it. "You who received the law as delivered by angels," he said, "and did not keep it." And he castigated them too for the role that they had played in effecting the death of Jesus. But that made no difference to them. They took him outside the city in order to stone him. The reason they did not do it inside the city was that the high priest, as had happened in the past, feared an uprising of the Jews if it was done in more visible surroundings, so much did the Jewish people favor our group. So they took him to an isolated place where the people would not see. Saul was there at the execution, and though he did not throw any of the stones, he guarded the outer garments of those who did, those people having removed those garments in order to make their work easier.

Saul watched, however, as he saw Stephen die. He saw the first stone reach its goal on the side of Stephen's head, and he saw Stephen, still standing with dignity, stagger under its impact. The next one hit Stephen in the chest, which only made Stephen thrust out his chest farther. As other stones struck him in other parts of his body, he continued to stand. He did not try to dodge the stones or turn his side to them or try to protect his head with his hands. Some of them missed him anyway, but soon too many of them found their mark. When one of them struck him in the forehead, he fell involuntarily to his knees. Then Saul saw the blood pouring down his face. If Stephen had let himself fall to the ground at this point, his executioners would have thrown a few more stones and then, if there were no more signs of life, would have considered him dead and left. Some people survived stoning in that way. But Stephen would not attempt such a ploy. He was too proud a man for that. He sat up on his knees for as long as he could and never once did he raise an arm to protect himself. Too many stones soon reached his head, and the blood began to flow in streams down his face. Another stone to the side of his head knocked him to the ground. He lay there senseless, his body slumped forward and his face immersed in blood. They formed a closer circle around him and threw a few more stones. Then, when they were certain that he was dead, they took back their coats from Saul, put them on and walked towards the city together. Saul lingered behind a short time, feeling a compulsion to stand there alone. He looked at Stephen's body and did not know why he was doing it. Then he walked away, catching up with his friends, and, as if wanting to ignore or forget what they had done, talked with them about other things.

The death of Stephen haunted him. Though he told himself repeatedly that the execution had been justified because the man had been an outright agitator, the dignity of Stephen and the conviction with which he had spoken before his death made Saul wonder about what it was that sustained such intransigence. He began to wonder if the Nazarenes knew something that he didn't. He was a Sadducee now. He worked for Caiaphas. Gamaliel and the Pharisees were behind him. But this particular variety of Pharisee called Nazarene, though it was his duty to suppress and imprison them, had held a fascination for him from the time that he had first heard about them from Machaiah. Now, however, they actually haunted him because of the memory of Stephen.

Even after Stephen was killed, Caiaphas did not stop. Having disposed of Stephen, he now set out to dispose of Stephen's followers, for, as I have said, they were the more militant branch of our movement.

Stephen's followers dispersed after his death, however, and sought refuge where they could. One of the places they went was the neighboring Arab country of Nabataea and its principal city, Damascus. The king of that place was Aretus of Petra, and he welcomed dissidents from all over the Roman Empire, as long as they submitted themselves to the authority of his government. But of all the dissidents who came, he welcomed those from Israel the most. To him, whether they came from Galilee or Judaea, they were all one and the same people, fleeing from the same despicable rulers. Herod Antipas, the tetrarch of Galilee and Perea, the man who was the king of the Jews, had grossly insulted him. That decadent monarch had been married to his daughter and had turned her away, divorced her, so that he could marry that opportunistic harlot, Herodias — she whose daughter was even more salacious than her mother, doing her half-naked lascivious dance in exchange for the head of that prophet named John the Baptizer. And the chief priests, those hypocritical lackeys of the Romans, were cast from the same mold as their king. Aretus felt that anything he could do to help the enemies of those people, he would do. If the Nazarenes intended to set up a new kingdom, that was fine with him. Nothing would give him more pleasure than to see Herod Antipas deposed. Thus, when Stephen's followers fled from Caiaphas' police, Aretus welcomed them into his country. Most of them settled in Damascus, and a sort of Nazarene community in exile, complete with synagogues, was formed in that city. As long as the refugees respected the authority of Aretus and his officials, they were welcome to stay.

Nazarenes, of course, were not the only Jews who lived in Damascus; other Jews lived there too. And those other Jews and the Nazarenes lived together as one people. The other Jews held the Nazarenes in high regard. One of the Nazarenes they esteemed most was a man named Ananias. He was renowned for his piety and adherence to the Torah, and his opinions were listened to with respect.

Caiaphas knew all this, and he wanted to better relations with Aretus, to surmount the ill will that Antipas had created. Then maybe Aretus would send him those Nazarenes who were hiding in Damascus. So he sent his daughter, Rabath, to perform the task of mending hurt feelings. She was to meet Aretus and to meet his daughter and to try to befriend them both. Caiaphas thought that his beautiful daughter might be a more effective emissary in a situation like this than any more conventional diplomat. Certainly a woman-to-woman commiseration with Aretus' daughter might be just the thing that was needed. And while she was there, she might also find out something about the fugitive Nazarenes.

So Rabath went and spent time in Damascus. When she returned, Caiaphas threw a party in her honor. It was at that party that Saul saw her again.

He came to the party and met Jacob, who pushed a cup of wine into his hand and proposed a toast to Caiaphas. Musicians on an elevated dais were playing, and people in the center of the room were dancing in a large circle. In the center of that circle was Rabath, dancing abandonedly, her long, dark hair flying in response to the turnings of her head as if her hair was being blown by the wind, her arms weaving with the sinuosity of waves and the jewelry on her ankles jangling barbarically with the light, swift movements of her feet. Though she was wearing a long dress, her body twisted and undulated in movements that bordered on the lascivious. Yet she seemed always to hold back, so that the propriety expected of a high priest's daughter was never quite transgressed but only challenged.

At the end of the dance, she walked to Jacob. She was breathing heavily, and her eyes still had the wild look of a woman who had seen her kinship with the untamed and had not yet pulled back from the brink.

"So, Jacob," she asked breathlessly, "has my dancing improved since I returned from Damascus?"

"Immeasurably, my dear Rabath,"Jacob replied. "You dance as I've never seen you dance before."

"So you see what my trip to Damascus has done for me," she said.

"Is this how they dance in Damascus?" he asked.

"Slave women dance like that for their masters. Shall I dance that way for you, Jacob?"

He felt too embarrassed to answer, so he changed the subject by saying, "You remember Saul, don't you?"

Rabath squinted, trying to recollect. "Are you the former chariot racer?" she asked.

"No, my lady," Saul answered. "I'm one of your father's policemen. I come from Tarsus."

"Oh, yes," she said. "You're the one who lives here with his sister."

"Yes, my lady. You do remember," he said.

Jacob interjected with, "How was your stay in Damascus, Rabath?"

"Quite good, I would say, Jacob. I was treated exceedingly well."

"Did you improve relations with King Aretus?" he asked.

"Not completely," she answered, "but he did seem pleased with my visit. I was treated very well by him. I was regaled with food and wine, and he took great pains to see that the food met our Jewish standards; I was given a tour of the city; and I even had a few men propose marriage to me."

"Marriage! How wonderful, Rabath. Did you accept any?"

"Alas, no, Jacob," she said teasingly. "They were all wealthy merchants, and I, you see, prefer more scholarly men."

"Really?" he said, knowing she was only dallying with him.

"Yes, scribes and secretaries, men of that sort, are irresistible to me."

Jacob cleared his throat and changed the subject. "Did you get the chance to do any reconnaissance for your father while you were there?"

"You mean for Nazarenes?" she asked.

"Yes, for Nazarenes."

"Yes, Jacob, I played the part of the spy very well. I learned all about their secret hiding places — which really are not so secret, since Aretus lets them live there openly — and I learned the names of their leaders and who their members are. There's a man named Peter. He's one of their leaders here in Jerusalem, and he travels to Damascus from time to time."

"We all know him," Saul interjected. "He was brought up for trial once, and the Pharisees set him free."

"Well, apparently, he's important to them," Rabath said. "And there's another one, a man named Ananias, and all the Jews out there, whether they're Nazarenes or not, hold him in high esteem."

"Are you telling us that all the Jews out there respect the Nazarenes the same as they do here?" Jacob asked.

"Unfortunately, yes, Jacob," she answered. "My father shouldn't expect any help from them if he's planning to capture Nazarenes in Damascus. The only Jews in Damascus who might help us are Sadducees, and they're few in number, I'm afraid."

Caiaphas and Annas entered the room, and Rabath went to greet them like the dutiful daughter and granddaughter that she was.

Jacob turned to Saul. "What do you think of her?" he asked.

"Magnificent," Saul said. "She's like no other woman alive."

"Well, she *is* beautiful," Jacob said, "but I think she's too much for any man to handle."

"Like a wild wind," Saul said.

"Yes," Jacob said, "and, like the wind, unmanageable."

"And yet, if a man tried," Saul said, "wouldn't the prize be worth the effort?"

"At the risk of losing my job?" Jacob asked and then answered his own question by saying, "No! Dealing with an unpredictable wife is bad enough; losing my income because of it is too high a price to pay."

"And yet," Saul said, "*I* would pay the price. To me, the prize would be worth the risk."

Jacob was totally surprised by this, and after a moment's silence to absorb the meaning of it, he said, "Saul, I do believe you're smitten. The wild charms of our high priest's daughter have ignited a fire in you."

Saul was embarrassed that his secret desire had been so carelessly revealed. "Oh no," he protested, trying to deny the meaning of what he had said, "I was just speaking hypothetically, in a general way."

Jacob said, "In a general way? Oh, I see. Well, be that as it may, I would advise caution before I would let that general way become a more specific way. Just in case you might find yourself thinking more specifically in the future, I mean. Our high priest has his own ideas for his daughter, her streak of independence notwithstanding, and I would think twice before I would do anything that might thwart those ideas."

"Yes, of course, you're right," Saul said. "But, all the same, if it were the right man, might he not convince them both?"

"Perhaps," Jacob said. "But neither you nor I are the *right man.* So do yourself a favor, and don't waste your time pining for something that can never be. We are what we are, and she is what she is, and not all the desire in the world can change that. Remember what I say."

"Yes, I'll remember it," Saul said. "Don't look so concerned, Jacob. I'll remember it. I will."

CHAPTER VII

It was because Saul had proved himself to be the most effective police officer in Caiaphas' police force that Caiaphas considered him the right man for the job. Saul had proved himself through the hounding, beating, arresting and imprisoning of political troublemakers, many of whom had been Nazarenes. But not all Nazarenes had been subject to such treatment. The quiescent ones, the socially obedient ones, had been left alone. For even the high priest could not arrest people at random: there had to be a legitimate justification for that. And it was precisely because of that restriction, the need for a legitimate reason to arrest someone, that Caiaphas had not been able to touch our revered leader, James, who was revered not only by us but by all the Jews of our nation — except for the Sadducees, of course. That was why Caiaphas, unable to get James legally, attempted to have him assassinated. If you should wonder why there was such hostility towards James — after all, he was in the Temple praying every day, and he was permitted into the innermost sanctuary where only the holiest people, such as priests, could go — the reason was not religious. James was too pious, too obedient to the Torah for that. The reason was political — and, one might even say, personal. James was not only the leader of a group that promised there would be a new kingdom in Israel, he was the man around whom the lower priests flocked as they increasingly extended their Pharisee beliefs into the Nazarene movement.

Saul had not been part of the assassination attempt, however. The men Caiaphas had assigned to do that job had failed in their mission, and Caiaphas had regretted not having given Saul the assignment, since Saul had had an exemplary record of success. The men whom Caiaphas *had* sent had followed James to a woman's house and had seen him enter, but when they themselves had entered, they had found him gone. Someone must have warned him, they felt. And to Caiaphas, the single act that he thought could have stopped the rebellious Nazarene movement dead in its tracks had been foiled, and the leader of the movement would now be on his guard. Caiaphas needed a compensatory success to assuage his feelings. So he turned his eyes to Damascus. The Nazarenes *there* were legitimate targets, since they, unlike James, had shown themselves to be militant, many of them having been followers of Stephen. If a capable man could bring some of them out, Caiaphas could bring them to trial and could get the Romans to execute them with legitimate reasons under the law. And since Saul previously had expressed to Caiaphas his own interest in pursuing Stephen's followers there, Saul appeared to be the best man for the job.

Consequently, Caiaphas and Jacob met with Saul to discuss the assignment. It was an assignment that needed courage, tact, cunning and, above all, loyalty. And Saul was the man who could do it. He was the man who could go into King Aretus' country and get the fugitives out and bring them back for trial. And he was the man who, if arrested by Aretus for violating Nabataean sovereignty, would deny any involvement with Caiaphas in spite of anything that Aretus might do to him.

"If you were to be caught," Caiaphas said, "I would have to deny that you were acting on my authority; I would have to say that you were acting on your own. You do understand that, don't you?"

"Of course," Saul said. "I understand it completely."

"Then choose the men you want to go with you," Caiaphas said. "I'll give you letters to some of our Sadducee friends in Damascus. Rabath will give you details of the information she has gathered. And may God be with you, Saul."

"And with you, Caiaphas," Saul answered.

Caiaphas left then, and Jacob and Saul were alone. Now Saul, because he was going on a dangerous mission, confessed to Jacob the secret that had been burning within him from the day he first met Rabath. He was in love with the daughter of the high priest. No denials now, no claims of speaking in generalities. He was in love with Rabath, as he had loved nothing else in his life. And so overwhelming and desperate was that love that no mention of its hopelessness could prevail over Saul's determination to win her.

Jacob looked at his friend. He observed that Saul was a short, broad-shouldered man with bandied legs and thinning hair. He saw the hooked nose and the bushy eyebrows that swept without separation across the tops of his friend's small eyes. But he also saw the glowing intensity in those eyes, as if some raging fire inside his friend's body was burning but not consuming it and showing itself through those tiny apertures to the agitated soul within. And there was that rumor among the Temple guards that Saul, for all his vigor and physical strength, was afflicted with epilepsy, something that Jacob had never seen in him and which may or may not have been true but which Rabath must surely have heard about and taken as a possibility. All this hardly cut a handsome figure to compensate a young woman for the lack of wealth and position that her father would demand of a prospective son-in-law. Unquestionably, the situation was hopeless.

That hopelessness became even more apparent when Saul revealed to Jacob that he was not a full-fledged Jew. A Jew in spirit, yes; a God-fearer who had taken Jewish vows and recited Jewish prayers and eaten Jewish food but who had never taken the final step of circumcision that would have made him irrevocably a member of the people he so admired. So Jacob, with compassion for his friend, and notwithstanding the improbability of Saul ever winning Rabath as his own, said to him, "Saul, I think her father already has other plans for her, but with God's help, all things are possible. There's no chance at all, though, if you're not a Jew. You must become a Jew in every sense of the word. That much you must do, or you'll have no chance at all." So Saul, out of his love for Rabath, submitted himself to Jacob for the ritual act, and Jacob secretly performed the ceremony, catching the severed foreskin in the silver bowl, saying the sacred prayer of dedication and binding up the wound of his friend.

A short time later, Saul met with Rabath in a garden in her father's house. It was a warm evening, and a light breeze blew through the trees and played with Rabath's long black hair as she sat next to him on a bench. She gave him the names of Nazarenes and maps and locations of their leaders' homes. And all the time, Saul absorbed the sight of her and adored her beauty.

"I hope the maps will ensure your success," Rabath said in a very businesslike way.

"They will certainly make my work easier," Saul said.

"We're counting on you, Saul. My father thinks that you can do it if anyone can."

"I'll do my best, Rabath, for you as much as for him."

"For me?" she said, laughing. "Why for me? Do you think I want this as much as my father does?"

"Yes, I do," he said.

"And if I do," she said teasingly, "are you as anxious to please me as you are to please him?"

"Yes," he answered simply, averting his eyes as he did.

"Really? I'm flattered. May I ask why?"

"Don't you know?" he said. "Can't you guess the reason?"

"No, I can't. Tell me."

But he did not answer. So she said to him again, "Tell me!" But still he did not answer. So now she said, "Will you please stop sitting there like a stone statue and tell me why you want to please me as much as you do my father?"

He paused before saying it, so irretrievable would be the words, once spoken. And then he said, "Because I love you."

And now it was Rabath who could not speak. She had to assess the implications of this unexpected development and decide how to respond. She did not want to jeopardize Saul's loyalty to her father, but she had to neutralize this situation.

"I see," she said. "Well, Saul, I hardly know what to say. I am flattered, of course, but I had no idea. I had no suspicion you felt that way."

"Since the first day I met you," he said. "I haven't been able to think of anyone but you since then. Everything I've been doing, I've been doing to impress you."

"I'm touched by your affection, Saul. I'm sure you must know that. Any woman would be. I hope that — we can become friends and that my respect for you can be returned in kind."

"I'm not speaking of respect, Rabath; I'm speaking of love," he said.

Rabath tried to be tactful. "Yes, but after all, you hardly know me. What you call love is only a superficial attraction, a mere fascination, as one might have for a bauble that one sees for the first time."

"No, this is not superficial," Saul said. "What I feel for you is very deep. When I first saw you, I knew that you had touched something deep in my soul. I knew that I loved you and that I always would."

"Now, Saul, be reasonable," she said. "You can't be touched in your soul by someone you've just seen and have hardly spoken to."

"And yet, I was," he said.

"But it's just a physical attraction. Believe me, if you would get to know me, all that would be gone. I'm self-willed, I'm unpredictable and I'm very undependable when it comes to romantic relationships. Believe me, I'm speaking the truth."

"And yet, I love you," he said.

She was utterly frustrated. "Look, you go to Damascus, and do a good job for my father. When you come back, he'll reward you handsomely. Believe me, I know him, he will. And with the money you receive from him — and maybe even a promotion of some sort — you'll be able to interest all kinds of girls in yourself. And you'll see, when they're young and pretty, how easy it will be to fall in love with one of them."

"Rabath," he said, "the only reward I would ask of your father, the only reward I would ask of God, is to grant me you as my wife."

"As your wife!" she ejaculated.

"Yes, Rabath, as my wife," he said.

"This is really going too far," she said. "In the first place, you don't go around asking a girl to marry you. You ask her father first."

"I intend to," he said.

"Well, if you do, I can tell you what he'll say. He'll say 'no.' And I'll tell you why. He has plans for me to marry one of his wealthy landowner friends."

"Who?" Saul asked.

"I don't know who. I don't even know if he has the man picked out yet. I just know that he intends for one of those men to be my husband."

"I see," Saul said. "I didn't think that one of them would be my rival. At one time, I thought that Jacob might be, but now I know that that's not so."

"Jacob?" she said. "Why Jacob?"

"Because of what you said to him at the party, that you preferred scribes over merchants."

"That? But I was just joking. I was teasing him just for fun. I wasn't serious. I thought that would have been obvious to anyone. It was to Jacob. He knew he couldn't have me even if he wanted me."

"And why is that, Rabath?"

"Because of the difference in our positions, that's why. We're too far apart. Can't you understand that?"

"Does that mean that you and I are too far apart, Rabath?"

"Oh, what am I going to do with you? Yes, if you must know! I'm the daughter of the high priest, and you..." She stopped herself before saying the rest.

"And I am merely a policeman. A man who loves God, serves his high priest and has no wealth."

"You're putting me into an awkward position. Are you aware of that?"

"I'm sorry, Rabath, but I love you too deeply not to try to win you. And as for my position, I may not always be a policeman. I feel a burning desire within me to do more with my life. And I will. Somehow I will. And when I do, you'll look at me differently than you do now. You'll see, Rabath."

"In all likelihood, I'll be married by then," she said.

"I ask you to give me a chance, Rabath, a chance to show you what I can do. Can't you give me a little more time to prove how much I love you?"

"And what of me, Saul? Have you stopped long enough to ask yourself if *I* love *you*? Are *my* feelings of no importance in all this?"

"Oh, Rabath, of course they are. They're the most important thing in the world to me. How could I love you and not care about your feelings? What is all this burning desire within me to do more with my life if not to impress you, if not to affect your feelings in such a way as to make you love me in return?"

"And if you do whatever it is you may do you achieve this higher position that you think you *can* achieve, and if after having done that, you find that I still don't love you, what will you do then? If, after all the trouble you've gone to, you find that you still have not touched my heart, what then, Saul of Tarsus? Will you leave me alone and seek another, or will you persist in harassing me with your endless declarations of love until I cry out for you to leave me alone?"

"I don't know, Rabath," he answered. "I know that I'll never stop loving you. I thought that, in time, with a better position, the persistence and depth of my love would affect you. I thought that my love for you would make you love me in return."

"But if I'm not attracted to you as you are to me, what then? If you were to become — the king of Nabataea, and if I did not find you attractive, and if I begged my father not to arrange a marriage with you, what then? Wouldn't you set me aside in your mind and wisely go off to seek another? Wouldn't that be the sensible thing for a man to do?"

"Not if the man loved you as I do, Rabath. If I were that king, and if I loved you as I do now, I would lavish you with gifts, I would plead for an audience with you. And if I were granted one, I would convince you of how purely and passionately I love you."

"Ah, there you have it! Passionately! Passion! That's what it's all about. Passion! You yourself have said it. You feel passion for me. You lust after me, and that's what it's really all about. Don't mix up purity with it. It's lust, pure and simple, and you can just as easily lust after another as you can after me."

"But I would give my life for you. Don't you understand that?"

"I don't want you to give your life for me. Don't *you* understand *that!*"

"I'll die if I don't win you!" he shouted.

"Then die if you must!" she shouted back. "But leave me alone. I don't love you, and I'm not attracted to you. And your being the king of Persia isn't going to change that. Don't you understand? I don't want you! Can't you get that through your head?"

"Am I ugly or something?" he asked.

And for just a moment, she paused and then said, "Yes, you're ugly! Your face is ugly, your body is ugly and the work you do is ugly."

"My work?"

"Yes, your work! You're my father's henchman, his trash collector. You do the work he wouldn't soil his hands with. You deal with people he wouldn't even touch."

"So that's what you think of me?" he said, abruptly subdued.

"Yes, that's what I think of you."

He tried hard to keep some measure of dignity, so shaken was he by her words. "Very well. Very well then. I go to do your father's dirty work, his trash collecting, as you put it. But do remember this, Rabath: I serve God first, not your father. I serve your father because he leads us in our service to God. If I am a henchman and a trash collector, as you say, then I am God's henchman and God's trash collector first, not your father's. And if ever I see that your father ceases to be God's instrument here on earth, then I will cease to be your father's instrument." And now his voice softened. "It's hard to accept that I don't even have a chance with you, Rabath. It's a shame that you can't see beyond the surface of my body to the soul inside. You might see more beauty there than you realize." He stood up and said, "Farewell, Rabath."

He walked away from her, but before he turned the corner of a bush to disappear from her view, she called to him. "Saul," she said, and he turned to face her, "it's a shame you can't see beyond the surface of *me*. What you see might not look so beautiful."

"I already have, Rabath," he said, "and still I love you."

He turned the corner of the bush, and he was gone. Rabath sat there, not stirring from the bench. The night air blew cool across her face and hair, and she sat immobile, apparently deep in thought. Then she heard a voice.

"Not wise, Rabath, not wise." It was the voice of Jacob. She could make out his silhouette emerging from the dense foliage. "You did well until you lost your temper and called him names."

"Jacob!" she exclaimed. "What are *you* doing here?"

"I was in the garden. I overheard your conversation," he said.

"You overheard? You mean you eavesdropped. You sneak!"

"Easy, Rabath," he said. "You've done enough name-calling for one day. I *overheard* your conversation. Your father is sending a man on a delicate mission into a foreign country, a mission in which he must take possession of people illegally. That means he has to do it without the authorities of that other country being aware of what he's doing. If he's caught, he must not reveal that he's your father's emissary. All *that* requires a keen mind — cleverness, tact, determination and, above all, loyalty. All this he does for your father, as long as he believes that your father represents the wishes of God. Now, into such a precarious mind, you instill disharmony. You make him doubt his own worth. Your rejection of him, my dear Rabath, should have been done *after* Damascus, not before."

"Would you have had me lie to him then?" she asked.

"Yes, I would have had you lie to him. I would have had you deceive him, lead him on, give him hope, entice him, allure him, tantalize him — anything to help the success of his enterprise, of your father's enterprise. Instead, like the self-willed, spoiled child that you are, you insult him. What stupidity! With what kind of heart do you think he goes to Damascus now?"

She sighed. "With a heavy one, I suppose."

"Yes, with a heavy one for certain, Rabath."

"I couldn't help it, Jacob. He seems so unrefined. And only a ruffian would do the work he does. How could he have presumed to think of me as his wife?"

"Perhaps because he really does love you and because he's one of those men who believes that love conquers all. He's a man of deep feelings and convictions, Rabath. He's not the shallow boor you make him out to be. And he has a determination about everything he does. I believe you've sent him to Damascus with a broken heart."

"Do you think it will make him fail?" she asked.

"We'll see," he answered. "We'll see what Damascus brings?"

CHAPTER VIII

Saul took four other policemen to Damascus with him. They dressed like ordinary wayfarers and made the journey on foot. There were times when the road was crowded with people, some of them traveling with caravans carrying goods between Damascus and Jerusalem. At other times, there were only the five of them, walking together in a cluster or else separating themselves so that they looked as if they were strangers.

It was during one of those times when they were partially separated that something happened to Saul that was to change the entire course of his life. I don't know if his despair or his resentment or whatever it was he was feeling after that last encounter with Rabath was a factor, but there is no doubt that he was in a state of agitation and that she was on his mind as he advanced along the road. He had become a Jew for her, and she had rejected him.

They had almost reached Damascus, and he was straggling behind the others when a sudden radiant light appeared before his eyes, a light so brilliant that everything else was extinguished from his sight. It was so intense that it completely overwhelmed him, and he fell to the ground because of it. He closed his eyes to escape from the light, but that didn't help. Even with his eyes closed, the light persisted. It was as if the light was something inside his mind rather than something outside himself that could be escaped through darkness.

And then, from within the light, he heard a voice. It was the voice of a man, and it said to him, "Saul, Saul, why do you persecute me?" And with fear in his heart, he answered it and said, "Tell me, lord, who are you?" He called it "lord" because he could not imagine it being anything other than an angel — or God Himself — for what else could speak and radiate out of nothing as this did? And the voice answered him and said, "I am Jesus, whom you are persecuting. It is hard for you to kick against the pricks."

Saul was trembling with fear now, and he said, "Lord, what do you want me to do?"

And the voice said, "Get up and go into the city, and you will be told what you have to do."

Then the light disappeared, but Saul did not open his eyes immediately. He kept them closed as he rose from the ground and stood up. Then he opened them, and what he saw was only blackness, and he knew then that he had been blinded.

In his need to have the reality of his experience confirmed by others, he asked each of the other men if they had seen anything or heard anything. None of them had seen the light, but each of them had, indeed, *heard* something. The two men who had been nearest to Saul said that it had been the voice of a man, although they told their other companions later that they could not be sure if it was Saul's voice or someone else's voice that they had heard; the two who had been farthest from him said that, while they could not be sure, the sound that they had heard could have been the sound of a man's voice.

They entered Damascus, and the other policemen led Saul to the house of a man named Judas, who was a Sadducee. The house was located on a street named Straight, and it was the place where it had been arranged they should stay while they were in the city. Saul was laid on a bed, and he stayed there for three days in a state of utter despondency, unable to eat or drink anything, so unnerved was he by what had happened. After those three days, at an hour when Judas happened not to be at home, there was a knock at the door, and a man named Ananias asked to be admitted. They let him in. He said that he was looking for someone named Saul of Tarsus. The other men were suspicious. They were in Damascus on an illegal mission, and they had to be careful about every person who saw them.

When the first policeman asked Ananias why he was seeking Saul, Ananias said it was because he had been informed that Saul needed help.

"By whom?" the first policeman asked.

"I have been informed," was all he would say. "I have been informed that this Saul has been blinded and that he needs my help."

"Are you a physician?" the first policeman asked.

"Not by training," Ananias said. "But I do heal people. I have a way that helps sometimes."

The second policeman spoke: "Even the blind?" he said.

"Even the blind," Ananias answered.

"What do you think?" the second policemen asked the others.

"Are you a Jew?" the third policeman asked.

"Yes, I'm a Jew," Ananias answered.

The policemen looked at each other, unsure of whether to trust the stranger.

Then the fourth policeman spoke and said, "What harm can he do?"

The first policeman echoed that. "That's right. As long as *we're* here, no harm can come to Saul."

So they led Ananias into the room where Saul lay, and Ananias began to question him. Saul told him about the blinding light and about the things the voice had said and about whose voice it was. The other policemen confirmed having heard the voice, some saying that they had heard some of the words and others saying that they had heard a sound that could have been a voice but that they had not been able to make out any words.

Ananias sat down on a stool next to the bed and said, "Saul, can we be alone? There are things I must say to you that should only be between us."

"I suppose so, if you think it's necessary," Saul said.

But the first policeman, listening to the conversation, said, "Saul, don't be a fool. We don't know anything about this man. How do we know he won't harm you the moment we leave?"

"Oh, sirs, I assure you, I'm a man of peace," Ananias said. "And I'm unarmed. Please, search me, I beg of you."

So they searched Ananias, feeling the outside and inside of his robe and garments. When they found no weapons, they were reluctantly satisfied.

"All right," the first policeman said. "But we'll be right outside the door, Saul. If you need us, just shout. We'll hear you."

They went out, and Saul was left alone in the room with Ananias.

"Now, Saul of Tarsus, let me tell you who I am," Ananias said. "I'm a member of the Nazarene sect, a follower of Jesus of Nazareth. And I'm well aware of what you've done to our people. I'm well aware that you've persecuted them even to the point of death sometimes. And yet, what you've just told me convinces me that Jesus has come to you. If I can bring back your sight through him, will you then be convinced that he is the Messiah, the Chosen One, the leader who will return to free us from the Roman yoke and restore God's kingdom to Israel?"

"Ananias," Saul said, "if Jesus can take my sight, as I know he has, and then restore it to me again, how can I think anything else of him? Can you really bring back my sight through him?"

"Jesus healed people," Ananias said, "and before he left, he told his disciples that all the things that he had done, they would be able to do. And so, I learned from them. And someday, if you wish, you can learn from me. But for now, you must do as I tell you. If you believe, if you believe all the things I tell you, you will be healed. I'm going to touch your eyes, Saul." He placed his fingers on Saul's eyelids and closed them. Without removing his fingers, he prayed: "Oh, Jesus, healer of men's bodies, hear my prayer. This man, who has heard your voice and seen the light of your glory, asks for the return of his sight. Let his eyes be opened to the light of the world, as his heart is now opening to you. Let your spirit embrace him, let your love pervade him, let your power restore him."

He turned to Saul. "Do you believe, Saul of Tarsus, that Jesus of Nazareth can heal you?"

"Yes, I do, " Saul answered.

"And if the use of your eyes is returned to you, will you acknowledge Jesus as the Messiah?"

"Yes, I will. I swear it," Saul said.

"Then say the words, Saul of Tarsus. Say that you acknowledge Jesus as the Messiah."

"I acknowledge Jesus as the Messiah," Saul said.

Ananias removed his hand from Saul's eyes. "Now open your eyes, Saul of Tarsus — and see."

Saul opened his eyes and, through the unaccustomed brightness, made out the kindly, bearded face of Ananias. "I can see," he said. "Oh, God be praised, I can see." He began to cry, and his tears were tears of joy. Then he closed his eyes and said, "Oh, God, how can I thank you?" He fell to his knees at the side of the bed and bent his head in prayer. "What words can I find to express my awe at your greatness, that you can dazzle me into blindness through your anointed one and then restore my sight again? Oh, God, how could I have persecuted his followers? How could I have persecuted the followers of your anointed? Thank you, God, thank you." Then he opened his eyes and saw Ananias kneeling in prayer beside him. "And you, Ananias, thank you too."

"No, my friend, do not thank me," Ananias said. "It is not I who has healed you but the power of God. Your belief is what has healed you."

Then he told Saul that he would baptize him, and he explained that that was the symbolic washing away of sin through repentance, something that was done by all Nazarenes and what John the Baptizer had done for Jesus. They went to the mikvah pool, and Ananias washed Saul with the water, and Saul repented his sins. Then he told Saul that, under the circumstances, he thought it would be best if he came to his house to stay for a while. Ultimately, he wanted Saul to meet Jesus' brother, James, and Jesus' first disciple, Peter, in Jerusalem.

Now they considered the men outside. "We've been sent here to search for Nazarenes," Saul said, "and maybe even find Peter. I don't know how my friends will respond to all of this. They don't know you're a Nazarene. Why tell them?"

"But we're safe here, Saul," Ananias said. "This is not Jerusalem; we're in Damascus. King Aretus rules this country, and his governor rules this city. They give us sanctuary. It's your friends who are in danger. If the governor were to learn that a band of abductors has come into his city, he would not take kindly to it. He would have them arrested immediately. And that includes you, since he would think that you're still one of them. You need have no fear of your friends retaliating against you. We would report them to the police if they did. And we'd find a way to hide you at the same time. I think we should make their position clear to them when we tell them about you."

"Very well," Saul said. "Call them in. I'll tell them in here."

Ananias went to the policemen and announced that Saul was healed and that he could see again. They rushed past him and crowded around the bed where Saul sat blinking at them with a smiling face. One of them, to satisfy himself that Saul really could see again, held up some fingers and asked Saul to say how many he saw. Another turned to Ananias and said, "You're amazing. And yet you say that you're not a physician."

"That's right," Ananias said, "I'm not."

"Are you a sorcerer then?" the man asked.

"No, I'm not that either."

"Then how do you do it?"

"I'm a man of God."

"As all of us are. Yet *we* can't do such things."

"But I can."

"Do you have some natural power to heal?"

"If a man believes strongly enough," Ananias said, "and if God grants him the power, it can be done."

"Ha! Do you expect us to believe that?"

"Saul was blind, was he not? Now he can see, can he not?"

Another of the policemen spoke up: "All right, let me put you to the test. For the last two days, I've had a pain in my tooth. Make it go away."

"I can't," Ananias said.

"Why not?" the man protested. "If you can cure Saul's blindness, why can't you cure my toothache?"

"Because you don't believe," Ananias said.

"Believe? Believe what?"

"That Jesus of Nazareth is the Messiah."

There was a moment of stunned silence and then another policeman shouted, "He's a Nazarene!"

They murmured among themselves as the realization of this occurred to them. The first policeman, who had more or less become the leader of the group during Saul's incapacitation, said to Ananias, "Is this true? Is that what you are?"

"Yes, that's what I am," Ananias said.

"Do you know who we are?" the policemen asked.

"I do," Ananias answered.

"Then you know that we've come here to take people like you back to Jerusalem with us."

"I know that too," Ananias said.

"And I suppose it would be futile for us to tell you to take us to the others so that you can avoid the bodily harm we'll inflict on you if you don't?"

"You know that that's true," Ananias said. "I'd die before I'd betray my friends."

Then the policeman with the toothache said, "Wait! If you can't cure my tooth pain because I don't believe Jesus is the Messiah, does that mean you cured Saul's blindness because he *does* believe it?"

"Why not ask him yourself," Ananias said.

The first policeman did that. "Is this true, Saul? Do you believe that this Jesus person is the Messiah?"

"I used to think it was foolish," Saul said. "But I don't anymore. I heard his voice. It came out of the light. And now I know that he'll return and lead us. I'm sure of it now."

"A dead Messiah, Saul. Are you out of your mind?"

"He isn't dead! He was, but God raised him and exalted him. And he'll return to us. I know that now."

"And what are we supposed to do about the Nazarenes we've come after?"

"I'd advise you to forget them."

The man with the toothache drew his knife. "You'd advise us!" he said. "Maybe I should give *you* some advice." He advanced threateningly towards Saul.

"Stop!" Ananias shouted. "Don't harm him, I warn you. I took the trouble to tell my friends where I was going. If I'm not back in an hour, they'll come after me — with the police."

"He's bluffing!" one of the policemen shouted.

"I'm not!" Ananias said, turning to him. "I speak the truth. If you harm him or me, it will be your undoing. You can depend on it."

The first policeman spoke up and said, "Let him be, let him be. He's a small fish." Then he turned to Saul. "Well, Saul, what can we say? You've had some sort of experience, and it's changed your way of thinking. There's nothing we can do about that. Our high priest will not be too happy over this, but what can we do? For old time's sake, Saul, go in peace. We won't try to stop you."

Saul gathered together his meager belongings and left with Ananias. The policemen stood in the room in silence. Then one of them said to the first policeman, "Why did you do that? We could have taken them prisoner and been on our way before any of his friends could have acted."

"No," the first policeman said, "I have a better idea for Saul. We're going to find the chief of police and tell him that an agent of the high priest has come from Jerusalem to do some illegal abducting in his city. We'll let *him* take care of Saul."

The others smiled in approval. It would be an ironic retribution for that to happen to the man who had betrayed them. They left the house on their mission.

CHAPTER IX

Saul stayed with Ananias and his wife. They fed him and housed him during his time in Damascus. Because Ananias was so highly regarded by the Jews in that city, his name alone gained Saul access to speak before the congregation of any synagogue he wished. Saul spoke in them about Jesus and tried to convince those Jews who were not Nazarenes to accept Jesus as the Messiah. The reactions were mixed: some believed, some doubted, but all were respectful. After all, this was a man who was approved by Ananias, and Ananias was revered by all. In the evenings, after they had eaten, Ananias taught Saul about Jesus' teachings and about his promises and the Nazarene hope for what Jesus would accomplish when he returned.

One night, Ananias told him about Jesus' charge that we love our neighbors and even our enemies, just as Moses and Philo had written, and that if someone strikes us on one cheek, we should turn the other cheek to him as well.

"And yet," Saul said, "you told me that he checked to see that his followers were armed when he was with them in that garden in Gethsemane just before he was arrested."

"Yes he did, but it was for self-defense. If the group of them had been attacked with swords, they could not have allowed themselves to be hacked to pieces."

"But he himself surrendered without a fight."

"Because he knew his fate beforehand," Ananias said. "He didn't want to defend himself against what he knew God had in store for him."

"Then why the sword?"

"Because of the others who were with him. They *did* have a reason to defend themselves; he was the only one who didn't."

"Then it's all right to fight in self-defense?" Saul asked.

"Yes. And let me tell you, when Jesus returns, if he *can* convince the Romans to leave peacefully, he will do that. But if he has to fight, he will fight. He welcomed Zealots into our group and not without reason."

They were interrupted by a knocking on the outer door of the house. Sarah, Ananias' wife, opened the door and admitted Nathan, a Nazarene friend. He was a tall young man with a dark beard.

"Ananias," he said, puffing from having run to the house, "the police are searching for Saul."

"Why?" Ananias asked.

"Saul's former friends have told the governor that Saul has come here as an agent of the high priest to abduct Nazarenes and take them back to Jerusalem. They're questioning people now. They'll be here by tonight, I'm sure."

Ananias responded quickly. He was a man with experience in dangerous situations. "Saul," he said, "we must get you out of here tonight. Maybe even out of the city. They're not going to believe that you've given up your job with the high priest to become a Nazarene. They'll think it's a trick. And even if they did believe it, Aretus might just pretend not to, because you're his way of getting back at the high priest, and he'll want the high priest to know that his secret police officer has been apprehended."

But Nathan discredited the plan when he said, "They're watching every gate, Ananias. Saul's former friends are there with the police in order to point Saul out if he tries to leave the city."

They were stymied by this, and rather than try any further to solve what seemed to be an unsolvable problem, Saul suggested they pray for God's help. The three men sat at the table, closed their eyes and prayed. Sarah, meanwhile, took a tall, woven, cylindrical-shaped basket from her kitchen and placed it on the table. The noise made Ananias open his eyes. "Sarah," he said, "why have you put a basket in the middle of the table?"

The others opened their eyes.

"It's a nice basket, isn't it?" Sarah said.

"Yes, Sarah, it's a lovely basket. But must you put it in the middle of the table just when we're praying?"

"Do you know how I got that basket?"

"No, Sarah, I don't."

"You did, but you've forgotten. I got it from the old woman at the marketplace, the one who sells cloth. I traded her this for some clothes I made." She spoke to the others. "I'm very good at making clothes, you know. And mending too. If you ever need any help like that, let me know. I'll be glad to help in any..."

"Sarah!" Ananias interrupted. "We're trying to help Saul in a crisis, and you're bothering us about mending."

"You think I'm not trying to help him?"

"How is this basket helping him?"

"It's a strong basket, isn't it?"

Ananias did not answer. He gave her an exasperated look.

"It's strong enough to hold a man, isn't it?" she said.

They suddenly understood, and a smile crept onto Ananias' face.

But then Nathan said, "At the gates, they're searching any bundles large enough to hold a man. They're not stupid."

"Then why use the gates?" Sarah said.

"What else do you do with a man in a basket?" Nathan asked.

"You attach a rope to the basket, and you let the basket down the side of the wall," Sarah answered.

There was a stunned silence. It was a flawless solution. Before the night had passed, Saul was lowered down the side of the city wall to the safety of the darkness below and soon, cloaked in the sheltering shadows of the night, was gone.

CHAPTER X

There was a question now of what to do. Saul was not so naive as not to realize that news of his betrayal would reach Caiaphas quickly. The high priest would respond, predictably, with anger and a desire for revenge. If Saul showed his face now in the vicinity of Jerusalem, his life would be in danger. Caiaphas, and even more, Caiaphas' father-in-law, Annas, were powerful people in that city, and one way or another, they would find a way to get him. He could not go back now.

Then he thought of Rabath. What would she think of him? Probably less than what she had thought before. Yet it did not seem to make any difference in what he felt for her. He could not stop loving her, he could not stop wanting her, in spite of what she had said to him. It was as if she was *in* him, a part of him, pervading and haunting his soul. Her presence seemed entrenched and inexpugnable, a living force too powerful for his own poor powers of resistance to expel. He wondered if he would ever see her again, now that he had done what he had done.

No, he could not go to Jerusalem. At least not now. But where else could he go that would make any sense in light of this new, unexpected turn in his life? Damascus — the officials there — were on the lookout for him. Where else could he go that was not an escape into nothingness? Where could he go that would give some forward meaning and direction to his life?

He sat in the shade of an olive tree on the morning of the next day and nibbled at some fruit that Sarah had given him to sustain him on his journey. He knew that he had been through a profound religious experience and that he had responded to it by becoming a forceful speaker for the movement in which he now believed. He asked himself if that was to be his new task, the new work he was to do in the service of God and his country. As he sat there trying to decide the answer to that, he saw three men walking towards him along the sunlit road. By their dress, he recognized them as Essenes. As they came opposite him, he greeted them, and they, wary of strangers as Essenes sometimes are, nodded cautiously in return. He felt something in him, an exigent feeling, that told him not to let them go.

He stood up and said, "Are you Essenes?"

"Yes, we are," the tallest of them replied. "Who are you?"

"Saul," he answered. "I am a Nazarene."

Their countenances brightened. "A follower of Jesus?" one of them asked.

"Yes, a follower of Jesus," Saul answered.

"We knew him," the tall man said. "He was with us for a time."

"When?" Saul asked, excited at the thought of speaking to people who had actually known the man he now called the Messiah.

"About seven years ago," the tall man said. "And we knew his cousin, John the Baptizer. He was with us too."

"We heard that Jesus was crucified and resurrected," another Essene said.

"He was," Saul answered.

"And that he promised to return as the Messiah."

"Yes," Saul said, "and he will."

"I hope so," the tall man added. "It would be good if he did. Many of *us* think he will too."

The third Essene entered the conversation with, "Some people think his cousin, John, is the Messiah. John was baptizing three miles from our home about six years ago."

"Where is your home?" Saul asked.

"We live in a community near the Dead Sea."

The tall man added, "We're going there now. Would you like to join us?"

"To tell you the truth," Saul said, "I have no place else to go right now. I'm a fugitive."

"That's common enough these days," the tall man said.

To himself, Saul ruminated, "Why not?" Then to the others, "Of course I'll come. I would like very much to come. Thank you for your invitation."

And with that, the four of them walked southward in the hot sun towards the Essene community near the Dead Sea.

Along the way, Saul learned about the Essene way of life — their practices, their beliefs, their aspirations. They pervaded the towns as well as the deserts, and they hated the Roman occupiers of our sacred and holy soil. Their hatred, however, was not confined solely to Romans. They were xenophobic in the extreme and hated anyone who was a Gentile. The Essenes in the cities were less extreme, but those in the desert, if they could not drive the Romans out of our land, could at least separate themselves from their contaminating presence. And as for our chief priests in Jerusalem, who did whatever the Romans said, they considered them corrupt and sinful and worthy of the strongest condemnation. They felt that the Messiah should rid the land not only of the heathen Romans but of the iniquitous chief priests as well. The Essenes, Saul now learned, were not passive weaklings, buffeted by every wind that came along; they were militant men who knew how to fight and awaited the day when they could. Because of that, it was not unusual for Zealots to visit them. They and the Zealots shared the common goal of ridding our land of the Romans. Zealot leaders would come from their own desert and mountain retreats to confer with these Essenes about military matters. Or they would simply come to find spiritual replenishment, for among these Essenes, the spiritual and the military stood side by side, the one sustaining the other.

When Saul and his friends arrived at their destination, Saul saw the sparse structures of the community, the simple dwellings of stone built around — and even in — the cliff caves of the region. He saw the rampart and the defensive towers and the forge for making weapons, and he realized that here was a people prepared to fight against any hostile intruder. He saw some men working and others sitting in the shade of palm trees, reading and talking quietly. He saw only a few women and children at the time, the women carrying water in jugs from a cistern and the children playing at being warriors. He met Abram, the leader of the community, who accepted him into their midst. And just as Jesus and John the Baptizer had stayed and learned from these Essenes, so did Saul remain with them now to learn and absorb what he could. Abram, particularly, took a liking to him and put him under his wing, as if he were a son, and taught him personally the secrets of the sect.

Paul learned of the different beliefs about fate that set the Essenes apart from the Pharisees and Sadducees. The Essenes believed that fate governs all things and that nothing happens to anyone that is not preordained. The Sadducees, at the other end, did not believe in fate at all but that whatever happens to us is determined by our own actions, so that we ourselves are the causes of the good or evil we receive. And the Pharisees, in their view of the nature of things, stood somewhere between these two extremes, believing that some things, but not all, were the workings of fate while others were caused by our choice.

He learned that the Essenes and Nazarenes and Pharisees had at least one thing in common besides their being Jews: they shared together the common hope for the restoration of the kingdom of God. And the Essenes, like their co-religionists, the Pharisees, accepted the possibility that that might come about through Jesus and that time, that merciful rewarder of patience, would let us know about that soon enough. They felt, as we Nazarenes did, that the Messiah would appear while most of us were still alive. They likened the Messiah to a star, and when Saul asked them why they had chosen that particular symbol, they said it was because of Moses having said that a star would come from Jacob. The Essenes, Saul also learned, believed in a new covenant — one with the strictest adherence to the Torah. Second only to God, they believed, was Moses, who had brought us the law.

This, they said, they had taught to Jesus and also to his cousin, John. They felt that the chief priests, for all their avowals of being Torah-adhering Sadducees, were the most hypocritical and irreverent of men. On the other hand, they revered Jesus' brother, whose fame was widespread now, and they called him the Teacher of Righteousness and also a doer of good. Because of the legendary goodness of James, they said to Saul, Israel was being made worthy of a Messiah.

They did not marry very often, these men of the desert, not because an Essene could not do so — many of the Essenes who lived in the cities had wives and children, as did some of the men in this Dead Sea community — but because this particular group of Essenes considered celibacy a higher spiritual state than marriage, which explained to Saul why he saw so few women and children in the vicinity as he went about the place. But even for those men who did not marry, children were important, so that it was not uncommon to see these men adopting children and raising them as their own, as Abram, albeit belatedly, seemed to be doing with Saul.

Saul learned from them about sacred meals — the ritual of bread and wine and the prayers that are said before them. The prayers, Saul learned, were almost the same as those he had learned from Ananias in Damascus. The prayer of the Essenes, it seemed to Saul, was like the prayer of the Nazarenes. And so was the structure of leadership between the two. For just as Nazarenes had twelve apostles and a primary leadership of three men — James and Peter and John, the son of Zebedee — so did the Essenes have twelve who made up their council of elders, with three other men above them. And their baptism, too, was the same as ours, the same as John the Baptizer's. But these Essenes did not do it just once, as all the Nazarenes did, but every day, renewing afresh the washing away of their sins. And when they sinned, they had prescribed penances to follow to atone for them. In general, they atoned by practicing justice and suffering affliction. But, also, they believed that those who made a covenant with God to obey all His laws, as given to us by Moses, and who then were obedient to that covenant, were

74

cleansed of all their sins. But making such a promise did not relieve them of the need for specific atonements. A man who deliberately lied, for example, had to do penance a full six months. Forgiveness was something in which they believed but not to be given too lightly. Yet one crime to them seemed greater than any other and was considered a capital offense: so staunch was their love of Mosaic law that anyone who spoke against Moses was worthy of being killed.

He learned of their contempt for pain, which they could tolerate as if their bodies had no feeling, and he learned of their disregard of danger in any enterprise that served God. To them, an honorable death meant more then prolonging their lives.

Their lives were intentionally austere, but, because of that, they seemed more prone to higher spiritual experiences. They studied the Book of Enoch, with its apocalyptic predictions and its visions of the unknown. They meditated, and some had visions and saw things with their inner eyes about the world beyond and about the world that was to come and related them to the others, who marveled at their descriptions. It was said that their predictions of the future were seldom off the mark. Saul told them of his own vision and of the voice that had spoken to him out of the light. And in time, through the cultivation of the arts and skills that they taught him, he began to have more visions of his own. He was caught up and lifted to a higher spiritual realm, wafted upward into a level of awareness that he called the Third Heaven, and he was allowed, through the grace and generosity of God, to see what he called Paradise. How pale then the lust that he felt for the woman who haunted his soul. How inconsequential did earthly pleasures seem compared to the bliss he had briefly glimpsed. He was changed, he was changing, in this dry, dusty, rocky place. He felt that he was evolving into something different from the man who had spoken to Rabath in the garden that night. Yet, in spite of that, something of her still remained — smaller, purer perhaps, more suppressed than before, but still there, ineluctable, and as permanently entrenched in his body as the marrow in his bones.

He stayed with the Essenes almost three full years before he was ready to leave. Then he went to each of them, one by one, and bid everyone goodbye. He waited for Abram last, because Abram was the hardest one to leave, having taught him so much and having become almost like a father to him.

"I am going," Saul said, extending his hand.

"I know," Abram answered and took Saul's hand into his own. "I think you're ready now. Remember all that you've learned from us."

"I will," Saul said. "I'm not the same man who came to you three years ago."

"I know that too," Abram said. "You're a good man, Saul. Do good things. Remember the Torah, and follow it. Shun the influence of Gentiles unless they accept God — the one true god — and swear to follow His laws. Marry if you must — the lure of the flesh is strong — but if you find yourself losing your desire, let it happen as it will. Men who live as we do do not force themselves into continence. It is something that comes slowly, without effort or suppression. It is something natural and effortless. Work every day for the goal that we share, fight for it if you must — the goal of freeing our people from their slavery to Rome and restoring the kingdom of God. Remember, we were chosen to be God's people, not for special rewards or privileges but for special work. We must show the people of the world what it means to be a nation of God, so that they can look in wonder and copy us; we must show them the Torah, so that they can use it as a guide for their own lives." He squeezed Saul's hand and then embraced him. "Now go, my boy. You have been like my son. I will pray that God be with you and guide you wherever you go."

Saul left the Essenes a changed man, as he had said. He was filled with some inner strength that he had not had before. And yet, for all that had happened and all he had learned, he was not completely changed. For he knew that his inner strength, as strong as it was now, was still not strong enough to expunge from his soul the love he still felt for Rabath. He had seen Paradise in the world to come, but she was Paradise in the world that was now. He would go on to fulfill his destiny, whatever it was going to be, but she would be with him wherever he went and whatever he was going to do.

He made straight for Damascus to see Ananias once more. He knew that no one would be seeking him now since so much time had elapsed, and he entered the city safely, with no difficulty at all. He knocked on the door of Ananias' house, and Sarah, overwhelmed with surprise and delight, almost dragged him through the door. There was nothing short of exultation from Sarah and Ananias both, and Sarah, typical of her warm-hearted nature, immediately offered him food. She soon had a warm meal on the table, and they gave thanks to God and ate together. Sarah showed Saul the basket they had used to lower him down the wall, and they laughed when Saul said that too much of Sarah's good cooking would render him too heavy for the basket to hold him a second time. Then Ananias gave him a letter, a letter addressed to me. Ananias and I knew each other, having met when he had been in Jerusalem for a time and having formed a warm friendship that we had been keeping alive through correspondence. This letter recommended Saul highly as someone whom we could trust and said that I should not hold Saul's past activities against him. Fortified with that letter and filled with dedication, Saul left Ananias and Sarah after a few pleasant days of rest and made his way to Jerusalem.

CHAPTER XI

In the meantime, Pontius Pilate was working his way into the final act that would lead to his expulsion from office. Someone who claimed to be the Samaritan version of the Messiah led a group of Samaritans to Mount Girizim, because the sacred vessels of Moses were supposed to be hidden at the top, and the hiding place was about to be revealed to him. Some of the pilgrims took weapons, but only for the purpose of protecting themselves against robbers. Pilate sent his soldiers to quell what he considered a brewing rebellion, and many of the Samaritans were killed and the others taken prisoner. Yet all this killing at the mountain was not enough to satisfy him. He turned to the prisoners next. Like the beast that he was, he executed them. No trials; no explanations heard.

The remaining Samaritan leaders went to Vitellius, the legate of Syria. They had never intended to rebel, they said. Pilate's reaction had been unwarranted. Vitellius believed them, and deposed Pilate and replaced him with his own friend, Marcellus. He ordered Pilate to go to Rome to explain his actions to the emperor. Though Tiberius, the emperor, was not particularly well-disposed towards Jews, having expelled them from Rome some eighteen years before under the prodding of his anti-Jewish advisor, Sejanus, and also because of Fulvia, Senator Saturninus' wife, having become Jewish and then having had some of her property purportedly stolen by Jews, he was still enough of a politician to want a procurator who could keep the Jews of Judaea tractable. That meant a procurator who did not stir up passions as Pilate had been doing, something that Pilate would now have to answer for.

Vitellius knew that the Samaritans were not the only ones who hated Pilate; he knew that all the Jews did too. The removal of Pilate was the removal of a reign of terror. But he knew that Pilate was not the only one the Jews hated. He knew that our high priest, Caiaphas, was not far behind the governor in our affections. For things that Caiaphas had done on his own as well as his close association with Pilate, he was a man abhorred by his own people. Vitellius knew this and, somewhat deceptively at first, acted on it. First, as a general gesture of goodwill, he released the sacred vestments of the high priest, which had been taken from our people in the time of Herod the Great, and he returned them to Caiaphas just in time for Caiaphas to wear them on the upcoming Passover holiday. This pleased us very much, not because of Caiaphas but because of our religion. But then he acted on our hatred of Caiaphas and deposed him, putting the chief priest, Jonathan, one of Annas' sons who had not been appointed to the high priesthood previously, into his place. We were even more elated over this, and Vitellius basked in the warmth of our gratitude for a time.

But we were not so enamored of Vitellius that we would violate our religious laws for him. We proved this in the matter of the Nabataean expedition, which began before a year had passed. You will remember that our king, Herod Antipas, had been defeated in battle by our neighbor, King Aretus, and that Antipas had appealed to Emperor Tiberius for help. Now, in response to that, Tiberius ordered Vitellius to send a punitive force into Nabataea against King Aretus. He wanted to show Aretus how costly it was to attack a Roman-appointed king. To accomplish that task, Vitellius wanted to send his army from its base at Ptolemais through Judaea. But there was again the problem of sculpted images on the standards of the army. To have them come so close to Jerusalem would be a religious offense to us. Previously, with Pilate, we had asked that those images not be brought into Jerusalem; now we expanded our request and asked that they not be brought into Judaea. Vitellius was accommodating; he granted our request and sent his army through a less-convenient route in the Jordan Valley. Then, to show his goodwill even more, when the time of the Passover Festival came, he visited us in Jerusalem, and he and King Herod Antipas made a religious sacrifice together. Then he announced that he was rescinding the tax on fruit and vegetables. He could not rescind the poll tax because that was the prerogative of the emperor, but he relieved us where he could of the burden of taxation. As a result, he was warmly welcomed by our people. Flushed with all that adoration, having gained our favor because of his dismissals of Pilate and Caiaphas and because of the vestments and the images and the religious sacrifice and the reduction of taxes, he now decided that so much accommodation to a subject people might be construed as weakness. So to remind us that Rome was still the final authority, he discharged Jonathan from his post as high priest and replaced him with Jonathan's brother, Theophilus, this change from Jonathan to Theophilus taking place in less than a year. Still, that did not change our opinion of him. He was a breath of fresh air after the beatings and thefts and unbridled crucifixions we had known under Pilate.

He stayed with us for three days, and during that time, unexpectedly, word came that Tiberius had died. Gaius Caligula was the new emperor. For Pilate, that was fortunate, for, after delays and a purposely prolonged trip, he arrived in Rome just when that occurred. Had he had to face Tiberius, his fate would have been a nasty one to say the least. But with Caligula in charge, it turned out that Pilate's crimes were ignored, and he was allowed to live peacefully in Rome.

Vitellius, upon getting the news of Tiberius' death, immediately did the required thing and made us swear allegiance to Caligula. Then he left to attend to the Nabataean campaign. But that campaign was soon annulled when Caligula, seemingly anxious to reverse all of his predecessor's policies, gave Nabataea independence and freedom from Roman rule. How fortunate that was for King Aretus!

And now Caligula deposed Herod Antipas and exiled him to Spain. The reason for that was that he believed that Antipas, who had gathered enough arms to equip seventy thousand troops, had been plotting with the Parthians to make war on the Romans. The Parthians were those bellicose warriors whose empire in the east was separated from Rome's by the Euphrates River. Rome had learned to respect them after one disastrous attempt by Crassus to invade their land almost a hundred years before. They had shown the Romans the effectiveness of mobile horsemen shooting arrows at them from a distance. They were a fierce and capable people whom the Romans had learned to fear. The banners they carried at the tops of their poles when the Romans first faced them in battle were made of a material from China called silk, and, in spite of the wary animosity between the two empires, they traded with the Romans for that. And these Parthians had a means of dipping metals into watery mixtures that coated them with gold for jewelry. The Romans traded them for those things too. But trade and commerce did not do away with the vigilance that both sides had to keep, for the slightest sign of weakness was an invitation for the stronger of the two to step in. Hence Rome's fear of a conspiracy that might open its eastern frontier. Hence its concern about Antipas.

Though Antipas *had* gathered arms, it had not been for the purpose of rebellion or of uniting with the Parthians. But Caligula could not be convinced of that, especially since his friend, Agrippa, had sent him false letters to the contrary. To Herodias, Antipas' wife, however, he offered freedom, because she was Agrippa's sister. Yet she declined and, with a show of loyalty not demonstrated when she had left her husband, Philip, to marry Antipas, said, "It is not right that I stay with the man I love only in prosperity and leave him when times are bad. I will accompany him." So these two, who had broken the laws of Moses and killed our beloved John, lived out the remainder of their miserable lives in the rude discomforture of Spain.

Agrippa now became king over some of our land. Caligula favored him because Agrippa had once expressed the hope that Tiberius would die so that Caligula could become the emperor. Tiberius had then imprisoned him for that supersessionist remark. Those had been dark days for Agrippa. Tiberius' centurion had led him to prison on a scorching day, still in his purple robe, and Caligula's slave had given him water when Tiberius' centurion would not. He had stayed in prison for six long months, not knowing if he was to die. But he had friends allowed to bring him food and bedding and accompany him to the baths every day. Then one day, when he briefly had been allowed outside his cell, he had seen an owl land in a tree. An old German prisoner, skilled at divining, had told him that it meant he would be freed and honored. "But when you see that owl again," the man had said, "in five days more, you'll be dead." But the owl had not appeared again, and, after Tiberius' death, Caligula gave Agrippa the title of king and the lands over which the deceased Philip had ruled: Ituraea, Trachonitis and others. And he gave him something else as well: the privilege of naming high priests. That privilege had formerly belonged to the procurators; now it would belong to the king.

CHAPTER XII

When Saul arrived in Jerusalem, instead of coming to me first, he went straight to one of our synagogues, anxious to announce that he had seen the light and was joining us. But no one believed he had changed so drastically from a dedicated pursuer of Nazarenes into the devout follower of Jesus he now claimed to be. They thought it was a trap.

So he came to me then and presented me with Ananias' letter. I interviewed him at length before I dared introduce him to everyone; I had to be sure it was safe. He told me everything about himself that he thought I should know, especially about his vision on the road to Damascus and his three years among the Essenes. Then, in an easy conversational mood one evening, he told me about Rabath. I could sense that he still loved her, though his voice sounded bitter about how she had treated him. And I wondered what influence she had had — or was still having — over this dramatic change in his life, which had started on that Damascus road. He told me, too, that he had been married briefly when he was younger. His wife had died unexpectedly of some kind of fever, and he had never again felt attracted to a woman until the day he had met Rabath.

I took Saul to our next meeting and introduced him to our brothers. James was reluctant to meet him, because he still did not trust him and because he still resented him for his involvement in Stephen's death. So I did not press an introduction between them. But Peter met him and spent time talking with him. They talked about Saul's experience in Damascus and about Jesus and all he had said and done. From Peter, Saul learned that all the things that had been foretold about the Messiah had come true in Jesus: his descent from King David, the recognition of him as king, his suffering at the hands of heathens. And soon, he said, the only part that had not yet occurred *would* occur: his triumphant return to claim Israel as his kingdom and return it to God. Peter traced the lineage of Jesus from the time of Abraham onward. He traced it generation by generation, name by name, from Abraham to King David to Joseph to Jesus. Hence, he said, the prophecy that said that the Messiah would be descended from King David was fulfilled. And then he spoke of Jesus' resurrection after the cross and of his marvelous appearance to Mary Magdelene and to some of the disciples. And he spoke of Jesus' imminent return, for which they had to prepare as many Jews as possible.

That led to the question of Saul's work. What kind of work was he to do, and how could he best serve the cause? While the leaders of our group, James, Peter and John, the son of Zebedee, deliberated over this, Saul did not hesitate to speak publicly about Jesus. That resulted in Caiaphas learning he was back and in Caiaphas speaking to our new high priest, Theophilus, who then sent out his minions to find Saul. Then, also, in Saul's public speaking, he allowed himself to get drawn into debates with Greek-speaking Jews, who tended to be more accommodating to the Romans than other Jews and who disputed the entire claim of Jesus' messiahship. As a result of the influence of the Essenes, Saul had become more zealous about politics and was now more ardent in his denunciation of the Romans and the chief priests. So cogent and forceful were his statements that he angered these Greek-speaking Jews, whereupon they decided to kill him for what they considered his radicalism. Then, too, the new procurator, Capito, who had been sent by Caligula to replace Vitellius' friend, Marcellus, was not very tolerant of agitators. Because of Caiaphas and Theophilus seeking Saul, and because the Greek-speaking Jews were plotting to kill him, and because it was only a matter of time until Saul's public statements reached Capito, our leaders considered Saul's life to be in too much danger to allow him to remain in Jerusalem. They, therefore, had him spirited off to Caesarea and then sent him on to Tarsus, the city of his birth, to carry on the work there. He was to gain entrance into the synagogues and to convince as many Jews as possible to prepare themselves, both physically and spiritually, for the arrival of our king. When that day arrived, he was to tell them, the world would change, and a new era would be ushered into existence; every knee would bend to our new king, and Israel would be a light to all nations, and goodness and mercy and prosperity would reign. That was the message he was to deliver, and Jews had to purify themselves and gird themselves for battle if necessary to help overthrow the heathens and establish the kingdom of God.

So Saul left to do *his* work, and I went back to mine in Jerusalem. Yet I could not help thinking, after he had left, that twice now he had had to leave a place for fear of his life and that he was paying a price for his belief in Jesus. I admired him for that.

The work in and around Jerusalem went on, and on one occasion, Peter traveled to Lydda. There he was taken to the home of a man named Eneas who had been bedridden for eight years with a palsy.

Peter cured him of his condition, and the man immediately left his bed. Peter accomplished that through the power that God had given him, and so many Jews were impressed by what he had done that they became Nazarenes without hesitation.

Meanwhile, in the neighboring city of Joppa, a Nazarene woman named Tabitha died. Some of the men in Joppa, hearing that Peter was nearby, hoped that he might be able to bring her back to life, so they hastened to Lydda to ask him to try. He went to Joppa with them and, in an upstairs room, found the dead woman surrounded by wailing women. He sent the mourners away and then kneeled down to pray. Then he turned to the dead woman and said, "Tabitha, arise!" And with that, she opened her eyes and saw him and sat up. He took her hand and walked her outside to present her to the mourners. They saw her and rejoiced. And when news of that spread through Joppa, almost every Jew in the city became a Nazarene.

And now Peter went to Caesarea because a centurion named Cornelius, who had become a God-fearer and who had given much to the poor, asked him to come. The centurion had heard of Peter's work and wanted salvation for himself and his family. Peter, without getting into the political aspects of Jesus' work, baptized Cornelius and his family and accepted them as Nazarenes. Though Peter usually encouraged full conversion to Judaism before granting anyone acceptance as a Nazarene, in this case he was so touched by Cornelius' ardor and sincerity that he forewent his usual practice.

And now *I* received a new assignment. It had to do with the followers of Stephen. After his death, they had fled. The Romans considered them rebels who deserved the same fate as their leader. They had fled to such places as Damascus and Cyprus and Phoenicia and Antioch. Some of them had come originally from Cyprus and Cyrene and were accustomed to communing with Greeks there. So it was not so strange that when some of them went to Antioch, they spoke to Greeks as well as Jews. What *was* strange was that, like Stephen, they were speaking to these Greeks about Jesus. A number of these Gentiles had become Nazarenes, but the problem was that they weren't Jews, and how could anyone who wasn't a Jew become a Nazarene? That was what I was sent to find out.

When I got there and when I spoke to them — the Gentiles who had become Nazarenes, I mean — I realized how sincere they were. The new era that was to come appealed to them as much as it did to Jews, and they were determined to be loyal subjects of Jesus when he assumed his throne as king. I rejoiced at the sincerity with which they embraced our cause, and I could not find it in my heart to refuse them acceptance because they had not first become Jews. If they would help us, work with us, even fight alongside us if necessary, then they were worthy of our brotherhood now. So I welcomed them with an open heart.

I knew that Jesus taught against this. I knew that, once, when a Gentile woman asked him to heal her little girl, he refused and said that his help was only for us Jews, whom he called "the children", who had the right to be fed first, and that it was not right to take the children's bread and throw it to the dogs. And I knew that only after the woman conceded that she and her daughter were, indeed, dogs and again appealed to him to heal her child, to give the dogs the crumbs from the children's food fallen under the table, as it were, did he relent and do the healing.

And I knew that, another time, when he sent his original disciples to evangelize the whole nation, he instructed them to limit their activities solely to Jews. "Go nowhere among the Gentiles," he said, "and enter no town of the Samaritans, but go rather to the lost sheep of the house of Israel." And another time, he said, "Do not give dogs what is holy; and do not throw your pearls before swine, lest they trample them underfoot and turn to attack you." From all this, we knew he meant Gentiles, and we knew that he did not want us to go to them. Part of it, I knew, was the influence of the Essenes, with whom he had lived for a time and whose disdain for Gentiles must have affected his thinking. But part of it also was that there was too much to be done among Jews, and Jews were our first priority. But just as Jesus had finally not refused the woman who had begged him to heal her child, how could I now refuse these Gentiles when they were so devoted to us? If they would just become Jews, of course, I would have no problem, but without their becoming Jews, I was in a quandary. Yet I made the decision to accept them and hoped I could convince James back in Jerusalem that I had done the right thing.

I traveled then to Tarsus and stayed with Saul for a while. He seemed happy and confident in the home of his youth and even happier to have me with him. He had been spending his time not only teaching about Jesus but also absorbing other ideas.

He had met the Epicureans and had listened to them profess their cherished beliefs. That group, for some three-hundred and fifty years, had been following the teachings of Epicurus and his later exponent, Lucretius Carus. Though they allowed that there were gods, their gods did not care about men, and even less did they care about evil and good and punishments and rewards. So no prayers or sacrifices had to be made to these gods, and no priests or temples had to exist for them. This conflicted, of course, with what Saul had learned from his Jewish teachers, such as Machaiah — and even Gamaliel during the brief time that they had been together. The exponents of Epicureanism, Democritus and Leucippus, said that all bodies came into existence from empty space in the form of tiny particles called atoms and that these would exist for a time and then disappear for good.

Saul could find nothing in common with these people except for their self-restraint and their considerate attitude towards others. They liked physical and mental pleasures but not overindulgence in them; they thought it was good to love pleasure but not to become enslaved by it. Self-restraint and moderation were good. Helping others was good — for as Epicurus had said, "It is better to do kindness than to receive kindness". Right and virtuous deeds brought tranquillity to the soul.

Interestingly though, there was something else about them with which Saul found he could agree: they discouraged marriage and family, since it disturbed and troubled the spirit. And here Saul saw a common theme with that of the desert Essenes, who, even if they married, believed that celibacy was superior to marriage and sex and that it indicated a higher spiritual state. But another reason for Saul's agreement with that aspect of their philosophy may have been his feeling that the end times were coming soon and that a long-term commitment to marriage would not be very productive.

Politics they also avoided because it, too, caused trouble and strife. But on this issue, Saul stood as a man unsure, because he himself had been agitating for an end to Roman rule. Yet he wondered now if the Nazarene movement, stripped of its political aspect, would make people respond to him faster. Not in Jerusalem, of course, because there, it was the political theme that was partly responsible for so many people becoming Nazarenes. But elsewhere, throughout the Roman Empire, he wondered if an apolitical Jesus would gain adherents more quickly. It was something to think about.

He met the Stoics in Tarsus too, and here were people who struck a more resonant note in his soul. For though he found himself at odds with some of what they said, he found one of them, Posidonius, on common ground with him when it came to the subject of God. This Stoic believed, as do we Jews, that there is one and only one god — a rational, unperceived spirit concerned with the actions of men. Posidonius of Apamaea, he was called, and he had started their trend of thought almost two-hundred and fifty years before, and his followers could boast that Cicero and even Pompey had studied their beliefs. The eternal soul is a piece of God, Posidonius had said, remaining bound to its progenitor throughout the life of a man. But then, with death, it returns to its source and joins with God again. And that god, according to Posidonius, is always around us and is the cause of all that is good. Evil comes from wicked men and not from the will of God. And in contrast to the Greeks, who thought that courage was the highest virtue, Posidonius held that greatness of soul was more important than that and that such greatness is achieved by leading a moral life. Homer, he said, was wrong in attributing human natures to gods when he should have been attributing divine natures to men.

So the idea of leading a moral life and of a single, caring god had also started among the Gentiles — even among those who were not God-fearers. Our venerable Jewish beliefs, having persisted now for so many centuries in spite of all the pagan efforts to eradicate them, were finally exerting their influence, it seemed. But the idea that men had natures that are divine, coming off as pieces of God, as it were, ran dangerously close to the pagan belief that certain great men are gods, Roman emperors being the foremost recipients of that obsequious and spurious belief. And then Saul learned that the foremost proponent of Stoicism, Lucius Annaeus Seneca, was alive and residing in Rome and holding there a position of importance. (He was to become even more important later, when he became the teacher of the future emperor Nero.) This scholar expounded the teachings of Posidonius and added to them those of Chrysippus and Zeno, both considered the formal founders of Stoicism. Saul, ever seeking to expand his knowledge of the great concerns of the day, listened to Seneca's writings and absorbed that philosopher's ideas.

Man is weak, Seneca said, and his body is the prison of his soul. Saul thought on this and mentally tested its validity on himself. Was not his soul striving to be pure within the lustful immurement of his flesh? Was not his spirit longing to be virtuous beneath the carnal grating of his bones? He tested Seneca on the man he knew best and found that the writer was right.

Seneca said we must follow God in a righteous and upright way. And that made Saul remember the Jewish sages who told us to "...cleave to the standards of the Holy One, blessed be He" and also made Saul remember Jesus, who said that we should all adhere to the Torah. Did this idea occur to Seneca in a void free of all other people's thoughts, or had the many centuries of Jewish belief pierced the curtain of pagan mistrust and made this teacher of a future emperor see the way and the nature of things?

Seneca echoed Posidonius by saying that death frees us to return to our source. And he echoed the ancients and Jesus when he adjured us to love even the erring and to remember that we all have done wrongs at one time or another. For it was Ben-Sira, in our ancient Jewish tradition, who said, "Do not reproach a man who repents of sin; remember that all of us are guilty." And it was Jesus, in my own lifetime, who defended an adulteress against a crowd that would have stoned her by saying, "Let him who is without sin cast the first stone." Better, said Seneca, to be fatherly towards wrong-doers and to summon them back to the right path.

Do not return evil for evil, he said. And if a wise man receives a blow on the cheek, he does what Cato, the Roman, did: he does not flare up, he does not avenge the wrong, he does not even forgive it, but, instead, says that no wrong has been done. And when Saul told this to me after one of the meetings he had attended, I remembered that Jesus had gone even beyond this and had said that if a man strikes you on the cheek, give him your other cheek to strike as well.

As for the doing of good, intention, wrote Seneca, is more important than the deed itself. And, also, one should do good without any motive of reward.

For women who paint their faces and wear the kind of clothes that only better reveals their nakedness and hides their pregnancies and induces miscarriages — for these he had the strongest words of reproach.

The good person fears nothing, he wrote, not even pain or humiliation. Pain can be beneficial because it strengthens a man, and virtue without adversity grows weak. We should receive all that comes to us with love and not complain, he said. And here I remembered our Jewish sages, who wrote that a Jew recites a prayer of thanks to God on hearing good news and on hearing bad news.

We went together, Saul and I, to hear the Stoics speak. We sat in silence, listening to their discussions, absorbing their ideas. At one of these meetings, they read aloud some letters that they had from Seneca. In one letter, an older one written when Augustus had been the emperor, Seneca said that Augustus was one reputedly born from the gods and that he was destined to give birth to gods. This, of course, conflicted with the concept of one god that Posidonius had previously espoused. Seneca was reflecting the pagan idea that there was more than one god and that men could ascend to be gods. This idea, Saul and I knew, was part of what pagans believed. The Egyptian pharaohs were considered incarnations of the gods, Amon and Re. When Alexander conquered Egypt, he called himself the son of Zeus-Amon. The Greek kings of the house of Ptolemy, who ruled Egypt, were all considered divine. And for the Persian king, it was exactly the same: he was considered a god. Then, forty-eight years before our beloved Jesus, an inscription in Ephesus called Julius Caesar "...the god who sprang from Ares and Aphrodite, the manifestation of deity on earth and the readily accessible savior of human life." Then, six years after that, the Roman Senate declared Caesar divine. Two years later, Octavian called himself "Son of the Divine" and later "the Holy", and thus he too became a god. People referred to Octavian as "god and savior" and looked to him for salvation. The only exception to all these divine politicians seemed to be Tiberius, who seemed content with being just the ordinary decadent human being that he consistently was.

As we talked to other pagan philosophers living in Tarsus, we also learned about the Egyptian mystics and their custom of drinking and eating the blood and bodies of their gods, of putting their gods into their bellies, to become a part of them.

The pagans believed in all kinds of gods — a whole procession of them stretching from Egypt to Asia. Some had been killed and returned to life, which at least requires us to give credit to the pagans for recognizing some degree of truth, for although their gods were non-existent, their recognition of resurrection as a true and natural phenomenon deserves some commendation.

Thus, aside from the non-resurrected gods, such as Egypt's Isis and Serapis; Persia's Ahura-Mazda, Anahita and Mithras; and Phrygia's Attis-Cybele — aside from these and other non-resurrected gods, recognized by the pagans under one name or another, there were the resurrected gods, the ones who had been killed on earth, who had died and risen again: Egypt's Osiris; Greece's Dionysius; Phoenicia's Adonis; Phrygia's Attis; and Babylonia's Baal-Bel-Marduk.

Baal-Bel-Marduk was arrested and sentenced and beaten and sent for execution along with another prisoner, while yet another prisoner was freed. His heart was pierced by a spear, and his wound was washed by a woman. But, later, he came back to life and was well and whole again. The story of Baal-Bel-Marduk, who never actually existed, of course, was a presage and presentiment by pagans of an actual future event. For the things that transpired in that ancient myth actually happened later to Jesus. It was as if God was trying to prepare these pagans for a significant event in their lives, so that when the event finally did occur, they would recognize its source.

Osiris was killed by his brother, and his body was found by his wife, Isis, floating in a coffin on the Nile. After much tribulation in which his brother regained the body and dismembered it and then Isis gathered its parts, reassembled it and floated it on the Nile, letting it be baptized in a sense, Osiris returned to life.

And the young and handsome Adonis, loved by the goddess Aphrodite, died when a boar he was hunting attacked him in the forest. And he too was resurrected, some say repeating the life-and-death cycle annually, so that his repeated deaths and resurrections brought the changing of the seasons.

And Dionysius too followed the path of the others by dying and returning to life.

And the handsome shepherd, Attis, beloved by the goddess, Cybele, she the great mother of gods, consorted with a nymph, thus arousing the goddess' jealousy, so that she killed the nymph and drove Attis mad. He castrated himself in his madness and died because of his wound. But Cybele, still in love with him, felt compassion and restored him to life.

The followers of Attis saw his death as a propitiation for their sins, and saw his rising from the dead as an indication that he was not a man now but a god. His followers mutilated themselves to emulate his actions, and the statues of his hanging, beaten and bloody body permeated Phrygia and Cilicia. His votaries went to his sanctuary, and there, inside a dark cavern, they were buried in the ground up to their necks to symbolize their deaths. The others present sang funeral songs until a light suddenly appeared in the cavern, and a priest told the votary he had been saved and that he, like the god, Attis, would rise to eternal life.

None of these gods existed, of course, except in the minds of pagans, but the concepts that some them had in their minds showed an inchoate understanding of God.

Concepts of God aside, however, the Stoics at least preached morality. And since their morality had been preceded for centuries by the morality of the Jews, the earlier having surely influenced the later, was Seneca, then, appropriately respectful of our Jewish religion, owing so much of his morality to it? It would surely seem that he should have been. But such was not the case in a world of politics and national pride. The truth of the matter is that Judaism was making inroads into the highest pagan circles, and that was something that Seneca and other traditionalists didn't like, because along with the religion that came with the Jews was a sense of nationhood too. We heard a letter by Seneca read by the Stoics in Tarsus. He wrote of the Jews and their religion. Our religion was popular everywhere, he said, and this was something bad. "The customs of this accursed race have gained such influence," he said, "that they are now received throughout the world." How different the seething tone of this from his lofty words about righteousness and the doing of good and loving even the erring and not returning evil for evil! "The vanquished," he protested, "have given their laws to the victors." We Jews had lost to the Romans on the battlefield, so we should have lost in the temple as well. And the unspoken corollary to that, I suppose, is that the triumph of a religion should be decided not by reason but by superior force of arms. Whosoever's army is bigger and wins the war is the one whose religion is right. This was Seneca, the head of the Stoics, proclaiming his high, noble morals in the abstract and showing his true barbarian self in practice.

"He doesn't seem to like us very much," I said to Saul as we left that meeting.

"His religion is faulty," Saul said. "There's a lot of paganism in it."

"Of course," I said, concordantly. "And I don't know what those people think about God. Posidonius speaks of one god, and Seneca speaks of many."

"But then," Saul said, "their morals are in many ways like ours."

"They are," I said, "but do they practice them? You heard what he said about Jews."

We talked more about the Stoics as we walked along the street. Saul seemed to reject what they believed and yet seemed to dwell on their ideas. He seemed to want to absorb everything he could about every philosophy of the day. It was as if his convictions were still not complete and he was still seeking answers to things; or as if they *were* complete but that he wanted to know what the pagans believed so that he could argue against them better.

He showed me around the city like a buoyant, excited child. I saw the places where he had played as a boy; I saw the tree under which he had sat and meditated and dreamed his dreams of becoming a learned man. And, too, I saw the icons of the pagan god, Attis, whom the Gentiles of Tarsus worshipped and whose image was fashioned as a hanging, sacrificial man, his flayed body dripping blood to fertilize the fields below. And I saw Attis' frenzied and ecstatic worshippers, who flayed and castrated themselves in order to experience the same suffering as their god and, thereby, enter into him, as they put it. And I looked, too, at the work that Saul had done, and I met several Jews whom he had won over to our belief in Jesus' messiahship, and I was impressed. Whatever else one might say of Saul, there was no question that he was a convincing and effective speaker. I decided he could help me sort things out in Antioch, and I asked him to return there with me. He accepted, and we went there together. Once there, he looked at the issue of Gentiles becoming Nazarenes, and he agreed wholeheartedly with my decision not to reject them.

THE CHRIST-KILLERS

CHAPTER XIII

While Saul and I indulged ourselves in the leisure of philosophical reflections, Jews elsewhere in the world suddenly found themselves having to fight for their survival. This happened in Alexandria when the Egyptians attacked the Jews.

The reason for the hostility was complex, and much of it was derived from history. To understand how it all began, we must go back a few hundred years to a time when Gentiles respected Jews. There were Gentile writers back then — Hecataeus, Theophrastus, Megasthenes, Clearchus, Hermippus and Ocellus — who called us a nation of philosophers and admired us from afar. Some two-hundred and twenty years before Jesus, one of them, Hermippus, wrote of us in that way. He reported that Pythagoras, three-hundred and twenty years before him, had copied the teachings of the Jews and Thracians and introduced Jewish law into his philosophy. Another writer, Hecataeus, said Moses' laws were a political and religious ideal. And closer to our own time, Strabo, in writing of our exodus from Egypt, said we were right to have left, unhappy as we were with Egyptian theology and ritual, and that the Hebrew religious philosophy reflected the more enlightened thinking of the time. Longinus, too, wrote favorably of Moses, having one of his characters say, "He was no ordinary man," and having the character praise Moses' concept of God. Nicolaus of Damascus, the tutor of Anthony's and Cleopatra's children and, later, an advisor to King Herod, wrote of how pious and virtuous we were; he extolled our customs, especially the Sabbath. Diodorus of Sicily praised Moses as a lawgiver and our religion as divinely revealed. Pompeius Trogus, another Gentile, also touted our ways.

All these writers were Gentiles, and all of them saw Judaism as good. As a result, our religion found converts at every level of pagan society. Some became Jews and some became sympathizers, but even those who did neither felt the influence of Moses.

But still there were exceptions to all these favorable words. One of these was Mnaseas of Patara, who wrote that we worshipped the golden head of an ass in our temple in Jerusalem. But most people perceived his claim as a lie and did not take it seriously.

After all this pagan admiration occurred, there came the time when we followed Judah Maccabee and defeated Antiochus Epiphanes. Then the inimical feelings began. How the Gentiles could have expected us to do anything but fight when Antiochus was trying to destroy our religion — the religion that they had so much admired until then — I do not know. But it was after that event, which even those Gentiles who were distant from Antiochus saw as a defeat for themselves, that some of their writings began to change. Now they seized upon a casual remark by Hecataeus, in which he said that some of our customs were peculiar and antisocial and hostile to foreigners — that remark never having been meant to detract from his general admiration of us, which I have just mentioned — and used it to represent the sum total of the author's opinion. Then Cicero spoke ill of us, calling our religion a "barbaric superstition," calling our people "a nation born to slavery" and, like his teacher, Apollonius Molon, saying that the practice of our ancient rites was antithetical to the glory of the empire, the dignity of the Roman name and the customs of his Roman ancestors. Then, other Roman authors begin to write against circumcision, against the Sabbath and against our abstinence from pork.

And yet, in spite of such prevarications, many Gentiles still studied and practiced our religious beliefs and ways. Indeed, the success of our religion in winning new converts seemed now to be the very thing that made the new pagan writers so hostile. Thus did the praetor, Cornelius Hispanus, issue an edict expelling our people from Rome because they were introducing our rites to the Romans and, purportedly, infecting Roman morals. And some one-hundred years later, that was why the emperor Tiberius did the same. So, along with whatever it was that attracted pagans to us, there was this envy and fear that made some of them want to keep us away.

But among the Egyptians, religious rivalry was only one of the things that aroused them against us. When Augustus defeated Mark Anthony some eighty years before this Alexandrian uprising that I have referred to, Rome emerged as the ruler of Egypt and all the Mediterranean. Though Romans put a special tax called the *laographia* on anyone who was not a Greek citizen (Egyptians and Jews being among those who were not), they gave religious freedom to the Jews. Not only that, but they actually were the protectors of Jews against any abuses that the Egyptian majority might try to commit against them. The Egyptians resented this seemingly favored status that the conqueror was giving the "foreigners", and their writers fed that resentment with fresh new libels of their own. Chaeremon, a teacher of Nero, said of our exodus from

Egypt that two-hundred and fifty-thousand polluted persons were driven out along with their leaders, Moses and Joseph, who were renegade Egyptian priests. Later, some of these undesirables returned again, he said. Lysimachus also wrote of our exodus. An oracle, he said, had advised the king to expel all unclean persons, and one of the groups that the king expelled was led by a man named Moses, who taught his people not to show anyone any kindness and to give bad instead of good advice to others and to overthrow the altars and temples of the Egyptian gods. Moses led this group across the desert, he said, and into the land of Judaea, where they then abused and plundered the people and set fire to their temples. Finally there was Apion, the head of the Alexandrian library, who wrote that we were driven out of Egypt and contracted a disease of the groin, the Egyptian name for which is the same as the word for the Jewish Sabbath. He repeated Mnaseas' lie that we worship the golden head of an ass in our temple in Jerusalem and said that when Antiochus Epiphanes entered that temple for the first time, he found a Greek being fed and fattened there for our annual sacrifice of a Gentile. Circumcision, he said, and eschewal of pork were wrong, as were all the laws of Moses. To the claim of the Jews that they were Alexandrian citizens, he answered that they were "foreigners", outsiders from Syria, unsavory people who lived in a slum and failed to make statues of emperors or worship Egyptian gods. As proof of their peregrine status, he cited the Ptolemaic actions against them and their exclusion from the grain dole by Cleopatra and Germanicus.

The Egyptian resentment of its conquest by Rome found its outlet in the hatred of Jews. They saw our people not only as foreigners but as proteges of the Romans. When King Agrippa was given his throne after Caligula exiled King Herod Antipas, he stopped in Alexandria on his way to northern Galilee. Here he made public appearances and spoke in favor of the Jews. But this just fanned the fires of hate among the nationalistic Egyptians. Added to that was the attempt by Jews to obtain Greek citizenship in order to avoid the foreigner's tax. The gymnasium, where exercise and discussion took place, was the center where citizenship was determined. Isidorus and Lampo were the leaders there and opposed these attempts by Jews. Both of them were known for their anti-Roman activities, Lampo having been tried for disloyalty to Tiberius, and Isidorus having fought against Flaccus, the Roman governor of Alexandria. Those two, along with the anti-Jewish demagogue, Dionysius, filled the hearts of their people with hate, while the writings of Lysimachus, Chaeremon and Apion aided them in their work.

Now the Alexandrians formed anti-Jewish clubs. They persuaded Flaccus, in spite of Isidorus' previous opposition to him, to downgrade the status of Jews. And Flaccus, ignoring Isidorus' anti-Romanism, took away synagogues and labeled our people as "aliens and strangers"; he made them live in a segregated neighborhood and arrested all their elders; he meted out punishments harsher than what ordinary "citizens" received. Inspired by this, the Egyptian anti-Jewish clubs then pillaged and destroyed Jewish homes. They beat our people and tortured them and then killed them. These atrocities lasted for two or three months until Rome put a stop to it all. And all of it — the misery and pain and suffering, the ending of human life and negation of people's life's work for the future, the truncating of families and mutilation of flesh — all of it had as its unconfessed cause the resentment of Rome and its rule. Incredible as this contention may seem, we Jews appeared to the Egyptians as the symbol and presence of Rome. Both Jew and Egyptian were victims of Rome, yet one looked upon the other as the conqueror's pet and sought to hurt the conqueror by hurting the pet.

CHAPTER XIV

A great debate now took place in Jerusalem. It was the brainchild of Gamaliel. Yet one might say that Caiaphas brought this debate on himself. Caiaphas was no longer high priest at this time, but as a chief priest he still wielded power. He was driven by some sort of inner compulsion to destroy the Nazarene sect. So obsessed was he with this that I suspected an ulterior reason for it. The general Jewish population still looked at him with contempt. His role in having taken Jesus to Pilate was seen as an act of betrayal against his own people. Since so many thousands of Jews considered Jesus the Messiah, and since so many more thousands considered it a possibility, Caiaphas found himself despised and reviled by most of the Jews in his country. To counteract this opprobrium, he felt that he had to do more. Instead of repudiating what he had done, he felt that he could justify himself by going beyond it. If he backed away, if he did something less, it might be construed as a doubt on his part or even an admission that he had done something wrong, and he could not allow that to be thought. So he became the most ardent adversary against the Nazarenes and denounced us wherever he could.

It was during one of his harangues before the Sanhedrin, when he was railing against the impunity and Temple privileges that had been given to James, and in which Joseph of Arimathea was defending the messiahship of Jesus, that Gamaliel, the leader of the Pharisees, serenely aloof and secure in his reputation for fairness, suggested a public debate. Caiaphas was taken aback by this. He was accustomed to being insulated from having to defend his views, and, besides, a public debate would put him on an equal footing with the man he had once tried to have assassinated. That would be an embarrassment. To have to stand on the same platform as his nemesis and bear the ignominy of trying to refute him — or even worse, of being refuted by him — was an insupportable degradation that he felt he could not abide. And yet, to refuse, to bow out, to decline that debate, would appear to be capitulatiing. It would appear that he had some fear of meeting James on a par.

"I will let you know," Caiaphas said, not committing himself to the proposal. "I must consider whether the dignity of my office would permit me to lower myself to that level."

"Perhaps the dignity of your office should not permit you to refuse," Gamaliel quipped, which elicited snickers from some of the Pharisees in the room.

"You make light of it for only one reason," Caiaphas retorted defensively, "and that is because you lack such dignity yourself."

A murmur of disapprobation spread through the Pharisee ranks. But Gamaliel, good-humoredly calmed injured prides by saying, "Caiaphas, I think you are right," and smiling, which then made the Pharisees smile, because no none in the room had more stature than Gamaliel, unofficial as his leadership might be, and no one in the room was more painfully aware of that than Caiaphas, who had just tried to insult him.

Caiaphas then slinked home like a beaten hound with his tail between his legs. He caviled to his daughter, Rabath, about Gamaliel.

"Father, don't let him annoy you," she urged, her dark eyes flashing fire. "You're a bigger man than he is, and he's jealous of what you are. You're a former high priest. You're among the elite." His daughter's words gave him strength.

The next day, conferring with Jacob, Caiaphas said, "A public debate? How can I do it? How can I prepare for it?"

"I'll help you," Jacob said. "There's no need for us to get emotional about this. You can speak in a rational way and prove everything he says is wrong. But the one thing you cannot do, in my opinion, is to decline the offer. You must not appear to be afraid of him. There is, of course, the possibility that James will decline. That would solve our problem entirely."

But, unfortunately for Caiaphas, James did not decline. He accepted the offer with alacrity. Word went out throughout the city that a great debate was to take place. An air of excitement took over Jerusalem, as if Jesus himself would be there. Many people hoped to see Caiaphas belittled, bested, by their favorite, who was James. They hoped to see Caiaphas defeated in a logical, civilized way. While it was true that Caiaphas had made himself the agent of prophecy by taking Jesus to Pilate, he had not escaped the contumely and hatred of the people for what he had done.

At midnight, the night before the event, under a clear sky and a bright moon, a massive crowd gathered at the Temple. People secured positions as near to the bottom of the stairs as possible, since they wanted to hear the speakers, who would be arguing at the top. They stood, they sat, they slept on the ground. They reserved their small plots of land by remaining fixed to them. They came even from the city's environs to hear the debaters speak. They talked and joked among themselves as they spent the night waiting. They mantled the Temple grounds like a restless army forced to keep its position. No space, no spot, was left exposed, there were so many people there. There were actually too many of them to fit inside the walled grounds of the Temple, and many of them had to stand outside. Those outside hoped for progress reports to be shouted to them by speakers or orators from the walls.

Then dawn came like a knife on the horizen, slicing away the darkness in layers. Gamaliel came out of the Temple and stood at the top of the stairs. The people applauded and cheered him. He raised his hands for silence and spoke as loud as he could.

"Today we will hear two different opinions about whether Jesus of Nazareth is the Messiah, whether Jesus of Nazareth is the one whom Moses said God would send. We have Jesus' brother, James, who leads the Nazarenes and who says he is. We have our former high priest, Caiaphas, who says he is not." At the mention of Caiaphas' name, some people made deprecating sounds. "We will have none of that," Gamaliel said. "Each man must be permitted to state his views without comments from the audience. I am the moderator, and if I find you making sounds or interfering with a speaker, I will end the debate immediately. Now pass the word along that Gamaliel means what he says."

This was done, and the crowd settled down to a respectful silence. Then James came out from one side and Caiaphas from the other. The contrast between them in the way they dressed was as great as were their views. James wore a white linen robe. His hair was somewhat disheveled. Caiaphas, in contrast, wore a robe of black with a headdress that matched it in color. The crowd, obedient to Gamaliel's command, made no sound as the men appeared.

"Now one thing more," Gamaliel said. "I know that large numbers of you here are followers of John the Baptizer. I know that those of you who are his followers think that John and not Jesus was the one whom Moses promised. I promise you that you will have your chance to speak. There will be more public debates like this. For today, we will limit ourselves just to the views of James and Caiaphas. We are planning more debates in the future."

Then, as a cool, morning breeze migrated from the surrounding hills and the sun broke refulgent from its nocturnal grave, the great debate began. James started off by enumerating those things that we would expect to see in a Messiah. Then he reviewed what Jesus had done: his miraculous healings, his increase of the available food supply, his walking on water, his restoring the dead to life. These things, said James, were surely not the work of an ordinary man. And besides that, he said, in righteousness and goodness, Jesus was unsurpassed. James did not mention resurrection because he did not feel it was necessary to do so in order to make his point. But Caiaphas soon forced him into doing that when Caiaphas' turn came to speak.

Caiaphas gave the opinion that anyone who knew the prophecies about the Messiah beforehand could have contrived to make himself fulfill them. But what is the Messiah to do, James asked, if he does them without contrivance? If we follow Caiaphas' thinking, he argued, then the real Messiah will always be considered a charlatan. Then Caiaphas went on and said that the miraculous things attributed to Jesus had only hearsay evidence to support them. People could have made them up if they wished. He had never seen those things himself; he had only heard about them from others. He doubted they had ever really happened, he said, thus discounting all testimonies to the contrary. "I think people just made them up to make Jesus seem more than he was." But James objected and said that these things had not been reported by just one or two people. Many different people had witnessed them, he said. Was Caiaphas calling all of them liars? Caiaphas said yes and then went on to make what he considered his strongest point of all: Jesus, if he was the Messiah, he said, would not have suffered death. The Messiah, if he had been threatened with death, would have been able to save himself. He would not have allowed himself to be treated the way the Romans treated Jesus. He would not have allowed himself to be pinioned to a cross. He would have smitten his enemies with the power that God had given him. But James had an answer for that too. Jesus could not have done that yet, he said. He first had to fulfill Isaiah's prophecy. He had to suffer, he had to be killed, so that the prophecy could be fulfilled.

"That is not so!" Caiaphas shouted. "Jesus himself knew that that is not what should have happened. That's why, when he was on the cross, he asked God why He had abandoned him."

"A momentary human weakness," countered James. "And God did not abandon him. God restored him to life. That is the proof that God did not abandon him — the fact that He restored him to life!"

"Another of those miracles that only his closest followers saw!" mocked Caiaphas.

"Enough people saw it to make it more than just one person's word," James said. "Are all of them liars too? Is everything that shows a man to be the Messiah to be considered false by you? How can we ever acknowledge the real Messiah if everything that's supposed to prove that that's what he is is considered a lie by you? What will it take to make you acknowledge him when he does come? What characteristic do you have to see in him that you haven't seen in Jesus?"

"At least that he doesn't get crucified!" Caiaphas shouted.

"But I told you, that was only temporary. He was restored to life after that."

"I don't believe it," Caiaphas said. "This whole idea of resurrection is absurd!"

In saying that, Caiaphas was leaving the limited subject of Jesus. He was now introducing the larger question of whether resurrection was or was not a true phenomenon. Jacob had told him the night before to avoid getting into that.

"Stick to the subject of Jesus," he had said. "Don't get into resurrection. If you want to say that Jesus himself was not resurrected, that's all right. But don't get into the issue of whether resurrection itself is valid. Don't get into the subject of whether resurrection can or cannot occur. Too many people believe that it can, so why get involved in that?"

But Caiaphas, in the heat of his convictions, forgot his secretary's advice and ejaculated the Sadducee line, thus opening extraneous wounds. Most of the people, as I have said before, believed in resurrection, and the Pharisees, especially, more than any other group, held it as one of their beliefs. Yet Gamaliel, as an unbiased moderator, did not allow his personal opinions — either about resurrection or about Jesus — to affect the impartiality of his actions. But the people, though they obeyed Gamaliel's instructions not to give any vocal responses, turned and twisted and sighed and frowned and looked at each other with obvious annoyance.

By noon, the debate drew to a close. Gamaliel asked the mass of Jews arrayed before him how many thought Caiaphas had won. Scattered hands were raised like spindly trees on an arid plain. When he asked how many thought James had won, a virtual forest of arms sprouted up at once with a roar of approval from the crowd.

Gamaliel thanked both speakers for having given their time. Then the people went off to get water and to find themselves shade from the sun.

The effect of the debate, as I saw things unfold after that, was, first, a strengthening of the Nazarene belief among the Jews of Jerusalem and, second, a vicarious form of revenge on Caiaphas (and perhaps all the chief priests) for his past hubris and persecutions.

And now more pagan hostility occurred, and this within our own land. It started in Jamnia, when the Gentile inhabitants of that city learned that Caligula considered himself divine. His liberal beginning as emperor was completely reversed when a fever so badly affected his mind that he rose from his bed a madman. He was actually obsessed with a belief in his own divinity. The sycophants around him acted their roles accordingly. Vitellius, for example, when he returned to Rome after his term as legate of Syria was over, insisted on wearing a head veil in the presence of Caligula and prostrated himself when he appeared before him. Caligula, on his part, ordered all the statues of gods that were famous for their beauty or their venerableness to be brought to Rome so that their heads could be removed and his own head substituted for them. He also started a temple with priests and with victims sacrificed to his own divinity and had a gold statue of himself placed within the temple. Priesthoods in his temple were purchased at tremendous prices.

Since there were always strained feelings between Gentiles and Jews because of different points of view on religion, the Gentiles of Jamnia seized on the emperor's belief as an opportunity to provoke their Jewish neighbors. They built an altar to Caligula so that they could worship him. To Jews this was a sacrilege. No man could be looked upon as a god; that was an insult to God. They tore down the altar and destroyed it, just as Moses had destroyed the golden calf.

The procurator, Capito, reported this to the emperor, and the emperor took it as an insult. For revenge, he ordered Petronius, the new legate of Syria, to build a huge statue of Zeus in the Jewish Temple in Jerusalem, and, because he knew Jewish reaction would be strong, he ordered him to use troops to back him up.

To a people for whom even the smallest statue within the city was enough to start a riot, a statue of such a size and of a pagan god and placed within the Temple would have started a revolution. Petronius knew that, but he also knew that to disobey the emperor would mean his death. And he knew, too, that if he got involved in a war with the Jews, the Parthians on the eastern frontier would take advantage of his weakened Roman force and invade Syria and that they would have the aroused Jewish population of Mesopotamia to support them.

So he played for time. In the winter, he moved two Roman legions and a large auxiliary force of Syrians into Israel and stationed them in

Ptolemais. He ordered the statue to be started in Sidon and negotiated with our leaders to accept Caligula's command peacefully. But our people could not do that. They flocked to Ptolemais by the thousands, camping on the plain near the city, to tell Petronius that there would be a general massacre on both sides if the statue was built. Petronius again delayed. He ordered the artists to slow their work, telling them that they must aim for exactness of detail. Then he wrote to Caligula, saying that the goal of perfection as well as the need to oversee the harvest were delaying things a little. Caligula accepted the excuse but was secretly enraged by it.

But now, as if all this was not bad enough, Caligula suddenly announced that *he* was Zeus existing in human form and that the Temple in Jerusalem must be turned into a shrine to his own divinity. The fact that we already sacrificed to *our* god in his behalf would no longer be enough; now we had to sacrifice to Caligula himself. This, of course, made things even worse, and Petronius could see the impendency of a bloody revolution against the entire Roman presence in Israel, all caused by this issue of a sculpted piece of stone. It made no sense to him. But, also, it made no sense to King Herod Agrippa. Agrippa, you will recall, was Caligula's friend; he had suffered imprisonment on Caligula's behalf when Tiberius had been emperor, because he had openly expressed his desire that Tiberius would die so that Caligula could replace him. Agrippa went to Rome to speak with the emperor and to seek an alternative way. He had to counter the anti-Jewish influence of the emperor's advisor, Helicon, when he did this. But his appeal was effective, and Caligula decreed that work on the statue should be stopped. But as a price for that, he ordered that the Gentile communities in Israel must erect pagan altars and that they must not be hindered by the Jews from doing so. To Agrippa, the nation was saved. But Petronius, not knowing any of this because the entire thing was taking place in Rome, made his own try at peace. At the risk of his own life, he wrote to Caligula, asking him to rescind the order for the statue. Caligula was insulted anew. He flew into a rage. He nullified his agreement with Agrippa. He ordered a new statue to be started in Rome, which he would send in its completed form to Judaea. And he sent a message to Petronius, advising him to kill himself.

Then Flaccus, too, incurred the emperor's wrath: he had mishandled his governorship in Alexandria. In his case, however, the emperor's displeasure was for another reason besides ineptitude. Years earlier, poor Flaccus had supported Caligula's rivals in the political maneuvering in Rome and had been involved in the exile of Caligula's mother. Not a wise thing to have done, in retrospect. Now he was being summoned to Rome. He was going to have to explain to Caligula why he had deviated from established Roman policy and permitted the slaughter of all those loyal Jews in Alexandria. Things, to say the least, did not look good for him. In addition to Flaccus, an Egyptian delegation, including Apion and Chaeremon, went to Rome to plead the case for the Egyptian side, while a Jewish delegation, including Philo, the writer, went to plead for the Jews. The Jews had lesser hopes, however, because of the emperor's anti-Jewish advisor, Helicon, and because of the affair of the statue in Jerusalem.

Now, Pontius Pilate, true to form, became involved in an intrigue against the emperor. He was, I suppose, unable to live with just his wealth and nothing more. That he, who had mastered the unruly Jews, who had stopped rebellions before they began, who had conceived of building an aqueduct in Jerusalem with Jewish Temple money so that Rome would not be bothered, should now be consigned to some trash heap of unneeded, anachronistic officials was an insult, an unbearable slap, in the face of an eminent man. He was determined that the world should hear from him again and that he should rise even higher than before. If Caligula was so blind as not to realize his worth, another emperor would. He involved himself in an assassination plot as a means to reach his goal. The conspirators would surround Caligula and stab him with daggers, just as others had stabbed Julius Caesar in the past. The new emperor would reward Pontius Pilate and give him authority again.

But Caligula, for all his maniacal insanity — perhaps because of it, I might say — was alert to any threat to his life and responsive to any rumor. When a spy informed him of the conspiracy, he had all the conspirators arrested. Pilate went into a cold, wet cell with as little light squeezing through the slit in the wall as the food and water they gave him. His wife was not permitted to see him. His jailer was mute. In a week, he lost all sense of time; in two he began to babble. Then a messenger came from Caligula and handed him a knife. "The emperor is kind," the messenger said. "He sends you this as a gift."

That night Pilate slashed his wrists. In the morning he was dead. Was this retribution from God, a punishment from heaven? The man who had sentenced Jesus to death was forced to kill himself! Was there any thought of remorse for the people he had killed? Did he think of Jesus or any of them with regret? Or did he see himself only as an honorable, mistreated man? Without speech or writing, there are only thoughts, and those are known only to God. Whatever Pilate did think

106

died with him: private, secret, concealed, inaccessible to the inquisitions of men, interred to curiosity. He died, dark in death as in life, with only corpses in his wake.

But Caligula's reign ended abruptly anyway when another assassin killed him. What a sense of relief pervaded the empire when that occurred! The Egyptian problem would be something for the next emperor to decide, but, more important for us Jews, the affair of the statue was ended. Yet the memory of it still lingered and reminded us of our helplessness as a conquered people. It was bad enough to compromise on the paying of tribute, as many of us did for the sake of peace, but there could be no compromise on the statue of a pagan god or a pagan emperor being placed within the sacred walls of our temple. And what one emperor had tried to do, another might try to do as well. Zealotism in Israel increased after that.

This entire affair reminded me of another pagan conqueror some two-hundred years before: Antiochus, the Syrian, who stamped coins with his face on them and called himself Antiochus Epiphanes — God Manifest — and who built altars to Zeus in our land. He burned our holy books, banned all Jewish observances and forced our people to eat swine or die. He murdered forty-thousand of our people, including mothers with their babies. In front of him, Hannah and her sons refused to bow to Zeus, and each was killed in his turn.

But then Mattathias and his sons started the Maccabean Revolt, not so much because they objected to Antiochus as king but because he would not allow us to practice our religion. In the battles that ensued, Antiochus once attacked on the Sabbath because he knew Jews could not fight on that day, and that cost us one-thousand men. Because of that, Mattathias decreed that, henceforth, Jews could *defend* themselves on the Sabbath; they just could not attack. Then Mattathias died, and his son, Judah Maccabee, took over. Maccabee means the Hammerer, and he was a man aptly named. He won many battles, using sticks and stones and farm tools fashioned into weapons, using them against the swords, javelins, spears and elephants employed by the Syrians. And out of his final victory near the town of Ammaus came our festival called the Feast of Dedication.

So just as we had prevailed against Antiochus' attempt to push a false god upon us, so had we prevailed against Caligula's attempt to do so. But our victory over Antiochus had been a military one that left us free of foreign rule, while our victory over Caligula had been a passive one that left the Romans still in power. So we made no festival to commemorate our victory over Caligula. We were still a subject people.

THE CHRIST-KILLERS

CHAPTER XV

When news reached Alexandria that Caligula was killed, the Jews there responded to it by fighting against the Egyptians. They may have felt that Helicon, Caligula's anti-Jewish advisor, previously had kept the emperor from acting sooner or more forcibly in their defense and that now, without that man's influence in Rome, they could act without fear of reprisal.

Claudius became the emperor, but the trouble in Egypt remained. So Claudius wrote the Egyptians and warned them to behave gently and kindly toward the Jews and not to dishonor any of the Jews' customs in the worship of their god. He restored the Jewish privileges that Flaccus had so peremptorily removed but then warned the Jews not to aim for more than they previously had had, by which he meant the citizenship that some of them wanted, and also not to bring into Egypt more Jews from other parts of the world. Apion, meanwhile, though unsuccessful in getting Claudius to suppress the Jews, remained in Rome as an important literary figure and exerted his influence there. But Lampo and Isidorus, those two anti-Jewish Alexandrian agitators, made an unwise and fatal mistake. They made it publicly known that they were enemies of Agrippa. They had forgotten, perhaps, that Agrippa had been not only Caligula's friend but Claudius' friend as well. Agrippa was one of the people who had helped Claudius acquire his new position. Claudius did not take kindly to this public disparagement of his friend, and he had Lampo and Isidorus executed as enemies of the state.

Alexandria then stayed quiet during Claudius' reign, but the bitter feelings remained. Chaeremon, Lysimachus and Apion; Lampo, Isidorus and Dionysius — all had inscribed their malice and hate onto the Egyptian mind; while Flaccus and Rome's inconstancy had left their marks on the Jews. The Egyptian still hated the Jew in his midst, and the Jew now cared less for the Roman.

Meanwhile, across the desert, in our own land, things were improving for Agrippa. Because Agrippa had helped Claudius to power, Claudius now rewarded him by adding Judaea, Galilee and Perea to the territories over which he already ruled. Rewarded now by two emperors, first Caligula and now Claudius, Agrippa's lands became as vast as Herod the Great's had been, and our entire nation knew for a time the rule of a Jewish king, albeit under Roman supervision. For three years after Claudius did this, there was no procurator in Judaea, and things were easier for the people. Agrippa, who had been raised with his two half-brothers, Herod and Aristobulus, and who had sired five children with his wife, Cypros, now looked at his oldest daughter, Bernice. She had lost her husband, Marcus, recently. Agrippa decided that she needed a new husband to look after her. So he turned to his half-brother, Herod. Herod readily agreed to the marriage. Bernice was an attractive young woman, and Herod did not need much convincing. Because Agrippa was now grateful to him for having taken Bernice as his wife, he now spoke to Claudius on his half-brother's behalf and secured for Herod the territory of Chalcis. Herod was now to be called, Herod of Chalcis, a step up in the world for him.

Also, Agrippa, having now also been given the authority by Claudius to appoint high priests, gave Simon Kantheras, son of Boethus, that post.

I have said that things were better for Agrippa, and that indeed was true. But Agrippa felt that he had to prove he was worthy of all this Roman largesse, so he looked at the political turbulence that still beset his domain and set about to end it by a show of force and determination. It was not just the Zealots who struck fear into his heart but the Nazarenes as well. Those Nazarenes who were quiescent he could leave alone but not those who were public agitators. He knew that all the Nazarenes opposed his rule and wanted to set up a new kingdom. He knew what Jesus' followers were after when they said to Jesus, "Will you be restoring the kingdom to Israel at this time?" To them Jesus was the rightful king and would return to claim his throne. Agrippa saw in this a potential unseating of himself by an increasingly popular movement, so he took steps to suppress it before it got out of hand. In fairness to his name, however, he was somewhat a religious man; he did study the Torah. Yet he saw no sin in supporting a pagan master, which was contradictory to all that we believed.

Within our group were men disposed to aggressive action. They were the ones the Romans and the king and the Sadducees feared the most. Certainly, Simon the Zealot, one of Jesus' disciples, was one of them, and certainly Peter himself was another. And the brothers, James and John, the sons of Zebedee, who were also Jesus' disciples, were so vehemently demonstrative about the kingdom that was to come that they earned for themselves the title, Sons of Thunder or Sons of Fiery Zeal. Two years into his reign, Agrippa, who was aware of these activities, arrested James, the son of Zebedee, and had him executed by the sword.

The only blessing in all that, I suppose, was that there was no Roman procurator on the scene, for if there had been, James would have been killed by crucifixion, a slower and more torturous death. The execution, of course, pleased the Sadducees. It meant one less Nazarene leader for them to have to deal with. But for the people in general, it was another tragedy in a long line of tragedies that seemed never to end until the coming of our Messiah.

Now, either to show his power or simply because he wanted to give someone else a turn at the helm, Agrippa deposed Simon Kantheras from his post as high priest and offered it to Jonathan, the son of Annas, for whom it would have been the second time in that office. But Jonathan declined and said that he was unworthy of having that honor twice and requested that it be given to someone else, such as his brother, Matthias. So, instead of Jonathan, Agrippa appointed, Matthias, who accepted the post enthusiastically.

Then Agrippa turned his attention to us Nazarenes again and went after Peter next. He had Peter arrested and put into prison. We had no doubt that he intended to execute him just as he had James, the son of Zebedee. But it was the time of the Passover Festival, and crowds of pilgrims were now filling the streets, just as they had done during the time of Jesus' imprisonment. Peter was a popular man (you may recall how many thousands of people had become Nazarenes because of his healings, just as thousands had become Nazarenes because of Jesus doing that), and the things that Peter preached about were popular too. Agrippa knew that. He knew how many thousands of Jews had joined the Nazarene movement, and he realized that the execution of such a person at a time when national pride was running so high was a dangerous thing to do. So he decided to delay the execution until after the festival was over. He ordered four quaternions of soldiers to guard Peter, so dangerous did he consider him, and at night, he had Peter bound with chains between two of the soldiers and had two other soldiers guarding the door. Yet, in spite of all these precautions, Peter escaped from them, just as he had escaped when Annas had taken him prisoner before his trial with the Sanhedrin. Some unidentified person got Peter out at night while the guards were asleep. Even Peter was not sure of who it was, but there are some who say, and perhaps rightly so, that it was an angel from God. In the morning, when Agrippa learned of Peter's escape, he took out his anger on the guards and had them all put to death. If they were innocent, he felt, then they deserved to die for dereliction of duty. But he had a strong suspicion that they were not innocent and that they were either Nazarene sympathizers or Nazarenes and that they had freed Peter themselves. Religious as he was purported to be, his understanding of the Torah was not deep enough for him to have learned about the virtue of mercy and forgiveness and the preciousness of human life. Peter told some of our friends about his escape and told them to inform James, Jesus' brother. Then he sought out Simon, our Zealot disciple, and spoke to him about what to do next.

"When things get too hot in one place," Simon said, "it's a good idea to withdraw and strike somewhere else."

"Where could I go?" Peter asked. "Agrippa has his agents everywhere."

"I'm talking about leaving the country," Simon said. "I'm talking about putting some distance between you and Agrippa. What would you think of Alexandria?"

"Alexandria!" Peter exclaimed. "Do you realize how far that is, Simon? I wouldn't be able to see Rachel or my son. I wouldn't be able to help James in making policy decisions."

"Rachel and your son could go with you," he said. "And as for James and making decisions, he'll do all right without you. You could work in Alexandria, the same as you do here. We have plenty of friends there who will see that you're safe."

Peter placed his elbow on the table and rested the side of his face in his palm. He remembered his promise to Rachel that he would be careful and stay alive. But if he parted from her for a lengthy time, it would be as good as if he were dead. And aside from that, her own life and the life of Marcus, their son, might also be in danger. Agrippa might take both of them hostage in order to force Peter out of hiding, or he might kill them both, as he had Peter's guards, in a state of unrestrained savagery.

"Can you get a message to Rachel secretly for me?" he asked.

"Of course," Simon said. "Agrippa's men are probably watching your house, so I'll send some of the older women. Do you want her to come here to you?"

"Yes," he said, "and have her bring Marcus too."

What Agrippa's men saw when they watched Peter's house from a distance that night were two elderly women, one of average height and one rather short, the hoods of their cloaks partially adumbrating their faces, paying a neighborly visit to Rachel. What they saw a short time later were the same two women leaving the house, their hoods held more closely to their faces, and each carrying a bundle that might have been a gift of food or clothing or some other such item with which women are commonly concerned. But these second figures were Rachel and Marcus, deceiving Agrippa's men.

In Simon's house, Rachel and Peter talked alone in a room while Simon, ever the warrior, played bow and arrow with Marcus outside.

"So it's come to this," she said to him. "Another arrest, another imprisonment and another threat to your life. And this time there's no Sanhedrin or Pharisee leader to set you free. Peter, what kind of life is this? We had a decent income when you were a fisherman in Galilee. We had enough to eat, and you earned enough at the market to give us a few small luxuries. It wasn't that much, but it was enough to keep us alive and safe. And we had peace. I could go to sleep at night knowing that you'd be there the next day. But now, ever since the Nazarene talked you into following him, we've had to live with danger every day. We left what we had in Galilee, and now we live in a city with all kinds of people from all over the world. We had a simple life, a peaceful life, and now all we have is trouble. And now you're telling me that we have to move again, because if we don't, you're going to get killed. And John's brother, James, he's already been killed. God, what his wife must be feeling! I have to remember to send her something. And the soldiers who were guarding you, they were killed too? What kind of a life is this, Peter? What kind of a life is it?"

"Rachel, we've been through this before," he said. "I told you, I don't have a choice. If you had seen him do the things he did, if you had heard him say the things he said, you wouldn't have any doubt. I have to do what I'm doing now. It's a call from God, believe me. The abilities, the powers that have been given me, they haven't been given without reason. There are things I have to do because of them, and getting our people ready for him is one of those things. There's going to be a new kingdom when he comes back, Rachel, and I've been chosen to spread the word about it. That's it, pure and simple. I've been chosen to do it, and I'm going to do it. I love you and I love Marcus, but I can't let that stand in my way. You must understand, Rachel. I would protect you and Marcus with my life, I love you both so much, but I must do what I've been chosen to do."

She stood with her back to him, not wanting him to see the tears in her eyes. "All right, all right," she sighed. "If you have to, you have to. Where is it that you want us to go? Where is this place, this haven, that you think will be safe for us?"

He hesitated a moment, because he knew the effect it was going to have on her when he said it, and then said, "Alexandria."

She whirled to face him. "Alexandria? Peter, that's in Egypt!"

"I know it's in Egypt," he said. "I know where Alexandria is."

"You want us to go to Egypt? And to live there?"

"Yes," he pleaded. "It's far enough away to be safe from Agrippa."

"But Egypt, Peter. It has all those strange people with strange customs. They worship strange gods. They even eat their gods and drink their blood to make their gods a part of them. How can we live among people like that?"

"You won't have to," he said. "There are more Jews in Alexandria than you can count. You'll be among Jewish people. You don't have to worry. It'll be all right. You'll see. They'll help us, they'll support us."

A sigh, a nod and a capitulation, and Rachel agreed to make the move. She brought in Marcus to tell him about it.

Simon arranged for Zealot guards disguised as traveling merchants to accompany them to the coast. There the three fugitives boarded a ship bound for Egypt and watched the dim bulge of Judaea recede behind them like a shriveling pomegrante in the sun. The leadership of our group then fell almost entirely to James.

Agrippa, with a fickleness worthy of a Roman procurator, then changed high priests again. This time the honor of that office went to Elianaios, who was as inconsequential as the others during this non-Roman reign of a Jewish king.

Meanwhile, Peter and his family arrived safely in Alexandria and were succored there by our friends. In my opinion, he would have remained a hunted man even there if it had not been for Agrippa's sudden death. It was said that that happened — or, at least, started to happen —while Agrippa was pronouncing a judgment from his throne and some fawning courtiers were flattering him by saying, "The voice of a god and not of a man!" I think those people must have been very surprised at how quickly this god of theirs left the earth. I am ashamed to have to tell you that Jews resorted to this kind of sacrilegious sycophancy, but not all of us are as strong as others.

It happened in Caesarea. Agrippa was there celebrating the quadrennial games being held in honor of Augustus. As he sat enthroned under an awning, his silver robes glistening in the sun, his obsequious followers seized the opportunity to curry favor with him by calling him a god. Yet he did not object to this, as he should have. To a Jew, it is blasphemous to call a man a god. Instead, Agrippa just beamed his approval and let the adulation go on.

Then, as he looked up to heaven, the dwelling place of God, he saw an object silhouetted against the sun. The sight made him blanch with fear. An owl was sitting on a rope of the awning above his head. "The

114

German," he muttered, remembering his fellow prisoner and the prophesy eight years before. Abruptly, he moaned and clutched his chest. Then he fell to the ground in pain. They carried him back to his palace, and five days later, as had been predicted, he died.

Agrippa, I should tell you, had had two sons and three daughters by his wife, Cypros. Agrippa and Drusus were the names of his sons, and his daughters were Bernice, Mariamne and Drusilla. Drusus had died before reaching puberty, so the young Agrippa was now heir to the throne. But this young Agrippa, who was now just seventeen, was considered much too young and inexperienced to handle the affairs of government, so the emperor Claudius had to look elsewhere for a ruler. Also, an audit revealed that the elder Agrippa had indulged himself in unrestrained spending and that the kingdom was now in debt. Claudius had no reason to think that the young Agrippa was any more capable of handling money than his father. For that reason, also, he did not allow him to rule the entire land.

This new Agrippa, however, was not so young that he was unaware of his responsibilities as the head of his family. He had to see that his sisters were married and taken care of henceforth. Mariamne, his middle sister, was now ten years old and was betrothed already to Julius Archelaus, a Jewish commoner, but the son of the commander-in-chief, Helcias. So there was no problem there. He gave Mariamne to Archelaus and saw the two of them married. His sister, Bernice, who was now sixteen, had already gotten married again, you will recall, this time to her uncle, Herod of Chalcis, so there was no problem there either. But Drusilla, who was now six years of age, was having a problem in securing a mate. Their father, Agrippa I, when he had been alive, had arranged with King Antiochus of Commagene that Antiochus' son, Epiphanes, would marry Drusilla, but with the understanding that Epiphanes would accept circumcision and adopt the Jewish religion. Epiphanes had accepted these terms, for Drusilla's wealth and her promise of future beauty as she grew into womanhood had seemed a prize worth having, even if it did mean some temporary discomfort. But somewhere along the road between betrothal and wedlock, the ardor of the bridegroom had waned, and Epiphanes had said that he would marry the girl but not on the previous terms. The elder Agrippa had been determined that his daughter would marry no one but a Jew, so he had withdrawn his offer and had started looking elsewhere for a match. But he had died before a suitable mate could be found, and the responsibility for marrying Drusilla to someone had fallen now to his son. Young Agrippa, green as he was, was determined to do what he must. He spent time looking about for a mate for his youngest sister.

Agrippa I, when he had been alive, had spent much of his own money to help Caesarea, Berytus and Sebaste. He had done much to rebuild those cities and had not only constructed baths and colonnades in them but even pagan temples in which the Gentiles could worship. One might have thought those Gentiles would have been grateful for that and would have lamented Agrippa's death. But the very opposite actually occurred. They cursed Agrippa foully as they celebrated his death in the streets, and a large group of their soldiers raided Agrippa's house in Caesarea and carried off the statues of his daughters and placed them on the roof of a brothel and performed indecent sexual acts with them in full approving view of the people. So much for the Gentiles and Agrippa.

You may well ask why a Jewish king had statues in his house, since that was a violation of Mosaic law. But Agrippa, you see, though he had adhered to the Torah up to a point, had felt comfortable in ignoring it when it inconvenienced him. Statues were the rage in Rome; all the best people had them. Agrippa, anxious to modernize his country and bring it into the current century, had commissioned these sculptures to be made in order to show his Roman masters he was one of them. He had done as much with the coins of his realm, for they had his and the emperor's face on them. And to celebrate the buildings that he had built for the Gentiles, he staged gladiatorial shows, in which men by the hundreds fought to the death or were thrown to wild beasts to be eaten. Impieties? Violations of Jewish law? Yes, all these things were his. Yet he adhered superficially to the Torah enough to convince some Jews that he was good.

Herod of Chalcis, the deceased Agrippa's half-brother, seeing that the young Agrippa was not going to be given any responsibilities by Claudius, now petitioned Claudius for control of the Temple treasury and for the right to appoint high priests. Claudius, feeling that the young Agrippa could not handle even that much responsibility as yet, gave Herod the privileges he wanted. Immediately, Herod, like a child that had been given a new toy, exercised his newly won power by deposing Elianaios, son of Kantheras, from the high priesthood and appointing Joseph, son of Camus, in his place.

The governing of all the territory of Agrippa I, however, was another matter entirely, as I have said, and Claudius decided to give control of that domain to the procurator whom he would appoint. Before Agrippa I, only Judaea had known a procurator's rule; Galilee had been left under the king. Then, when Agrippa I had become the king, the entire nation had been placed under him. Judaea had then had a much-needed respite from the harshness of direct Roman rule. But now, everything was going the other way. The entire nation over which the deceased Agrippa had ruled directly was now being placed under the direct control of the procurator. Galilee, which had been spared the harshness of such rule in the past, was now to know it first-hand. The effect of this on the Zealots was to make them even more active than before. And Peter, whose life had been in danger under Agrippa I, was now too inconsequential for the new rulers to pursue in the rush of all these events.

When word of these things reached Peter, he knew the danger was gone. He said to Rachel at dinner one night, "Would you like to go back to Jerusalem?"

Rachel, who had started to accept her new life, looked at her husband and smiled. "I feel like a woman who takes a breath in Egypt and exhales it in Jerusalem. Yes, I'd like to go back," she said. "Maybe someday even to Galilee." So they packed their bags, as they had before, and returned to the city of God.

Cuspius Fadus became the procurator now, and he immediately set out to make a name for himself. At the borders of Nabataea and Idumaea, a famous Zealot named Tholomais was successfully harassing the Romans. Fadus pursued him and caught him. Tholomais' execution was Fadus' first success.

Then came a man named Theudas. He claimed to be a prophet. Many people believed in him, and he exhorted them to gather their belongings and follow him to the Jordan River, which would divide as the Red Sea had divided for Moses, after which they would cross into the desert and wander like the ancients into the new promised land. Unfortunately for them, since Zealots operated out of the desert as well as out of the hills, Fadus perceived this pilgrimage as the beginning of a new Zealot force, and he had his cavalry attack it. Theudas was caught and beheaded, and many of his followers were killed. Thus Fadus followed in the footsteps of Pilate by killing without asking questions.

Though some had thought Theudas was the Messiah, we Nazarenes, of course, had not. A prophet, perhaps, but not the Messiah. The Messiah, we knew, was Jesus, and he would return to lead us again.

Cuspius Fadus did not stay long in his post as procurator. The man who replaced him was Tiberius Alexander, the son of Alexander, the Jewish alabarch of Alexandria, and the nephew of the historian Philo.

117

Tiberius had been a Jew, but he had renounced his faith to gain favor with the Romans. He would now be governor of all of Israel. His uncle, Philo, had tried to forge a compromise between his love for Greek culture and his loyalty to the Jewish religion. His nephew, Tiberius Alexander, had not bothered with that. He had severed the one and adopted the other and become a true adherent of Rome.

One of the first things Tiberius did was to capture Jacob and Simon, two of the sons of Judas of Galilee, and execute them. By that he showed his Roman masters how formidable an adversary he was against Zealots. For most of us, it was another in a long line of set-backs we were to endure before God would restore our freedom. These were troubled times, and we were not a compliant people, and the Romans had their hands full with us.

CHAPTER XVI

Visitors from Jerusalem came to us in Antioch. Their words held great importance for us not only because of the news they brought but because they were prophets. One of them, a man named Agabus, predicted that a great famine would come to the land. Later, when it did — primarily in Judaea — we decided that it was our duty to help our brothers there. Claudius, as I have mentioned, had just replaced Fadus with Tiberius Alexander as procurator, and we heard that Tiberius was not too well disposed towards Jews, even though Philo was his uncle. The situation in Jerusalem, we feared, might be even more unpleasant than before. The execution of Judas of Galilee's sons did not presage well for our cause, and that, coupled with the famine that had come upon us, suggested difficult times ahead. Saul and I collected money from our followers in Antioch to take back with us to Jerusalem. But before we went, Saul left me for a day to conduct some private business on his own. Later, he told me that it was to purchase a Roman citizenship. He had used some of the money we had collected from our followers to purchase what he felt might be a valuable protection as we did our work in the future. I raised no objection to this, for I felt that it was a justifiable expenditure.

We left for Jerusalem and, along the way, saw evidences of the famine: a man giving his sword for a loaf of bread; a woman with her starving baby at the roadside; an old man in a ditch breathing his last. We helped where we could, giving small amounts of money here or there, so that the hungry person could buy whatever meager supply of food was still available. We heard that the Jewish converts, Helena, Queen of Adiabene, and her son, Monobazus, were spending large sums of money in Egypt to buy food for the hungry masses. They were people, you see, who did not just study Mosaic law but practiced it as well.

Then we came to Jerusalem, and there we met with our brothers. The money that we poured onto the table before them brought tears to some of their eyes. Pangs of hunger are not pleasant to experience, and many of them had been experiencing that lately. James was not there at the time, but Peter was, having returned to Jerusalem, and he expressed his gratitude to us.

Later, when empty bellies had been filled, we sat and talked about Antioch, and Saul and I revealed that some of those who had contributed money were Gentiles. No one really was shocked by this, as we had thought they were going to be, and the reason for that was that Peter had started preaching to Gentiles too. Our brothers told us that James had been skeptical about this at first, considering the fact that Jesus had instructed us to go only to Jews, but that since Peter was encouraging these Gentiles to convert to Judaism, which meant the Torah, circumcision and all the dietary rules that go along with that, James had agreed to it. As he saw it, the more people who followed the Torah, the better off the world would be; and the more people who followed his brother, the more likely it was that his brother would be successful when he returned. For those who were not Jews, however, even for those who had made a partway conversion to Judaism, acceptance as Nazarenes was denied. It was that way with the Cutheans, who practiced the Torah up to a point. When their leader came to Peter and said, "We wish to become Nazarenes," Peter placed his hand on the man's shoulder and said in a friendly but resolute manner, "Not until you become Jews. Only those who follow the Torah completely can be followers of Jesus."

Saul and I did not reveal that we were not doing the same as Peter; we did not reveal that we were *not* encouraging our Gentile followers to become Jews, that their mere acceptance of Jesus' forthcoming kingdom was all that we were requiring, although we were teaching them basic morality to which they should try to adhere. And the reason we did not reveal what we were doing — or not doing — was because we feared that James would disallow it. We feared that James would insist that Gentiles become Jews if they were to be accepted by us. And Saul and I knew that most of the Gentiles would not accept that. Circumcision and food restrictions alone were enough to turn them away. And if most of them left us, the strength of the movement that we had created in Antioch would be gone. To have the Jews of Antioch join us was one thing; to have the Gentiles join us meant a much wider range of influence. So we said nothing except that these people had joined us; and our brothers, thankful enough for the respite from hunger that we had brought them, did not think to question us further.

After that I went to my sister Mary's house, and Saul visited his sister too. Mary was elated to see me. After hugs and kisses and squeals of delight, she sat me down and fulfilled the universal female imperative of feeding guests. The food which, in this time of famine, was kept secretly hidden in the house, had been obtained through her husband Joash's work. He was a merchant, whose employees transferred food from the coastal areas to the city. He would ensure that all the familes of his workers as well as his own had enough to eat before he would sell any food. When my nephew, John, surnamed Mark, tried to ask me about my travels, my sister said, "No, not until after he's finished eating. Then you can ask him what you want."

But while she could successfully limit my own oral activities to the silent ingestion of food, she could not prevent her voluble son from telling me that he had joined the Nazarenes. His father interjected that it had been a decision made without his parents. They had not wanted him to get involved in a revolutionary movement as I had done. These were perilous times, and revolutionaries were fair game for both Romans and high priests.

"I did it because of you, uncle," my nephew proudly announced. "You inspired me to join them."

I swallowed the food in my mouth and turned to my sister. "Have I eaten enough to be allowed to speak?" I asked.

She looked at the food still remaining before me. "Speak," she said magnanimously.

"Thank you," I answered. Then to my nephew, "You don't become a Nazarene because someone else has done it. You do it because of a deep belief inside yourself."

"Which I have!" he answered, looking directly into my eyes, and I could see in his face that he was sincere.

My nephew, I should mention, was not much younger than myself. We were both young men, and for anyone who did not know our family relationship, we appeared to be just contemporaries and friends. And, I suppose, in the way that we actually related to each other, that is exactly what we were.

Late in the evening, when my sister and I were alone, she talked about our uncle in Cyprus.

"Uncle Daniel writes to me," she said, "and he always asks about you. He feels responsible for you since father died. I think he's even forgiven you for selling the land and giving away the money."

"How is his health?" I asked.

"Good, as far as I know. I think his biggest problem is that he's lonely. His wife is gone, he has no children and you seem to be like the son he never had."

"Well, maybe I can find a way to get back there," I said.

I had no idea of what that way might be when I said it, but I think the thought entered my mind unwittingly at that moment and that I started looking for the opportunity from then on.

Saul and I left Jerusalem, and we left with a feeling of relief as well as a feeling of freedom to continue our work in the same manner as before. This time, however, my nephew, John (Mark), who, I was discovering, was quite an independent thinker, went with us. And instead of going back to Antioch, the three of us went to Cyprus. It was my suggestion that we do that, my stated reason being that we had not preached our message there yet. Though that was true, the opportunity that it presented me to see my uncle, of course, and to introduce him to the son of his niece, whom he had never met, was certainly an influence as well.

I planned to meet my uncle at his home in Salamis. I did not want to shock him by making an unannounced appearance, so I sent a message to tell him that I had arrived in Cyprus and would come with friends in two days. When Saul, John (Mark) and I entered his house, I was greeted by old friends and schoolmates whom my uncle had contacted and invited to the house for a party. I felt like a long-absent son returning. It was obvious that my uncle had gone to some expense to do this. The food and wine were plentiful, and the musicians were very accomplished. It was also obvious that my uncle was doing this to impress me — not with his wealth, which I knew he had, but with the attractions of Cyprus over Antioch and Jerusalem. Among those attractions were unwed young women who had come with their parents to the party. How could I tell my uncle that, beautiful as they were, they held no allure for me? I decided that if I said it, it would hurt his feelings, so I left it unsaid and smiled my way through the endless introductions and flashing eyes, until I could briefly corner him in the courtyard and say, "Uncle, I have a surprise for you."

"For me?" he said, opening his eyes wide. "What is it?"

I pointed to John (Mark). "That young man over there, do you know who it is?"

"Your friend," my uncle said. "Your traveling companion."

"He's your grandnephew, uncle. He's Ruth's son. He carries your blood in his veins."

My uncle's mouth opened wide. Tears began to fall down his face. "Oh, oh," he moaned tremulously, like a man who was having a seizure. "God be praised! God be praised!" He covered his mouth with the palms of his hands and inhaled audibly between his fingers. Then again, "Oh, oh," like a lowing calf. Because the sounds of joy and the sounds of pain are sometimes so much alike, I could not tell at the moment if my uncle needed help or if he was just exulting over the unexpected news I had given him. Then, when he said in a fragile voice, "Take me to him, take me to him," I knew that he was all right and that his sighs and effusions were ones of happiness.

I took him to John (Mark) and introduced them to each other. John (Mark) kissed my uncle's hand and then his cheek and then received my uncle's warm embrace with supple compliance. My uncle then did to him what he previously had done to me. He subjected John (Mark) to repeated introductions to young women and their families, submitting him to a gauntlet of marital possibilities, until John (Mark) looked over his shoulder to me for help, and I, with a perverse smile on my lips, turned my face away.

When I introduced Saul to my uncle a little later in the afternoon, Saul was rather reserved. My uncle tried to put him at ease in the hope of making him smile, but Saul remained serious and formal, and my uncle finally gave up. My uncle spared him the array of eligible young women because he sensed immediately Saul's imperviousness to their charms. Saul seemed to have such important things on his mind that even an afternoon's diversion could not swerve him from thinking about them.

In the evening, after the guests and musicians had gone and the servants were cleaning the house, we talked to my uncle about our work and our desire to speak in the synagogue.

"You still feel the need to do this work?" my uncle asked me, making a feckless appeal to my reason.

"Yes, uncle, even more now than before," I said.

"Ah," he sighed, "do you know what you're giving up?"

"I know," I said, "but I have to do this. All of us who are in this movement feel the same. Even John (Mark) here has joined us. He's going to be preaching too."

"Even him?" my uncle said. "A peaceful life, that's what you should try to have. You go from city to city, and you never live in one place. You remind me of Moses wandering in the desert."

"We *are* like Moses," Saul interjected. "But we're leading people to a *new* promised land, a new kingdom, one that will cover the entire earth and not just Judaea and Samaria and Galilee."

"We want to speak here in Salamis," I said. "Can you arrange for us to speak in the synagogue?"

"Of course I can," my uncle said. "Maybe I'll even learn something from all of you. I'll arrange for you to speak this next Sabbath." Then, like the surrogate parent he was to us all, he said, "Now boys, you must get some rest."

In the synagogue at Salamis, we preached our message. We were nicely received and encountered no problems. And since we were preaching to Jews, the issue of Gentile conversion never arose.

After that we said goodbye to my uncle and went to the island of Paphos. The deputy there was a man named Sergius Paulus. When he heard about us and the things we were teaching, he invited us to appear before him. We went together to meet him and found him to be a very gracious man. He had an open mind about Jesus and listened attentively to all we had to say. Saul seemed to relate especially well to him, and that, perhaps, was because Sergius Paulus was a Gentile, and Saul himself had been a Gentile at one time. He asked us to return the next day, but because we had promised to speak in a synagogue at that time, John and I kept our appointment at the synagogue while Saul went to see Paulus alone. We had no idea that Paulus had intended to test us in some way, but that is precisely what he did. When Saul arrived, Paulus presented a Jewish sorcerer named Bar-Jesus or Elymas, who immediately started to refute all that we had said the previous day. But Saul was undismayed. He waited until the man had spoken and then, when Saul's turn came to speak, rather than degrade himself by engaging in polemics, he stared at the man and taught him a lesson by blinding him, telling him that he would not see the sun again for the space of one season. Someone then led the astonished sorcerer out of the room. Such action may seem drastic, but it was not unjustified. Elymas was not only challenging Saul, he was insulting Jesus as well, and it had been necessary to refute his arguments in a way that could leave no doubt about who was right. So Saul, rather than waste his time in futile rebuttals, did something that would, at once, silence the man and at the same time convince Sergius Paulus about who was right. He caused the man no permanent damage, for the blindness was only temporary, but, undoubtedly, it had its effect, and Sergius Paulus was greatly impressed. Whatever else one might say of this event, it was now apparent that Saul had attained a degree of power almost as great as Peter's.

He told us about it when we met that evening, and I, like Paulus, was greatly impressed. But John did not seem to share my enthusiasm, and I suspected he was skeptical about whether this entire affair had happened at all, although he was polite enough not to say that to Saul to his face.

Sergius Paulus regaled Saul royally all the next day. He took pains to respect Saul's special dietary needs and had all of Saul's food prepared by Jewish cooks. Saul was equally impressed by his host, and he told us that evening that he was changing his name from Saul to Paul in honor of the man who was treating him so well. We respected his wish and started calling him Paul from that moment on, and, out of respect for his wishes, I will use his new name henceforth in this account.

We left Paphos and traveled to Perga in Pamphylia, and it was there that John saw for the first time how we dealt with Gentiles. He saw that we welcomed them into our fold without requiring them to become Jews. He could not understand that, and, when we were alone, he asked us how we could do this, since Jesus' mission had been entirely for the Jewish people and since the promise of his kingdom could have meaning only for Jews. If these Gentiles *became* Jews, then their becoming Nazarenes would make sense. But without that, how could they become Nazarenes? How could anyone who wasn't a Jew become a Nazarene?

Paul explained that most of them could not bring themselves to follow every jot and tittle of the Torah, especially when it came to circumcision and dietary restrictions, but that all of them believed in the one god, as we Jews did, and wanted the acceptance of that god, just as Jews did, and accepted the general morality of the God-fearers, and longed for the new era of peace and prosperity that would come when Jesus returned. All that, Paul said, should not be denied them. John agreed that our Gentile converts should have those things but said that they had to be worthy of them. That worthiness would be earned when they became Jews, he said.

But Paul was firm. "Are all those who are not Jews to be denied acceptance by God?" he asked.

"Not at all," John answered. "If they want acceptance by God without becoming Jews, let them become God-fearers. God-fearers are just as acceptable as Jews are to God. But if they do that, then you still must understand that they can't become Nazarenes, because only Jews can become Nazarenes. Jesus as king can't have significance for anyone but Jews."

I was intrigued by John's reply. To be honest with you, I had not thought about Gentiles becoming God-fearers, which would have given them a moral code without the Torah. But that still would have made no difference, according to John, since even God-fearers could not become Nazarenes.

An argument ensued. John and Paul were adamant in their views, and John made it clear that he intended to report this to James. But Paul did not care. He was not in Jerusalem now, he said; he was in the field, where he had to assess every situation for himself. And in his best judgment, *his* path was the right one.

So John (Mark) left us. He went off to Jerusalem to talk to James. The leader of our movement had to be told what was going on, he said, after which James could decide for himself what to do.

Meanwhile, Paul and I went to Antioch and rested there for a time. Some of our followers there took care of us until we were ready to travel again. While we were there, Paul had time to meditate, and he began to develop further his concept of Jesus. Sometimes, when he told me things, I asked him how he knew them, and he told me that he had visions. I considered him blessed. He who had done so much to hurt us in the past was becoming God's chosen messenger now.

He told me that he was beginning to realize that Jesus was more than we had thought him to be. He was beginning to realize that Jesus' death was not just the fulfillment of prophecy about what would happen to the Messiah but an actual human sacrifice that God had required in order to forgive us for our sins. Up until that time, I had thought that the only reason for Jesus' death was that it had been necessary to fulfill the Scriptures. And I also believed that he would return. Now I was being presented with a new reason for his death. Or at least an additional reason to the one I had clung to until now. I thought about Attis, the god whom the pagans of Tarsus worshipped; I thought about his tortured body dripping blood and about how his suffering and sacrifice were supposed to help his worshippers fare better in the world. I wondered if Paul, who had been raised in Tarsus as a child, had had the exposure to that idea so ingrained in his mind that he could conceive of God's blessings as coming only after a ritual sacrifice of some sort. I thought he may have found justification for this in Abraham's near sacrifice of his son, Isaac, in obedience to God's command. But then God had commanded that only as a test of Abraham's obedience and had never intended for Abraham to go through with it. When God saw that Abraham would obey, He stayed his hand and ordered an animal sacrifice instead. So, in all our Jewish tradition, we never more heard of a human sacrifice being necessary to satisfy God. Indeed, the sacrifice of Isaac also had not been necessary, since, as I have said, God never intended Abraham to go through with it.   The protection and preservation of human life had become the tradition of Judaism, not the taking of it on God's altar. So the idea that God needed Jesus' death to forgive the sins of men was a new one to me and one that suggested a pagan idea. I had thought that repentance after baptism would gain for us the forgiveness we sought, that the doing of good deeds and obedience to God's commandments would render us pure to God. That was why the commandments had been given to us, I thought. That was why James back in Jerusalem had taken the Rechabite and Nazarite vows and had made himself as pure as the purist Essene. But Paul said no: all the good deeds in the world, all the obedience to the Torah, could avail us nothing without the sacrifice of Jesus' death. He told me that we were born into sin, that sin was ingrained in our flesh from the moment of our births and that good intentions and good deeds could not rid us of that stain no matter how hard we tried. Only the death of Jesus could do it. Jesus had done the penance for us. That was God's gift to us: forgiveness for our sins through the taking of Jesus' life. But that gift was only available to us if we believed that this was true. If we did not believe it, then the gift was not ours to have.

"But why Jesus?" I asked him. "Why did God choose Jesus to be sacrificed and not someone else?"

"Because Jesus is God's son," Paul said, "and God needed the sacrifice of someone special and not just some ordinary person."

"But we are all the sons of God," I said. "Didn't Jesus himself say that?"

And I remembered all those times when he *had* said it. I mean all the stories I had heard about him saying it: how we should let our good works shine so prominently before men that, in appreciation, men would glorify our father in heaven, by which we understood him to mean that we were all the children of God; how if we love our enemies and bless those who curse us and pray for those who persecute us and use us despitefully, we really would be the children of our father, by whom he meant God, the father of all; and when he made that statement, we understood him to mean not our individual earthly fathers, who may have died and gone to heaven, but our spiritual father, our heavenly father, who was God; how we should be perfect even as our father in heaven is perfect, meaning that we were the children of God; how we should give alms anonymously without earthly recognition, so that we might be rewarded by our father in heaven; how we should pray secretly to our father, so that our father might reward us openly; how we should begin our prayers by saying, "Our father, who is in heaven...", meaning that we are the children of God; how we should forgive men their trespasses against us, so that our heavenly father could forgive us *our* trespasses; how we were not to fret as Gentiles do about how to get food and clothing, because our father would provide those things for us; how if we were brought before the high priest or his council of judges, we should not be concerned about what to say but should let our father do the talking through us. "A sparrow," he had said, "does not fall to the ground without your father." And, of course, before either Jesus or I were born, our sages taught us that those who follow the spirit of God are the children of God. For did not Solomon say that the righteous man boasts that God is his father and that if the righteous man is a son of God, God will defend him and deliver him from the hands of his adversaries? And in the Book of Deuteronomy, does it not say, "You are the children of the Lord your God?" And did Nathan not speak for God when he said of King Solomon, "I will be a father to him, and he shall be a son to me?" And did Ben-Sira not say, "And God will call you 'Son'" and also, "I exalted the Lord saying, 'You are my father'?" And did not Philo call God, "the father of all" and those who were righteous, "the sons of God"? And didn't Paul himself, as I then recalled, once say that all who are led by the spirit of God are the sons of God and that we are fellow heirs of God with Christ? Didn't he tell me once that to Israelites belongs the sonship? Didn't they all, including Jesus, say that God was the father of us all? Yes — they did. And from all of them, I had come to understand that we were all the sons and daughters of God and that God was the father of all.

But Paul said no: we were the sons of God, the children of God, in a symbolic sense or adopted sense, but Jesus was the son of God in an actual one. And, in fact, he was the only son of God in that way.

And then I remembered the story of the Exodus, and I said, "But Paul, didn't God say to Moses, 'Israel is my first-born son'?"

"He wasn't speaking about His actual son. Jesus was His first-born son," Paul said.

"But why couldn't God forgive us our sins without Jesus' death?" I asked.

"Why did God need Isaac's death by the hand of his father, Abraham?" Paul answered.

"But God *didn't* need that!" I said. "He only demanded that to *test* Abraham. He didn't let Abraham do it."

"But in Jesus' case, He *did* need it," Paul said. "It was the fulfillment of prophecy in the Bible."

These ideas were very new to me, and I needed time to absorb them. I always had been taught that the Messiah would be a man who would be chosen by God to be king and that this king would not be beyond our scrutiny and criticism if he deviated from the path of what was right and that he might even be accompanied by a prophet like Elijah, who would reprimand him if he failed in his duties. But Paul's ideas were different. To him the Messiah was more than a mortal human; to him the Messiah was divine. To Jews, of course, that was offensive; not only to themselves but to God. It was not that I wanted to challenge Paul; I liked him and admired him too much for that. But the idea that a human being could be divine was one of those pagan beliefs that a Jew could not tolerate. Even Moses had not been considered divine, and from Moses we had gotten the Torah.

All this reminded me of the beliefs of other people, and I wondered if Paul, unconsciously, was fitting Jesus into the substance of those other beliefs. There were the Gnostics, who talked about a descending savior coming to bring enlightenment to the earth. There were the mystery religions, that spoke of a deity whose sacrificial death confers salvation to all through the symbolic sharing of his death with men. And there was, of course, that Attis, whose hanging, flayed, bleeding, immolated body could be likened to Jesus hanging on the cross. Paul had been exposed to all these beliefs. Some of them may have been imbedded in his mind since childhood. Was he using Jesus to fulfill them? And did he not realize how paganistic they were? But beyond that, was he right? Was he saying these things because God was telling him to say them? A man who had been given the powers that Paul had been given by God — the power to blind people for one thing — is not likely to have been given false information too.

I was in a quandary over this and did not know what to think. Here was one concept of God built up by our people through thousands of years, and here was another one revealed to a chosen messenger through visions. I doubted Paul, yet I feared to doubt him, because I thought he might be right.

"In the Psalms," Paul said to me, "doesn't God say to David, 'You are my son, today I have begotten you'? And doesn't Enoch speak of the son of God, and doesn't Solomon do the same?"

"Yes, Paul, they speak of the son of God, but they don't mean what you mean when they say it. If the Messiah *is* the son of God, that doesn't mean he's divine. If he is the son of God, then he's the son of God because he's exalted above everyone else. But he has a mother and father the way all of us do, and then God takes him to His bosom and loves him as a son. But he's still human, Paul. He's someone to respect and revere; he's not someone to worship."

"No," Paul said to me, "he's more than that. He came to us in a human form. Yes, that's true. But he's the offspring of God, Barnabas. He's the issue, the progeny of God, and that means that he's divine."

"Does that mean we should worship him?" I asked.

"Is that so hard to do?" Paul asked me almost paternally.

I began to pace the room we were in, struggling to find words to express the upheaval I was feeling. The son of God: what did it mean? I had heard the expression all my life but never the way that Paul meant it. If we now called Jesus the son of God, what would that mean to everyone — that he was superior and elevated above everyone else, or that he was a deity, made of the same spiritual stuff that God Himself was made of? I chose to withhold my judgment on this. I needed more time to think.

Paul then did something else that caused me much concern: he gave a new name to our followers. Drawing on the word, Christ, which is the Greek word for Messiah, he called our followers Christians and thus gave them the feeling that they were different from Nazarenes. I asked him why he was doing that. We were Jews, and our movement was Jewish, so why not use a Jewish word to describe it? Besides, the word Nazarene had served us well until now. What was the need for a change? Paul shrugged off the importance of this by saying that it was merely an accommodation to our Gentile friends of a word derived from their own language. It was meant to make them more comfortable with Jesus by giving him a name from *their* language rather than one from an alien tongue. He wanted them not always to have to think of Jesus as a Jew because of a Jewish title that had been ascribed to him; he wanted them to feel that Jesus belonged to them as well. A Greek name, he felt, would help to do that.

But I saw more than this in the change. Since Paul was now teaching repentance through Jesus' death, and since he was now calling Jesus divine, it seemed to me that he wanted the people who believed *those* things about Jesus to have a different designation than those who believed the way the Nazarenes in Jerusalem did. The Nazarenes did not believe that Jesus was divine nor that his death wiped out their sins. Not only was I seeing two different concepts of Jesus; I was seeing a different name being given to each of them: a Greek name for Paul's concept and a Jewish name for the Nazarene one. But even that was not to last, because as we talked further in the weeks that followed, Paul began to use both words synonymously, using each of them to designate his new idea.

Messiah and Christ were supposed to be the same words in two different languages. The way Paul used them at first, they weren't. But then, as I said, he made them synonymous but used his *new* definition for each of them. The Jews back in Jerusalem, meanwhile, were using the old definition, not knowing that a new one even existed. When a Nazarene or any other Jew used the word, Messiah (or its Greek translation, Christ), they meant a king, a human being, chosen by God to lead the Jewish people — someone who matched the oracle's description given by Philo. But when Paul and our Gentile converts used it, they meant a divine being, a special and exclusive son of God, someone who was beyond just respect, as was due a God-chosen king, someone who was worthy of much more, namely worship and adoration, as was due a god. This could only mean future confusion and that as much time was going to be spent on what these two words meant as on which of the two concepts was right. To avoid such wasteful polemics, why hadn't Paul chosen a different name entirely? To call two different things by the very same name was not conducive to clarity. But then it occurred to me that it was not really clarity that Paul wanted but credibility.

Messiah was a venerable word. It evoked thoughts of lengthy tradition, of honored belief, forged and tested in the crucible of time. To use it gave the appearance of continuity, of a flow of purposeful events leading to their apogee in Jesus. Indeed, this was so. Jesus was the Messiah, and he was the climax of all those events. But to Jews, at least to those Jews called Nazarenes, that climax was in the form of a future king, a liberator of the people. To the new Jesus-followers called Christians, it was in the form of a divine being, the only son of God, who had come to the earth to enlighten us and whose death, if we but believed it, could free us from penance for our sins. That the word meant one thing to one group and another thing to another group seemed to make no difference to Paul. The word served his purpose, and he used it.

But there was yet another reason for using it. The foremost authorities on Jesus' life, those whose credibility could not be challenged because of their close personal associations with Jesus, were using the word Messiah to describe him. Paul could not use another word to label *his* conception of Jesus. To do that would be to set himself apart from those authorities, would make him appear as an independent interpreter, at odds with the leaders of our movement, giving a completely fanciful and imaginary picture of the man he was asking people to follow. No, he needed that word, he needed Messiah, to show he was in accord with the leaders in Jerusalem.

And he also needed our religion. He needed Judaism to give meaning to his interpretation. Jesus had talked too frequently of the law and the prophets, had used Jewish teachings too often, for Paul to try to separate Jesus now from his Jewishness. Jesus' own words, just his adjuration that we go only to Jews to preach, made it necessary for Paul to link his own interpretation of Jesus with older Jewish thinking. And he was true to this, either out of a sense of duty or out of a necessity required for his own credibility, for he taught our Gentile followers that they were like wild olive shoots or side branches off the main branch of the tree, which was Israel.

CHAPTER XVII

In Antioch our purpose was to gain more followers by speaking in the synagogues. In one particular synagogue, we were welcomed as guests, and, after the customary reading of the Torah, we were invited to speak about our beliefs. Paul, who, I must confess, was superseding me now in leadership, did the talking for us. He spoke of our history in Egypt and of the land that God had given us; he spoke of our judges and of Samuel, the prophet; he spoke of King Saul and then of King David; he spoke of David's seed giving us our savior, Jesus; he spoke of John the Baptizer, who foretold the coming of Jesus. And then he spoke of our people in Jerusalem — not just the leaders, by which he meant the high priest and his entourage, but the people, the Jewish people, all the people who lived there — and said that they had desired Jesus' death and had wanted Pilate to kill him. Since he went on speaking about other things after that, my mind could only linger on that statement for a moment. And since I knew how warmly our people had welcomed Jesus into Jerusalem, how much they had grieved over his death and how much they hated the chief priests, I wondered momentarily about the complete contradiction to those facts that Paul's statement constituted. Then he spoke of Jesus' crucifixion and of his resurrection before witnesses. Then he said who Jesus was, that he was God's son, and that his death had been necessary for the forgiveness of our sins. I trembled at his boldness. But he spoke with such conviction, with such certainty of his claim, that I found myself again being drawn to believe him.

But now he said something else, something that he had not told me before: he said that the forgiveness of sins, the path to salvation, need no longer be gotten through the Torah. The expiation of sin through Jesus' death was all that was now required. I already knew of Jesus' death being necessary for God to forgive us for our sins, but I had thought of this in conjunction with the Torah. I had never thought of it as annulling the Torah. I was stunned by this disclosure. The Torah was the foundation of our entire religion; it was the basis of our covenant with God. If I understood Paul correctly, that sacred text was now obsolete. How could this be? Jesus himself had defended the Torah. He had said to us that if any man sets aside even the least of the

133

Torah's demands and teaches others to do the same, he will have the lowest place in the kingdom of heaven, whereas anyone keeping the Torah's commandments and teaching others to do the same will stand high in the kingdom of heaven. Did Paul not know this? Did he not know how sacred the Torah was to Jesus himself that he would presume to say that it was no longer necessary for salvation? And what of the things he had learned from the Essenes? Could any group of people have been more loyal or more stringent followers of the Torah than they? What of their belief that God forgives our sins when we make a new covenant to follow the Torah? Or was this a part of God's plan, something revealed to Paul through a vision: a new pathway that God had decided was now to supersede the old?

The congregation was undecided, and the members asked us to come back next week to repeat these views. So the next Sabbath, we returned. But now the crowd was much larger, and when Paul spoke of his views this time, most of the people spoke out against him. They rejected his claims and said that they were lies. To claim that Jesus' death was a required sacrifice to expiate sin was one thing; to claim that the Torah was no longer necessary was another. But Paul stood his ground and returned anger for anger. His conviction was like a rock. He answered the voices of rejection by saying that it had been necessary for us to go to the Jews first but that since they were rejecting their chance for salvation, he would offer it, henceforth, to the Gentiles. I did not contradict this statement of his that we had to go to the Jews first, but I knew that there was no such requirement. Neither James in the flesh nor Jesus in the spirit had ever imposed on us a stricture that said that before we preached to Gentiles, we first had to preach to Jews. That, especially, would have been a strange regulation to have given to Paul, since repeatedly he had told me that his primary mission was to preach to Gentiles not Jews.

In any event, he did what he had threatened to do and went just to the Gentiles now. I followed his lead to these people and saw many of them accept his words.

But now, some of the Jews decided to go the Roman authorities. Using the revolutionary nature of our movement as an excuse, they told the authorities that we were political rebels who sanctioned a new Jewish king and that we were arousing the people accordingly. We were forthwith arrested and expelled from the territory, and we found ourselves traveling once again.

Undaunted, we went to Iconium where we spoke to Greeks as well as Jews. Many from both groups believed us as we spoke in the synagogue and elsewhere. But some of the Jews who did not believe us used that same tactic that the unbelieving Jews of Antioch had used: they turned the Gentiles and the authorities against us by reporting that we were agitators against Rome. We were almost stoned this time, and we left hastily for other parts.

We traveled now to Lystra and Derbe, two cities in Lycaonia, and to the environs surrounding them. Once again we preached about Jesus. But an interesting event occurred shortly after our arrival in Lystra that gave us a better chance for success than we had had in Iconium, and it also gave me pause for thought not only about the increasing abilities of Paul but about the people to whom we were speaking. It happened in the street. We were walking along it one day, and we came upon a man who was not able to walk because he had been crippled in his feet since birth. Paul, sensing that the man was ready to believe in our message about Jesus, said to the man in a loud voice, "Stand up on your feet!" And, immediately, the man did that and was even able to leap upward and walk about.

My admiration for Paul increased after that, but it could not compare to the awe in which some of the witnesses in the street held him. Or the awe in which they held me for that matter, for they attributed the healing to both of us. The Jews among those witnesses were duly impressed, but the Gentiles went even further: the Gentiles believed that we were gods. They thought we were gods who had come to earth in the likenesses of men, and they knelt on the ground in adoration of us. The Jews, of course, could not believe that, first, because Jews believe there is only *one* god (Paul and I were two) and, second, because Jews cannot accept *any man* as being divine. I remembered how many Gentiles had looked upon Gaius Caligula as a god, and I saw how many of them now looked upon Paul and me as gods, and I realized then that Paul's concept of Jesus as the one and only son of God was going to find more fertile soil among Gentiles than among Jews, because Gentiles were accustomed to accepting *some men* as being divine. For me, though I did not show it to Paul, there was never a time when I was more torn between loyalty to my traditional Jewish beliefs and the blissful beatitude of Paul's new way.

The Gentiles identified me as the pagan god, Jupiter, and they identified Paul as the god called Mercury. And a pagan priest of Jupiter heard about us and came to the gates of the city with oxen and garlands to worship us along with the people. When we were informed of this, we were astounded. We felt irritated, chagrined, enraged — it is so hard to say just what we felt at that moment — we actually rent our clothes and ran out amongst these Gentile worshippers and expostulated with them about what they were doing.

"We are men like you!" we shouted. "We are not gods! We have come to tell you about the real god, who made heaven and earth and the sea and everything else, who has given us rain and fruit, who has filled our bodies with food and our hearts with gladness. *He* is the one you must worship, not us!" But they hardly listened. They were in a state of delirium over us. It was only with difficulty that we were able to restrain them from making sacrifices to us and to convince them that we were telling the truth. I think they were disappointed at this, but they finally did come to their senses and agree to accept us as the mere men that we were.

But, oh, it was still a propitious time for us. It is no small thing to be thought of as a god. And when people are ready to think that much of you, they are ready to welcome you enthusiastically about anything you have to say. The Jews were certainly impressed with how we had affected their Gentile neighbors, and they invited us readily to speak in the synagogue. We were preparing ourselves to do just that, but then a new and dangerous threat appeared and, with the suddenness of a lightning bolt, it eradicated all the recent good that we had done. It came in the form of disgruntled Jews who had traveled from Antioch and Iconium and who were determined to discredit us among the people of Lystra. They convinced the Jews that we were religious blasphemers because we preached rejection of the Torah, and they convinced the Gentiles that we were dangerous revolutionaries because we preached of a new kingdom that was to come. How quickly do loyalties change, how brief was our apotheosis! The very people who had invited us to speak, the very people who had worshipped us as gods, now turned against us and threatened our lives. I ran for help to those whom I knew would be loyal to us, but I did not get back in time. While I was gone, the mob, both Jews and Gentiles, grabbed Paul and stoned him mercilessly. And then, when they thought he was dead, they dragged him out of the city and left him in a desolate place to rot.

But he was not dead. He was unconscious but not dead. We found him where they had left him, and we revived him and gave him drink. I thought of Stephen then, whom Paul had had a hand in killing in the very same manner as this. Later, Paul told me that he too had been thinking of Stephen when he had felt the pains of the stones. The worst thing of all, he said to me, was not knowing when one of them would hit — or where — so he could never prepare himself, even mentally, to receive the missile's blow. But now he stood up and, in spite of his injuries, walked back with us into the city. By any measure, he was an unusual man. I remember thinking that only a person who had been touched by God could have survived and recovered as he just had.

The next day we went to Derbe and delivered our message there. Then, since things had quieted down again, we went back to Lystra, then to Iconium and then back to Antioch. In all these places, we appointed leaders of the groups we had created and told our followers not to expect the path to be easy and that only with much tribulation would they finally enter the kingdom of God. Our own recent tribulations were proof enough of that.

From Antioch, we traveled elsewhere in Pisidia. Then onward to Pamphylia, and in Perga preached again, and from there into Attalia. Back again to our home base in Antioch, and we stayed there for some time with our loyal followers, recounting our successes to them. We learned, while we were in Antioch, that the Temple had a new high priest, appointed, as the previous one had been, by Herod of Chalcis. This new one was Ananias, son of Nedabaios, and father of Eleazar, the childhood friend of Rabath's. We did not know it then, but Ananias was destined to be decisively involved in Paul's life and well-being in the future.

About a year after that, a new procurator came to Judaea to succeed Tiberius Alexander. This was Cumanus, in whose inglorious reign thousands of Jews were killed. But before the events that led to that, Herod of Chalcis died. This was in the eighth year of Claudius' reign. Bernice, who had married Herod after the death of her first husband, Marcus, now became a widow for the second time in her life, and she went to live with her brother, Agrippa, as she had lived with her father before. The territory over which Herod of Chalcis had ruled, Claudius now gave to Agrippa, and the privilege of assigning new high priests, he gave to him as well.

It was at this time that Agrippa discovered the one great love of his life. It came unexpectedly, as such things do, and it came in the form of Bernice. Just as King David had been struck by Bathsheba when he first had observed her at her bath, so did this young Agrippa succumb to desire when he saw Bernice at hers. It was not premeditated or intentional. It was simply that he had been accustomed to walking through this particular bathing area on his solitary, meditative wanderings through the house, because it and the apartment associated with it had been unused and empty for so long. He had forgotten that he had just given it to Bernice, and he now meandered aimlessly into it while cogitating about the inexperience of the new procurator, Cumanus.

When he walked into the room that contained the sunken pool, he was suddenly aware from the corners of his eyes that there were people standing there. He looked up and saw two young serving women, scantily clad, drop to their knees at the sight of him and Bernice, completely nude, walking out of the pool. Her body was shining and glistening in the adumbrated daylight that sent shafts through the windows in the walls. Agrippa stood immobilized by this unexpected sight, and Bernice, her body dripping water onto the tiled floor, stood equally motionless, surprised at her brother's sudden appearance. He saw her entirely — her flat abdomen, her firm thighs and her breasts that were upright and pointed. Without realizing what he was doing, he focused his eyes on them. She could see at that moment that he was looking at her with interest. A woman perceives such things instantly in the eyes of a man. She followed the line of his staring and dropped her eyes to her breasts, realizing that that was where his eyes were now resting. Instinctively, she raised her head and drew back her shoulders and held one leg slightly forward on the ball of her foot.

"May I clothe myself, my lord?" she asked superciliously and awaited his protracted reply.

"Oh," he stammered, as if discovered in a criminal act that he had been performing in a trance. "Of course," he said, "of course."

He turned his face so as not to see her, while her attendants, one on one knee and the other now standing, dried their mistress and covered her with a toga, in the fashion of the Romans.

"Did you wish to see me?" she asked him once she was clothed.

"No," he faltered, "I...Bernice, I'm so sorry. I...I walk through here occasionally, and I forgot that this is your apartment now."

She turned to her servants. "You may go," she told them, not even bothering to wave them away.

The two girls hurriedly left the room, impressing the young Agrippa with their barely concealed nubility.

"Come, brother," she said, taking command of the situation. "Walk with me to the patio outside." She took his hand in hers and led him numbly along.

Agrippa now recovered himself. "Bernice, I'm so sorry I came upon you that way," he said, trying to show proper respect for her privacy.

"Actually," she said, releasing his hand and stopping to face him, "I didn't mind."

Then she walked away, reaching the patio without him, and stared at the setting sun. She was fully aware of what he was feeling. Young as she was, she had had two husbands and had learned from them the

+effect a beautiful woman can have on a man. The fact that Agrippa was her brother did not diminish her pleasure in this. The awareness that she could make a man desire her was not only a satisfaction but also a reassurance of her own self-worth. Then, looking at the reddening discus descending behind the clouds, she thought for the first time of how attractive her brother was, of how his strong, youthful limbs might look if she saw him as he had seen her.

She turned as he approached her and said in a sultry tone, "'Oh that you would kiss me with the kisses of your mouth, for your love is better than wine.' Do you know what that's from?"

"No," he whispered, the desire to hold her growing strong within him.

"It's from the Song of Solomon. You should read the Bible, brother."

"I'm sure if I did," he sighed, "it would tell me that what I'm thinking now is a sin."

"It's not a sin to love," she said.

"But you're my sister, and I'm your brother."

"I know," she said, "but you've aroused me. Have I done the same to you?"

"When I saw you just now coming out of your bath, I thought that I had never seen anything so beautiful in my life. I hadn't realized how beautiful you are."

"And I hadn't realized how handsome my brother is, how wonderful his eyes look — or his lips or his shoulders."

She could hear his breathing deepening now. She saw him walk to her and felt his arms embrace her and his lips upon hers and the warm soft melting within herself. She was his and he was hers, and she recited from the Song of Solomon, "'My beloved is mine, and I am his.'"

He removed her toga and let it fall to the floor where it surrounded her feet like water. Then he watched as she peeled from his body all his clothing down to his feet. He lifted her in his arms and carried her to the couch in the neighboring room. He stayed with her most of the night.

The two young women who had washed and dried their mistress observed all this from behind the edge of the doorway, so that what Bernice and Agrippa thought was secret was known at least to these two.

But now events of significance occurred under Cumanus. They would leave their mark on our people. The first occurred outside the Temple at the time of the Passover holiday. A Roman soldier was on guard duty on the roof of the Temple when the people were gathering for worship. Soldiers were always assigned such duties at festivals because the crowds were so huge that rioting was always a danger. The soldier made an indecent gesture to the crowd: he pulled up his garment and showed his buttocks and private parts. The crowd went wild. The younger men and the more riotous of the people began to throw stones at all the soldiers who were there. Others rushed to Cumanus and appealed to him to punish the soldier. But so tumultuous was the crowd that approached Cumanus that he feared the crowd itself would attack him. So he ordered out his heavy infantry to disperse them. Upon seeing all those troops, the people, who were unarmed and who had come to appeal and not attack, panicked and fled, and, in the rush of the crowd, thousands of people were trampled to death. All because of a foolish obscenity from one Roman soldier.

Our nation mourned this incident. The tragedy of the Roman occupation could never have been more apparent. We all knew it had to end.

Another incident occurred on the road to Beth-horon. A servant of the emperor named Stephen was conveying some furniture on the road when bandits swooped down and seized it. Cumanus had the people of the nearby villages brought to his headquarters in chains and blamed them for not pursuing and capturing the bandits. As his soldiers were breaking into people's homes, one of them found a copy of the Torah. The soldier tore it in two and threw it into a fire. The people became outraged at this, for the Torah is a sacred book. As word of this violation spread, they flocked to Caesarea by the thousands, coming in from all directions to tell Cumanus that the man who had so insulted God must be punished. This time Cumanus chose appeasement. Perhaps the death of all those thousands of people in Jerusalem, all started by the act of one soldier, made him want to avoid a repetition of such a thing. He ordered the offending soldier to march between two lines of his accusers so that the people could see him, and then, at the end of the line, he had his soldiers execute him.

I don't think the people had wanted Cumanus to go that far. They had wanted the soldier punished, not executed. But, apparently, Cumanus had wanted to leave no further room for complaint, so he had had the man put to death.

These events will apprise you of the tenor of the time. It was a time in which the smallest event might spark a revolt. It was a time of nervousness for Romans and frustration for Jews. It was a time that could not last.

CHAPTER XVIII

Emissaries came from James. John (Mark) had told James about our activities, and James had sent his representatives to make his own position clear. These men spread the word throughout Antioch that, according to Jesus' brother, no one could be accepted as a follower of Jesus unless that person was circumcised in accordance with the law of Moses. This, of course, was contrary to what Paul and I were teaching, and we disputed with them about it.

I remember thinking at that time that they could not have realized fully the ramifications of what they were demanding. They wanted all Gentiles who followed Jesus to become Jews: circumcision, dietary laws, adherence to the commandments, everything. They wanted everything that the Torah demanded of a Jew to be demanded of a Gentile who followed Jesus. In short, they were saying that you had to be a Jew — or become one — in order to follow Jesus. Others were preaching to Gentiles, including Peter himself, and they were encouraging those Gentiles to become Jews. The case of Cornelius was the one time that Peter hadn't done that, so righteous and sincere had Cornelius been. But in all other instances, as far as I knew, he urged them strongly to become Jews, which they did.

This idea that all followers of Jesus had to first become Jews came from Jerusalem, from James and Peter and John, the son of Zebedee, and the first disciples, all of whom still thought of Jesus as the Jewish Messiah, as the deliverer of Israel from the Romans, just as Moses had been its deliverer from the Egyptians. But did they realize the consequences of doing what they said? Did they realize that the Gentiles would fall away from us and that the promise of turning large numbers of them into loyal subjects of Jesus would be ended before it began? Did they realize that all those people who worshipped Jupiter or Zeus or Attis or some other such god could be turned to the one true god if only the way was not made too hard for them? Paul and I were giving them something they could accept, something that had meaning for them, something that was not so strange to their customs and beliefs that they would totally reject it out of hand. To demand something different from them now than what we had demanded previously would lead either to their turning away from Jesus and returning to their pagan beliefs or to their forming their own groups of adherents who followed Jesus in their own way, which was different from the way of the Jews.

And then I realized that Paul and I already had done that last thing. Though the revelations and ideas had been his, the promulgation of them to our listeners had been the work of both of us. And I hoped that I was doing the right thing.

But we had no desire to challenge James. We simply had to make him and the others understand that the golden opportunity that was being presented to us to make Jesus the leader of the world was being threatened by this unaccommodating ultimatum of theirs. We told this to the emissaries, but they were adamant: no Torah, no Jesus; no circumcision, no Nazarene. We Nazarenes, they said, are not called the Zealots of the Torah without good reason.

There was nothing to do in the end but to put the question to James. So they suggested that Paul and I return to Jerusalem to present our case to James in person. Otherwise, they would go on publicly refuting us, and they reminded us that they had the authority of James behind them. So we agreed to go, and once again Paul and I were on the road together. For myself, I trusted to God to guide me and to continue to reveal His will to me through Paul.

Along the way, we passed through Phoenicia and through the sometimes-hostile Samaria. We spoke where we could because we did not want to miss any opportunity to spread the word, and we concentrated mainly on Gentiles. It was surprising how many of them believed us. We were giving them something they wanted: a god who, unlike Jupiter, was merciful and loving, benevolent and sacrificing, and who would give them something better after they died. And what they had to do for that something was not hard, the way the Torah was, but easy, as befitted the demands of a compassionate father. They had only to believe, to believe and accept, and to do just those few basic moral things that we felt should be required of them. What we did not give them was a Torah. Whether we were right or wrong, we did not give them a formal body of work as a guide for their earthly conduct; we did not give them a reference book to which they could look when the question of how to behave in a particular situation arose. In essence, Paul told them that if ever such a question should arise, they were to ask him for the answer. And yet, interestingly enough, when he gave them his answers, he used the Torah to frame them. As I have said, whether we were right or wrong — I certainly thought we were right at the time, for I had made up my mind to accept what Paul said — we told the Gentiles that if they accepted the divinity and saviorship of Jesus and fulfilled the minimum requirements of human decency and morality, they could enter the kingdom of God. And though that did not stop their present sufferings, it did give them something to look forward to. For lives that were hopelessly hard, that was enough.

And then we entered Jerusalem, taking the same street to the same private house where we had gone before when we had come there during the time of the famine. Our Nazarene brothers greeted us warmly and fed us an evening meal, which we shared in fellowship with them. At this meal, we recited together the Eucharist prayer that Nazarenes always say before eating. We raised our chalices and said, "We give thanks to you, our Father, for the holy Vine of your servant David, which you have made known to us through your servant, Jesus. *Glory be to you, world without end.*" Then we took the piece of bread that the host gave to each of us and said, "We give thanks to you, our Father, for the life and knowledge you have made known to us through your servant Jesus. *Glory be to you, world without end.* As this broken bread, once dispersed over the hills, was brought together and became one loaf, so may your Church be brought together from the ends of the earth into your kingdom. *Yours is the glory and the power, through Jesus Christ, for ever and ever.*" I should mention here that no one who was invited to eat with us was permitted to drink the particular wine that was blessed nor to eat the particular bread that was blessed unless that person had been baptized. We based this on Jesus' own words: "Give not that which is holy unto dogs."

Then after we ate, we thanked God by saying, "Thanks to you, holy Father, for your sacred name which you have caused to dwell in our hearts, and for the knowledge and faith and everlasting life which you have revealed to us through your servant Jesus. *Glory be to you for ever and ever.* You, O Almighty Lord, have created all things for your own name's sake; to all men you have given meat and drink to enjoy, that they may give thanks to you, but to us you have graciously given spiritual meat and drink, together with life eternal, through your servant. Especially, and above all, do we give thanks to you for the mightiness of your power. *Glory be to you for ever and ever.* Be mindful of your Church, O Lord; deliver it from all evil, perfect it in your love, sanctify it, and gather it from all the four winds into the kingdom which you have prepared for it. *Yours is the power and the glory for ever and ever.* Let his grace draw near, and let this present world pass away. *Hosanna to the god of David.* Whosoever is holy, let him approach. Whosoever is not, let him repent. *O Lord, come quickly, Amen.*"

This was our Eucharist prayer, which we said before each evening meal. You see, the breaking of bread and the drinking of wine at the beginning of an evening meal was a custom performed by Jews everywhere. The Essenes had shown Paul their way of doing it and had taught him the prayers that they said. We Nazarenes did it the very same way, but our prayer also recognized Jesus as the servant and Messiah of God. And I should mention too, that in this prayer, we did not call Jesus the son of God, as Paul was teaching us to do, but rather the servant of God and that alone.

Our hosts took us to our beds. We were tired after our long journey. At night, in the dark, I lay with my eyes open. I was too apprehensive to sleep. I turned my head to the bed on which Paul was lying and whispered his name to see if he was awake.

"Paul," I said.

Almost immediately, he answered, "Yes?"

"You can't sleep either?" I said.

"No," he said. "I'm praying."

And I said nothing more, but I prayed too.

In the morning was the meeting. James, our leader, presided. So that you may understand the stature of the man, I will tell you first that everyone stood up when he entered the room. And it was not just because he was Jesus' brother, although that would have been reason enough for them to have done that, but also because he commanded respect in his own right. James was revered because of his religious purity, because of the goodness with which he endowed his every act and because of his courage in standing up for what he knew in his heart was right. Though he walked in the shadow of his brother, he did so with pride. He felt tremendously his responsibility in being the brother of the Messiah. While he held things together until Jesus returned, he felt it incumbent upon himself to be the best example of what a follower of Jesus should be: above reproach, pure in thought and deed, kind and compassionate towards all men and women, courageous in the face of adversity, and obedient to the laws of God as written in the Torah. I do not believe that there was any Jew alive at that time who better exemplified those characteristics than James. He ate no meat, and, in contrast to what Paul would later tell us to do, he drank no wine. He did not go to the public baths or anoint himself with oil. He did not shave his hair. He had only one article of clothing: a garment made of linen. He never wore anything made of wool. He was, in practice, a spiritual man, and he very much looked like an Essene. His every act, his every thought, reflected obedience to God and love of mankind. He was true to what Jesus would have wished all his followers to be.

The room was filled with Nazarenes. Among them was the group of seventy-one teachers whom James had appointed to help make judgements, much in the fashion of the Sanhedrin. We all stood when James entered the room, and then as everyone sat down, Paul and I remained standing, since we were the ones being questioned.

James greeted us cordially and expressed to all of those present his gratitude for the help Paul and I had given in the past (and by this we knew he meant the money we had brought during the famine) and then said that John (Mark) had returned with disturbing news about the nature of what we were preaching. He asked us to recount for the assembly the places we had been and to explain what it was we were teaching, especially about the Torah and the need — or lack of need — for followers of Jesus to adhere to it.

Paul did the talking for both of us, for he, unquestionably, was the more convincing speaker. He told the story of our experiences in Salamis, in Paphos, in Perga, in Antioch, in Pisidia in Iconium and in Lystra and Derbe and related the kind of reception we had encountered in each of those places. But the enmity that we had experienced was not a total surprise to James, for John (Mark) had informed him about our teachings. James pointed out to us that such animosity from our own people was not being experienced by Nazarenes in Jerusalem, that in Jerusalem we were highly respected by everyone (except for the Sadducees, of course), and he wondered why we had experienced such animosity in the places where we had gone. Could it be because of what we were teaching? Were we, as John (Mark) had reported, teaching something different?

"Two of my Pharisee friends saw me in the Temple," he said. "They asked me if we were preaching to Gentiles now. I told them that some of us were, but I asked them why they thought that unusual. After all, Jews have been preaching to Gentiles for some time.

"'Yes,' one of them said, 'but I thought your brother didn't want his message to be for anyone but Jews.'

"'True,' I said. 'But if a Gentile converts to Judaism, is he not a Jew?'

"And then the other said, 'Oh, but we have heard that your emissaries in Antioch are teaching Gentiles that they don't have to *become* Jews to follow your brother, that they can follow him without accepting the Torah.'

"That I could not answer. Or perhaps I should say, I dared not answer. John came back to us after he left you in Perga and told us that that very thing is what you are saying to Gentiles. I have called this meeting because of that, and I want to ask you as straightforwardly as possible, Is that truly what you are teaching?"

Paul answered for both of us. "You knew we were preaching to Gentiles when we came to you at the time of the famine, when we brought you gifts of help from the very people you now question me about."

"Never doubt that we are grateful for the help you brought us at that time," James said. "Those were hard days for us, and the memory of them is still painful for us to bear. And yes, we knew you were preaching to Gentiles, but we thought you were having them become Jews. We had no idea that you were having them join us without that."

"Why do you want me to make it hard for them?" Paul asked. "Why make demands that are certain to drive them away? Take circumcision, for example: to us it's sacred; to them it's a mutilation. Look at our dietary restrictions: to us, they're essential; to them, they're burdensome. Why not make it easier for them? Don't you think Gentiles seek God just as much as Jews do? Don't you think they long for an eternal life? Shouldn't it be available to them too?"

"But it always *has* been available to them," James said. "God-fearers are Gentiles. They follow the minimum moral laws for Gentiles, such as the ones that God gave to Noah and his sons, just as Jews follow the moral laws of Moses, and they are as acceptable to God as any law-abiding Jew. No one has denied Gentiles salvation. *Are* you turning them into God-fearers?" he asked.

"Not in a formal way," Paul said, "but I tell them to turn from idols and to love God and their neighbors as themselves, just as Jesus taught us to do. Isn't that enough? I don't want to make it hard for them to become followers of Jesus."

An elderly man stood up, signaling for recognition.

"Yes, Isaac," James said.

And now Isaac spoke and said, "I do not think that if Paul *did* turn these people into God-fearers that even that would qualify them to be Nazarenes. Nazarenes are zealous for the Torah. No group of Jews excels us in this. The Essenes may equal us, but they do not excel us. This is what makes us worthy of having someone like Jesus as our leader. Remember, he told us that the highest virtue is to follow the Torah and to teach others to do the same. How then can people who do not adhere to the Torah become followers of such a man?"

146

Isaac sat down and waited for someone to answer. His question was valid. I had asked myself that question when Paul had first told me that the Torah was no longer necessary.

John, the son of Zebedee, stood up, and when James acknowledged him, he said, "Of what importance is it to a God-fearer that our nation be freed from the Romans? Such a thing is of concern to Jews, not Gentiles. Why should a Gentile, God-fearer or otherwise, be concerned about who rules in Israel?"

Then Peter stood up and offered *his* thought: "We can't deny Gentiles the right to be God-fearers. That's as legitimate a path to God as Judaism is. And if a God-fearer wants to follow Jesus, must he stop being a God-fearer and then become a Jew in order to do that? Wouldn't that take away his God-given right to be a God-fearer?"

Then John, the son of Zebedee, responded and said to that, "We're not denying them the right to be God-fearers. We're only saying that if that's the path to God that they choose, they can't become Nazarenes. Only Jews can become Nazarenes. You can't be a Nazarene without being a Jew."

Paul opened his arms as if to gather them all close to him and said, "Do all of you realize what we would be giving up if we adhered to that? Most of the Gentiles will not join us if we tell them they must become Jews, and many of those who already have joined us will leave us if we tell them that. The influence that we might have had in the Gentile world would be lost to us, and the money that they send to sustain our center here in Jerusalem would be lost too."

"At what price do we gain all those people?" John said.

"What do you mean?" Paul asked.

"I mean, do we gain them by distorting — or at least diluting — what a true follower of Jesus should be? It's fine to talk about having more and more people turn to Jesus — the more numerous we are, the more influential we become — that's fine. But if the price we have to pay for that is to give up the very thing that Jesus is coming back for, then what's the use of it? If we give up the Torah, then we give up being Jews. If we do that, then we might as well give up Israel. And then what's the purpose of Jesus' return?"

"I don't know why we're putting up such restrictions," Paul said. "I'm not doing anything different from what Peter had the centurion, Cornelius, do, am I?" He looked towards Peter for an answer.

"No, you're not," Peter said. "But you must understand that Cornelius was an exceptional case. First of all, he was a Roman with a lot of authority, and I thought it would be to our advantage to have him on our side. But that wasn't all of it, I assure you. He was an exceptional man, so exceptional that I allowed more leeway for him than I have ever allowed for anyone else. He was already such a paragon of virtue and so respectful of me as a Nazarene leader that I could not find it in my heart to demand anything more of him. I haven't dealt with other Gentiles in the same way. I've encouraged everyone else to become Jews. I could have had the entire Cuthean people join us if I would have been willing to compromise on that. They were good people, and they had gone half-way towards becoming Jews. But I told them no, if they wanted to join us, they had to go all the way and become full-fledged Jews."

It was going to be up to James. We all knew that from the beginning. The issue was the Gentiles and whether they needed the Torah. It was James who had to decide.

There was silence now in the room. No one else had anything to say. Everyone's eyes turned to James. He sat looking downward, with his face showing the deepness of his thoughts. It took a while for him to speak.

"Do you have them follow our dietary laws?" James asked.

"No," Paul said, "I don't. I don't want to make it hard for them."

"I think you must do something minimally along that line," James said. "I think it's obvious that I cannot allow a situation in which people join us without any formal moral obligation or commitment in their lives and without the recognition of the election of Israel as the nation of God. Those who join us must be moral, and those who join us must accept that Israel and its people are the example of what a moral, God-obedient people should be."

"We do that!" Paul said. "We tell them that in no uncertain terms. I tell them about Jesus' moral teachings, and I tell them that they are extensions of Israel, like wild olive shoots off the main branch of the tree, which is Israel."

"Well," James said, "then there is only the matter of the Torah to consider. Do we require it of them or not? I have heard different views about this expressed today, and I have given serious consideration to each view. I think of a Pharisee synagogue, where I see not only Jews but also God-fearers sitting in prayer. Every Pharisee synagogue I know of has its circle of God-fearers as well as its congregation of Jews. And there is always love and mutual respect between them. Can we Nazarenes do the same? Can we have God-fearers who join us just as they join the Pharisees but who also accept that Jesus will return to rule over them? I think we can. Jesus will be king of the Jews, but that does not mean that he will not be king over others as well. If these Gentiles become God-fearers, then I believe we can accept them, just as the Pharisees do. Can you have them become God-fearers, Paul?"

"Yes," Paul answered. "I can do that."

"Then tell them that they must follow the minimum laws of Noah. They are to abstain from anything that has been polluted by having been offered to idols or by having been in contact with idols; they are to avoid fornication or any such unchaste behavior; they are to avoid eating any animal that has been killed by strangulation and that hasn't been drained of its own blood; they are to abstain from shedding the blood of their fellow men through murder. Now — Paul, Barnabas, will you do that?"

"We will do it," Paul said.

"Yes," I echoed, "we will do it."

James nodded approvingly. "Good," he said. "I'm glad that we could resolve that. Now, also, you must tell them to remember the poor. It is essential that they help those who are less fortunate than themselves."

"They already do that," Paul said, "and they will continue to do it."

"Good, good," James said. "I'm glad to hear that. We'll send letters to those who have already joined us that these are the things they must do. Now, let me say a word to the rest of you. Many of you are concerned that the Torah will somehow fade away if so many Gentiles who are with us fail to follow it. Have no such fear. The Torah and everything that Moses taught us have never lacked spokesmen anywhere over all our past generations. Moses is read Sabbath by Sabbath in every synagogue that exists. And always will be. As long as there are Jews in the world, there always will be the Torah." He allowed that thought to settle on the minds of everyone there, and then he said, "Does anyone else wish to speak?" No one answered, so he said, "Then there is nothing else to say. If we are in agreement on this, let us wish Paul and Barnabas a safe and prosperous journey on their trip back to Antioch."

If there was anyone who disagreed, that person did not speak. James was an imposing figure, and he was the brother of our Messiah. And though he was loving and generous and understanding to us always, he also was firm and resolute once his mind was made up. His judgments, once given, were conclusive with us, and we accepted them without further discussion.

"Very well then," he said, "let us pray."

We all rose, and we bowed our heads, and we said in unison, as Jesus had taught us, "Our Father, who is in heaven, hallowed be your name. Let your kingdom arrive, when your will will be done on earth as it is in heaven. Give us this day our daily bread and forgive us our trespasses as we forgive those who trespass against us. Lead us not into temptation, but deliver us from evil. Amen."

And then we parted. It had all been so easy. Paul had pointed out the obvious advantages of having large numbers of Gentiles join us, and James had attenuated our demands on them because of that. It had been so easy. But I knew that it had not been complete. We had not told James everything. But then James had not asked us everything. We had not told him that we were also telling Jews, not just Gentiles, that the Torah was no longer necessary for them. If we *had* told him that, perhaps he would have been a little less certain about the future of the Torah in the world. And we had not told him about Jesus being the only son of God, in that special way that Paul had taught me to understand it, and that Jesus was divine because of it. And we had not mentioned the savior. We had not talked about the death of Jesus as the human sacrifice that God required to enable God to forgive us for our sins. We had not said that good deeds were not enough and that only a *belief* in that sacrificial death would afford us the salvation we sought. We had not said those things. It had seemed better at the time to leave them unsaid and to accomplish for ourselves an agreement on one thing at a time. The Gentiles and the Torah was the issue we had addressed, and we had emerged from that battle victorious.

Now that we were in Jerusalem again, Paul and I had to visit our sisters. It was going to be easier for him to do that than for me. John (Mark) would be at my sister's house, and John (Mark) had reported Paul and me to James. There was a strained feeling now between us because of that. I had seen John (Mark) sitting at the meeting, but we had not greeted each other there. If I went to Mary's house now, he would be there. When I saw him, what would I say? Perhaps I wouldn't have to say anything. Perhaps I could just talk to Mary and her husband, Joash, and avoid saying anything at all to John (Mark). So, resignedly, I went there, jauntily walking up to the front door of the house in order to put myself into a lighter frame of mind. It was my good fortune that Mary answered the door. She almost ululated at the sight of me.

"John told us you were here, and I couldn't wait to see you," she rejoiced.

She hugged me over and over again, then pulled me into the house. She summoned Joash, who smiled broadly at the sight of me. He never said much, but I knew that he liked me. He was like a silent caryatid, supporting his family through every vicissitude of life and never saying much about it. Yet he expressed his feelings as much with his eyes as others do with words. As usual, I had to do some obligatory eating and tell Mary everything I had been doing.

John (Mark) entered the room while I was talking and sat down and listened to the account of my travels. We did not look directly at each other. After questions and answers and still more food, Mary turned to John (Mark) and said, "John, you haven't even greeted your uncle. Aren't you going to say hello?"

John (Mark), apparently just as concerned as I not to let his parents know there was friction between us but still too proud and unyielding to give me an effusive welcome, even for show, said perfunctorily in a cold and monotone voice, "Hello, uncle, how are you?"

And I, with only a little less reserve, responded, "Fine, John. It's good to see you again."

The silence that followed was more eloquent than our greetings, and Mary sensed there was something wrong. She sundered the silence by saying, "What's the matter with you two? Are you friends or enemies? You sound as if you don't want to speak to each other."

Mary was right. We were behaving like children. I decided then to reach out to John, to put our past differences behind us.

"What do you think, John?" I said to him, smiling. "Do you think your mother is right?"

"What do *you* think?" John (Mark) tossed back to me. "Do *you* think she is right?"

"No," I said, "I don't think she is. I think we do want to talk to each other."

"About Paul?" he asked.

"Yes, about Paul, if you wish" I said.

Mary and Joash realized now that something really was wrong between us and that they were about to hear what it was.

"Do you still think he's a man who tells the truth? Do you believe all those things that he says?" John (Mark) asked.

"Why is what he says so wrong? What is so terrible about them?"

"They're wrong because they don't agree with what we Nazarenes say. That's what's so terrible about them.."

"Is it so incredible, so impossible to your way of thinking, that God might give us additional information, new information that He hasn't given us before?"

"How do we get that information?" he asked, pointing a finger at me. "Through the visions of a single person who tells us something? Through the visions of a man who tells us that everything he says is true and that he alone is the trumpet through which God's voice is speaking to us? That fifteen-hundred years of a covenant with God should be thrown out the window just because he says so? Well, maybe that's good enough for you, but it isn't good enough for me. For all I know, the man could have butterflies in his head."

"Then how would you have us get information?" I asked him. "How did the prophets get *their* information? Didn't they get it in the same way? How did Abraham get *his* information? How did Moses get his? Or David or Jesus, how did they get theirs? Haven't there always been people selected by God to be recipients and conveyers of information? Why is it so hard for you to believe that Paul might be one of those people?"

"Because of the Torah!" he ejaculated loudly. "Because of the Torah, dear uncle. Because with it, we're like children of God, and without it, we're like savages. And Paul tells us to abandon it. That's why I can believe Moses and Jesus and not believe him."

"But he hasn't told us to be savages," I shouted.

"But he's trying to take away from us the one thing that keeps us from..."

But that was as far as he got, for now the booming voice of Joash thundered, "Stop it, both of you! This house is a house of peace. Is this how relatives act to each other? Is this how the Nazarene would want you to act? Remember what it is you claim to be — both of you — and show me how you're supposed to behave. I've heard of Nazarene love. Is this it? Is this how people behave when they have it?"

I laid my forehead into the palm of my hand. I realized he was right. "I'm sorry, John," I said. "I'm sorry I shouted at you."

"I'm sorry too," he said, his father's reproval — and perhaps my apology — affecting him too.

We walked to each other and embraced, feeling that whatever our differences were, they were not worth our turning against each other. Besides, James had made a compromise, and it was one that we both could live with. The two of us became friends again, and Mary and Joash smiled.

CHAPTER XIX

Strengthened by our leader's decision, Paul and I set out again for Antioch. With us, at James' behest, went two of James' personal representatives: Judas (surnamed Barsabas) and Silas. Their task was to write letters and to openly assert James' new policy towards Gentiles. John (Mark), in spite of his having left us in Pamphylia to report our doings to James, followed soon after to help us with our work. In the spirit of love that Jesus had taught us as well as the love I had for a member of my own family, I welcomed him when he arrived. Soon our old ties were renewed, and we spent much time together.

John met with Paul too, and in the quiet times before we set out on our missionary work, they spoke to each other about what they believed.

"You tell everyone the Torah is no longer necessary," John said. "Yet, recently, I heard you brag to some Jews that you're a student of the Torah."

"If I'm to win people, I must be flexible," Paul said. "I must adapt myself to the situation at hand. To those Jews whom I can see are going to fight me on this Torah issue, I act like a Jew to win them over. Since most Jews consider themselves subject to the law of Moses, when I am in their presence, I put myself under that law to win them — even though I myself am not subject to that law. To Gentiles, who are outside the law of Moses, I make myself like one of them, even though I myself am not outside God's law, since I am actually under the law of Christ. To people who are weak, I become weak in order to win them. To other people, I become what they are for the same reason. I've become every sort of person imaginable in order to make myself just like the person I'm approaching so that, in one way or another, I might save that person."

John thought that too accommodating. "You can't believe one thing one day and another thing another day, depending on which person you happen to be with," he said.

"Why not?" Paul answered. "I have a mission: to win followers for Jesus. To do that, I have to present myself in whatever way is most appealing to the person I'm talking to."

"But you can't go around telling one person one thing is true and another person that the opposite is true just to accommodate what each person wants to hear."

"Why not, if it turns people to faith in Jesus?" Paul said.

"The gospel," John answered, "the interpretation of what Jesus was here for, can't be changed from one person to another!"

Then Paul said, "When James allowed me to preach differently to Gentiles, wasn't he allowing there to be two gospels? Wasn't he making Peter's gospel the one for those who are circumcised and mine the gospel for those who are not?"

John was amazed. "Is that what you think? Is that what you think James was saying? One gospel for Jews and another for Gentiles? He never said that! All he did was make a different set of requirements for Gentiles to join us. He required them to become God-fearers if they didn't want to become Jews, and he excused them from observing the Torah in that case. But he didn't allow there to be two versions of Jesus' mission. He didn't allow there to be two gospels."

"Why do you dispute with me on this?" Paul asked. "Is what I teach so terrible? I acknowledge the Torah as a spiritual ideal. I'm simply saying that we're not spirits. We're made of flesh. And that flesh is born with sin as an inherent part of its make-up. When I know what's good spiritually and I can't measure up to it because my flesh makes me do the opposite, then I'm a prisoner of my flesh. How can I escape from that prison? The law — the Torah — doesn't help me. What does? What can? Jesus' sacrifice is what saves me. Jesus' sacrifice is what saves me from my prison."

"I don't know what you're talking about," John said. "What sacrifice did Jesus make that saves you from this inherent sin in your flesh that you're talking about?"

"His death," Paul said.

"His death gets rid of the sin in your flesh?"

"Yes," Paul said.

"I don't really understand it, but it sounds like a way out for people who are too weak to follow the Torah."

"Exactly," Paul said. "And we're all too weak. We're born too weak."

"Not all of us," John said. "James is not too weak."

Paul shrugged his shoulders rather than say that John was right. James was a touchy subject with him. James had power and authority in our movement, and he was a staunch adherent of the Torah. Paul resented him inwardly because James could tell him what to do. And if

Paul's visions were fully revealed to James, and if James did not believe them, then James' emissaries would discredit everything that Paul was saying.

John walked away, his head bowed deep in thought, and then he raised his head and said to Paul from across the room, "You say the Torah is too hard, too hard for men to follow. Yet I remember in the Bible that God says to us that the commandment He gives us this day is not too hard for us and is not far off; that it's not in heaven, making it necessary for someone to go there to bring it back so we can hear it and do it, but that it's close to us, in our own mouths and hearts, so we can do it readily. Why would God give us commandments and make us incapable of following them? Different people have different capabilities in following the Torah. Our Pharisee sages always have said that the Torah could be met at different levels. That's what spiritual growth is all about. You seem to think a person has to be perfect or else he's damned."

"If he's not perfect, he is. Unless he accepts Jesus," Paul said.

"That's misleading, Paul. You mean, unless he accepts what you claim about Jesus — this business about his death freeing us from inherent sin. But I don't accept what you claim. And you make it sound as if anyone who doesn't accept what you claim is rejecting Jesus. James won't accept this claim of yours; you know he won't. Maybe that's why you didn't tell us all this in Jerusalem. And now you're trying to tell me that if he rejects your claim, he's rejecting his brother? He's the leader of a movement that's preparing to set his brother up as king!"

Paul had not told all, of course; he had only touched on Jesus' death as the penance for our sins, and he had not mentioned divinity at all.

It was the next day that Peter came to visit us. Though he did not say it, I suspected that the reason he had come was to see if we were adhering to James' instructions about what we should tell the Gentiles. Since Peter was accustomed to preaching to Gentiles, he must have seemed the most appropriate person for the job. We knew, though, that Peter was taking a different approach to the Gentiles to whom he spoke; we knew that he was encouraging them to make a full conversion to Judaism. If they couldn't bring themselves to do that, then he was telling them to become God-fearers. But Paul wasn't doing either, in spite of James' instructions; he was giving Gentiles only the Christian way of following Jesus, which did not require the Torah or the formal set of laws ordinarily required of God-fearers. For one thing, in contrast to what he had told James he would do, he was telling the Gentiles that they could eat any food they wished, including animals that still contained blood and also food that had been offered to idols, and only to show restraint in this if the person with whom they were eating was going to be made to feel uncomfortable or guilty by it.

In an effort to find out more about what this Christian way was, Peter accepted a dinner invitation from some of our Gentile converts. The invitation extended to Paul and myself and a few other Nazarene Jews. We met in a house in which an especially long table had been set up for us. Of the food placed on the table, some, such as bread and fish and vegetables, was acceptable for any Jew to eat. But the rest of it, especially the meat, was not. Peter offered no objection to this mixed variety of food, since he wanted to win the friendship and confidence of our Gentile hosts. And though he wanted to learn more about what they believed about Jesus, he did not immediately enter into the subject of religion, since that, he felt, would make his presence seem too entirely investigative. He talked instead of the dire political situation in Judaea and about personal things, such as his wife and son.

The opportunity to discuss Christianity, however, as Peter had planned to do later in the evening, never arose, because, shortly after the dinner began, two serious-faced emissaries from James arrived and, after apologizing for their intrusion, asked to see Peter alone outside. Peter excused himself and went out with them.

Once there, the two messengers announced that they had a personal message for Peter but that they first wanted to tell him how shocked they were to find him eating forbidden food with Gentiles.

"The Gentiles," Peter said, "are followers of Jesus like ourselves. I think we should give more consideration to them than to others. And besides, the fact that *some* of the food on the table is forbidden doesn't mean that we ate that food."

"But even if you didn't eat it," one of the emissaries said, "your presence at a table where such food is being served is enough to make people think that you *did* eat it. We're called the Zealots of the Torah because we follow the Torah so zealously. But now, because we're bringing so many Gentiles into our movement, there's a suspicion that we're getting lax about that. Do you want to feed such suspicions by eating at a table where forbidden food is being served?"

"Whether you eat the food or not," the other emissary said.

"All right," said Peter, "for the sake of appearances, I'll accept what you say. But we really have to be careful not to offend our Gentile friends. They're good people, and they add strength to our movement."

Peter went back into the house and asked the rest of us who were Jews to join him outside, apologizing to our Gentile hosts for the interruption of the dinner necessitated by an unexpected emergency.

When we stood outside with Peter and the emissaries, Peter explained the situation to us. All of us except Paul agreed to follow his orders and, for the sake of appearances, to desist from eating with Gentiles again if there was any forbidden food on the table. This, of course, had nothing to do with communing with Gentiles in all other ways. Paul objected and said to Peter that we had not done anything wrong, so he could not see why we should leave. He told Peter and me in the most adamant terms that both of *us* were wrong.

"And besides," he said, "what difference does it make anyway? Even if we *had* eaten forbidden food, what difference would it make?"

"We are Jews!" Peter said. "That's what difference it makes."

"Would you want all Gentiles to eat like Jews?" Paul asked.

"Ideally, yes," Peter answered. "But... "

Paul drove in his point before Peter could continue. "You admit that you did nothing wrong and that you're just giving in for appearances. Then if you did nothing wrong, you're willing to live like a Gentile. So if you're willing to live like a Gentile, why won't you let the Gentiles live like Gentiles? Why do you insist that they live like Jews?"

"I don't expect Gentiles to live like Jews," Peter protested. "I never said that. And I don't expect them to *eat* like Jews. If they're going to join our movement and still remain Gentiles, there are only two dietary restrictions that James requires of them, and that is that they avoid eating blood and the meat from which the blood hasn't been drained — strangled animals in other words — and that they avoid eating food that's been offered to idols."

"And I say, why bother about such things? Is God really concerned about food? Why not let them eat what they wish?"

"Dietary laws were commanded by God," Peter said. "They're not whimsical. They were given to Noah after the Flood, and they were meant for everyone — Gentiles as well as Jews. Our law doesn't permit us to eat fat. Shall we disregard that as well? You promised James that you would have the Gentiles abide by the dietary restrictions that he mentioned. Are you going back on your word?"

"I'm telling you that we're wrong to burden them with this!"

This was the first time I had seen Paul openly defy Peter. I doubt that he would have spoken that way to James, because James had more authority than Peter, and he was also Jesus' brother. But to Peter, Jesus' first disciple and the man who had been Paul's teacher at one time, Paul said openly and to his face that he was wrong.

I sided with Peter in this, but I could see Paul's frustration at being asked to widen the gap between Gentile and Jew when he had wanted to narrow it, even if it meant discarding some of our sacred laws. Now it was the rift between Peter and Paul that was widening, and it seemed that it would widen further with the passage of time. Peter left Antioch, I am sure, with the belief that this would be so.

In spite of our differences that evening, Paul came to me and suggested that we return to the cities we had visited previously to see how our fellow believers were doing. Because I had gotten so friendly with John (Mark) again, I immediately suggested that he go with us. But Paul demurred. He said that John had shown his disloyalty to us by what he had done in Pamphylia and that he was not the person for us to work with anymore. I disagreed. I said that John had been entitled to his opinion even if it differed from ours but now that James had established our policy, John would adhere to it. But there was no swaying Paul; he was adamant. Our discussion about it led to an argument between us, and soon Paul and I were so much at odds that we decided that *we* could not work together either. As a result, John and I stayed together and went to Cyprus to teach, and Paul took Silas with him and went to Syria and Cilicia to work.

This split between Paul and me was painful. I could not understand his inflexible resentment of John. If we all agreed on James' new policy — something I still hoped was true but was beginning to doubt because of the dietary argument between Peter and Paul — why should there be contention? And then John told me about the last conversation he had had with Paul, and I realized what it was. Paul had not been concerned about the Torah and how it related to Gentiles (James had settled that issue for all of us); he had been concerned about the things that he had not revealed in Jerusalem: the divinity of Jesus and the concept of a savior. He had only *begun* to reveal the savior concept to John, and John had disagreed so forcefully that Paul had decided not to go on with it. The little he had said might be reported to James, and Paul was anxious to get more converts before a new confrontation with James took place. In the person of Silas, however, I believe Paul felt that he had found another Barnabas, another willing ear to listen and learn from him as I had.

So we went our separate ways, and I felt the loss of a friend.

Since I, like Paul, believed in Jesus' divinity and in the sacrifice of his life for our sins, it now fell to me to explain these things in full to John.

I would be teaching them soon enough in Cyprus. John was attentive and very respectful, as was proper for a friend and a nephew to be, but he could not accept these beliefs. He felt, as most Jews did, that to claim divinity for a Messiah was an affront to God. Though he readily acknowledged that Jesus had been sent by God, he continued to maintain that Jesus had been a man — a man with a special mission, a man favored by God, a man who had been resurrected from the dead, and a man who would return to us again, but not the son of our god in some familial way that the rest of us were not. And as for Jesus' death being the ransom for our sins, as he put it, he considered that belittling to every God-fearer or Jew who was trying to compensate for his sins by doing good deeds. Paul's idea that man was born with sin before he had actually *done* anything wrong and that all the good deeds in the world could not exonerate him from that did not sit well with John. And, furthermore, the idea that the Torah, the book of good deeds, could now be forgotten by Jews as well as Gentiles was nothing short of blasphemy to him. Jesus himself would object to this, he said.

I could not answer all his objections at once, so I concentrated first on Jesus' death.

"John," I said, "the idea that one person might die as a penance for the sins of others is not totally new to us. You do realize that, don't you?"

"When did that ever occur?" he asked skeptically.

"It's not that it actually occurred," I answered. "It's that our people suggested it in the past. Do you remember Eleazar in the time of Antiochus? Ninety years old, and after that tyrant Antiochus tortured him and burned his flesh to the bone trying to get him to eat pig meat, and when Eleazar was resisting him to the end, because no amount of pain was going to make him disobey God's commandment, do you remember what he said just before he died? Do you remember the words of his prayer?"

"Vaguely," John said.

"Well, let me make it less vague for you. He said, 'You know, oh God, that though I might have saved myself, I die in fiery torments for your law's sake. Be merciful to your people and be content with our punishment on their behalf. Make my blood a purification for them, and take my life as a ransom for their life.'"

"You memorized all that?" John asked me.

"Yes, I memorized it," I said. "I memorized it because when Paul first presented me with the savior concept, the idea that Jesus died for our sins, I objected to it. But because I wanted to be fair to Paul, I started looking for precedents for it. And I found one in Eleazar. Obviously he believed that *he* could die to propitiate the sins of our people."

"What sins had we committed that needed propitiation?" John asked. "Antiochus was the culprit and the villain. He was the one who had sinned. He was the one who needed forgiveness, not we. If God wanted propitiation from sinners, don't you think He should have started with Antiochus before He turned to us? And when He got finished with Antiochus, then how much fault was He going to find with us when we were willing to fight and die for His law? Eleazar wasn't the only one who died under Antiochus, you know. And those who didn't die fought. Wasn't death and the risking of life an expiation for whatever sins we had committed? Was Eleazar's death the only death that counted?"

"No, you're right," I said. "The deaths and the resistances of other people counted too. I'm only saying that Eleazar was *asking* God to take his death as an atonement for all the Jewish people. Even if there wasn't anything to atone for, Eleazar thought there was, and he thought that one person might be sacrificed so that God would let the others alone."

"The idea of human sacrifice ended with Abraham and Isaac, Barnabas, and that was a long time ago. A very long time ago."

"That's exactly what I said to Paul when he first told me this idea. But out of fairness to him, I started looking for precedents. And I found that Eleazar wasn't the only one who thought of that idea. The writer who wrote the book about the Maccabees said it too. When he talked about the people who died under Antiochus, he said, 'They became as it were a ransom for our nation's sin, and through the blood of these righteous ones and their propitiating death, the divine Providence preserved Israel.' And in Isaiah we find propitiating suffering. So you see, other people have had this idea about one good person sacrificing his life to atone for what the rest of us have done wrong."

John began to squirm agitatedly. "Pontius Pilate crucifies innocent people without giving them even so much as a mock trial, and you say that *we* are the sinners! And we're such bad sinners that our own Messiah — the man who is going to lead us to victory over the Romans — has to die so that we can be forgiven for these sins. Is that reasonable? I ask you, Barnabas, is that reasonable?"

"Yes," I ejaculated, "it's reasonable! Are you going to tell me there was no adultery, no theft, no idolatry going on in Israel?"

"Of course there were. But by whom? Yes, some of our people committed adultery and theft and the other sins that Moses warned us about, but that wasn't the *mass* of the people. Most of our people *weren't* doing those things. So because a few weak or errant individuals broke the law, does that mean that the whole nation has sinned? And going by your reasoning, Barnabas, whose death did God need to atone for the sins of Pontius Pilate and his Roman killers or for the sins of Antiochus and his?"

Oh, how we argued, the two of us, loving each other and wanting desperately to win our respective points of view. We were like two typical Pharisees, like the more liberal School of Hillel and the more conservative School of Shammai, arguing back and forth in search of truth. We stayed together and looked for a compromise. He did not leave me as he had in Pamphylia; he stayed and listened, and I did too. Somehow, somewhere, we both believed, the answer would come.

In Judaea, meanwhile, the turbulence grew worse. Some Galileans who were en route to Jerusalem were killed by the inhabitants of a Samaritan village. Other Galileans appealed to Cumanus, the procurator, for justice. But the Samaritans bribed Cumanus, who then refused to do anything to the Samaritans. The Galileans were infuriated, and they appealed to the Judaean Jews to take arms in their behalf. The Galileans and Judaeans then sought the help of Eleazar, the son of Deinaios, a Zealot who was fighting the Romans from his mountain hideaway. Led by Eleazar, the Jews attacked and massacred the inhabitants of a number of Samaritan villages. Cumanus responded by sending out troops, who captured some of the Jewish rebels and either took them prisoner or killed them. Eleazar and his Zealots, however, got away and went back to their mountain retreat. The number of people who joined the Zealots increased after that, and resentment by the Jews of how unfairly they had been treated continued.

The Samaritans then appealed to Numidius Quadratus, who was the legate of Syria, at Tyre. He came to Judaea to investigate. He sided with the Samaritans and had the rebel prisoners crucified and other captured revolutionaries crucified as well. The crucifixions were many, and Jewish hatred of the Romans grew worse. But Quadratus did not care. He went from Caesarea to Lydda and listened to the Samaritans again. Then he sent for eighteen Jewish prisoners who were accused of having taken part in the fighting and had their heads cut off. Then he ordered Ananias and some of the other chief priests, along with the commander of the Temple and other prominent Jews, to be put into chains and sent to Rome. With them went Cumanus, the procurator, and an anti-Jewish tribune named Celer and the angry Samaritan leaders. Quadratus then went to Jerusalem and, finding the inhabitants celebrating Passover peacefully, went from there to Antioch, feeling confident that he had made the right decision.

But now the king, Agrippa II, intervened with the emperor, Claudius, and the Jews got a favorable verdict. Cumanus, the procurator, was sent into exile, and Celer, the tribune, was sent back to Jerusalem in chains with orders that he be given to the Jews for torture and that he be dragged around the city before he was finally beheaded.

But that did not bring back the people whom Cumanus had crucified and beheaded, and a festering resentment remained and did not bode well for peace.

Felix became the new procurator, and Claudius expanded the area of his authority. To Judaea and Galilee, he added Samaria and Peraea. He became the most powerful man in our nation, and we waited to see what he would do.

CHAPTER XX

In the meantime, Paul and Silas went to Derbe and Lystra. There they met a young man named Timotheus. His mother was a Jewess who believed in Jesus as the Messiah, and his father was a Greek who believed the way pagans do. Timotheus believed as his mother did, and our followers in Lystra and Iconium reported to Paul that he was strong in his belief and commitment. Paul decided to take him with him as a disciple. He felt that this youth, having reached one level of belief so firmly, could be brought to the next higher level with ease. But Timotheus had never been circumcised, so Paul decided to circumcise him first. Years later, when I asked Paul why he had done this, since a rejection of the Torah would have made this no longer necessary, he said that it was because of the Jews to whom they would be speaking. He still hoped to bring more Jews as well as Gentiles into our movement, and, to be acceptable to Jews, a teacher, such as Timotheus was going to be, would have to be a bona fide Jew himself. Eventually, they were going to be telling Jews to reject the Torah (something that James had never suspected they would be doing, since he had thought we would be saying this only to Gentiles who didn't want to become Jews), and such an instruction would sit better with Jews if it came from a Jew and not from a Gentile.

For myself, after discussion with John (Mark), I intended to speak of Torah rejection only to those for whom James had intended it: Gentiles who did not want to become Jews and who preferred the God-fearer path instead. I would not speak of Torah rejection to Jews.

Paul, Silas and Timotheus preached throughout Phrygia and Galatia. But when they came to the border of Asia and were preparing to cross it, Paul had a vision. In it, Jesus told him that he was forbidden to go into Asia to preach. Paul did not say *why* Jesus had prohibited this, but it had not been necessary to tell Silas and Timotheus why: the fact that Jesus *had* prohibited it was enough. So, even though they were opposite Mysia and wanted to go to Bithynia, they did not go. Paul's vision of Jesus stopped them, and they went instead to Troas.

In Troas, Paul had another vision. In this one, he saw a man from Macedonia, who pleaded with him to come into that country to help the people by teaching them. As Paul had done with his other visions, he related it to Silas and Timotheus, and, accordingly, they set off together again.

They traveled now to Samothracia and the next day to Neapolis and the day after that to Philippi, one of the chief cities of Macedonia. They stayed in Philippi several days and, on the Sabbath, went outside the city to a riverside place where people customarily prayed. They talked to the women there, and one of them, a woman named Lydia, who sold purple cloth and who lived in the city of Thyatira, responded enthusiastically to what they were teaching. She brought her family to them and had the family baptized. Then she invited Paul and Silas and Timotheus to stay at her house, which they did. "You are men of God," she said to them as she showed them to their rooms, "and my house and everything in it is yours."

A few days later, as the three of them were on their way to prayer, a young slave girl followed them in the street and began to announce in a loud, shrill voice that these were the servants of the most high God and were showing the way to salvation. That, in itself, would not have drawn much attention, but the girl was a well-known soothsayer who earned money for her masters by telling fortunes; therefore, her words were listened to with much respect. Paul explained to Silas and Timotheus that a divining spirit was in her. He was not disturbed by what she was saying, for, after all, what she was saying was complimentary to them, but he *was* disturbed by the loud, somewhat hysterical way in which she was saying it. Paul tolerated it for several days, no doubt enjoying the attention they were getting but then decided it had gone on long enough. On a day when he and Silas were walking and Timotheus was not with them, he commanded the divining spirit within the girl to leave in the name of Jesus, the Christ. It did so immediately, and her obstreperous promulgations ceased. But now she could no longer divine, and this meant that she could no longer earn money for her masters. Those pecuniary gentlemen became upset at this, and they organized a group of men to seize Paul and Silas and bring them to the magistrates of the city.

They told the magistrates that Paul and Silas were Jews and that they were teaching the people that there was only one god and about a Jewish king who was going to take over soon and that this king was the son of that god. All this, they said, was sacrilegious to the customary beliefs of the people, who, being Roman citizens, believed as the Romans did. In front of this large crowd of people, the magistrates went up to Paul and Silas and tore off their clothes. Then they ordered the guards to beat Paul and Silas publicly, and the guards did so with rods. This was not the first time, of course, that Paul had been beaten publicly. At Lystra, they even had stoned him and left him for dead. But now, under orders from the magistrates, the guards dragged Paul and Silas into the prison and told the jailer to secure them there safely. The jailer put them into the innermost part of the prison and placed stocks on their ankles to make sure they couldn't escape.

At midnight, Paul and Silas lifted themselves painfully off the floor and prayed for deliverance. They sang songs of praise to God, but they sang so loudly that they awakened the other prisoners. These prisoners now shouted and complained that their sleep was being disturbed. But all this was minor compared to what happened next, for now, as if in answer to their prayers, an earthquake began, and it shook the foundations of the prison to its core. It was so severe that the prison doors sprang open and the shackles of all the prisoners loosened enough for many of them to get free.

The chief jailer was awakened by this, and he rushed into the prison to see what had happened. He could see only by the moonlight coming through the windows, but it showed him enough to put him into a panic. He saw that the cell doors were open, and he immediately thought that all the prisoners had escaped. His punishment for this would be severe — more severe than he felt he could stand — and he readied his sword to kill himself rather than face it.

But Paul saw him starting to do it and immediately sensed why.

"Don't!" Paul shouted. "Don't harm yourself! All the prisoners are here."

How Paul knew that, I don't know, for the prison was dark and Paul had not looked into the other cells to see who was there and who wasn't. But somehow, he did know it and shouted it out to the jailer.

The jailer stopped. Paul's voice, coming out of the darkness, was like something supernatural, and he obeyed it implicitly. Then he called for his guards to get a light. When one of them returned with it, the jailer took it from him and sprang into the cell where Paul and Silas were being kept. He stood trembling before them and then knelt on the floor to show his respect, for he was certain that the earthquake had occurred because of them. Then he led them out of the cell and into a more comfortable room.

Now the jailer, because he had heard about their teachings of salvation and about Paul's exorcism of the divining spirit from the girl, asked about their philosophy and said, "What must I do to be saved?"

"Believe in Jesus, the Christ," Paul answered. "Do that, and you and everyone in your household — your family and your servants — will be saved."

"From what will we be saved?" the jailer asked.

"From the punishment you will otherwise have to suffer for the sins of which you are guilty," Paul said.

The jailer summoned everyone in his household — his wife, his children, his servants — and made them listen to Paul and Silas. Paul told them about Jesus; about his goodness and his love for all people; about his special position as the son of God; about his cruel crucifixion, which had been the necessary sacrifice that God needed to forgive us for our shortcomings and our sins, these being so integral a part of us that no amount of good deeds could eradicate them; and about God requiring us to *believe* that Jesus had died for this reason before he could grant us forgiveness.

The jailer took Paul and Silas home with him and washed their wounds. Paul baptized the entire household that night. Then the jailer brought meat for Paul and Silas to eat.

Unlike Peter and unlike the new compromise policy that John and I were trying to forge, Paul had not given these Gentiles the choice of becoming Jews and, therefore, Nazarenes, nor had he spoken to them about the set of laws we had gotten through Noah, which would have made them God-fearer followers of Jesus, as James had intended, nor had he even spoken to them about the minimal moral standards required of a non-Jewish follower of Jesus. He had spoken to them only about the new concept of Jesus: about Jesus being the son of God and about a belief in the sacrifice of his life being the means by which we could expiate our sins and become acceptable to God. These were the concepts of Christians, and Paul had given these Gentiles only that way to become followers of Jesus; he had not told them there were other ways.

In the morning, the magistrates were told about how the earthquake had affected the prison. They were understandably fearful that Paul and Silas had caused this to happen or that some god had caused it for them. They sent soldiers to tell the jailer to release the prisoners. The jailer then told Paul and Silas they were free to go. But Paul refused to leave. He knew the magistrates were afraid of him now, and he decided to teach them a lesson. He told the soldiers that he and Silas were Roman citizens and that the magistrates had acted illegally by beating them and imprisoning them without a trial.

"We're not going to leave," Paul said. "Do they think they can treat us this way and then cast us out without apologizing as if we're some sort of vagabonds to be pushed around? They won't get off so easily. If they want us to leave, let them come down here themselves and ask us to do so politely. Otherwise, we're staying here where they put us, and when word reaches the higher authorities about this, let the magistrates take the consequences."

I was not aware that Silas was a Roman citizen, but I was aware that Paul was one, for I knew that Paul had purchased a Roman citizenship with some of the money he had collected for the famine in Jerusalem.

When Paul's response was conveyed to the magistrates, they became even more fearful than before. Now they were concerned not only about the god who had caused the earthquake but about a Roman authority who might accuse them of having acted illegally. Forgotten now were their previous concerns about the sacrilegious teachings of Paul and Silas. Paul's boldness alone was enough to convince them that he was a more important personage than they had realized. They hastened to the prison and personally escorted Paul and Silas out of it, beseeching their pardon and pleading with them to leave the city peacefully.

Had Paul and Silas decided to stay, I think the magistrates would have accommodated them out of fear. But, as it was, Paul and Silas wanted to go anyway, so they accepted the magistrates' apologies and went to Lydia's house to say goodbye and then left with Timotheus for other parts.

CHAPTER XXI

They passed through Amphipolis and Apollonia and entered Thessalonica, where they stayed at the house of a man named Jason. In the synagogue in Thessalonica, Paul was invited to speak and present his views. This was a common enough event, for the synagogue was not only a place to pray and praise God but also a place to thresh out ideas. He spoke there and conversed for three Sabbaths in succession, and many Jews accepted his teachings and became avid followers of Jesus. But these Jews did not become Christians, for Paul had not gone so far as to tell them to reject the Torah. With these people at least, he was true to the policy that he had told John about in Antioch: that when he was with Gentiles, he would teach in such a way as to cater to *their* needs, but when he was with Jews, he would cater to theirs. He had told *me* about this when he spoke of his conversation with John (Mark), and he had said that there would be some Jews that he would tell to abandon the Torah but that he would be selective about which ones they would be. When he felt that he was among Jews to whom the Torah was foremost, he would tell them to obey it, though privately he did not feel bound by it in any way.

But some Jews in Thessalonica rejected Paul. Though he had not said to abandon the Torah, he *had* told them that Jesus was the son of God and that that made Jesus divine. Had he just said that Jesus was the son of God, all of them would have understood Paul to mean that in the symbolic sense, in which the Messiah is a human being, chosen and anointed by God and so favored in God's eyes that God loved him as a father loves a son. But by saying to these Jews that Jesus was divine, he was imparting to the venerable expression, "son of God", a meaning that they had not expected. It was blasphemy to some of them; it was what Romans and other pagans did to aggrandize their prominent men. The Jews who rejected Paul wanted to stop his preaching, so they seized upon the political issue to get the Romans to order him out of the city. Paul was later to say to me that they did this out of jealousy. "Jealousy over what?" I asked him when he told me about it. "Over my having gotten so many people to accept me as their leader and advisor," he said. But I, personally, suspect it was because of the divinity idea and about some of the savior concept that may have leaked out in his talks.

The disgruntled Thessalonian Jews got some rather tough fellows to go with them, and they went to the house of Jason with the intention of dragging Paul and Silas out of the house and bringing them to the Romans. But Paul and Silas weren't there at the time, so these ruffians pulled Jason and some of the other Jesus-followers out instead and took them to the Roman authorities for judgment.

"These men are turning the world upside down," the leader of the crowd announced. "They're going against the laws of Caesar. They're saying that another king — someone named Jesus — is coming to rule over us." These were not the issues that the crowd really cared about, of course; the religious issues were what concerned them. But since those issues would not be very important to the Romans, they chose the political one in the hope of using the Romans to get rid of the blasphemers.

The Roman authorities soon came to understand that Jason and his friends were not the instigators of this rumor about a new king but the recipients of it. So they took bail money from them and let them go for the time being.

Meanwhile, other followers of Paul and Silas and Timotheus got *them* out of the city secretly by night.

The three of them went to Beroea. Once they were there, they went to the synagogue. They usually did this when they arrived in any city, because they had to establish themselves with a house and a source of food before they could start their teaching. In the synagogue would be Jews, and Jews could not refuse hospitality to fellow Jews (or to any stranger, for that matter) since the law of Moses forbade it. Mosaic law required Jews to treat strangers as their own and to love them as much as they loved themselves. So Paul and Silas and Timotheus had no difficulty in finding food and lodging among the Jews in the cities they visited.

They spoke in the Beroean synagogue on the Sabbath. They were well received by the people, just as they had been well received when they had first arrived in Thessalonica. Paul later referred to these people as a nobler group of Jews than the ones in Thessalonica, but I asked myself why. I don't believe that people are less noble because they doubt what we have to say. I had many Pharisee friends at the time who had doubts about what I believed, but I did not consider them ignoble because of it. Gamaliel, the leader of the Pharisees, reserved his judgment about whether we were right or wrong, but I did not consider him ignoble because of that. Was it because the Thessalonian Jews had tried to get Paul imprisoned or evicted? Was that the reason he considered them ignoble? But what of the Thessalonian Jews who had not tried to do that? What of those who had accepted his teachings and those who had helped him escape? Were they also less noble than the Jews of Beroea? And if they were not, and, presumably, that was the case, why blame *all* the Jews of Thessalonica for what only a few of them had done? But this was a pattern I was to see over and over again in the writings and teachings of Paul and his followers: the habit of blaming all members of a particular group for the things that only a few of the members had done.

The Beroean Jews accepted Paul well, and many of them accepted Jesus in the way that Paul was presenting him. But it was never made clear to me just what Paul was teaching. Was he telling them that Jesus was the Messiah and the future Jewish king, who would return to defend the Torah as he so often had done in his life, or was he telling them that Jesus was the savior, whose death had wiped out their sins, thus making the Torah obsolete, and who stood unique in the annals of men as the divine son of God?

I never knew the answer to this, at least not insofar as what he was teaching at that time. When I saw him years later, and we talked about so many of the things that had happened to us, I never asked him about how much of the new doctrine he was teaching in each specific city that he had visited. Certainly, some of the new things must have crept in, perhaps inadvertently or perhaps because he was testing the waters to see just how much of it the Jews would accept.

So the Beroean Jews accepted him, but what was the reason? Was he being more careful, more circumspect now, after the trauma of his Thessalonian experience? Was he making his presentation more acceptable to a Jewish audience by praising the Torah and sticking only to the Messiah concept of Jesus? Whatever the reason, all that eclat was short-lived, because now some of the Thessalonian Jews, who had heard where he was, came to Beroea to discredit him.

As before, when Paul told people about this some time later, he was to say to them, "The Thessalonian Jews came to discredit me." When we did meet again years later, I asked him why he had said this. Only *some* of the Thessalonian Jews had come to discredit him; most of them had not. Why then was Paul telling about this episode in such a way as to imply that *all* of them had come? Was this, as I mentioned before, a new policy of Paul's: to blame all members of a group for what just a few of them had done? And was he applying this new policy only to Jews?

The agitating Thessalonian Jews turned many Beroean Jews against him, and his friends in Beroea then took him away by boat to protect him against any possible violence. Silas stayed behind in Beroea, however, and preached again after the Thessalonians had left. And Timotheus, defying danger, went back to Thessalonica to strengthen our followers there.

Paul and those who had sailed with him made their way, meanwhile, to Athens. From there Paul sent word to Silas and Timotheus to join him. And then, while he waited, he spoke in the synagogue. It was customary for synagogues to allow people to speak. That was because synagogues, as I have said, were places for discussion and argument as well as places for prayer and worship. And Jews, especially Pharisees, loved to argue among themselves. They said it stimulated the mind and led to greater wisdom. So Paul spoke in the synagogue.

But soon he encountered the Epicurean and Stoic philosophers, who were Greeks. And here he found people who loved argument and discussion just as much as Pharisees did. These philosophers were pagans, but they searched for answers too, and they looked for them in the same way as the Pharisees. Paul knew much about them, of course, because of his past encounters with them in Tarsus. Once they learned that Paul was a religious teacher, they brought him to Mars Hill to one of their leading philosophers, a man named Areopagus, and asked Paul to speak to them about his beliefs. Whether they were genuinely interested in what he had to say or whether they were just baiting him, I cannot say, but Paul, upon seeing the graven images of their many different gods, spoke to them about the one true god. He told them that this one god had created the world and everything in it, that He did not live in altars or shrines, such as the ones that they had built, and that He wasn't one to be served by human hands, as though He needed anything, since He had everything to give, and that He had given men life and breath and everything they needed. And he told them that we all were the offspring of God. This last thing is what Jews have always claimed, of course, but it stood in sharp contradiction to the thing that Paul had said and taught to me previously; namely that Jesus was the one and only son of God.

One of the Greek philosophers asked Paul, since God needed nothing from man because God had everything He needed, why God had required Jesus' death in order to forgive the sins of man. To this Paul answered that that was the one thing that God had needed.

Some of these Greeks, including Dionysius and an Aereopagite and a woman named Damaris, were convinced that Paul was right. But others were still not sure. The doubters among them questioned the resurrection of Jesus, while others among them believed it. Still, they all agreed to consider the matter and to listen to Paul again.

But that opportunity never came, because Paul now went to Corinth. Why he didn't wait for Silas and Timotheus to arrive, and why he didn't meet with the Greek philosophers again, I don't know. It may have been his restless spirit, which seemed never able to stay in one place too long, or it may have been that he wanted to reach as many communities as possible and to win them over to his Christian way of thinking before James found out what he was doing and sent emissaries to discredit him. Paul knew a simple truth: Whoever reaches an uncommitted mind first always has the advantage over the latecomer who tries to convince the listener of the opposite view. Invariably, one sees this throughout life: that the uncommitted mind becomes committed to the first convincing view that is presented to it and then resents the presenter of an opposite view. It is all a question of who gets there first. So perhaps that was why Paul scurried so impatiently from province to province and city to city, lining up as many followers as he could.

In Corinth he stayed with a fellow Jew named Aquila, who worked in leather just as he did. Aquila and his wife, Priscilla, had come to Corinth from Pontus in Italy when the emperor, Claudius, had ordered all foreign Jews out of Rome. (It is interesting, I think, that this expulsion occurred not because of a spreading of Jewish religious beliefs, which had been going on in Rome for some time, with many Romans converting, but because of the political threat that the Romans perceived from those who looked to Jesus as the Messiah. "They are continually making disturbances," said Claudius, "at the instigation of Christ." I tell you this so that you will clearly understand that the Romans considered Jesus-followers to be Jews, and, moreover, politically threatening Jews in a way that other Jews were not.)

Aquila spoke of all this when he and Paul first talked together. "I'm a Jew, and I work in leather," he said. "That's it! I did my work, and I minded my own business. I observed the Sabbath, and I followed the Torah. When I lived in Italy, did I bother anybody? No! I minded my own business. Did some of the Romans become Jews? Sure they did. A few here, a few there. Some of them were even important people. But so what? That didn't hurt anybody, did it? Look, a person should be able to believe what he wants to believe without anybody bothering him. Right? And as far as I was concerned, it wasn't my business to try to convince anybody of anything. If somebody wanted to ask me about being a Jew, I'd tell him. But if he didn't ask me, I would leave him alone. Let him believe what he wants to believe, and I'll believe what I want to believe. I minded my own business. I didn't bother anybody.

"Then, all of a sudden, we started hearing about Jesus, that he's the Messiah, that he was dead but came back to life, that he's going to come back and kick out the Romans, that he's going to set up a new kingdom with God at the head of it. All right, fine. But what did that have to do with me? If he does it, he does it; if he doesn't, he doesn't. Look, I'd like to see all those things happen. Believe me, I would. But what could I do about it, one way or the other? I had to earn a living for me and my wife. So I did my work and minded my own business. Right?

"And the next thing I know, the emperor orders all Jews to leave the country. Why? What did we do? It's because of Jesus, they said. All those Jews who think he's the Messiah are demonstrating in the streets about him. And they're trying to convince other Jews to join them, and they're saying that Jesus is going to take away every authority from the Romans when he comes back. So the emperor gets upset about this, which I can understand — Wouldn't you get upset if you were the emperor? — and he says all Jews have to get out. Why? I said. What did I do? Did I challenge somebody? Did I disobey a law? No, they said, nothing like that. You're a Jew, and all Jews have to get out. But some of us aren't part of this Jesus movement, I said to them. That doesn't make any difference, they said. They can't tell which Jews belong to it and which Jews don't. So they get rid of the whole problem by getting *all* the Jews to leave.

"Do you know how much property we lost when we left? We got out with my tools and some clothes, and that was it. I really resented that, I really did. I hadn't done anything wrong, and they made me get out.

"So then I started thinking, if I'm going to be punished for being a Jesus-follower when I'm not one, then I might as well become one if I think that what he said was good. Either way I'm going to get punished. So then I started thinking about what he said. I started to go to meetings, and I started to listen. And let me tell you: what he said made sense. And what all the Jesus-followers were saying made sense too. So if you're a teacher or a leader or something like that in this movement, you can count on me to support you. If you want someone who knows how to work and can get the job done, I'm your man."

Paul accepted him; he accepted Aquila and also his wife. He baptized them and taught them to be Christians. Then he went into the streets and also into the synagogue, and in many places in this city of Corinth, he continued to do his preaching. He spoke to Greeks as well

Jews, but mainly he spoke to Jews. And then Silas and Timotheus arrived, and they all did their preaching together.

But the Jews of Corinth opposed him, and many of them reviled him. It was probably the new philosophy. I was sure now that he was going beyond what he had said he would preach to Jews, that he was not teaching respect for the Torah but, rather, its irrelevance in the light of Jesus' death. As was proved by the situation in Jerusalem, the claim that Jesus was the Messiah and that he was resurrected after death elicited no animosity from Jews. That is what the Nazarenes in Jerusalem were claiming, and they enjoyed not only respect but status among the Pharisees of that city. But the claim that Jesus was the exclusive son of God, that a belief in his sacrificial death was enough to wipe out all our sins, that no amount of good deeds could accomplish that expiation and that the Torah, therefore, was obsolete — those claims elicited anger, and that is what I think Paul was getting closer and closer to saying, with less and less dissimulation and more and more boldness. And for that reason, I believe, the Jews of Corinth opposed him.

Paul's response to that opposition was disgust, and he shook off his garments and said to them, "Your blood be upon your heads! I am innocent. From now on, I will go to the Gentiles." With those words, he had called a curse on them — a curse because they disagreed with him. This, I think, was excessive. But not only was there a curse but also a promise not to preach to Jews anymore! A promise not to preach to the very people that Jesus had ordered us to preach to!

It was significant to me that those Jews of Corinth did not strip Paul in public and have him beaten, as the Gentiles of Philippi had done, and that they did not imprison him in the deepest dungeon as those Gentiles also had done. Yet, notwithstanding that these Jews had done far less to him than those Gentiles, he swore that he would not preach to Jews anymore but that he *would* continue to preach to Gentiles. It was the same thing he had done in Pisidia six or seven years earlier, when the Jews in that place had rejected him. Then, as now, he had sworn never to preach to Jews again. But, of course, he *had* preached to them again in spite of it.

Paul's response did seem strange at first. Why was he not swearing that he would never preach to Gentiles after what the Philippian Gentiles had done to him? And, conversely, why *was* he swearing that he would never preach to Jews in spite of the fact that the Corinthian Jews had done so much less? But then I saw again the pattern that I previously have described: the pattern of blaming *all* members of a group for what a small number of them had done, and the application of this principle only to Jews. A blow from a Gentile was tolerable to Paul and made him only want to talk to Gentiles more; but a slur from a Jew was intolerable to him, and made him want to shun *all* Jews because of it.

Now I began to see the pattern of an underlying animosity towards Jews. Gentiles, to Paul, were to be judged by one standard, and Jews were to be judged by another. But from where did this animosity come? What seed had started it? What rain had nurtured it? And then I saw the answer: I saw Rabath and Gamaliel and Peter and James. And from all of them I saw the source of what had happened to Paul. Rabath, who had spurned him after he had undergone the full conversion to win her; Gamaliel, who had rejected him because he did not know enough about the Torah; Peter, who was now his rival in getting new followers for Jesus; and James, who lorded it over him and told him what to do, and who was able do that not because he had worked harder than Paul or knew more than Paul but only because he was related to Jesus and nothing else.

All these people were Jews, and from all of them had come rejection and pain. And now the Jews in all the synagogues he visited were doing the same to him. It began to seem to Paul that Jews in general were inimical to him, and so, apparently, he decided to be the same to them. But not openly. What he did would be done more subtly and more circumspectly than that.

And while all this development was going on in his mind, while all this unfolding of the pages of his life was turning like a book as yet unread, the lives of others, the destinies of those in high places, were turning with leaves of their own.

Agrippa's political fortunes were improving: Claudius gave him more land. Though Claudius took Chalcis away from him (he had had it for more than four years), he gave him even more territory than before in the form of the old tetrarchy of Philip and also Batanea, Trachonitis and Abila. This was far less land than what his father had had, but it was still a step in the right direction. He resented that Claudius did not have enough faith in him to give him the entire nation, but he kept his thoughts to himself.

He felt that he could prove his maturity to some extent, however, by being a capable head of his family. He was obliged to find a husband for Drusilla, but he was having some difficulty with that. The frustrating effort was taking him years, and he wondered if he would ever be successful. Then, as if in answer to a prayer, he found a mate for her. You may wonder why Drusilla, as beautiful as she was, had to wait so long for a man. The reason, at first, was because she wanted someone who wasn't a bore. But the field of choices was somewhat limited by the requirements of her royal position. A princess, after all, could not marry just any man; the man, of necessity, had to be either of royal birth or from a family of stature and means. But, beyond that, to make things even more difficult for her, he had to be a Jew. No one in her family would tolerate anything else. What finally wore her down, what made her accept one of Agrippa's proposals at last, was not so much the paucity of good specimens her brother was bringing her but the erosion of her sanity from having to live with her sister, Bernice. Bernice had been somewhat fearful that her own recognized beauty might be eclipsed by that of her sister, so she had treated Drusilla meanly at home and had made her life miserable there. (At least that is what the people said when they talked about this in the streets.) Drusilla then resigned herself to a fate of marital dullness over one of domestic persecution and accepted as her husband a man named Azizus, king of Emesa, who had promised Agrippa that he would get circumcised and learn to be a Jew. To Azizus, unlike his predecessor, Epiphanes, that was a small enough price to pay for the acquisition of such a prize.

In the public view, then, there remained only Bernice who ostensibly needed a husband. But Agrippa did nothing to abet that goal, so much did he want her for himself. He did make some token, some superficial gestures, for appearance's sake, but none of them were really serious, and Bernice continued to stay with him, sharing his bed at night.

Felix, the procurator, had now been in office about a year. One evening he accepted an invitation to a party, and it was there that he saw Drusilla for the first time. Felix was a soldier who had worked his way up from the ranks. He knew how to seize what he wanted. He knew, too, the importance of time, so he was not a patient man. He was sometimes brusque and sometimes charming, but he was always intense about his goals. Life to him was a battle. A person either won it or lost it by the degree of his cleverness and courage.

When he was introduced to Drusilla, he knew immediately that he wanted her. He knew only one way to go after anything, and that was by a direct frontal assault. So, over the edge of his wine cup, when he had her to himself for a moment, he said, "Queen Drusilla, I have not been able to take my eyes off you all evening."

Drusilla flashed him a smile. "I am flattered, Governor Felix. Perhaps I remind you of someone in Rome."

"No, dear lady," the governor said. "I have never seen anyone as beautiful as you in my life."

"You're a man of pretty words, your excellency. A woman should be wary of you," she said.

"I'm not a scholar in the use of words, your majesty, so I'm compelled to tell the truth. Your beauty, if I may say so, is something fit for a god."

"My husband sees me every day, Governor Felix, and I can assure you that *he* is not a god."

"Then the sight of you should make him feel like one," Felix said.

"My husband is concerned with affairs of state, and we are not together very often. I think he still feels more like a busy man than a god."

This was the soft spot that Felix had been seeking. "If you are not together very often, your majesty, then a gift of the gods is being wasted."

"You may not be a scholar, Governor Felix," she said, "but you flatter very well."

"Still, I am more a man of action than a man of words, I assure you, your majesty."

"Yes, governor, I sense a certain energy in you."

"Would that I could spend that energy on you, dear lady. As your subject for the rest of my life."

The boldness of that remark made Drusilla pale with fear. But the fear that she felt was not from Felix but from the feelings within herself. She separated from him to talk to others, but soon he waylaid her again. They talked; he aroused her anew, and again she had to tear herself away from him. That night, she could not sleep for thinking of him. What woman does not love a bold lover? She felt drawn to him by a force too powerful to resist and too mysterious to understand. She wanted to see him again.

In the morning, Felix sent his friend Simon to see her. Simon pretended to be a magician. Through entertaining her first and then speaking in Felix's behalf, he convinced her to leave her husband.

There was a scandal, of course. When Felix and Drusilla married, she violated Mosaic law. Not only was she breaking her vow to her husband, she was marrying a Gentile too. But there were some who sympathized with her; there were some who saw in her situation the dilemma of a young woman who had been treated badly at home, who then had married a man to escape from that, and who had then met another man who inspired her love, a man whom she should have met years before.

I mention this so that you will understand the lives of those powerful people who were to have a direct effect on Paul and our nation as the events of the future unfolded. At the time that all this was happening, however, it was of little importance to Paul. He was dealing with intensities of his own. For him, living away from such royal ordeals and petty affairs, being concerned with things of much deeper significance, life went on steadily in Corinth. He still lived in the house of Aquila and continued his work from there.

He now wrote a letter to our friends in Thessalonica. His intention was to give them reassurance, since the tribulations they were experiencing were enough to rattle anyone's belief. He wrote to them to be steadfast and not to buckle under the weight of their trials. He mentioned some of the God-fearer laws and told them not to fornicate lustfully the way pagan Gentiles do (for neither Jews nor God-fearers nor Christians do that) and not to defraud anyone, for God avenges such wrongs, and to love each other, and to practice the quiet pursuit of one's daily business activities, and to work each with his own hands, so that they could have enough for themselves and enough to give to the poor, and to have faith that Jesus would return in glory, and that the righteous who are dead and the righteous who are alive would be raised up into the clouds to live with him forever.

The day of Jesus' return would come unexpectedly, he said, like a thief in the night, and overwhelm the unprepared with distress, like a woman in labor. But *they* were not to worry, for they *were* prepared; they were children of light, who watch and wait and are sober and put on breastplates of faith and love and, for helmets, wear the hope of salvation.

He spoke of Jesus and called him, "our lord", which was the first time I had heard of him doing this since his experience on the road to Damascus, because that is a term that Jews usually reserve for God; not even a king or an emperor is called that by us. But for Jews such as myself, who believed that Jesus was the only son of God, the term, I suppose, seemed appropriate for Jesus too, since he was part of the divine family.

In his letter, he told the Thessalonians to esteem their spiritual authorities, even when those persons admonished them, and to be at peace among themselves and to warn the unruly and comfort the retarded and support the weak and be patient to all and avoid the appearance of evil and to never return evil for evil but, rather, always to follow what was good, among themselves and with all other people. "Greet all your brothers with a holy kiss," he wrote.

These were the words of a great man, and I tell you, in spite of any disagreements between Paul and myself, he was a great man. Hillel would have been proud of him, Gamaliel would have been proud of him, and James and Peter, too, would have been proud of him, for the things I have just told you he wrote to the Thessalonians.

But marring these noble words and ideas was another part of his letter that betrayed his own weakness, which he himself acknowledged frequently, and showed me again his animosity towards all Jewish people. In the first part of his letter, he told the Thessalonians that they were members of the same church in Judaea that accepted Jesus as the Christ and that the believers there had suffered the same kind of persecution from the Jews of that country as the Thessalonians were suffering from their own countrymen. And I asked myself which Jews in Judaea were persecuting the Jesus-followers there — or in any part of our country, for that matter. It could not be the Jews in Galilee, who had tried to make Jesus king; nor could it be the Pharisees there, who had tried to save his life; nor could it be the Pharisees in Judaea, who held James in high esteem and who considered the Nazarenes part of themselves and who had even joined the Nazarene movement; nor could it be the thousands who had flocked to Peter when he healed so many Jews and then restored Tabitha to life; nor Gamaliel, who counseled patience to see if Jesus returned; nor the lower priests, all of whom had joined us and were Jesus-followers now; nor the Zealots, who had had one of their own members become one of Jesus' disciples; nor the Essenes, from whom Jesus had drawn so much of his philosophy and who, tentatively, considered him the Messiah; nor the unaffiliated mass of Jews who had hailed him into Jerusalem and who had struck fear into the heart of Caiaphas if he dared arrest him during Passover; nor could it have been those Jews who made Judas Iscariot afraid if he betrayed Jesus openly; nor the masses of Jews who had followed Jesus to his death on Golgotha and who had pounded their breasts with weeping as they returned to their homes afterwards. And if it could not be all those tens of thousands, then which Jews could it be?

The Sadducees, of course, were the ones; it was they who persecuted Nazarenes. Yet Paul had chosen not to distinguish them from the mass of the Jews in Judaea. He had chosen to lump all Jews together and to have the Thessalonians believe that the sentiments of the Sadducees were the sentiments of all Jews. And, beyond that, he had made the Thessalonians think that the church that he had formed with his gospel was the church of the Jesus-followers in Judaea. It was not! And no one knew that better than Paul, and no one knew it better than I.

But now he said something else in his letter that was so egregious that it shocked me. After saying that "the Jews" had persecuted the Jesus-followers in Judaea, he then said that "the Jews" had killed the lord, Jesus. I have just mentioned some of the instances in which Jews — Pharisees, Zealots, any Jews but Sadducees — had favored Jesus and his followers. How could these Jews have revered him so much and then turned around and killed him? With all the lower priests now having become Nazarenes, how could *they* have killed him? And by what means did "the Jews" do it? Did "the Jews" nail Jesus to a cross? That was not even the Jewish method of execution. Did Paul mean, perhaps that "the Jews" had taken Jesus to the arch-killer, Pilate, and that that is how they had killed him? But the people who had done that had been the chief priests. Was Paul calling them "the Jews"? And if he was, what name would he give to the rest of the Jews who had *favored* Jesus? Or did he wish the Gentiles to think that there weren't any? Did the people who had flocked to Jesus and favored our movement not exist for Paul? Or did he think they should be called by some other name than "Jews"? This is what he had touched on so fleetingly when he had spoken in the synagogue in Antioch. Though he had not said at the time that the Jews actually killed Jesus, he *had* said that they *desired* his death. But now, to the Thessalonians, he was going beyond that. He was telling the Thessalonians that the Jews had actually killed him.

This was the first time I had heard what was to become an oft-repeated canard: that "the Jews" killed Jesus of Nazareth. Incipient now but later to flower, all Jews would be blamed for the death of our Messiah. Throughout all the Christian communities of the world, this is what would be taught. And all because Paul had said it and not because it was true.

What was his purpose in doing it? Was it because of his resentment against those Jews who had hurt him? Or was it because the Nazarenes were Jews, and because it was only a matter of time until James learned everything about what Paul was teaching and sent emissaries to refute him?

The Jews killed Jesus! Was this to become part of Christian doctrine, part of what I myself would have to teach? And what of the Romans? Had they kissed Jesus with a holy kiss of love? Had they momentarily become weak and ineffectual, so that they could not protect an innocent man against "the Jews"? Had Pilate, the Crucifier, become Pilate, the Coward? Had he fearfully bent to pressure from "the Jews", as he had not done on any other occasion when Jews wanted something from him, and crucified a man he preferred to let go? Or was it just expedient to spread that idea, so that the Romans would see that Christians were not calling them bad, in which case they would see that Christians were not fomenting hatred against Romans for having killed their savior, which would give the Romans less reason to persecute them?

News of this letter reached me in Cyprus, having been brought to me by fellow Christians who traveled there, but it never reached James in Jerusalem. So, at this time, not only did James not know that Paul was telling Jews to abandon the Torah, but he also did not know that Paul was accusing all Jews of having killed Jesus. Peter, too, did not know about this. Word reached me that he was passing through Rome. Paul's claim that the Jews killed Jesus and Paul's abandonment of the Torah had not reached that far as yet.

Paul's adjuration to our Gentile converts that they remember that they were wild olive shoots off the main branch of the tree, which was Israel, was not being mentioned anymore, because to do so would be to suggest that Torah-following was better, since that is what the main branch did, and many might be tempted to join the main branch and become Nazarenes instead of the side branch to become Christians. Where then would be the belief in salvation through Jesus' death?

And now for the first time, I felt fear — fear that all I had come to believe of the things that Paul had taught me were wrong. I still believed, yet I had doubts. For if Paul was beginning to denigrate all Jews for what he felt a few of them had done to him, or, if he was trying to denigrate all Jews in order to weaken the position of the Jewish followers of Jesus in Jerusalem so that they could not compete effectively with *his* gospel among the Gentiles, the effect on me, in either case, was monumental. Jesus would never approve of this. And I could not support a philosophy that misrepresented my people. I was a torn man from that moment onward.

But Paul's vow not to preach to Jews anymore was soon forgotten by him, just as it had been forgotten in Pisidia. He left the house of Aquila, where he had been staying, and went with Silas and Timotheus to the house of Justus to stay. Justus' house was located next to the synagogue of Corinth. Paul got to know Crispus, the chief of the synagogue, and convinced him of the messiahship of Jesus, so that Crispus and his whole family now became followers of Jesus, with Paul baptizing them first.

Because of the rejection Paul had experienced from other Jews in Corinth, he was careful, when he presented Jesus to Crispus, not to deviate too far from traditional Jewish beliefs. He gave Crispus and his family the same material that James and Peter and John were giving to people, in order to win them over. Then, once people became comfortable with that, he could gradually give them more. This is certainly how I became convinced. It was not a bad way to do it. People can't take too much of a change at once without becoming angry at it. But a little change at a time, they can accept. Because of Crispus' influence, other Corinthian Jews also came to accept Jesus as the Messiah, and Paul baptized them as well.

He found the time in Corinth, too, to write a letter to the Christian community in Rome. Now his gospel was being spread by his own group of emissaries even to that arrant bastion of unbridled paganism, and there were plenty of people there who looked to him as their spiritual leader. Because it was his intention to carry his gospel into Spain, he wrote to them that he might visit Rome on his way there.

His letter was one of instruction and explanation. He began by mentioning that Jesus came from the seed of David (for Jesus had come from Joseph, who had come from Jacob, who had come from Matthan — and so forth back to David).

Then he seemed to compliment the Torah, for he said that just hearing the words of the Torah was not enough and that one had to do the things it required as well. He asked if we could continue to sin after we had received expiation through Jesus' death, and he answered that question with a no. Then, to establish again that Gentiles need not be circumcised in order to follow Jesus, he asked, if Gentiles did the good and moral things required by the Torah, didn't that make them as good as circumcised? And of course it did, for that was what being a God-fearer was all about.

But then, later in his letter, he said that a man fulfills his duty to God not by doing the deeds that the Torah requires but by believing the things about Jesus that he, Paul, was preaching. This seemed to contradict what he had said earlier in his letter: that it was not enough just to hear the words of the Torah but that you had to do the things it required as well. In any case, faith was more important than deeds, and believing was everything. Needless to say, if people *believed* what Paul taught, regardless of what they did, they would become members of a group that looked to him as its spiritual leader. For that reason alone, believing must have meant a great deal to him. But now, by saying that a man does his duty to God not by deeds but by faith in Paul's gospel, it seemed that Paul was calling the Torah obsolete. Yet, to that very question of whether freedom from punishment from sin by Jesus' death made the Torah null and void, Paul said that it did not but that it actually established the law. (Since Torah and law were words used interchangeably, I thought at first that he was upholding the Torah, and that made me feel good, because I had been teaching that a belief in either the Torah or the God-fearer rules was necessary along with a belief in Jesus as savior.) And Paul seemed to reinforce this when he said that the law and the commandments were holy and just and good and that the law is spiritual while man is carnal.

But my elation over this apparent compatibility between the Torah and the savior concept was short-lived, because now Paul asked what it was that made a person who believed in Jesus — by which he meant his gospel about Jesus — acceptable to God. Was it the law of the Torah and the deeds or works that that person did in obedience to that book? No, it was the faith in Paul's gospel that made a man acceptable and not any deeds. So then I understood that when Paul had said earlier in his letter that Jesus as savior established the law, he did not mean that it established the Torah but rather that it established a new law — what Paul called the law of faith. So all the good things he had said about the Torah earlier in his letter seemed to be wiped out by what he said later. And this was confirmed when he said to the Romans that Christ had ended the law.

I was again and again driven to ask myself why Paul was so against the Torah. Was it because he wanted to give the Gentiles an easier way to follow Jesus, or was it because he had such difficulty in mastering that book and adhering to its rules of behavior? Perhaps it was both; I was not sure. But the latter reason seemed apparent later when he wrote about his own lust and concupiscence. For whom could he have felt such passion? I asked myself. For whom indeed? I answered. He still carried within him his unrequited love for Rabath, and his impression of life was being formed by his irrepressible desire for her. The Torah demanded that he respond a certain way to someone like that, and his own inability to do so made him feel that no one else could do so either and that the Torah, therefore, was too hard to follow and that a merciful God had to offer an easier way. He exonerated his own lack of will power by saying that it was not he who performed the sins (of which the Torah at least had made him aware) but the sin that dwelled within him that did it. No good thing dwelled in his flesh, he said. While his mind had the will to do what the Torah called good, he could not do it because the sin contained in his flesh did otherwise, meaning that sin could do things independent of a person.

I thought of how much he must have loved her, of how much he must have hungered for her, to be undergoing such a struggle within himself that what he called good and what he called evil wrestled like two contestants for possession of his mind. Men love, and when love is not fulfilled, they usually forget. But sometimes they don't; sometimes they love without hope or sense or reason and carry that sweet pain secretly with them through the long, far pathway to the grave. That's how I think it was with Paul. And that's why I think he despised himself: he could never expunge her from his thoughts or destroy what he considered his lustful desire for her flesh. He was too hard on himself. He was a great man, but he was only a man, and he expected himself to be more. I wondered if his concept of inherent sin had come from a revelation from Jesus or from his inability to suppress his desire for Rabath.

I have said that he was a great man. He showed that greatness when he conveyed to the Romans some of the great lessons that Jesus had taught. He told them not to return evil for evil but to give back good instead; he told them not to seek revenge but to leave that up to God; he told them to live peacefully with all people; he told them to do what was good; he told them that if they loved their neighbors and did them no harm, they had done all that they had to do to fulfill the law; and he told them that we all would have to give an accounting of ourselves to God.

Would the Romans who became Christians have heard these great truths if it had not been for Paul? He carried Jesus and the message of love to the far places of the earth and made himself great when he did so. He *was* a great man because of that, but he was a troubled and tortured one too; and what he taught when he went to those far places of the earth was not the same as what they taught in Jerusalem. It just was not the same.

He would go to Jerusalem, he said to the Romans, before traveling to Rome or Spain, because he wanted to bring the offerings he had collected from the different Christian communities to the leaders who lived in Jerusalem. He would minister to those saints first, he said, and by that statement, he showed his loyalty to them. But I am sure he wanted to impress them too; he wanted them to appreciate and acknowledge all that he had accomplished.

And now Paul had a vision. In it, Jesus told him not to be afraid to speak. Jesus told him to tell everything without fear, saying that he was with him and that no one could hurt him, since he (Jesus) already had many people in the city of Corinth who were his followers.

Such visions were becoming increasingly important to Paul. They were giving him Jesus' most current thoughts. He was receiving directly from Jesus himself the latest things to be done. And that, when he compared it to the absence of such communications to the others in our movement, made him feel every bit as important as the others, even superior to them, including even the first disciples, for it was to him and not to them that Jesus had chosen to speak.

As a result of this latest vision, Paul stayed in Corinth a year and a half and, gradually, began to explain the full story about who Jesus was. He began to venture farther from Jewish tradition than wisdom would have dictated. He was an impatient man who felt that he had much to accomplish, and this business of weaning Jews from the Torah gradually did not sit well with him. So he preached belief in the death-sacrifice as the only way to expiate inborn sin, and he preached the divinity of Jesus. And also, he preached rejection of the Torah, a book that he now seemed almost to resent. And perhaps he did resent it. You see, because I now perceived his hidden resentment of Jews, I began to understand his resentment of the Torah. Though he might feign respect for it in circles where it was politic to do so, his rejection by Gamaliel because he had not mastered its meanings and his own inability to abide by its rigid codes of behavior had led him to the easier path of deprecating it, of saying that it was just a book of ritual, unworthy of the effort of following it, and in that way, dissembling the moral and ethical precepts that the book contained. The influence of Rabath, of course, was there as well.

The reaction of the Jews was predictable. As had been done elsewhere, they sought to silence Paul. And who better to do that than the Romans? Led by Sosthenes, the leader of the synagogue, they took Paul to the Roman deputy of this Achaian province, the proconsul, Annaeus Gallio, and complained to him that Paul was causing a public disturbance by trying to persuade Jews to worship God in such a way that was contrary to Jewish law and to believe things that were contrary to that law. Gallio could have cared less. What difference did it make to him which way the Jews prayed to their invisible god?

"See here," he said to the crowd, "if this man has done something in violation of civil law, or if he has done something lewd or outrageous, then I am inclined to go along with you. But if it's a question of names and titles and matters of religious law, then I'm not your man. You can't expect a Roman authority like myself to rule on matters of religion. That's *your* business, not mine. I'm going to have to ask all of you to leave. I consider it highly improper that you've brought this man before me today. Highly improper."

The Jews felt rejected. They had not been as clever as Jews elsewhere, as the ones in Thessalonica, for instance, who, when they wanted to use the Roman authorities to get rid of Paul, had raised the political issue of Jesus as king instead of the one that really concerned them, which was the religious issue of Jesus as savior and son of God and the rejection of the Torah. Thus the Achaian Jews were frustrated by Gallio's punctilious adherence to the separation of religious and state matters.

The Jews began to disperse, letting Paul go his own way. When the crowd was gone, Sosthenes, the leader of the synagogue, his head bowed deeply in thought, stood alone before the judgment seat on which Gallio still sat looking down at him. It may have been that he wanted to say more, but he never got the chance. Some Greeks appeared suddenly and, seeing Sosthenes alone, seized him and beat him, while Gallio sat impassively looking on. Why they beat him, I was not told. Whether it was because they were followers of Paul or because they just didn't like Jews, I don't know. But I do know that Gallio did nothing to stop them. Maybe these Greeks just didn't like Jews, because if they had been Gentile followers of Paul, and if they had not been God-fearers but, rather, Christians, they could not possibly have beaten anyone; for Paul, presumably, was teaching his Christian followers Jesus' lessons to return only love for hatred and to turn the other cheek when one cheek is slapped.

Of course the other factor in Gallio's passivity (and, for all we know, complicity) in Sosthenes' beating may have been the fact that Gallio was Seneca's brother, and Seneca, as I have mentioned before, hated Jews. It seems unlikely to me that Seneca's attitude did not influence his brother to some extent. And finally, Gallio, in a general misanthropic way, having been banished from Rome by the emperor Claudius and dumped into this provincial outpost of Achaia as the governor, was probably not well disposed towards anyone.

But now I wondered something else, and that was why Paul had not been able to stop Sosthenes and the crowd himself. For that matter, why he had not been able to stop the hostile Jews of Thessalonica or the hostile Gentiles at Philippi? Paul had the power to blind people. He had blinded Elymas, the sorcerer, on the island of Paphos. Why did he not blind these others who threatened him now? I cannot say, of course. Paul had his visions and the instructions that came with them, and I am sure that he had his reasons for not using all the powers that he had at his disposal.

But he was safe now, and he stayed in Achaia a while longer and then set sail for Syria, taking Silas, Timotheus, Aquila and Priscilla with him.

CHAPTER XXII

The emperor Claudius died. Though he had exhibited wisdom when he extended Roman citizenship to worthy people throughout the empire, he had exhibited just the opposite when it came to his choice of wives. The last of these was his own niece, Agrippina, who pushed him into adopting Nero, her son by a previous marriage, and then into favoring Nero over his own son, Britannicus, for the line of succession to the throne. Once that was done, Agrippina served Claudius a dish of mushrooms, which she knew he liked, and Claudius promptly died, since the mushrooms, it seems, had been poisoned. So this emperor, who had passed over King Agrippa II and who had made Rome the ruler of both Judaea and Galilee and who later had expelled Jews from Rome (as the emperor Tiberius had done some thirty years earlier) and in whose reign even Britain was conquered, now passed away from the scene. Nero replaced him.

Yet all this intrigue and villainy transpiring in places of power did not seem to affect the work of Paul — or the trend of things in Jerusalem. One emperor was much like another, and the work for our Messiah and the struggle for freedom went on, barely noting the change. But even more than this, Paul was becoming convinced that the end was drawing near — the time when kings and wealth and marriage and success would simply not matter anymore. The appointed time was coming, and the day of deliverance was soon, so all these changes in Roman rule meant as little to him as dunes of sand shifting in the desert wind.

For Agrippa, however, the change in emperors was more significant, because Nero added to the places of his authority. He gave Agrippa four cities along with their toparchies: Abila and Julius in Peraea, and Tarichaea and Tiberius in Galilee. This was an improvement over what Claudius had given him, and though it was still a far cry from what his father had had, Agrippa felt better about Nero than he had about Claudius.

Meanwhile, Paul, along with Silas, Timotheus, Aquila and Priscilla, stopped at the city of Cenchrea. There Paul decided to take a sacred vow, which required him to shave his head. This was common among Jews. Fasting, shaving of the head and ritual baths were all common in

Judaism, and the taking of a vow was a way to dedicate oneself even more strongly to a sacred duty.

When they reached Ephesus, Paul entered the synagogue alone. Forgotten again was his vow never to preach to Jews. He spoke to the congregation about Jesus, and just how much he said I don't know, but the Jews received him well and asked him to spend more time with them so that they could hear even more of what he had to say. But Paul, ever restless, declined. He said that he had to get to Jerusalem in time for the Passover Feast but that he would return to them in the future if God willed it.

He left Aquila and Priscilla in Ephesus and sailed with Silas and Timotheus to Caesarea, staying with some of our Christian followers there, and then went to Antioch to strengthen the ties with our followers there too. Then the three of them traveled throughout Galatia and Phrygia, doing the same. His statement to the Ephesian Jews that he could not remain with them because he had to get to Jerusalem in time for Passover was forgotten now. He was busy in the field again, and Jerusalem could wait a while longer.

In the meantime, a man named Apollos came to Ephesus, where Aquila and Priscilla were now living. This man had been born in Alexandria and had become a Nazarene in that city when Peter had gone there to preach. He was an eloquent speaker and was well versed in the Torah. He had felt the call to be a teacher, and he was traveling from city to city to teach Jews about Jesus. What he was teaching was what Paul had called the Gospel of the Circumcision — the gospel for the Jews. It was the version of Jesus' mission that was being taught by Peter, for, as Paul himself had said, "Peter's is the Gospel of the Circumcision and mine is the Gospel of the Uncircumcision." Apollos taught that Jesus was the Messiah, that he had been resurrected and that he would return to be king. And he preached adherence to the Torah. As a result of Peter's work in Egypt and James' work in Israel, the Jews who accepted Jesus in those places believed in Peter's gospel and not in Paul's. But now Apollos was preaching Peter's gospel in the places where Paul had taught his own.

Apollos spoke in the synagogue in Ephesus, and Aquila and Priscilla met him there and were very impressed with him. They complimented him on the extent of his learning and on his skill as a speaker and then told him that his knowledge of Jesus was incomplete. They told him that Jesus was the one and only son of God and that because sin was inherent in man and could not be dispelled with good deeds alone, God had required Jesus' death as a sacrifice in order to forgive men their sins, and that because Jesus had made that sacrifice, the Torah was no longer necessary. They called this salvation through grace, and they explained that salvation can be achieved only through grace and not through deeds. Apollos accepted some of these things but not without some skepticism, and though he began to teach some of them himself, he did so cautiously, not fully rejecting the Torah. He was looking for the same kind of compromise that I was looking for, and, because he knew the Torah so well, he began to show in how many different places that book described Jesus as the Christ. Fortified with his slightly expanded doctrine, he traveled to Corinth and continued his teaching there. In time he became Paul's rival for the loyalties and affections of the Corinthians.

In the meantime, Paul left Phrygia and returned to Ephesus and saw how much had been accomplished in bringing people from the Gospel of the Circumcision into the Gospel of the Uncircumcision, by which he meant, of course, the gospel without the Torah. In essence, this meant changing people from Nazarenes into Christians. Many had been so changed.

Aquila and Priscilla had been responsible for that, and at first Paul felt glad that he had chosen them to do the work in his absence. But then, like a man who plugs a leaky hole in a wineskin only to have a previously plugged one open up, he saw that there were just as many people being diverted away from his gospel to Apollos' teachings as there were being diverted away from the Torah and coming to him. While many Jesus-followers were forsaking the Torah to qualify for salvation-through-grace, many of those who already had made that change were going back to the Torah because of Apollos. This meant that nothing was being gained. Success was measured by the number of people you convinced, and if the number stayed the same, you were stagnant.

"How could you have allowed this to happen?" Paul asked Aquila and Priscilla one day.

His question betrayed his displeasure and made them feel defensive. "We tried to prevent it," Priscilla said. "We dealt with it at its source. We made friends with Apollos and even complimented him on his knowledge as a scholar. Then we taught him the same things we teach everybody else. And to be frank with you, we thought he accepted it. He was so attentive and thoughtful about what we said."

"He even began to change what he taught a little," Aquila said. "He began to talk about Jesus as the son of God. So we thought, if he was starting to say that — and we were the ones who taught him that, you know — he wasn't saying that until we taught it to him — we thought if he was saying that, then he was going to go on and say everything else we had taught him. But he didn't do that. He stopped with that and then taught everyone to follow the Torah. He said that that's what Jesus had wanted us to do — to follow the Torah, I mean."

"And how could we stop it?" Priscilla asked. "We couldn't stop people from listening to him if they wanted to. You know there isn't much entertainment here in Ephesus...".

"Not the way there is in Rome," pined Aquila. "Now *there* is a place for entertainment, let me tell you. What don't they have there! Circuses, races, musicians, singers, jugglers, magicians. Whatever you want, they have."

"Aquila!" Priscilla interrupted in an intense whisper. "He doesn't want to hear about that. He wants to hear about Apollos."

"All right," Aquila whispered back. "I didn't think there was anything wrong in just mentioning what it was like back there."

Priscilla pursed her lips and then sucked her tongue against the roof of her mouth with an audible click of disapproval. She turned to Paul. "People like to hear public speakers. It's entertaining to them," she said. "So when Apollos decided to make public speeches, we couldn't stop him from speaking and saying what he wanted. And we couldn't stop people from going to listen to him, could we?"

"We thought we'd convinced him," Aquila said.

"That's right," Priscilla echoed. "We thought we'd convinced him about salvation through grace."

"But I guess we hadn't," Aquila went on. "We convinced him of some things but not of that."

"And how could we know what he was thinking," Priscilla asked, "when he didn't say anything back? When he didn't say anything to argue back with us, we thought that meant he agreed."

Then Aquila: "And when he started talking about Jesus as the son of God — and remember, we're the ones who taught him that — we thought he accepted everything else. But I guess he didn't. So the next thing you know, he's telling everyone to follow the Torah."

Paul reflected soberly on this. "We must counteract what he's done," he said. "We just have to try harder, that's all." He cupped Aquila's shoulder in his hand. "I know you tried, my friend. It's not your fault. We just have to try harder, that's all."

And they did that. They started again as they had before and spoke wherever they could. There was not a place of public gathering, not a synagogue, not a marketplace, where Paul and Aquila and Priscilla did not proclaim their beliefs and exhort people to join them.

Outside one synagogue, Paul encountered about twelve men who were disciples of John the Baptizer, and he asked them how they had been baptized.

"We've been baptized the way John baptized all people," they said. "We repented our sins while he washed them away with water."

It was their view, as it was of all the disciples of John, that John, not Jesus, was the promised Messiah and that John had made a mistake in thinking that Jesus was the one.

"You are wrong," Paul said. "John did not make a mistake. He knew who Jesus was. Furthermore, your way of being baptized is no longer the way. Yours was the baptism of repentance, and even though it was the way that Jesus was baptized, it is not the way any longer. Now you must be baptized by the Holy Spirit, the spirit of Jesus himself. John himself stipulated this, because he himself said that a Messiah would come and that we should follow him. Jesus is that Messiah. John recognized that, and so should you."

And Paul explained the reason for Jesus' death and that because of that reason, they must now be baptized in accordance with salvation through grace.

They listened and became convinced and were baptized anew by Paul. Paul told me later that, at that moment, Jesus' spirit descended on all of them and that they all began to speak in strange, unknown languages and that they prophesied about things that would happen in the future.

Paul spoke for three months in the synagogue in Ephesus. A lot of discussing and disputing went on. He said of those who disagreed with him that they were speaking evil of his gospel. What he did then was to keep our Christian followers away from the synagogue, so that they might not hear any views that were contrary to his, and to have them go, instead, to the meeting place of a sage named Tyrannus to carry on the discussions there. Paul's work in Ephesus covered a period of two years. And from Ephesus as his base of operations, he spread the Gospel of the Uncircumcision throughout Asia, even though an earlier vision had forbidden him to go into Asia. And he healed people even without touching them, just as Peter had done, for as Peter had healed with just his shadow, so did people take handkerchiefs and aprons that had merely touched Paul's body and bring them to the sick to heal them.

And Jerusalem was still waiting. His need to get there for Passover was forgotten now, and the delay was covering years.

THE CHRIST-KILLERS

CHAPTER XXIII

In Ephesus now, Paul began to show some of his old powers again. He performed miraculous healings by exorcising evil spirits. Once, when a traveling Jewish exorcist named Sceva, along with his seven sons and a Sadducee priest, attempted to do the same as Paul by calling forth an evil spirit in the name of "...this Jesus whom Paul is preaching about," the spirit actually answered them and said, "I know Jesus and I know Paul, but I don't know you. Who are you?" The sick man then went wild and attacked them and tore off their clothes, so that they had to run from the house to get away.

News of this got around Ephesus, and it became apparent that not everyone could effectively use the name of Jesus to heal. This event had the effect of causing fear and awe in the hearts of Greeks and Jews alike. Respect for Jesus and his followers increased. People who had practiced magic arts considered those things worthless now, and they publicly burned volumes of books on that subject.

Paul told the disciples who traveled with him — for now there were more than just Silas and Timotheus — that the spirit of Jesus had directed him to go eventually through Macedonia and Achaia to Jerusalem. "After that," he said, "I must see Rome." So he sent Timotheus and a new disciple named Erastus to Macedonia to prepare things for him there while he himself stayed for that year in Asia, the place where Jesus previously had forbidden him to go.

And still no Jerusalem. The place where he had told the Ephesian Jews he had to go in order to attend the Passover Feast, and to which he had not gone for years now, the place where Jesus was again telling him he had to go, and to which he still delayed going for yet another year, would have to wait a while longer. In retrospect, I think he was delaying because of James, because of the ultimate confrontation that he knew he would have to face when he was there. That confrontation could change everything, and Paul was anxious to establish the Christian concept as strongly as possible before he faced it.

In Ephesus, an interesting event occurred that, when I heard about it, taught me a cogent lesson in commerce. Demetrius, a silversmith in that city, made silver shrines for the pagan goddess, Diana, and earned a sizable sum on each one he sold. He was a pagan Gentile, and graven images were revered among his people. The fact that Jews eschewed such things did not stop Jews and Gentiles from living peacefully together in that city. Each let the other's religion alone. But now Paul had come, and he was telling Gentiles that Diana and the other Greek gods were false and that there were no gods fashioned by human hands. Paul, of course, was interested in getting the Gentiles to accept Jesus as their savior from inherent sin. The acceptance of one god and only one god was the first step in getting there. Those who did take that first step no longer wanted to buy statues of Diana, and that made Demetrius angry. His sales had dropped. And all because this itinerant Jew had broken the silent pact of letting each other's religions alone. It was one thing to tell Jews to accept this Jesus person in some particular way; it was another to tell Gentiles to forsake their own gods. Demetrius gathered other silversmiths around him and told them what Paul was doing.

"He's endangering all our livelihoods," he said. "And it's not just here in Ephesus. He's trying to get Gentiles all over Asia to worship this invisible god of his. Who will want to buy our statues then? And it's not just for ourselves that we should be fighting him; it's for the goddess, Diana, too. Some people are beginning to despise her temples. Her magnificence is being destroyed. Out of respect for her, we have to stop this troublemaker."

And the silversmiths, inspired by Demetrius, began shouting, "Great is Diana of the Ephesians," over and over again in affirmation of their belief. But also, I suspect, in support of their incomes.

The city was thrown into confusion. The silversmiths ran to Paul's dwelling place and found two of Paul's newer traveling disciples from Macedonia, Gaius and Aristarchus, and dragged them out of the house and into the city theater. Paul heard about this and ran to the theater to help them. But near the theater, he was stopped by his own friends and disciples who dissuaded him from entering.

Many Jews and Gentiles had followed the silversmiths into the theater, and there was a great deal of noise and confusion, with everyone shouting something different. When it finally became known why this gathering was taking place, the Jews present selected a man named Alexander to speak for them. It was their intention that he should convince the Gentiles that this attempt to divert Gentiles from their gods was the act of a few errant Jews and not reflective of all Jewish people. But as soon as Alexander stood before them and they recognized him as a Jew, the Gentiles began to shout in unison, "Great is Diana of the

196

Ephesians," and they continued this for a long time, not letting Alexander speak.

Those who formerly had practiced magic arts and who publicly had burned their books on that subject after Sceva's unsuccessful attempt to exorcise in the name of Jesus could not help Gaius and Aristarchus in this melee. Though they supported Paul and his followers now, they were too few in number compared to the massive crowd of hostile Gentiles assembled in the theater. The widespread awe at Paul's exclusive ability to heal in the name of Jesus was forgotten by the Gentiles now, just as his elevation to the status of a god had been forgotten by the Gentiles at Lystra when it had pleased their imaginations to do so.

Finally, the town clerk, a Gentile, stood up. The crowd quieted and listened to him, if for no other reason, than because their throats were hoarse after shouting for so long.

"Men of Ephesus," the town clerk began, "what man among you doesn't know that our city worships the great goddess, Diana, and the statue of her that fell down from Jupiter? You all know it! And seeing that no man can really speak against this — not effectively, that is — you all ought to be quiet and not do anything rash. These two men you've brought here haven't robbed our temples or even spoken against our goddess. Now, if Demetrius and the other silversmiths have a grievance against these two men, let them state it in a proper court of justice, where each side can present its case. And if you yourselves have a grievance against them, then that too should be aired in a lawful assembly. What you've done here today, this wild uproar, is unlawful, and I'm afraid we may be called to account for it. Now let's disperse and go our separate ways before all of us get into trouble."

With that the crowd did disperse, and the immediate danger to Gaius and Aristarchus was over. Paul was informed of all that had happened and how the Gentiles had been so hostile. Yet he swore no oath never to preach to Gentiles again because of it, as he had done previously in the face of Jewish rejection. That contrast, to me, was significant.

He decided to leave Ephesus, because it still was a dangerous place. The silversmiths were still agitating too much over their loss of business. They said it was for Diana, of course, and not in the least for themselves. But leaders in suppressing others for the public good always seem to be those who benefit most from the suppression, and the people whom they suppress always seem to be their competitors. So Paul decided to leave, but before he left, he found time to write another letter. This one was to the Corinthians, for he wanted to strengthen his ties with them even though he could not be there in person.

He told the Corinthians he would visit them on his way to Macedonia and said that, in the meantime, they were to keep faith in the gospel he had taught them and, above all other things, to practice love.

He told them too that since he was the one who had taught them about Jesus, if they were to have ten thousand instructors about Christ, they would not have many fathers and that he had begotten them like a father by means of the gospel that he had taught them. Twice in his letter, he told them to be followers of himself. These were the children that Paul could not have through marriage with a woman. He looked upon them as children. They were his handiwork and the fruits of his labor, and woe to the person who might try to take them away from him.

He had given much thought to the sexual relationship between men and women, and he told the Corinthians that it was good for a man not to touch a woman. But because he knew the exigence of that part of human experience and because he did not want unmarried people to fornicate, he advised the Corinthians to get married — if they could not be abstinent like him, that is. Celibacy, though, was better than marriage, since in celibacy one could concentrate on pleasing God, whereas in marriage one had to concentrate on pleasing a spouse. And besides that, one of the main reasons he was so pessimistic about marriage was that he believed, as we all did, that the day of reckoning, when marriage and material wealth and all worldly considerations would become irrelevant, would be upon us soon and that one might just as well be spared the troubles of a married life when its span would be so short. Meanwhile, for those who were married, he said that husbands and wives should not deny each other the satisfaction of their sexual needs, unless it was for the purpose of fasting or prayer, and *that* to be done only by mutual consent. But then, afterwards, they were to join again, so that Satan might not tempt them to go elsewhere because of incontinence.

I believe to this day that Paul could never have married anyone but Rabath and that he stayed unmarried because of that. And I believe that he loved her so much that he never felt desire for another woman. And yet, being a man, he had to deal with the physical urges that tore at his body and pressed on the solidity of his constraint. But he did deal with them; he dealt with them by suppressing them and channeling his energies towards traveling and speaking and creating a following. Out of his self-confessed struggle with the impulses of his flesh and his self-confessed failure always to win in that endeavor, and out of the expiation for that failure that Jesus' death had given him, he found the inner strength to write great thoughts and teach great things to people who struggled like himself. So that when he wrote of love, for example, he could say with poetic beauty, "Though I speak with the tongues of men and of angels and have not love, I am become as sounding brass and a tinkling cymbal; and though I have the gift of prophecy and understand all mysteries and all knowledge, and though I have all faith, so that I could remove mountains, and have not love, I am nothing." These were eloquent words, and he was an eloquent man. He had the power to express things loftily. And, as I have said before, he was a great man. And yet — he was *only* a man, and, like all men, he had flaws and weaknesses and foibles, as if to show that God's highest creation, except in Moses and Jesus, was still incomplete.

In spite of my belief in his greatness, in spite of my admiration for his eloquence, in some things I thought he was narrow. That a woman's hair should be long and a man's hair not long was important to him. That style of coiffure was customary for our time, but Paul wanted a more cogent reason than that for advocating it, so he based it on what he said nature itself taught us about such things. But for myself, who saw the short hair of the lioness and the long hair of the lion, nature could just as well have taught us the opposite. And towards women, too, he seemed narrow, for he said that they were required by God to be obedient and to be silent and not speak in the churches but to ask their husbands for information at home if they desired it. In many synagogues, women spoke, but Paul chose not to allow that among Christians, and I sensed in that a clandestine wish that Rabath, whose power he resented, could be put into that condition.

And he seemed to want to create visible differences between his Christian followers and traditional Jews, as if by doing that, he could ensure the non-visible differences he was creating between them. As Jewish men covered their heads when praying to God, he wanted Christian men's heads to be bare; and as Jewish women uncovered their heads, so Christian women's heads should be covered.

And in this letter appeared something else I had not heard Paul say before. You will recall that Jews recite a ritual prayer over bread and another one over wine before a meal. Paul had repeatedly witnessed this no matter which Jewish circle he was in. And each particular group, he had observed, had a prayer uniquely his own. To the Essenes in the desert, for example, such a meal prayer was very important, and Nazarenes, as I have mentioned earlier, had a lengthy and similar prayer as well. And the Nazarene prayer, you may recall, thanked God not only for the bread and wine but for having sent his servant, Jesus, to us. You may also remember that people who were not prepared by baptism were not to partake in that prayer. Now in this letter to the Corinthians, Paul revealed something new. He revealed that he had received directly from God (or from Jesus, since I was never sure whom he meant when he said "the Lord") information about what Jesus had said at the last supper that he had eaten. This information, I must assume, came to him through a vision or through a voice that spoke in the spirit. The information did not come from speaking to those who had been present at the supper that night but from a revelation, which was how much of Paul's information was derived. The information he received was that Jesus took bread and thanked God for it and then broke it and said to his disciples, "This is my body which is for you. Do this in remembrance of me," and that he took a cup of wine after the dinner and said, "This cup is the new covenant in my blood. Do this as often as you drink it, in remembrance of me." Paul wrote that this acceptance of the food and wine as the body and blood of Jesus was the way to show the significance of Jesus' death until Jesus returned — which, of course, we all felt would be soon. And just as our original Nazarene prayer prohibited an unworthy (unbaptized) person from participating in it, so did Paul now say that if an unworthy person participated in this new ritual prayer, that person would be guilty of profaning the body and blood of Jesus.

How could I so admire a man and yet find such points of disagreement with him? And yet that's what I did. Only by hearing him speak could anyone understand that. He had a gift for words such as is given to few of us on earth, and at times, as he himself put it, he spoke with the tongues of angels. But though the *way* in which he spoke was uplifting to the soul, were the *things* of which he spoke the sentiments of God? That subject had become the greatest mystery of my life, the greatest question for which I sought desperately for an answer.

Paul, with the breath of the silversmiths still hot on his neck, went to Macedonia and, after that, into Greece. Then, after three months in Greece, he prepared to sail to Syria. But he learned that some Jews were planning to waylay him at the waterfront. These, no doubt, were men who were disgruntled over his rejection of the Torah. So he changed his plans and went back into Macedonia. With him went some of his disciples; namely Sopater, Aristarchus, Secundus, Gaius, Timotheus, Tychicus and Trophimus. Some of them traveled ahead of him to his next stopping place at Troas to prepare things for him there.

Paul and his remaining traveling disciples were now at Philippi, the city where the Gentiles had beaten and imprisoned him. There they celebrated the Passover Feast along with other Jews in that city. Then they sailed to Troas, which took them five days, and then stayed in Troas for a week.

After he had been in Troas for a week, Paul preached to his many disciples at breakfast one morning and told them that he would have to leave the next day. This being his last opportunity to speak to them, he preached from that early morning hour until midnight. This long disquisition was delivered in a large , brightly lit room on the second floor of one of the disciple's houses. One of the group was a young man named Eutychus, who sat in a window that was on the second floor and listened. The hour growing late, he fell asleep and lost his balance. His body went plummeting downward and fell with an audible thud onto the ground. Two of the disciples looked down and saw what had happened. "Eutychus has fallen down!" they shouted, and they rushed down the stairs, with the others following them. Those who got to him first felt him all over for signs of life and tried to arouse him by shaking him. But to no avail. He was dead, and they hung their heads in despair. They carried his lifeless body into the house and laid it on the floor. Then Paul knelt and took the body into his arms and said to everyone, "Don't be troubled; he's alive." And whether it was because Eutychus really had not been killed or whether Paul, like Jesus and Peter before him, could now restore the dead to life, Eutychus breathed and opened his eyes and lived.

After that, they went upstairs and ate and drank and spoke together until dawn.

From Troas, the traveling disciples took a ship without Paul and went to Assos. Paul made the trip by land. At Assos, Paul met the ship and boarded it, and they sailed together to Mitylene, past Chios to Samos, and Trogyllium to Miletus. Though he knew they wanted to see him again in Ephesus, Paul sent word that he could not come there because he wanted to get to Jerusalem by Pentacost. No doubt Demetrius and the other silversmiths were also a factor in his not wanting to go back to Ephesus. But his compulsion to get to Jerusalem was undoubtedly sincere, for, as he had told his disciples when he had been in Ephesus, Jesus had ordered him to go there, and also he knew that it was only a matter of time until news of what he was teaching reached James and that he would have to explain it to James or suffer the discrediting by emissaries who were bound to come and say that Paul was wrong. For James still had the position and the power to do that.

201

If the brother of Jesus said that Jesus was the Messiah and that he *was* resurrected from the dead but that he was *not* the exclusive son of God and not a savior whose death pays for our sins and that the Torah or the Noahide laws were still the only legitimate paths to God, then all Christians would become confused and would question the truth of Paul's doctrine. But, as it was, James still did not know all of what Paul was teaching — or all that I was teaching, for that matter, although my own Christian message was somewhat a compromise between John's strictly Nazarene gospel and Paul's new Christian one, and even that was troubling me, because I didn't know if an anti-Jewish belief was going to become part of it.

Paul summoned the elders from Ephesus to come to him in Miletus. There were Gentiles and Jews among them, but now all of them were Christians.

When they were gathered before Paul, he made a speech to them and said, "All of you know what I've been like since the first day I came into Asia. You know that I've served God with humility and tears and that I've suffered temptations to do some wicked things against the Jews who lie in wait to attack me."

And here the Jewish Christians among the elders winced, for though they were now Christians, they still considered themselves Jews, and this one-sided slur against all the Jewish people offended them. For they knew well what the Gentiles of Philippi and their own city of Ephesus had done to Paul and the disciples. Why then did Paul not cast aspersions on all Gentiles as he now did on all Jews? (My own thought about this goes further than that, for why cast aspersions on all of any people because of what some of those people have done?) And here again was confirmation of my growing suspicion that Paul sheltered hatred of Jews, that his resentments of Rabath and Peter and Gamaliel and James made him hate all those who belonged to the group from which those people sprang, and that while Jesus himself had belonged to that group, the people that belonged to it now were no longer worthy of Jesus' love, because some of them had hurt Paul and many of them refuted what Paul was saying Jesus was. Yet Gentiles who hurt Paul and Gentiles who refuted what Paul said Jesus was, were not to have all members of their group similarly disparaged. Why this double standard? I wondered once again. Was it because Gentiles offered easier pickings than Jews, because Gentiles could more easily relinquish their multiple gods than Jews could relinquish their Torah? And was it because Paul was the first authority to Gentile converts, while to Jewish converts, he was only James' emissary? And was it because the beatings he received from Gentiles did not hurt him as much as the rejections he received from Jews, most especially Rabath and Gamaliel, who had denied him the two things he wanted most in his life? And was it because, in the final analysis, Christianity was the Gentile way of following Jesus and not the Jewish one?

And Paul said, "You know that I never held back on teaching you anything that could be of benefit to you and that I taught you publicly and privately in your homes that you should repent your sins to God and have faith that our lord, Jesus Christ, will save us by his death. And now," he said, "filled with the Holy Spirit, I am going to Jerusalem, not knowing what will happen to me there."

That statement had an ominous ring to it, and it surprised them, for what harm could befall him once he was in the safety of our brothers in Jerusalem? But of course, Paul knew what they didn't know; that he had converted Gentiles without making them either God-fearers or Jews and that James would be upset by that. But more than that, James would be upset by the idea of Jewish rejection of the Torah, for as the Jews of Judea said of James, "He is strong for the Torah", and Nazarenes were not called the Zealots of the Torah without reason

"Jesus knows," Paul went on, speaking to these Ephesian elders who had come to him in Miletus, "that in every city, I am arrested and afflicted. But none of these things affect me. I don't even count my life as precious compared to the completion of my work and the ministry that I received from the lord, Jesus, to spread the gospel about the forgiveness of sins through grace, by which I mean the sacrifice of Jesus' life. And now I tell all of you that you will not see my face again."

And there was a murmur of despair from the elders, who wondered again at this dark presentiment of ill.

"I ask you to remember that I have never harmed or killed anyone and that I never held back on telling you about what God was advising. I'm leaving you to be the caretakers of the church of God, which has been bought with the blood of Jesus, and I'm warning you to be wary of disparagers, who will come to you like wolves trying to disperse the flock. And under their influence, even some of you will change from what you are and speak perversely and draw away some of our followers. For three years among you, I've warned you of this, even shedding tears over it."

All of them thought about Apollos when Paul said this, for Apollos had preached in their city. But all of them had rejected Apollos' teachings, which was why they were here with Paul now. So who were these disparagers that Paul was talking about, and what would they be teaching that would draw some of them away? They were not aware that Nazarenes interpreted Jesus differently from Christians and that James, who was leader of them all, could send messengers to say that.

"I leave you with God's blessing," Paul said, "and the gift that has made you holy, I have wanted no man's silver or gold or clothing. I have worked for my daily needs with my own hands, and I have tried to impress upon you that whatever you earn that way should be shared with the poor, for as Lord Jesus said, 'It is more blessed to give than to receive'." That also, of course, is what Epicurus had meant when he had said, "It is better to do kindness than to receive kindness," and also what the Torah had been saying for centuries before that.

Then they knelt and prayed and hugged Paul and kissed him goodbye and wept over his departure. They walked with him to the ship and saw him off.

The ship took Paul and his traveling disciples to Coos and then to Rhodes and Patara. At Patara they boarded another ship bound for Phoenicia. They passed Cyprus, where I was still working with John, and sailed to Syria and landed at Tyre, where the ship's cargo was to be unloaded.

In Tyre they found Christians and stayed with them for a week. These Christians told Paul not to go to Jerusalem as he had planned. Unlike the elders from Ephesus, they knew the differences between what Paul was teaching and what James was allowing to be taught, and they feared that Paul would suffer great disappointment if he went to Jerusalem again. But Paul did not say whether he would or would not heed this warning. He went with these Christians and their families to the seashore, where they all knelt down and prayed.

Then he and his traveling companions boarded a ship and went first to Ptolemais, where they stayed at the house of Philip, who was traveling with them now. Philip had four daughters, all of whom could prophesy the future. Yet Paul did not consider them possessed by demons because of that as he had with the slave girl in Philippi, and he did not remove the divining spirits from them as he had from the slave girl. I never knew why the difference, but it may have been because they did not embarrass him in public the way the slave girl had done.

But now Agabus, the prophet, came to see Paul. He was the same man who had come to us in Antioch years earlier, predicting that a famine would come to Judaea. And, of course, it *had* come, confirming that he was right. To demonstrate the meaning of what he was going to predict now, he undid Paul's girdle from Paul's waist and tied it around his own wrists and ankles and said, "Do you see this? The spirit of Jesus says that the man who owns this girdle will be tied like this by the Jews in Jerusalem and will be turned over to the Gentiles by them." Agabus, like Paul, could now receive communications from Jesus that James and Peter and the other apostles still had not received.

Paul interpreted these "Gentiles" to be the Romans. He knew, of course, that he would have to give an accounting of himself to James, but he had not thought that Nazarenes would betray him to the Romans, since Nazarenes were on the edge of safety with the Romans themselves. Paul wondered if Agabus was talking about the Sadducees when he talked about the Jews in Jerusalem.

Paul's followers intruded on this contemplation by urging him not to go. They got emotional about it and even wept over it. But Paul knew that though Jesus was telling him through Agabus how he would be treated in Jerusalem, Jesus also had spoken to him directly back in Ephesus and had told him that he must go there.

So Paul said to his friends, "Why are you doing this to me? You break my heart when you act like this. Surely you know that I'm willing to suffer more than being just bound and imprisoned. You know that I'm willing to die for Jesus. And if I do suffer, I suffer for you. I rejoice in those sufferings for your sake. Whatever was lacking in Jesus' sufferings in your behalf, I will make up. I will take on whatever suffering he was unable to complete for you. That's my fate. You can't change it, so don't try."

But they did try. They tried again and again to dissuade him, but he would not be deterred. Jesus had told him in Ephesus that he had to go, so, after all the delays and all the misgivings, he would go to Jerusalem at last.

CHAPTER XXIV

It was time for me to report my activities to James. Unlike Paul, who had traveled so extensively, John and I had worked only in Cyprus. We had made an impact there — there was no question about that — but we had not reached nearly as many people as Paul. Perhaps the reason that John and I had not traveled farther was because of my uncle. It could have been, without my realizing it, that I had lingered in Cyprus because of him, that I had wanted to give him his surrogate son for as long a time as I could. But now it was time to leave; it was time to report to James.

I say that it was time to leave, but to be honest with you, that is not all there was to it. If I had decided to make the trip to Jerusalem even a year later, it would not have made much difference to James. I was writing to him regularly, since all of us, even Peter, were required to send him at least an annual report, and I was telling him most of what he had to know. So my physical presence in Jerusalem was not really essential. No, the real reason I chose to leave at that time was because of a girl. Let me assure you that she was no ordinary girl. She had qualities that were exceptional. She was the daughter of one of my uncle's friends, and her name, like the fertile plain of Israel, was Sharon.

My uncle, you see, was getting tired of waiting for me to get married. My daily work of preaching, discussing and helping needy families left me no time for involvements with young women. But my uncle was convinced that his duty to my father would not be fulfilled until he saw me married and siring children, so he decided to take things into his own hands and to dangle someone of his own choice in front of me. He found that someone in Sharon. It was easy enough for him to find reasons for visits to her parents' house or to have Sharon or me deliver bags of food or clothing as gifts. On each of these occasions, of course, the two of us saw each other, and, gradually, I started to notice the lure that my uncle had so dissemblingly put before me.

She was truly beautiful. She had a delicate, angelic appearance, with eyes that were strangely dark and mysterious but without a trace of guile. When she raised her head to search my face with that innocent, worshipful look of hers, I felt ensnared, entranced, enchanted, as if a spirit of purity and beauty had found its home in her body and was focusing itself on me.

I had never fully realized the delightfulness of human speech until those moments when she spoke to me. If I tell you that her voice was the song of a bird and her laughter the tinkling of bells, you will say, with a knowing smile on your face, that I exaggerate. You will say that such sounds were in my ears alone, that others who heard her speak would not have heard her that way. But you can say that only if you had not heard her yourself, for those who had could never scoff at my description. There were those qualities in her voice.

And the words that she spoke and the thoughts that she expressed were filled with such delicate wisdom, with such gentle kindness, with such tender compassion for all living things — and with such a capacity for absorbing the woes of others while taking nothing for herself — that one could not help but wonder at how much love the hand of God must have felt to have fashioned such a creature as she.

You think I extol too much perhaps. Do not think so. She was all that I have said and more. If you had been there, if you had seen her face and heard her voice, you would not think my description unwarranted. Rather you would say that my words fall short, that they do not do justice to the truth of what she was and that only by feeling and being in her presence could anyone know that I speak the truth.

Yes, I came to love her. I came to love her very much, and in doing that, I came to face the only real threat that I had ever had to face to my chosen mission in life. I knew the work I had to do. I felt that I had been created for it. I knew that others, even Peter himself, could do this work while they were married. If Peter could do it, I asked myself, then why couldn't I? Peter even had a child, and he could do it. But then I remembered Rachel's life, how unstable, how insecure it was. I remembered her traveling, being always on the move, running alongside her husband, escaping with him from dangerous situations to sanctuaries of ephemeral longevity. One day I, too, would be on that road again. I would be expanding my field of operations just as Paul had been doing. Could I ask Sharon to share that kind of life with me? Could I ask her to live not knowing where she would be sleeping next, not knowing where her next meal was coming from? Rachel already had been married to Peter when he had heard the call from God. If they had not been married and he had heard that call, would he have asked her to marry him then? Would he have asked the woman he loved, the woman whose happiness he desired, to share with him that kind of life? I think not. I do not think he would have done it. And so, how could

I, who loved this Sharon, ask her to lead that kind of life with me? I could not do it. I just could not. I could not ask this gentle, this lovely creature to walk with me on such a path.

And then there were also the words of Paul, whose influence had never left me, that in marriage we must be pleasing to a spouse, which takes time away from our service to God, while without a wife, we can spend all our time devoting ourselves to God.

And then there was also our common belief that the end times were coming soon and that marriage was one of those transient things that would mean nothing when the end times came.

So it was that, months later, on a sunny day when we were climbing a hill (so she could be closer to the clouds, she said), and when we looked out across the hills from our high vantage point and Sharon laughed at the breeze that blew her long brown hair back from her face, she turned to me and said as nonchalantly as if she were asking me the time of day, "Do you love me, Joses?" using the name by which I was still called by all my friends in Cyprus.

I turned to her and answered with far less nonchalance than she, "Yes, Sharon, I love you."

"Do you want to marry me?" she asked.

I swallowed when I answered her then. "Sharon, I can't," I said. "I'm committed, devoted, to this work that I do. I can't take on a wife."

I decided to leave it at that, because I knew that if I told her that I loved her too much to subject her to the life I was going to lead, she would, in her goodness, protest and tell me that being by my side was all the happiness she desired and that there was no hardship or danger she would not face in order to be with me. So I let it sound as if my concern was only for myself, that my concern was only for the busyness I would be incurring in this work I had chosen to do, which would allow me no time to give to a marriage, to a wife and to children.

She answered with her usual sweetness and serenity, "I understand, Joses."

But, of course, she did not understand. She did not understand at all, and it was my intention that she not understand. I loved her enough to have her think less of me, to have her think that my concern was only for myself, that she meant so little to me compared to my work that even the love I felt for her would not allow me to make some space for her in my life. No, she did not understand or even suspect my concern, and I did not want her to either.

And John (Mark) also did not understand. A week later, presumably after he had spoken to her, when I asked him about a trip we had planned to make to preach in a different part of Cyprus, he growled with obvious discontent and said, "You're a fool. Do you know that? You're a fool."

"Why do you say that?" I asked him, not knowing what was in his mind.

"She loves you, you fool. That perfect creature loves you. She would devote her entire life to you, and you turn away from her as if you were turning down a cup of water."

"John, you don't understand," I said. "It's not the way you think."

"Oh, yes it is," he protested. "I don't know why it is that the best women seem to want men that don't appreciate them."

Then, all at once, I understood. I understood why he was saying this to me. "John, you love her yourself," I said. "You love her, don't you?"

I didn't have to say anything more, because his silence in the face of what I had said confirmed that I was right. He just walked away and didn't answer me, and that told me that I was right.

There was strain between us then. There were hidden thoughts that had not been there before, and I felt that I had to leave that place, because the air itself pressed down on me now with such a heavy and dolorous weight that I did not think I could bear it. I told this to John, that I thought it would be better if we separated for a time, until this ponderous door that had come between us had time to open again. He agreed. Things were not the same as they had been, and it seemed better to him too that we part.

I said goodbye to my friends. I did not go to see Sharon. I told John to tell her I had to go and that I might see her again one day. How cold and indifferent I made those words sound. How much I regretted them later.

I said goodbye to my uncle last. We walked together to the ship. I did not know what to say to him, because I knew what was in his heart. I simply turned to him before I boarded and said, "Uncle, I am truly sorry."

"Don't be," he said, grasping my arm. "You were meant to do other things."

He hugged me then, with such love that I felt encircled by it. I could not hold back my tears. I feared I might never see him again. I did not look back when I got on board, but later, when the ship was a short distance away from the shore, I did look back, and I saw him standing there, and I saw, too, by his side, a girl with long, brown hair and eyes that were strangely dark and mysterious but without a trace of guile.

I returned to Jerusalem. It seems more than chance that I should have done that at the same time as Paul. We seemed destined to meet more than once in our lives.

In the same room in which James had allowed the Gentiles to follow Jesus without becoming Jews and in which he had told us not to fear the demise of the Torah, since that book would be read and revered as long as there were Jews in the world, he now stood facing the man who had introduced his brother to much of the Roman Empire, although, unbeknownst to him, in a new and different light.

James was a man of stature. He walked with dignity wherever he went, and the eyes of the people were always on him. The Sadducees actually feared him because of the respect the people had for him. They would like to have arrested him or even eliminated him, the loss of the lower priests to his leadership being only one reason for that, but just as they had feared an uprising of the people if they arrested Jesus, so did they fear an uprising now if they arrested James. For the people still resented the chief priests for having taken Jesus to Pilate, who, because of his record of crucifying so many people without trial, they knew would, more than likely, do the same to Jesus. But now there were so many more Nazarenes in Israel, and the chief priests had even more people to fear.

Paul of Tarsus also was a respected man. For him, the respect was from the Gentiles and the Jews of the Diaspora who had accepted the Christian belief that he had taught them.

James spoke first and welcomed Paul for us all. Then he said, "Paul, before you tell us all about the places you've visited, I want to tell you about a rumor that has come to us. I heard it first from some Pharisee friends who told it to some of the Pharisees in our own movement when they met them in the Temple recently. They say that you're going all through Galatia, Greece, Macedonia and Asia telling Jews to ignore the Torah. You know that we've had thousands of Jews join our movement and that all of them are zealous for the Torah. And now we hear that you're trying to dissuade Jews *away* from the Torah, telling Jews to forsake Mosaic law, not to circumcise their children, not to observe our customs. Is this true?"

Paul had not wanted it to start this way. He had wanted to discuss the Torah later. First, he had wanted to tell them about how many Gentiles and Jews he had gotten to become followers of Jesus. But the Torah question, put to him so directly by James, could not be avoided.

He said, "I tell them that the Torah isn't necessary for salvation. You yourself said that that was all right."

"I said it was all right for Gentiles; I didn't say it was all right for Jews. Are you trying to turn Jews into God-fearers?"

"I'm trying to turn Jews into Christians," he said, "followers of your brother."

"We Nazarenes here in Jerusalem are Jews, and *we* are followers of my brother. But we are not Christians. What *are* Christians?"

"They are followers of Jesus."

"Gentiles?"

"Jews and Gentiles."

"Do the Jews who are Christians follow the Torah?"

"No," said Paul, "they don't."

And here there was a general murmur of astonishment.

"Then," James said, "you're trying to turn Jews into people who don't follow the Torah?"

"Why do they need it if they have your brother?"

"What are you asking me? Even my brother needed the Torah! They're Jews! That's why they need it! How can Jews exist without the Torah?"

"Your brother frees them from the need for it. The Torah doesn't save them, your brother does."

"Save them from what? The Romans?"

"From the price they must pay for their sins."

"I don't understand what you're talking about. My brother is the Messiah. He'll return to complete his work; he'll save us from the Romans; he'll establish God's kingdom here. How does that save anybody from a personal accountability for sin?"

"*That* doesn't. But the *death* of your brother does."

James, in a measured incredulous tone of voice, repeated what Paul was saying: "The death of my brother saves people from being accountable for their sins?"

"Yes," Paul said, "but only if they believe it. If they don't believe it, then they're doomed."

"Doomed?" James said. "No man is doomed if he repents his sins and does good deeds afterwards."

"No amount of repentance and no amount of good deeds can counterbalance our sins," Paul said.

"Are our sins so many then?"

"We're born with sin in our flesh."

"Can a newborn baby sin?"

"The sin is in our flesh. That's why men are weak. That's why even though their spirits want to do good things, their flesh always succumbs to temptations. The issue isn't how to behave — behavior can't save us — it's how to find salvation from the damnation this ingrained sin has put us into."

"So we're damned no matter how many good things we do?"

"Unfortunately, yes."

"And good deeds can't help us?"

"Not alone they can't, no."

"Then the Torah, which teaches us how to do good deeds, can't help us either?"

"The Torah is a magnificent book," Paul said, "but it isn't meant so much to teach us good behavior as it is to show us how impossible it is for us to reach that state of perfection while we're in our earthly bodies."

"Are we not supposed to do good deeds then?"

"Of course we are," Paul said. "But that alone is not enough. We must also accept that the death of the Messiah is the way we're forgiven for our sins."

"God is the only one who forgives sins," James said.

"Of course," Paul said. "And he required Jesus' death as the price for that forgiveness."

This was as far as Paul went in telling James about the new idea. He had not told James that Jesus was the son of God and the only son of God and that, therefore, he was divine. That would have made James' father not the real father of Jesus, and Paul was not sure how that would affect him. So he left it unsaid. He had given James enough of a problem with the Torah, and he had to see how that would be resolved. James, after all, was renowned for his adherence to the Torah. James the Just, as he was called, was considered "...strong for the Torah", and the Nazarenes were known as the Zealots of the Torah. How could all that be reconciled now to Paul's rejection of that book?

I didn't envy James. He was in a difficult position. The last time Paul had faced him, there had been the question of the Gentiles. James had seen the obvious advantage of having large numbers of them following his leadership, and, to the problem of their lack of a moral code because they would not follow the Torah, he had found his solution in a minimum number of the Noahide laws of the God-fearers. But now the issue was more difficult. It concerned not Gentiles but Jews. And it concerned the book of Mosaic law that was the basis for the Jewish religion. And all this conflict was being created by a driven man, whose motives seemed completely sincere.

Why had Paul done it? James could understand Paul not being able to bring Gentiles into the group if they had to get circumcised and avoid

213

certain foods and follow other things in the Torah. But why Jews? Why try to take Jews away from the Torah, since they accepted it already? I, of course, knew the answer to that because I was closer to the situation than James. I understood that as long as there were Torah-adhering followers of Jesus, Paul's contention to the Gentiles that Jesus' sacrificial death was a replacement for adherence to the Torah as a means of salvation would be questioned by those Gentiles, who would wonder why some Jesus-followers were following the Torah if they didn't need it anymore. It would give them an alternative way to follow Jesus that might make Paul's own unique way seem invalid.

We waited for James to speak. When he finally did, it was in a voice filled with gentleness.

"Paul," he said, "there are those in this room who, like myself, lived with my brother. We spoke with him and listened to his words. Never did he tell us the things you're telling us. You never met my brother. From where do you get your information?"

"It's revealed to me," Paul said.

"By whom?" James asked.

"By Jesus. He speaks to me in visions."

"But why did he never tell *us* these things when he was alive?"

"I don't know," Paul said, "but he tells them to me now."

"I had a vision of my brother once," James said. "I was never sure if it was real or just my imagination. But, assuming yours are real, was there ever a vision in which my brother told you that we should no longer follow the Torah and that sin is inherent in us from birth and that his death was required for the forgiveness of our sins?"

"No, I can't say that he ever told me those things directly, but they follow reasonably from what he did tell me. He told me to preach to Gentiles, obviously for the purpose of getting them to join us. If I then find that they won't join us if they have to follow the Torah, I have to do something about that."

"But we solved that problem last time you were here," James said. "I told you to just have them follow the minimum number of the Noahide laws. But here we're talking about Jews and why Jews have to abandon the Torah."

"They don't have to abandon it," Paul said. "They can still follow it if they like."

"If they like?" James ejaculated. "If they don't follow it, they're no longer Jews."

Paul shrugged his shoulders. "Then let them be Christians. Do you realize that if we eliminate the need for the Torah, we will eliminate the differences between Gentiles and Jews who follow Jesus?"

And here the members of the audience murmured disconcertedly; they spoke to each other in intense whispers.

When they quieted, James said, "Is that the choice then? Are you telling Jews that they should stop being Jews if they want to follow my brother?"

Paul said, "No! They can *be* Jews or *not* be Jews, as they wish."

James walked slowly in front of Paul, his head bowed deeply in thought. When he stopped, he looked about the room at all our faces. He spoke in a slow, measured pace that suggested careful deliberation.

"I want to tell all of you that whatever happens in the future, whatever words of mine are repeated among men, whatever is written about me and whatever is said of me, this much must be remembered: we are a people of faith, and by that I mean that we trust that certain things will happen in the future. But faith means different things to some of us, and, as Gamaliel said when Peter was at the Sanhedrin, only time will tell which of us is right. But whatever we have faith in, whatever it is we believe will happen in the future, we cannot be justified by faith alone. Whether our faith is in Paul's concept of my brother's mission or in the concept that we have held for so long here in Jerusalem, the faith itself is not enough. A man must also be justified by good works. If he claims to have faith but has done no good works, his faith will not save him. Faith without works is a thing that is dead. The word — the Torah — should be our guide. But to hear the word and believe it is not enough. We must be doers of the word as well. Remember that I have said this, and be sure to tell it to all who wish to know the words of James, the brother of Jesus."

He turned to Paul. "And now, Paul, I understand why so many of our Jewish people have rejected you. You are not teaching what we teach. Here, in and around Jerusalem, we don't experience this kind of rejection. People either join us or are in sympathy with us. Except for the Sadducees, of course, but we all know what they are. But the general population is *for* us, which is why our high priest does not lay a hand on me, much as he would like to. But farther away, in the synagogues of Greece and Macedonia and Galatia and Cilicia and Asia, they reject you. And now I know why. They would not reject us if we taught them. What can I say to that? You herald the name of my brother throughout the world, and you bring gifts of money from all who believe you. And yet, what they believe is not what we believe. Honesty demands that I say that openly.

"I must act on the Jesus I knew in the flesh. I am the leader of our movement, and I must protect it. I must preserve it as I know it. I tell you, therefore, that you must not preach these doctrines of yours anymore. And you must go back to those you've already taught and re-educate them. If you don't, I'll have no choice but to renounce you. I will see to it that word is spread far and wide that the brother of Jesus and the leader of the Nazarenes abjures what you teach. Please don't make it necessary for me to do that.

"And now there's one other thing you must do. You must help us save our reputation among the people here in Jerusalem. They ask whether we've abandoned the Torah and whether we tell Jews who join us to abandon it as well. They ask it because they've heard that you have been telling this to Jews throughout the world. In addition, there are Jews who have come here from distant places — Asia for one. I've heard that some of them might want to harm you. And now I understand why. It's because you've been telling Jews, not just Gentiles, to ignore the Torah. You must show all these people that you still respect the law. We have four men who are under a vow. Take them with you to the Temple tomorrow, help them with the recitation of their prayers, go through the ritual of purification with them, pay their expenses and help them shave their heads afterwards, as I heard you did to yourself in Cenchrea. Then everyone will know that you're a practicing Jew and that you keep the law yourself."

He turned to the assembly. "And to everyone here, let's not speak to anyone outside this room about the differences that we've had here today. Let's make Paul's demonstration of his adherence to the Torah look like just a routine matter."

And now he turned to Paul. "Do you agree to these things, Paul?"

And Paul answered, "Yes, I agree to them."

With that, James concluded the meeting with a prayer, and we went our separate ways.

Outside the house, I stopped Paul to talk with him. The argument we had had about John (Mark) was long past, and we both had the feeling of old friends again. I embraced him and told him about my work in Cyprus and the vacillating nature of my gospel there. I was going to have to tell James about that in the future. I did not tell him about Sharon or about why John (Mark) and I had separated. Paul then told me about *his* work and all his experiences and about his increasing conviction that James was wrong and that all followers of Jesus should adopt the new interpretation.

"You didn't tell him everything," I said.

"What do you mean?" he asked.

"You didn't tell him that Jesus was divine, that he was the one and only son of God."

"No," Paul said, "I didn't tell him that. I thought it would be better if he got used to one new revelation before I presented him with another. Besides, Jesus' relationship to his family is probably a sensitive issue with him."

"I've heard about your letter to the Thessalonians," I said to him.

"They're a fine group of people," he said.

"You told them that the Jewish people killed Jesus," I said.

"I never said that to them, did I?"

"You told them that the Jews had killed our lord, Jesus."

"I meant the chief priests when I said 'the Jews'. I didn't mean *all* the Jewish people. Surely you must know that."

"*I* know it. Of course I know it. Anyone who lives here knows it. But *they* don't know it, and that's the problem. You're making them think that our people hated someone they really loved."

"But any knowledgeable person will know what I mean."

"It's the unknowledgeable ones I'm concerned about, Paul. It's the ones who don't know what really went on who are going to think you mean *all* the Jews. Can't you see the hatred you could start?"

"The people I teach will not hate," he said. "They can only be capable of love."

"Then even if they love," I said to him appealingly, "they'll love the Jews *in spite of* what they think the Jews did to Jesus. They'll still be believing a lie."

"I'll try to make it clear to them when I see them again," Paul said. "I'll be more specific about what I meant."

This statement to the Thessalonians was troubling me so much, and yet Paul seemed so casual about it. I had no choice but to take him at his word and to hope he would do what he said.

"Where are you staying?" I asked him, changing the subject, because I could feel that if I didn't, I was going to say more about his attitude towards Jews and start arguing with him all over again, as in Antioch.

"With my sister and her family," he answered.

"Will you see Rabath?"

"I hadn't planned to," he said. And then he added, "But I might see Jacob. I think I can trust him not give me away to Caiaphas. He still works for Caiaphas, you know."

"I've heard some of the things you say about women, Paul, how they should be silent and totally obedient to their husbands. And I've heard what you say about marriage: that if you're married, stay married, but if you're not, try to avoid it." I was feeling resentful against him because those words, which had had such an influence over me, were partly responsible for what I had done to Sharon. "It's because of Rabath, isn't it? I know how much she hurt you. Do you hate all women because of her?"

"No, of course not," he said. "I don't hate women. I don't hate anybody."

"Nobody?" I asked, suddenly feeling a perverse compulsion to make him tell me the truth about the other subject again.

"No," he answered.

"Not even Jews?" I asked.

He looked surprised. "What makes you ask such a thing? How could I hate Jews? I *am* one."

"Because of Rabath and Gamaliel, who rejected you. Because of James, who tells you what to do, and Peter, who is your rival for Gentiles. He's out there now someplace, preaching his own gospel, maybe in Antioch or Alexandria or Corinth. Because Jews are more difficult to convince of the Gospel of the Uncircumcision, since they keep the Torah. Because Peter's gospel threatens everyone's belief in *your* gospel. And because of things I've heard that you said: that when Gentiles do something mean to you, it's just those who have done it who are bad, while all other Gentiles are good, but that if Jews do something mean to you, then all Jews are bad; that when Jews reject you, you swear that you'll never preach to Jews again but that when Gentiles reject you, you don't swear the same about them. That's why I can ask the question."

"Do you think I would let personal affronts like that affect my attitude towards everyone?"

"Yes, I do," I said. "Just as you let them affect your decision about John when we argued about him in Antioch. And all that you've taught me, and all that I believe of what you've taught me, I find myself doubting because of that. I start asking myself if the visions you told me about, and which I believed with all my heart, are worth believing anymore. The things you taught me were given only to you. Jesus didn't give them to James or Peter or anyone else. Why you? Why did he choose you, Paul?"

"I don't know," he said. "I don't know why he chose me. Maybe because I sinned so much against him that my working for him the rest of my life became my penance. Maybe that was it. But he revealed things to me, some of them so secret that human lips dare not even repeat them. And I became a part of him. I was *in* him to such an extent that now I even carry his crucifixion marks on my body."

"His wounds?" I asked.

"Yes, his wounds," he said. "Here, look!"

He pulled up the sleeves of his cloak and showed me the clotted wounds on his wrists. Then he showed me his feet, and I saw the same kinds of wounds there. Then he opened his cloak and tunic and showed me a clotted wound on the side of his torso. I was stunned at the sight of them, and I hardly knew what to think for a moment. I turned away from him and tried to collect my thoughts. My mind raced from memory to memory across all that I knew of Paul — of his childhood and his manhood and his experiences and all that I knew of his nature.

And then I said, "You and I traveled together. And what I didn't know of Cilicia, you showed me, because you had been raised there and knew much more about the place than I. You showed me the icons of the pagan god, Attis — Do you remember that? — and you showed me his followers too. Do you remember them? Do you remember that when they would get frenzied and ecstatic, they would castrate themselves in order to experience the same suffering their god had suffered, so they could enter *into* him the same way that you say you entered Jesus? Do you remember that?"

"Are you saying I did this to myself?" Paul asked.

"The Corinthians say that you beat yourself with your fists to subdue your flesh. Is that true?"

"Yes, but what does that have to do with this?"

"Did you wound yourself too, Paul?"

"No!"

"Then how did the wounds get there? None of the rest of us have had this happen to us."

"They came by themselves," he said.

I grew excited and said, "Are you sure that *you* didn't do it and then forget you did it? Are you sure you aren't so influenced and caught up by all that you saw in your childhood that you aren't trying to turn Jesus into your own personal manifestation of Attis? Is that what's happening, Paul? Is it?"

CHAPTER XXV

I had lost him again, and I berated myself for having handled it as I had. We had separated in Antioch because of an argument, and now we were separating in Jerusalem because of one again. Yet I still felt close to him, because he had given me something I still thought could be right, in spite of my disagreement over how he was handling it or his attitude towards our people.

Paul went to his sister's house and sent his nephew with a message to Jacob. Jacob kept his confidence and met him secretly. At the meeting, Jacob told him that Naomi, Rabath's mother, had died of a fever and that Rabath had become even closer to her father after that. But then Rabath had married. As had been expected, it was to a wealthy Sadducee.

"Does she ever speak of me?" Paul asked.

"Yes," Jacob said. "She told me once that she had found you the strangest and most intriguing man she had ever met. And then when you betrayed her father in Damascus, she resented you. But then, when she heard that so many people were starting to pay attention to you, she told me that she had never realized the kind of man you were. I don't know if that was a compliment or not, but I think she feels a certain regret that she didn't get to know you better. I think you fascinate her now. More than you did when you worked for us anyway."

"Is she happy?" Paul asked.

"Happy? No, I don't suppose she's happy. The man she's married to — what can I say of him? — he's wealthy, and he's dull. And she — well, you know what she's like. No, I can't say that she's happy, but she is his wife."

"Will you tell her you saw me?"

"Yes, I'll tell her," Jacob said.

Paul squeezed his friend's arm to thank him.

"You still love her, don't you?" Jacob asked.

"Thoughts are powerful things," Paul said. "I try not to think about her, but it's hard. My flesh craves her, and I try to suppress it, but it's hard. That's why I tell people that sin is in our flesh and that, try as we may, we can't eradicate it. All the good deeds in the world can't eradicate it. All the good deeds in the world can't expiate the sin that's in our flesh. That's why we needed Jesus to die — so his death could do it for us."

"You're too hard on yourself, Paul. None of us is perfect. We practice the Torah as best we can."

"We don't need the Torah anymore, Jacob. When Jesus died, that was the offering that God needed to forgive us for our sins. Jesus was divine, Jacob. He was God's only son. And God needed the sacrifice of someone that precious and that dear to Him in order to forgive us for our sins. But it all worked out all right, because Jesus was resurrected; he came back to life! And after he spoke to his disciples and gave them instructions about what to do, he left. But he promised to return to establish God's kingdom here. And he will."

"You say he left," Jacob said. "How did he leave?"

"He ascended to heaven."

"You mean his whole body floated up?"

"Yes!"

"I thought maybe he left his body behind, the way people always do when they die, so his spirit could be free to join God."

"No, that's true for most people but not for him. There's an earthly body and a spiritual body, and for most of us, we leave our earthly bodies when we die and ascend with our spiritual ones. But for Jesus it was different. He was resurrected from death with his earthly body, and when he left us, he left with that same earthly body. But it was during his ascent that he became a spirit."

"Did his earthly body just disappear then?"

"Yes, of course. If it hadn't, we would have had something left to bury or entomb, wouldn't we?" Jacob didn't answer. "You think it's all foolishness, don't you, Jacob? But let me remind you that the wisest men of our time — the sages — believe in the resurrection of the dead."

"You know that I'm a Sadducee, Paul. I just don't believe in such things. And you know that I come from Alexandria. And because that's in Egypt, it's only natural that I should know something about Egyptian history. Did you know that the Egyptians, about twenty-five hundred years ago, had a sun god called Re? He was the lord of eternal light. And Re had a son named Osiris, who was resurrected after he was killed. And in Babylon, wasn't Baal-Bel-Marduk arrested and beaten and pierced with a spear and then resurrected after he died. It's sort of like Jesus, don't you think? And Attis, didn't he suffer and then die and then come back to life?"

"You can't get rid of it that simply, Jacob. There were too many witnesses to what happened."

"Yes, well, there's no arguing that, is there?" He patted Paul on the back of the hand. "Good luck to you, my friend. God be with you in whatever you do."

"He always is," Paul said.

"I'll tell her I saw you," Jacob said, and he left.

Paul went then to his sister's house and spent time with the young man who was his nephew. From him Paul learned about the latest events in Jerusalem. A new group of freedom fighters was present on the scene. These were a branch of the Zealots who were known as the Sicarii, which was the name the Romans gave them, because in the Roman language *sica* means dagger, and *Sicarii* means one who murders with a dagger. The Sicarii were impatient men who wanted immediate results in their quest for freedom. They were highly religious, and they were zealous to establish God's kingdom in place of the Romans, just as Zealots, Nazarenes, Essenes and Pharisees were. But their particular method of operation was to mingle with crowds at religious festivals and to draw short daggers from beneath their robes and to assassinate Jews who collaborated with the Romans.

The Sicarii — and the Zealots in general — usually operated in companies throughout the country, urging the people to resist the Romans. If a village was uncooperative in this, the Zealots burned it. That may seem drastic, but a revolution cannot be won if the people are not of one mind and purpose. The Zealots entered the homes of the wealthy and killed or pillaged them, because the Zealots resented the wealthy for prospering under an oppressive foreign rule. And the mass of our people, the lower priests included, resented the chief priests for prospering under it too.

And another thing about the Sicarii: like all Zealots and Nazarenes, they were not afraid of crucifixion. The Zealot saying, "Pick up your cross and follow me," which later was preached by Jesus when he said, "If any man would come after me, let him deny himself and take up his cross and follow me," was the motto that accompanied the *sign* of the cross, which was the symbol of the Zealots.

Paul realized what a political hotbed Jerusalem was in this day of Felix as procurator and Nero as emperor, and he saw that heaped on that was the religious fervor of the people, who believed that an increased devotion to God would hasten the day of deliverance for Israel. It was not a good time or place to tell people to forsake the Torah. It was a time for caution.

Paul did as James had ordered and helped the four young men with their vows the next day. He was seen doing this by a number of other people in the Temple, which was the general idea, for now word would spread that he had prayed from the Torah. What he thought while he was doing this, I can only imagine. He had preached the irrelevance of the Torah, and now he was being forced to make a public demonstration of his adherence to it. If he felt any resentment over that, he must surely also have realized why James had required it. The fervor of the people to rebel against Rome was being lit by religious zeal. It was not the time to say to them that what they believed was wrong. For the sake of Paul's own safety as well as the reputation of the Nazarenes, James had ordered Paul to do this. And while Paul might dare to challenge James in the field, he dared not do it in Jerusalem, lest he be expelled from the movement and publicly denounced.

Paul continued to assist the young men and to pray from the Torah over the next few days, and, in the afternoon of the third day, he parted from the young men, promising to join them again the next day.

You must understand that this public appearance that Paul was making was dangerous. Caiaphas had never abandoned his goal of revenge on Paul, and if Caiaphas should see him in the Temple, all might then be lost. I don't know if James realized the danger to which he was having Paul expose himself by making a public appearance in the Temple, but Paul was aware of it, keenly so, and he blended himself as much as possible into the large crowds of people who came into the Temple and made himself as inconspicuous as possible. And since the lower priests were physically close to the people and the chief priests farther away, Paul was able to recite his prayers unnoticed by any chief priest. And, too, the lower priests, being Nazarenes, could protect him by telling him if Caiaphas was anywhere nearby.

He had gone there successfully for three days now, and he was leaving the Temple for the day. As he walked alone in the outer area of the Temple, five men, standing in a cluster, observed him. They were Jews from Asia who had come to pray in the Temple. When they saw him, they moved quickly towards him. They surrounded him, and two of them grabbed him roughly and held him.

"You're the blasphemer, aren't you?" one of them said.

Paul looked at the scowling faces of the men and realized that they were dangerous.

"Blasphemer?" he answered. "Why do you call me that?"

"Because you tell Jews to give up the Torah. It's true, isn't it? We know all about you."

"How can you say that?" Paul said. "Haven't I shown my adherence to the Torah these last few days? Didn't you see me in the Temple

224

praying with the young men who were taking their vows? Didn't any of you see me there?"

"I did!" one of them said. "I saw him."

But another said, "So what! What does it mean? How do we know he didn't make a public display in order to deceive us? What he shows us is one thing; what he teaches outside Jerusalem is another."

During this fracas, two Jews who were natives of Jerusalem came out of the main part of the Temple. When they saw the Asiatic Jews shaking and pushing Paul, they felt obliged to help him.

"Hey," one of them shouted, "why are you pushing this man?"

"We'd like to do more than push him," one of the Asiatic Jews answered.

"Why?" said the Jerusalem Jew. "What has he done?"

The Asiatic said, "He's been going around telling people to forget about the Torah, telling them that we don't need it anymore. That's what he's done!"

"But I just saw him praying from the Torah in the Temple," the Jerusalem Jew said.

"A deception!" the Asiatic answered. "And besides that, he brings Greeks into the Temple."

"When?" Paul protested. "When did I bring Greeks into the Temple?"

"Trophimus of Ephesus!" shouted another Asiatic Jew. "We saw you walking with him, and we found out his name!"

"Yes, I was walking with him, but that doesn't mean that I brought him into the Temple. Why should I?"

"Because you believe there's no difference anymore between Jews and Gentiles," another Asiatic shouted.

Now two more Jerusalem Jews came onto the scene.

"But that doesn't mean I brought him into the Temple," Paul said. "I didn't!"

One of the new Jerusalem Jews said, "What's going on here?"

"They say this man preaches against the Torah," an earlier Jerusalem Jew said.

"He does!" shouted an Asiatic Jew. "He ought to be killed!"

"Wait a minute," said another Asiatic. "We never talked about killing."

"How else would you treat a Jew who teaches against his own religion?" the first Asiatic said.

"This is getting out of hand," said another Asiatic.

"Killing is too good for him," said another.

"Remember where you are!" shouted one of the Jerusalem Jews. "This is the house of God."

"Then let's take him to the high priest," said an Asiatic. "He'll know what to do with him."

The arguing and tumult continued and increased, and it grew even worse as more Asiatic and Jerusalem Jews chanced to come by.

But now, some Roman soldiers appeared: Lysias, the captain of the guard, with two centurions and two soldiers. They moved quickly through the crowd towards Paul and freed him from the two men who were holding him.

"Is your name Paul?" the captain asked.

"Yes," Paul answered.

Captain Lysias then turned to the crowd. "What has this man done that you're trying to attack him?"

The Asiatics shouted things like, "He's preaching against our religion and causing people unrest! He's a troublemaker! He's a liar about our sacred law book!"

Lysias got the gist of their meaning, and he shouted back, "All right, quiet down, quiet down. I don't know what this is all about, but I don't want any more disturbances like this. Is that clear?" He turned to the two soldiers who were holding Paul. "Put a couple of chains on him and take him along." The soldiers chained Paul's hands behind him.

Lysias spoke to the crowd again: "I am Captain Claudius Lysias, and those of you who know me know that I do not deal lightly with troublemakers. I want you to disperse, and that means now."

The crowd, with a low, mean grumble, broke up slowly. But many followed at a safe distance as the Romans took Paul to their headquarters. And the crowd seemed to pick up sympathizers as it moved along the streets.

An hour later, Lysias sat at a table in his office and looked at Paul and the two centurions standing before him.

"Your name is Paul. Is that right?" he asked.

"Yes, captain," Paul answered.

"I was told about you. Your nephew and your friend, Trophimus, came to me today to warn me there might be trouble because some Asiatic Jews were out to get you. You caused quite a commotion out there."

"I was not the cause of it, I assure you," Paul said.

"You're not that same Egyptian fellow who caused us trouble here before, are you? The one who led all those people to the Mount of Olives?"

Paul knew the captain was referring to the Egyptian Jew who had gathered four-thousand Sicarii at the Mount of Olives, promising them that, at his command, the city walls would crumble, as the walls of Jericho had crumbled for Joshua, and that he would then lead them to the slaughter of the Roman garrison. Paul knew that that man's followers had considered the man the Messiah and that Felix, the procurator, had gotten news of this and had sent his troops, who had killed or captured the Jews, except for the Egyptian, who had gotten away.

"No, captain, I'm not that man," Paul answered. "I'm a Jewish citizen of Tarsus in Cilicia. Do you happen to know it, captain? It's no small city by any standard."

"Yes, I know the place," Lysias said.

"Captain," Paul said, "do you see the crowd that has followed us?"

"Yes, I see it. Of course I see it. I'd have to be blind not to see it. They seem to be out for your blood."

"Would you allow me to speak to them, captain? I might be able to pacify them."

Captain Lysias looked at his two centurions, one of whom shrugged his shoulders as if to ask what harm there could be in that.

"Take him outside," Lysias said. "Take off his chains, and let him speak to them."

The one who had shrugged his shoulders took Paul outside, and Lysias and his other centurion sat and talked.

"Marcus," the captain said, "this whole country is mad. You know that, don't you? They spend half their time arguing about religion and the other half trying to figure out how to get rid of us. It's a wonder they have any time for their women." Marcus laughed. "A little while ago, a Greek fellow named Trophimus comes to see me. He's a friend of this Paul, he says. And with him is a young fellow who says he's Paul's nephew. They say to me that there might be trouble outside the Temple because some Jews from Asia are out to get this Paul, and they say that this Paul deserves my protection because he's a Roman citizen. So I go there. And when I get the man out of trouble and bring him back here, what does he tell me? That he's a Roman citizen? No! He says he's a citizen of Tarsus. Now, why did I go to all this trouble to help a citizen of Tarsus? And now he wants to appease the crowd. Well, who's going to appease me? Who's going to get rid of this pain in my stomach? I'm damned upset about this, I don't mind telling you. When I took this assignment, I thought I'd have some fun — you know, some adventure — foreign places, exotic women. You know what I mean. Instead, I find this hellhole. Everyone is always fighting around here."

Suddenly the centurion who had left with Paul rushed into the room.

"Sir," he exclaimed breathlessly, "I'm afraid that appeasement speech didn't work."

"What happened?" Lysias asked.

"This Paul starts off by telling the crowd he's a Pharisee."

"What's a Pharisee?" Lysias asked.

"One of their religious sects, sir," Marcus explained.

"And then he tells them that he used to be a student of Gamaliel's, that he was brought up at the feet of this man, Gamaliel."

"Who's Gamaliel?" Lysias asked.

Again, Marcus was the one who answered. "He's the leader of the Pharisees, sir. A kind of religious philosopher. His family has been here a long time."

"Well, we all have to be good at something," Lysias quipped. But Lysias was having trouble with this, for he found himself wondering why a man who had lived in Jerusalem from the time he was a child (which is where Paul would have to have lived to have been brought up at the feet of Gamaliel) was calling himself a citizen of Tarsus instead of a citizen of Jerusalem. And why, beyond that, was he calling himself a citizen of Tarsus if he actually was a citizen of Rome?

The centurion continued: "Someone in the crowd shouted that he was a liar and that he never had been a student of Gamaliel's. Well, he ignores the heckler and goes into this story about how he used to work for the high priest, Caiaphas, as a policeman, arresting Nazarenes. As soon as he says that, someone else in the crowd shouts out that that proves he wasn't a student of Gamaliel's, because no self-respecting Pharisee would ever have gone to work for a Sadducee."

Captain Lysias turned to his other centurion, Marcus. "I take it the Sadducees are another religious sect?"

"That's right, sir," Marcus replied.

The other centurion went on: "But he ignored that heckler too. And he tells them that he used to persecute Nazarenes."

"Nazarenes? Another sect?" Lysias asked.

"Another sect, sir," said Marcus. "They believe their dead leader came back to life and that he's going to return and kick us out and set up a new kingdom here."

"And, as it happens," the other centurion went on, "a lot of the Asiatic Jews in the crowd are Nazarenes themselves. And he tells them that when he was on an official mission to Damascus to capture

Nazarenes, he had this blinding vision that convinced him that he should become a Nazarene himself."

"Well, as far as I'm concerned," said Lysias, "that clinches it about his being a Roman citizen. No Roman citizen is going to join a group that wants to end Roman rule."

The centurion, having more to tell, said, "Someone in the crowd shouts out that he can't possibly be a Nazarene, because he preaches against their sacred book — they call it the Torah — while Nazarenes always defend that book. 'The Nazarenes are the Zealots of the Torah,' the man shouts."

"Look, I'll tell you what to do with this man," Lysias said. "Take him out and give him a good flogging. Then ask him why all those Asiatic Jews are against him. I still don't understand what all this is about."

"You definitely want him flogged first, sir?"

"Absolutely! It's always been my experience that people give you a more honest answer after they've been flogged."

The centurion left to do his duty, and Lysias and Marcus continued their talk. But that was short-lived, because the other centurion soon returned with a heavy face and said, "Our prisoner, sir, we were getting him ready for flogging when he says to me, 'Is it lawful for you to flog a Roman citizen who hasn't been found guilty of anything?' So I said to him, 'Speak the truth! Are you really a Roman citizen?' And he says, 'I am,' and then he shows me this paper as proof."

Lysias looked at the paper. He could see that it was authentic. "Then it's true," he said. "His friends weren't lying this morning."

"Under these circumstances, I thought we should be careful how we treat him."

"You're right, you're right," Lysias said. "I'll tell you what to do. Don't flog him, but do keep him in custody overnight. I still want to find out why all those people are against him."

"It's probably all religious," Marcus opined.

"It's interesting," Lysias said. "A man who formerly works for the high priest, Caiaphas, and arrests Nazarenes for him becomes a Nazarene himself. Then other Nazarenes turn against him — for reasons unknown. As I say, it's a crazy country. But maybe we can arrange a little drama here — a little amusement. Send word to Ananias, and tell him to convene the Sanhedrin tomorrow morning to interrogate a man named Paul of Tarsus, who has been causing some public disturbance which may be religious in nature. It promises to be good sport. Caiaphas will be there, reunited with his turncoat policeman. What a scene that should be. Yes, this definitely should be good sport."

CHAPTER XXVI

In the meeting hall of the Sanhedrin, the members sat in their tiered seats and looked at Paul of Tarsus and the high priest, Ananias, standing before them. Two guards stood to the side. For Caiaphas, who sat in the front row, this was a moment of triumph. Whatever else had occupied his mind these last several years, the embarrassment of Paul's betrayal certainly had not been forgotten. And now he was to have his revenge. In a completely legal manner and over an issue that had nothing to do with the betrayal, he would teach Paul what a heavy price one pays for crossing him. His friend, Ananias, who was now the high priest, would help him do it.

Paul looked around and saw in one mosaic mass the white robes of the chief priests, the gray robes of the bearded Pharisees and the stern faces and belted whips of the heavily muscled guards. He prayed inwardly for God's help. In the front row he saw Caiaphas, the man who had sent him to Damascus, the father of the woman he still secretly loved, glowering at him with obvious hatred. This was to be Caiaphas' day of revenge. And Paul saw another chief priest standing in front of the audience not too far from him, but he did not know who that was.

This other chief priest was Ananias, who now began to speak. He told the members of the Sanhedrin that they were to consider a charge of blasphemy against the man who stood before them. But not only were his *religious* teachings offensive, he said, he also was stirring up the people to such an extent as to cause public disturbances and unrest.

"He preaches about a new kingdom that will replace Roman rule" Ananias said, "and that puts us in danger with the Romans. And he also preaches against the Torah. So from a political *and* religious standpoint, he deserves the severest penalty we can impose. After you have heard the evidence, I can see no other decision for us to make except the death penalty. Death by stoning is the sentence for which I ask."

Paul could not let this go unchallenged. He had little to lose by speaking. "Men and brothers," he proclaimed, "I beseech you, do not allow hearsay evidence to convince you of what is not true. To this very day, I have lived in all good conscience before God."

Ananias turned angrily to his guards. "Shut his lying mouth! Immediately!"

One of the guards walked to Paul and smacked the back of his hand across his mouth.

Paul, with a trickle of blood coming from his lip, remained defiant. "God will smite you, you blank white wall!" he shouted to Ananias, still not realizing who the priest was. "You claim to sit in judgment of me in accordance with the law, and yet you command this guard to strike me in violation of that same law. Is it lawful to strike a man who hasn't been found guilty of anything?"

With that, the Sadducees stood up and shouted to Paul about his disrespect.

"Curb you tongue!" said one.

"Do you revile the high priest?" said another.

Until that moment, Paul had not realized that the chief priest who was speaking against him was the high priest himself. To have spoken against a chief priest was one thing; to have spoken against the high priest was another. So Paul said, "I am sorry. I didn't realize this was the high priest speaking. It is written that we must not speak evil about the rulers of our people. I apologize, therefore, for the impoliteness of my remark."

Ananias turned to the audience and said, "This man betrays his own religion and his own people. Hear the witnesses against him!"

The guards left and brought back one of the Asiatic Jews. Ananias established who the man was for the benefit of the audience and then pointed to Paul and said, "Do you know that man?"

"Yes," the Asiatic said, "he's the one who preaches against the Torah."

"There you see?" Ananias said to the audience. "And he's not the only one. There are other witnesses."

He began to gesture for the guards to see the Asiatic out and to bring in the next witness when one of the Pharisees stood up.

"A moment, Ananias, a moment, if you please," he said. "I would like to ask the witness if he himself has ever heard this Paul preach against the Torah."

"No, I never heard him myself," the Asiatic stammered, "but everyone knows it. It's all over Asia."

"But that's hearsay evidence," the Pharisee said, "and we shouldn't base our decision on that. What this witness *believes* to be true because of a rumor he has heard should not be the basis for our decision."

Frustrated, Ananias had this witness removed and had the second witness brought in — another Asiatic Jew. And with him, it was the same. The Asiatic reported what he said was common knowledge, but he had never heard Paul preach. And with each subsequent witness, it was the same: none of them had heard Paul's blasphemous teachings with his own ears. And for the Pharisees, that was not enough evidence; they needed more proof than that.

Caiaphas saw the success he had planned being threatened by the punctiliousness of the Pharisees. Ananias was not being effective enough.

Caiaphas stood up and said, "This man standing before you threatens everything that we hold sacred. He threatens our very relationship with God, our covenant with God, the obedience of our people to the will of God. Are you Pharisees going to let him go on doing what he's doing without lifting a finger to stop him? On this matter, the Pharisees and Sadducees must stand together. We must forget our differences and be of one mind concerning this threat to our people and our religion." Then he sat down.

Paul had felt optimistic when he had seen that the Pharisees were not going to accept Ananias' witnesses. But in Caiaphas' speech, in the force of that man's power to sway people just by what he said, and because Caiaphas' power along with Ananias' and Annas' was so great throughout the land, he saw a renewal of the threat to his life. He knew that the Pharisees and Sadducees had differences in their beliefs, and it was by those differences that he saw a way to save his life. He had nothing to lose by speaking out now.

"Men and brothers," he shouted, " I beg the chance to speak to you now."

"Be silent, you lying serpent," Ananias said. "You'll get your chance to speak when you're told."

"No, Ananias!" one of the Pharisees shouted. "Give him a chance to speak."

"I want to hear what he has to say," another Pharisee shouted.

And soon more voices came from the Pharisees, encouraging Paul to speak.

"Thank you," Paul said back to them. "Thank you for letting me speak." And now, he directed his remarks to the Pharisees. "Men and brothers," he said, "like many of you here, I am a Pharisee and the son of a Pharisee." (The latter, of course, was not true, but I cannot begrudge Paul this attempt to align himself as much as possible with the majority group in order to save his life. Still, he did not say that he had been raised as a student at the feet of Gamaliel, as he had said to the crowd the day before, because now Gamaliel was present in the room and would have refuted what he said. If he could have gotten away with making that claim, it would have given him an even closer alignment with the Pharisees, but he avoided saying it this time because Gamaliel himself was there.) "I would ask you to ask yourselves the real reason I have been brought here today," Paul went on. "Is it because of the Torah and the things I am purported to have said about that marvelous book? Or is it because I am a believer in Jesus of Nazareth and in his resurrection from the dead? I say it is because of my belief in resurrection that I have been arrested — a belief that I have because I am a Pharisee and for which the Sadducees hate me. Yet so many of you here are Pharisees like myself and believe, as I believe, in the resurrection of the dead. Just because the Sadducees disagree with us is no reason for them to persecute me. Am I to suffer, am I even to be executed, because I believe that Jesus of Nazareth was raised from the dead and that he'll return to us to prove he's the Messiah? Resurrection is the issue here today, not the Torah and not anything else. Pharisees, we share the same belief! Save me from those who would take my life because of that belief."

"That's not true!" Ananias shouted. "That's not the reason for his arrest. Yes, I disagree with many of you about resurrection, but I would never give my consent to arresting somebody because he believed it. If I were to do that, I would be arresting every Pharisee and most of the people in our nation, and that would be ridiculous. No, it's not because of resurrection that this man is on trial; it's because of the Torah. But since the witnesses that I have brought before you seem unable to convince you that this man preaches against the Torah, let me ask you about the other charge against him: sedition — arousing the people to rebellion."

One of the Pharisees stood up. "On what grounds do you make that charge, Ananias?"

"On the grounds that he's a Nazarene," Ananias said, "and the fact that Nazarenes advocate the overthrow of Roman rule."

"We've been through this before, Ananias," the Pharisee said. "We can't prove a man is guilty of sedition just because he's a Nazarene."

"That's right," said another Pharisee as he stood up. "If you're going to do that, then you're going to have to arrest every Zealot and every Sicarii in the country."

"And some of us Pharisees too," another Pharisee said. "It's no secret that we're against this continued Roman occupation."

"Do you have any witnesses," asked a Pharisee, "who can testify that this man actually tried to overthrow the Roman government or that he openly — or even secretly — encouraged others to do it?"

Ananias answered, "No, we have no such witnesses. But he's a Nazarene!"

"So what!" another Pharisee retorted. "There are a lot of Nazarenes around these days. Joseph of Arimathea, one of our own Pharisee members sitting right here in front of you, is one. As long as they don't *do* anything to try to overthrow the government, we shouldn't do anything against them."

"Besides," said another Pharisee, "sedition is a matter for the Romans, not us. The Romans had him, and they sent him to us. They didn't find him guilty of sedition."

"That's right," another Pharisee said. "Let's not send him back on a sedition charge the way Caiaphas did with Jesus."

Caiaphas stood up indignantly. "I didn't do anything wrong when I did that. That man was preaching that he would set up a new kingdom and that we shouldn't pay taxes and that he would destroy the Temple. He even took possession of the Temple one day and decided who could go in or out. I did what any law-abiding citizen should have done: I took him to the Romans to let *them* deal with him."

"You took him to a man you knew would crucify him without a trial," one of the Pharisees said.

"Were you ignorant of Pilate's record of crucifixion when you took him there?" another Pharisee asked.

"The most murderous procurator we ever had," said another. "You knew what he would do when you took him there."

"And you made the decision without the full Sanhedrin. We're tired of you and your clique trying to run things without involving the rest of us," protested another.

"And today you won't get away with it," said another.

The Pharisees began a murmur of subdued conversations in which they grumbled their displeasure at the Sadducee party's arrogation of power.

"Are you punishing him, as he says, because he believes in resurrection?" one Pharisee asked.

"Are you trying to teach *us* a lesson by killing this man?" asked another.

An argument began in which many voices were raised simultaneously. The Sadducees protested that Paul had raised the resurrection issue in order to conceal the real reason for his being there.

The Pharisees, refusing to accept that, railed against the Sadducees for persecuting Paul over his belief in resurrection. This was unusual for the Sanhedrin, this scene of emotional outbursts and personal recriminations. This usually austere and dignified body of men were shouting their polemics and vituperations at each other with mounting vehemence.

It was clear, however, that no matter what else happened, Paul was not going to be executed. The Pharisees were not going to allow it. As for Paul, he had successfully changed the subject and used a well-known point of contention between the Pharisees and the Sadducees as the means by which to escape Caiaphas' revenge.

Into this highly charged atmosphere, suddenly, walked Captain Lysias and his two centurions. The room immediately quieted.

"I am sorry for this intrusion," Captain Lysias announced, "but I received word that this man's life was being threatened." He did not say who had brought this information to him, but, of course, it would have had to have been someone in the room who had seen what was going on. "I sent him to you to investigate his religious teachings, to see if they were in any way fomenting civil disorder; but I did not send him to you to have his life placed in jeopardy. This man is a Roman citizen, and, as such, he is entitled to certain protections." There were murmurs of surprise around the room. "I am taking him back from you, and you can all go about your business after that." The centurions took Paul into custody and walked out of the room with him.

So rapid had been this transformation from Paul, the captive, to Paul, the liberated, that no one could move or speak for a moment. Then, individual Pharisees stood up and left, one of them remarking to Caiaphas something about vengeance being the prerogative of God and not of man. The Sadducees left too, except for a small number of chief priests who stood around, numbed by the defeat of their effort.

An Asiatic Jew entered the room and came to them to speak. "Which of you is the high priest?" he asked.

"I am," said Ananias.

"May I speak to you alone?" the Asiatic asked.

"We all are chief priests here," Ananias said. "You can speak freely to all of us. Aren't you one of the men who was going to testify today?"

"Yes, I was," the Asiatic answered. "But I was never called. And the reason was because of the lies of that man when he spoke to all of you."

"If you weren't in the room, how do you know what he said?" Ananias asked.

"Because I overheard him talking to a young man when the centurions brought him out. He told the centurions it was his nephew, who had been waiting outside for him, and he asked to be allowed to speak to the fellow for a minute. The centurions allowed it, and he told his nephew, privately, that he had just gotten out of a difficult situation, that he had been sent to the chief priests on a charge of causing public unrest because of preaching against the Torah and that he had turned it into an argument between Pharisees and Sadducees over resurrection. He said that he had turned the Pharisees in his favor over that and that they had protected him from Caiaphas' revenge. But if you will help us, your eminence, he will not be able to escape what we have planned for him."

"What is that?" Ananias asked.

"Forty-two of us," the Asiatic answered, "forty-two of us from Asia have taken a vow not to eat or drink anything until we kill him. We have called a curse on ourselves if we fail in this mission."

The chief priests looked at each other in amazement.

"Are you Sicarii?" the high priest asked.

"I would rather not say, your eminence," the Asiatic answered, "but whether we are or not, we will be effective in what we do."

"And how do you think I can help you in this?" Ananias asked.

"If you would send a message to the Roman captain that you want to interrogate Paul again tomorrow, but privately, in order to get more details about his religious views, we will be nearby, and when the man is left alone with you, we will attack and do what has to be done."

Ananias thought for a moment. He looked at Caiaphas. "It could work," Caiaphas said. "And the deed would never be attributed to us. The Pharisees would never be able to say that *we* did it. We would be innocent bystanders who could not stop what the Pharisees will call an atrocity. It could work. But there must be one or two witnesses present — preferably Pharisees. The Asiatics must hold all of us down while the others kill Paul."

Ananias shook his head. "I will send a message to some of the Pharisees tonight and ask them to join me in the interrogation tomorrow. Can we all agree on this?"

The Asiatic Jew and all the chief priests said yes.

"Come back to see me tonight," Ananias said to the Asiatic. "I'll have the time of day when he'll be here tomorrow."

That night Paul had a vision. Jesus appeared to him again and told him to have courage and that just as Paul had preached about Jesus in Jerusalem, he must also do that in Rome.

237

And that night, too, Paul had a visitor, a man who told the Roman jailer he was a friend of Paul's and that he had come from a distant place to see him. The soldiers searched the man for weapons and, finding none, admitted him. When Paul looked up from the bed on which he was lying, he saw the gray-bearded face of Abram, the dust of the desert still caked on his eyebrows and the effect of the sun evident on his tanned and wrinkled face.

"Abram!" Paul exclaimed, rising from his bed to greet him.

He held Abram's arms in his hands and felt, beneath the dusty frayed cloth garment, the hard sinews of a man who had spent his life laboring with his body as well as with his mind.

"Why are you here?" Paul asked. "What has brought you?"

"You," Abram answered, "you have brought me."

"Why?" Paul asked. "Is there some news? Do you have a message for me?"

"Sit," Abram said, pointing to the bed on which Paul had been lying.

Paul sat on the side of the bed, and Abram sat beside him.

"You have traveled much since you lived with us," Abram began.

"Yes," Paul acknowledged, "I have."

"We receive frequent news of your whereabouts and your activities. We Essenes, as you know, are scattered over many places, and our network of brothers sends us a constant flow of information. Since the time you left us, much of it has been about you."

"I'm flattered," Paul said. "What do they say?"

"That you've become an important man — at least in the places where people believe what you teach."

"An important man? That's not true," Paul said, self-effacingly. "I'm simply a humble servant of God. And what I do, I do for Him."

"A servant?" Abram asked.

"Yes, a servant," Paul answered.

"The way Jesus was a servant?" But the question had a challenging ring to it.

Paul looked at him and did not answer. He wondered why Abram was asking the question in such a manner.

"Or was Jesus more than a servant?" Abram continued. "Would you like to tell me that?"

Now Paul saw the slant of it. He would have to answer Abram — out of respect if nothing else. Abram had been his teacher for three years — and more than a teacher too. Paul looked down at the floor from side to side, as if to find the words he needed there.

"I — had this vision," he stammered. "More than one."

"And what did you see or hear in these visions, Saul?"

"As you suggest in your question, Abram, I saw that Jesus was more then a servant. He was — he was the son of God. God's only begotten son."

"And what does that mean?" Abram asked.

"It means that he's divine, Abram. He's the offspring of God."

"Did he actually say that to you? In words, I mean?"

"No, but by everything else he said to me, I knew it."

"Did he ever tell you that the Torah was no longer valid?"

"It was the only way I could get the Gentiles to follow him."

"I ask you again: Did he ever tell you that the Torah was no longer valid? In words! Did he ever say that?"

"No," Paul admitted, "he never said it in words."

"In the three years that I taught you, I taught you how to bring visions into your mind more easily, didn't I?"

"Yes. Yes, you did teach me that."

"And I taught you something else too, didn't I?"

"What do you mean?" Paul asked.

"I taught you the Torah. And I taught you the significance of the Torah. I taught you, did I not, that the Torah is God's instruction to us about how we should live our lives? Did I not teach you that?"

"Yes, but can't God change? Can't God give us a new way if He wishes?"

"By doing what? Requiring a human sacrifice in place of the good behavior the Torah demands of us? What are we, pagans? Are we going to revert back to that kind of barbarism? You've betrayed everything I've taught you. You've betrayed Judaism. You've betrayed God."

"I have not!" Paul protested. "And I haven't betrayed Judaism. I've advanced it! I'm making it progress from where it was into something better."

"No!" Abram shouted. "You haven't advanced Judaism; you've advanced yourself. That's why you've done this: to advance yourself! So you could impress that Sadducee harlot you lust after."

"She's not a harlot! Because she's beautiful, that doesn't make her a harlot."

"*I* have visions too, Saul. Do you know that? *I* have visions too. And do you know what they tell me? They tell me that you're a liar, that you're a spewer of lies, that you've founded your own separate religious communities and that you've founded them on deceit, that you deceive the people who trust you! That's what they tell me!"

"I don't believe you," Paul said, astounded.

"No, Saul, it's I who don't believe you!" Abram answered. "Do you see these hands? Do you see these arms? I could kill you with them here and now. I could twist your neck or bash your head against that wall and end it here and now. And the only reason I don't is because I'm not a murderer. I could kill you in battle but not like this. The Torah — the book that you say is obsolete — stops me. At this moment, the Torah, Saul of Tarsus, has saved your life. Be sure of it. But I can still talk, and I can still write. And I will tell the world what you are."

"What *am* I, what *am* I?" Paul shouted, feeling now that he had to fight back.

"A liar!" Abram shouted. "That's what you are! A liar!"

"I am not!" Paul retorted. "I follow the orders that are given me."

"You follow yourself," Abram said in a subdued but contemptuous tone. "But I won't contemn you. Jesus has already done that for me."

"Jesus?"

"Yes, Jesus, Saul. He said that anyone who taught people to forsake the Torah would have the lowest place in the kingdom of heaven. And by his very words, Saul of Tarsus, that's where you will be."

Abram turned and started walking out of the room, and Paul called after him, saying, "Abram, I am not a liar! I am not a liar! I tell them what I see in my visions. I do!"

But Abram could not be swayed. He continued walking down the corridor with Paul's parting words of protest reverberating in his ears.

CHAPTER XXVII

The nephew of Paul, his sister's son, had seen the Asiatic listening nearby when Paul had revealed how he had turned the Pharisees and Sadducees against each other. The nephew became suspicious of the eavesdropper, and he followed him when he went to the chief priests. Playing the Asiatic's game, the nephew, unseen, listened to the Asiatic's conversation. Thus he came to know the entire assassination plot. He went with that information to Claudius Lysias. While he was giving it to him, a message came for Lysias from the high priest. As Paul's nephew had predicted, Ananias was asking Captain Lysias to send Paul of Tarsus back to him for an additional interrogation the next day. The captain told his young informant to leave and not to worry; his uncle would be kept safe. Then he summoned his two centurions and told them what was going on.

"Look," he said, "this whole affair is getting too hot for us to handle. I want you to get this man out of Jerusalem and over to Caesarea to Governor Felix. I want you to take — let's see — two-hundred foot soldiers, seventy horsemen and two-hundred spearsmen as an escort."

"All that for one man?" the centurion, Marcus, asked.

"Yes," said Lysias, "all that for one man. My informant tells me that forty-two men have sworn to kill this Paul of Tarsus. Does that mean that forty-two are all there are? Of course not. This man seems to be upsetting a lot of people. I don't know why, but he seems to be. So forty-two may not be all there are. I want to play it safe. Maybe the escort *is* excessive, but I want to make sure the man gets to Felix alive, and then I'm finished with it. Because if anything happens to him between here and Caesarea, I'm the one who will have to answer questions, such as why I sent such a small escort when the party that attacked us was so large. No, it has to be a large escort. I want a show of force large enough to scare off any would-be attackers.

"And you had better leave at night. Say about three hours after dark. The less attention you call to yourselves, the better. Get some extra horses, and let this Paul ride in the middle of the horsemen, so that he'll be more protected."

Then he told them to send in his scribe on their way out. He was going to send Governor Felix a letter, which he wanted them to deliver.

241

He said that in that letter he was going to explain all that had happened to this Paul of Tarsus and that he, Claudius Lysias, had found nothing to warrant the execution or imprisonment of the man. And then he said that he would send a message to the high priest to tell him where Paul was and that if he wanted to make any accusations against him, he could go to Caesarea to do it. And he said that he would wait until Paul was well on his way to Caesarea before he sent the high priest that message.

It was the plan of a good military commander, and it went well. Saul was delivered safely to Felix. Ananias got the message and realized that now, in order to get Paul, he would have to talk to Felix. So he engaged the orator, Tertullus, to do the talking for him, thinking that Tertullus would be a more effective speaker than anyone else.

The group that traveled to Caesarea included Ananias, Tertullus, Caiaphas, Ananus and others from among the chief priests. When they gained their audience with Felix, Paul was brought in, and Tertullus began his presentation with a lengthy oration about the greatness of Felix.

"Oh, noble Felix," he began, "munificent light of our age, beneficent judge of our actions, radiant inspiration to our souls, how grateful we are, how blessed we feel, how fortunate we consider ourselves, to have as our governor such a one as yourself. Under your illustrious rule, our nation has prospered. Peace has reigned, public order has prevailed and our economy has thrived. The magnanimous gift of your wisdom has led us to heights we have never before attained, the grace of your kindness has spared us the penance for our shortcomings, the firmness of your hand has lifted us to the highest pinnacles of success, the brilliance of your decisions has astounded us beyond our wildest expectations. In you, noble Felix, our people have the gift of a true leader, who rules yet inspires, who commands obedience, not through coercion but through the forceful persuasion of his immaculate reason, through cogent adherence to his irresistible logic, through willing submission to his glorious pronouncements."

Felix, growing uncomfortable under this effusive laudation, said, "Orator!"

But Tertullus heard nothing, so caught up was he in the torrent of his address.

"Oh, great star of reason...," he continued.

"Orator!" Felix cried out.

"Oh, great moon of compassion..,"

"Orator!"

"Oh, great illuminator of our thoughts...,"

"Tertullus!" Felix shouted.

And now Felix's voice penetrated the wall of words, and Tertullus said, "Yes, your honor?"

"I am not the emperor; I am only the procurator. You don't have to go through all this for me. Just tell me what the charges are against this man."

"The charges, your honor?"

"Yes, Tertullus, the charges — the things that this man has done wrong, his transgressions, his violations, his perpetrations. Do you understand?"

"Why yes, of course, your honor," Tertullus said. "Well, in short, this man, this nefarious malcontent, spreads discontent among our people. First of all ,he spreads sedition by telling people there will be a new kingdom with a man named Jesus of Nazareth at the head of it. This man is one of the ringleaders of the Nazarene sect, which spreads this belief. I need not expound on how such an event would affect the glorious Roman government, which has so benefited our lives; I need not expound on how it would grieve our people to sustain such a loss; I need not expound on how it would pain our dear emperor to be parted from his subjects and how it would sadden the heart of every Roman soldier to leave this land in which his presence has been so welcomed and his protection so cherished."

"No, Tertullus," the procurator said, "you need not expound on that. Now, is that the only charge you wish to bring against this man?"

"Ah, no, there is more," Tertullus said.

"I was afraid so," said Felix.

"He has profaned our religion and has attempted to profane our Temple."

"Well, Tertullus," Felix said, "you do understand that religious matters are not something I want to get involved in, unless they are adversely affecting the tranquillity of the people, in which case I might then concern myself with them."

"Then, Governor Felix," Tertullus said, "you must concern yourself with this. This man's religious teachings do that very thing. He profanes our religion and our Temple by adjuring Jews everywhere to abandon the law of their fathers. This has caused immeasurable discontent among our people, especially in places outside Judaea, where he's done all his preaching. We would have condemned him ourselves had your Captain Lysias not wrenched him from us."

Felix asked each of the chief priests if they agreed with the charges. Each one said that he did. Ananias, however, went further than the other chief priests and said what Tertullus had said: that they would have executed Paul themselves had Captain Lysias not interfered. That prompted Felix, who knew more about this affair than he had revealed, into teasing the powerful Jewish priest.

"Would you really have executed him?" he asked.

"Yes, we would have," Ananias answered.

"Well, can you tell me how you could have done that when the majority of the members of your Sanhedrin were against doing it? Or so I've been told."

Ananias gave no answer. No doubt he needed time to think of one. But before he could do that, Felix went on.

"I have not given you enough time to think of an answer, I fear. I apologize for that. It was inconsiderate of me. You must forgive my blunt Roman-soldier ways. I served in the army in less-civilized surroundings than these before I became a public official, so I attribute the specious inconsistency between *your* claim that your council would have executed him and *my* information that your council would not have allowed that — I attribute that to my inexperience with the more civilized way of interpreting things. I will attribute it to that because I cannot conceive that a high priest would try to deceive a Roman governor.

"But now I would like to ask Paul of Tarsus if he will respond to the charges brought against him."

Paul, having listened to Tertullus' flowery praise of Felix before getting to the issue, decided that he should be no less eloquent in *his* opening remarks. So he said, "Your honor, I know your reputation for being a fair-minded judge. You have had this reputation for years. So I welcome the opportunity to answer these charges to you especially."

"Thank you," Felix said, "but I believe that Tertullus has expounded my virtues adequately today, don't you think?"

"Yes he has, your honor," Paul said.

"Then let us get on with the charges."

"Well, your honor, it's all made up. In the first place, I'm not against the Roman government. I've always respected Roman authority. I even became a Roman citizen."

"Yes," Felix said, "but aren't the Zealots interested in getting rid of us?"

"The Zealots?" Paul said, not knowing why the procurator was mentioning them.

"Yes, the Zealots, the movement that Judas of Galilee started years ago. Aren't they committed to getting rid of us?"

"Yes, I believe they are, your honor."

"And among the leaders of the Nazarenes, isn't there a man named Simon, who is known to be a Zealot?"

"Yes, your honor, that is true," Paul said, "but I myself am not a Zealot."

"But your movement does allow Zealots into it?"

"Yes, your honor, but only because we don't want to deny God's salvation to anyone."

"I see. And it's not because your movement wants to replace the king that we've appointed with this Jesus of Nazareth when he returns?"

"No, your honor, it isn't."

"Well, that's interesting, because I've heard otherwise from certain circles." He looked at the chief priests and then back to Paul. "I'm curious," he went on. "Have you heard of this group called Christians?"

"Yes, your honor," Paul answered.

"Aren't they also waiting for this Jesus of Nazareth to return?"

"Yes, your honor, they are."

"Well, this dead leader of yours seems to be quite popular. A lot of people seem to be waiting for him. But I think I should tell you that these *Christians* who are waiting for him are not very popular with our emperor right now. Nero, I've heard, has a particular dislike for them."

"I'm sorry to hear that, your honor."

"But his wife, Poppaea, you know, is rather sympathetic towards your Jewish beliefs, so that may be tempering him to some extent. But, be that as it may, in your own case, I do concede that men can have the same religious views but different political ones. Perhaps your movement has non-rebels in it as well as rebels."

"Your honor," Paul said, "it's been about twelve days since I went to worship in our Temple. While I was there, I did not do any preaching nor did I enter into any arguments or even discussions with anyone. I did not go into any synagogue or onto any street to preach or discuss anything. They cannot produce one witness to say that I did.

"And as for my beliefs, which Tertullus says are heretical, I tell you that I worship the god of my fathers as a good and faithful Jew and that I believe in our religious laws, as they are written in the Torah and the books of our prophets. And I tell you also that I hope to God, as *they* do," and here he pointed to the chief priests, "that the dead, both the just and the unjust, will be resurrected. My conscience is clear insofar as my having acted without offense towards God and towards my fellow men."

At this point, the chief priest, Ananus, one of the sons of Annas, raised up his hand and said, "Your honor, forgive me for interrupting, but *we* do not believe in the resurrection of the dead."

"Well," Felix said with a playful grin on his face, "he didn't say that you did; he only said that you hoped for it." Whereupon he signaled Paul to continue.

"Well, your honor," Paul went on, "after years of being away, I came recently to Jerusalem to bring financial help to our brothers from the offerings that our other brothers had made in the places I had visited. And also to worship and make offerings in the Temple. Well, outside the Temple, some Jews from Asia accosted me. And frankly, your honor, if they think I have done something wrong, they should have been here today to make their accusations and to offer their proofs. But are they here? No, your honor, as you can see, they are not. Because they have no proofs and because their accusations are false."

Felix looked at Ananias. "Well, high priest, that's a legitimate point, don't you think? If these Jews from Asia found enough fault with him to attack him on the street, I mean if they felt that strongly about it, why didn't they come here today to testify?"

"Because," Ananias answered, "your Captain Lysias chose not to tell them about this hearing. He told *me* and left me just enough time to get here. But he chose not to tell *them*."

"How unfair of him," Felix said with barely concealed sarcasm. "I'm surprised at such biased behavior by one of our officers. I can't imagine what was in his mind when he did that. Unless, of course, it was because of that rumor he heard, the one about some Asiatic Jews who had sworn not to eat or drink anything until they killed Paul of Tarsus. Have you heard that one, high priest?" He did not wait for an answer. "It was foolish of him to give credence to such an absurdity, of course, if that's what he did, and I would have to attribute it to his youthful gullibility. When you're inexperienced, you'll believe anything, won't you ? Oh, and do you know what else that rumor said? A fantastic story! It has to do with you, high priest. It seems that you sent Captain Lysias a message to send Paul of Tarsus back to you the day after your Sanhedrin meeting so that a small group of you could interrogate him further. And the story that our captain heard was that *you* had conspired with those Asiatic Jews to have them come in during the interrogation and to overwhelm you and the others and to kill Paul of Tarsus. I told him, of course, how ridiculous that was. But youth is youth. If I had been there, you understand, I would have given no credit to that story at all. The high priest of the Jews does not go around assassinating people. We all know that."

Felix now turned to Paul. "And as for you, Paul of Tarsus, as you can see, you cannot fault the Asiatic Jews for not being here today to accuse you. If they weren't told about the meeting, they couldn't be here, could they?"

Paul answered, "Well, your honor, you have the high priest to make the accusations for them. And I've already been examined on these charges. I was examined by the Sanhedrin. And I challenge the high priest or Tertullus or any of the priests here today to say that the Sanhedrin found me guilty of any evil. They didn't! The majority of the members said I was innocent. I told them then, as I tell you now, it is because of this question of the resurrection of the dead that I am called before you today."

Ananias had expected Tertullus' brilliance and the stature of himself and his colleagues to carry the day. But Felix seemed to be toying with them. And now Paul was again trying to obfuscate the real issue by bringing up the unrelated subject of resurrection. Ananias could not let this happen again.

"That is not true," he declared. "Resurrection is not the issue here at all. It's because he preaches against the Torah and spreads sedition. He brings up resurrection to divert us from the real issue. When Tertullus presented the charges, did he once mention resurrection?"

"But he has just said that he *believes* in your Torah," Felix said.

"He tells you that here, but he preaches the opposite all over Antioch and Tarsus and Athens and Pamphylia and all the other places he's visited. It's true that we Sadducees do not believe in the resurrection of the dead, but the Pharisees and Essenes do believe it, and if a belief in resurrection were an offense, I would have to arrest every Pharisee and every Essene in the country. That would be ridiculous, not only because our religion allows for such variations in thought and belief but because the majority of the judging body believes in the very thing that we would be bringing the person to trial for."

Felix conceded Ananias' point, but, apparently, he had had enough for the day. He suspended further discussion, saying that he wanted to get Captain Lysias' information first-hand. He would keep Paul in custody in the meantime. He dismissed the priests and Tertullus and gave his centurion instructions to keep Paul under arrest but to give him the freedom of the city. If his friends wanted to visit him or minister to him, they were to have ready access to him. He then made Paul promise on his honor that he would not leave the city. Then he dismissed the centurion, saying that he wanted to speak to Paul alone.

When the centurion had left, Felix said, "Now, Paul, are you satisfied?"

"You mean with your decision, your honor?"

"Yes, with my decision as it stands at present," Felix said.

"Oh yes, your honor. I think that you're fair and that you'll continue to be fair."

"Well, such fairness is not easy to find, you know."

"Oh, how right you are, your honor," Paul said.

"And once you find it, it certainly is worth preserving if you can."

"I agree with you completely," Paul said.

Felix poured two cups of wine and gave one to Paul. "Regretfully," he said, "we sometimes have to pay for fairness in this world."

"You mean pay a price for it, your honor?"

"Yes, Paul, a price. Everything, you see, has its price: food, women, fairness. Everything has its price."

"What sort of price does fairness have, your honor? I thought people should be fair to each other just for the sake of being fair."

"Ah, then you thought wrong, my dear fellow. Even fairness must be paid for sometimes."

Paul was beginning to understand. "And how might I pay for the fairness I wish for, your honor?"

"I'm glad you asked me that," Felix said. "Each of us, surely, must pay with whatever resources he has available. Some with service, some with goods, some with money. Friendships are cemented that way, you know. And I would like very much to be your friend."

And now Paul understood why Felix had been so unaccommodating to the priests. "Have you selected a particular means by which I might cement our friendship, your honor?"

"Why yes, I *have* chosen the means," Felix said. "What *we* must discuss is the amount."

"You're speaking of money," Paul said.

"Yes, Paul, I'm speaking of money."

"And where would I get the money that would ensure my freedom?"

"Oh, I'm not speaking about freedom," Felix said. "The price of freedom might be higher than you could afford. I'm speaking about fairness."

"Well, where would I get the money to ensure this fairness?" Paul asked.

"I'm told that you have collected large amounts of money from your followers throughout the empire."

"That money was meant to help our leaders in Jerusalem," Paul said.

"But not all of it. Surely not all of it," Felix said. "Surely some of it — justifiably you understand — has been held back as a protection and a security for the collector himself."

"All of it is for the cause," Paul said.

"Of course, my dear fellow, of course it is. But aren't you a part of that cause? To a great extent, doesn't the cause require the continuation of your work? Shouldn't some of the money, then, be set aside to ensure your safety?"

"I have taken only what I needed to survive," Paul said.

"Of course! And with complete justification for doing so. That's why you used some of that money to purchase your Roman citizenship, isn't it? Oh, please don't think that I'm saying that critically. You had every right — even an obligation — to do that. You bought the Roman citizenship to protect yourself, and you were protecting yourself for the good of the cause. Completely justified! Now I'm saying that you should do the same thing again."

"To protect myself?" Paul said.

Felix made an open-handed gesture, as if to say that the answer should be obvious.

"All right, your honor, I understand," Paul said.

"I'm so glad," Felix exulted. "You're a man of the world. I knew that when I first laid eyes on you. I'm sure we'll get along famously, you and I. Oh, and I would like to bring my wife, Drusilla, to meet you. She's a Jew like yourself, you know. Right out of the royal family. And she adores religious philosophy. It would please us both to know more about yours."

"I would be honored to have the opportunity to tell you, your honor," Paul said.

And Felix then promised to bring her after he and Paul had completed their financial transactions the next day.

That evening Felix told Drusilla about Paul. What made him fascinating to her was not that he was a Jesus-follower, for there were plenty of those around from whom she already had learned about this interesting new movement, but that he was a particular Jesus-follower, one who was disliked by some of the members of his own group. That made him intriguing in his own right.

She said to Felix, "When you finish whatever business it is you have with him, arrange for me to meet him. I love unusual people like that. They make life more interesting, don't you think?"

"Whatever you want, my love," he said. "Your wish is my command."

"Do you know," she said, kissing his cheek, "you're the one man in this world who makes me feel like a queen."

"You are a queen," he said. "You rule my heart, and that makes you my queen."

"Oh," she said, throwing herself into his arms, "what am I going to do with you? You and your words that make me melt. What am I going to do with you?"

"Well, would my queen allow me to kiss her?" he asked, holding her captive in his arms.

"Oh, Felix," she pleaded, "please not now. You know what your kisses do to me. We have to go to dinner in a few minutes. We have guests this evening."

He released her from his embrace and allowed her to straighten her dress.

"Speaking of guests," he said, "have you heard from your brother and sister?"

"Agrippa and Bernice?" she asked, and then without waiting for his acknowledgement, said, "No, I haven't. This is the third time I've invited them to visit us here, and they never even answer me."

"Why are they so unresponsive?" he asked.

"Oh, Felix, you know why. It's because I left my husband and married you."

"A woman can change her mind, can't she?"

"I violated one of our religious laws when I did it. And they say that I ruined our family's reputation when I did that. They say that people lost respect for our family name. But I'll bet there were as many people who sympathized with me as there were who didn't. Anyway, I don't care whether they did or not. I don't care what anyone thinks. I love you, and that's all that matters to me."

"Do you know what a hypocrite is?" he asked, apparently changing the subject.

"Of course," she said, "of course I do."

"Then tell me if that's what your brother and sister are when I tell you the latest news about them."

Drusilla looked at him inquisitively and formed a half smile on her lips. Felix's introductory remarks portended something important.

"One of our centurions has just come back from an inspection tour of Galilee. He tells me there's whispering in the streets about your brother and sister."

"What kind of whispering?" she asked, delighting in his protracted release of information.

"They say that your brother and sister are lovers, that they have sexual relations together."

The half smile on Drusilla's lips broadened into a full one. "I see," she said, stretching out the words, as if some enlightenment had come from above. Then excitedly, "Oh, Felix, I see, I understand now. Don't you see? Don't you see what happened? She wanted him for herself all the time that I was living there, and she was afraid he'd be attracted to me. She thought I might take him away from her. That's why she was so cruel to me. That's why she treated me the way she did." And then, as if an even greater light had broken through, "And he — he must have wanted her too. That's why he let her do the things she did to me. Oh, Felix, my love, thank you. Thank you for telling me this. Now I understand it all."

"Why are you so happy?" he asked. "Haven't they also broken these laws of yours?"

"Yes, yes," she cried as she danced about the room. "That's why I'm so happy: because they've committed a sin."

"And yet they won't accept an invitation from you because they say that *you've* sinned."

"Yes," she laughed, "but that's the beauty of it. My sin was committed in the open. They think theirs is secret, and it's not."

"So they break this law of yours in secret and then set themselves up as judges over you when you break it in the open. Isn't that what a hypocrite usually does?"

"Yes, my husband, you're absolutely right. Oh, revenge is sweet! We have a saying in our religion that we shouldn't seek revenge on anyone who does us a wrong, that revenge is something we should leave to God. But I'll tell you, my love, when God does do it, it's sweet to the person who's been wronged. Oh, Felix, I love you so much. I think I'm going to enjoy the dinner this evening better than anything in a long time."

CHAPTER XXVIII

Jacob reported to Rabath his secret meeting with Paul. He took a chance when he did this, because her father's hatred of Paul had not diminished even a little, and she, dutiful daughter that she was, might tell the former high priest that his private secretary had had a friendly meeting with the man whom her father wanted dead. So Jacob swore her to secrecy before he revealed anything, and only then did he tell her about Paul. She seemed to become vivified when he mentioned him. She seemed to be interested beyond the casual response that he had expected her to show.

"What does he look like now?" she asked. "How does he sound when he talks? Does he ask about me? Does he mention me at all?"

"He does speak of you," Jacob answered, "and if you want my opinion, I think he still loves you?"

"Did he tell you that?"

"Yes. But he's found something else too — something that seems to have taken him over — the way you once did — and still do sometimes."

"And what's that?" she asked.

"This Messiah business. This belief in the resurrection of Jesus, the man your father took to Pilate. He really does believe that the fellow is going to come back. He really believes it."

"Come back and do what?" Rabath asked.

"Who knows? Establish God's kingdom on earth; make everything beautiful; make everybody love each other. Who knows what's in his mind? I'm not even sure that he or the others who believe this business know themselves what they mean or what they expect. They're all so pitiful."

"But it is rather beautiful, isn't it?"

"Well, so is every fanciful tale that a storyteller wants to tell, but that doesn't make it true."

Rabath leaned forward and looked intently into his eyes. "Jacob, I've seen some of those people — the ones who believe that this Jesus is the Messiah. They seem — they seem supremely content. Oh, I know they don't like us. We're decadent and corrupt to them. But even if they *are* misled, they seem so — so blissful. I've started to wonder if they know something that we don't."

253

"Well, I'm at your service as always. What are you saying to me —
that you want to know more about them?"

"Could I?"

"If that's what you want?"

"You won't tell my husband or my father?"

"Do you have to ask me that?"

She breathed deeply. "All right then, yes, I want to know more
about them."

"All right," he said, "I'll arrange it. Do you want to see Saul — or
Paul, as he's now calling himself?"

"Could I?"

"I'll see," he said, and he squeezed her hand reassuringly.

He went to inquire about Paul the next day. He learned that the
Romans had taken him to Caesarea. Caiaphas, he learned, had left
hurriedly too, along with Ananias and some of the other chief priests.
Rabath was not going to be able to see Paul unless she traveled to
Caesarea, and that might prove to be very embarrassing because that
was where her father had gone, and he might see her there and want to
know why she had come. And she also would have to explain to her
husband the reason for such a trip. But there were others in Jerusalem
who could satisfy her newly acquired curiosity, and the foremost of these
was James. So Jacob sought out this reputed paragon of righteousness
and told him that a Sadducee woman wanted him to teach her about his
brother. He did not reveal who the woman was — that she was the
daughter of the man who had taken his brother to Pilate — but simply
said that she was a woman of means (he used the name Ruth to identify
her) who wanted to learn in secret. James agreed to meet with her, and
they set a time for the next day.

When Jacob told Rabath that she would not be able to see Paul, she
was very disappointed. It was obvious that her motive in wanting to see
him involved more than just religious philosophy. But she agreed to see
James, because he also had piqued her curiosity, and all this secrecy and
intrigue seemed to appeal to her too.

So Rabath, the next day, found herself in the presence of James the
Just, the leader of the Nazarenes and the brother of the man whom her
father had taken to Pilate. He told her of the prophets and of the
predictions they had made concerning the Messiah. He told her about
Jesus and all the things he had done that fulfilled those predictions. He
told her of Jesus' goodness and, as he did so, seemed to radiate a
goodness of his own. When they finished their meeting that day, she
asked to see him again. She knew that he was occupied with so many

254

responsibilities, but she felt drawn to him and, perhaps for the first time in her life, needful of the things he was teaching. He agreed to see her, and as the days passed into weeks, she went to him again and again — and gradually she changed.

Jacob, as he watched her from afar, saw the inevitability of her conversion. The day came when she sat with him and told him what she believed. In her heart, she said, she was a Nazarene, and she asked him not to tell anyone about it, at least until she was ready. He could see that there was something in her face that had not been there before. She looked at him with that same radiating warmth that she had told him she had seen in James. There was something in her now that was different than before.

She had two things to accomplish, she said, and she would do the easier of those things first. She went to see James, and, in a quiet moment alone with him, she said, "Teacher, my name is not Ruth. I am Rabath, the daughter of Caiaphas, the man who took your brother to Pilate."

"I know that," said James. "I know who you are. I've known it from the first day you came."

She was stunned. "And still you took me as your student?"

"Yes," he said. "It would have been wrong of me to deny you this knowledge. You had done nothing to warrant my hesitation about teaching you. But even if your *father* had come to me — even if he were to come to me now — I would bear him no grudge. I would teach him as I have taught you. I was flattered that you had come."

She left him after that, feeling that she had caught a glimpse of something — something beyond. A glimpse perhaps of heaven. Maybe a glimpse of God.

But now she had this other thing to accomplish, and she went to see her father, who had long since come back from Caesarea.

"Do you remember that man you took to Pilate?" she asked when she had him alone in a room.

He remembered. How could he not remember? The ubiquitous Nazarenes were a constant reminder, curse their stupid souls!

"Is it possible — just possible," she asked, "that the man really was the Messiah?"

"Are you out of your mind?" Caiaphas asked. "The man was a charlatan. He was trying to make a name for himself. Or at best, he was deranged, thinking himself the fulfillment of a childish notion. Of course he wasn't the Messiah. How can you even ask that?"

But the nature of his response, she observed, betrayed a certain nervousness. It was as if he was saying one thing but thinking another.

"They say that he did many good things? Do you think that that's true?" Rabath asked.

"Perhaps," Caiaphas answered, shrugging his shoulders unconcernedly. "But he did some bad things too. And that was why I arrested him."

"What bad things, father? I'm just curious. I would just like to know."

"He was stirring the people into a frenzy," Caiaphas said. "They would have revolted under him if I hadn't stopped him. He knew the Zachariah prophecy, and he arranged things to do what it said. The Messiah is supposed to come riding on a donkey; he got himself a donkey. There's not supposed to be any commercial business in the Temple on the day the Messiah arrives; he drives out the moneychangers, and has his men block anyone from coming in. He took over the Temple for the day. Who knows what he would have done next? I saved our people from a catastrophe. Believe me, I did."

"They say he was resurrected, but *we* don't believe that, of course."

"Of course we don't. It's a stupid superstition. It's not worthy of an intelligent person to believe that such a thing is even possible."

"Why do you think the Pharisees believe in it so strongly then?" she asked.

And now Caiaphas began to suspect that there was something more behind his beautiful daughter's questions than casual curiosity.

"Who's been talking to you?" he said. "We haven't talked about this Jesus person for years."

"I met his brother recently," she confessed.

"James? That untouchable lunatic? What were you doing with him?"

"I just met him."

"And talked to him?"

"Yes."

"What did he do to you, Rabath? Put some of his crazy notions into your head?"

"Father, did it ever occur to you that Jesus may have been who he said he was?"

"Are you out of your mind? I didn't bring you up to be stupid! The man was a charlatan — or a lunatic — or a combination of both. But one thing he was *not* was the Messiah."

"Are you sure of that, father?"

256

"Rabath! You will not even suggest such a thing in my presence again. Is that clear? It's obvious that James has worked on you and twisted your thoughts. When you've twisted them back into sanity, then come to see me again."

He turned angrily and walked away.

She called after him: "You sent a holy man to Pilate, father! You sent a holy man to a murderer!"

He whirled angrily. "I saved our nation from destruction! That's what I did! I saved our people!" he shouted.

And then he was out of the room, leaving Rabath with her second task only partially completed, because she had hoped to change her father's mind and bring him to that same state of repentance that Paul had reached over *his* persecution of Nazarenes.

CHAPTER XXIX

Peter wrote a letter to James. Peter had left Jerusalem after the meeting with Paul and was once again in the field, working to gain adherents to Jesus, just as Paul had been doing. In the past, though he had done some traveling, he had spent most of his time in Alexandria, the city with the biggest Jewish population outside Israel. This was a place where Paul had not gone, perhaps because he had considered it Peter's territory. There Peter had preached the gospel that Paul attributed to him — the Gospel of the Circumcision. As it happened, Peter had been so busy in this place that he had not had time to travel to the places where Paul had been, as Apollos had done. But, finally, he was able to do that, and he did.

Among the places he visited were Antioch and Corinth. There, for the first time, he learned exactly what Paul had been teaching. He was understandably shocked. He already knew that Paul had not been offering the Gentiles the chance to become Jews nor requiring them to become God-fearers; he knew that Paul had been telling them to forsake the Torah and to accept salvation through grace. And he knew that Paul had been saying that not just to Gentiles but also to Jews. And he knew that James had told Paul to retract all that and that Paul had agreed to do it and, as a first step towards that goal, had publicly prayed from the Torah with the young men who were taking their vows in the Temple. But now Peter learned about something else that Paul had been teaching: that Jesus was the only begotten son of God and that he was, therefore, divine. And even beyond that, Peter learned what was being said about himself. Paul, apparently, had not wanted to give the impression that the original disciples and the Nazarenes in Jerusalem disagreed with him. That would have weakened his credibility wherever he went. So he had collected money for them, which had showed his audiences his oneness with the Jerusalem group (and which also had given that group a reason to support him), and when he had been questioned about their belief, he had said that it was the same as his. That meant that they rejected the Torah, and it meant that Peter did too. Peter was astounded when he heard it. He felt compelled to write to James. How could he be preaching what Paul himself had called the Gospel of the Circumcision and yet be against the Torah? The Gospel of the Circumcision required obedience to the Torah. Did Paul not know that? And Jesus himself had repeatedly cited Mosaic law as the basis for his rules and instructions. Sometimes, when Jesus had told us what to do, he had added the phrase, "...as Moses commanded." Did Paul not know that too?

Peter wrote his letter. He wrote to the man who was "strong for the Torah", to the leader of those who were "the Zealots of the Torah", and told him that he was being falsely credited with *rejecting* the Torah and with being afraid to say so openly. He called Paul's doctrine "absurd" and referred to Paul now as "my enemy". He was afraid that if people were bold enough to falsify his statements while he was still alive, they would be even bolder about it after he was dead. So he suggested to James that the record of his preachings be entrusted only to the most worthy of the brothers, so that his words would not be altered in the future as he saw them being altered now. He wrote this letter so that James would know the true nature of his beliefs:

"Peter to James, the lord and overseer of the holy congregation: Peace be with you always from the Father of all through Jesus the Messiah.

"Knowing well that you, my brother, eagerly take pains about what is for the mutual benefit of us all, I earnestly beseech you not to pass on to any one of the Gentiles the books of my preachings which I (here) forward to you, nor to any of our own tribe before probation. But if some one of them has been examined and found to be worthy, then you may hand them over to him in the same way as Moses handed over his office of a teacher to the seventy. Wherefore also the fruit of his caution is to be seen up to this day. For those who belong to his people preserve everywhere the same rule in their belief in the one God and in their line of conduct, the Scriptures with their many senses being unable to incline them to assume another attitude.

"Rather they attempt, on the basis of the rule that has been handed down to them, to harmonize the contradictions of the Scriptures, if haply some one who does not know the traditions is perplexed by the ambiguous utterances of the prophets. On this account they permit no one to teach unless he first learn how the Scriptures should be used. Wherefore there obtain amongst them one God, one law and one hope.

"In order now that the same may also take place among us, hand over the books of my preachings in the same mysterious way to our seventy brethren that they may prepare those who are candidates for positions as teachers. For if we do not proceed in this way, our word of truth will be split into many opinions. This I do not know as a prophet, but I have already the beginning of the evil before me. For some among the Gentiles have rejected my lawful preaching and have preferred a lawless and absurd doctrine *of the man who is my enemy.* And indeed some have attempted, whilst I am still alive, to distort my words by interpretations of many sorts, as if I taught the dissolution of the law and, although I was of this opinion, did not express it openly. But that may God forbid! For to do such a thing means to act contrary to the law of God, which was made known by Moses and was confirmed by our Lord in its everlasting continuance. For he said: *'The heaven and the earth will pass away, but one jot or tittle shall not pass away from the law.'* This he said *that everything might come to pass.* But those persons who, I know not how, allege that they are at home in my thoughts wish to expound the words which they have heard of me better than I myself who spoke them. To those whom they instruct they say that this is my opinion, to which indeed I never gave a thought. But if they falsely assert such a thing whilst I am still alive, how much more after my death will those who come later venture to do so?

"In order now that that may not happen I earnestly beseech you not to pass on the books of my preachings which I send you to any of our own tribe or to any foreigner before probation, but if some one is examined and found to be worthy, let them then be handed over in the way in which Moses handed over his office of a teacher to the seventy, in order that they may preserve the dogmas and extend farther the rule of the truth, interpreting everything in accordance with our tradition and not being dragged into error through ignorance and uncertainty in their minds to bring others into the like pit of destruction.

"What seems to me to be necessary I have now indicated to you. And what you, my lord, deem to be right, do you carry fittingly into effect. Farewell."

It was interesting to me that in this letter Peter broke our usual Jewish tradition of not calling anyone but God, "lord", and referred to James as the lord of our congregation and to Jesus himself as "the Lord". But in connotation, I do not think that those appellations implied that he considered anyone but God the supreme authority. Also in this letter I saw that he called God the father of all and did not refer to God as the father only of Jesus. And I saw too that he confirmed what we already knew about Jesus and the Torah: that Jesus averred its validity and its "everlasting continuance".

This letter was revealing to James and was important enough to be preserved among the Nazarenes and to be formally named, The Epistle of Peter to James.

From this and other sources, James learned the teachings of Paul. He knew about the Torah, and he had taken measures to have Paul give public evidence of his adherence to it. But he had not known that he himself and Peter were also said to have turned from the Torah. And he had not known about Jesus' divinity and that while his mother was Jesus' mother, his father was not Jesus' father, the latter relationship being God's. He wondered, then, why they had gone to all the trouble to trace and publicize Jesus' lineage from Joseph back to King David. The prophecy that the Messiah would come from King David could not be fulfilled if Jesus was not Joseph's son. But soon he learned from other sources that Paul's followers, in order to circumvent that problem, were setting up a new lineage — one that showed that Mary, Jesus' mother, was also descended from King David. Yet the original lineage outlined by Peter had been traced, name by name, through Joseph. Those who were trying to trace Jesus' lineage through Mary would have to say that Peter's lineage, though correct, was irrelevant and that Peter had listed those names because he hadn't known their irrelevance, which means that Peter hadn't known that God was Jesus' father and that he had thought all along it was Joseph. "After all," the Nazarenes would say to the Christians who claimed that Peter had recognized Jesus' divinity, "if Peter had known that Jesus was God's son and not Joseph's, why would he have traced Jesus' lineage through Joseph? For that matter, why would any Nazarene have done it?"

Meanwhile, while James was being made aware of these things for the first time, Paul was in Felix's custody, and while he could not leave Caesarea, he had many people visit him there. From them he learned what was going on in the Christian communities that he had started. As time went on, he learned that men were going there and teaching that his gospel was wrong and that many of his followers were accepting the other gospel in place of his. This is what he had feared when he had spoken to the elders from Ephesus. During the two years that Felix had him in Caesarea, he heard reports of this again and again, and he knew who was behind it all. It was he who would have to act now, to save all that he had created. He could not travel, but he could write. So he wrote letters to reach out again to the people whose hearts and minds he had won.

One of these was the Galatians, the descendants of the immigrants from Gaul who had come into Greece three-hundred years earlier. Because he knew that James' emissaries were teaching the gospel of Peter, he saw the possible loss of this entire Galatian Christian community to the Nazarenes, so he wrote to the Galatians, as to his children, about his disappointment in their shifting to the other gospel.

"I am astounded," he wrote, "that in such a short time after I taught you and convinced you of the gospel of Jesus Christ," (by which he meant the gospel of the freedom from the penance for sin by believing in the sacrificial death of Jesus), "you are turning to another gospel. Not that there *is* another gospel," (and here I saw the denial of the very thing he had told me earlier, because he himself had said that there *were* two gospels, his and Peter's, and he had named them, the Gospel of the Circumcision and the Gospel of the Uncircumcision), "but there are some who shall trouble you and pervert the gospel of Christ" (meaning the emissaries from James), "but if we or an angel from heaven preaches any other gospel to you than the one we preached originally, let that person be accursed; and as I said before, so I say again: If any man preaches any other gospel to you than the one I preached originally, let him be accursed."

So strongly did Paul resent the intrusion of James' and Peter's influence into the communities that he had won that he would curse an angel from heaven for preaching their way instead of his. He then said in his letter that he wasn't interested in gaining anyone's approval, by which I know he meant James, and he said that the gospel he preached wasn't learned from men but by a revelation from the departed Jesus himself. He said that when he left Damascus, he didn't go to Jerusalem to learn the gospel from the apostles but went for three years into Arabia. He did not mention specifically what he did during those three years, but, of course, that was the time he spent with Abram and the Essenes and in which he learned more about having visions. He said he went back to Damascus and then made his way to Jerusalem. In Jerusalem, he said, he met with Peter for fifteen days but not with anyone else. He said that he saw no one else except for Jesus' brother, James, at the time. Of course, in Jerusalem, besides Peter, he *had* spent time with me, but I was not an original apostle, so I was never one who could tell him anything about Jesus from personal encounters as the others could. But by his own statement in this letter, Paul had not learned about Jesus even from them; he had learned about him independently through his own revelations.

And speaking of personal encounters, James' emissaries never hesitated to point out Paul's lack of such encounters with Jesus as a serious deficiency in his credibility. But Paul always countered that by saying that his revelations were superior to the apostles' encounters, that his encounters with Jesus in the spirit were superior to their encounters with Jesus in the flesh.

As he recounted more of his personal history to the Galatians, he mentioned that James and Peter and John, the son of Zebedee, had given him sanction to preach the Gospel of the Uncircumcision to the Gentiles, just as Peter had been sanctioned to teach the Gospel of the Circumcision to the Jews. So there it was again: the admission that there *were* two gospels, which he had denied in the beginning of his letter.

Then he wrote about his disagreement with Peter and me over the issue of dining with Gentiles and made it sound as if Peter was a weak and effete individual, shrinking under Paul's reproachment. But that simply was not true.

And then he said that obedience to the laws of Judaism and the deeds that we do because of them could not achieve salvation for us and that the only thing that could achieve it was a faith and belief in Jesus Christ, by which he meant a belief in his own portrayal of Jesus as our savior from the punishment for sin. And by pitting a belief in the Torah against a belief in Jesus Christ, he made it seem to the Galatians that those beliefs were mutually exclusive, where in truth they actually were not. The Nazarenes, for example, believed in both Jesus and the Torah, but *their* Jesus, of course, was not the Jesus of Paul. And Paul, in spite of his having told me that in the presence of Jews, he respects the Torah, and in spite of his having prayed from the Torah when James had told him to do that, and in spite of his having said to the Sanhedrin and also to Governor Felix that he followed the Torah like any devoted Jew, now wrote to the Galatians that if a man can achieve righteousness through the Torah, then Jesus Christ has died in vain. For Paul felt strongly that the only thing that could have made Jesus not die in vain was Jesus' immolating death for our sins. That the Nazarenes followed the Torah and that to them Jesus also had not died in vain, but not because he had died for our sins but because his death was a necessary fulfillment of prophecy preceding his return to triumph over pagan oppression, Paul chose not to reveal to the Galatians. He wanted them to think that the acceptance of the Torah constituted a rejection of Jesus and that if acceptance of the Torah was right, then Jesus was irrelevant. By this means, those Galatians who wanted desperately to follow Jesus were led to believe that the only way they *could* follow him was by rejecting the Torah. Paul called them foolish if they did or thought otherwise and then went further and said that those who persisted in trying to follow the Torah were under a curse, because it was written that anyone who did not follow everything in the Torah was cursed, and since no one *could* follow everything in it, those who tried were unavoidably cursed; whereas those who did not try but, instead, had faith that Jesus' death would free them from that curse were blessed and saved and redeemed.

Yes, it is true that we were under a curse if we failed to adhere to the morals that God demanded of us through Moses: how to treat the poor, how to treat our enemies, how to treat our neighbors and our wives and husbands and children, how to deal with adversity and disease and business and trade, how to deal with sex and cleanliness and health and food, how to dress with decency and speak the same, how to organize our society and render justice to each other, how to worship God and walk before Him with humility and obedience. Yes, all those things we had to do or suffer the curse of God's displeasure. Moses had written it, Jesus had said it and James had taught it in our daily gatherings. And now Paul was writing and telling the Galatians how difficult those things were to follow and telling them, too, that God in His mercy was easing the load he had given us and offering us another way to find favor in His eyes. No, it was more than just another way: it was now the *only* way, with the other way now being wrong. But oh, I say from the depths of my soul, how beautiful this world would be if all men and women could adhere to these laws and walk in the shadow of God. And how beautiful, too, if they could love Jesus, our king, our Messiah and our savior too, and prepare for him a world like the Torah to rule over when he returns. The Pharisees had taught me, and I believe it's true, that the *effort* is worth something to God and that men achieve perfection in life as they adhere to the Torah by degrees.

But that was my view. For Paul, it had to be one or the other. And with this letter to the Galatians, his break from the Torah was made complete. But in breaking from the Torah, he also was breaking from Judaism. And in breaking from that, what else could one say of the Christian doctrine other than that it had become a new and separate religion?

I had taught this doctrine in an attenuated form but as a variant form of Judaism. Now that it was to exist as a thing apart from Judaism, I felt more torn and doubt-ridden than ever.

In this same letter, I found the answer to a question the Nazarenes had raised with Paul. Paul had said that Jesus was the only son of God, and this had conflicted with his other statements that we are all the children of God, as he had said, for example, to the Athenian Epicureans and Stoics. He told the Galatians that we were the children of God, but he referred to us as adopted sons. I had heard him say it

265

before, of course: Jesus was the only begotten son of God while the rest of us were adopted.

And with the belief that we were all God's children, Paul said, all differences between us were over. No more Greek or Jew, no more man or woman, but all the same and equal. But elsewhere, he did not say the same about women; elsewhere he did not make them equal but rather subservient to men in general.

He wrote to the Galatians as to children who had misbehaved. Circumcision, he told them, and a full conversion to Judaism would make them ineligible for the salvation and forgiveness of sins that Jesus' death was offering them. If they became Jews, as James' emissaries were suggesting — and those despicable men would have a lot to answer for to God when their time came, and he wished they would mutilate themselves by castration — then they would have to accept the Torah. If they accepted the Torah, then they had to follow every law in it or be damned. But the only law that Christians needed was to love their neighbors as much as they loved themselves.

All this made me feel that Paul hated the Torah. And I wondered if he hated it because of his inability to abide by its restrictions or because his deficient knowledge of it had made Gamaliel reject him as a student. Or was it because the Torah was the foundation of Rabath's religion, the religion that he had entered because of her and the one that constantly reminded him of the woman who had spurned him. But I've spoken of this before, and I still had no answer to it.

He wrote to the Galatians of the flesh and of its various sins: adultery, fornication, lasciviousness, uncleanness, idolatry, witchcraft, hatred, strife, seditions, heresies, envyings, murders, drunkenness, revellings and things of that sort. These were the sins of the flesh. In the face of these sins, salvation could not be achieved by good deeds as listed in the Torah but only through faith — the acceptance of the belief that Jesus' death expiated our sins. Thus again he pitted the one against the other. He wrote that those who urged the Galatians to get circumcised did so only so that they could glory in the flesh, so that they could feel an accomplishment in having gotten others to do what they had done or what had been done to them. And I thought, if that was the reason, then why had Paul circumcised Timotheus? But I, better than anyone, knew the answer to that. It was because when Paul had circumcised Timotheus, he had not yet fully developed his belief that an acceptance of the Torah meant a rejection of Jesus; he had not as yet realized that the followers of the Torah might take away *his* newly won followers. Back then, an acceptance of Jesus' messiahship was all that

266

either of us wanted from anyone. Back then, we saw nothing wrong with a Gentile follower of Jesus becoming a Jew.

But now things had changed. All the Gentiles that Paul had won as Jesus-followers *without* the Torah and *without* the God-fearer laws might now be changed into Jesus-followers *with* the Torah or *with* the God-fearer laws if those imperious emissaries from James had their way. And where would Paul's influence be then? His position as spiritual leader of the Galatians — or of any of the Christian communities for that matter — was being threatened, and he had to become more aggressive to keep them. Since the Nazarene gospel was competing with his own, and since the Nazarene gospel kept the Torah as its guide, he now had to attack the Torah to discredit his competition. He could no longer afford to say that the Torah was an acceptable alternative to salvation through grace, lest Christians turn to the Torah and he lose all the influence he had gained. So he told the Galatians it was either Jesus or the Torah and that choosing one meant a rejection of the other.

Almost as an afterthought, he told them to do good to others, especially to those who believed as they did. He told them to help the poor, as James had instructed him to do. And then he wrote that he was crucified with Jesus and that Jesus lived in him and that, henceforth, no one should trouble him with trivialities because he bore the crucifixion marks of Jesus on his body, implying that that singled him out for important matters and not just trivial ones. Those marks — he had shown them to me in Jerusalem — he wore like a badge of distinction. They set him apart from everyone else, even James and Peter and John, and gave him an importance that no one else could have.

I was still in Jerusalem at this time, and when news of this letter came to me, I knew there could be no more compromise. I had stood with one foot as a Christian and the other as a Nazarene Jew, and now I could no longer do that. I prayed to God for guidance, and I looked for an answer or a sign.

Paul wrote to other communities. In a second letter to the Corinthians, he called them his children and expressed to them the same fear he had expressed to the Galatians: that just as the serpent had beguiled Eve, they, the Corinthians, might be beguiled into believing another gospel by false apostles, deceitful workers, men who appeared righteous on the surface but who really were ministers of Satan. He called his own gospel the gospel of God. And if any detractors claimed to be more authoritative than Paul, he asked on what basis. Were they Hebrews? So was he. Were they Israelites? So was he. Had they suffered more than he? No, he had suffered more. He had more stripes from beatings than they; he had received thirty-nine lashes from "the Jews" on five occasions and had been beaten with rods three times and stoned once and shipwrecked thrice and spent a night and a day floating on the sea. He had journeyed through all kinds of perils, and among these were the perils of false brothers.

It was interesting to me that he did not mention one of the worst beatings of all, the one he had received from the Gentiles at Philippi. He spoke only of the beatings from "the Jews", implying by the use of the word, "the", that this was from all the Jews as a group. But he did not mention the Gentiles as a group and recount what *they* had done to him; he did not mention them at all. He did not mention his stripping and beating and imprisonment from the Gentiles at Philippi or the affair of the silversmiths at Ephesus. Was he trying to create an anti-Jewish sentiment among the Corinthians? Was it a way of fortifying the belief in his gospel to make all Jews seem bad, so that the itinerant Jews who disputed his gospel would be disdained before they spoke?

And when he wrote to the Corinthians about false brothers, I knew that he meant the Nazarenes, who themselves were saying that *he* was false.

He said with pride to the Corinthians that he had preached to them without asking for money, that he had earned his living at his usual trade without bothering them about his needs. But then he said that he had taken funds contributed by others and had used that money to feed himself while he was teaching the gospel to them. "I robbed other churches," he said to them, "taking wages from them that I might minister to you," and later, "...the brothers, when they came from Macedonia, supplied the measure of my want," the money having come from other Christian communities.

It was interesting to me that he would say that to them, because in his farewell speech to the Ephesian elders, he told them that he had wanted no man's silver or gold or clothing and that he had worked for his daily needs with his own hands (just as the sages in the synagogues did who never earned their livelihoods by teaching). But then, as if he resented having had to do that, he had asked the Corinthians in his first letter to them, "Do we not have the right to our food and drink? Do we not have the right to be accompanied by a wife, as the other apostles and the brothers of the Lord and Peter? Or is it only Barnabas and I who have no right to refrain from working for a living?" And then later he had said to them, "If we have sown spiritual good among you, is it too much if we reap your material benefits? If others share this rightful claim upon you, do we not still more?" And later still he had said, "...the Lord commanded that those who proclaim the gospel should get their living by the gospel." Thus having established his *right* to ask them for money, he had said that he would not do so. He had written to the Corinthians in that first letter to them, "...in my preaching I make the gospel free of charge, not making full use of my right in the gospel." So in that first letter, he had made it clear that he was not asking them for money (just as he had told the Ephesian elders he was not asking it of them and just as, as he was to tell me later, he had not asked it of the Thessalonians). But now in this second letter to the Corinthians, he said that though he was still not asking them for money, he had gotten money from other Christian communities and had not earned it with the labor of his hands. So while he was not exerting his "right" to ask for money (from either the Ephesians or the Corinthians or the Thessalonians), he *was* getting it from other Christians to help him give the gospel to the Corinthians "free of charge". But Paul's claim that he had the right to ask for money if he wished was not in accordance with what Jesus had taught, for Jesus, I knew, had said to his disciples, "You received without pay, give without pay," and in that had been true to the Pharisee sages who took no money for their teachings.

For myself, I think that Paul was right. It would have been unreasonable to expect him to spend so much time traveling and preaching and not to be given sustenance while he was doing it. I think that Jesus may not have realized how much time his followers would be spending on teaching when he told them to give without pay. James and Peter and John and I — all the apostles — received contributions. The precedent had been set by James, so I believe that Paul was right.

In telling the Corinthians about the things he had suffered, he mentioned how King Aretus' governor in Damascus had had soldiers out looking for him and how he had had to escape through a window and through being let down the side of the city wall in a basket.

The point of all this was that *his* tribulations, being greater than those of his detractors, established *his* claims as superior.

There came into my possession now a carefully copied letter from Paul to Timotheus. You must understand that, in spite of my disagreements with Paul, I was still a Christian of sorts and, as such, was privy to information in the Christian communities.

In his letter, he wrote to Timotheus as to a son and expressed his fear of another gospel, just as he had done to the Galatians. He said that he had given to the Devil two of his former disciples who had turned to this other gospel, and he called the gospel a godless and silly myth. Yet, in spite of that, some Christians, he predicted, would follow those doctrines of demons in the future. I had heard that he was using names like that to label Peter's gospel, that he had once called it the doctrine of the Devil and said that those who taught it were liars; that he had told his followers to look out for such dogs and evil-workers and mutilators of the flesh and had said that such people were enemies of the cross of Christ. Yes, I had heard that he was saying that, and I saw in it his gradual transition of thinking about Jews and the Torah and the gospel. What had started out as a mild disagreement had developed now into a war. It was a war being fought without swords or spears; it was a war of words. And the words were of concepts and cherished beliefs and were used to praise or disparage or extol or curse, depending on which side you were on.

He told Timotheus, also, not to bother with lengthy genealogies in regard to Jesus, since that might lead to questions and controversies about their accuracy. (Peter, at that meeting in Jerusalem, had cited Jesus' lineage back to King David and even back to Abraham.) At first I did not know why Paul was saying that, since the Messiah was supposed to come from King David, and if we showed Jesus' lineage back to King David, that would support our claim that Jesus was the Messiah. Paul recommended *faith* in who Jesus was rather than genealogy. Later, of course, I realized again it was because of Jesus' father and whether it was Joseph or God. And later, too, I was to learn that Paul would tell Timotheus in no uncertain terms that Jesus was descended from King David. Was faith, then, superior to genealogy in proving that simple fact? And who was Paul saying that Jesus' father was? If he said that Jesus came from David and accepted that on faith, was he still discounting Joseph as Jesus' father? And if he was, then was he thinking that Jesus' mother was descended from David? Or were we not even to think about that but simply to state the conclusion and not know why?

Paul reminded Timotheus that Jesus had come into the world to save sinners (in contrast to Peter's and James' and the first disciples' belief that he had come to establish his kingdom in place of the Romans), and he said that he, Paul, was the greatest sinner of them all. Again, I say that he was too hard on himself. There had been far worse sinners than he, and Pontius Pilate and some of the other procurators come immediately to mind when I think of that. But now, because we were sinners, an intermediary was necessary to sit between man and God, to plead for man to God as it were, and the person who did that was Jesus.

He wrote to Timotheus about women. They were to dress modestly, he said. They were not to embroider their hair or adorn themselves with gold or pearls or wear expensive dresses. They were not to teach; they were to remain silent. They were not to overstep their subservient positions to men. He would permit no woman to have authority over men. And I could see him trying to put Rabath into that mold. And I could see that he did not consider them one and the same with men, as he had said they were in his letter to the Galatians.

Then I saw his letter to Titus, another disciple whom he called his son. He told him, as he had told Timotheus, to avoid genealogies and also questions about the law. And he warned him, too, about the other gospel. Those who taught circumcision were unruly and vain and deceivers and taught falsely in order to get money, and their mouths ought to be stopped! The other gospel was a Jewish fable, and the Torah contained only the commandments of angels, not of God. Those who did not believe *his* gospel were corrupted; they claimed to know God, but they were detestable.

I noticed that he had not disparaged circumcision to Timotheus as he was now doing to Titus, but *that*, I knew, was because he had circumcised Timotheus. As I have said, I think when he did that, he had not realized how much influence he was going to gain *without* his disciples being circumcised. He certainly had not realized that the Torah, which *demanded* circumcision, would become the nemesis of his Christian belief. But he realized it now and proceeded to act against it, as James, seeing the threat to *his* belief, was proceeding to act *for* it.

CHAPTER XXX

About a year before the end of Felix's procuratorship, Ananias stepped down as high priest. His influence was getting too great, and Agrippa replaced him with Ishmael. Then the Sicarii did something that had never been done before: they killed the former high priest, Jonathan, by cutting his throat. Jonathan, you may recall, was high priest when Vitellius, the legate of Syria, came on his three-day goodwill visit to Jerusalem in the days when the Romans were invading Nabataea. And you may recall that Vitellius deposed Jonathan and appointed his brother, Theophilus, in his place, just to remind us that Rome was still our master. It happened just when the emperor, Tiberius, had died and Gaius Caligula had taken his place. And you also may recall that Jonathan showed a degree of humility not common among chief priests when he declined to accept the high priesthood for a second time when Agrippa needed a replacement for Simon Kantheras. While it was true that the people hated our chief priests and the Sadducee party because that group collaborated with the Romans and had contributed to the death of some of our revolutionary leaders, not the least of whom had been Jesus, still it also was true that no one had ever carried the hatred of the chief priests to such an extreme.

There was a rumor that Felix had been so irked by Jonathan's admonitions that he rule justly that he had bribed Jonathan's friend, Doras, to get the Sicarii to kill him. But that rumor had no basis in fact and was started, I think, by the Sadducees to make the Sicarii look like nothing more than assassins for hire instead of the religious patriots they were.

But now Ishmael, as I have said, replaced Ananias as the high priest. But while Ishmael held the post, everyone knew that Ananias wielded the power. Ananias was a very wealthy man, and to get his way, he bribed Felix with one hand and Ishmael with the other. He was a power to be reckoned with in Jerusalem at this time.

But Felix seemed too preoccupied to care who wielded the priestly power as long as he got his money. As he began to approach the end of his eighth year as governor, the conditions he had to contend with grew even worse. He previously had suppressed a revolutionary movement led by the Egyptian who had taken the Sicarii to the Mount

273

of Olives. But now the activities of the Zealot and Sicarii raiders were increasing, and Felix could not predict where they would strike next.

Then trouble broke out in Caesarea, with fighting between the Jews and Syrian Greeks who lived there. The Jews claimed that the city was theirs, since it had been built by the Jewish king, Herod the Great, in the time of Caesar Augustus. But while the Greeks acknowledged that the founder had been a Jew, they said that the city belonged to them, since Herod obviously had meant it for them by virtue of his having built statues and temples in it. The city — white stone buildings; polished stone houses around a wide, bustling harbor; the king's costly palace, with its Roman columns and central pool ensconced on a promontory next to the sea; a theater of stone and a capacious, circular amphitheater looking out upon the cargo-laden ships; and the temple dedicated to Caesar, the fawning symbol of Jewish defeat and compliance with the wishes of Rome — stood as a living testimony to the incompatibility between any two religious groups unless one is dominant and the other acknowledges it.

Arguments and battles ensued. The Jews could have prevailed easily over the Greeks, since the Jews were the better fighters and were better equipped, but the Roman soldiers, most of whom had been raised in Caesarea and who were pagans like the Syrian Greeks, sided with the Greeks and helped them. Felix himself sided with the Greeks, but his whippings and imprisonments of dissident Jews did not stop the Jews from fighting. On one particular day when the Jews won a ferocious battle, Felix stood up and ordered them to pull back, with the threat that he would have them killed if they didn't. But the Jews refused to give up what they had fought so hard to gain, so he sent in soldiers, and they killed many Jews. And then the soldiers plundered where they could. But even that did not stop our people, for now they fought with even greater determination than before. Felix could see that the Roman army was not going to stop the Jews of Caesarea, so, in his frustration, he chose leaders from among the Jews and the Greeks and sent them all to Rome to present their arguments to Nero.

Then, at about this time, which was two years after Felix took custody of Paul, Nero replaced Felix with Porcius Festus. When Felix told Drusilla about this, his face was drawn and despondent. "My term of office is being ended," he said. "I've been ordered to return to Rome." Drusilla looked at him, and because she did not speak, he felt obliged to explain further. "It's because of the situation here in Caesarea. Nero doesn't think I can handle it. I've tried to keep your people in check, but they're impossible to control. So I sent that delegation of Jews and Greeks to Nero — you know the one — to let *him* make the decision about who owns this city. Well, it seems that that was a mistake. Apparently, your Jewish countrymen have convinced him that I did something wrong. And, besides, our emperor doesn't like being disturbed by what he considers minor affairs like this. He expects his procurators to handle things like this for him. So, because he's being forced to listen to arguments from both sides in this affair, he punishes me for having disturbed him by removing me from office. Apparently, he was going to do worse than that, but my brother, Pallas, is one of his favorites, and he talked him out of doing anything more."

"Why are you so sad?" Drusilla asked. "Don't you realize how wonderful this is?"

"Wonderful?" he exclaimed, totally surprised by her response.

"Of course it's wonderful, you silly man. We're going to live in Rome."

"But I'll have no authority there, no soldiers under me."

"What's the difference? We have enough money to live well, and we can spend more time with each other. Oh Felix, I've always dreamed of living in Rome. This is a time to be happy."

Felix saw his transfer in a completely different light by the time Drusilla got through with him, and he began to think of this relocation to Rome as a step towards a better life.

For Paul, the immediate consequence of this change in procurators was that he no longer had to pay money for his safety. But as Felix left office, he put Paul into prison. He had him bound like any ordinary prisoner and had him delivered to Festus like that. Then Festus, after only three days residence in his chambers in Caesarea, traveled to Jerusalem to see his garrison there. Ananias, whose pride and reputation were still smarting from Paul's elusiveness two years before, saw an opportunity to get this new procurator to do what the previous one had not. He organized a delegation, with Caiaphas and the high priest, Ishmael, and some of the other chief priests as a part of it, to approach Festus about Paul. They brought the same charges against him that they had brought two years earlier, only this time they added that Paul's belief that the crucified Jesus of Nazareth was alive was also a crime. They asked Festus to bring Paul back to Jerusalem to stand trial before them there. But Festus had read the report about Paul. He knew of the old plot by the Asiatic Jews to waylay him on the road between Jerusalem and Caesarea, and he knew of the plot to assassinate Paul during an interrogation by the high priest. He suspected that such plots might still be in existence, so he refused to grant Ananias' request. He suggested, instead, that the chief priests come to Caesarea to bring their charges against Paul. Then, after almost two weeks in Jerusalem, he left to return to Caesarea. The chief priests now went there too.

Festus had Paul brought to the hearing room and had the chief priests come there as well. They made their malevolent accusations just as they had to Felix, and Paul answered them by saying that he done nothing offensive to the Torah or the Temple or the emperor. But Festus, being new to his job and not knowing whom he should favor for his own advantage, thought it best not to be as chaffing towards the chief priests as Felix had been. Under their prodding to have Paul stand trial in Jerusalem, he went so far as to ask Paul if he would be willing to do that, the threat of an assassination apparently being no longer a consideration in his mind. The reason he *asked* Paul rather than ordering him was because Paul was a Roman citizen and, as such, deserved certain privileges.

To Paul, a return to Jerusalem was tantamount to turning him over to the chief priests for execution. This time they would find a way to prevent the Pharisees from saving him.

"When I stand before you," Paul said to Festus, "I stand before Caesar's judgment seat, which is where I ought to be judged. You know I haven't done anything against the Jews. If I have done anything worthy of death, then I refuse not to be executed. But if I haven't done any of the things they're accusing me of, then I shouldn't be turned over to them. I'm a Roman citizen! I appeal to Caesar!"

Festus, upon hearing this, conferred with the chief priests and then turned to Paul and said, "You've appealed to Caesar? Then to Caesar you will go."

The chief priests left, and Paul's fate was in the hands of the Romans now. But Paul was aware, as all this occurred, that by exercising his right to appeal directly to Nero, he was doing what Jesus had told him to do in the vision that night after the Sanhedrin meeting, when Jesus had said that Paul must now go to Rome to preach his gospel there.

Felix and Drusilla, meanwhile, left for Rome. Their departure utterly delighted Bernice. Though Bernice had long since ceased to think of her sister as a rival for her brother's interest, the old hostility still remained like a dormant disease that erupts in bad weather. Her ostensible reason for not responding to Drusilla's and Felix's invitations was that Drusilla's and Felix's marriage was an affront and a sacrilege and an embarrassment to the family. One does not visit and dine with sinners! She said this openly to all who might ask her, thinking that her own sin with Agrippa was a well-kept secret. Her real reason for not accepting these invitations, of course, was because of her rivalry with Drusilla. Drusilla's transgression with Felix had merely provided a convenient excuse.

But now that Drusilla and Felix were gone, it seemed only proper for the king and his sister to pay their respects to the new procurator. So when Festus sent them an invitation to visit him in Caesarea, they readily accepted. Laden with gifts and attended by soldiers and servants, they made the trip to see him.

A few days later, Agrippa and Bernice, arrived in Caesarea. Festus entertained them grandly, and they talked at length about the increasing unrest in the country. Then Festus mentioned his prisoner, Paul, and that Felix had delivered him in chains when he had left office, after having allowed him to be a prisoner without chains and with freedom to travel the city for the two years preceding that.

"When I went to Jerusalem," Festus said to his royal visitors, "the chief priests wanted me to find this man guilty of some crimes worthy of death. But I told them it was not customary for Romans to execute someone without letting that person face his accusers and answer the charges against him."

That claim was far from the truth, of course, although Festus may have been unknowledgeable enough to believe it. Pontius Pilate had earned his reputation as the great crucifier because of all the people he had killed without trials. So bad had he been that even Agrippa's father, Agrippa I, had had to write to Gaius Caligula complaining about him. And, also, other Roman governors had slaughtered the innocent without giving them even a chance to speak. So Festus could make his noble statement about Roman fairness if he wished to, but history, if told as it actually happened, showed a much different picture than that.

"And I could not grant their request that I bring this Paul to Jerusalem, because two years ago there was a plot to assassinate him on the road and another plot to assassinate him during an interrogation. I was concerned that those plots might still exist. So I had the chief priests make their accusations here in Caesarea. Well, they made them, and this Paul denied them, and then they pressed me to make him stand trial in Jerusalem. So I asked him if he would do that, and he said that rather than subject himself to that, he would appeal for a hearing with Nero. I granted it. The man's a Roman citizen, and he's entitled to such an appeal."

"I'd like to meet the man myself," Agrippa said.

"I'll arrange for it tomorrow," Festus answered.

Then Bernice asked, "Why did Felix keep him in custody for two years without rendering any verdict?"

To that Festus could offer only the rumor of continued extortion.

"And if Felix let him roam the city for two years, why did he bind him and imprison him just before he delivered him to you?" she went on.

"At first," said Festus, "one of my centurions thought it was to please the Sadducees who live here. But I said that if that's what he wanted to do, why hadn't he done it two years earlier when he first took this Paul into custody?"

"Maybe because now he wasn't going to be getting any more money from the man, and he felt that he no longer had to indulge him," Bernice suggested. "Or maybe it was because he wanted to impress *you*."

"Impress *me*? How would that impress *me*?"

"By showing you that he wasn't soft on prisoners and maybe to counteract the rumor that he was being lenient because of the money he was getting."

Agrippa then told Festus how much their family despised Felix. He said that Felix was a common freeman, a lowborn soldier turned procurator, who had seduced their sister, Drusilla, away from her husband, so that she had married Felix in violation of Jewish ancestral law.

"The two of them blackened our family's name," Bernice said.

And Agrippa explained that their family's position and good reputation had been hard won; that when Tiberius had been emperor, he had resented their father's friendship with Gaius Caligula and had imprisoned their father for that; but that when Caligula had become emperor, he had released their father and had rewarded him with land; and that when Claudius had become emperor, he had rewarded their father's loyalty to him with additional land — all of Judaea, in fact — so that their father's domain had become as great as Herod the Great's had been. Their father's renown had increased with his land, but he had worked hard to achieve it. And their father had had a reputation for piety too, being very respectful of Jewish ancestral law.

"I myself don't care for religion much," Agrippa said, "but my father did, and our people respected him for it. His reputation among our people was very high."

What he did not say to Festus was that many people had *not* respected their father, because their father had executed James, the son of Zebedee, and had tried to execute Peter after that and had executed Peter's guards after Peter's escape. But that disrespect had been on political grounds, their father being close to the Romans. In the religious sphere, some of the people thought that he had been a staunch Sadducee, a strict adherent to the law, and for that they had respected him; still not so strict an adherent, it seems, that he did not succumb to some of the Roman influence by having statues made of his daughters and placed in his palace in Caesarea, and not so strict an adherent that he did not check himself from smiling delightedly when some of his lackeys called him a god. And while it was true that Drusilla, with her one abandoned transgression, had made those people think less of their family, at least where religion was concerned, the whispered rumors about Agrippa and Bernice were not helping matters either; their incestuous affair was becoming more known. But Bernice avoided bringing that up, for it would have made Drusilla appear less culpable.

Apologetically, Festus commiserated with them over their father's tribulation from the emperor, Tiberius, who had imprisoned him. But that was how Tiberius treated everyone, Festus explained: he executed people just for murmuring about him, and when he died, there was jubilation in the streets of Rome. Then, in at least a perfunctory defense of Felix's record, something that Festus must have felt he had to do for a fellow Roman procurator, Festus reminded them that Felix had done *some* good things: he had captured the Zealot leader, Eleazar, and had crucified many of the Zealots and ordinary people who followed that man and had sent Eleazar in chains to Claudius in Rome; he had stopped the insurrection of the Egyptian who had led the Sicarii to the Mount of Olives with the promise that the city's walls would crumble at his command, after which they could slaughter the Roman garrison.

"But didn't he have our former high priest, Jonathan, assassinated by some of those very same Sicarii?" Bernice asked assertively, anxious to find fault with the husband of her sister.

"That is a rumor I heard when I first took office," Festus said, "but we've never had proof of that, your highness. In any event, whatever you feel you've lost as a result of Felix's presence here in Judaea has surely been compensated by the friendship you've enjoyed from our emperors in Rome."

"I'm afraid that's not so, governor," Agrippa said with a tone of bitterness in his voice. "My father ruled all of Galilee and Judaea; now *you* rule most of that. Claudius took it all away from me when my father died. I was too young and inexperienced, he said. He gave me only minor provinces to rule. He sent Cupius Fadus to be procurator, and I'll admit that Fadus did a decent job of putting down revolts along the borders. And then came Tiberius Alexander, one of our own — a Jew even though he had renounced Judaism — and he did well when he crucified Simon and Jacob, two of the sons of Judas of Galilee. But then — then came Cumanus, and that man was a catastrophe. One of his soldiers made an obscene gesture to a crowd of our people who were gathering to worship. The crowd rioted, Cumanus sent in troops, and the troops killed thousands of our people. So much for establishing good relations between Romans and Jews! And one day when an imperial servant was attacked by some robbers on the road to Beth-horon, Cumanus decided to punish all the local inhabitants for it. One of his over-zealous soldiers burned a copy of the Torah, and the people got so outraged that Cumanus had to execute the soldier to appease them. All that was unnecessary. A Jewish king would have known how to handle his people better than that. Nero, I must say, gave me more than Claudius did, but Judaea still belongs to you."

Festus could see that Agrippa had seized this opportunity to complain about his personal disappointment, and he could see that it was a sensitive topic with him.

Diplomatically, he said, "*I* will certainly consult with you on matters like that, your majesty. Your knowledge of your people would be invaluable to me. That's why I wanted your opinion about this Paul of Tarsus."

Such words gladdened Agrippa's heart. Here was a procurator who knew how to treat him like more than a figurehead.

And Festus was true to his promise. The next day, with much pomp and ceremony, Agrippa and Bernice entered the hearing room in the presence of Roman captains and the leading citizens of the city. Festus sent for Paul, and once Paul was present, Festus announced that this man had been accused of capital crimes by the chief priests but that he, Festus, had found no guilt in him. All that, though, was not germane, said Festus, because the man had appealed for a hearing with the emperor.

"But I don't know what to write to the emperor when I send the man," Festus said to Agrippa. "What crimes am I to say he's charged with? I don't really understand the religious charges, and I haven't found that he's done anything seditious. What am I to say he's charged with?"

Agrippa looked at Paul. He was not unaware that this man came from the same sect as James, the son of Zebedee, the violent revolutionary orator whom his father had had to execute, and the same sect as the man called Peter, whom his father had *almost* executed because the man was spreading stories about a new king, a resurrected Messiah, taking over the country. But he also knew that some members of that sect were moderate, that they prayed quietly for this phantom king and waited patiently for the appearance that the man obviously was never going to make. If this man was one of those harmless types, then he posed no danger to the kingdom.

Agrippa said, "You have our permission to speak for yourself, Paul of Tarsus. What do you have to say to these charges?"

Paul stretched out his hands so that Agrippa could see that they were bound. "Your majesty," he said, "I am happy that I am permitted to speak before you this day and to answer the charges that the chief priests and the Sadducees have brought against me. I know that you are knowledgeable about our Jewish customs and laws, and so I ask you to hear me patiently. Everyone knows how I've lived my life from the time I was a youth here in my own nation at Jerusalem." (But Paul, I knew, had been raised in Tarsus.) "And they know, if they would just tell the truth about it, that I lived in the strictest manner required of a Pharisee." (Except when he worked for the high priest, of course, because then he had become a Sadducee, high priests not hiring Pharisees to do their police work for them.) "And like a Pharisee, and like all Jews, I believe in the promise that God made to our people long ago — the promise for which we hope and for which the twelve tribes of our people work day and night to serve God. It is because of my hope for that promise that I was accused of wrongdoing."

"Because of your hope?" Agrippa said. "Surely not just that alone. Especially if, as you say, it's the same hope that everyone else has."

Paul ignored that question and went on with a question of his own. "King Agrippa, why should you think it so incredible that God should raise the dead?"

Agrippa answered, "I haven't said anything about that. I haven't said anything about the subject of raising the dead — whether I believe it or don't believe it. "

"King Agrippa," Paul said, "do you know the name, Jesus of Nazareth?"

"Yes, his name is familiar to me," Agrippa said.

"Well," said Paul, "we who follow him believe that he was resurrected, that God brought him back to life after he had died physically."

"I've heard that," Agrippa said.

"I used to work for Caiaphas when he was high priest, and, under his direction, I used to persecute the people who believed that. I used to hunt them down and force them to renounce their belief; I beat them; I imprisoned them, and I even supported the on-the-spot-execution of one of them. I hunted them down in other cities — cities in which I had never been before.

"Then one day, I was on the road to Damascus, on my way to find some of the militant members of this group, when I was stopped by a light more radiant than the sun. It was all around me and all around the men who were with me. We all fell down, and I heard this voice say to me in Hebrew, 'Saul, Saul, why are you persecuting me?' And I said, 'Who are you, lord?' And it said, 'I am Jesus, whom you are persecuting.' And then it said, 'But stand on your feet. I have appeared to you in this way in order to make you a minister and a witness to what you have seen today and a witness to those times when I will appear to you in the future. I am going to protect you from all people who might threaten you, whether it be Jew or Gentile, so that I can send you among people to open their eyes, to turn them from darkness to light, from Satan's power to God, so that they can receive forgiveness for their sins and the inheritance that is due to all those who are sanctified by faith in me.' And I was not disobedient to that heavenly mission, King Agrippa. I spoke to Jews in Damascus and Jerusalem and all along the coasts of Judaea; and then I spoke to Gentiles and urged them to repent their sins and to turn to God and to do the things that are proper for repentance." His voice rose and became impassioned. "That's why those Jews from Asia accosted me at the Temple and tried to kill me. But I had God's help to save me, and because of it, I continue to this day bearing witness to everyone, great or small, to the things that I have seen, and saying no other things than what the prophets and Moses said would happen." His voice now reached a high-pitched intensity. "And by that I mean that Christ should suffer and that he would be the first to rise from the dead and to show light to our people and to the Gentiles."

Festus could see the state of feverish agitation that Paul had reached, and he restrained him by shouting, "Paul, you're getting carried away. All this learning and knowledge you have is making you mad. Control yourself."

Paul calmed down and said, "Most noble Festus, I am not mad. I speak words of truth and soberness. I am sure the king knows about these things that I have related to him so freely. These things have not been hidden from him. They are not the kinds of things that are done in a corner." Then he turned to Agrippa and said, "King Agrippa, do you believe in the prophets?"

"Yes, I believe in the prophets," Agrippa said, "and you are right that I know at least something about what goes on these days. And because

I do know something, I have to ask you, first, about this prediction of Moses and the prophets you just mentioned: that Christ would be the first to rise from the dead. Just who is this Christ person?"

"Jesus, your majesty," Paul answered. "Jesus is the Christ."

"Oh, I didn't understand that," Agrippa said. "He has two names then?"

"Christ is a Greek term, your majesty," Paul said. "It's something like Messiah in our language."

"Oh, I see," Agrippa said. "Well, I'll get back to that in a moment. But first let me ask you, did Moses really make this prediction you're referring to — that Christ would be the first to rise from the dead?"

"He did, your majesty," Paul answered.

"I was not aware of that," said Agrippa. "But you're more learned in the Torah than I, I'm sure. But wasn't there a man named Lazarus who was brought back to life by Jesus?"

"Yes, your majesty, that's true," said Paul.

"And didn't this Jesus of yours also make a dead child and also a young man from Nain come back to life?"

"Yes, your majesty. The most trustworthy people have reported it."

"Well, if all those people came back to life *before* Jesus, then Jesus wasn't the first to whom it happened, was he? And if he wasn't the first, then one of those others — whichever *was* first — should be called by this Christ name from the prophecy. Isn't that right?"

"No, your majesty," Paul answered, "Jesus was the one whom Moses and the prophets were talking about."

"Well, then somebody wrote it down wrong," Agrippa said, "and I think you should get it corrected. But now let me ask you: Nazarenes are said to believe in a new kingdom that will be formed when this Jesus of yours returns. Nazarenes are said to have Zealots among them. Now surely you can understand that beliefs like that — about a new kingdom — and people like that — Zealots I mean — make people like me — and like Governor Festus here — a little uncomfortable. You can understand that, can't you?"

"Yes, of course I can, your majesty," Paul said.

"And you can understand that we are duty-bound to resist any new kingdoms that might upset the present government."

"Of course, your majesty," Paul answered. "But the kingdom that *we're* talking about is not a kingdom of this earth. It's a heavenly kingdom — a kingdom of God."

"Well, we must all submit to *that* kingdom, of course. But if it's not a kingdom on this earth, then why must this Jesus return to establish it?

283

If it's a heavenly kingdom, why doesn't he just stay in heaven to rule over it?"

"We believe that the heavenly kingdom will be brought to us here on earth," Paul said, "that God's will will be done on this earth just as it's done in heaven. You will not cease to be king and Governor Festus will not cease to be procurator when that happens. It's just that a new spirit of brotherhood and love will pervade everyone. That's what we mean by a new kingdom."

This, of course, is not what Nazarenes believed. Nazarenes believed that the new kingdom would be one without the Romans and one in which the Herodians would be out of power. Paul himself had said as much in his first letter to the Corinthians, when he wrote that Jesus would destroy every rule and power and authority before he delivered the kingdom to God. I could only conjecture that Paul was saying what he was saying in order to circumvent a charge of sedition, a means of taking from the Romans a reason for their suppression of Jesus' followers.

"It's a relief to hear that your Jesus doesn't want to overthrow us," Agrippa said. "My father thought your movement threatened his position, and he executed one of your Nazarenes — a man named James, the son of Zebedee — because of it. The man was an original follower of your Jesus, I think. He and his brother, John, were notorious for their violent tempers. 'The Sons of Thunder' my father told me they were called. Well, one of them is not thundering down here anymore. But my father wasn't the only one who believed that you Nazarenes want a kingdom to replace ours. A lot of others believed it and still do."

"I know that, your majesty, but they are wrong," Paul said. "Many of us who follow Jesus understand his mission in the way I have just described it. Those of us who do understand it that way call ourselves Christians."

"Well," Agrippa said, "you're a very convincing speaker. The kind of ideal world you describe is very beautiful. You almost make *me* want to become a Christian."

"Oh, King Agrippa," Paul said, "I wish that everyone who is here listening to me today could be in the same state that I am in." Now he held out his hands again. "Except for these bonds, of course."

Agrippa had heard enough, he said. He had the guards take Paul away. Then he said to Festus that while the man had some strange religious beliefs, he did not appear to be seditious.

"Why not let him go?" Agrippa asked. "Is it because he appealed to Rome and because you have no choice but to send him there once such an appeal is made?"

"*That*," said Festus, "and something else too." The other reason was Ananias and Caiaphas. Those influential priests appeared to have some unusual interest in the man, and releasing Paul outright might turn them both against him. Knowing Ananias' capacity for conspiracy, Festus did not need the additional trouble.

As for the charge with which they would send Paul to Rome, one of the leading citizens who was present said that, in his opinion, they had to create one and that the most appropriate charge would be sedition. And as for sending Paul to Rome rather than letting him go free, if Festus found him innocent, Ananias might complain to the emperor, but if the emperor found him innocent, Ananias could not blame Festus for that. So sending him to Rome on a charge of sedition seemed the best thing to do with Paul.

With that having been decided, the meeting came to an end. Polite goodbyes were said by all, and they went their separate ways. Except for Bernice and Agrippa, that is, for the two of them left together. In the hallway, when they found themselves alone, she spoke to him but not about what had just taken place. She had something else on her mind.

"The people are talking," she said. "They're talking about *us*."

"Let them talk," Agrippa said. "They know nothing, nothing at all."

"The servants talk," Bernice persisted. "We can't afford to have another scandal in our family. One is enough."

He looked at her intensely. "All the talk in the world isn't going to stop me from loving you," he said.

"I have to leave you," she pleaded. "I have to leave for the sake of our family's reputation."

"And go where?" Agrippa asked.

"I've made an arrangement with Polemo, the king of Cilicia. He's agreed to marry me. And he'll get circumcised and make himself a Jew."

"He's agreed to marry your money. That's what he's agreed to do," Agrippa muttered grumpily. He could not allow the obscenity of his sister sleeping with another man to pass unscathed by detraction.

She smiled at him. "Don't you think he might find me attractive?" she asked, tossing her hair with a turn of her head. It was a smile of self-assurance, a certainty about herself. After two ardent husbands and a lover, she knew her power over men.

Agrippa took a long look at his sister's face. "He'd be a fool if he didn't find you beautiful," he said.

He took her into his arms, not caring if anyone saw them, and she bent to him limply and offered him no resistance. He kissed her full on her lips. "I'll come to you tonight," he said.

She hesitated only a moment and then sighed resignedly. "All right," she whispered. "Tonight."

She had no thought about the fact that she was breaking Mosaic law in this affair she was having with her brother. She had sneered at her younger sister for violating that law, and yet she was turning from it herself with her brother. She felt helpless to resist, however. She loved Agrippa, and she felt that God would forgive her because of that. And Agrippa, who cared nothing for the Torah, gave of himself that night as he had never given before, hoping to sway her from her resolve to leave him for someone else.

She stayed until dawn. He was asleep by then. With the first faint glow of morning light, she slipped from the bed and dressed. She gave him a lingering look, as if kissing him from afar, and then left and went to Cilicia.

CHAPTER XXXI

After they sent Paul to Rome, Agrippa decided to build a dining room extension onto his palace in Jerusalem. But the site of that structure was highly controversial, since it would overlook the Temple and allow Agrippa to see some of the activities going on inside. The chief priests countered this by building a wall to block Agrippa's view. The wall, however, also blocked the view of the Roman guards who kept watch on the Temple during festivals. So Festus ordered the chief priests to take down the wall. The chief priests refused to do this on religious grounds and asked leave to explain this to Nero. The people too, on this one occasion, agreed with the chief priests and grumbled with dissatisfaction about Agrippa. Agrippa, in the meantime, stood his ground and refused to change the location of the new structure. It was apparent that while he sometimes made token gestures towards being a Jew, he really didn't care much about his ancestral religion. The insult of putting his eating place where it would look down on the Temple meant nothing to him at all. I strongly suspect that his wretchedness over Bernice's departure was a factor in all this too. She had left because of the gossip of his uncompromising people, and I think he may have wanted to hurt us in return. The fact that he was causing discontent and sowing the seeds of revolution over this affair did not seem to concern him at all. He was a king, and a king could do what he liked. As the controversy grew more intense and the objections more trenchant and numerous, Agrippa stood firm as a rock, impervious to advice or threats. He would not change his plan in order to placate the people. He was a king! A king could do what he wished.

So the high priest, Ishmael, and some of the chief priests pleaded their case before Nero. The empress, Poppaea, sympathetic towards the Jewish religion, intervened on the chief priests' behalf, and Nero allowed the new Temple wall to remain. Poppaea kept Ishmael and the chief priest, Helcias, as hostages, however, while allowing the other chief priests to go home.

The rapport with the people that Agrippa had claimed he had when he had talked to Festus at Paul's interview seemed as ephemeral now as the shape of a cloud, if it ever had existed at all. Though it would not be true to say that the people *hated* their king — not the way they hated the chief priests and the Romans — it would still be correct to say that they disliked him. His contempt for his religion — or at least his indifference to it — did not endear him to a people whose entire lives were devoted to God.

He learned at this point about Ishmael being kept in Rome, so he changed high priests again. He deposed Ishmael, whom he had appointed two years earlier, and put in his place Joseph Cabi, the son of Simon.

Then, in that same year, Agrippa's good fortune came back — at least in his eyes it did. Bernice, unenamored of her husband, King Polemo, and missing the presence of her brother, said farewell to Cilicia and joined Agrippa again. Polemo was outraged at this. It meant the loss not only of Bernice but of her sizeable fortune. He had undergone circumcision for her and had made himself into a Jew! Now he had to face the realization that she had used him deceptively. In resentment, he turned from his newly adopted religion and spoke against it wherever he could. Because of what had happened to Paul with Rabath, I had wondered if a man who accepts another religion for a woman might later hate that religion if the woman rejects him. In Polemo I saw that it could. Here were Paul and Polemo each getting circumcised and the women for whom they had done it turning from them. If this could make Polemo hate Judaism, why could it not do it to Paul? I could more easily believe that Paul's hatred of Jews was partly because of Rabath, since I saw that Polemo's reason was entirely because of Bernice.

When Bernice came to the palace in Jerusalem, attendants led her to her apartment. They told her that Agrippa would see her that evening sometime after dinner. When he did come, she was alone. Her room was dark, illuminated only by the warm, soft light of a full moon creeping through the outdoor windows.

"I've come back because I love you," she said, as he stood in silent awe before her.

"I hoped and prayed that you would," he said.

"But I must tell you about these thoughts I've had. I had time to think while I was away. I..." — she spoke falteringly now, unsure of what she wanted to say — "I don't know how to describe them, because they aren't always clear. But...I find myself wondering if what we've done is right."

"Right?" he said. "I don't know what you mean."

"Well, the old laws, they say it's wrong, wrong for us to be lovers. They say that what we're doing is a sin. And I've started to wonder if they're right."

"What's right for other people is not necessarily right for us," Agrippa said. "I recognize that most of our people need some kind of restrictions in their lives. It keeps our society in order. If someone tells them the restrictions come from God, all the better. They'll obey them better than if they came from me. But you and I are above that, Bernice. We were born to be above it. We have royal blood, and we can do whatever our hearts desire. Don't believe those imaginary stories about punishment for doing this or that. They come from people's imaginations, and they keep the masses in line."

"But then what about children?" she asked. "You know they say that the chances of a child being born abnormal are greater if it comes from close family members. Don't you want to have a child, an heir to your throne?"

"There's plenty of time for that," he said. "My love for you is more important to me right now. I'm overjoyed that you've come back."

Whatever misgivings she had about this affair were forgotten under her brother's touch. The Torah and all its restrictions once again ceased to exist.

Then, in that same year, as if the blood of the family contained an inborn spirit for change, Mariamne, the middle of Agrippa's three sisters, abandoned her husband, Archelaus, and gave herself in marriage to Demetrius, the alabarch of the Alexandrian Jews, whose family and wealth brought her more than her previous husband had done. All three of these Herodian ladies (Bernice, Mariamne and Drusilla) seemed unconcerned with the restraints required of pious women by the Torah. It was not a good example to set for their Torah-following subjects.

During this time, too, the activities of the Zealots and the Sicarii increased even more. Festus did not know where to turn next to stop the needle-thrusting blows that the Jewish patriots were inflicting. It was a tactic of hit-and-run, and the Roman force could not be everywhere at once. The lower priests not only were Nazarenes now, but many of them were Zealots, and the chief priests had to wonder each day which of the lower priests who performed his sacerdotal duties before them was a secret fighter against the legitimate government that ruled. And added to this undermining of priestly political power was the insulting presence of the leader of the Nazarenes each day in the Temple. But not only *in* the Temple but in the innermost sanctuary of the Temple, where only those who had taken special vows and who had earned respect for their knowledge of the Torah and whose reputations for piety were above and beyond the ordinary were permitted to enter. And James, the leader of the Nazarenes, had been given that status — an honorary priestly status accorded to few and which the chief priests had been unable to deny him. The people called him by the epitaph, "the Just", and they called him "the Rampart of the People and of Righteousness", and his influence with the people was growing so great that the Sadducees, especially the chief priests, were growing fearful of the power he could wield. Just as his brother had stirred the people to a frenzy of devotion and expectation, so did James now stir them to a rising loyalty of hope. He told them that Jesus would return soon, and that when he did, a new order would prevail. Jesus, the Messiah, would have the full power and authority of God behind him, and the wicked would not withstand it, and evil men would fall.

From the time that Festus took office, from the time he sent Paul to Rome, this seething cauldron of agitated hopefulness simmered throughout the land. Festus, as procurator, and Joseph Cabi, as high priest, dealt with this situation as best they could but always with limited success. But the man who dealt with it most was Ananias. For Ananias, by bribing Festus on the one hand (just as he had previously bribed Felix) and Joseph Cabi on the other (just as he had previously bribed Ishmael) controlled what he wanted to control and practically ruled the land.

And then, two years after taking his office, Festus suddenly died. Word immediately was sent to Rome, and it was expected that Nero would send a new procurator soon. Ananias, meanwhile, visited the king, and the king suddenly thought it best for the nation that a new high priest should reign. Thus it was that Agrippa deposed Joseph Cabi and appointed Ananus, the son of Annas, in his place.

Ananus now pursued an aggressive policy against the forces that disturbed the land. He could do nothing about the Zealots and Sicarii — that task was up to the Romans — but he *could* do something closer to home. He turned to the lower priests. If they could turn against the powers that gave them sustenance, he, likewise, could turn against them. The money that came into the Temple each day — the tithe money that came from the people — went in part to the lower priests, but it passed through the hands of the chief priests first, and they doled it out after that. To punish the lower priests for their betrayal in becoming Nazarenes (and, as I have said, in many cases, Zealots), Ananus stopped giving them money. The sole source of their livelihoods was thus cut off. They had themselves and their families to feed, and how could they do that now?

James, who was their leader and who felt responsible for their welfares, now openly spoke against Ananus. In public meetings, in open forums, the usually quiet and dignified leader of the Nazarenes spoke in passionate tones, like a venerable prophet, of the injustice and cruelty of the high priest and his selfish and merciless clique. And the people, already responsive to the words of this paragon, this righteous and holy man, now shouted and grumbled and demonstrated against what Ananus had done to the lower priests.

More than ever, Ananus felt threatened. More than ever, Ananias, the instigator of this whole affair, saw the possibility of a popular movement against the Sadducees, or at the very least, against the chief priests. That he and the other chief priests could be killed, as Jonathan had been killed, became a real possibility, and the man who had started it was James.

There was no procurator now. The new one from Nero was yet to arrive. So there was no one to give permission for the Sanhedrin to be convened, and that was good as far as Ananias was concerned. He would get Ananus to convene the Sanhedrin on the pretense of an emergency, a matter so pressing that they could not wait for the new procurator to arrive. But they would not call *all* the members to meet. They were not going to get outvoted on this by the Pharisees, as they had been with Peter and Paul. Just enough Pharisees to make it look good but not enough to carry the day. James was too dangerous now, and he had to be stopped. Quiescently waiting for a Messiah was one thing; arousing the people to act against the chief priests was another. They would arrest James on a manufactured charge, find him guilty and destroy him, and there would be no procurator to ask for permission to do it.

So Ananus sent his guards, and they arrested James and some of his companions and had a brief, perfunctory trial, with the verdict decreed in advance. The charge against James was almost ludicrous in light of the man against whom it was brought. They charged him with defamation of the Torah, based on evidence of the preachings of one of his emissaries named Paul. On that basis they found him guilty and quickly condemned him and the others to death. So, on the charge of his being against the Torah, the man who was said to be "strong for the Torah", the leader of the group whose members were called "the Zealots of the Torah", was executed by stoning along with his companions on the order of the high priest.

And the nation, I can tell you, grieved. When word of this spread through the city, the people descended to despair. A gloom, a darkness, pervaded the voices of men as if a pall had muffled all sound. People, their tenebrous faces drooped and forlorn, spoke in hushed whispers of the tragedy. James the Just was gone from the earth, and Israel was diminished because of it.

But some did more than talk among themselves; some decided to protest. Some of the leading citizens of the city, Pharisees but not Sadducees of course, protested what Ananus had done. One group of them went to Agrippa. *He* was responsible for having appointed Ananus, and look what his appointee had done. A pious man of high religious standing had been executed on a false charge. The king must not allow that to happen again, and the man who had done it must be punished. And another group of the same leading citizens, some of them Pharisees who had not been summoned to the Sanhedrin meeting, met with Albinus, the new procurator from Rome, and told him the same thing: without the procurator's permission, a limited membership of the Sanhedrin had been called, and an innocent man had been executed; the charge for which the man had been killed was false.

From both these political leaders, a favorable response was received. I don't believe it was because they each had a sense of justice but because they realized that the feelings of these petitioners were the same as those of the people, and they wanted things quieted down. So Albinus rebuked Ananus severely, and Agrippa removed him from office. Ananias, while he may have been able to use his influence to prevent a more serious penalty from being applied, could not prevent at least something being done. Jesus, the son of Damnaios, was appointed the new high priest, and Ananias now gave *him* bribes to get the things done that he wanted.

But we Nazarenes had no leader. We conferred about this, and we agreed that our new leader had to be a blood relation of Jesus. None of the disciples, not even Peter, who was back from his travels, could qualify. James had been Jesus' eldest brother, but Jesus' other brothers were no longer alive. We decided to ask a cousin of Jesus, a man named Symeon, son of Cleophas, who was Jesus' closest living relative. He had worked hard in our movement and was known to be honorable and pious. We proposed this to him, and he accepted. Now we could go on. The important thing was that a blood relation of Jesus now stood at the head of our movement again to inspire and sustain us with hope.

While this was taking place, Paul was being taken to Rome. The large ship he was on went through a storm, and Paul's reassurance to the centurion who was escorting him and to the others on the ship that they would survive the danger helped sustain them through the difficulty. When they got to the island of Melita, the natives built them a fire to warm their wet, cold bodies. When Paul threw a bundle of sticks onto the fire, a viper came out of them and bit Paul's hand and clung to it. Paul threw the viper into the fire and, afterwards, suffered no ill effects. This made the people think he was a god, but that was because of the kind of people they were; they were accustomed to thinking that men could be gods and that gods could appear in the bodies of men. They were pagans. Jews, God-fearers and Christians would not have thought that, for they knew there was only one God, and Jews and God-fearers also could not have thought it because they could not think of humans as gods.

Paul then healed the father of one of his hosts, curing him of a disease that had been causing fever and a bloody discharge. When word of that got around, others came with their sicknesses, and Paul healed all of them too.

After that, he and the centurion traveled further by sea and, with various stops along the way, made their way to Rome. Once there, the centurion turned Paul over to the captain of the guard. The captain permitted Paul to rent a house, as long as he lived there alone, except for a soldier who was assigned to guard him. But Paul was not to be treated as well here as he had been under Felix. Not only was he confined to his house, he was also made to wear chains.

But Paul was ever restless, even when confined to one place. After only three days of solitude, he sent messages to the leaders of the Jewish community and asked them to meet with him. Because Christian groups already were existent in Rome, and because Paul's name was prominent among them, these Jews responded out of curiosity if nothing else. Paul told these men that, although he had done nothing against our people and nothing against our customs, he had been delivered as a prisoner out of Jerusalem into the hands of the Romans. This made it sound as if he had been *taken* to the Romans by some Jews, instead of having been arrested by Captain Claudius Lysias as he had been. And then he said that the Romans had found him guilty of nothing that had warranted a death penalty and that they had been prepared to let him go, but because "the Jews" had spoken against that, he had been forced to make an appearance before the emperor. And again he was saying "the Jews", meaning all or the majority of Jews. But, of course, there had been no accusing Jews in the room that day when Paul had met with Festus and Agrippa and Bernice; the chief priests had not been invited. And, of course, he hadn't been *forced* to go to Rome at all; he was there at his own request. Why then was Paul speaking as if this trip had been forced on him by "the Jews"? Was this trip not something he ardently desired in obedience to Jesus' assignment to him in that vision that night after the Sanhedrin meeting? Indeed, when Christians were later to tell of these events, they would say that it was Paul and not the chief priests who had demanded the trip to Rome and that the Romans would have let him go had it not been that Paul's demand (made under the rights of his Roman citizenship) had compelled them to send him to the emperor. The Christians would say that Agrippa had said that very thing to Festus: "This man might have been set free if he had not appealed to Caesar." Why then was Paul accusing "the Jews" of having forced this on him? It was something he wanted himself! Yet here was Paul telling the Roman Jews that "the Jews" had objected to his release and that *they* had forced the Romans to send him to Rome. He told them nothing about his own demand that this be done. Why was he lying? He was saying something contradictory to what his own followers would say when they told this story in the future. Did he see here another opportunity to attribute something bad to Jews even though that something wasn't true? And how was he going to explain that all the Jews were against him when the Pharisees in the Sanhedrin had demanded his release?

Then Paul said to the Roman Jewish leaders, "I am not accusing my nation of anything, but I have asked you to see me today so that I can say that if it wasn't for the hope of Israel that I be found guilty, I wouldn't be wearing this chain today."

And now there could be no more doubt. Where previously Paul had said "the Jews" whenever the Sadducees had done something bad, even accusing "the Jews" of having killed Jesus, and where he previously could explain away my challenge to this by saying that he had not meant *all* the Jews but just those few who were among the chief priests, now he could not say that. For now he had said that "Israel", the entire Jewish people, had wished him ill and was responsible for him wearing a chain.

I no longer could doubt that Paul intended to disparage all Jews, even those who had saved his life, and to disparage them even to Jews themselves; that for all the reasons I have mentioned before, he was determined that Jews — all Jews — should be seen as bad and should be believed — as incredible as this may sound — to be the killers of Jesus the Messiah; that all the Jews who had flocked to Jesus and saved Peter and Paul from death, who had protested the killing of James and joined the Nazarenes in droves; that *they* should be seen as Jesus' killers and the haters all of his followers. He could get away with that in Rome; he could never have said it in Jerusalem. No longer could I doubt his intent; no longer could I accept what he was saying as an innocent misuse of words.

The leaders of the Roman Jews told him that Jerusalem had sent them no letters about him and that those Jews who had come to Rome from there had not said anything negative about him. What they could not understand was why, if *all* the Jewish people had found fault with him and had forced him to go to Rome, those Jews who had been arriving from Judaea were not reporting all this in their news. Nevertheless, these Roman Jewish leaders were very interested in knowing more about the Christian sect, in which they knew Paul was prominent, since everywhere people were speaking against it.

On a subsequent day they met again, and Paul told them about Jesus and that Moses and the prophets had written of him. When he finished, some Jews believed and some didn't, but those Jews who did were now his. Because some of them did not believe, however, he angrily quoted Isaiah, the prophet, about Jews who had eyes and ears but would not use them, and he said, as he had on those other occasions when Jews had not accepted his teachings, that he would preach to the Gentiles and bring salvation to them and that they would hear and believe, as these unbelieving Jews would not.

And he did just that for the next two years, with many Gentiles coming to him and hearing his words and becoming Christians. And no one interfered with his work.

THE CHRIST-KILLERS

CHAPTER XXXII

The Sicarii did not take kindly to the execution of James or the denial of income to the lower priests. They increased their activities even more now. Albinus imprisoned many of them, but always there were more to find. The Sicarii, from their standpoint, considered the chief priests to be in the camp of the Romans. To them, a blow against the chief priests was a blow against the hated occupiers of their country. Their opportunity to do that came soon enough.

Ananias' son, Eleazar, who was Rabath's childhood friend, was now the commander of the Temple guards. One of Eleazar's servants went to a festival, and the Sicarii took the servant prisoner there. Then they sent a message to Eleazar that they wanted ten Sicarii prisoners released in exchange for their hostage. The servant was a member of Eleazar's family, and Eleazar could not let the demand go unheeded. He went to his father, who then went to the procurator, Albinus, and Albinus, for a price, let the prisoners go free. This meant more fighters for Jewish freedom, but Albinus was more interested in lucre than in how many revolutionaries were roaming the land. The Sicarii success with the taking of this hostage led to repeats of this tactic again and again and, invariably, with success.

And now Agrippa, ever anxious to remind us of what otherwise might have been his inconsequential existence, changed high priests again. Jesus, son of Damnaios, stepped down from his position, and Jesus, son of Gamaliel, (not to be confused with our Pharisee leader, Gamaliel) replaced him. For Ananias, with all his riches, it made little difference. Through bribery, he still got whatever he wanted.

Now came more social eruptions, in a land already inundated with them. The Levites, who did the singing in the Temple services, demanded that they be allowed to wear the same linen vestments as the priests. They were no longer going to be looked upon as if they were something less than the priests. They were just as good, and their vestments were going to show it. This may seem to have been petty at a time when so many more important matters were pressing the nation, but status seems to want its way under all sorts of circumstances. And then it may have been more than status: the Levites had wanted to bring the chief priests down a peg or two for some time, and the vestments were one way of doing it. King Agrippa had been having differences with the chief priests at that time, so he granted the Levites what they wanted just to spite the priests.

Another problem was unemployment. For some time the Temple had been undergoing more construction, but now that project was completed, and thousands of men were out of work. They were employed temporarily paving Jerusalem with white stone, but that could only last for so long. Here were more disgruntled men for the ranks of the Zealots. We were like a volcano burning fiercely, broiling toward some explosive denouement.

And Agrippa, like a small boy with limited power, ever anxious to make his presence known, changed high priests again. Jesus, son of Gamaliel, descended, and Matthias, son of Theophilus, took his place. As always, with Ananias, the change was of little concern. He could pay off one high priest as well as another and get done whatever he wished.

Albinus, with all his pecuniary crimes, was with us for all of two years. In the year when his tenure was over, a fire broke out in Rome. This was the great conflagration that destroyed so much of that city and took so many Christian lives in its aftermath. The fire started in the lower parts of the city and rose upward into the hills and then went downward again to the lower parts. It burned for almost a week, the black smoke billowing across the sky and permeating the air with the choking dust of cremated houses.

Nero, when all this occurred, was not present inside the city. He was at Antium nearby, taking a respite from his duties in Rome. When he returned to the smoldering ashes of the city, he looked for someone to blame.

As a result of the work of Paul's missionaries in Rome and then of his own presence there, Christians had been growing in number in that city, just as Nazarenes had started to grow again in Judaea. Nero had heard of their dead leader, Jesus. Reports from Jerusalem said that this man's followers expected him to return to set up his own kingdom in Judaea. The potential for revolution that that posed was of concern to him. And now the man's followers were here in the city, infesting the heart of the empire itself.

Paul had tried hard to dispel that fear. He knew that if the Romans saw the Christians as a revolutionary group, they would move to destroy them. He had to deliver a clear and certain message to the Romans that Christians were not their enemies and that they sought no political change. (He knew with certainty within himself that the change would come when it would come and that Christians would not have to revolt against Rome to make that change occur.) But he had before him the problem of the disciples having asked Jesus, "Lord, will you be restoring the kingdom to Israel at this time?" That was a clear indication of the political and even revolutionary nature of the movement. And he had before him the problem of one of Jesus' disciples being a Zealot, another indication of politics and revolution. And he had the problem of Christians predicting that the kingdom of the world would become the kingdom of the Lord and his Christ. That, too, was something political. And, as I have mentioned before, there was the problem that he himself had created when he had written his letter to the Corinthians, in which he had said that the day would come when Jesus "...delivers the kingdom to God the Father after destroying every rule and every authority and power." There was no question that the "authority and power" that Jesus was going to destroy was Rome. And here was Paul having to find a way to conceal those things or to change the political threat that they posed. So when he spoke of Jesus' kingdom, he spoke of it as being in heaven; when he spoke on the question of taxes, he made Jesus depart from his usual objection to them, and even contradict one of the reasons that Caiaphas had brought him to Pilate, by having Jesus say that they should be paid; and he himself concurred with that as the wisest thing to do; he took the crucifixion of Jesus by Romans, an act that the Romans might well have understood would make Christians dislike them, and blamed it all on "the Jews", as if to say to the Romans that if Christians were going to hate anyone for Jesus' crucifixion, it would be the Jews and not the Romans they would hate; he took the great crucifier, Pilate and made him a merciful man, one who had been pushed unwillingly into the killing of Jesus by a frightening Jewish mob, the soldiers who had tortured Jesus having been disobedient and exceptional to the merciful nature of their leader; he made Jesus an envoy of peace and removed from him any affiliation with those revolutionary Zealot ideals that sought the ousting of Rome. Peace and love were all that Christians had on their minds, and they respected the authority of Rome. Appeasement of Romans was behind it, so that Christians would not be attacked.

But Nero did not believe what to him was all that pacific pretense. Or if he did believe it, he chose on this occasion to act as if he didn't. He equated Christians with Jews, and a particularly rebellious branch of the Jews at that. And you will recall that his attitude towards Jews had been inculcated into him by his anti-Jewish teachers: Seneca, who called us an accursed race, and Chaeremon, the Alexandrian, who said that we were a polluted people, driven out of Egypt.

It was being rumored that Nero had started the fire himself. He had to divert attention away from that belief. The Christians could be said to be revolutionaries, based on this kingdom of Jesus they wanted. So he blamed them for starting the fire. Their motive for doing such a thing? The destruction of Rome itself! They were enemies and had to be destroyed. He fomented hatred against them.

As Paul once had hunted the militant members of the Nazarenes, going from house to house and town to town, so did the Romans now hunt the Christians, placing those they captured into the arena to be devoured by dogs for the sport of the populace. And Nero, not satisfied with that creative way of disposing of these troublemakers, outdid himself one evening by having Christians tarred and tied to stakes in his garden and then having them torched so that their burning bodies could illuminate the scene. This was a man who had poisoned his stepbrother and who, later, had had his mother assassinated. This was the man whom Romans and Greeks called "the good god." This was the leader of the Romans, and these were the people who, Paul would have had us believe, wanted Jesus not to be killed.

But Paul was not there when the fire occurred, and he was spared the persecutions that followed. Prior to the outbreak of the fire, he had been given permission to travel to Spain, with the understanding that he was to return to Rome after a time. The emperor, preoccupied with other things, had not yet been able to attend to him and would hear him upon his return. So shortly before the fire began, Paul was traveling to Spain to spread his gospel there.

CHAPTER XXXIII

Now came the time of Gessius Florus, who vied in our estimation with Pilate for being the worst procurator of them all. Though he did not crucify with quite as much abandon as Pilate, he did other things to compensate for that deficiency. He took bribes, as Felix and Festus had done, but, beyond that, he randomly accused innocent people of being bandits, with all the penalties attendant thereto unless they gave him the amounts of money he demanded. Yet more profitable than dealing with individuals was the plundering of entire communities, which he engaged in routinely. Some of them became so impoverished by him that the inhabitants had to leave Israel to live in foreign places. These were Jews having to leave their ancestral lands because a Roman invader wanted to get rich.

When Cestius Gallus, the legate of Syria, came to visit Florus in Jerusalem, a mammoth crowd surrounded them both and beseeched Gallus to stop Florus' outrages. Florus laughed contemptuously at this, but I think, inwardly, he was struck with fear over being reprimanded for the things he had done. Gallus quieted the crowd by promising that Florus would act better in the future. Then he and Florus, like two old friends, went off together to Caesarea, and then Gallus went to Antioch. Their open friendship made Gallus' promise suspect.

Florus' plan was actually to foment revolt, to persecute the people into such a state of frustration that they could not do other than to take arms. If peace prevailed, the Jews would take their grievances to Nero, who might then punish Florus for abusing the power of his office. But if Jews began to fight because of the unbearable things being done to them, their complaints would carry no weight, because then they would be branded as rebels.

More trouble came after that. A delegation of Greeks from Caesarea returned from Rome with a written decision from Nero that Caesarea was to be controlled by the Greeks. Trouble between Jews and Greeks in that city had started when Felix had been procurator, the Romans always siding with the Greeks. You may remember that Felix had sent representatives of both groups to Nero to present their cases. Now that the decision had been made, Jewish resentment was intense. Warfare between Jews and Greeks began when a Greek who owned property next

301

to a synagogue started building a factory right up to the dividing line, thus making it impossible for the Jews to get around the synagogue. Young, angry Jewish men interfered with the builders, but then Florus suppressed the young men. Then John, a Jewish tax collector, gave Florus a large bribe to stop the construction. Florus took the money and then left Caesarea for Sebaste, the bribe, in his mind, apparently, serving not to help the Jews by stopping the construction but only to allow the Jews to fight without Roman interference.

The next day, a group of Gentiles, itching for a fight, sent one of its members to sacrifice birds on the steps of the synagogue for the purpose of insulting the Jews and provoking them. The Jews restrained their young men — one does not fight on the Sabbath! — and a Roman cavalry officer named Jucundus had his men try to hold back the Gentiles. But the Gentiles pushed back the Romans, so that the Jews, prohibited from fighting on the Sabbath, seized their Torah and escaped to Narbath, a Jewish area seven miles away. Then John, the tax collector, and seven influential Jews went to Sebaste to see Florus. They complained about the Gentiles and tactfully reminded him of their bribe. Florus grew angry at being told about his end of the bargain, and he put the Jews into prison for the "crime" of having taken their Torah from Caesarea! So much for bribes to Florus.

During this time, Jerusalem was quiet, and King Agrippa was confident it would remain so. Because Tiberius Alexander, the former Jew and former procurator of Judaea, had now become governor of Alexandria, Agrippa traveled there to congratulate him. He left Bernice behind.

Bernice, left alone to think without being distracted, became plagued with the feelings of guilt that she had expressed previously to her brother. She felt that she needed advice, and she chose for this not a Sadducee priest, which is what a Sadducee princess might have been expected to do, but rather a Pharisee sage. Since she was a royal personage, she felt she should have the foremost of these, and that, of course, meant Gamaliel. She arranged to visit him.

At the meeting she told him everything. Gamaliel listened and pondered and spoke. He understood that she loved her brother immensely, and love, wherever it occurred, was not to be discouraged. But the form that that love took, the way it which it was made manifest, was in her case very wrong. He respected her love for her brother. He found that admirable and good. But that love, he said, should rise above lust, should express itself in a higher, purer, spiritual form. She should walk with her brother by her side and work for the good of the people.

"You broke the law," he said, "and you didn't care, because you thought you were above the law. You thought the law was for the rest of us but not for you. And look what such thinking has brought you. Has it brought you peace? Has it brought you happiness? Or has it brought you doubt and uncertainty and restlessness and guilt? You sinned when you slept with your brother. You sinned when you left your husband. But I'll give you credit for this at least: that you came to realize that you were doing wrong, which brought you here to me."

Bernice was crying now. "And yet I love him," she said. "I love him so much."

"Then put your love on a higher plane," Gamaliel said. "Go and sin no more."

"Those were the words that that Nazarene used to the woman who had broken the law," she said.

"You mean Jesus?" he said. "When he spoke to the adulteress?"

"Yes," she said. "I heard the story. Those were the words he used."

"Yes, I heard the account too," he said, "and those were the words he spoke."

"I even heard that he's coming back. Do you really believe in such a thing?"

"I believe he may," Gamaliel said. "I would welcome the day if he does."

Then he told Bernice that if she truly repented her sins, she should not only cease to do them again but should do penance for the ones she had committed. He advised her to shave her head, to go without shoes for an entire month and to abstain from wine during that time. These things she accepted and these things she did while she awaited her brother's return.

News of Florus' treatment of the Caesarean Jews now reached Jerusalem, and the smoldering hatreds grew even worse. But Florus was not satisfied with smoldering; what he wanted was open rebellion. His next move would satisfy his desire for money and also advance his secret goal of forcing the Jews to rebel. He had a large sum of money taken from the Temple treasury on the pretext that the emperor needed it. We Jews were behind in our taxes, he said, and that money would partially cover it. The response was quite as expected. People ran to the Temple, and with piercing shrieks and outraged yells, called on Nero to free them from Florus. Some shouted obscenities about Florus, and one group sarcastically collected copper coins from the crowd to help what it called their pitiful, starving pauper of a procurator. Such mocking, when news of it reached Florus in Caesarea, made him vengeful towards those in Jerusalem.

Caesarea was still in an uproar, but attending to that was not going to make Florus richer, and getting rich was the one thing he cared about more than anything else. Vengeance, of course, was another, and provoking rebellion too. Jerusalem looked ripe for squeezing, so he left Caesarea in its chaos and went to Jerusalem with his cavalry and infantry to ply his intimidations there. Another rumored reason for his coming was that because we were still in arrears in our taxes, he was going to get the money we owed from the Temple once again. The people heard he was coming, and some went out with friendly intentions to shame him back with a show of docility. Florus would not be outwitted by this. If he let a show of submission turn him back, he would be thwarted from getting his money — either through threats and intimidations or through outright confiscation from the Temple — and also from getting revenge. So he sent Capito with fifty horsemen to tell these people that their specious friendliness had come too late, in light of their previous abuses against their procurator, and that if they had any self-respect, they would make fun of Florus to his face and then show their love of liberty by fighting him and his soldiers. He wanted us to go to war, you see, so that when we complained to the emperor about his crimes, we would be criminals ourselves. Capito's horsemen now charged into the crowd and sent it scurrying home in disgrace.

The next day, outside the palace, Florus sat and received the chief priests and prominent citizens and told them that he would severely punish them if they didn't produce the men who had come to the Temple to mock him and curse him after he had ordered the money to be taken from it previously. They couldn't do that, they said, because they didn't know who the men were, just some juvenile hotheads in contrast to the mass of people who were peacefully disposed and loyal. Florus grew furious at this. He told his soldiers to sack the upper marketplace and kill anyone they saw. But the soldiers exceeded their orders. They entered houses, stole what they could and killed everyone inside, including infants. The people, of course, were unarmed and could not defend themselves very well. And the infants — well, the infants also did not prevail against those courageous Roman soldiers. Those people who fled and who were not killed were captured and brought before Florus. These innocents were scourged and crucified, stirring memories in us of Pilate. A few thousand people were killed that day, including high-ranking Jews of equestrian rank, who had gained their status by siding with Rome. Men of high station along with the rest of the victims were pinioned to wooden posts for the personal whim of this man.

King Agrippa, as I have said, was gone at the time; he had traveled to Egypt to congratulate Tiberius Alexander. But Bernice was in Jerusalem, and she felt for the plight of her people. Again and again she sent her cavalry commanders to beg Florus to stop what he was doing. But Florus cared nothing for people, not even of the highest rank, and he had his soldiers torture their prisoners to death before Bernice's very eyes. Then his soldiers turned menacingly toward Bernice, and she fled within the palace where her guards could discourage any attack for the night.

Because she was doing penance, because she was under the holy vow that Gamaliel had told her to take, with its thirty-day abstinence from wine and her head shaved and her feet bare, she went in that manner to Florus to appeal to him in person. Even like that, she was beautiful, but Florus was unaffected. "If I don't get what I want, then even *you*," and here he pointed his finger at her, "are going to get a taste of my anger!" His response was so threatening that she left quickly in fear for her life.

The next day, crowds shrieked over their dead in the streets and cursed Florus for what he had done. And the chief priests and prominent citizens begged them not to do even that, lest Florus be provoked to do more.

Florus now demanded this: he had two cohorts of soldiers coming to the city, and he wanted a Jewish crowd to welcome them outside the gate at the north wall. Why he was bringing in so many more soldiers, we didn't know. The chief priests appealed to the people, and arranged this over the objections of the young revolutionaries. Meanwhile Florus had ordered the soldiers to attack if even one curse was heard.

The people saluted the soldiers, but when the soldiers did not respond, as would normally have been expected, some people uttered profanities. That was the signal to attack. The soldiers surrounded the people and clubbed them down; the horsemen trampled those who fled; in the congested mass that rushed through the gate, many were trampled by friends. The soldiers pushed through the gate and moved south through the city towards the Temple. And Florus, from the palace on the west, sent his own men towards the Temple as well. And now the purpose was clear: Florus wanted the Temple treasure. Now we knew why he had sent for two cohorts. And now the people turned and blocked the Romans in the narrow streets; they climbed on roofs and pelted the Romans from above. The Romans pulled back and camped near the palace, having done enough work for one day.

The Temple had been built with a fortress called the Antonia that stood before it for defense. The Jews cut a gap in the connection between the colonnades, thus making entry to the Temple more difficult. That dampened Florus' ardor, and he told the chief priests and the Sanhedrin that he would leave the city for Caesarea but would leave a Roman garrison behind. They promised to keep order and prevent a revolt, and they breathed with relief when he went.

He had come to Jerusalem for only one purpose: to get money from wherever he could. He left with so little for his work. But he left monuments to his presence behind him: mangled arms, flattened chests, crushed faces and slashed bowels; hanging sculptures of rotting flesh and the dented sides of children's heads. And in the streets and in the houses, there were ravaged women with clotted hairs between their open legs, lying as silent and immobile as the statues of Rome. Everywhere there was crimson and the stench of dead bodies keeping us away. These were the tributes to Roman greatness; this was the triumph of Rome. This was our governor, Florus, who, as I have said, did not crucify as many as Pilate but compensated in other ways.

Caesarea was still upheaving when Florus returned to it. The Jews and Greeks were still fighting it out, with small skirmishes becoming almost a daily event. But Florus was more concerned with protecting his position than in establishing order in the city. He was concerned about what Gallus would think about his recent trip to Jerusalem. So he wrote to the legate and told him that the Jerusalem Jews had revolted and that he had had to put them down. When we heard of this in Jerusalem, Bernice and the chief priests were appalled, and they wrote several letters to Gallus. They denied what Florus had said and told him what Florus had done. Gallus didn't know what to believe, so he sent a tribune named Neapolitanus to investigate. When this tribune stopped for a night at Jamnia, he happened to meet Herod Agrippa, who was stopping there too on his way back from Alexandria. They were both then approached by the chief priests and Sanhedrin who aired their complaints against Florus. All of them went to Jerusalem and, seven miles outside the city, were met by a wailing throng, led by the widows of the men who had been killed. They took Agrippa and Neapolitanus to the marketplace, to the sacked houses, the wooden crosses, the blood-stained patio of the palace itself and showed them the people, bitter towards Florus but loyal to Rome. From the outer court of the Temple, Neapolitanus praised an assemblage for their unshaken loyalty and bowed to the Temple sanctuary to show his respect for our god and our religion.

His praise was not totally warranted, however: the loyalty was not universal. It was certainly not there with the Zealots and Sicarii and Essenes and certainly not there with us Nazarenes. The Zealots and Sicarii, although present in large numbers as individuals, had not had time to organize into their fighting units to counter the Roman attack. Now though, they prepared to do so in the future. Many Nazarenes had died under Florus, and many of us could not be passive after that. We began to feel, as Stephen had felt, that it was going to be better to prepare the way for Jesus ourselves rather than wait for Jesus to do it for us. It was becoming more common to see people who were both Nazarenes and Zealots at the same time. The lower priests were certainly foremost in that. And the ranks of the Zealots were swelled even more by the thousands of unemployed workmen who, having finished the Temple and the laying of white stone throughout the city, were now without work or livelihoods. Even my brother-in-law, Joash, who had plied his food-importing business aloof from revolutionary involvements, now descended from his privileged pedestal and became a secret supplier of food to the Zealots. How could any of us remain uninvolved any longer after what Florus had done?

After Neapolitanus left, the people asked Agrippa and the chief priests to complain not just to Gallus but to Nero himself about Florus, detailing his outrages and showing that they themselves had not rebelled. But Agrippa was cautious. To complain about Florus might arouse more violence from that man and, in a world of whimsical autocracy, might make the emperor angry as well. He counseled restraint and forbearance instead of angry complaints. Then, having disposed of his responsibility to his people by giving them his advice, he felt that he had time for Bernice.

He almost failed to recognize her at first because her head was shaved. That alone told him that something was wrong, and he asked her what it meant.

"Do you remember those feelings of guilt I had when I came back from Cilicia?"

"Yes," he said, "and I told you to forget about them."

"You told me we were privileged and didn't have to abide by the law."

"Yes, and that's true," he said.

"No, it's not true," she countered. "We're as subject to the law as everyone else."

"Who says so?" he asked.

"Gamaliel," she answered. "I visited him, and he said so. But even before I visited him, I knew it was so. My own conscience told me it was so."

"Bernice, I love you, and I would indulge you anything, but I don't agree with you about this. What does all this mean?"

"It means that I can't sleep with you anymore."

"No!" he said. "That's too much! I won't agree to that."

"You must," she pleaded. "You must, my love. What we've done is offensive to God."

"Oh, how I hate this religion of ours!" he uttered. "I know it's important to our people, so I tolerate it for them. But I hate it because of what it does to us. It takes away our freedom and our happiness."

"You must not say that, my brother," she chided. "I think God wants us to show restraint. Maybe He wants *us* to show it more than anyone else because He's given us so much. You must not curse God because I won't be yours in bed. I will always be yours in love."

This softened him and made him think. When he was alone without her that night, he wondered if there was something to what she had said, something he had failed to see. Was there something to this religion of theirs after all?

The Zealots were starting to organize now, and it seemed not just for defense. Agrippa could almost smell revolt in the air. And revolt would be dangerous to him. So he summoned a large crowd of people into the gymnasium, which sat between the Temple and his palace on the west and put Bernice, who was now a heroine to the people, on the roof of the palace where she could be seen. He then made a lengthy oration in which he counseled the people to peace. He asked them to resist the freedom fantasies of their inexperienced young men; he asked them to distinguish between tyrannical officials and the Roman people and the emperor. Bad officials did not last forever and would surely be replaced by better ones. Nero had not sent what turned out to be a tyrant on purpose. Roman rule was a fact of life, and we should accept that and learn to live with it. Freedom, if we had wanted it so badly, should have been fought for years ago when Pompey first invaded our land, when we had an army that could have resisted the Romans. Now it was too late. We could not muster now what our forefathers had had then, and the Roman force back then was much smaller than what we would have to face now. He spoke then of nation after nation and of their futile resistances to Rome; he spoke of how people with natural land and water defenses and some with a natural fierceness had fallen before the

Roman legions and how few Romans in those places were now needed to administer Roman law. Even God, he said, was in favor of this, for the Romans could not have achieved their victories and maintained their power without the approval of God.

This last declaration flew in the face of the Zealots, for their claim had always been that Roman rule was offensive to God and that it was their religious duty to remove it. And it flew in the face of us Nazarenes too, who believed that God did not want this Roman kingdom and that He would replace it with His own through Jesus.

But Agrippa went on with his speech and said that if we fought, we would have to fight on the Sabbath and that that would be offensive to God. He had no doubt forgotten that we Jews had suffered slaughter from that restriction when we fought the Syrians under Mattathias, the father of Judah Maccabee, and that we were never going to give an enemy that advantage again, for Mattathias had ruled afterwards that we could defend ourselves on the Sabbath but just could not attack. And Agrippa said that if we rebelled here in Jerusalem, it would result in massacres of all the Jewish communities throughout the empire, which would be unfair to those other communities. If we took the path of revolt, we would take it without him, for it would take us all to our doom, and he would not accompany us there. He burst into tears; Bernice burst into tears. It was obvious that they both were sincere.

Some people shouted that it was Florus and not the Romans they hated. And Agrippa said that while that well may have been true, they were acting as if they were threatening *all* Romans.

"Rebuild the colonnades to the Antonia, and pay Nero the taxes we owe. The money will not go to Florus; you can be sure of that."

Many of the people heeded him, and they, with Bernice and Agrippa by their sides, began to rebuild what was broken. Agrippa also sent magistrates all around the city and into the surrounding villages to collect the taxes. They told the people what the king advised, and many gave their money until the full amount owed was collected. But the Zealots and Sicarii did not pay. In fact, the payment of this tax by others infuriated them. They began to agitate and threaten, they urged rejection of Roman authority, and it looked as if the burgeoning revolution that Agrippa had thought was gone was still alive and well.

So Agrippa summoned the people again and adjured them not to revolt but to accept Florus' rule until Nero sent someone to replace him. But hatred of Florus was just too high for that, and this time, the people shouted abusively at Agrippa and even threw stones at him. They declared him banished from the city for even suggesting what he had.

Agrippa was hurt by this; he felt that the people did not appreciate the good he was doing them. He performed a last duty by sending some of the leading citizens to Florus so that Florus could choose future tax collectors from among them, and then he left with Bernice for his own kingdom, leaving the ingrates in Jerusalem to fend for themselves from then on.

CHAPTER XXXIV

The roiling volcano in the hearts of our people now erupted uncontainedly. Events moved inexorably towards war.

Rising upright from the land near the sea, like a giant fist thrust upward from beneath the earth, stands the impregnable fortress of Masada. Here, in complacent security, sat a Roman garrison. But in the summer of Florus' second year as governor, Menahem, one of the sons of Judas of Galilee, led his men stealthily into this stronghold and massacred the soldiers. This was an act of war.

At the same time, in Jerusalem, Ananias' son, Eleazar, the commander of the Temple guards and Rabath's childhood friend, turned from his father's position and took a stand against Rome on his own. How much was patriotism and how much filial revolt I cannot say, but I am sure that there were elements of both in what he did. He convinced the lower priests not to accept any Temple gifts from foreigners. His brothers, his father and all the chief priests demurred. We had always accepted gifts from foreigners, they said; the sanctuary had been built with such gifts; the acceptance of them did not defile anything, and the refusal of them would only insult the givers. But Eleazar went beyond that: he had the lower priests stop their daily sacrifices and prayers for the emperor and the Roman people. That was an act of rebellion, a declaration of independence, a rejection of Roman rule. These offerings had been the symbol of Jewish loyalty to Rome. Because of Eleazar and the lower priests, that symbol would now be gone.

The high-placed citizens wanted no part of this; Roman rule had been good to them, Florus' excesses notwithstanding. They sent delegations to Florus and Agrippa, the one to Florus including Ananias' own son, Simon, and the one to Agrippa including one of the king's own relatives, and asked them to suppress the rebellion. Florus gave them no reply. To him, the deeper the hole the Jews dug for themselves, the more complete would be their destruction later and the more unnoticed or ignored would be his own misdeeds. But Agrippa, temporarily forgiving the insulting banishment he had suffered at Jerusalem and anxious not to see Roman might destroy the city, sent two-thousand horsemen to suppress the revolt. It was not solely altruistic, though, for a devastated Israel would be bad for him too.

In the upper part of the city were the Sadducees and the other anti-revolutionaries, and that was where the king's men went. In the lower part of the city, which included the Temple, were the Zealots and Sicarii and Pharisees and Essenes and Nazarenes and all the other people who had joined the revolt. Our side drove into the city and forced most of the king's men out, but the Antonia still remained in their hands. Eleazar then led his men to burn down his father's house and the palace of Agrippa and Bernice. It is significant for those who are not from our country and who have been misinformed about us to know that these were the majority of Jews who were acting against the former high priest and the king and that, in contrast to what was later said about the one-mindedness of the Jewish people and their leaders, the two rarely had agreed. Our forces burned down the records office with its list of taxpayers and debtors. Some of the chief priests and other Sadducees fled for their lives into the sewers. Other chief priests, including Ananias and his brother, Ezekial, along with some of the king's soldiers and some Romans, escaped to the Upper Palace and bolted the doors.

The next day, the Zealots and Sicarii attacked the Antonia and besieged it for two days before it fell. They killed the defenders and set fire to the fortress. Then they turned to the Upper Palace and attacked it from four different sides. The defenders threw down stones, and many attackers fell. Ananias, bolted within, could reflect on the course of his life and the irony of having one of his own sons leading the destruction of his house and the attack against him now. What he did not know was that Eleazar had not wanted him to be killed. But as the leader of the revolt, Eleazar could not show weakness or favoritism in front of his men, so he had burned his father's house to prove his resolve.

The revolt was directed against Rome. Why then were we attacking the Sadducees and chief priests and soldiers of the king? It was because they would have suppressed our revolt if they could have done so for their own vested interests and because we knew that they were more loyal to Rome than they were to us. By attacking them, we were removing one of the impediments to our Messiah who now would surely come soon, we believed.

But now Menahem, armed with Roman weapons, left Masada and came with a force of men to Jerusalem. When he entered, he entered in triumph and called himself King of the Jews. As his father had declared himself king at Sepphoris before that ill-fated march to Jerusalem, so did

Menahem say that he was king and Messiah — Menahem, King of the Jews!

Eleazar relinquished command of the revolutionary army to him. Menahem's father, Judas of Galilee, was a hero of Israel and had never been forgotten. That one of Judas' sons could be the Messiah appealed to many who had been inspired by Judas' example. And Eleazar, either because he believed in Menahem or because he had little choice in the face of such overwhelming popularity, relinquished command to the man who had proven himself at Masada and whose father had inspired the founding of the Zealot movement.

But Menahem was not accepted by those of us who followed Jesus. We were Nazarenes, and we knew that he was not the Messiah. Though he might continue to be victorious in battle, he was not God's chosen for king. We Nazarenes would not support him because of his claim, and we lessened his ranks when we withdrew.

Menahem now led the siege against the Upper Palace. Because he had no engines to breach or surmount the walls, and because his men could not undermine the walls without being stoned from above, he dug a tunnel from a distance. When the tunnel went under a tower, he supported the tower with wooden props. Then he set fire to the wooden props, and the tower collapsed. The defenders had surmised this plan and had built a barrier to prevent the tunnel from going any further, but they knew that it was only a matter of time until that would be broken through. So they sent an appeal to Menahem, asking for a truce and amnesty. Menahem granted it to any who were Jews or soldiers of the king, but he would not grant it to the Romans. As the Jews and the king's soldiers came out, the Romans fled to the three King's Towers, but some of them were captured and killed. Ezekial, the brother of Ananias, came out with the Jews, but Ananias himself did not. Ananias feared for his life, not only because he was the leader of the anti-revolutionaries but because of his past activities against the common people. He sneaked off and hid for the night.

In the morning, they caught him hiding in a canal next to the palace. They took him and Ezekial inside to Menahem. And Menahem, in the presence of some of his soldiers, spoke to them thus: "Ananias — and you too, Ezekial — the Lord has appointed this day for you to answer for your crimes."

"Why me?" said Ezekial. "Am I guilty because I'm his brother?"

"No," said Menahem, "you've done enough on your own, Ezekial. You and your whole clique of Roman-loving priests."

"Are you going to allow us a trial before the Sanhedrin?" Ananias asked.

"Which Sanhedrin?" Menahem answered sarcastically. "The Sanhedrin that you always put together whenever you want the vote to go your way, or the Sanhedrin that includes all the Pharisees? No, I'm not going to call the Sanhedrin. Every Sadducee in it is a Roman-lover. Every one of them should be on trial himself."

"Whatever I did, I did as a legally appointed authority of the government. If I acted against you Zealots and Sicarii and Nazarenes, I did it to save our nation. Your insanity will ruin us. It will bring destruction on us all."

"God wants His nation back, Ananias. I'm going to give it to Him," Menahem said.

"Do you think the Romans are going to sit back and let you do it?"

"No! But when they come, we'll fight them."

"And lose!"

"If it's God's will. But I don't think it is. I think we'll win."

"The way your father won? Judas of Galilee, the great Torah teacher! He called us cowards because we paid tribute to Rome and accepted mortal masters instead of God. He told us to resist the census and to help him fight. He called himself the King of the Jews. Everyone said that he was the Messiah. And where did it get him? He wound up on a Roman cross with all his followers. Or the way your brothers, Jacob and Simon, won when Governor Tiberius Alexander killed them? Or the way Jesus of Nazareth won? They called him the Messiah too. And the Romans nailed him to a cross the same as they did your father. Or the way Theudas won? He was supposed to be the Messiah too. Or that Egyptian who was going to make the city walls crumble the way Jericho did for Joshua? Or that Samaritan who led the pilgrims to Mount Girizim? They were all supposed to be the Messiah. And every one of them got killed. You Zealots are right to use the cross as your symbol, because that's where you're all going to wind up in the end."

Menahem answered him: "My family has preserved the Zealot cause for sixty years so that this day could be fulfilled. Jerusalem is ours."

"For how long?" Ananias asked contemptuously.

"For as long as God wills," said Menahem. "But certainly long enough to take care of you."

"Where's my son?" Ananias asked frantically. "Where's Eleazar?"

"Your son can't help you now," Menahem said. "He's relinquished his command to me."

"But he's the leader of this revolt!" Ananias exclaimed.

"Not anymore, Ananias. I'm the leader now."

"It can never be the will of God that you kill his chief priests."

"Ananias! We Zealots have seen our friends and our parents tortured, and we have not given in. We have seen them killed, and we have not shrunk from our duty to call no mortal man 'Master' and to call only God our lord. Our people have waited many years for the Messiah to come, to deliver them from foreign rulers and to restore the kingdom of God. They have waited for those who persecuted them to be punished. The servant of God must strike down the wicked, and I am God's servant today."

He nodded his head as a signal, and two Sicarii who were standing with the Zealots moved forward, one towards Ananias, the other towards Ezekial. They drew their knives and plunged them into the sides of their victims, then withdrew their knives and plunged again. They did this several times until the two men fell. Ezekial issued a low moan as he dropped; Ananias was silent. The powerful leader of the pro-Roman aristocracy died like a Roman emperor in a pool of blood on the floor of a palace. With him died the major symbol of Jewish compliance.

When we Nazarenes heard of it, we prayed. We prayed for the souls of Ananias and Ezekial as if they had been one of our own. We had never approved of what Ananias had done, but he still was a fellow Jew. He had been our enemy, but we followed Jesus' teachings and loved this enemy as we did ourselves. We had fought for the revolution, but we had never approved of the killing of those whom we could have taken prisoner. And once Menahem had declared himself Messiah, we had withdrawn and stood aside. Jesus would come in his time, we said, and prove that Menahem was wrong.

Eleazar, upon hearing of the death of his father, became distraught. He went to talk to Rabath, who was visiting Bernice at the time. Rabath, secret Nazarene that she was, could not approve of this continued Roman occupation of her country, so she sympathized with the revolution, though she could not say that to Bernice. But also, being a Nazarene, she could not approve of unnecessary executions, so she asked Eleazar how he could have allowed such a thing to happen, especially since the execution had been of his own father. She spoke to him, as she had since they had been children, like an older sister scolding her younger brother. And he, accustomed to being spoken to that way by her when he had erred, listened sheepishly, without protest, to her words.

Although Rabath had not in any way encouraged him to do it, he returned to Jerusalem with an inner determination to avenge his father's death. When he got there, he found the people in distress. Menahem was now in control and was ruling with the same merciless disregard for human life that the Romans had had. Sadducees were hunted down and killed, among them the husband of Rabath. All who were not *for* the revolution were against it. Caiaphas went into hiding and successfully eluded those who were looking for him. Private property was confiscated by Menahem's men as the need (or desire) for it arose. It seemed that we had exchanged one tyrant for another.

Eleazar gathered about him a loyal coterie of soldiers and spoke to them of killing Menahem. Not only were *they* with him in this, they said, but the people would be too.

So the plan was made, and one day when Menahem, dressed in a royal robe, went to the Temple to pray along with a personal bodyguard of armed Zealots, Eleazar struck. Before Menahem got into the Temple, Eleazar and his men rushed the Zealot guards, while the people threw stones at Menahem. Menahem and his men defended themselves, but as they saw the number of people against them increasing, they scattered. Some were killed; some were found hiding and were killed; some escaped. A different Eleazar — Eleazar, son of Jairus — a relative of Menahem, escaped and went to Masada and took command of the Zealot force there. Menahem himself got to Ophales, but his pursuers found him hiding in a house and dragged him into the open air and tortured him until he died.

I think that was unnecessarily cruel. I am against killing if at all possible, though I know sometimes it is necessary. But to torture someone to death, the way Florus did to his victims in front of Bernice, for example, or the way Antiochus did before the Maccabees stopped him, or the way the Romans do in general before they crucify people, is not worthy of godly men.

But Eleazar had done what he had planned to do; he had avenged his father's death. He had used the people's displeasure with Menahem as the means by which to achieve it. And the people, thinking only that they were ridding themselves of a tyrant, had not known that they were serving Eleazar's private purpose as well, though I do believe that those with any imagination must have suspected it.

Now he could turn to the Romans. They were still in the Herodian Towers, and he could concentrate on laying siege to them. The Romans saw their position was hopeless, so their commander, Metilius, sent a messenger to Eleazar, saying that they would leave their weapons and belongings behind if they could just leave Jerusalem alive. Eleazar sent three messengers to say that he accepted these terms and that he guaranteed the Romans safe passage. On the Sabbath the Romans came out with their weapons, and we kept our distance and watched. Then they laid down their weapons and warily marched away. And now Eleazar's men attacked. The Romans could not defend themselves without weapons, so they cried out about the agreement and how unfair it was to break it. They were thinking about their equally armed gladiators fighting it out in an arena and expecting themselves to be treated the same. But they were forgetting about how often fully armed Romans had attacked unarmed Jews and about the women and infants who had died on the shafts of Roman swords.

The Roman commander, Metilius, was the only one who asked for mercy, and when the attackers shouted that they would show him as much as he had shown the infants he had slaughtered, he tried a different tack and begged to become a Jew. Eleazar thought that ironic. After all the attempts by Romans to force their pagan religion down the throats of Jews, a Roman captain, to save his life, was now begging to become a Jew. Eleazar spared his life and presided over the formal ceremony in which Metilius was circumcised. Now at least one Roman would know how it felt to be pushed into a religion because of military might.

Eleazar had killed on the Sabbath, and there were those who thought that was wrong. But Eleazar, remembering Antiochus' Sabbath attack in the days of the Maccabees and the slaughter of one-thousand Jewish men who would not fight on that day, refused to be restricted as they had been. Besides, if the Pharisees were right that it was acceptable to heal on the Sabbath when the need for it was great, then it must be equally acceptable to fight on that day when the need for that was great. Agrippa's warning that we would be defeated by the Romans because we could not fight on the Sabbath was not going to be true as long as Eleazar was in command.

CHAPTER XXXV

While Eleazar was ridding Jerusalem of Romans, the Syrians in Caesarea, with the Romans to help them, were trying to rid that city of Jews. Flushed with their paper from Nero, which said that Caesarea belonged to them, and strengthened by the support of Florus and his anti-Jewish soldiers, just as they previously had been supported by Felix and his, and already brought to a fighting pitch by the incident at the Caesarean synagogue, the Gentiles in Caesarea killed more then twenty-thousand Jews. Those who were not killed and were caught were sent in chains by Florus to work as slaves in the dockyards. This was Romans and Syrians fighting hand-in-hand to rid the city of Jews. Whereas previously, Jewish weapons, supplies and skill at arms had enabled the Jews to beat the Syrians, now, with Roman soldiers against them too, the Jews could not prevail.

But this began a series of reprisals, and then reprisals against the reprisals. When news of the Caesarean massacre reached other parts of the empire, Jews in Gentile cities killed Gentiles in their midst. In Philadelphia, Sebonitis, Heshbon and Gerasa, in Pella, Scythopolis, Gedara and Hippos, in Kedasa, Ptolemais, Gaba and Ascalon, in Anthedon, in Gaza, in the district of Gaulonitis and the neighboring Syrian villages, Jews massacred Gentiles to pay for the twenty-thousand slain Jews in Caesarea and the enslavement of almost all the rest. Samaritans and Jews now joined together as one, and in Sebaste, they destroyed the Roman garrison and burned that city to the ground. Ascalon, Anthedon and Gaza were also destroyed. Even Caesarea got a taste of Jewish rancor, for armed bands of Jews extracted a price even from Caesarea for the thing that it had done. Looting was rampant everywhere, and captured adults were killed. But we Jews did not kill the children; the lives of the children we spared. That, at least, gave some small measure of humanity to the heartless butchery of the time. An-eye-for-an-eye pervaded our hearts, and the Pharisee teachings against this practice and Jesus' turning his other cheek were forgotten or ignored in the heat of pride and honor and reputation, in the fire of Jewish revenge.

In Scythopolis, the Jewish residents sided with their Gentile neighbors against the rampaging Jews. One of these Scythopolitan Jews was Simon, son of Saul, so powerful in battle that, in the daily defense of his city, he sometimes singlehandedly drove off the entire invading Jewish army. But in spite of their Jewish champion, the Gentiles feared being betrayed, so they asked their Jewish neighbors to prove their fidelity by taking their families to a grove. The Jews did so warily, wanting to show their sincerity to the Gentiles but, at the same time, cautiously posted guards at night. After two peaceful nights, the Jews felt safe, so they no longer posted their guards. The watching Gentiles saw their chance and attacked the sleepers at night. They killed thirteen-thousand Jews in all, including old men and women and children, and looted their property afterwards. Simon, seeing the mistake he had made in putting his trust in the Gentiles, would not give them the satisfaction of killing him and his family. He drove his sword into his father and then his mother, into his wife and children, and then into his own bowels. But even greater was the mistake of the Gentiles, for they had lost their one-man army, and now the invading Jews poured in and slaughtered them.

But now Gentiles would again have their chance, for when news of these slaughters spread farther, Gentiles in Alexandria and some Syrian cities retaliated by killing Jews: in Ascalon, twenty-five hundred; in Ptolemais, two-thousand; and those not killed were imprisoned. In Tyre and Hippos and Gedara, the same. But in contrast to that, in Antioch and Sidon and Apamea, the Jews were left alone, and in Gerasa, the Gentiles even helped the Jews leave if they wished to go elsewhere for safety. Perhaps it was because many Gentiles in those places were God-fearers or Christians — Christians who had not yet heard that the Jews killed Jesus — and were thus sympathetic towards Jews. In the places where killing did occur, it was always followed by looting and piles of naked corpses, mephitically fouling the air.

In Cypros overlooking Jericho, Jews killed the Roman garrison and burned down the headquarters. In Machaerus the Romans surrendered peacefully and left under an agreement of truce. But in Alexandria, a tragedy occurred. Both Greeks and Jews lived there with, as you know, a long history of clashes between them. The governor at this time was Tiberius Alexander, the Jew who had given up Judaism in order to become a Roman and the man who, when he had been governor of Judaea, had executed Jacob and Simon, two of the sons of Judas of Galilee. The Greek citizens of Alexandria were holding a meeting in an amphitheater to consider sending a delegation to Nero about some dispute they were having with the Jews. A stream of newcomers came in, and some of them were Jews who thought the meeting was a general one involving all the citizens of the city. When they were recognized for what they were, one of the Greeks shouted that they were enemy spies, and other Greeks picked up the cry. The Jews turned and fled for their lives, but the Greeks caught three of them and took them from the amphitheater and tied them to posts for the purpose of burning them alive, in emulation of Nero, who had burned Christians tied to posts in his garden.

Word spread quickly among the Jews about what was going to happen, and the Jews grabbed torches and rushed to the amphitheater and threatened to burn everyone in it alive. But then word of this got to Tiberius Alexander, and he sent prominent Jews to the Jewish crowd to get it to retreat, on threat of a Roman attack. But the Jews would not retreat, and they cursed Alexander for not telling the Greeks to desist and to release the three Jewish men, who had done nothing more than walk into what they had thought was a public meeting. Alexander would not do that. He chose to warn only the Jews, and he responded to the crowd's intractableness by loosing on all the Jews of Alexandria, not just the crowd at the amphitheater, two legions of Roman soldiers plus two-thousand more added to that, with orders to kill and plunder and burn down Jewish houses as they wished.

The Jews fought well against the Romans, holding their line of defense for some time. But when the line finally broke, the Romans poured in; the slaughter began in earnest. Just as the Romans had done in Jerusalem under Florus, they killed infants and the aged indiscriminately. They killed in houses, they killed in streets, and, before they were done, fifty-thousand Jewish bodies lay dead in red, congealing puddles of blood, putrefying the smoke-filled air.

The Greeks followed close behind as the Romans hacked their way through the Jews. Those Jews who lay bleeding and wounded, the Greeks finished off themselves. What possessions the Romans did not take, the Greeks took. As the Romans penetrated deeper into the Jewish section of the city, the Greeks lingered over the bleeding Jewish bodies, stabbing them if they were still alive and looting them, as vultures and hyenas pick the flesh off the bones of dead animals after the lion has walked away.

The remnant of the Jews still alive sent a message to Alexander begging mercy. Alexander called off his troops, and the troops immediately obeyed. But the Greeks who hung over the dead had to be dragged away by the Romans, so thirsty were they to taste the sweetness of their victory, their triumph over the Jews. And the Greeks who had taken the three Jews, intending to burn them alive, paid no penalty for having done that or for having sparked a demonstration that resulted in so many deaths. As for Tiberius Alexander, the former Jew, he had proved his transformation to his Roman superiors by showing that he would sooner side with Greeks than Jews regardless of which side was right.

A significant thing in all these events in all these different places was that Romans were not the only Gentiles against us; almost all the Gentiles were. Because most of the Gentiles were pagans and believed in their multiple gods, they stood together against Jews, who believed in only one god. The exceptions among the Gentiles were the God-fearers and Christians, but they did not fight alongside the Jews in these present upheavals. Though pagans everywhere lined up with the Romans, not all believers in one god lined up with the Jews.

Meanwhile, in King Agrippa's kingdom, Rabath sat in relative safety with Bernice and heard of her husband's death in Jerusalem. He had been killed because he had been a Sadducee who had favored the Roman presence. She grieved for him because he had been good to her, even though she had secretly disagreed with his politics. Of her father she heard nothing, so she assumed that he was safe. Though she and her father had not spoken to each other since their last disagreeable encounter, she still loved him and cared about his safety, especially since Eleazar's father, Ananias, had been killed by that false Messiah, Menahem. For the king, the tragedy of all this killing in Israel (he had not heard about Alexandria yet) was driven home when he saw its effect on Rabath: her eyes red and sunken, her expression long and drawn, a look of desperation on the pale, gaunt face of this beautiful woman. He felt driven to find a way to end what he considered a national insanity. He decided to go to Antioch to discuss the state of affairs with the legate, Gallus, in the hope of finding a means to end it. He left his friend, Noarus, who was also related to King Soaemus, to rule while he was away. That proved to be a tragic mistake. Noarus ordered the king's soldiers to kill a peaceful delegation of seventy prominent Jewish citizens from nearby Batanaea, who had come to ask for troops to discourage any uprising from starting in their district. From that outrage he went to others, taking people's possessions as he pleased and threatening any objector with death. Bernice sent word to her brother about what was going on, and Agrippa removed Noarus from office even before returning home, not venturing to do more than that lest he offend King Soaemus. While that stopped any future perpetrations by this imitator of Florus, it did not end the resentments that his rule had created among the people who lived under Agrippa. The king now had discontent in his kingdom that he had not had before.

Florus meanwhile, inwardly delighted that we Jews had gone as far as we had in Jerusalem, now started the final part of his plan for our destruction. He sent word to Cestius Gallus that although his forces had quelled the Jews of Caesarea, they were inadequate to do the same in Jerusalem. It was up to Gallus to punish the Jews for their impudent, offensive revolt.

Gallus was forced to act. Agrippa's recent visit, which had sought a peaceful solution to all the chaos, was still fresh in his mind. But the finality of the Jews taking over Jerusalem required a forceful response; the empire had to be preserved.

Gallus gathered an army. To the twelfth Roman legion he added two-thousand troops from other legions; to these he added six cohorts of infantry and four troops of cavalry; King Antiochus sent two-thousand horsemen and three-thousand bowmen; King Agrippa sent two-thousand infantry and almost as many cavalry; and King Soaemus sent four-thousand troops, both horsemen and bowmen. An army of prodigious size. Enough to reconquer the Jews.

After three months of organizing, they marched to Ptolemais, with Gallus and King Agrippa in the lead, Agrippa being there to guide and advise. Caesennius Gallus, the commander of the twelfth Roman legion went with them. Along the way, Gentiles with minimal fighting skills but a strong hatred of Jews joined the army, the incongruity of being led by a Jewish king not disturbing them any more than the Jewish king seemed to be disturbed by leading an army of Gentiles against his own people.

As the Roman drive began, the Gentiles in Damascus decided to do their part. They were more numerous than all the Jews, God-fearers, Nazarenes and Christians who lived there, and they could do things by force because of their numbers. They felt justified in suspecting the Jews of plotting rebellion against Rome, and they pushed all of them into the gymnasium, where they could detain them for a while. Nazarenes, being considered Jews (which they were), were pushed in there too. God-fearers were not because they were not Jews, although it was known that they admired the Jewish religion. (Interestingly, the wives of many of these Gentile pagans had become Jews or God-fearers and were at odds with their husbands about religion. They exerted a restraining influence on their husbands at home.) Christians posed a special problem, because some of them were Jews and some of them were not. Circumcision was sometimes used to identify the former, and those who *were* circumcised were classed as Jews and pushed into the gymnasium too. And here was one of those times when it was better for Christians to disavow themselves from Jews; when it was better to deny that they were wild olive shoots off the main tree of Israel, which, though he had said it originally, Paul had not been saying in recent years; when it was better to deny that Jesus was going to create a new government to replace that of the Romans; when it was better to present themselves as being loyal and obedient to Rome (in spite of what Nero had done to them) and to say that Jesus had felt that way too.

Meanwhile, in Israel, Gallus and his army first attacked the town of Zebulon with its ubiquitous, colorful flowers and found the fortress and town deserted, the Jews having fled to the hills. He allowed his soldiers to take the rich treasures the Jews had left behind, and then, in spite of the beauty of the place, he had them burn it down and the neighboring villages as well. He returned to Ptolemais, leaving the Syrians from Beirut to continue looting whatever they could in Zebulon.

When the Jews saw that only a few thousand soldiers remained in the town, they swept down from the hills and killed two-thousand of the Syrians, thus lessening the enemy's army by that amount.

But Gallus continued his task. He sent part of his army to capture Joppa, while he and Agrippa marched to Caesarea with the main force. The separated portion attacked Joppa by land and sea and took the Jews by surprise, breaking into their houses and killing them before they even had time to grab their weapons. They killed eight-thousand, four-hundred Jews, the infants and aged included, for the greater glory of Rome.

Gallus went on with his work. To Narbatene near Caesarea he sent large numbers of horsemen, who dutifully killed large numbers of Jews and looted and burned down the neighboring villages. Rome was on the march; you could smell it in the air: blood, decaying flesh and smoke, so that a blind man could tell you where they were. And Herod Agrippa II, the king of the Jews, was paying back his people for their insulting rejection of him in Jerusalem. They would have more respect for him now.

Now Caesennius Gallus, one of the commanders previously mentioned under the legate Cestius Gallus, led part of his twelfth legion into Galilee, the region of Jesus' boyhood. In Sepphoris, the city where Judas of Galilee had seized Herod's armory and joined with Zaddok, the Pharisee, to march on Jerusalem, the people welcomed the Romans; hypocritically, I think, because they really despised them in their hearts and wanted only to avoid being attacked by them. This happened in other towns as well. But those disposed to resist went to Mount Asamon near Sepphoris, gathering there with light weapons and stones. The Romans attacked them in an uphill fight, and the Jews drove them back, killing two-hundred. But with a flanking attack, the Romans got higher, and their heavier weapons carried the day so that they killed two-thousand Jews.

Galilee was now secured for Rome, so the army left Caesarea for Antipatris, where it scattered a Jewish force without a blow being struck and where it burned the town and the neighboring villages to the ground. Then onward to Lyddia, which was almost empty because the Jews had gone to Jerusalem for the Feast of Tabernacles. The fifty Jews who did appear were killed, and the town was then burned down. Then through Beth-horon to Gibeon, six miles from Jerusalem, where the Roman army camped.

The next day, which was the Sabbath, the Jews attacked the encamped Romans. It took Gallus by surprise, first because he had expected only a defensive posture from the Jews and, second, because Agrippa had told him that the Jews would not attack on the Sabbath. But Agrippa had not been aware that Eleazar, the Jewish commander, had killed Romans on the Sabbath and had made it clear that he would not be constrained militarily by that day. The Jews drove a wedge through the Roman army and, at the cost of twenty-two Jewish lives, killed four-hundred Roman infantry and one-hundred fifteen cavalry. And Agrippa suffered disappointment too, for some of the neighboring kings who had served with their men in his army were now on the side of the Jewish defenders.

The Romans retreated to Beth-horon. And some of the Jews followed them and damaged their rear and took their pack animals back to Jerusalem. The Romans stayed in Beth-horon three days, and the Jews took positions in the hills outside Jerusalem, threatening any Roman advance.

Agrippa was surprised at the Jewish strength, having become accustomed to easier victories over his people. But informants came to tell him that some Jews wanted peace. Agrippa advised Cestius Gallus to offer a peace treaty, thinking that even if the militants said no, the pacifists would argue with them and cause internal dissension. Gallus sent two messengers forthwith, offering amnesty for past offenses if the Jews would lay down their arms. The advance guard of Jewish officers who received the messengers from Gallus were from the more militant branch of the defenders, although some pacifists were among them too. The militants feared the offer reaching the populace, lest the majority accept it out of fear. So they assaulted the messengers, killing one and wounding the other. The pacifists present objected to what had been done, so the militants attacked them with clubs and stones and drove them back to the city. The wounded Roman messenger saw all this and escaped to report it to Agrippa and Gallus.

Gallus sensed division in the Jews, and that renewed his confidence. He had his whole army attack the Jewish forward guard, and he drove it back to the city. Then he camped for three days outside the city and had his soldiers seize corn from the surrounding villages while he waited. He would give the Jews time to surrender if they would or to weaken themselves through dissension, as the sight of the invincible Roman army arrayed against them worked its effect each day.

But Gallus waited in vain, for the Jews did not surrender. So on the fourth day he attacked and entered the city of God. The Jewish defenders drew back and moved to defend the Temple. Gallus burned buildings as he advanced. At the walls of the Temple, he stopped, aligning his men in rows, so that the Roman soldiers covered the approaches to the Temple like a mantle of restless beetles.

Ananus, son of Jonathan (not to be confused with Ananus, son of Annas, the man who had executed James), and his prominent Sadducee friends within the Temple feared the impendency of their destruction. They sent a message to Gallus, saying that they would open the gates in exchange for the lives of all within. Gallus sent word that he would consider the offer, while, perfidiously, he continued to organize his troops for an assault. The messages that traveled between Ananus and Gallus were discovered by Eleazar, who still commanded the revolt. Angrily, he had Ananus and the Sadducees who had conspired with him thrown down from the walls of the Temple and pelted from above with stones, so that they ran off to their homes, happy to have escaped with their lives.

With the absence of Ananus and his group, Gallus saw that the pacifists who might have helped him into the Temple were now out of the picture. His choice of two strategies was narrowed to one. Immediately then, he attacked. His men attempted to surmount the walls from every direction, but every time they did, they were driven back by the stones of the defenders. They tried repeatedly for five days, always to be repulsed. On the sixth day, Gallus led a large group of infantrymen backed by all the Roman archers in an attack on the north wall of the Temple. The Romans lined up in rows at the foot of the wall and placed their shields above their heads, overlapping them, so that they formed a shell like a giant tortoise. This protected the soldiers from the stones coming down from above. Under this shell, they began to undermine the wall and prepare to set fire to the Temple gate. Some of the Jewish defenders saw what was happening and lost courage; they escaped unseen over the walls and fled from the city for their lives. But the majority of the Jews remained and continued to pelt the Romans from above and to prepare to repulse them if they broke through at the gate.

In the evening, before the day of the final breakthrough, Ananus, son of Jonathan, and his evicted fellows left their homes and went to speak to Agrippa. Their fear, they said, was for the Temple, which the Romans seemed poised to destroy. When they had been inside, they said, they had offered to open the gates for Gallus, but he had delayed his decision until it had been too late. Now they begged Agrippa to prevent the destruction that seemed certain to come with the dawn. He should do it, they said, out of pity for his people and in honor of his father's memory.

Agrippa, for all his cooperation with Rome, was still a Jew, and the plea of Ananus touched him deeply. He went to speak to Gallus. Why had Gallus not told him about Ananus' offer when it had come from inside the Temple? Why had Gallus not accepted it? Gallus said that it was because it would have required him to spare all their lives. He was not going to let rebels go free. The Jews must be taught a lesson.

"And what of the Temple?" Agrippa asked. "Do you intend to destroy that too?"

"Of course," Gallus said. "We've burned cities and villages on our way here. We've burned parts of this city already. Why shouldn't we burn down this one symbol of Jewish unity?"

"Because it's religious and not political," Agrippa said. It was interesting: Agrippa, casual as he was about religion, and with enough disregard for the Temple that he built a new section of his palace overlooking it, still had enough respect for it — if only as a mollifier of the people — that he drew the line at its destruction.

"My dear King Agrippa," Gallus responded, "let's not be naive. You know as well as I that religion and politics are so tightly entwined with your people that you can't affect one without affecting the other. If we destroy this one great center of the Jewish religion, we'll be destroying the thing that holds Jews together politically. Your people persist in thinking of themselves as a nation apart from Rome. We want them to become loyal Roman subjects. Like you! You're an example of what a Jewish subject of Rome should be. Why can't they all be like you?"

"I admit they need chastising," Agrippa said. "If I didn't think so, I wouldn't be here. But we don't have to destroy the religion. The religion gives them a reason for living. If we destroy the Temple, we'll be destroying them as a people."

Cestius Gallus leaned back in his chair and stretched his legs languidly. "Agrippa, my dear fellow," he said, "I do believe you exaggerate. As long as you Jews continue to worship and believe as you do, you'll be seen as a separate and distinct people wherever you are, Temple or no Temple."

"I'm afraid in this I must insist," Agrippa said. "When it comes to killing rebels, I'm with you; when it comes to destroying the Temple, I'm not."

Agrippa was well aware that he was challenging the Roman commander, but he felt strongly compelled to do so. He had chosen to minimize religion in his life as a rebellion against his father, to whom, up to a point, it had meant so much. That was common enough between children and parents. Eleazar, Ananias' son, had shown his independence of *his* father by taking an anti-Roman position as opposed to his father's pro-Roman one. But just as Eleazar had drawn the line at his father's death, so was Agrippa now drawing it at the destruction of the Temple. Though religion did not mean that much to him, the preservation of his people did. The tears he had shed in Jerusalem after his long speech in which he had urged the people to tolerate Florus had not been insincere.

"You say you must insist!" Gallus said. "Do you realize to whom you're speaking when you say that?"

"I do," Agrippa said. "And do you realize who is speaking to you as well?"

There was a weighty moment of silence and then Gallus stood up and walked casually about the room, as though merely stretching his legs.

"Well, King Agrippa, since you feel so strongly about the matter, I'll order the troops not to burn down the Temple when they take possession of it tomorrow. How's that? Will that satisfy you?"

"Unfortunately, no," said Agrippa.

"No? What more do you want?"

"If they take the Temple..."

"Not *if, when,*" corrected Gallus.

"Very well, *when* they take the Temple tomorrow, they still may burn it down."

"I'll be issuing orders not to. Roman soldiers obey their orders." Agrippa shrugged his shoulders. "Are you suggesting that I won't give that order when I say I will?"

"Even if you give that order," Agrippa answered, not wanting to accuse the legate of lying, "they still may burn it down. And then you'll come to me and say that you're sorry but you couldn't control the troops because they just got out of hand."

"What would you have me do then?"

"Leave Jerusalem. You've proved your point. The Romans are still the greatest military power in the world. I'll get Ananus, the son of Jonathan, the man who contacted you when he was still inside the Temple, to convince the more reasonable elements among the people that you've spared them, and he'll get them to reject the rebels."

"Leave Jerusalem when we're on the verge of bringing down its last stronghold?"

"Yes," Agrippa said.

"And if I refuse?" Gallus asked.

"I have almost five-thousand men under my command, horsemen and foot soldiers both."

"Are you threatening to withdraw them?"

Agrippa nodded his head affirmatively and then said, "I've already issued a tentative order. And besides that, King Antiochus is a friend of mine; he has five-thousand troops under him. And King Soaemus is also a friend; he has four-thousand. And your Syrian legionnaires are not too well disciplined; it's known throughout the army. They've done all right so far, but they can be easily swayed."

"And you think you can get them all to withdraw?"

Agrippa made an open gesture with his hand, as if to say that that remained to be seen. "*My* troops will certainly obey me," he said. "They alone could hurt your flank."

"Hurt my flank? Are you suggesting they'd attack?"

"Troops do get out of hand," Agrippa answered, "whether it's burning down temples or attacking the flanks of their allies. In spite of what their commanders order."

"I see," said Gallus. "I see, I see, I see. Well, it seems we will have to withdraw. I hope, King Agrippa, you can make good on your promise to get Jerusalem to stop fighting. I certainly hope you can."

Agrippa said he would try and that Gallus could depend that he would. He went then to see Ananus, the son of Jonathan and urged him to do his part in getting the people to lay down their arms and acknowledge the authority of Rome. Then he left Jerusalem for his own kingdom, leaving his army commander, Philip, son of Jacimus, in charge of his troops.

In the morning, the Romans pulled back and started to leave the city. The Jews in the Temple could hardly believe their eyes. The Romans had been on the verge of victory, and now they were withdrawing. But Agrippa's soldiers did not leave with them. Philip, their commander, had ordered his men to defect. Since Agrippa had told him the night before that he might want to do that, Philip, seeing that the king was no longer in the city, interpreted that to mean that he was to go ahead with the plan. He sent a message to the Jews that his army would not attack them, and he stayed in the city when the Romans withdrew.

The Zealots, of course, were elated. They seized this opportunity and left the Temple. They followed the Romans and killed infantrymen and cavalrymen in the rear of the Roman army.

The Romans camped at Mount Scopus for the night and the next day withdrew even further. But the Zealots continued to follow them and killed even more Romans in the rear. Then the Zealots sped unseen along the flanks of the Roman force, appearing abruptly at prearranged places and hurled spears at the Romans and killed them. But the Romans kept marching in tight ranks, not daring to break formation, lest they be picked off one by one. They had no idea how big the Jewish army was behind them, and they could see that Jews on their flanks were quick and mobile, able to strike and run with impunity. After suffering many losses, the Romans abandoned most of their baggage and moved quickly back to Gibeon. But the Jewish attacks increased in number, and, after two days, Gallus saw how untenable his position was. His main concern now was to save the army. The Jews were swarming around him. He discarded anything that would slow him down. He killed mules and wagon horses (except for those carrying missiles), and he moved quickly towards Beth-horon.

Through open spaces they passed relatively unmolested, but where the road went down into a ravine, the Jews were waiting in hiding; the Romans marched into a trap. In front of the exit to the ravine stood a mass of Jewish fighters preventing the Romans from going forward. At the rear of the ravine, another group of Jews prevented a Roman retreat. And all along the high mounds that bordered the ravine on both sides, Jews appeared and threw down a continuous shower of missiles that killed and wounded devastatingly. The Romans could not climb the steep, high sides of the ravine; they could not move forward or backward. They were trapped and could only use their shields to ward off the stones and rocks that rained on them from above. Men and horses fell; moans and whinnies rose upward; shouts of joy echoed back. The slaughter went on until dark, and then — only then, under the cover of darkness, could the Roman army escape.

They quickly ran to Beth-horon. The Jews, upon discovering the Roman escape, followed just as fast and encircled them. Gallus knew he could not remain there in Beth-horon. He posted four-hundred sentries on the roofs of the houses and had them shout watchwords throughout the night while the bulk of the army sneaked silently off to a place three-and-a-half miles away. When the Jews discovered this, they killed the deceptive sentries with javelins and started off after the Romans. The Romans, attempting to increase their lead, discarded their engines of war as they ran, and these were then taken by the Jews. The retreat then became a debacle as the Romans ran for their lives.

The Jews chased the Romans as far as Antipatris, but they could not catch them, so they turned back and took from the Roman dead whatever useful things they could find and then marched to Jerusalem singing hymns to God and to victory.

CHAPTER XXXVI

The Zealots had proved that the Romans were not invincible, though they had to admit that the Roman withdrawal from the walls of the Temple, which was the turning point in the fortunes of this war, was something they simply could not explain. Encouraged by this victory, many who had been reticent about joining the ranks of the Zealots now joined them. But there were others who saw in this humiliating Roman defeat the danger of Roman retaliation. Philip, the son of Jacimus, the commander of Agrippa's troops, was one of them, and he quietly left the city with a goodly portion of his men and headed northward to join Gallus. He would tell Gallus that he had acted only on Agrippa's orders and that his sentiments had been with Gallus all along.

Gallus himself had to explain his defeat to Nero, so he sent a messenger who was instructed to say that the Jewish revolt had been too much for an army of his size and that the reason the revolt had been so widespread and intense was because of Florus' excessive persecutions, which had gone far beyond what had been necessary. As for the reason he had called off the siege at the Temple, his messenger was instructed to say that his top officers had advised it militarily but that they, as he later discovered, had been bribed by Florus, who had wanted the attack called off so that an even greater Roman army might be dispatched in the future to more completely wipe out the Jews. It was a strained explanation at best, but he hoped it would divert criticism from himself to Florus, their previous friendship having little meaning for him now. He dared not tell Nero that he had made the final decision himself and that he had done it because of Agrippa. Agrippa might deny it, and Nero might believe him. After all, Agrippa was a king whose family had a long history of loyalty to Rome, and legates and procurators were more expendable than people such as that.

When news of the Roman defeat reached Damascus, the Gentiles there sought to kill the Jews who were being detained in the gymnasium. Since many of the wives of these Gentiles had become Jews, the husbands of these women had to act in secret, lest they have chaos at home. These wives, incidentally, though they had adopted Judaism, had not been interned in the gymnasium, because their husbands had been classed as pagans, and it was felt that when the final test of loyalty came, they would always follow their husbands. So the pagan Gentile men, including those whose wives were Jewish, armed themselves in secret and went to the gymnasium where they unflinchingly slaughtered thousands of unarmed Jewish men, women and children.

The carnage was horrible. Armed Gentiles blocked the doors so that no one could escape. Women shrieked as their babies were skewered like plump wine sacks, the blood gushing from them like fountains. Barehanded Jewish men grappled with armed Gentiles, who hacked at them with swords or lunged at them with daggers. Children clung to parents, who stood before them for protection. Husbands took piercings intended for wives. Men took sword cuts intended for friends. A film of blood spread on the floor, so that people slipped and fell as they ran. Exsanguinating bodies reeled dizzily, as if engaged in a drunken dance. People whose visions were dimmed from loss of blood tripped on bodies that lay before them on the floor. The dead became cushions for the dying. Bodies heaped on bodies. The slaughter was prodigious and whole.

Ananias of Damascus, the protector of Paul, was there with his wife, Sarah. He watched almost detachedly as the butchery started. Screams and bellowings assaulted his ears, but he could not move. The odor of blood filled his nostrils. He stood petrified, incapable of believing what he was seeing: the violent rage, the riotous savagery, unleashed like a beast that tore at everything — anything within the sphere of its reach. And he, the mortared spectator, unable to do anything but watch, to observe, with incredulous wonder the capacity of man to hate. Only when Sarah emitted a scream did he waken from his trance and act. A dagger upraised in the hand of a man was poised and about to strike her, and Sarah, her feckless palms held out for defense, was preparing to fend the blow. Ananias, with an effort worthy of a man one-third his age, threw himself in front of the dagger before it was halfway down. He took the blow in his chest, the blood spurting from his punctured heart, and he grabbed the man's wrist in an attempt to withdraw the knife. But the man drove Ananias to the ground by pushing the knife in further. Then Sarah leaped onto the assailant with a primeval scream that even she did not know she possessed and clawed at the man's eyes with her fingers. She was gored in the back by another man with a sword, who shouted above the din to his friend, "I got the bitch! I got the Jewish bitch for you!" With the few brief moments of life that were left to them, Ananias and Sarah lay with their heads close together and, though their bodies were stretched at an angle to each other, found each other's fingers and held each other's hands as they bled. There in that abattoir, in that former sanctuary of enlightenment where men had exercised and discussed philosophy and where butchers and victims now drenched themselves in gore, the man who had restored Paul's sight and the woman who had devised Paul's escape bled to death like sacrificed lambs on an altar to pagan gods.

Why? Why had the Gentiles done this? They were Greeks, not Romans, so why this hatred of people with whom they were not at war? It was because of religion, you see. The relative sameness of the Greek and Roman religions made them feel together in this all important aspect of life. It gave them something in common against Jews. Jews were different because their religion was different, and differences lead to hate.

There is a tendency in all of us to like those who think like ourselves and to dislike those who do not. And there is a compulsion to make the world think the way we think, either through conviction or enlightenment or social advantage or coercion, so that what we think may not be challenged, or, if it is challenged, so that we can claim we are right because so many more people agree with us than with our challengers, the more who do, the more valid our belief, and so that those who believe our way may, by dint of greater numbers, have the power of coercion over those who do not. That is why the Gentiles of Damascus, some of whose wives were Jews, sneaked off from their homes in secret to kill the Jews in the gymnasium.

In Israel, however, we Jews had won. When our soldiers returned from their pursuit of Gallus' army, our joy at their victory was immense. We knew that the Romans would come back again, but we were confident now that we could win. Opposition to the war disappeared. Even those who had been pro-Roman now joined in the preparations for war. Sadducees, Pharisees, Essenes and Nazarenes all joined the Zealot cause. We began to organize in earnest. We chose generals and governors for each part of our country. We knew that when the Romans returned, they would first go into Galilee, so we chose Josephus, who was a capable soldier and administrator to govern there. He built walls and fortifications for defense. We chose, among others, Rabath's friend, Eleazar, son of Ananias, to lead our forces in Idumaea. In Jerusalem we chose both Joseph, son of Gorion, and, over the objections of us Nazarenes, the former high priest Ananus, son of Annas, to govern. We objected to Ananus, of course, because he was the one who had killed James. The others told us that our past differences with Ananus should be forgotten now, because this was the time for Jews to unite against our common enemy — Rome. Those who had been against Rome all along were not to be given a greater voice than those who had been *for* Rome in the past. Even Caiaphas could come out of hiding and appear publicly without fear. The walls of the city were built higher and were strengthened.

In Galilee, according to what we heard from Josephus, not everyone acted for the good of the country. Some Jews sought to profit from all this expenditure for defense. Josephus reported later that he had to deal with one such man, whom he considered an unpatriotic profiteer. This was John of Gischala, the son of Levi. Josephus, when he would speak of this man, would not have much good to say about him, but it was only later that we found out why.

Other things that Josephus considered misdeeds occurred soon after that. When one of King Agrippa's ministers was passing through their region, Josephus' men stole money from him. This seemed perfectly acceptable to them, because they felt that Agrippa was on the side of the Romans. But Josephus had other thoughts about it. Agrippa had power and an army of his own, and though Agrippa was on the side of the Romans just now, his actions in the past had intimated that he might be swayed if conditions were right. Certainly his sister had not been treated well by the Roman governor, Florus, and Josephus thought that the memory of that and a favorable attitude from the Jewish people, sprinkled with a little Jewish victory here and there, might convince Agrippa to change his side. So he made it known publicly that he would return the stolen money to Agrippa. But he had forgotten how the people might react, and react they most certainly did. Agrippa was their enemy, and they did not take kindly to treating him with consideration and respect. John of Gischala led the protest against this and, by doing so, gained popularity with the people himself, which led Josephus to say all sorts of vile things about him, which really were not true. But Josephus weathered the storm of dissent and managed to stay on top. His endorsement by our leaders in Jerusalem and his fabled prowess as a soldier were enough to keep him in power.

Nero now ordered Vespasian to retake Israel for Rome. Vespasian was a career soldier, who had quelled the rebellious Germans and also had conquered Britain. Vespasian sent his son, Titus, to Alexandria to get one Roman legion from there, while he himself went to Syria to raise an army of Romans and soldiers of the neighboring kings. Agrippa, who desperately had wanted to save the Temple (and all of Jerusalem if he could have) from utter destruction now gave up all hope of making his countrymen see things his way, and he presented his army to Vespasian.

From Jerusalem, meanwhile, we Jews sent an army to take Ascalon from the Romans. We felt encouraged by our recent victory, and we all joined together in the common cause. Even some of the Essenes left the isolation of their desert communities and armed themselves to fight. But, alas, in Ascalon we failed miserably. The Romans sent out their cavalry, whose maneuverability on the plain before the city proved devastating to us. We pulled back and left many dead. But that victory over Gallus was still fresh in our minds, so we attacked Ascalon a second time. But this time the Romans were waiting in ambush, and again we lost many men. Those of us who were left alive retreated to Belzedek. But the Romans came after us there and set fire to the fort and killed many of our men who were in it.

Now Vespasian started his move. He marched into Galilee, as we had expected, and entered its main city, Sepphoris. The people there pusillanimously welcomed the Romans and allowed them to take over the fortifications that Josephus had built. Thus, when Josephus and his soldiers subsequently attacked Sepphoris, they found themselves unsuccessfully assailing the very walls that they had built to keep the Romans out. From their stronghold in Sepphoris, the Romans sallied forth repeatedly to raid and burn villages, to kill and enslave the people. Galilee reeked with smoke and blood, always the signs of Rome.

The Roman tribune, Placidus, commanded the Romans in Sepphoris, while Vespasian and the bulk of the Roman army went to Ptolemais to meet Titus and the legion from Egypt. With three Roman legions and more troops from Caesarea and Syria, as well as the armies sent by King Agrippa, King Antiochus, King Soaemus and Malchus the Arab, the Roman army was a formidable force. All this to conquer the Jews.

While Vespasian was forming this army with Titus, Placidus, anxious to show his commander what he could do on his own, left Sepphoris to attack the Galilean city of Jotapata. But what he had thought was going to be an easy victory turned out to be an embarrassing defeat. Josephus' forces were in Jotapata, and they fought hard and drove the Romans back.

But now Vespasian and his huge army entered Galilee, and many of Josephus' men, upon seeing or hearing of this horde arrayed against them, abandoned the cause of freedom and fled. Josephus' army was so diminished by this that he and his men had to take refuge in Tiberias.

Vespasian entered the city of Gabara. He easily overwhelmed its few Jewish defenders and killed all the inhabitants except for small children. (This was a departure from past Roman practice, in which all, including infants, were killed.) Josephus was still in Tiberias, and he heard about the downfall of Gabara. Now he sent messages to Jerusalem: either sue for peace or send him an adequate number of troops to enable him to fight; the Roman army was just too large.

Vespasian left the smoke of Gabara and marched for Jotapata, eager to avenge the defeat of his tribune, Placidus. Josephus, hearing of this move, returned to Jotapata, being convinced that he had to take a stand against the Romans in that city once again.

When the Romans arrived, they positioned themselves and attacked. Their archers sent showers of arrows over the heads of their assault infantry, which was led by Vespasian, who charged with his men up the hill to the city's walls. The walls were not that high and would be easy to surmount, they thought. But Josephus came out with his men and drove the Romans back. The Jews were desperate for survival against this huge Roman army, and the Romans were chagrined that they had just been repulsed by such a small Jewish force. The next day, the Romans attacked again. Again the Jews drove them back. For five days the Romans persisted, and each time the Jews did the same thing to them. Vespasian built catapults; he built platforms, rising ever higher against the outside of the walls. Josephus countered this by having his stone masons build the walls to greater heights. The Romans then pulled back and waited for the Jews to run out of drinking water, for they knew that the town depended on rain water and that it had not rained for some time. But the Jews, to deceive the Romans, wet their garments and flung them over the tops of the walls to dry, making the Romans think that there was no water shortage. Then the Jews came out of the city and made some bold attacks, again confounding the Romans. Day after day they burned the Roman platforms.

Vespasian brought forth his battering ram to batter down the wall. The ram, a thick pole like the mast of a ship, had a metal ram's head at one end. The ram was suspended horizontally from fixed beams and posts and was swung back and forth by the soldiers for the purpose of pounding down a wall. The Romans swung their ram, and every thud was followed by the shrieks of our Jewish women inside the walls. The Jews lowered stuffed sacs down the outside of the wall to divert the head of the ram. The Romans then used curved knives attached to the ends of long poles to cut the ropes off the sacs. The Jews then rushed out and burned the Romans' war engines and more of the Romans' platforms. One Jew threw a huge boulder down on the head of the ram and broke it. Then he jumped to the ground outside the wall and picked up the head. The Romans shot arrows at his armorless body, and five of the arrows found their mark. Yet the man climbed up the wall with the head in his arms and brought it to Josephus like a trophy.

The Jewish sorties continued, with more burning of Roman war engines. But the Romans brought up a new battering ram, and the pounding proceeded anew.

Then a Jewish arrow grazed Vespasian's foot, and the Romans seemed to resent that more than they had anything else. They previously had sought to avenge both the humiliating defeat of Cestius Gallus in Jerusalem and the more recent defeat of the tribune, Placidus, at these very walls. Now they sought to avenge their commander's wound. Their mechanical stone-throwers and spear-throwers were employed in sending missiles flying into the city with great force. One Jewish man was decapitated by a flying stone; the baby of a pregnant woman was pushed out of its mother's belly by another. The Jews threw their corpses down to the ground outside the walls, and the corpses piled up so high that one could almost climb them to the top of the wall. This is how a people fought, this is how a people died, who chose God to be their master rather than a group of pagan tyrants.

When news of Jotapata's resistance reached the Galilean city of Japha, the people were so inspired by Jotapata's stand that *they* dared defy the Romans too. Vespasian, still at Jotapata, sent Trajan first and Titus next to subdue this new rebellion. Japha fell but not without a fight. In the end, it was house to house fighting, with women pelting the Romans from the roofs. All the men were killed, and only women with infants were spared and were taken to be sold into slavery.

And these were not the only places in Galilee where fighting occurred. In Samaria, a large group of Samaritan men gathered at their sacred Mount Girizim. Vespasian sent soldiers to disperse them. The soldiers surrounded the mountain, and the Samaritans ran out of drinking water, so that some of them died in the heat. The weaker-willed surrendered to the Romans. The Roman commander told the others that he would guarantee their safety if they would throw down their weapons. But they refused. They had reached that state in which men prefer to die fighting rather than submit anymore to a tyrant. So the Romans fell upon them hard and massacred all of them that remained.

And Jotapata still held on. A Jew one day was captured by the Romans and tortured for information about conditions in the city. He refused to speak; he refused to give any aid to the enemy. When other tortures failed, they burned his skin with fire, but still he would not tell them anything. Vespasian, vexed and frustrated at the man's intransigence, ordered him to be crucified. And the man, when they were nailing him to the cross, smiled esoterically as if he had won a victory rather than suffered a defeat at the hands of the pagans. And Jesus, I know, welcomed that man after his days on the cross as the hero and patriot that he was.

But another Jew turned traitor and told the Romans how desperate the situation was inside the city, how little sleep the defenders had had and how low the food and water was. Reassured by this knowledge, the Romans climbed the walls quietly before dawn, disposed of the sentries, and began their massacre by first light. The sleepy, exhausted Jewish men were caught off guard and were slaughtered, and the women and children were pushed into cages, to be sold in the future into slavery.

Josephus and some of the city's leaders hid in a cave but were discovered there. Vespasian offered them their lives if they would come out, ostensibly because he admired the stand the Jews had put up and wanted especially to meet the leader who had proved such a capable adversary. Josephus was inclined to accept, but the others with him were not. For one thing, they didn't trust the Romans; for another, they thought it would be hypocritical to surrender like cowards after having exhorted everyone else to fight to the death. Josephus rationalized by saying that to fight at this point would be committing suicide, which God would not want them to do; that if they accepted whatever fate God now gave them and waited until God was ready to take them from this earth in His own good time, He would reward them for their forbearance, and they would remain with Him in heaven until He was ready to send them out again to occupy some new body on the earth. (In this he spoke like one of those mystics from the East, who tell us that souls come back again and again to occupy some new body in order to learn and grow. But such thoughts are not limited to the East, as you see, for here was Josephus, a Jew, expounding them too.) But his companions were unconvinced, and they each threatened to kill Josephus for what they considered his treachery and his cowardice. Josephus then said that since they were determined to die, they should draw lots and kill each other, with the last man killing himself, so that the Romans would not have the satisfaction of killing them. But Josephus knew secretly which lots to pick, and he picked them in such a way that he would be one of the last two men. The men cut each other's throats, and Josephus did not have to kill anyone until he stood and faced the last man, with whom he would have to draw lots to see which should kill the other and then kill himself. Though Josephus could have picked the one that would have made him do the final killing (he could have killed the man and then not killed himself), he talked the man out of this course, and they surrendered to the Romans together.

The Roman soldiers crowded about to see this commander of the Jews, who had fought them so well for so long. Some hated him; some admired him. Titus was among the latter, and he led Josephus to his father with a plea to spare the prisoner's life. Vespasian did that but said that he would send Josephus to Nero. Josephus asked Vespasian not to do that but to keep him prisoner for himself.

"For the day will come," Josephus said, "when you will be emperor in Rome, and the day will also come when Titus will sit on the throne after you. I would rather be the prisoner of both of you than be the prisoner of Nero."

"How do we know this prophecy of yours is accurate?" Vespasian asked.

"I predicted to my followers that Jotapata would fall in forty-seven days and that I would be taken prisoner. All that has come to pass."

They asked the other prisoners if Josephus had predicted that, and the other prisoners said that he had (though they may have said it just to give their commander greater status among the Romans). Vespasian now thought that he had not only a knowledgeable general in his hands but an accurate prophet as well. Therefore, he did not send Josephus to Nero but kept him with himself.

For the winter that was now approaching, Vespasian put two Roman legions in Caesarea, where the Jew-hating Greek population applauded the Romans' success and clamored (unsuccessfully) for the execution of Josephus, and he put the other Roman legion in Scythopolis, the city where Simon, the Jewish one-man army had fought the invading Jews for his Gentile neighbors and where those neighbors had then betrayed him and where the Jewish invaders had then, unimpeded, killed the triumphant Gentiles.

This lull in Roman activity gave some Jews a chance to act without hindrance. The seacoast town of Joppa had been destroyed by Cestius Gallus in spite of his ignominious flight from Jerusalem. The surviving Jews in that city, as well as Jewish survivors from burned-down villages thereabouts, rebuilt the city and formed a pirate fleet that raided ships on the sea route to Egypt. Vespasian sent infantry and cavalry to put an end to that. The Jews fled to their ships and sailed them out of the range of the Roman arrows. But a storm arose and drove some ships against each other, breaking them up, and drove other ships against the rocks close to the shore. Those Jews who were washed to shore alive were killed by the Romans who were waiting there. And Joppa was destroyed a second time along with the villages that had been rebuilt.

CHAPTER XXXVII

News of this and other tragedies reached us slowly in Jerusalem. When we heard that Jotapata had fallen, we were told that Josephus had died there too. For a month afterward we mourned not only the loss of friends and relatives in Galilee but our respected northern commander as well. Josephus' wife and his mother and father were in Jerusalem, and they now grieved at his loss. But then, when news came that Josephus had surrendered and was living like a pampered pet with the head of the Roman army, the grief of many of us turned to hate, and the desire to defeat the Romans was spurred anew, this time not just for liberty but to get at Josephus as well. For Josephus' wife and mother and father, their grief turned to outward shame at his betrayal but inward delight that he was still alive.

Agrippa, meanwhile, tried to keep the war out of his territory. As he had done in Jerusalem, he counseled peaceful acceptance of Roman authority. Many of his citizens, accustomed to obeying their king in whatever he said, followed his advice — or perhaps I should say, his command. But some did not. Some, still resentful over what Agrippa's appointee, Noarus, had done, and sensing that the time of liberation was at hand, armed themselves and formed groups for the purpose of fighting. To counter this, Agrippa decided to ask for Vespasian's help. At Agrippa's invitation, Vespasian and his soldiers came from Caesarea on the coast to Caesarea Philippi in Agrippa's domain. Agrippa regaled Vespasian with banquets, and Vespasian offered prayers of thanks for his victories.

Two of the cities in revolt in Agrippa's domain were Tiberias and Tarichaeae. To those of us who thought revolution, a strike against Agrippa was a strike against Rome, and that was why the Zealots who lived in his lands rose up. But Agrippa felt confident. The greatest army on earth was on hand to help him re-establish his power. He asked Vespasian for help.

Vespasian, who knew that wherever Agrippa ruled Rome ruled, gave it. He sent a group of cavalrymen to Tiberias to speak to what he had heard were peaceful members of the community about their giving pledges of loyalty to Rome and resisting any revolutionaries in their midst. The cavalrymen dismounted as they approached close to the city.

Was it because they were confident about their indestructibility or because they wanted to show their peaceful intentions? I do not know. But whichever it was, the revolutionaries saw it as an opportunity. Led by Jeshua, the son of Shaphat, the revolutionaries rushed out at the Romans and caused them to flee, with some of the Romans even abandoning their horses as they did. Yet, in spite of that first successful encounter, some of the Sadducees in the city sneaked off to the Romans to tell them that they were not revolutionaries and that they were on the Roman side. That defection led Jeshua to question how many citizens of Tiberias could be depended on when the time finally came to fight. Because he had his doubts about this, he left Tiberias with those whom he knew were loyal and made his way to Tarichaeae.

Vespasian sent Trajan to Tiberias to do what his first cavalry unit had not been able to do. But Jeshua and the Zealots were all gone from there, and those people who remained in the city opened the gates to Trajan so that the Romans could enter without a fight. And because Agrippa now guaranteed the loyalty of these remaining citizens, Trajan did not permit plundering by his soldiers. So much for Tiberias.

In Tarichaeae, on the other hand, more and more Zealots came in and prepared to make a stand. In the recent past, Josephus had directed the construction of a defensive wall for this city, just as he had for Tiberias and other cities in Galilee when he had first taken command of the north. It was ironic, then, that the man who had done that should now be advising the Romans on how to breach that very same wall.

Vespasian camped his army near Tarichaeae in sight of all the defenders. He wanted the Jews to see how large an army he had. But the Zealots, led by Jeshua, could not be daunted by that. They came out of the city and made a lightning attack on the Roman encampment and then fled as the Romans pursued them. The city was situated next to a lake, so Jeshua and his men got into boats and sailed out on the water and then shot arrows at the Romans on shore.

Another force of Zealots was on the plain in front of the city. The Romans attacked it with cavalry and bowmen. The Zealots, who had no armor to protect them from the Roman arrows and lances and who fought on foot against their mounted enemy, held back the Roman attack for a while. But, eventually, the Roman advantage in equipment wore them down, and they ran to the safety of the city. The Romans seized the moment and rode their horses into the shallow water on the lake side of the city and entered by that route. Some of the inhabitants tried to swim for the boats, which already were on the lake, but they were killed by the Romans as they made that attempt. Others were slaughtered in the streets. Jeshua and a number of his Zealots, when they saw that defeat was inevitable, got their boats to the safety of land and fled the city in the hope that they could fight another day.

Now the Romans went after the remaining boats. They built rafts and steered them towards the boats on the lake. The Zealots on those boats had nothing left to fight with but stones, and these proved harmless against the armor of the Romans. In contrast, the Zealots, who were completely without armor, fell victim to the Roman lances, arrows and swords. When their flimsy boats were crushed by the stronger Roman rafts, those who survived tried to swim for the rafts, intending to be taken prisoner. But the Romans were taking no prisoners. The Jews in the water were shot by arrows, and any Jew who clung to a raft had his hands or head cut off by Roman swords. If a Jewish boat did make it to shore, the Jews on board were shot by arrows as they tried to escape. The lesser weaponry of the Jews took its toll, and the Jews suffered total defeat.

Of those Jews who were still alive, Vespasian gave some to Agrippa for execution, some he executed himself and some he sent to Nero to work on the digging of a canal at Corinth. The most tractable survivors he left alive to serve as chastened Roman subjects. They were to dispose of the stinking corpses that were piled in the streets and along the shore of the city of Tarichaeae.

With the fall of Jotapata and Tarichaeae, most of the remaining cities and towns in Galilee surrendered to the Romans. But a few did not, and one of these was Gamala, a city on the opposite side of the lake from Tarichaeae. This city was surrounded by defensive trenches on land and had had a wall built around it under Josephus' orders in the past. Now it was filling with Zealots and other Jews who had escaped being killed by the Romans. It was located in Agrippa's domain, but its inhabitants had not surrendered to Agrippa as had the inhabitants of other cities, and it now became the new center for Galilean resistance. For seven months Agrippa's troops had tried to capture it and always had failed in their attempts. So Agrippa now turned to Vespasian.

Vespasian marched to Gamala. He camped his men at different points around the city and had them work on siege platforms and war machines and on filling in the city's outer trenches. Within the city there was a limited supply of water, but the defenders overcame their despondency over that hardship and prepared themselves to fight. Then Agrippa, who never seemed to lose hope that his powers of persuasion might sway rebels to lay down their arms, went to one of the walls and tried to discuss surrender terms. Someone slung a stone at him, and it hit his elbow, and that terminated any discussion.

The Romans attacked. They used platforms, catapults and battering rams, as they had at Jotapata. They broke through the wall and entered the city with the sound of trumpets urging them on. The defenders stood their ground and stopped the attackers at first. Then they moved to the upper parts of the city into narrow alleys, with the Romans close behind them. But then, unexpectedly, the Jews turned and attacked the Romans, and the Romans, caught by surprise, tried to retreat back down the streets. But the press of other Roman soldiers moving forward from behind prevented this, and the retreating Romans climbed onto the roofs of houses to avoid the close man-to-man combat with the Jews that they would otherwise have had to endure. But under the weight of so many men on the roofs, the roofs collapsed. And if the house was more than two levels, as many of them were, the roof caved into the floor below, and that floor caved into the next one, and so on, until the Romans fell to their deaths or were buried under the debris. Those Romans who were in the narrow streets reeled and fell under the storm of arrows and stones that rained on them from the Jews on the roofs. Everywhere, houses collapsed and dust filled the air. And our people acquired new weapons and ammunition in the form of stones from fallen houses and swords from fallen Romans.

Vespasian himself was there in one of the steep, narrow streets and stood in danger of losing his life. He realized this, so he had his soldiers surround him and link their shields together to ward off the hail of stones and arrows being rained on them by the Jews. The Zealots then attacked Vespasian and his men with swords, and the Romans moved back in an orderly fashion, since they saw that they could not beat the Jews in this situation.

The Romans were driven back, and some of them who had not retreated in time were trapped in the network of Jewish houses. One of these, a Syrian centurion named Gallus, took ten soldiers with him and hid in a house. Since the battle was over, the Jewish residents came in to eat their supper. Gallus overheard them talking about their strategy for fighting the next day, and he made a mental note of it tell Vespasian. Then, at night, when the inhabitants were asleep, Gallus and his men sneaked out from their hiding place and cut the people's throats and then made their way back to their camp.

But notwithstanding such isolated incidents, it was a terrible defeat for the Romans. Yet, as stunning as that victory had been, the defenders were concerned that they might not win again. Food and water were low, and some people were actually starving. Some left the city under cover of night, and some left through tunnels which had been built as escape routes some time before.

And then, as Vespasian sat outside Gamala, contemplating what his next move should be, word came to him that a new flare-up had occurred in Galilee. The mountain fortress of Mount Tabor was now in revolt. Vespasian sent a detachment of Roman troops there, and their commander, finding ascent to the fortress impossible without the annihilation of his soldiers, sent word to the Jewish defenders that if they came down and surrendered peacefully, he would treat them with favor and respect. The defenders took him at his word and came down to the plain below. Now the Romans had them. They had never intended to keep their word. They attacked the Jews on the plain. The killing was easy in the open, with the Jews having no armor or horses. But though many were killed, many escaped to tell their tale in Jerusalem.

This victory at Mount Tabor encouraged the Romans outside Gamala. They forced their way into that city again and this time avoided the high, narrow streets in the upper sections. The Jewish defenders, short on ammunition, retreated to the high citadel which towered above the city and which stood next to a ravine outside the wall. Unlike the Romans, our people had children and wives to protect, and these hampered their effectiveness as fighters. Those who did not make it into the citadel died under Roman swords, and that included children and their mothers as well. From the citadel itself, our people threw down rocks and shot arrows and killed many Romans below. But the food and the water finally ran out, and the Jews knew that the end was near. Large numbers of them hurled themselves out of the citadel to their deaths rather than allow the Romans the satisfaction of killing them or of selling their wives and daughters into slavery. Those who remained to fight succumbed to the Roman attacks, and Gamala, after its bloody and heroic defense against the foreign and pagan invader, finally fell to the Romans after a hard, full month of resistance.

Who was left in Galilee to fight? Josephus, who had been our hope for success in the north, was now on the side of the Romans. Our major cities in Galilee were lost. Who could lead us, and *where* could he lead us, now that our cause was so low?

Out of that state of despair, out of that condition of unprosperous hope, came John — John of Gischala — the man whom Josephus had feared and disliked, who had threatened Josephus' primacy in the early days of the fight, whom Josephus had labeled a thief and an opportunist but who, when the test of loyalty came, proved himself more staunch

347

and courageous, even in the face of likely defeat, than his weaker-willed detractor had been. In his own town of Gischala, he gathered about him a determined group of Zealots. In spite of the terrible odds against them, they would fight for the kingdom of God. They prepared themselves for battle.

Vespasian sent Titus there at the head of a large group of horsemen. Titus offered them peace if they would merely submit to Rome. John said he needed time to consider this proposal, especially with the Sabbath approaching the next day. Titus gave him the time, and John and his men discussed the situation. They decided, in the face of such a superior Roman force, that it would be better to leave Gischala and go to Jerusalem, where they could join the growing Jewish army and fight more effectively against the Romans. They did not, as Josephus had done, surrender.

Under cover of night, they left with their wives and children (a responsibility the Romans did not have), a long, slow stream of them strung out along the road to the south, vulnerable to attack by Titus' fast-moving cavalry as soon as their flight was discovered. Those who were left in Gischala were disinclined to fight. They opened the gates to Titus, and he and his men rode in. It did not take him long to discover the exodus that had taken place during the night. Now he and his men gave chase. They found the column disjointed and unprotected, families separated by the huge numbers of people, and they killed the stragglers, who were mainly women and children. Yet many of the people did get through, and we welcomed them into the city with jubilation when they arrived.

Yes, we had lost Galilee, but Jerusalem was still strong. Fighters were everywhere. They were coming from every part of Israel to fight for the city of God. Men who had suffered defeat in the different cities of Galilee were coming in as were men who had not yet seen battle. Here in Jerusalem, on this sacred and holy soil, we would make our stand for the greatness and glory of God. For us Nazarenes, we vowed that when Jesus returned to be king, this city would be his.

CHAPTER XXXVIII

I was in the city before the Romans came. Letters were still getting through. One day, while I was attending a meeting with Peter and Symeon, I received one from my uncle, and I read it slowly and meticulously, savoring each sentence, as though I could feel my uncle through his words. He wrote of his continued good health and of my friends and their doings. He asked if Mary and Joash wanted to leave Jerusalem for a while and come to stay with him. Then, as if it were just another piece of casual news, he wrote that John (Mark) and Sharon were to be married. I could not go on with the letter. The life I had loved her too much to ask her to share with me she would soon be sharing with John.

What regret I suffered then, what a sense of devastation pervaded my soul, what misery and remorse I felt! I turned to God and asked Him by what error in judgement, by what blindness of thought, by what quirk of fate, I had made the decision I had. I went into a room where I could be alone, and I fell to the floor, I was shaking so much with emotion. A vast emptiness, such as I had never known, filled me and drained me. I felt an overwhelming sense of loss, the prodigious weight of my mistake, and I cried and lamented audibly over it.

Peter was in the next room, and he heard me. He came in to see what was wrong. He found me trembling, my body rocking back and forth like an infant being cradled by its mother. This was how the Jews at Golgotha swayed when they cried over Jesus.

"What's wrong, Barnabas?" he asked me, deeply and sincerely concerned.

I spoke fragmentedly, my tears and moans like erratic punctuation marks, inapposite and excessively placed. "Peter... Peter... I loved this girl... oh, I loved her so much, and... I would not marry her because... I didn't want her to live... with insecurity and... and danger... the way I know Rachel must live with you... I loved her too much... to subject her to that... I thought someday when things were quieter... or when Jesus returns and things change... I would go back to her... and ask her to be my wife... because I knew she loved me... and also I believed Paul... and I thought if the end days were soon... then what was the use of marrying her... and I believed him that without a wife... we could devote more of our lives to God... and now John (Mark) is going to marry her... because he loves her enough to take her... into our kind of life... no matter what the risks... oh, Peter, I made a mistake!... oh, God, I feel so miserable... she's so pure and so good and so beautiful... oh, Peter, I've lost her... I've lost her as if she had died... and I love her so much."

He knelt on the floor and took my swaying body into his arms and rocked me like a baby. I felt his arms, his strength, encircle me. He did not say a word. He held me and rocked me and let me cry. He held me until my tears abated and I could lean against him quietly. I was so exhausted that I almost slept. Then I disengaged myself and stood up. He did too. He looked at me with that radiant look of his that could cure all ills and said, "Come, Barnabas, from now on, we will walk together, you and I." Together we left the room.

Vespasian, meanwhile, gave his men rest. They ate, drank and sported themselves before that inevitable march to Jerusalem they knew they would have to make. After they had rested, he trained them for fighting. He wanted to have the greatest army ever assembled to fight against the Jews.

In Jerusalem, the leadership had changed. The Zealots were now under the joint command of Eleazar, son of Simon, and Zachariah, son of Amphicalleus. These leaders needed a strong, united people to fight the coming onslaught; they could not tolerate underminers, lest their effort be weakened by dissent. The Roman army had no dissenters in it; it had no group of men agitating to make peace with the Jews and to let them have Israel. And the leader of the Romans, the emperor himself, had no opposing party advocating giving Israel back to the Jews. The Jewish army could afford no less than that. If Roman soldiers were to be of one mind, Jewish soldiers must be the same. Relatives of Agrippa, who counseled surrender and submission, were quickly silenced and killed. Chief priests, long the advocates of Roman rule, were stripped of their power, and the ancient custom of choosing a high priest by lot was revived in place of the inherited familial system that had prevailed for so many years. As a result, a simple country priest, Phannias, son of Samuel, from the village of Aphtha, came to be chosen to replace the present high priest, who was Matthias, son of Theophilus. The long tradition of high priesthoods chosen only from a small select group of families was thereby bought to an ignominious end.

Outraged at this was Ananus, son of Annas, the man who had executed James. Somehow he, like his colleague, Caiaphas, had managed to survive the campaigns against the chief priests that had been going on sporadically in the city, and now, still feeling the power of an office that he had held for only three months before the Pharisees forced him out, he began to speak openly against the Zealots and to gather an army of his own. He got enough followers together to do battle in the city's streets. The Zealots were caught by surprise, for they had not expected their own people to turn against them; they had no weapons to defend themselves. Their main force ran into the Temple and barred the doors. Among them, of course, were many Nazarenes, for many of the Zealots believed that Jesus was the Messiah and that he would come to save Israel in the end. For Ananus, it was not just the regaining of priestly power that motivated him; it was also the desire to surrender to Rome. For under Jewish rule, he would have no power at all; but under Roman rule, he would have it secured by Roman might. Secretly, he made arrangements to send a delegation to Vespasian, asking the Roman general to hasten to Jerusalem to take over the city and informing him that the "loyal" citizens would be on hand to help him.

John of Gischala pretended to be on Ananus' side. Thus he was welcomed into Ananus' private meetings. But John reported the details to the Zealots in the Temple, for it was with them that his loyalty lay. His spying lasted for only a limited time, however. Ananus discovered what he was doing and severed all relations with him. Many of us wanted to help our Zealot leaders in the Temple, but Ananus' forces were too strong and well organized to allow us to do that effectively.

Our beleaguered Zealot leaders then sent messages to the Idumaeans, those converts to our religion whose territory was nearby, and asked them for help in freeing them from the Temple and in defending Jerusalem against Rome. The Idumaeans responded with alacrity, and they quickly raised an army of twenty-thousand men. When this army arrived outside Jerusalem, the former high priest, Jesus, stood on the wall of the Temple and tried to convince the Idumaeans that they should be *attacking* the Zealots instead of trying to *help* them. And that was not because he was pro-Roman anymore, he said (because it was obvious that war with Rome was inevitable now), but because he and Ananus were more qualified to lead this fight than were Eleazar and Zachariah and their loathsome Zealots. And when some of the Idumaeans shouted that Ananus had just tried to send a delegation to surrender to Rome, this priest retorted that that was a lie spread by the Zealots and that the proof of its falsity was that no such delegation had ever been sent. (But we knew that it was the truth, for John of Gischala had been present at the meeting when Ananus had tried to do that and had witnessed Ananus' own people refuse to sanction surrender even though they preferred Ananus to lead them over anyone else.) Since one

351

good speech deserves another, one of the Idumaean generals answered Jesus with a cogent speech of his own and accused this chief priest of hypocrisy and of not being on the side of liberty.

Meanwhile, some of the Zealots, in spite of their lack of weapons, escaped from the Temple under cover of a storm and opened the city's gates for the Idumaeans. They freed the other Zealots and gave them weapons with which to fight.

Now the Idumaeans and Zealots together attacked Ananus' forces and vanquished them. They killed any Sadducees who had been advocating a return to Roman rule. They caught Ananus and Jesus and some of the other chief priests and executed them. They killed these puppets of Rome, these decadent sycophants who had murdered Nazarenes and Zealots and Sicarii. They removed them from our midst for all time. So much did the Idumaeans hate Ananus and Jesus that they stood disdainfully upon the corpses of those two, as if killing them had not been enough and as if something more had to be done. Ananus was hated not only because he would have surrendered Jerusalem to the Romans but because of what he had done to Jesus' brother, James. James had been so loved by our people, and Ananus had actually murdered him. James had been so strong for the Torah, and Ananus had accused him of being against it. And though we had strongly protested to Albinus and Agrippa the egregious wrong that had been done, the removal of Ananus from his position of authority had hardly seemed enough. So here were the Idumaeans doing more, and even *that* didn't seem enough. Now that he was dead, how could one show him the terrible wrong he had done? He was beyond being shown anything now — except by God, of course — and the Idumaeans, by doing what they did, were only showing themselves and others the depth of their contempt. The chief priest, Jesus, because of his lengthy speech extolling Ananus, had brought upon himself the overflow of the people's hatred for Ananus. The Idumaeans, after they had vented their anger on the insensible remains of these two, would not even allow their corpses to be buried but threw them into a ditch instead.

We had ended the tyranny of the high priests. Never again would we run the risk of a holy man who wanted us free from Rome being taken by one of our own authorities to the alien occupiers of our land for punishment. Never again would there be a Caiaphas to bring Jesus to Pilate or an Ananus to cause the killing of a James. We had despised these priests for years on end, and now they would be no more. Though we had not killed every last one of them, we had ended the office that had given them authority. We had killed many of them, though. The

Sicarii had started it when they killed the high priest, Jonathan; Menahem had continued it when he killed Ananias; and now Eleazar and Zachariah had almost completed the job when they killed most the chief priests who remained. The few who were left after that stayed out of sight in order to protect their lives. Among these, almost forgotten by all but the Nazarenes, was Caiaphas, who had gone into hiding again. Paul and his Christian followers, who were spreading the claim that our people and the high priests were all of one mind and that the majority of the Jews had wanted Jesus killed, would have to answer why these purported abettors of the sacerdotal aristocracy had executed three high priests and almost all the chief priests as well. They would have to explain to all of us who knew what the Jewish people had done to their chief priests why these same Jewish people had, according to Paul, favored those priests when it came to Jesus. Paul's lie would be exposed for what it was by the very facts of history. And Paul's attempt to elevate his own gospel over that of the Nazarenes by describing all Jews as the killers of Christ and thus making anything Jewish seem bad (the Nazarene gospel being one such bad thing for it was the gospel of the Jews) would be thwarted by the incredibility of his claim in the light of all the facts.

But the chief priests were not the only ones to feel the effect of this long-term resentment; other wealthy Sadducees felt it too. It was not their wealth, however, that tipped the scales in favor of our acting against them (although many of them had prospered under Roman rule while the mass of us had suffered) but rather their pernicious attempts to betray us to the enemy, so that their Roman benefactors could exploit us again and give them a part of the spoils. Such a one was Zechariah, the son of Barachiah, who tried to send a surrender proposal to Vespasian but whose message was intercepted. The Zealots put him on trial. They used seventy prominent citizens — all wealthy men, so that wealth could be shown not to be a factor in this — that had been suggested to them as judges. But when the judges unanimously found Zechariah innocent, the Zealots suspected bias. They found out the judges were Sadducees, so they refused to honor the verdict. They refused to brook any further delay, and they summarily executed Zechariah there in the middle of the Temple.

Therein lies a lesson in choosing judges, for when they all come from the same group as the accused, more often than not they vote for the accused regardless of the facts of the case. Of course, the opposite is also true: when the judges are all from the opposite group, the judges vote against the accused. In each case, the judges vote for their group;

they do not vote on the facts. How do we find fair judges then? The answer is that we don't, unless — and this is the only exception I know — they are truly men of God.

Now, however, even though we were no longer burdened by the disruption of the chief priests, the internecine fighting among ourselves continued with other factions and groups. The Idumaeans, for example, had a falling out with the Zealots, which led the Idumaeans to free two-thousand prisoners from the jails and then quietly walk out of the city.

Vespasian heard of this and nurtured the hope that we would weaken ourselves so much from such dissipation of our energies that we would save him the trouble of having to fight. He decided to spend his time subduing other cities around us while he waited for us to exhaust ourselves.

In the city of Gadara were Zealots who were planning strategies for both attack and defense against the Romans. The more cowardly elements in that city, however, were frightened about being killed, and they secretly invited the Romans to enter and tore down part of their wall to show their pacifity. The Zealots inside were taken by surprise and had to flee the city as the Romans came in, but not without first killing the pacifist leader who had betrayed them and the nation. They fled to the village of Bethennabris, with the Romans pursuing them on horse and foot. Ill-equipped as they were, these Zealots came out of the village when the Romans arrived and attacked the Roman cavalry and infantry, not caring for the danger and odds against them but only for the winning of God's kingdom. They literally hurled themselves at the Romans, as if their very bodies were missiles, and in dying, died fighting. For the liberation of Israel and the greater glory of God, these Jewish men fought bravely and without concern for their safety against the unclean and pagan invader that was Rome. But the Romans drove them back and took the village and burned it to the ground.

The people in the neighboring villages feared that they would be next, so they abandoned their homes and fled for the city of Jericho. To do that, they had to go south and cross westward over the Jordan River. But the river was swollen and difficult to cross, and the Romans caught them strung out along the eastern bank and slaughtered them en masse. Men, women and children, and most of the men without weapons, all of them slaughtered on the bank of the river, their corpses floating down to the Dead Sea itself. Fifteen-thousand Jews in all, another massacre for the glory of Rome.

Symeon summoned some of us to meet him. Jerusalem, he felt, would be next. Jesus, he said, would not come just yet, and the movement that preserved the belief in his messiahship and the belief that he *would* come again had to be protected from annihilation. He wanted some of us to leave Jerusalem and to go to other parts of the empire to teach and to counsel patience for the return of the Messiah. What he well understood now, too, was that there were people elsewhere in the empire who were preserving the belief in Jesus as the Messiah but that the Messiah that they envisioned was of a different sort than ours. The very word meant something else to them. While *our* Messiah was a man who would return to save Israel from the pagan oppressor and establish the kingdom of God, theirs was a divine being whose death had wiped out their sins and who would return to establish God's kingdom on earth while the Romans remained in power. *Our* Messiah was a liberator; theirs was a savior. I say "our", but I must confess that I had never fully disengaged myself from my adherence to Paul's belief. There was something in me that clung to it — by my fingertips, as it were — because it had given me something precious, uplifting and exalting, something that went beyond my love for my nation and my people, something that made me feel with rapturous certainty the loving presence of God. But I could not tell this to Symeon, and I could not tell it to Peter. This was something deeply personal that I had to work out for myself. For, in spite of this marvelous feeling, I could not give up the Torah, for I still believed it was God's book and that Jesus had wanted us to follow it. I could not accept Paul's more recent claim that if we accepted the Torah, we could not have God's gift of repentance through Jesus' death. Why, I asked myself, could we not have both?

Symeon sent us to different places, some of us to Pella and Philippi but Peter and me to Rome. I think Peter must have told him that he wanted to work with me from now on. He wanted Peter and me to find Paul and to seek some way of bringing Paul's Christians and us Nazarenes together if we could. If we could not do that, then we were to teach in the strongest terms that Paul's new doctrines were false and to try to persuade Christians to change into Nazarenes. We left just one at a time so as not to bring attention to ourselves and went where we had been assigned. For our group, it was not just Peter and me who had to leave but Rachel and Marcus, Peter's son. Wherever Peter traveled now, they went with him.

I said that Symeon had summoned only some of us to meet him. Those of us whom he had summoned constituted only a small segment of the total number of Nazarenes in Jerusalem at this time. You will recall that all the lower priests had joined us and that many Zealots had done the same. If everyone who believed in Jesus' messiahship would

355

have left Jerusalem at this time, our defenses would have been diminished tremendously. Symeon did not want that. He wanted us to fight, because he felt that victory might still be ours. But in case we did not win, he wanted there to be a cadre of teachers who would keep the torch burning, who would teach the lessons of love and morality that Jesus had taught and the real meaning of his ministry among us. Symeon himself would stay and fight, because if we won, there was a chance that the Nazarenes in Jerusalem would press the population to make him temporary king in anticipation of Jesus' imminent return. He had to give an example of courage to the others; he had to be an inspiration to those who would stay and fight.

For those of us who were not to stay, we could not leave in the open. Since the mass departure of so many Idumaeans, no one was being let out. The only exceptions I knew of to this were those who were old or who were assigned to forage for food. Desertions were like draining blood from the army, and our commanders could not allow that to continue. Anyone capable of even throwing a stone was now required to stay.

One of our conservative Pharisee teachers was Johanan ben Zakkai. He did not agree with our war with Rome, and he asked our leaders for permission to leave. He was a seer who saw the Temple being destroyed and Vespasian becoming the emperor. He did not want the Pharisee teachings to be destroyed with everything else, so he asked our leaders to give their assent, to give him permission to leave. Our commanders, however, could not allow that. It would set a bad example for everyone else, they said. They were obliged to do what they had to do, and they knew that Johanan would understand.

But Johanan felt obliged to do what *he* had to do. He was just as determined as our leaders, and he looked for a way to leave. He found it at last by pretending to die and having his "corpse" put into a coffin. His followers then asked for permission to take the coffin out of the city, so that they could bury their teacher's last remains somewhere that was quiet and pleasant. This our commanders did allow. A corpse could not throw stones! So Johanan left in a wooden box and thwarted the Zealots' precautions. The Romans, I heard, gave him leave to start a Pharisee school in Jamnia. And I suppose, when one thinks of how much learning and wisdom he had, he may have served God much better that way than by fighting at the walls of the Temple.

When the time came for Peter and me to leave — and the others whom Symeon had assigned — we knew that we too would get no official consent from our leaders. We decided, therefore, to leave one at a time, to avoid bringing attention to ourselves. We could not use the coffin ploy, for that device had since been uncovered. But we did do something else. We went through the gates when we knew that the guards on duty would be Nazarenes. These guards, these young Nazarenes, were willing to fight and even to die for God and Jesus; but they knew, just as Johanan had known, that there was a certain wisdom in preserving the teachings of the group. This was considered especially true in light of how those teachings were being changed elsewhere in the world. So while most of the Nazarenes stayed behind, those who had been made emissaries left — and as imperceptibly as possible.

We left — Peter, Rachel, Marcus and I and those who had been assigned to different communities. We bid our sacred city farewell and wondered if we ever would see it again. It was a sad — even tearful — departure, but we did it because it was necessary.

We traveled by land and sea and visited different communities along the way. We learned that some of the Nazarenes in these communities were taking vows of poverty in obedience to Jesus' adjuration that we sell all we have and give it to the poor. We learned, also, that because these people were Nazarenes and, therefore, loyal to the Torah, Paul despised them and contemptuously called them "Poor Men", meaning that they were poor in spirit and character. But these people turned the tables on him: they adopted his derogatory appellation with pride and used the Hebrew word for poor, which is *ebion*, and called themselves Ebionites — the true followers of Jesus in the way that Jesus had desired. Peter and I spoke to these Nazarenes (and to the Ebionite branch of the Nazarenes) about Peter's personal experiences with Jesus and about my experiences with Paul. In this way, they came to know about Jesus and Paul from persons who had had intimate contact with each of them. And if anyone came to them preaching Paul's gospel, they could refute it by saying that Peter's gospel was the right one because it was based on a personal association with Jesus, and they could say that Paul had hidden reasons for saying the things he said, especially about Jews, since his former ally, Barnabas, had revealed those reasons to them.

But not all the communities were receptive to us, not everyone believed us. On that arduous, enlightening trek to Rome, we learned how entrenched Paul's ideas had become. We visited Pontus, Galatia, Bithynia, Cappadocia and Asia, and in all of them preached to Jews. These were the people whom Peter called lovingly, the "Jews of the Dispersion", those outside Galilee and Judaea. He called them that because he still believed that Jews, ideally, belonged in their native land, that Jews outside their country were dissipated unnaturally. He had forgotten, perhaps, that such disseminated Jews were not only people who had migrated from Israel but also Gentiles in other lands who had converted to Judaism; that so many Jews lived in other nations now that Judaea, Samaria and Galilee could not contain them all. Peter told these Jews about Jesus. He preached his gospel fervently: Jesus as the Messiah; salvation through the Torah. It was the message of the Nazarenes. He stood as a living testimony to God's ordination of man. He was the first authority on everything Jesus had said and done. Many were drawn to him because of that, as they had been in Jerusalem and Lydda and Joppa and Alexandria. But others, it seemed, were not so moved. Some Jews simply could not believe that Jesus was who we said he was. The fact that the Romans had crucified him instead of succumbing to him was enough to prove us wrong. And some Jews, even if they did believe it, were afraid of rebelling against Rome. They knew that Jerusalem was under siege, and they knew that our movement stood for freedom. They knew that their Gentile neighbors were loyal to Rome and would attack them at any sign of insurrection.

For those Jews who followed Paul, however, it was another matter entirely. These people were Christians, and, while they respected Peter because of who he was, they were astounded at what he was teaching. They had thought that Peter believed the same as Paul and that the errant gospel that Paul had warned them about would come from some vague, irresponsible travelers and not from the first disciple. There was a flurry of confusion because of this. They had thought that Peter was a Christian like themselves. But when he preached adherence to the Torah, when he rejected a belief in sacrificial death as the pathway to salvation, he challenged what they had come to believe as true, and, what was worse, he embodied what they had come to expect in the perfidious liars whom Paul had told them might come. Understandably, they were confused.

As an example of how they responded, I will tell you about the Galatians. Remember that they had turned from Paul's gospel when Jame's emmissaries had come. Then some had gone back to Paul's gospel after Paul had written them from Caesarea. In that letter, you may recall, he had told them that there was no gospel but his and that if he or his disciple or an angel preached a different one, that person was to be accursed. And here was Peter doing just that. Here was Peter preaching the errant gospel that Paul had warned them about.

They had a leader among them named Julius, a white-bearded man who, formerly, had gained stature because he had adhered to the Torah.

Now, of course, he did not follow that book, because now he was a Christian.

"Paul warned us this might happen," he said. "He warned us that someone might come preaching another gospel — a gospel that wasn't true." He was speaking to us both, but his eyes were on Peter.

"Do you think what I've told you isn't true?" Peter asked.

"I know it's not," Julius replied. "Forgive my candor, but how could you have lived with him without knowing the meaning of his death? I mean no disrespect to you, you understand — I look up to you because you were his disciple — but I can see now that even a disciple could have missed knowing everything. Paul said the Jesus of his visions was more reliable than what others knew in the flesh. Either that or your mind has become possessed. Yes, perhaps that's what it is: you're possessed by an evil spirit. You're saying things you'll regret having said once that spirit leaves you. Paul knew that this was possible — even for himself, he knew it. That's why he told us to detest even him if he preached a different gospel from the one he had preached to us originally. He or his disciple or an angel should be accursed if they preached something different to us."

"I say only what is true," Peter announced in a calm, equable voice. "We had many private talks together, Jesus and I, not all of them revealed to others. I tell you he never told me he had come to die to save people from penance for their sins. He never told me that his death would make the Torah obsolete."

Julius dropped his head. "Then perhaps Jesus himself was unaware of the full meaning of his mission. After all, he was encased in a human body, with all the limits that that incurs."

"There was no such limit when he healed the sick," Peter protested, "or when he walked on water or..."

"But suppose, just suppose, that he did not become aware of everything until he was a spirit again. And then, once he was, he could see everything clearly and could give that information to Paul, information that he couldn't give to you while he was in his earthly body because he wasn't even aware of it himself at the time. Now, isn't that possible? Don't you think that *could* be the reason he didn't tell you he had to die as a penance for our sins?"

Peter sat at the table, supporting his cheek with his fist. I stood a discrete distance away, not wishing to influence his answer. I had mixed feelings about this that I had not revealed even to Peter: the belief in Jesus' sacrificial death was still in me, and yet I could never accept it as a replacement for the Torah.

Peter lifted his head and said, "No, it is not possible."

Julius had hoped for the opposite. He lowered his eyes and left the room. I knew he was unswayed. He belonged to Paul and not to Peter now, and he must have felt that any further discussion with us would have been unproductive and painful. The first disciple had come too late to dislodge the roots of the tree that Paul had planted. Christians now were the children of Paul, and no one could change their minds.

It was that way with the other communities that we visited as well: mixed responses from Jews. Some uncommitted Jews and some Christians became Nazarenes after listening to Peter, but other Christians clung to Paul's gospel, offended by Peter's claims.

While we were making this slow, laborious journey to Rome, two others were making their way there as well. These were Rabath and Jacob. They had left the kingdom of King Agrippa to join Agrippa's sister, Bernice, who was now the guest of Nero. Because the army of Gallus had not conquered Jerusalem, there was a fear that the army of Vespasian might not do so either. And if the Zealots won again, Agrippa's kingdom would be vulnerable to attack. Agrippa had felt it better that his sister not be present in such an event. And if the Roman army won, then Florus would still be procurator, and considering how *he* had treated Bernice when she had appealed to him, she did not feel safe with him either. So she had gone to Rome as the guest of Nero to ensure her personal safety. And now Rabath was joining her there too. And Jacob, who had become Rabath's protector and who knew her secret Nazarene belief, was accompanying her there. When Rabath and Jacob finally arrived, Bernice treated Rabath like her sister, and these two beautiful women conquered Roman society. If the Jews could produce such beauties as these, thought the Romans, they could not be totally bad. But among the common people, the people who had no contact with the two of them, there was no such placating effect. Roman patriotism was running high since the Jews had started their revolt, and Jews in general were not liked in Rome. The popularity of Judaism as an alternative to paganism was arrested now by the war.

Jacob, as was his custom, insinuated himself into various circles of people. It was through them that he heard about Paul: that Paul was the leader of the new group called Christians (but he already knew that) and that Paul was not safe in Rome's present environment. Jacob casually mentioned this to Rabath, and she, with sudden alacrity, said that she wanted to see Paul again. She had lost her husband and the security of her home. The world that had made her so happy was crumbling around her, and she had become aware of the tenuousness of wealth and the impermanence of power. The suffering she had experienced had made her more sensitive to the sufferings of others, and she felt remorseful over the pain she must have caused Paul years ago. She had been hearing about him over the years, about his teachings and his activities, and she wondered how much of that had been caused by the way she had acted. She had to make amends, if only to say that she was sorry. And since she had become a Nazarene, a believer in Jesus like him, she also wanted him to know that.

"I'll arrange a meeting," Jacob said, "but not an open one. Things have changed for Paul. Nero reprieved him once, but he won't do that now. Christians are hated around here. The Romans don't like the idea of this Jewish king called Jesus that the Christians are talking about, and Nero finds it convenient to blame the Christians for every problem Rome has. He thinks they're part of the reason — maybe the main reason — for the war in Galilee and Judaea. So it wouldn't look good for a guest of the emperor to be seen talking in public with Paul."

She agreed to do as he said and to put the matter entirely into his hands.

Jacob was true to his word. He found out where Paul could be found. He walked with Rabath through dingy streets, with her cloak and hood concealing who she was, and, when they arrived at the place where Paul was staying, he stationed Rabath outside and told her to wait there while he went in alone. She waited in the street — a street so narrow that a person living on one side could reach out and touch the hand of someone on the other, a street which, because of the height of the multi-level buildings and the clothes that were hung between them to dry, kept the sun out most of the day, so that the street seemed like no more than a thin crevice in a wall of cracked stone. Rabath pressed herself against the three-level house to let two men pass by unimpeded. She was concerned about being left alone. This was not the kind of place for a woman to be left standing, unaccompanied by a man.

Inside the house, Paul was reading a letter when his attendant told him that Jacob had come. All was now set aside with the excitement of seeing an old friend.

"Jacob," he said when Jacob came in, "Jacob, is it really you?"

Jacob assured him that it was and that his eyes were not deceiving him. They gave each other concise accounts of what had happened to them since their last meeting in Jerusalem, Paul interspersing his remarks with exclamations of how good it was to see Jacob again.

And then Jacob said, "There's someone who wants to see you."

"Who?" Paul said.

"An old friend," Jacob answered mysteriously, and he went outside to bring in Rabath.

When she entered, she held the side of her hood over her face so that Paul could not see who it was, and Jacob left discreetly so that Paul and Rabath could be alone. When she took down the hood, those long-remembered cascades of black hair fell about her face — a face that had ripened from insouciant smoothness into the slightly creased countenance of a mature woman. It was a chastened Rabath who faced him. But though her eyes were deeper with the meaning of life, they still showed that fire that had made her the proud spirit that she was, and Paul, still mortal, felt captivated anew by her beauty. But he quickly recovered himself and remembered who he was.

"Rabath," he said with quiet composure, "I'm — overwhelmed."

"How are you, Paul?" she asked, using the name that she knew he had adopted for himself instead of the one he had had in the past.

"I'm fine, I'm fine," he said. "I'm surprised that you've come to see me."

"I had to," she said. "I realize so many things now that I didn't realize before. I understand what you felt. And I didn't know what kind of man you were then. There was more to you than I thought. I've lost my husband and my home, and my world has fallen apart." She began to cry. "Oh, Saul, I'm so sorry," she said, forgetting to use his adopted name now and using the one that she had associated with him in the past. "I'm so sorry I hurt you. I've come here to apologize and to beg you to forgive me."

He walked to her and wiped her tears. It was the first time he had ever touched her.

"Don't cry, Rabath. Please don't cry," he said. "It was destined it should be this way. I lost the love of woman when I lost you, but I found the love of God. It was destined it should be that way. God had something else in store for me."

She turned away from him and walked to the table where she saw the letter. "You're writing another one of your letters?"

"Reading," he said. "This one was sent to me."

"I've heard about some of the things you say, especially the things about women."

"What sorts of things?" he asked, actually flattered that she had heard of his work.

"That women should be silent in the synagogues and obedient to their husbands, that they should even fear them; that people shouldn't marry if they can resist the urge for sex. Is that what *you've* done, Saul?

362

Have you resisted that gift of God because I turned down your offer of love?"

"You know my secret. I could never love any woman but you. And, yes, you were the reason at first; you were the reason I could never seek anyone else. But then I learned another reason, and this one was more than that: I learned what it meant to serve God to the exclusion of everything else. The joy it gave me is more than I can describe to you. It surpassed the love of a woman. And it always — always — was there."

He did not tell her that once, for a short time, he *had* known the love of a woman, that he had married a girl, that he had slept with her and that she had died in her youth of a fever.

"Do you think sex is all there is between a man and a woman, Saul? Do you think that's all there is to marriage? I mean aside from it being an economic arrangement, which I admit is why my father had me marry the man he did, don't you think there can be something spiritual in it? You know about the marriages between spiritual men and virgins, where they never have any sex together. Don't you think there can be any spiritual love between a man and a woman?"

"I found my spiritual love with God, Rabath."

"Are women so inconsequential, then, Saul?"

"They're not inconsequential at all, Rabath. Women have their place just as men do."

"But a woman's place is to be silent and obedient, is that it?"

"Yes, Rabath. It's God's plan; it's the law."

"What law, Saul? The law of the Torah doesn't demand it."

"The law of the Torah is no longer in effect. The law of Christ demands it."

"But I've heard that Jesus himself had women disciples."

"He did. And each of them knew her place."

"They were *Jewish* women, Saul. What do you think their place was? Our women have held positions of importance for as far back as we can remember. Elijah and Elisha taught women to be teachers. Even the Pharisees give legal status to women. They don't relegate women to silence — in religious matters or anything else. Wasn't Miriam a prophet who taught us, and didn't Deborah do the same? Don't our women sit beside their men in the synagogues? Don't we have women who are synagogue elders, whom we call *presbytera*, and women who are heads of synagogues, whom we call *archsynagogissa*? Jacob told me that when you were in Caesarea, you stayed in the house of Philip, who was one of your traveling companions, and that he had four daughters who could prophesy. You didn't silence them because they talked about religion, did you? I'm the cause of what you said; I know it. And you're going to make other women pay for what I did. You don't even want men to get married because *you* couldn't marry the person you wanted."

"No, Rabath, that's not true. If I want that for those who are strong — and only for those who are strong enough to do it — I want it for them because there's a greater ecstasy in serving God than in serving a wife or husband."

"There's also an ecstasy in loving a woman, Saul."

Paul sighed at this. "Maybe it doesn't matter anymore, Rabath. The end times are coming soon, so maybe it doesn't make sense to start a long-term commitment to something like marriage."

"That's what James said to me: that the end times were coming soon and that that's when Jesus would come back."

"You spoke to James?"

"Yes, I went to him because I wanted to know more about this movement of yours. That Roman captain, Claudius Lysias, had sent *you* off to Caesarea, so I went to see James instead. I saw him several times."

"And what did you think?"

"I thought he was the most righteous man I had ever met. Maybe the most righteous man in the world. He made me feel ashamed of myself. I listened to him over and over again, and I became convinced that he was right. When my uncle, Ananus, had him stoned to death, that was the biggest sin in my uncle's life. I hated my uncle for that, just the way every Jew who wasn't a Sadducee hated him. You see, Paul, secretly, and without telling anyone except Jacob, I became a Nazarene because of James."

Paul looked at her, astounded. He suddenly became excited.

"Did he baptize you?" he asked.

"Yes," she answered.

"How?"

"With water, at a mikvah."

"Did he baptize you in the Holy Spirit?"

"He baptized me the way John the Baptizer baptized people. That's what he told me. I repented the things I had done wrong, and he baptized me."

"You did well, Rabath. You did very well. Now you must be baptized anew. You must be baptized in the Holy Spirit."

"James didn't tell me about that. But if I come back here again, will you do it for me?"

"Nothing would give me more pleasure," he said.

"Then I'll submit myself to you. That's something I never did for any man in my whole life — until I met James. Now I'll submit myself to you the way I once did to him."

For Paul, this was one of the crowning moments in his life, the fulfillment of something he had never dared even to dream. These words from Rabath made everything seem right. All that he had worked for, all that he had hoped for, seemed to congeal into this one supreme moment of time. The heaven he had glimpsed in his vision with the Essenes seemed to burst itself into the room.

She walked to him and kissed his cheek. "Jacob says your life's in danger. I know the emperor now. Would you like me to speak to him?"

"No, Rabath." He kissed her hand. "I have God now, and that's enough. He'll take me when I finish my work, and it might as well be Nero as anyone else who does the job for Him when the time comes."

"I'll come back to you," she said.

She left him and joined Jacob outside. "I love him," she said with tears in her eyes.

"I do too," Jacob said.

The two hooded figures walked silently through the narrow back streets of Rome as dusk descended on the city.

CHAPTER XXXIX

When Peter and I arrived in Rome, we went to the home of my nephew, John (Mark), who was living there now with Sharon and who was not only teaching the Nazarene gospel (Peter's gospel) but also absorbing the Christian one and trying, as I had been, to find a compromise between them. He had been spending some time with Paul, and he was more conciliatory to Paul's concepts now than he had been in the past. There in the house, of course, was Sharon. She greeted me with that look of perfect peace on her face. The life I had feared to offer her did not seem to be having any adverse effect on her. She seemed tranquil and unperturbed.

"Hello, Joses," she said to me in her quiet and dignified way.

"Hello, Sharon," I said to her, keeping my composure as best I could.

There were others in the room, so I could not say anything more. But even if they had not been there, what more could I have said to her? Could I have told her that I loved her, that I always would love her and that it pained me to see her married to another man? I could not do that. It would not have been fair. I could not disrupt what she had. I had had my chance, and I had missed it, and I would have to live with that. Peter, the only one who knew what was in my mind, observed me from across the room and smiled at me reassuringly.

I saw John (Mark) and congratulated him on his marriage and embraced him warmly.

"How are my mother and father?" he asked.

"They're fine," I said. "They send their love. They would have come, but it's not easy to get out of Jerusalem now. They say they are waiting for your first child to be born, and then, Romans or not, they will come."

"Do you hear that, Sharon?" John (Mark) laughed. "We must do something about getting my parents here."

Sharon just smiled and dropped her eyes demurely, and I silently suffered my pain.

In the days that followed, Peter and I kept our profiles low. Sentiment against Jews was running high because of the war, and we did not want to draw attention to ourselves as Jewish leaders of any sort.

Quietly, we inquired about Paul and the general mood of the city. There were very few Nazarenes that were there at the time. The few that *were* there attended the Jewish synagogues. The majority of Jesus-followers were Christians, and the Romans, while they hated most Jews (because we were trying to take from them a territory they considered theirs by right of conquest), hated Christians even more. Christians, they said, heralded a new Jewish king and the end of Roman rule. They considered Christians a Jewish sect (something the Jews themselves did not do, since Jews followed the Torah while Christians denounced it), but that categorization was more political than religious, because the finer differences in religious thought were of no consequence to the Romans compared to what they said was our common political goal: namely, the end of Roman rule. So dangerous was it for Christians in Rome that they had to meet in secret places in order to avoid being arrested and killed. Not even John (Mark) knew where Paul was living from one day to the next. Paul had tried to change that Roman perception of Christians by preaching that Jesus' kingdom was in heaven and not on earth and that Jesus had favored Roman taxation. But the Romans did not believe it. They saw it as a dissemblance to stop the killing of Christians, and they continued their work undeterred.

As we inquired about where to find Paul, we naturally talked to Christians. From them Peter learned something that surprised him. These people held him in high regard. Paul had taught them that Peter was Jesus' most important disciple and that he was to be revered for that. But Paul also taught them that Peter was a Christian. As a matter of fact, he had taught them that all the Jesus-followers in Jerusalem were Christians. Thus, instead of these people feeling that they were some kind of fringe group at odds with the original Jesus movement in Jerusalem, they felt that they were very much a part of it. They believed that the concepts they had about Jesus were the same as what the "Christians" in Jerusalem had. They believed that they were part of a long stream of history in God's relationship to man, from His covenant with the Jews to His new covenant with Christians. They said that they were not, as certain lying travelers had told them, a deviant group from the true one of Jesus; that they were not following a myth that Paul had created about Jesus out of his own imaginative mind; and that it was not true that Paul's belief and Paul himself had no true relationship to Jesus. The people who spread such lies, they said, were atavistic "Judaizers" — people who would have them go back to the old Jewish way of following anachronistic rituals and of eschewing God's gift of forgiveness of sins through the death of His only son. Not only were these Judaizers to be rebuffed; all things Jewish were to be rebuffed as well. For Jews had committed the unpardonable sin: they had killed the lord Jesus himself. That sin meant that anything that Jews professed was as evil as the Jews themselves.

That attitude, of course, was Paul's. It was the most effective way he had of countering his Nazarene detractors. If Jews and Judaism were evil, then the savior concept was not. For, as I have said, Paul had made them mutually exclusive. If one was true, then the other was false, and you had to make your choice. My way, my weak compromise between the two, my attempt to allow both to be valid, was drowned in the vortex of certainty by one side or the other. So I kept silent about my idea and followed the lead of Peter, for, since there was to be no compromise between the two, and since a Jesus-follower had to choose between Peter's gospel and Paul's gospel, and since Paul's way had now incorporated hatred of Jews in addition to the divinity and savior beliefs, I chose the lead of Peter and stifled my hope of bringing both sides together.

The fascinating thing was that some of the Christians thought that Peter and Paul were in agreement. Naturally, that is what Paul wanted them to believe. If it could be believed that Peter, Jesus' most personal confidant, had changed from being a Jew into being a Christian, then it would have to be assumed that Jesus himself had done the same and that Christianity was not something that Jesus would have rejected had it been presented to him (as the perfidious Judaizers were saying) but actually something he had started. These Christians were saying that Peter had differed from Paul at first because Peter had not fully understood what Jesus was telling him but that Paul had then enlightened Peter about who Jesus really was and that Peter had then come around. They knew nothing about the Letter of Peter to James, in which Peter had written against what Paul was teaching the Gentiles, and they knew nothing of Peter's refutations of Paul in the Christian communities that Peter had visited. To them, Peter and Paul were the pillars of the church and stood together in the Christian belief. Nebulous and inconsequential in all this was James, who really had stood above us all. James was given little importance, and his differences with Paul, while not eliminated as Peter's had been, were minimized into insignificance in the face of Paul's overwhelming enlightenment.

So Peter, while flattered that these Christians revered him so much (for he had encountered some Christian communities, as in Galatia, where they had rejected him), felt compelled to change some of their beliefs. But first he would meet with Paul. He sent a message to Paul that we were in Rome and that he wanted to have a meeting. This was something that Paul had not expected. He had not expected Peter to come to Rome, considering how dangerous it was at the time. He had told his story and spread his beliefs without dreaming that Peter would ever be there to renounce them. Peter was in Jerusalem fighting the Jewish war. And considering how ultimately victorious Roman armies always were, he might well perish there with Symeon and the others. Peter's sudden appearance was not in Paul's plans at all. It was easy to deal with a Nazarene who might come and bleat his beliefs; it would not be so easy to deal with Peter, whose words carried so much more weight. So he sent a message back to us, telling us where we should meet and setting the time for two days later.

But Peter insisted on going alone. He wanted to speak to Paul like a brother, to discuss their points of disagreement, to remind him about what Jesus had said, and to end this hatred of Jews that Paul was instilling into Christians. He did not want me along because he did not want to give the appearance of an official delegation sent by Symeon to threaten him; he wanted a man-to-man approach, a one-on-one confrontation, in a friendly but resolute manner.

He spoke to me on that morning shortly before he left and handed me a letter. "We're in Rome, Barnabas, in the den of the lion. I feel danger wherever we go. If anything should happen to me and I don't reach Paul, see that he gets this letter."

I took the letter and uttered some platitude about fears such as his being groundless and about the aura of protection that had always been his no matter what he had had to face. He looked down from the summit of his lofty frame and smiled as if I had ensnared him in a foolish, capricious thought.

"You're right. I worry too much," he said.

He went to Rachel and Marcus and talked to them for a while. Then, kissing each on the cheek and patting my shoulder reassuringly, he left to meet with Paul.

It was a sunless, chilly morning, with dark clouds filling the sky like an ominous pall over the earth. It put me into a cheerless state of mind, and I occupied myself in reading his letter to help the time pass more easily. Rachel and Sharon were busy preparing food, and Marcus had found some young men to talk to outside.

"Though we have our differences," the letter began, "I hope we can end them with this. Though what I write to you may seem blunt at times, you must not take it as a personal affront. It is important to all of us who are Jesus' disciples that his words and his actions be known and that no false story about him be spread by persons who were not with him when he was here. You receive your knowledge through visions, and they may or may not be true. But when a vision conflicts with what *we* have seen, what am I to think? Though I consider visions subjective, when they correspond with what I have seen and heard directly, I take them to be true. But eyes and ears are objective, and when a vision is opposite from what they show, I must consider the vision a manifestation of an evil demon or a lying spirit. A personal acquaintance with Jesus in the flesh and a personal instruction from him provide certainty; visions provide uncertainty because they can proceed from a deceiving spirit who feigns to be what he is not. The righteous man does not need dreams or visions to tell him what to do. Truth does not come in dreams or visions but is granted to us in full consciousness. This is how Jesus, the son of God, was revealed to me by the Father. True visions can occur, of course, but how could a true vision of Jesus have appeared to you when you teach the opposite of what Jesus taught me and the other apostles?

"You oppose me in spite of the fact that my teachings come directly from what Jesus taught me. If, however, by means of an hour's instruction, you have become an apostle, then also proclaim his discourses and expound them. Love his apostles, do not quarrel with me, for I was with him. You have opposed me, a firm rock, the bedrock foundation of the church. If you were not my adversary, you would not slander me and revile my preaching, so that I am not believed when I declare that which I received directly from the mouth of Jesus himself, speaking of me as if I were a condemned man and you were the one who was highly extolled, or if you do not condemn me but elevate me, tell lies about what I believe. When you do condemn me, you indict God, who revealed his Messiah to me; you attack him who praised me as blessed on account of this revelation.

"If, on the other hand, you do in fact want to work for the truth, then first learn from us what we have learned from Jesus, and become as a disciple of the truth our co-worker. I hope you will deeply consider this, as I hope for our reconciliation."

It was necessary, of course, that these things be said, so that Peter could bring Paul into line. But for myself, I still kept concealed in my heart the question of whether at least some of the new things that Paul was saying had actually come from God. I still searched determinedly for the answer to this.

About an hour later, there was a knock on the door, and John (Mark) let in a breathless stranger who said he had come from Paul with a message for Peter and Barnabas. I told him who I was and that Peter already had left. With that he sank into a chair and uttered a low moan.

"What's wrong?" I asked. "Why are you so upset?"

He told me then that the Romans had learned that Peter and I were in the city and that they were interested in finding us. They were as anxious to find Peter, it seems, as they were to find Paul. Somehow they had found out about the meeting and had set a trap for us. A Roman soldier, who was a Christian in secret, had gotten to Paul to warn him, and now Paul was trying to warn us.

"How long ago did he leave?" the messenger asked.

"It's been more than an hour," I said.

And again the low moan, for Peter was as important to him as Paul was, and then the slow, lugubrious assessment: "We're too late. I couldn't get here in time. They've got him by now."

I was devastated at the thought of it. The Romans had Peter? And he had been so diligent about avoiding them. I had to find out for sure. I had to know if the man who had been closest to Jesus in life and who could testify to what Jesus had said was now in the hands of the savages who relished the killing of Jews. Over the objections of Paul's messenger, who warned of the danger, I set out for the place of the meeting. I told John (Mark) not to let Rachel know that anything was wrong.

A light rain was falling, and the damp, dreary climate seemed to presage the worst. As I came near the meeting place, I edged more cautiously towards a small crowd of people who were talking outside the house. I asked one man, whom I surmised to be a Jew by the nature of his dress and beard, what had happened. He told me that a man named Peter had been taken by the soldiers for crucifixion, that the arrested man was one of the leaders of the Christians and that the Roman captain had told him his fate.

"Did the man say anything?" I asked. "I mean, when he was arrested, did he say anything?"

"Yes," the man answered. "I heard him say that he was grateful that he was going to die in the same manner as his Messiah."

It was so much like Peter to have said that. He had adored Jesus, he had loved him, and any opportunity he had had to imitate him, he had welcomed. When the guards had beaten him after his trial before the Sanhedrin, he had knelt and thanked God that he had been allowed to suffer in the same way as Jesus. And now, no doubt, he was kneeling and praying in some Roman prison and thanking God that he was being allowed to experience his final suffering in the same way. I could just see him thanking the Roman guards as they drove the nails into his body, and I could see the Romans wondering if he was crazy — as they must have wondered at Jotapata if the intransigent, tortured Jewish prisoner was crazy when he smiled as they nailed him to a cross. I sneaked back to the relative safety of our hiding place and asked John (Mark) if there was any way we could get to see Peter.

"Not without exposing ourselves to the very same fate," he said.

"We have to tell Rachel," I said.

"She's been through this before," John (Mark) reminded me.

"Yes, but that doesn't make it any easier. I hate having to tell her this."

We went together to see her. She was chattering with Sharon as the two of them worked with the food. I stood before Rachel, and she could see by my silence and my rigid stance that something was not right.

"It's Peter," she said, "isn't it?"

"Yes," I said.

"How bad is it?" she asked.

"The Romans have taken him prisoner," I said.

There was not a flicker or twitch in her passive face, not a movement of her body that betrayed fear. "God's will be done," she said, and then to Sharon, "Come, let's finish our work."

So I stayed where it was safe and hoped that some word about Peter would come to me — through some Jewish or Christian spy, perhaps, who was there in the Roman prison. And, indeed, some word did come. The Roman soldier who was secretly Christian sent word that Peter was dead. He reported that Peter had died on a Roman cross. But not quite the same as Jesus. In order that his suffering be greater, he had requested that he be nailed to the cross upside down. The Romans had accommodated him, and he had died like that, with the sound of their laughter in his ears.

John (Mark) and I went to see Rachel again. This time she was alone.

"He's gone," I said and nothing more. There was nothing more to say.

"I have to cry," she said. "Please leave me. I want to be alone when I do that."

We did as she asked, and, outside the room, I said to John (Mark) confidentially, "That's what I wanted to spare Sharon, in case that should ever happen to me."

John (Mark) stood up straighter and held his shoulders back. "It won't happen to me," he said defiantly. "I'll see that it doesn't."

I envied him his certitude. And he was probably right. Self-confidence makes its way in this world better than vacillations like mine.

So the first disciple was dead, and the talk and negotiations that were to take place with Paul now fell entirely to me. I was still under orders from Symeon, as I previously had been under James, and after a short grieving time for my beloved friend, I sent a message through the secret network that I wanted to meet with Paul. Paul's residence always was changing now; he never stayed in one place too long. Since word about the meeting place with Peter had gotten back to the Romans, it was possible that word about a meeting place with me might get back to them too. When a messenger finally told me that a meeting was being arranged, I had to go to another house and stay there for one day while the place for the meeting was changed. When I finally was taken to a different house, it was one that had been chosen only at the last minute.

When I got there, I was taken to Paul. Though he greeted me warmly, he did so with haste and with obvious agitation and concern.

"Come," he said, handing me a cloak with a hood and putting one on himself. "We have to go to another place that only a few of us know about."

I did as he said, and the two of us left the house and slinked like criminals through a series of streets and turns and away from the houses up a rocky hill where, behind a large rock, we squeezed through a narrow opening into the mouth of a cave. It was too dark for me to see but not for Paul; he knew the way. He led me down a stairway of stone steps, then along a descending rocky path into a tunnel. There was a light at the end of the tunnel, and we stepped cautiously towards it. The tunnel opened into a cave, which was lit by an oil lamp sitting on a small table. The table had two chairs around it, and Paul and I sat down on them and removed our hoods.

"I had to take these precautions," he said. "The Romans have spies everywhere. Either they capture a messenger and torture him into revealing something, or else someone in our group is a spy; I don't know which. We live like hunted animals. I'm sorry, Barnabas, but that's the way it is these days. Peter is gone, but you know that, of course."

"Yes, I know it," I said.

"That leaves only a few of us to carry on."

"Yes, just a few," I said.

"And in Jerusalem, how are things there?"

"When I left, they were preparing for battle. Symeon sent some of us into the field, but the majority of us stayed there to fight."

"And Symeon, what did he do?"

"He stayed. He wanted to set an example for the others."

Paul shook his head. "It doesn't make sense. To live and do the work is more important than to die."

"I didn't say he was dying, Paul. I said he was fighting."

"If he fights in Jerusalem, he'll die," Paul said. "Sooner or later, the Romans will win that war. Jerusalem is the crowning prize of it all, and when the Romans get that, it'll be over. It won't make sense for any of the other places to fight."

"But what makes you think the Romans will get Jerusalem? The last time they tried, they failed."

"They failed because they turned away by themselves. The Zealots didn't drive them back. The Romans turned back on their own, and then the Zealots took advantage of their retreat."

"Even so," I said, "we won our battles against them in the field."

"We won't win again," he confided, as if in prophesy. "They're smarter and stronger this time. Do you know the prophesy of the Sybil? Do you know what she said about Nero and Jerusalem?"

"No, I don't," I answered, fearing to hear the words of a prophetess who may have spoken direly of our cause.

"She was speaking about Nero, and she said, 'When he died, the whole creation was shaken, kings perished, and those in whose hands the power remained brought ruin on the great city and the righteous people.'"

"And that was Jerusalem she was talking about?"

"Yes, that was Jerusalem," he said with a certain finality to his voice.

"So when Nero dies, Jerusalem will fall?"

"According to the Sybil, yes."

Sybil or not, I could not accept that Jerusalem would fall. Somehow I believed — I had to believe — God would intervene.

"I understand that Josephus has defected to them," Paul said.

"He has," I acknowledged, "but Josephus is only one man. In any case, whether we win or not, Symeon sent Peter and me to talk to you."

"Look, Barnabas," he said, "things are desperate these days, and it's not a time for niceties. I don't feel under Symeon's authority, and before James died, I didn't feel under his authority either."

"Then whose authority are you under?"

"No one's. Certainly not some sedentary puppet who happens to be Jesus' cousin. God and Jesus: those are my authorities, those are the ones I answer to."

"Then I won't speak to you as an emissary of Symeon," I said. "I'll speak to you just for myself."

"Good!" he said. "That's what I want to hear."

"Peter was against you. You know that, don't you?"

"Not in everything, he wasn't. In some things he was but not in everything."

"Well, in *some* things then. Doesn't that mean anything to you? Doesn't it mean anything to you that the man who lived with Jesus says that you are wrong?"

"I have given him a position of stature among all the Gentiles I teach."

" *You* have given him? His stature isn't yours to give or withhold. Are the only people who have stature the ones whom you choose to give it to? And even if that were so, the only reason you *would* have given it to him is because you had to have it appear that he supported your gospel, to have it appear that he approved of what you're teaching the Gentiles. To some people you ridicule him, because those people know what he's teaching, and you want to counter that and belittle it. But to those who don't know what he's teaching, you say he agrees with you —which you know is not true — and you give him this stature that you're talking about. Here, look at this, Paul." I handed him the letter. "He wrote this to you. He said I should give it to you if anything happened to him."

Paul took the letter and read it. Then he pushed back his chair and stood up. "Do you think Peter was the only one who knew anything? Don't you think that I could know something that he didn't know? Do you think I could have spent my life, my energy, my spirit, traveling until I was exhausted, do you think I would willingly have suffered beatings and threats to my life, do you think I could have done all that, for something I didn't know to be true? Look at me, Barnabas! Does a man do such things if his only purpose is to deceive? Does he do them for personal gain? I've traveled to more places than anyone. I've traveled to Spain, Barnabas. Spain! And if I could go to the Britons and speak to them, I would do that as well. Does a man do all that when he's driven by lies? Why would I teach things that bring me such suffering if I didn't know them to be true?"

"For Rabath!" I blurted. "That's why you could do it: for Rabath. To impress her, to show her that she had rejected a great spiritual teacher and a leader of men. That's why you could do it. For Rabath!"

"No!" he shouted. "Not for that! I could never have done all this for that. Yes, I loved her; yes, I wanted her; yes, I wanted to impress her. I admit all that. And yes, I fantasized about what it would be like to be a great teacher like Gamaliel, revered by all, with a following of disciples. Yes, I admit that too. I was weak, I was human, I was tempted. But then...", and now his voice dropped to a soft, ethereal tone, and his eyes stared glazed and distant, "...then something happened, something... How can I describe it to you, Barnabas?... something happened to me. I felt... I felt the presence of God. It flowed through me like a river, it cleansed me like a rain. I became a new man. I felt as if I had been born again, born a second time. Can you understand that? And Rabath and Gamaliel and all my earthly dreams seemed to be washed away by that feeling. And the thoughts that came to me then, I know they came from God. These visions of mine that some men seem to doubt, I swear to you from the depths of my soul, Barnabas, they came to me from God." Then he paused, and in a quiet, peaceful voice, he said, "Besides, Rabath has joined our movement. Did you know that?"

"No," I said, quite surprised.

"She is going to be coming to me for instruction. I will teach her to be a Christian."

What could I say to him? I was never sure he was right about the things he had said, and I was never sure he was wrong. He had told me things over the years that had had the ring of truth in them, just as the things he was telling me about his motives had. He had taken pains to say that the others with him on that road to Damascus had at least heard if they had not seen Jesus, but he never again tried to have others confirm the authenticity of his visions. He had told me about the spirit world, the one where we go after this life; that time does not exist there and that there, the past, present and future are all one in the same; that time is just an illusion and that the space of our lives is but a moment, so that what is going to happen already has happened; that we are neither male nor female there and that all of us are the same; that whatever we do will come back to us many fold; that the greatest virtue is love and that on that we will be judged.

Just as he could *feel* the presence of God in his visions, so did I *feel* that these words of his were true. But not *all* his words and not all that he did. He had first said that there were two gospels, but then he had told the Galatians that there was only one; he had told me he left Damascus because King Aretus' police were after him, but now he told the Christians in Rome that it was because the Jews had wanted to kill him.

"You've made them hate Jews, Paul. You've made them hate our people," I said.

"Who?" Paul asked.

"The Christians," I answered. "You've told them that Jesus told Jews who believed in him that they were out to kill him. The Jews who believed in him were out to kill him, Paul! And your people are saying that when these Jews who believed in him said that God was their father, Jesus told them that their father was the Devil! And that inside the Temple these Jews who believed in him picked up stones to throw at him, so that he had to run outside the Temple to escape from them. Since when were there stones *inside* the Temple, Paul? You've told them that Nazarenes are dogs and evil-workers and false brothers and false apostles and hypocrites and dissemblers and servants of the Devil disguised as apostles and mutilators of the flesh and enemies of the cross of Christ. You've ridiculed circumcision by calling them the amputation party. You've ridiculed our dietary laws by saying that our god is in the belly. Our god is in the belly, Paul! When you introduced your new Eucharist prayer — the one that you got by a revelation about what Jesus had said at his last supper — and you must have gotten that through one of your visions, Paul, because I checked with some of the apostles and with Peter, all of whom were there that night, and none of them remember anything about Jesus having said what your revelation says he said, which is why the Nazarene prayer for bread and wine is different from yours — so when you introduced this new Eucharist prayer of yours about Jesus saying that the bread was his body and the wine was his blood, and when your followers say — Are you aware of what they're saying, Paul, because I know that you, whatever else you've said, could never have said this! — when they say that Jesus wasn't just the servant of God or the son of God but that he *was* God, then isn't *their* god in the belly? Isn't he, Paul? I mean, if you're going to get all excited about undue emphasis on food and the stomach, why not look to your own followers?

"And I keep wondering if you purposely introduced the idea of drinking blood — even symbolically — because you wanted to defy the Mosaic commandment against it and James' orders against it and even God's command against it when he spoke to Noah.

"But worse than that, you've taught them that the Jews killed Jesus and that the Romans were forced into doing it unwillingly. At first, I thought you were teaching them that just to mollify the Romans. Pontius Pilate — Pontius Pilate, Paul! — they're calling him a merciful but weak man. There's even a story going around that Pilate gave a Jewish crowd — a mob, your Christians call it — a choice: he would follow the time-honored custom of releasing a prisoner on the Passover Feast day — there is no such custom, Paul, and there never was, but that doesn't stop your followers from believing it — but the crowd had to choose between Jesus and a man named Barabbas. Barabbas, the criminal, they call him, instead of Barabbas, the Zealot and patriot that he was. But you kiss the behinds of the Romans and call him what *they* call him — a criminal!   Because he *fought* against them, he's a criminal.   And then the story goes that the Jewish crowd was not satisfied just with choosing Barabbas; it also had to be sure that Pilate didn't just imprison Jesus or punish him and then let him go; it had to be sure that Pilate did nothing less than kill him. So the crowd shouted in unison — as one, your people say, *as one* — 'Kill him. His blood be on us and on our children.' They must have rehearsed it the night before if they said it as one, Paul. Those are too many words for people to say in unison spontaneously. Only a fool would believe that they did. But your people *do* believe it! Not only do they believe it was said as one, but — for God's sake, think of it, Paul! — the Jews demand the life of a man they believe is guilty and then call a curse on their children for doing it! If your Christians ever demand the death of Jews for having killed Jesus, will they then call a curse on *their* children because they made that demand? Isn't the curse one that *your* people are making, while they spread the story that the Jews wanted that curse for themselves?

"And then *all* the Jews are guilty.   The 'mob' that called for Jesus' death reflected what all the Jews in Israel wanted.   If all the Jews in Israel and Alexandria and Antioch and Damascus and all the other places in the Roman empire could have been pushed into the square that day, they would all have called for the death of Jesus and cursed their children for having done it! Is there no sanity left in the world? The people who hailed him into Jerusalem, who followed him to Golgotha and anguished when he was gone, *these* are the people who demanded his death! You've told your Christians that to make them hate Jews. Everything Jewish has to be made evil, so that when Jews come to present them with Peter's gospel, that gospel and the people who are presenting it won't have a chance. And you did it not just to appease

Romans (which at first I thought was the *only* reason: to make the Romans out to have been merciful when it came to Jesus so that they would see that you were portraying *them* as nice people) but because of the gospel — Peter's gospel — the one that competes with your own. That's why, Paul, in spite of all the good I found in you, in spite of my believing in your visions, I turned from you — and from the gospel that you teach. I taught it myself, and I turned from it. You teach love out of one side of your mouth and hatred of Jews out of the other. So your followers can now choose either — or both — and still be known as Christians. It's not a doctrine of love anymore, Paul. It was when we first started, when we walked together in our common belief and taught the Gentiles about God and Jesus. Oh, those were glorious days! Before the competition came from John and James and Peter and you had to find a way to stop them from tearing down what you had built. But the price is too high, Paul. In the minds of all your followers, you're making our people pay for something they never did, and you make your followers and yourself less by doing it. Your followers speak with words of love and secretly harbor their hate. But God knows everything, Paul. He hears the thoughts in our minds and the feelings in our hearts as if they were words that we speak out loud. And what will He think of you and your Christians when He hears what you think of Jews? Search your heart, Paul. You're a great man, and you've done great things. Be great enough to search your heart and answer my question for yourself."

He was looking away from me, staring into space, penetrating the blackness beyond the lamp and seeing such things that only his eyes could see and hearing such things that only his ears could hear.

"I will correct it," he said softly, as if speaking to someone in the darkness.

And then nothing more but just peering and seeing and hearing things that I was not able to know. But his words had been enough. He had seen that I was right, and he would change the message and story to rectify what was wrong. He was a great man, and he could do it. Just as Christians believed what he had taught them in the past, so would they believe what he taught them now.

"If anything happens to me," he said, "I will instruct my disciple, Luke, to correct it in my place."

"He can't, Paul," I said to him. "He can't and I can't. We don't have your influence. It's got to be you."

He nodded his head, acknowledging that I was right.

"What about our Jewish practices, Paul? Can a person be a Christian and still practice them?"

"Yes," he sighed, as if resigning himself to something he didn't like but would have to accept. "I'll tell them that those practices are not dangerous to the consciences of those who want to keep them even after they've come to believe in Christ, since they've received them from their parents under the law. I'll tell them it's all right to do that."

The question of which gospel was right, I didn't even try to discuss. It was enough for now that he was going to amend his gospel to tell the truth about Jews and that he was going to allow the continuation of Jewish practices — for Jews at least — without contemning them as evil.

Then, in a wistful, contemplative tone, he said to me, "Barnabas, do you think he'll return before we die?"

With that question, he encompassed the hope, the expectation and the fear of Christians and Nazarenes everywhere. For who among us was so strong in faith that a trickle of doubt did not sometimes seep through the impregnable wall of our certitude?

"Before we die?" I echoed. "Before we die?"

"Yes," Paul said, "before we die."

I actually felt my chest rise and fall, heard the air sough through my throat, and sensed, in my awareness of those normally unnoticed events, the brevity, the evanescence, the desperation of life — the stringent demand of inflexible time that all be done and all be achieved before the inevitable end.

"I don't know," I said. "I only know that he'll return."

"I thought it would have happened by now," he confessed. "I had planned on it happening by now."

"I had too," I said. "He told us we would not have gone through every town in Israel before he returned. He told us that some of us would still be alive when he came back."

"I thought it was futile to make long-range plans," Paul said, "to marry, to have children, to plan for old age, if the end days were so close at hand." I nodded comprehendingly. "But now I don't know. It may take longer than I thought."

"In which case you'll change what you've taught?" I asked.

"I would have to," he said. "It doesn't make sense to plan for the end if the end is so far away."

We sat in silence, this leaden question suspended between us, weakening the strength of our resolve, changing the nature of our plans. Then, without speaking, we knew it *would* take longer, that we would not be here to see it and that others, perhaps yet unborn, would witness that final return.

Then we talked of ourselves, and it was in the dank shadows of that underground room that I learned about where he had been, the places, the events all pouring out of him, filling in the gaps of what I knew of his life, so that, perhaps, in a broad and also intimate way, I came to know him better than anyone else. He had done what he had done and started what he had started, and his words now had a life of their own. And I hoped that the changes he had promised to make could be carried to the places he'd been. Spain, even Spain, he had said to me. Would his words reach that far again?

CHAPTER XL

The Romans found Paul on information that was given them by a Christian that they tortured to death. Paul accepted his capture quietly, I was told, and even blessed the soldiers who came for him. He had once said to me that he had learned in whatever state he was, to be content there, and I know that that same state of mind sustained him when they came to take him away. He did not use his power to blind an adversary in an effort to save his life. I think he must have felt that his time had come and that he was ready to join Jesus and God. The Romans gave him the privilege of a quicker death than crucifixion because he was a Roman citizen. Two days after he was taken, they cut off his head with a sword. The promise, which I know he made me sincerely, was washed away with the blood that drained from the stump of his neck, and the severance of his body seemed to symbolize the severance of the Jew from the Christian, which he and only he could have stopped.

I cared more about keeping Jews and Christians together than anyone. If there was anything that made me distinctive, it was that. Yet it was something I felt I couldn't do myself; it had to be done by greater men. Which meant, of course, Peter and Paul, for they were the only ones who could change the beliefs of the Christians about the relationship of Jesus to his people. But now they both were gone; the Romans had seen to that. And who was I and what was my voice against the howling winds of change? Paul had given the Gentiles something they could feel in their hearts was right. It was an easier path than the Torah and one that was solely theirs. But he had made it not just an acceptable alternative to Judaism, as the God-fearer path had been, but the *only* route for anyone who wanted a way out of sin. But that meant that anything or anyone that said or implied something different was worthy of Christian contempt, because if the Torah or Noahide followers were given respect and *their* paths were considered acceptable alternatives to Christianity, then the uncommitted or even Christians themselves might choose to be Jews or God-fearers while still accepting Jesus as the Messiah.

And, too, the old hatred of pagan Gentiles for Jews and their religion, competing as it did with the secret attraction of that religion for so many of them, need not be sacrificed if one became a Christian. Pagan Gentiles could accept the one God and still go on hating Jews, but now with an added reason, for the Jews had killed the man whose death had given them freedom for punishment for anything wrong they might do, if they would only believe it was so. Why they didn't *love* the Jews for this purported wrong instead of hating them, I don't know. But the hatred of Jews fulfilled its twofold goal: it allowed Gentiles to go on feeling as they had before about their ancient enemy, and it protected their new belief against any requirement that it be changed and made closer to the enemy's belief, which, secret admirers notwithstanding, they had openly disdained for so long.

Though I knew it probably would be fruitless, I made an attempt to do what I knew only Paul could have done. I spoke to the Christians and told them all that I knew about Peter and Paul and James. I tried to make them change, at least to change about Jews. But Paul had taught them too well. They called me a Judaizer and reviled me and drove me away from their midst. They would not hear words that deviated from their belief. I became a heretic and a pariah to them. They did not invite me to speak anymore nor did they welcome me if I asked. My previous involvement as a Christian did not help me anymore.

And meanwhile things in Rome were changing for the Romans. Nero had started to rebuild the city after the destruction of the fire, and the project was almost bankrupting the government. He started clipping the coins of the realm and hoarding the clippings for himself, which soon served to lessen the buying power of the coins, since the price of everything went up. But he added to his troubles by deciding to recall several provincial governors and to execute them for purported wrongs. These were not men to be trifled with; they commanded legions of soldiers. In Gaul, Africa and Spain, in response to Nero's threat, they led their armies to revolt. And in Rome, the Praetorian Guard, the elite soldiers who protected the emperor himself, took the side of the governors and announced its hostility to Nero. Nero then fled the city but was found like a cornered rat. As the soldiers closed in around him, he killed himself rather than face public humiliation.

When news of Nero's death reached Vespasian, he delayed his march to Jerusalem to see who the new emperor would be and to get any new orders from him. He soon learned it was to be Galba, the provincial governor from Spain. Galba had been invited to become emperor and had been hailed into office by his troops. Vespasian sent his son, Titus, to Rome to swear loyalty to him, and King Agrippa sailed along with him so that he could do the same. For Agrippa, there was to be the added pleasure of seeing his sister again. But while Titus and Agrippa were en route, Galba managed to earn the displeasure of the soldiers in Rome, and they assassinated him in the Roman Forum. He had lasted seven months and seven days as emperor.

Immediately, a new emperor appeared. This one was Otho, another of the provincial governors. Titus and Agrippa were traveling along the Greek coast in warships when they heard of these events. Agrippa decided to go on, for now he would swear allegiance to Otho. But Titus did not. In this sudden change in leadership, which might change just as quickly again, he saw the unfolding of Josephus' vision. He went back to Syria and then to Caesarea in order to confer with his father.

In Jerusalem, meanwhile, the Jews waited. Eventually the Romans would come. But soon, unexpectedly, the Jews found themselves forced to fight someone else.

Simon, the son of Gioras, a tall and sturdy man, had been removed as chief of Acrabatene by Ananus, son of Annas, when Ananus had controlled Jerusalem, before the Idumaeans had killed him. Resentfully, Simon had gone with his women to Masada to join the Zealots and Sicarii there. He was an eloquent man, and he tried to convince those Zealots to follow him in a takeover of Jerusalem. But they had had their fill of the people in Jerusalem after the assassination of their former leader, Menahem, and they felt that they would get no support there. So they refused to follow him. But also, I think, they had the decency not to start an internal war among Jews, which could only have benefited the Romans.

Simon, however, was not so disposed. When he heard of Ananus' death, he became encouraged. He left Masada and, through his lofty speeches, raised a large army of his own. He retook the toparchy of Acrabatene and then entered Idumaea.

The Zealots in Jerusalem recognized the threat that he posed to their own authority and marched out to meet him in battle. But Simon's forces prevailed in the field, and the Zealots had to withdraw back behind the safety of Jerusalem's walls. Simon then won over the Idumaeans and their leader, whose name was John, and they put the territory under Simon's influence.

The Zealot defenders of Jerusalem were fewer in number than Simon's troops, so they did not venture into a new battle in the field. Instead, they resorted to ambushes and, in one of them, caught Simon's wife and her servants. Simon came raging to the walls of Jerusalem and demanded the return of his wife. He killed or tortured anyone who ventured outside the gate, even old people or those who came out to get firewood. He sent some back with severed hands and swore he would do that to everyone in the city unless his wife was returned to him soon. The people grew fearful, for his army was large, and what good was there anyway in keeping the lady except to irk her husband? So they released his wife and all her ladies, and Simon then left appeased.

Titus now met with his father. They decided not to await further orders from Rome. They would finish their work in Judaea and decide what to do after that. They sent their troops to all the cities along the route to Jerusalem, burning and killing and occasionally taking prisoners. They hacked a path of carnage like a reaper scything through a wheat field. They entered Idumaea, and whatever they saw, they destroyed. In the end, besides Jerusalem, only three Jewish strongholds remained: Herodium, Masada and Machaerus.

Now Vespasian returned to Caesarea. He was anxious to learn of any new developments in Rome. What he learned was that the Roman legions in Germany had demanded that their leader, Vitellius, be made the emperor. Otho, who already was the emperor, had resisted. Otho's army and Vitellius' army had fought it out in northern Italy, and Vitellius' army had won. Otho, upon hearing of his defeat, had killed himself, having reigned for all of three months and two days. Vespasian learned that Otho's soldiers had sworn allegiance to Vitellius and had swelled that army's ranks. Then Vitellius and his army had entered Rome, and the army had ensconced itself in the houses of the citizens and had stolen whatever valuables it could. So Vitellius, although he was emperor now, was not very popular in Rome.

And in Israel, more vying for power. Simon came back to Jerusalem and surrounded its walls with a tight cordon of troops. No one could leave the city. But some of the citizens in the city secretly invited him in, preferring him to take command rather than unleash his army on them. When he entered with a large force of men, the Zealots, under John of Gischala, realized what had been done, and they retreated into the Temple, from where they fought Simon's attackers with stones and arrows. This was Jew fighting against Jew, and the Romans could not have been more pleased.

Now Mucianus, a provincial governor from Beirut, and some of Vespasian's officers beseeched Vespasian to make himself emperor. They took Vespasian to his soldiers, who shouted their support for this move. Vespasian remembered Josephus' prediction and the advice of his son, Titus, when Titus had turned back from his trip to Rome, and he saw that everything was falling into place. It was time, he felt, to accept his fate. He sent a letter to Tiberius Alexander, the governor of Egypt and Alexandria, telling him of his intent. He wanted to be sure of Egypt first, because it supplied so much corn to Rome. The control of Rome's food supply would be the first step in his campaign. Tiberius gave his support, and the people and soldiers in Egypt did so too. Now Vespasian left Caesarea and traveled to Beirut, where Mucianus was his host. Emissaries from Syria and other provinces came there to swear allegiance to him. Vespasian was extremely delighted. He showed his pleasure at this unfolding of Josephus' prophesy by having Josephus' chains removed and giving him full civil rights. Vespasian chose governors for each of the provinces and then traveled on to Antioch. He sent Mucianus with cavalry and infantry through an overland route to Italy. But even before Mucianus arrived, two opposing Roman armies confronted each other in the Gallic town of Cremona across the Italian border. The army for Vespasian was led by Antonius Primus; the army for Vitellius was led by Caecina Alienus, the man who had defeated Otho's army. Primus' force was larger, and Alienus saw the futility of fighting it. He, therefore, changed sides and had his troops swear allegiance to Vespasian. But by evening, some of his troops had changed their minds. They took Alienus, their former leader, prisoner and prepared to kill him. But their tribunes begged them not to, so the mutinous soldiers bound him with the intention of sending him to Vitellius so that Vitellius could do what they had not. But then Primus got word of this and attacked Alienus' captors. He slaughtered them as they fled for Cremona, then gave his soldiers permission to sack the town because it had fed Alienus' troops. Primus then sent Alienus to Vespasian to report their glorious victory.

Many in Rome favored Vespasian. One such was Sabinus. He led the night guards in a seizure of the capital, and the next day many nobles joined him. But Vitellius' soldiers from the German campaign were too many for them. They overwhelmed Sabinus' men and killed them. They brought Sabinus before Vitellius, and Vitellius had him executed.

But the very next day, Primus arrived and killed almost all of Vitellius' soldiers. Then Vitellius himself, stuffed with food and drunk with wine, like an indulgent man on his last day on earth, came staggering out of the palace. The soldiers took him and dragged him through the crowds of people, who reviled him and tormented him as he passed. In the end, someone stabbed him in the chest, and he died on a Roman street. He had lasted eight months and five days as the emperor of Rome.

Primus' men now searched houses for the remainder of Vitellius' men. They wanted to kill every last one of them. But the next day, Mucianus and his army arrived, having traveled the overland route they had been directed to travel by Vespasian, and, as they joined together with Primus' men, they restrained them and stopped all the killing. Mucianus then made Domitian, Vespasian's younger son, temporary chief of state until his father should arrive.

The people cheered Vespasian, and the Roman empire seemed saved. Vespasian went to Alexandria and received pledges of loyalty from delegations from all over the empire. With his position secure and the empire intact, he could now turn his attention to the one aberrant people who still defied Roman rule. He ordered Titus to take Jerusalem and to put an end to the Jewish revolt.

In Jerusalem, meanwhile, things had changed. The Zealots in the Temple under John of Gischala, who had been fighting the army of Simon, now split itself into two opposing factions. The faction that broke from John was led by Eleazar. Symeon joined with it. These Zealots and Nazarenes took the inner Temple and drove John's forces out. John's group was larger, and it started attacking them from outside the Temple. The defenders sent down missiles from their higher vantage points.

But Simon, the son of Gioras, was also still on the scene. He controlled all of the upper city and much of the lower one too. John was wedged between Eleazar on the higher ground and Simon on the lower, but John gave blow for blow to each and rigidly held his ground. He burned down buildings and houses all around the Temple and, in doing so, burned grain, which could have supplied enough food for years. I don't think that that was intentional, but the damage it did was severe, and its effect on events in the future was to prove very decisive indeed.

Now Titus arrived with his army, and with him was Tiberius Alexander. The Jews suddenly came to their senses. The fighting among our people immediately stopped. Internal differences were set aside, and our people united to fight the Romans together. Titus and a large body of horsemen rode around the walls of the city to ascertain our strength. A large number of Jews now dashed out from behind one wall and split up Titus' force. They dragged some Romans off their horses and killed them, and Titus had to withdraw for his life.

Then at night, the legion from Ammaus came, and the Romans now set up a camp. The next day, the Tenth Legion came from Jericho, and Titus ordered it to set its camp on the Mount of Olives, three-quarters of a mile from the city and separated from it by the Kidron ravine. But before that construction could get very far, our men poured out of the city and attacked the Romans at work. The Romans retreated and some of them fled, and it seemed as if the entire Tenth Legion might be killed or routed. Then Titus came with more soldiers and drove the Jews down the hill into the ravine and part way up the opposite side. But now more of our people came out to fight, and they drove the Romans back to the Mount of Olives. Again the Romans started to run but then turned about in shame and again pushed our soldiers down the hill. Our people returned to the city, and now both sides took a rest.

During this respite, there was more internecine fighting in the city, but it resulted in a reunification of the forces of John and Eleazar. The rivalry now between Simon's men, on the one hand, and John's and Eleazar's Zealots, on the other, did not prevent the defenders from acting concertedly against the Roman threat.

That concerted effort led to the question of the Temple treasure. The treasure was now at risk. Though everyone planned to be victorious, the Jewish leaders were realistic enough to envision the worst. If the Romans did break through and our people had to flee, the treasure would have to be left behind. That was unacceptable. The treasure — at least those items that were made of gold and silver and that could be carried comfortably — would have to be removed and taken to a place of safety. Simon and John of Gischala, Eleazar the Zealot and John the Idumaean met to discuss this problem.

"We can't take the heavy stuff," Simon said. "The gold table, the gold lampstand — things like that. There's no way we can get those things out of the city without being seen. And there's no way we can travel with those things slowing us down."

"All right, the lighter things then," said John the Idumaean. "There are hundreds of items like that."

"Who takes them, and where does he take them?" John of Gischala asked.

"Whom can we trust?" the Idumaean asked.

"Exactly," said John of Gischala. "Whom can we trust, and where can he hide all that stuff? You could have enough for three kingdoms with what we could carry out of the city.

"Abram is here," Eleazar said. "Abram is in the city."

"Abram?" echoed the Idumaean. "You mean Abram, the Essene, from the desert?"

"Yes," Eleazar said. "We have Essenes all over the city. You know that. They've come from everywhere. But Abram has brought a large group of them from the Dead Sea area. He left a lot of them behind in case their settlement gets attacked, but he brought a lot of them here because they want to fight."

"You're driving at something, Eleazar," Simon said impatiently. "Come on, get to the point."

"Well," Eleazar said. "I propose that we load everything we can onto Abram and his Essenes and get them out of the city."

"And then what?" Simon asked.

"And then they take the treasure into the desert and hide it somewhere there. There are plenty of remote places, and Abram knows them all. He can choose them and make a record of where they are."

"Can we trust him?" Simon asked.

The other three raised or turned their heads and looked at him in disbelief.

"He's an Essene!" Eleazar said.

And Simon then shook his head comprehendingly, as if he regretted having asked the question. For who better to protect gold and silver than someone who despised them both and for whom they held no allure?

So they approached Abram and secured his help. They took an inventory of the treasure, item by item, and divided it among Abram's men. They listed the inventory on copper scrolls and gave them to Abram too. Then they planned their escape.

Titus sent Josephus to make an offer of peace if the defenders would lay down their arms. In spite of all the benefits he posited in exchange for their passivity, they refused. It was better to be free fighting men than de facto Roman slaves. They had seen the benefits of Roman rule from Pilate to Florus, and they preferred to die fighting than to have that. Besides, it was the city of God for which they fought, and if *they* did not defend it from pagan defilement, who would? Josephus left disappointed. Not only had he wanted to be successful for his new master, but he had hoped to protect his wife and his mother and father, who were still living in the city.

The next day, a substantial body of Jews was forced out of the city. They huddled against the wall in fear, while those who had evicted them shouted to the Romans to destroy these warmongers and to enter the gates, which they, the loyal subjects of Rome, would open. A group of Roman soldiers, without waiting for orders from their officers, attacked the evicted Jews. But this was a Jewish trap! More Jews came out and attacked the Romans from the rear, while the Jews who had invited them in hurled rocks and missiles at them from above with devastating effect. Those Romans who extricated themselves from this trap had to face the wrath of Titus, for they had acted without orders. Titus, though he was angry, did pardon them, for he needed every fighting man for what he was planning next.

But during this entire incident, almost all Roman attention had been drawn to the evicted Jews. Inconspicuously, Abram's men, one by one, had eased over another wall and disappeared into the landscape. At night, more of them had gone, and the Temple treasure — most of it anyway — had been moved from the city of Jerusalem to secret, safe repositories in the desert. With them, too, went sacred writings to be hidden for safekeeping as well.

THE CHRIST-KILLERS

CHAPTER XLI

Titus prepared his army for attack. He kept the Tenth Legion in reserve on the Mount of Olives, and he prepared the other legions for an assault on the walls. He lined up his infantry and archers and cavalry, row after row, a huge alignment of fighting men.

In the city, the Jewish fighting forces numbered ten-thousand men under Simon; five-thousand Idumaeans under their leader, John; six-thousand men under John of Gischala; and two-thousand, four-hundred Zealots, including our Nazarenes, under Eleazar. In addition to these were many unarmed civilians. I should tell you, too, that though many Jews had not formally declared themselves Nazarenes, they still believed, either fully or tentatively, that Jesus would return as the Messiah. This belief and this hope pervaded our ranks no matter which group of Jews were involved.

Titus brought up his engines of war: quick-loaders, catapults and stone-throwers. He ordered trees to be felled for timber and high platforms to be built. Our people unleashed stones and arrows on the builders in an effort to stop the construction, and they made short dashes at them outside the walls. The Romans built canopies of wicker to ward off the missiles from above. They brought up three battering rams, and the pounding reverberated through the city like an ominous knocking on the door of a house. John of Gischala and Simon, son of Gioras, had combined their forces by this time, and our people fought united, as they should have done from the first. They threw down firebrands; they made sorties outside the walls to destroy the wicker screens covering the engines; they set fire to the engines and platforms; they overpowered the work crews. The Romans were in danger of losing all that they had built thus far. They sent cavalry to drive back the Jewish attackers and to save their engines of war.

In one of these several battles, the Romans captured a Jew. This unfortunate man they nailed to a wooden cross and then placed the cross upright before the walls of the city to terrify the defenders. This was the Rome we knew all too well: the Rome of crucifixion. Rather than frighten the defenders, it inspired them. It reminded them of what they were fighting. The cross, you will recall, was the symbol of the Zealots, and they were reminded why by this deed.

Now a stray Arab arrow that came from the Roman side struck John, the Idumaean leader, in the chest and killed him. The Idumaeans were heart-struck with grief. But they knew that they had to go on with the fight, so they placed themselves under the command of Simon, which is what they felt their dead leader would have wanted them to do.

The Romans completed three high towers, and now it was they who pelted the Jews from above with spears and arrows and stones. Then one battering ram broke through a wall, and the Romans came through the breach. The defenders moved back behind a second wall, and the fighting between exhausted men on both sides went on day and night without pause. After four days, the Romans took the second wall, and Titus and his bodyguard and two-thousand Roman troops entered the city in the part where the fabric-shops and forges were located. But the Jews continued to fight in the streets and the houses and continued their sorties outside the walls in other places. Gradually, the Jews who were fighting in Titus' section forced the Romans back past the second wall and back through the breach in the first. Titus had to employ his archers to cover the egress of his men through the breach, lest the Jews kill all his soldiers inside as they tried to leave. The Romans then tried to enter the breach again, but the Jews held them back for three days. On the fourth day, the Romans climbed over the wall of dead Jewish bodies that filled the breach and made it to the second wall again. But now a third wall, which had been newly built, stood in their way, so the city was still not theirs .

Now a new calamity began. Food was getting scarcer inside the city, and people were starting to go hungry. It was not easy to fight without food. The hunger led to starvation, and emaciated bodies began to appear. The less spiritual of our people fought among themselves for food, and soldiers claimed priority over civilians because it was they, the soldiers, who would keep the Romans out.

Titus heard of this and decided to flaunt the Roman strength before the defenders in an effort to demoralize them and convince them to surrender. On the pay-day of the Roman army, he paraded his well-fed troops and panoplied horses in front of a city wall and had each Roman soldier paid amid decorations and ceremony. This lasted for four days, but all this display of gold and silver and show of soldierly strength did not result in surrender. Titus was angry. He was angry not only at the Jewish intransigence but at himself for having failed to gauge their thoughts correctly. Josephus, who was his advisor in this, had failed to do it too. And Tiberius Alexander, who had been a Jew himself, had not been able to read the minds of the people he once had called his own.

Titus set his men to building platforms. But their work was hampered by the Jews. Simon's men and the Idumaeans attacked the crew of one platform while John and the Nazarenes attacked another. Also, in addition to throwing stones down at the Romans by hand, the Jews had now learned to use the three-hundred quick-loaders and forty stone-throwers that they had captured in the war against Cestius Gallus. These caused much damage to the Romans.

So again, Titus thought of convincing the Jews to surrender. Neither starvation nor the threat of death seemed able to stop them, and he perceived that it was because they believed that they were doing the will of their god. So he sent Josephus to appeal to them, not just on the basis of reason, but on the basis that surrender is what their god really wanted.

Josephus circled the wall on a horse and kept out of missile range. He was appealing for reason, he said. Since this resistance was based on religious belief, they should first remember that the Romans had always respected the holy places of their subjects and had never violated them. Those on the wall responded with laughter and derision, for they remembered that the high priest's vestments had been taken by the Romans and that Caligula had almost placed a pagan statue in the Temple and that Pilate had raided the Temple treasury and that Florus had done the same. But Josephus went on and said that it was a law of nature that the weak must submit to the strong. The Romans were obviously stronger. One only had to look to see that. But the Romans, though stronger, would bear them no grudge if they would sensibly surrender now, for a devastated city bereft of all people is not what the Romans desired. The Romans would be magnanimous in victory if the Jews would surrender, so why not do the sensible thing? But Eleazar reminded the people of the thousands of followers of Judas of Galilee who had been crucified when the Romans had won, and Symeon reminded them of the crucifixion of Jesus (he had not heard about Peter), and Simon reminded them of the crucifixion of the tortured Jewish soldier outside the city of Jotapata and of the one outside Jerusalem whom they recently had seen with their own eyes. And the people remembered all those things, and they remembered the women and children the Romans had killed or put into cages to be sold as slaves. And they did not give heed to Josephus.

But Josephus continued his lengthy oration, determined to have success. This greater Roman strength was the will of God, he shouted, for the Romans could not have conquered all the nations of the earth without God's help and approval. Did the Jews not see that when they fought against the Romans, they were fighting against God Himself?

But that factitious argument also had no effect, for the people knew better than that. They were fighting their fight in the name of God, and God wanted them to fight as they did.

"Stand your wives and children before you," he shouted, "and consider what you are condemning them to. And if you think I am saying all this to save my wife and mother who are inside the city, then kill them — kill them both! — but then give yourselves up and save your lives and save the life of the city."

That Josephus should care so much about the lives of others, even to the point of having his family killed to prove his concern, seemed inconsistent with his actions in the past. He certainly hadn't cared very much for the lives of the men he had tricked into killing each other when they had tried to prevent his surrender. But, in any event, no one had harmed his wife and mother, and though his father was kept confined (to prevent his fomenting surrender in emulation of his son), no one had harmed him either.

Most of the people did not believe Josephus. A man who encouraged others to fight to the death but did not do so himself was not a man to be trusted. Even the tears he shed at the end of his speech were considered part of his specious performance.

Yet some people did believe him, just as those who fought at Tarichaeae had, and they sold their property for a fraction of its worth and swallowed their gold and sneaked out of the city. Titus let them go through his lines and into the surrounding countryside. Later, when they felt they were safe, they retrieved their gold from their stools.

The people they left behind in Jerusalem were starving yet loyal to God. But they had to find food if they were to go on, so they foraged outside the walls at night. Titus set his cavalry the task of finding them. When they caught them, they did what we would have expected: they whipped them and tortured them in every conceivable way and then crucified them in front of the walls. But since Romans take pleasure in the sufferings of men, the screams of their bound victims writhing in pain under torture and their victims' agonies as they moaned on their crosses was not enough to satisfy the Roman lust. To show the defenders what horror would come to any defier of Rome, they nailed their victims onto the crosses in bizarre and grim attitudes of fear. The dying were aware that they served as tableaus, and this was meant to cause them greater mental anguish than just dying in the usual manner.

But the martyrs, though they moaned in their moments of weakness, still found enough breath in their lungs to praise the glory of God and give thanks that they died in His cause. And the Nazarenes among them gave thanks, as Peter had done, that they died in the same way as Jesus. And the effect on the people was just the reverse of what Titus had thought it would be. For rather than cowering and shrinking in fear at such sights, the people grew angrier at the Romans and strengthened their determination to fight against them.

Soon the crucified bodies encircled the walls so completely and so tightly that there was no more room to squeeze in new ones if they were to be seen and have a visual effect.

It was at this time that Caiaphas came out of hiding. It was his exigent need for food that made him do it. Since the time when the Idumaeans had killed Ananus and stomped contemptuously on his corpse, Caiaphas had kept out of sight. It had not been a good time for chief priests. Many of them had had their throats cut. But now the Sadducees who had been hiding Caiaphas could scarcely feed themselves, and it became apparent that, henceforth, he would have to find his own food. There was little enough of it to be had in the city, so Caiaphas made the decision to leave. He secured for himself a ragged, dirty cloak with a hood, which was easy enough to find on one of the many abandoned corpses that lay on the city's streets. Then, bending himself over like a decrepit man and using an unshaved stick as a cane, he hobbled and shuffled his way to one of the city's gates. The guards were not letting anyone out, except for special reasons. Caiaphas intended to tell them that he wished to leave the city in order to find food and that he did not believe the Romans would bother him because he was so old and obviously harmless. This scheme may have gone well for him had it not been for the perspicacity of a young Nazarene guard who recognized him through the disguise. All the Nazarenes in Jerusalem, even the children, had come to know who Caiaphas was. His appearances with the other chief priests at public functions and in the Temple had made him a well known personage among the people. But, understandably, he was of especial interest to Nazarenes.

Without revealing that he recognized him, the guard said, "Come with me, old man. I'll get you some food, and then we can see how best to get you out of the city."

Unsuspecting, Caiaphas followed the guard, limping along with simulated difficulty. The guard took him to a house where a number of people were involved either in stacking or sharpening weapons or participating in intense, whispered discussions. The guard left Caiaphas and then returned. Then he led him into a sparsely furnished room, which contained only a table and four chairs. A dark-bearded man stood in the center.

"This old man wants some food," the guard said, "and he wants to leave the city."

The dark-bearded man stared at Caiaphas with a penetrating, unblinking gaze that seemed to look into his very soul.

"I am Symeon," the man said, "the head of the Nazarenes."

I cannot say what Caiaphas felt at that moment, but I *can* tell you what he said. He knew now that he had been led into a trap, and he straightened himself up and said, "And you know who I am, don't you?"

"Yes," Symeon said, "I know who you are."

They looked at each other intently, Symeon trying to fathom the inner workings of the man who had led the Messiah to the slaughterer and Caiaphas trying to assess the intent of the man into whose hands he had been delivered.

Symeon said, "You are hungry." Then to the guard, "Joshua, would you find him some bread?"

The guard left the room.

"Are you going to kill me?" Caiaphas asked his captor.

"No," Symeon answered, "we're not going to kill you. We're going to feed you and then help you leave the city."

Caiaphas could hardly believe what he heard. "But I'm your enemy," he said.

"Yes, I suppose you are. But the man you took to Pilate told us to love our enemies."

Had Symeon drawn a bow and shot an arrow into Caiaphas' heart, the pain could not have been greater. Caiaphas, who had appeared calm and even dignified until then, suddenly became nervous and agitated. He began to move about and gesticulate as he spoke. He could accept revenge, he could even accept death, but he could not seem to tolerate this kindness from one of the followers of Jesus.

"I had to take him!" Caiaphas shouted. "The people thought he was the Messiah! They were cheering him in the streets! He took over the Temple! He would have started an open rebellion! I had to take him to save the nation! Do you know how many people the Romans would have killed if I hadn't done that? Do you? Do you think I liked Pilate? Do you think I didn't know he was a monster? I had to take him!" Tears began to flood his eyes, and he sank in despair to the floor. "I had to take him," he cried. "I had to take him to save our people, to save them from the Romans."

It was strange that Symeon's words of love had made Caiphas feel compelled to justify himself. More than any accusation or demand for retribution, this kindness, this forgiveness from those he had tormented, was more then he could bear. He was completely overwhelmed by it. He could defend himself against a sword, even with his bare hands, but he had no defense or armor against love. And when he felt Symeon's hand gently touch his head, and when he heard Symeon's voice say, "I do understand," he felt as if God himself had put the words into Symeon's mouth to tell him that everything was all right.

So he ate and drank and renewed his strength and thanked Symeon as best he could. Then Joshua led him to the gate that would give him the freedom he sought. It was night, and Caiphas was once again the withered man with a crooked stick for a cane. He passed through the gate, Joshua wishing him well, and he entered the Roman domain.

He limped a short distance and saw by the moonlight the grotesque statues of human flesh, which formed a cordon of silent sentinels around the city. He slipped between two of the closely stacked pillars and edged away from a nearby Roman campfire. To his misfortune, he bumped headlong into a patrolling Roman soldier.

"Hey, old man," the soldier said, laughingly, "aren't you out a little late?"

Caiphas' voice took on the high-pitched quality of the old man he was pretending to be. "I am trying to leave the city," he explained. "I have no desire to fight you Romans. I have always been friendly to Rome."

"Of course you have, old man. Of course you have," the soldier replied. "But I don't know if I can let you go through just like that."

Caiphas thought he understood what the man was hinting. "Gold?" Caiphas asked. "Do you want some gold? I will give you some gold if you'll let me pass."

"Well, we'll see," the soldier replied. "Let's call the captain over here and see what he says."

Caiphas feared getting involved with more than one person. "I could give the gold to you, and no one would be the wiser," he said confidentially.

The soldier just smiled evasively and then called out towards the campfire: "Captain! Captain Antonius, would you come over here and have a look."

The captain came with another soldier, and now three of them stood before Caiphas.

399

"What have we here?" the captain asked. "Demetrius, have you caught a fish?"

"Well," the first guard said, "this old man wants to leave the city and go on his merry way."

"Really?" the captain said. "Well, grandpa, we would like to let you go, but we're having a party tonight, and we have strict orders not to let anyone go through our lines without joining our party first."

"But I'm too old for parties," Caiaphas said. "You can see that just by looking at me."

"No, don't say that," the captain said. "Don't say that about yourself. You're not that old. You know you're not. It's all in the way you think." He spoke to the two guards. "Do you think he's too old to join out party, boys?"

"Oh, no," the two guards said, almost simultaneously.

"You see," the captain said to Caiaphas. "They don't think you're too old. And I think they'd love to have you." Then he said to the guards, "Wouldn't you like to have him as our guest, boys?"

"Yes, oh yes," the guards replied.

"I think you're going to disappoint them if you don't join us," he said to Caiaphas. "You wouldn't want to do that, would you?"

"I have gold!" Caiaphas said frantically. "I can let you have some. Think of all the nice things you can do with gold."

"Oh ho," the captain exulted, "so you're going to bring some gold to the party too, are you? That's very generous of you, old man. Very generous indeed."

"No, I want to give you the gold so I won't have to attend the party," Caiaphas explained.

"There you go again," the captain pouted, "acting as if you really don't want to come. You're going to hurt our feelings, and you don't want to do that, do you?"

"All right, all right," Caiaphas replied. "If you insist on putting it that way, I suppose I will have to attend."

"Ah, now that's more like it," the captain responded. "Now I'll tell you what we do with our guests. We like our guests to entertain us, but let me tell you just how. First, you give us all your gold..."

"All?" Caiaphas asked. "Surely you'll let me keep a little to buy some food after I leave. I don't want to starve."

"Well, we'll see," said the captain. "Maybe you can keep a little. Now, after you've given us *some* of your gold, you lie down on your back. And what you lie on are these two crossed pieces of wood. And then you let us connect you to them. And then after we've connected you nice and tight, we'll lift up the top part of the wood where your head is and stick the lower part into the ground. And then you can move your body around a little bit and do us a little dance. And when you get tired of dancing, we can talk. All right?"

Caiaphas straightened his body. He spoke now in his normal voice. "I am not an old man," he said. "I am the high priest, Caiaphas. I demand to see General Titus."

The captain said, "My, my, grandpa, look how young you've become! Look at how many years you've gotten rid of."

The two other soldiers laughed.

"I demand to see General Titus," Caiaphas said.

"Oh, I couldn't do that," the captain explained. "General Titus is asleep, and I don't think he'd like it if I disturb him."

"You tell him the high priest, Caiaphas, is here, and then he won't mind so much."

"But why should we tell him *that!*" the captain said. "Why just a Jewish high priest? Why don't we tell him you're the king of Nabataea and that you got detained in the city when you were visiting there and that now you want to go home? That might be even better, don't you think?"

"I am Caiaphas, I tell you. I am one of the chief priests. I am not just an ordinary person."

"I should have known it," the captain said, "by the nature of your clothes. We've got to treat him more respectfully, boys. How do we treat important people? Get him the clothes his rank deserves. Let's see some respect around here."

They took Caiphas to the campfire where the other soldiers were sitting. They took off his clothes and put a cloak on him. They fashioned a wreath of thorns and stuck it onto his head like a crown.

"Hail to the high priest!" they shouted. "Bow down before the high priest!" And some of them actually did that, kneeling in bogus respect before the ridiculously attired Caiaphas.

They whipped him and then burned him with hot metal from their fire. He screamed in agony over the sound of their laughter and cried out that he was the high priest and that General Titus would punish them for this. But they just laughed and burned him again, and he screamed and roared in his pain and, finally, cried out to heaven that he had served God all his life and asked God why He was letting these heathen do this to him.

He was limp with exhaustion when they finished. He hardly felt the pain when they nailed him to the cross, and he hardly heard their voices when they continued to call him their guest and to express gratitude that such an important individual had condescended to join their party. They stuck a gold coin into his mouth before they lifted him up, saying that they were giving him back some of his gold because, as he had said, he might need it for food or something after he left.

In the morning, Caiaphas hung suspended, his cross squeezed between those of two others who were already dead. What thoughts, what regrets, what resentments, what prayers pervaded his mind, I cannot say. Who can know what anyone thinks suspended on a cross? Jesus, when he hung like that, asked God, his father, to forgive those who were doing it to him, since they did not realize the wrong that they were doing. Of course, if they had not done it, then Paul's belief in God's forgiveness of sin through Jesus' death could never have been conceived. But Jesus, perhaps because he had expected God to reach down and save him at some point, and perhaps because he never really knew that his death was God's price for forgiveness of the rest of us, called out in his great despair, "My god, my god, why have you forsaken me?" So at least we know something of what Jesus was thinking when he died like that on a cross.

Caiaphas died. He died with the sight of his beloved city filling his eyes to the last, a prickly crown of thorns piercing the skin of his head and the mocking laughter of Romans resounding in his ears. They nailed a sign to the foot of his cross, which said, "This is Caiaphas, high priest of the Jews," thinking to ridicule him as they had ridiculed Jesus when they had hung a sign on his cross saying that he was king of the Jews, and not knowing that each man that they mocked was just what the sign said he was.

The supply of timber ran out. It ran out so completely that there was no more left to build crosses. But Titus would not permit such minor reverses to stand in the way of his terror. He would use a different means to make his point to these stubborn and miserable Jews. He took now to cutting off the hands of whichever Jews he captured. Thus assured that these people could not hold weapons to fight, he sent them into the city with messages to John and Simon to surrender, lest this be done to them all. When he went to the wall to see how effective these messages were, the defenders answered him with derision and told him that Jews were not afraid of death and that they preferred it to the humiliation of slavery.

Now arrived a group of young Macedonian foot soldiers under a leader whose name was the same as that of the hated king, Antiochus Epiphanes. They were surprised that their Roman allies were fearful of approaching the wall. They wanted to impress the Romans with their daring and prowess. With Titus' permission, they attacked the wall with the insouciant courage of youth. Those who returned alive learned the lesson that their older compatriots had learned earlier: that fighting Jews was not child's play and that those who engaged in it paid a price. I think what these Macedonians had not understood and what Titus and his Romans were just beginning to understand was that Jews really were prepared to die fighting and that they had no fear of death. To the Romans and Macedonians, this was unnatural. Sensible people were expected to act like Josephus and to grab the chance for life when it was offered to them. The Macedonians — what was left of them — made no more heroic assaults on the walls. Henceforth, the more methodical tactics of Titus would prevail.

The Romans finished building four huge platforms. All the legions were to fight, including the Tenth, which had been held in reserve on the Mount of Olives. They began to move their platforms forward, two of them in the direction of the Antonia, where John and his men were positioned. John's men dug a tunnel to the place where the platforms would finally be, and they widened it into a cave, using timber to support it. They waited until the platforms were over the cave. Then they brought in firewood laced with pitch and asphalt and set the place on fire. When the supporting timbers burned, the ground under the platforms gave way, and the platforms went crashing into the cave, collapsing and burning in what must have seemed a fire from the depths of the earth. Thus two of the platforms were destroyed, and the Romans began to understand that they were dealing with a people who were not only prepared to die but who were determined to win.

But the Romans still had two platforms, and they had their battering rams too. With the latter, they pounded the walls, determined to do their worst. From Simon's forces, three men, torches in hand, dashed bravely from behind the wall, past the Roman guards, and set fire to the platforms and the wickers above the battering rams. The Romans were taken by surprise, but they quickly recovered and began to throw stones at the three men and to thrust their swords into the men's bodies. But even that did not stop the three of them as they went about setting their fires. Then more Jews came from behind the wall, inspired by these three men, and they fought the Romans who were trying to obliterate the fires. The Romans tried to save their rams by pulling them away from the flames, but the Jews held the red-hot metal of the rams in their hands and refused to let go. Then the flames got so hot that the Romans had to withdraw. But the Jews did not let them off. They followed the Romans right up to their encampment and threatened to overwhelm it entirely. Now more Jews came out of the city and attacked the Roman camp. The Romans used quick-loaders to bombard the emerging Jews, but that did not stop the flow. The Jews attacked and attacked and hurled their bodies like missiles against the Roman soldiers and the Roman spears, just as they had done at Bethannabris when the Romans attacked them there. Our people were fighting for the city of God, and death held a glory for them that the Romans could not understand. Here was a starving people finding the strength to fight and fighting so well that they were driving back what the Romans had thought was the greatest army on earth. Who were they, the Romans wondered, that they fought like demons on empty stomachs with the name of their god on their lips? Who was this Yahweh and Moses and Judas and Jesus who drove them to fight with such disregard for their lives that the unbeaten pride of the Roman elite was laid low in the dust of their shoes?

Titus came forward and led an attack on the Jewish flank. But the Jews did not give way. A part of their force turned to fight on this flank and gave no ground to the emperor's son. Dust and shouting filled the air so completely that the men on both sides could hardly discern whether they were fighting the enemy or one of their own. But now the Jews, having carried the war into the Roman camp itself, grew weary from lack of food and began an orderly retreat to the city.

The Romans had lost their platforms, and Titus summoned his commanders to decide what to do next. Some wanted a massive attack on the walls; others wanted more platforms (but there was no more timber for that, since so much of it had been used for the crucifixes); still others wanted to sit out the blockade and wait for the Jews to starve. Titus did not want his soldiers to remain inactive for too long. Inactivity would make them lazy and less inclined to fight when the time came for them to do so. He knew that he could not prevent the Jewish sorties outside the walls nor could he afford to encircle the city with a line of men which would have to be thin and vulnerable as it stretched along the hills and valleys of the terrain. So he chose, instead, to have his men build a wall around the city and, at different points along it, a series of forts.

In the city itself, the hunger got worse. More and more people were dying of starvation. Swollen abdomens were becoming common. Those who tried to bury their dead sometimes died themselves as they worked. The air became vitiated with the smell of death, and rotting corpses were thrown outside the walls to get rid of the awful stench. Even speaking required an energy that was better preserved for fighting, so that silence became as much a way of preparing oneself for battle as the sharpening of a blade. The sudden sallies from behind the walls occurred no more. And the Romans, aware of the destitution within, took pleasure in displaying their plenty to the sunken eyes that could still see it. Yet still there was no surrender, no capitulation from the incorrigible Jew, who did not have the good sense to realize when he was beaten and to lay down his arms.

It was only a matter of time until starvation took them all, but Titus was not content to wait for that. To walk triumphant into a city of dead without having lifted a sword was not the glorious victory he sought. So, once again, he set his men to building platforms, these even bigger than the ones before. They had to go miles away to get the timber because, as I have said, they had used up all the trees around the city for their previous platforms and crosses. One small group of Jews who were defending one of the towers felt overawed by all this activity and decided to surrender their section and let the Romans in. Titus sent his infantry to accept their offer, but Simon got wind of it and got there first and executed the men before they could open the city to the enemy.

Then Titus sent Josephus to make another appeal for surrender with all the usual promises. But the will of the people could not be turned, and they answered Josephus with stones, one of which struck him off his horse and knocked him to the ground unconscious. The Romans dragged him away.

There were some successful desertions. It is hard to be strong when hunger gnaws like a beast inside your flesh. There were those who leaped over the walls and came to the Romans with their bellies swollen. The Romans gave them food. The wise ate it slowly and sparingly; the unwise gorged themselves like ravenous beasts, only to die as their bellies burst. In the Syrian camp, a Jewish deserter was discovered searching his stools for the gold he had swallowed before he had left the city. News of this spread quickly, and the Syrians and Arabs on that night slaughtered their Jewish prisoners and cut up their bodies in order to search their entrails for gold. But then Titus ordered it stopped. It was all right to do that sort of thing to people who were being tortured, as he had allowed to be done when they were crucifying everybody around the walls, but it was not all right to do it now that the policy had changed. But the slaughter continued anyway, albeit in secret so that Titus could not punish the perpetrators. By morning, there were fewer Jewish prisoners and some wealthier Syrians and Arabs.

In the city, the people ate garbage and even searched old dunghills for food. Water came from rain and from the Gihon Spring in the Kidron Valley outside the walls through the secret tunnel that Hezekiah had built over seven-hundred and fifty years earlier to withstand the Assyrian siege. John of Gischala took the sacred corn and oil from the inner part of the Temple where it was kept before being offered to God and gave it all to the people. Symeon assured him that God and Jesus approved of that. The people should not be made to starve when there was food to be eaten.

The Romans moved up their engines of war — their platforms and battering rams and quick-loaders — and moved them towards the Antonia. They covered their torsos with vests of armor and formed themselves into tight cordons around the platforms to ward off any Jewish attacks.

Somehow, from out of their destitute state, our people rose up to fight them. Like ones resurrected, they raised themselves up and dashed with their torches for the platforms and battering rams. The sight of the Romans gave them new strength. But this time, they were not successful; they could not break through the Roman line. And as more Jews came out to attack, the Romans hurled rocks at them and killed some of them. Now the Jews withdrew. But then, as the Romans brought up their battering rams, it was the Jews who pelted *them*. Rocks and firebrands rained from above and slowed the Roman advance. But the Romans again used their wicker shields and warded off the stones. Then the wall under which John had dug his tunnel on the previous Roman assault collapsed in a heap. The Romans rushed through the breach but now found that they were facing a second wall — a new one that John had had built while waiting for the Romans to start their assault. It looked weaker and low enough to scale if one just climbed up on the rubble of the previous wall that lay piled up against it. But no Roman soldier dared to do that, for he knew that a horde of Jews on the other side was waiting for him to try and that he would not survive if he did. Titus goaded his soldiers to be fearless and to make the attempt. Fate was on their side, he said, for hadn't the wall collapsed for them? Just as the walls of Jericho had tumbled down for the Jews, so were the walls of Jerusalem doing so now for the Romans. Did his solders want the ignominious victory of starving the Jews to death, so that the world could say the Jews were better fighters and only lost from lack of food? And did his soldiers not realize that if they did die, they would have immortality among the stars because of their courage?

406

A black-skinned, small-framed Syrian cried out that he would try, and he rushed for the wall alone. Eleven others, inspired by his example, followed him but could not catch up to him. The Jews used rocks and spears and arrows to counter this Roman charge and, at first, pulled back a short distance to let the Romans in. Then the Syrian, shot with arrows, tripped over a rock and fell down, and our soldiers came back and killed him and attacked the eleven others with rocks as they started to come over the wall. Three of the Romans were killed. The remaining eight limped back or were dragged back wounded. They had forgotten the lesson of Antiochus Epiphanes and his Macedonians when they had attacked the wall.

But the Romans, two days later, made another attempt. In the night, twenty-four of them including a trumpeter, acting on their own, sneaked onto the wall and killed the Jews who were sleeping. The trumpeter sounded his horn, and Titus, awakened by the signal, gathered his troops for an assault and charged with them to the walls. The Jews retreated into the Temple itself, and the Romans not only came over the wall but came through the tunnel that John had built.

Both John's men and Simon's men were there at this time, and they blocked the Roman entry into the Temple. The fighting was close and could be done only with swords. Retreat for either side was out of the question, because the press from behind by one's comrades would not allow it. It was the Romans who finally gave way. Those behind, seeing the death of their forward companions, lost heart and moved back to the Antonia, which they now possessed in any case.

The Romans started to flatten the Antonia, to make it possible for the Roman army to come up to the Temple. And again Titus sent Josephus to talk our people into surrender. He spouted the usual canard about God being on the side of the Romans, and the defenders vociferated their usual response and said that God could never be on the side of pagans. But a few Jews, weary of suffering and having been pro-Roman in the past, did slip out of the Temple and surrender to the Roman camp. Two of them were chief priests who had not been killed with the others, and the others were from priestly families or were Sadducees.

THE CHRIST-KILLERS

CHAPTER XLII

The Romans could not deploy their entire army in the small amount of space in front of the Temple, so Titus assigned Cerealius the task of leading a smaller Roman force against it. Titus stood in a remaining section of the Antonia and observed the assault from above.

His men attacked before sunrise, but the Jewish guards were not asleep this time as the Romans had expected. They were not going to make the same mistake that they had made at that newly built second wall. Certain guards stayed awake all night and were allowed to sleep only during the day. So when the Romans attacked, the Jewish guards sounded the alarm, and the Jews rose up in force. Now began a violent confrontation between men fighting at close quarters. And because it was dark and the voices were numerous, one could hardly tell his friend from his enemy. But the Romans had a pass word that they used to identify each other, and it helped them avoid costly errors until daylight enabled them to see. Yet even with the daylight, they were unable to gain any ground. The Jews never slackened their fighting in spite of their weakened physical conditions, and it was as much Jews attacking Romans as it was Romans attacking Jews. By noon, the Romans retreated to consider some other means by which to vanquish their intractable enemy.

Then the Romans tried again. They completed the flattening of the Antonia, and they built a wide road leading up to the Temple. Then they started building four platforms, and for this they brought timber from miles away. Yet their work was frequently hampered by sudden attacks from the Jews. And in the areas outside the city, even their horses would sometimes be stolen. And once, because the Jews were so daring, there was even an attack on the Roman camp at the Mount of Olives. But the Romans drove them back because the Jews lacked the bodily strength to fight as hard as they had before. And around the Temple, the fighting continued, and the defenders began to burn down some of the colonnades that connected the Temple to the Antonia.

One Jew named Jonathan, small and weak from lack of food though he was, came out one day to challenge any Roman to fight him in single combat. When no one responded, he called them cowards. A Roman named Pudens could not bear such impudence from a Jew, so he stepped forward to accept the challenge. Swords crossed and metal clanged and Jonathan ran Pudens through the chest. But as Jonathan stood there with his bloody sword over the prostrate body of his enemy, roaring his triumph as if it symbolized Jewish victory over Rome, Priscus, a centurion, unable to bear this defeat but too cowardly to come out and fight Jonathan alone, raised a bow and arrow and shot Jonathan through the chest. Jonathan fell upon Pudens' body and lay there till he died. This last occurrence demonstrated, I suppose, the Romans' ability to win on equal terms.

The Jews now stuffed firewood and asphalt and pitch between the parallel beams of timber that supported the ceiling of the western colonnade, but they made it appear to the Romans that they were engaged in strengthening the structure. Then they retreated from it as if they were tired, and the Romans, without orders from their commanders, let their zeal get the better of their caution and rushed after the Jews. When the colonnade was packed with Romans, the Jews exposed their trap. They set the colonnade on fire, and the Romans, being crowded together as they were, could not turn back and get out. They jumped into the city area behind them or into the mass of Jews or into their own compatriots, being either killed or suffering broken legs as they did. But most of them stayed where they were and either killed themselves with their daggers and swords or, if they were not quick enough, suffered the scorching pain of being burned alive.

Titus was angry once again, for again his men had acted without orders. But it really was not their acting without orders that angered him; it was their failure to win when they did. You will recall that when a group of Jews outside the city wall had feigned eviction and the Jews behind the wall had begged the Romans to enter, his men had acted without orders and succumbed to the Jewish trap. After they had been beaten by the Jews, he had shown anger, ostensibly at their disobedience and not because they had lost. But when a small group of Romans with a trumpeter had taken off on their own to scale the second wall that John of Gischala and his men had built, Titus had felt no anger against them, because those men had won their goal and carved the way for others to drive the Jews into the Temple. So it was not disobedience that angered Titus but failure. Disobedience was fine if it resulted in victory.

A Jewish woman with a suckling baby now killed her child and roasted its body for food. The Jewish soldiers in the street smelled the roasted meat and followed the smell into the house. The woman had eaten half the child's body by the time they entered. She presented the other half to the soldiers. They could eat it if they wished.

"What have you done?" one of the soldiers exclaimed. "You've committed murder and cannibalism both!"

The woman, with tears in her pitiful eyes, said, "What difference does it make? Was it better that he lived to be a Roman slave, to serve them their food and work in their quarries or die in their arenas as sport for their eyes? Better that he be dead than have that kind of life. Better that he not have come into the world at all."

"But you ate him, you ate him!" another soldier ejaculated. "You used your own child for food."

"What difference did it make?" the woman declared. "Once he was dead, what difference did it make if I used his body to live?"

"To live for what?" the soldier shouted. "So that *you* could be a slave for Rome? If it wasn't right for *him* to be a slave, then why is it right for you to be one? If you think we're going to lose this war, then we men should kill our women and children and then kill ourselves before we're captured."

"We should!" she cried, falling in a heap to the floor. "That *is* what we should do."

"But we're not going to lose," the soldier declared. "And even if we did kill each other, we wouldn't be eating each other's flesh."

"If you think we can win, then why shouldn't we eat each other's flesh? How can we win without food?"

The soldiers, hungry as they were and confident as they were of victory and needful as they were of sustenance to achieve it, could not do what the woman had done and eat the child's flesh. They left with a feeling of revulsion but with pity for the woman's pain. She knew the horror of what she had done, no matter how she tried to justify it, and the awareness of her sin in eating her child was penance enough, they thought.

"God will forgive her for what she's done," one of the soldiers said in the street. "It's the Romans who are at fault. God will punish *them*, not the woman."

News of this incident reached Titus, who acted scandalized when he heard it. "I am not responsible for this," he said. "It's the Jews who have brought this on themselves. They're the ones who are responsible."

But his response was all a sham, for he, like his father, had ordered the killing of children, and the fact that a Jewish mother had eaten one filled him with inner delight, for it proved the plight of the rebels and that they could not go on much longer.

Platforms and battering rams were moved forward, and the pounding of the Temple began. But days of this effort proved ineffective, so strong was the structure. The Temple wall was stronger than the other walls of Jerusalem. An attempt was made to undermine the wall by levering out stones, but the wall was too thick for that. Attempts were made to scale the wall with ladders, but the ladders were pushed back, and the climbers were killed. Titus then set the gates on fire and flattened a road to reach them while they were still burning. Then he held a council of war which included all his generals. Tiberius Alexander was there, that apostate Jew who had become procurator of Judaea and then governor of Alexandria. He was chief of the generals now. And the new procurator of Judaea was there too. His name was Marcus Antonius Julianus. Julianus had replaced Florus under orders from Vespasian, and Florus, no doubt delighting in all that he had started, was now in Rome enjoying the wealth that he had accumulated at our expense.

The defenders of the Temple made brief, sporadic attacks on the Romans, but these were quickly repulsed. The Romans drove the defenders back into the sanctuary. Then a Roman soldier set fire to the sanctuary itself, and now the defenders found a strength they did not know they possessed. They rushed to put out the fire, not caring if they would be killed in the attempt. The sanctuary was holy and had to be preserved. The dead piled up to the altar, and the blood from their bodies flooded the floor. The Romans stole what treasures they could find and killed any Jew they encountered, whether woman or child, aged or young. A hecatomb of Jews was offered for the greater the glory of Rome.

Yet some Jewish fighters, with the desperation of men who had nothing to lose, fought their way through the Roman ranks and made their way into the city. The Romans, however, were still unimpeded in their burning of every building. They looted the treasury, which held not only the Temple money but the precious possessions of wealthy Jews who had brought them there for safekeeping. To their chagrin, there was not as much there as they had expected. Abram and his men had done their job well. At least part of our national wealth was still ours, and the Romans, who lived by stealing, were not going to steal that part of it.

On the last remaining colonnade of the Temple, a large crowd of citizens gathered as they fled from the flames and carnage. They were mainly women and children, and they had come to the Temple because they had been told by a man who claimed to be a prophet that if they went there, they would see the signs of their deliverance. Not a few of them were Nazarenes, and the sign that they had hoped to see was Jesus. But the Romans set the colonnade on fire, and the people either leaped to their deaths or were burned alive in the flames, many women clutching their children as they perished.

The destruction was to be complete. When some starving priests surrendered and asked for their lives to be spared, Titus ordered them killed. The looting, too, was to be complete. When the Syrians, for example, returned to their own country after this war was over, so laden were they with gold in its various forms that the gold supply in Syria was doubled, and the purchasing power of the metal was halved.

John and Simon had sworn never to surrender, but they invited Titus to a meeting. Titus came if only to see what these intransigent Jewish leaders looked like. Simon did the speaking first and said that if Titus would allow him and his men to leave with their wives and children, they would relinquish the city to him. Titus refused. To him the Jews were incorrigible. Israel had never stopped rebelling from the time that Pompey had first conquered it, and he was going to end that once and for all. No one was to be spared; all were to be killed. These were the words of the emperor's son.

So John and Simon returned to their men and announced that the fight was to the death. But if they were going to die, they would take as many Romans with them as they could.

So now the fighting began again, and, to Titus' utter consternation, the Jews did not just stand to defend; they actually attacked. They drove the Romans out of the palace, killed one and took another prisoner. When this prisoner later escaped from his Jewish captors and made his report to Titus, Titus had him expelled from the army because he had allowed himself to be captured. The fact that the man had managed to escape held no weight with him at all.

The Romans drove the defenders out of the lower part of the city and burned it, but the defenders held the upper part. More appeals came from Josephus, but these by now were ludicrous. Our people continued to fight without pause and took to the sewers when necessary. The Romans moved up platforms, for, without them, they could not hope to take the upper part of the city. Once, some Idumaeans plotted to surrender, but Simon put a stop to that by imprisoning them. And those Jews who did surrender were usually sold as slaves if Titus did not order them killed.

When the Romans brought up their engines, some defenders left the wall and fortified themselves in the Citadel, while others took to the sewers to fight the Romans from there. Meanwhile, some of them stayed at the wall and tried to fight the battering crews. But there were too many Romans and too few Jews who still had the strength to fight. The whole west wall broke down, and some of the towers collapsed. The other towers could not be budged, however, and the Romans felt that they could not get the defenders out of them by any means other than starvation. But those inside the towers would not allow themselves to suffer that degrading destiny. They broke out of the towers and fled, some to the sewers to fight from there and some to an outside ravine.

The Romans in the city killed anyone that moved and set fire to the buildings and houses. But now Titus required prisoners, for he had slavery and entertainment in mind. So he ordered that, henceforth, only resisters and the old and sick were to be killed; others were to be taken alive. Some prisoners he chained and sent off for manual labor in Egypt. The better-looking ones he kept for the shows he was planning. These shows included not only a parade in Rome but the killing of prisoners in arenas by wild beasts or by each other. Many prisoners died of starvation anyway, either because the Romans refused to feed them (out of hatred) or because the prisoners refused to eat (out of pride) or because, when an inventory was taken of the available food supply, it was found that there wasn't enough corn to feed so many people. John and some of his companions were found starving in a sewer and were taken prisoner. Simon also was captured after trying to tunnel out of the city through a sewer and then making a pitiful attempt to frighten some of the Roman soldiers by dressing himself like a ghost. And Symeon and a remnant of Nazarenes hid in a sewer and there, by the grace of God, escaped detection.

The Temple was destroyed. No more would a priest stand on the roof of the priests' chambers in the late afternoon of every sixth day and signal with blasts on his shofar the ending of work for the Sabbath and do the same every seventh day to signal the Sabbath's end. The loss of the Temple symbolized the loss of the nation. But not our religion! Not our religion. There had been a time late in the war when Titus had threatened to destroy the Temple if we did not surrender, so precious did he think it was to us; and though it *was* precious, so was freedom, so that our leaders had answered him by saying that the world was a better temple for God than this one, if it was going to be destroyed. They had known, as all Jews knew, that the religion of the Jews, like the god of the Jews, does not reside in an edifice of stone but lives in the ubiquitous spirit of the people, wherever they might be.

Titus sentenced John to imprisonment for life. I think he didn't kill him because he secretly admired him for the ingenuity he had shown when he had dug his tunnel under the platforms and caused those structures to collapse. But Simon he kept as a prisoner for the big parade in Rome. He had the walls of the city destroyed except for the one on the west, which he wanted as a protection for his garrison. He had all the structures flattened except for three towers, which he wanted to stand as a reminder of what a great city Jerusalem once had been. Josephus found his family members still alive, and Titus gave them to him.

Titus congratulated his army and rewarded those he considered the most courageous. He left the Tenth Legion and some additional troops in the city to establish a permanent military presence. These troops gathered what Jewish women they could find and kept them for their sexual needs.

Titus marched with the rest of his army to Caesarea on the coast and from there inland to Caesarea Philippi. At this place he started his shows for the entertainment of the crowds. He did this, in part, to celebrate his brother's birthday. The entertainment consisted of throwing Jewish prisoners to ravenous beasts so that the audiences could watch them being torn apart; or they consisted of staging wars between two opposing Jewish "armies" in which battles were fought to the death; or they consisted simply of burning Jews alive in an arena so that their writhings and screams could entertain the audiences. Then Titus went back to Caesarea to put on more of such shows as this. It was like a large troupe of traveling players in which actors are dead in the end but do not rise when the play is over. He did the same in Beirut, with his Gentile audiences cheering with delight at the gory and agonizing deaths of the Jews. And he did the same in the Syrian towns for equally enthusiastic crowds. By the time he reached Berytus, the city in Phoenecia, it was time to celebrate his father's birthday. And because his father was worthy of even more adoration and respect than his brother, Titus now made his next shows even grander. Greater numbers of Jews now fought in his "wars"; greater numbers of beasts now ate living flesh; greater numbers of fires now burned Jews alive, always to the delight of the crowds. I say this so that you will understand that Nero was not alone, that Nero was not some isolated case of an emperor gone awry, but that most Romans and pagans, when given the chance, would act in a manner like this. These were people without a moral code, without a guide or a Torah like ours, with no fear of God or awareness of retribution, people on a spiritual level with the very beasts they used to open our flesh, to devour the people of God.

In Antioch, the Gentiles hailed Titus along the roads and called down blessings on his head. Then, knowing his displeasure with the Jews because of the costly war they had started, these Gentiles begged him to expel the Jewish citizens from their city and make it entirely Gentile.

"Remove the bronze tablets on which the privileges of the Jews are written," they implored. "And then remove the Jews themselves, because all of them hate Rome."

But Titus said that if he did such a thing, these Jews would have to be banished to their own country, which was nothing but a smoking ruin now, and that no other country would take them in after what their people had done against Rome. So he left things in Antioch just as they were and went back to see Jerusalem one more time before returning to Rome. When he got there, he found that treasures were still being uncovered under the charred remains of the city and that people moved about the ruins like shadowy scavengers picking at the bones of a skeleton.

"Let this serve as a reminder," he said, "of what happens to those who defy Rome."

But let it serve as a reminder, I say, of who the Romans are. For though buildings fall and walls decay, the history of man remains. They cannot love their neighbors, these Romans, and they certainly cannot love their enemies. No, I do not hate them, in spite of their having destroyed our city and killed our babies and nailed our people to crosses and burned them alive and thrown them to wild animals to eat. I do not hate them because I am a Nazarene, and I love even those who do such things. I hate what they have done, but I do not hate them, because I believe that in the heart of every one of them lies a capacity to love. They are not ready to release it yet, but someday they will be, and when they do, I think Jesus will return. Then Israel will be restored, and, ironically, such love will pervade the world that we will have no need of Jesus to guide us anymore.

But that day was not yet upon us, and Vespasian still ruled the world. They called him their savior, the Romans did, as he marched on the road to Rome — their savior and their benefactor, this conqueror of the Jews. And Vespasian's son now left Jerusalem and crossed the desert to Egypt. From there he went to Rome and was welcomed by his father. I was there in Rome when news of the destruction of Jerusalem reached us. I cried for my people and my nation; I cried for God, for whom we had fought and for whom we had failed to win.

And I was in Rome when the Romans came out of their houses like agitated ants and scurried to the central avenue down which the parade would come. And what a parade it was! What a spectacle to please the people and show them the greatness of Rome. The generals had spent the night in the Temple if Isis. Their troops came to them in the morning. Vespasian and Titus then appeared with wreaths of bay leaves on their heads and robes of red on their shoulders. They walked to that place called the Octavian Walks where senators and other dignitaries awaited them. On a dais in front of the colonnades, they sat down on ivory chairs, and Vespasian silenced the cheering crowd by standing and raising his hand. He spoke to the people of their victory, and then Titus did the same. Vespasian invited the soldiers to eat the food that their generals had provided for them. Then he and Titus went to the gate through which victory parades always passed and ate some breakfast themselves. They made a sacrifice to their gods, and that signaled the parade to begin.

We saw treasures of gold and silver and ivory, taken from all the conquered nations of the world. We saw embroidered hangings, precious stones set in gold crowns and animals adorned with trappings. And we saw traveling stages on which tableaux were displayed, some of them three and four stories high. Colored curtains woven with gold hung from them, and scenes of battles and victories were portrayed on them. Battering rams broke through walls, defenders pleaded for mercy, burning temples and houses collapsed on the heads of the victims. Even ships came down the avenue, each with a story of its own.

And then came the spoils from Israel, most especially from Jerusalem and the Temple. A massive golden table and an elaborate lampstand made of gold; the sacred vestments of our Jewish priests; gold and silver in abundance. And yet not so much gold and silver as would have been displayed had Abram and his Essenes not helped us. And then, most grievous of all to those of us among the spectators who were Jews, the sacred Torah from the Temple itself paraded down a pagan street. Then came Vespasian and, after him, Titus with his brother, Domitian, riding by his side.

In this procession, also, were Jewish prisoners, Simon among them. When the parade ended at the Temple of Jupiter, Simon was pulled out and a noose put around his neck. He was kicked and beaten as they moved him along to the place of his execution. They killed him as the Roman people cheered and the scattered Jews in the crowd kept silent.

We dared not speak, we dared not praise him for the gallant stand he had taken and the heroic battle he had fought, lest the crowd hear our dissent and turn its fury on us.

After that, the crowd dispersed. People went home to their victory dinners, and I walked the streets aimlessly with an emptiness that food could not fill. Jerusalem was gone and Israel was gone and our people were scattered and homeless. And I who loved Jesus and still expected him to return asked myself what it was he would be returning to. From where would he gather his army to restore Israel again and bring peace and love to the earth?

CHAPTER XLIII

There were victory parties throughout the city, many for the Roman elite. Felix and Drusilla were invited to one of these, as were the emperor's sons, Titus and Domitian. Drusilla's beauty, delicate and yet darkly sensuous, overshadowed that of the Roman ladies and made men's heads turn in fascination. One of those heads was Titus', and he found an opportunity to speak to her alone.

"You're the talk of the party," he said to her. "The men here can't seem to take their eyes off you."

Evanescently, Drusilla remembered another party, when she had been married to someone else, and a governor, strong of limb and handsome, had spoken to her like this. And she remembered that the answer she had given then was the same as what she gave now.

"You flatter me, General Titus. You credit me with more than I deserve."

"No, I don't think so," Titus replied. "I believe I speak the truth."

"I think, general, you are not only a military man but a man of words as well."

"I am not skilled in the use of words," he said. "I am just a simple soldier."

"Just a simple soldier?" she said, deciding to play the game. "The man who conquered Jerusalem? I think you are more than that, general."

"I am flattered that you think so, dear lady," he replied. "And perhaps you are more than a beautiful woman."

"More than that? If I am even that, general, what more could I possibly be?"

"A woman of intelligence, of knowledge, of experience," he said. "I need advice on the administration of Judaea and Samaria and Galilee. I have to know how your Jewish people think. Josephus advises my father in that, but I need a personal advisor of my own. Would I be imposing very much on your time if I asked you to fill that role?"

"You flatter me, general," Drusilla said, "but I would be happy to serve in any way that I can."

"You are more than kind," Titus replied. "I will send an escort for you tomorrow."

419

Felix had seen Titus talking to Drusilla and had decided not to interfere. If his beautiful wife could gain influence with the emperor's son, the benefits might redound to him.

"He wants me," Drusilla confessed to him that night as they prepared for bed. "He uses the excuse that he needs political advice about Jews, but that's just a subterfuge. He wants me. I'm a woman. I know."

"And how does that make you feel?" he asked.

"I love only you," she answered.

He turned and walked away. She surmised what he was thinking.

"Do you want me to go to him?" she asked.

"Would it be hard for you to do so?" he replied without looking at her.

"I will think only of you when I'm with him," she answered, and nothing more had to be said.

Within a week, Felix' pension was increased, and gifts in the form of expensive furniture and two young slaves arrived at the house. Felix and Drusilla became more popular, and their presences were sought in the best Roman houses.

It was not long before Bernice heard of this. Drusilla was getting to be known. Though Bernice had been known to Nero, she had not yet been introduced to Vespasian or his sons. Her rivalry with Drusilla was kindled anew by this. More important than her feeling for Agrippa, which she could not do anything about anyway from now on because of the vow she had taken in Jerusalem, and more important than her pledge to be chaste, which she had given when her head had been shaved, was this competition with her sister, which infected her like a disease. That feeling suppressed everything else. She could not let Drusilla get the better of her in anything. She would take Titus away from her sister. She made up her mind to that.

In Judaea, Lucilius Bassus took over for Cerealis Vitellius as the legate of Syria. The defenders of the fortress at Herodium surrendered to him without a fight. At Machaerus, they surrendered too and were allowed to leave. But in a forest where survivors of the Jerusalem siege had gathered to organize again, the Roman soldiers found them and massacred them all.

Vespasian sent a message to Bassus and the procurator, Liberius Maximus. They were to sell all Jewish property but not to sell it to Jews. Jews were not to have land or wealth, and their nation was to be sold out of existence. The Romans did not do this to other peoples who resisted and fought against them. The Germans and Britons, for all their defiance, still retained their lands. But those people, unlike ours, had surrendered to Rome in the end. Our people had not done that; they had fought against Rome to the death. Perhaps that is what had made all the difference to the Romans: that the Jews had never given in. Those Jews who were left alive were to pay as much tax to Rome each year as they previously had paid to their Temple. This special tax was called the *fiscus Judaicus*, and it was levied on all Jews and Jewish converts throughout the Roman Empire. Thus, it was not only the Jewish nation that was to be wiped from the face of the earth but its god and religion as well. And because Vespasian recognized the Jesus-movement as a political threat to the sovereignty of Rome, he ordered that all who belonged to the house of David were to be sought out and killed, so that no more claimants to the throne of Israel would remain. But Symeon stayed hidden until the furor subsided and thus escaped this Roman threat to his life.

What was left now was only Masada, the high fortress still occupied by Eleazar and his Zealots and Sicarii. They were joined by Abram and a group of his Essenes, determined to make a meaningful fight. The Essene community near the Dead Sea had been demolished by the Romans, and those Essenes still strong enough to fight would do so at Masada. Because Eleazar was related to Judas of Galilee, he was looked upon with great respect. Then Bassus, who had served such a short time as the governor of Syria, died. And also a new procurator of Judaea came onto the scene to replace Liberius Maximus. This new procurator was Flavius Silva, a Roman general of note. He started his procuratorship aggressively, and marched an army to Masada. He built a wall around the fortress to prevent any Jewish escape. He sent captive Jews to get food and water for his soldiers, since there was none in the vicinity. He built a huge platform and a battering ram. He used quick-loaders and stone-throwers to drive the Jews from the wall. Then he pounded the battering ram insistently against the wall. But the Jews within were not idle. They built a second, inner wall made of wood and earth. When the first wall was broken and the Romans came through, they found the second wall keeping them out. The battering ram was used on the second wall, and, against the compressible earth, it proved ineffective because the force always was being absorbed. Silva then set fire to the wood of the second wall, and the burning of it began.

Eleazar saw that the end was near, and he spoke to his people of their duty as Jews. The people of God were not to be slaves, he said. To serve heathens, to pay them taxes, to accept *men* as lords — especially pagan men — was an affront and an insult to God. The only lord for a Jew was God. To accept anyone else was a sin. He asked

421

them to kill their wives and children and then each other, to take from the heathen Romans the satisfaction of killing or enslaving them all. They agreed to his proposal and caressed their loved ones one last time and then tearfully slit their throats. Then only the men were left, each having killed his own family. Ten of the men, chosen by the drawing of lots, killed all the other men and then themselves before dawn.

In the morning, when the Romans came through the charred remains of the second wall, the Jews lay dead before them. Two old women and some children who had hidden from all of this came out now to tell what had happened.

Yet, even with the destruction of this last pocket of Jewish resistance, Vespasian still feared more Jewish revolts. So he ordered Lupus, the governor of Alexandria, to destroy the Jewish Temple at Leontopolis, even though the Egyptian Jews had done nothing against Rome to warrant it. Lupus did not tear down the building as one might have expected but destroyed its function instead. He did this by taking out of the building all the money he could find and then closing the doors to the public. And when Lupus died a short time after that, his successor, Paulinus, handled the building in the same way.

Now, throughout the Roman empire, wherever there were Jews in smaller numbers than Gentiles, the Gentiles started killing Jews. In all the towns of Syria, the Gentiles killed the Jews. The Romans themselves tortured their Jewish prisoners by putting them on the rack or whipping them. They threw them to hungry beasts in the arena, and when their bodies were partially eaten away, they pulled them out and gave them food so they could be thrown in again the next day. And the Roman people loved it. They cheered at the sufferings of the Jews.

Some Sicarii from Israel escaped to Alexandria and tried to start a rebellion of Jews there, saying that only God should be their master. But the Jews of Alexandria, accustomed to Roman rule and fearful of retribution, turned these Sicarii and their families over to the Romans. The Romans tortured their new prisoners in varieties of ways, trying to make them declare that Caesar was their lord. But fire and rack and clubs and knives could not force them to say it. God was their only lord, and they would not accept anyone else. Even their little children, battered and cut and burned as they were, refused to commit the cardinal sin of calling anyone but God their lord. So the Romans killed them too, for what good were they to the Romans if they would not become their slaves and if they always intended to rebel? It was a tribute to Sicarii courage that not one of them ever gave in.

In Rome, Rabath, in secret, prayed for the return of the Messiah. She lived in the same house as Bernice, a marble structure with columns and running water from one of the aqueducts and a garden of colorful flowers. In the house, she ate from gold and silver plates and dined on venison, ostrich, vegetables and fruit, and drank wine chilled with ice and snow from the mountains. The only thing that made this house different from other wealthy ones was the absence of statues and pork. Bernice had chosen, selectively, which Mosaic rules she would obey, and the strictures against statues and pork were among the ones she had chosen.

Jacob lived in the house too. He was Rabath's guardian in a sense, certainly her protector, and in some ways, voluntarily, her servant. Bernice, who prided herself on her knowledge of men, observed this relationship without comment, but she wondered from time to time, as she saw what went on, why Jacob was always as loyal as he was.

Without telling either Rabath or Bernice, Jacob started a business enterprise. He imported grain from Egypt. Through his personal contacts in Alexandria, he arranged for the grain to be delivered each week to the port of Ostia at the mouth of the Tiber River, twelve miles from Rome. From there, he had barges bring the grain to Rome, where his agents then delivered it to shops and private homes. Later, he erected storage bins to keep the grain until his buyers could come for it. All this he accomplished quietly and industriously, not mentioning it to Rabath.

One evening, in the garden, he sat with her and presented her with a gift: a sparkling gold necklace set with precious stones. She was totally unprepared for this.

"Jacob, I'm speechless! I don't know what to say. How could you afford...? Why? What's the occasion for this?"

"We've known each other a long time," he said.

"Yes, I know that. But why this?"

"In all that time, have you ever wondered why I never sought anyone for my wife?"

She looked at him, and the realization of his constancy and strength through the years, something she had always taken for granted and had never even thought about, appeared suddenly before her like a book that had always been open but whose pages she had never read.

"Jacob," she said, realizing everything all at once. "Oh, Jacob, all these years! All these years, and you've never said anything. Oh Jacob, what have I done to you?"

"You've done nothing but bring me pleasure," he said, "and given me a purpose in life."

"And this gift, Jacob — I know it's beyond your means — why, after all these years, have you given it to me now?"

"I thought, since I'm going to be spending the rest of my life with you, that I might as well do it as your husband."

"But why didn't you say something sooner? Why did you wait all these years?"

"I didn't have much money. I wanted to have more if I married you."

"And now you think you have enough?"

"I'm a successful merchant now," he said. "I import grain from Egypt."

"You do what? When did all this happen?"

"Did you ever wonder how I spend my days and sometimes my nights when I'm away from you?"

"Jacob, Jacob," she said in wonder, "you never cease to amaze me. Is there nothing, is there nothing that you can't do?"

He smiled and left the question unanswered.

Fleetingly she remembered another night, in a garden such as this, when another man who had loved her had asked her to be his wife. She had rejected him. Then, years later, she had come to appreciate that man and even to love him from afar, as he had loved her. She would not make that same mistake twice in her life.

She married Jacob in Bernice's house. Then they moved into a house that Jacob bought. He continued to be a Sadducee and she remained a Nazarene, but they kept her belief a secret because in Rome it was still disliked.

Bernice, now living alone except for her servants, sent a message to Titus. She invited him to dine with her in celebration of what she called his liberation of Jerusalem. Titus, in a sense, was obliged to accept. Bernice's brother had been his ally in war, and it was time he paid his respects to her. But also, because Agrippa had spoken of her so often when they had sat together in a tent on the battlefield, and because Agrippa had described her as the most beautiful of his three sisters (without ever revealing his love for her), Titus was curious to see her. Drusilla, to his mind, was the most beautiful woman he had ever seen. If her brother thought Bernice surpassed her, this was something he had to see.

The dinner was just for the two of them. It consisted of rarities in food. It was not enough that the food be unusual; it had to be prepared in an unusual manner. Bernice had her servants place spices and juices on the peacocks and pheasants they were preparing. Each food was mixed with another in some way in order to give a combination of flavors.

Bernice wanted to present herself in an unusual manner as well. It was not enough that she be beautiful; she had to be alluring and tantalizing too. The dresses of Roman women, even when slightly revealing, were not enough to set a man on fire. She decided to dress exotically, to wear something that Titus did not ordinarily see even among captive slaves from afar. She ordered for herself a lavish cloak covered with peacock feathers. The magnificent colors of the male of that species would cover her from neck to toes. She wore earrings and a head band, both of twisted gold, and placed henna on her lips and cheeks.

Dressed like that she greeted him. "General Titus, how glad I am you could come. You honor my house and all who are in it." A servant took his cape.

To Titus, Bernice seemed even more beautiful than Agrippa had described her. Her elaborate covering and the jewels and cosmetics on her face contributed to that no doubt.

The dining table was set on the white marbled floor with plentiful cushions for each of them. Four toga-clad young women attended to their needs. They hovered at discrete distances, their eyes watching for ways to make themselves useful while being as unobtrusive and unnoticed as possible. Musicians, hidden from view in an adjoining room, played slow delicate music on flutes, drums, lyre and cymbal. A young Nubian girl entered the room and began to dance. She was completely naked. Her brown-black skin was heavily oiled, and it shone metallically and refulgent in the light from the oil lamps in the room.

"I hope you don't mind some quiet entertainment while we dine, General Titus," Bernice said casually.

"Not at all, Princess Bernice. I'm an admirer of the arts."

The nudity of the girl did not disconcert Titus in the least. He was accustomed to seeing nude captive women, fearful for their lives — or their children's lives — performing for him in various ways to gain his favor.

The girl's dance was slow and sinuous, much of it conducted on the floor, where she crawled on her belly or lay on her back and weaved her arms in helical paths through the air. Not infrequently, she stroked herself on her breasts and hips and thighs. Occasionally, Titus glanced at her, allowing his eyes to linger for a few moments, and then turned back to his conversation with Bernice.

The meal was sumptuous, consisting of small portions of a variety of delicacies. I daresay Titus did not eat this lavishly even in the imperial palace. His father was economical and even parsimonious and did not indulge himself in unnecessary extravagances. While they talked of different matters during the course of the meal, neither of them mentioned Drusilla. Titus took it for granted that that affair was secret, or, if it was not, that those who knew of it dared not speak of it openly for fear of risking his displeasure. At the end of the meal, the serving girls brought bowls of scented water for Bernice and Titus to wash their hands.

"I see that an arch is being erected to commemorate your victory in Judaea," Bernice said.

"Yes, princess," he answered. "It seems that certain influential people in our government wish to honor me with a monument of some sort."

"An entire arch, General Titus! That's quite an honor. Have you seen the design for it yet?"

"Yes, I have, princess. There will be a band around it showing my soldiers carrying off some of the treasures from the Temple in Jerusalem." Then, as an afterthought, he added, "I hope you don't mind that, princess."

"Not in the least, General Titus," Bernice replied. "I'm grateful that you and my brother could stop the rebels. If you hadn't, my brother wouldn't be king anymore. Many of them were fighting because they expected some Messiah who was resurrected from the dead to come back and throw down all the lawful rulers and set himself up as king. There's a prophecy that someone from our country is going to become the king of the world, and whether it's that man or some other man, many of our people decided to rebel because of it. Not all them, of course, but many of them. I met one of them once who believed all this but said that he didn't want to rebel because of it. But what else could he say when he was our prisoner? His name — wait, let me remember — it was Paul of Tarsus. He said that this new kingdom would be in heaven and not on earth. Apparently Nero didn't believe him and chopped off his head." She sighed. "No, general, your soldiers did a good job when they beat the rebels. I saw the parade when the Temple treasures were displayed. It doesn't bother me in the least that you're going to commemorate that in stone. It's a small enough compensation for what your soldiers did."

"You're most understanding," Titus said.

"And will there be other monuments, general? Mucianus and your brother are subduing the rebel army in Gaul. Will there be an arch built for them too?"

"I haven't heard any talk of that, princess. In Gaul, the soldiers we're subduing are exceptions to the general population. In your country, it was the opposite. In your country, it was the loyal citizens who were the exceptions. I think the war in Galilee and Samaria and Judaea was the worst we ever had to fight — against anyone — and I think that's why our people want a monument to this particular war and not to any other."

"Will your image be on it?" she asked.

"Yes," he laughed, "riding in a chariot right at the top. I asked them not do that — the army deserves the credit, not I — but they insisted. So anytime you want to see me, princess, you'll only have to raise your head a little." She laughed at this. "Which reminds me," Titus continued, "I don't see any statues in your house. Don't you have any?"

"No, general," Bernice replied. "It's prohibited by our religion."

"A pity," Titus sighed. "A statue of you would enhance the beauty of any room."

"Thank you, general," she said, "but I suppose my people prefer real flesh and blood to stone replicas."

"Romans do too, princess, but when it is not available to them, they settle for stone."

"A man of your abilities, General Titus, should not have to settle for stone." She called to the dancer who was undulating on the floor. "Neftara, go to the general. Let him have a look at you."

The girl immediately stood up and walked obediently to Titus. He could not help but notice the firm, strong muscles of her legs. She knelt on the floor, face down, with her thighs apart and her arms stretched beyond her head.

"Sit up, Neftara," Bernice commanded her. "I want the general to examine you."

"Yes, mistress," the Nubian girl responded. She sat up on her knees with her legs still apart and placed the palms of her hands on her thighs.

"Look at her breasts, General Titus," Bernice suggested. "Touch them, please, and tell me if they're not better than stone."

Titus looked at the girl. She had a child-like face with a straight profile, a small and delicate nose, and lips that were slightly full. Her breasts were, indeed, a work of art, for they appeared uncommonly straight and firm.

"I think General Titus is afraid to touch you, Neftatra," Bernice said mockingly. "Maybe he thinks you'll break."

With that as a goad, Titus touched the girl's breasts. He felt her nipples harden under his fingers.

"Now I ask you, general, are my people not wise in this at least? Are those not better then stone?"

"Immeasurably, princess, but when it comes to someone like you, stone may be the most a poor beggar like myself could hope for."

"You conquered my people, General Titus," she said. "Do you not think you could conquer me as well? You would not have to settle for stone if you did."

"If your brother was right in all he described about you, it would be my greatest conquest of all."

"Then perhaps I should give you the opportunity, General Titus, to complete your conquest of the Jews."

She stood up and clapped her hands. The four serving girls fled from the room.

"Neftara," she said, "make the general more comfortable until I return."

"Yes, mistress," Neftara answered in an artless, ingenuous voice.

Bernice started to leave the room when Titus called out to her, "Bernice!" She turned. "Who is to be the conqueror here, you or I?"

Bernice smiled esoterically and left the room.

Neftara rose and proceeded to put out more than half the lamps in the room. From a corner she took a large bowl filled with oil and brought it to Titus' side. She sat on her knees and said to him, "May I remove your clothing, my lord?"

Titus allowed her to remove his clothing until he was as naked as she. Neftara dipped her cupped hands into the bowl and brought out a small amount of oil. This she placed on Titus' leg and rubbed it into his skin. She did this on his arms and back with a strength in her hands that surprised him.

The gentle music from the adjoining room had never stopped playing. Now it did but just for a few moments. When it started again, it was different. The drums, which previously had been more subdued and accessory to the other instruments, were now more prominent than before. The flutes were played with more emotion, like sounds from a human voice.

There was a clash of small cymbals, and Bernice appeared in the doorway. Her body was mostly uncovered. It was oiled, as Neftara's was, but adorned as well with jewels. On her arms and wrists and ankles

428

were bracelets of rubies and gold. A jewelled necklace hung between her breasts. Her eyes were outlined with a dark cosmetic. A silken covering was wrapped around her hips. Dressed like this, the sister of King Agrippa danced for the emperor's son.

Her arms were stretched above her head, with her wrists crossed and her fingers spread open like a fan. She moved one leg forward on the ball of her foot, then dipped and rolled her hip. She repeated this with her other leg and slowly moved towards him in this manner. When she had covered half the distance, she dropped on her knees to the floor. With her thighs open wide, she arched herself back like the drawn bow of an archer, so that her hair touched the floor behind her. Then she twisted herself onto her belly and slithered towards him as if scaling a wall. There was an exigent look on her face.

"Titus," she whispered, "do you want me?"

"Yes," he roared, like a man restrained by shackles who wants desperately to break free.

"Then take me now," she entreated.

Titus tore himself away from the Nubian girl and took Bernice into his arms. He carried her to the pillows and kissed her mouth. Then, with Neftara still in attendance, he took Bernice and made her his. And in this way did a woman of Israel conquer the emperor's son.

Drusilla's delicate beauty could not compete with Bernice's creative imagination. Titus would never know from one week to the next what new theatrical experience or what new erotic device might await him in Bernice's house. Though she was thirteen years his senior, she became his mistress to the exclusion of anyone else.

Severed from Bernice's mind when she did this was all thought of Mosaic law. Only her triumph as a woman and her predominance in Roman society mattered to her now. When Agrippa came to visit her after this and chided her for disobeying with Titus the very law she had found it necessary to obey where he was concerned, she answered lightheartedly, "Wasn't it you, brother, who told me that the law wasn't made for people like us?"

"Do you no longer love me then?" he asked.

"I will always love you — more than anyone else," she said.

"Then how can you give your body to him and not to me?"

"Some sins are greater than others, more forgiveable in the eyes of God. Ours — ours was more frowned upon than this. So maybe that's one reason that I can do it with him and not with you and still call myself a Jew. And also I wanted to take him away from Drusilla, that conniving little bitch. I never had that problem with you. You love me to the exclusion of anyone else. I never had to compete with Drusilla to get you. And that's one of the reasons I love you now and could never love him in the same way. But I couldn't let Drusilla get the better of me with Titus. I had to show her that I could beat her. So I guess that's the second reason I can sleep with him and not with you. But there's a third reason too, my brother, and it's not one that I can tell you. It's something private between me and God, but maybe it's the reason He'll forgive me for all this when everything is over."

It was said of Titus, after he started this affair, that his nature seemed to soften. It was said that he became kinder and more compassionate towards other people after he started seeing Bernice. This man, who had crucified Jews and burned them alive in the arena, became more understanding of others, it was said, as a result of Bernice's influence.

This was true with one exception though, and that exception was Florus. With Florus, Titus' conversion to benevolence did not manifest itself as it did with other people. With him, it seemed that benign neglect — even incognizance — was the policy that prevailed. It was not a matter of money, because Florus did not need a government pension. He was wealthy enough on his own, having stolen so much money from us. But he did need to feel that he was safe and secure, accepted by the new imperial family. He remembered Flaccus, the governor of Alexandria. Flaccus had helped exile Caligula's mother. But then Caligula had become emperor and had ordered Flaccus' execution. The specious reason given for that was that Flaccus had allowed Egyptian Gentiles to massacre Alexandrian Jews. Now that Bernice was Titus' mistress — something that Titus did not try to hide as he had his affair with Drusilla — Florus was concerned that the same fate should not befall him. He had threatened to kill Bernice in Jerusalem. Would she now threaten to kill him in Rome?

It seemed to him that she would not, because nothing seemed to change. Life went on as it had before. He enjoyed his wife, his slaves and his friends. Of course, he had not been invited to Titus' party, given for the social elite, but then Felix, who was also a former procurator, had not been invited either, so Florus saw nothing significant in that. But then Florus began to notice that his friends were not inviting him to their homes anymore. And when he extended invitations to them, they always had scheduled engagements elsewhere. He tried impromptu visits to their homes and was always informed that they were out. He tried sending them messages that asked for replies, but the replies never came. He knew that he was being ostracized, excommunicated in a sense, cut off from his peers, and he suspected that Bernice, in a covert desire for revenge, was behind all these different things.

Then, one day, the centurion, Priscus, who had served with Titus in Jerusalem — he was the man who had shot an arrow through Jonathan, the Jewish hero, after Jonathan had beaten the Roman, Pudens, in single combat — this Priscus stepped forward and made the accusation that Florus had approached him with a diabolical scheme to assassinate the emperor. Florus, he said, had told him that he had enough military support behind him to become the emperor himself. Priscus said that he had deceptively agreed to Florus' plan but had then reported it to Titus. The guards then came for Florus at his home and took him away for trial. Florus protested that it was all a lie, that there wasn't a word of truth in it. "Why," they asked, "would Priscus lie? What did he have to gain from it?" Nothing that he knew of, Florus said, but still, it was all a lie! It became one man's word against the other, and they could not find Florus guilty without more solid evidence than that. So they let him go but gave him a warning to watch his behavior henceforth.

Florus went back to his house in fear and lived from then on like a troglodyte. He was fearful of talking to anyone, lest they accuse him of conspiracy. Yet, even with that much caution, he saw his house being watched. If he went out just to walk in the market, he could see that he was being followed. He began to grow nervous. He feared for his life. Yet that very life he feared losing was becoming unbearable. He found himself increasingly unable to eat. His body began to lose weight. He had been somewhat flaccid and paunchy before this; now he grew thin and bony. The skin on his formerly cherubic face now hung in folds like a curtain. His eyes receded into his skull; his forehead became more prominent. His voice grew weaker and higher in pitch. He seemed to be aging quickly.

One day he sat in one of his marbled rooms next to a pool of water. He felt that he had had enough of this game and that it was time to make it end. He had a slave write a message to Bernice, saying that he wanted to see her. Another slave delivered the message. When the second slave returned with Bernice's answer, it said that Bernice would see him, but only on condition that he shave his head, wear a sackcloth and be barefooted. He considered that a small enough price to pay for the termination of his misery, so he did it. He shaved his head, removed his shoes and cut a long tunic out of a sack. Then, accompanied by a slave who helped him walk, he went to Bernice's house. He was taken to the kitchen and was told to wait. Bernice was occupied at the moment, but she would see him presently. They did not offer him a chair. Bernice's servants looked at him askance as they scurried about the kitchen doing their work. Finally, after what seemed to him a long and painful wait, Bernice came into the room.

"You wanted to see me?" she asked superciliously, as a servant brought her a chair.

"I have come to ask you for pity," he said. "I know you are behind what is being done to me."

"Pity, dear Florus? What do you mean? I don't understand what you mean."

He understood that she needed revenge, and he was willing to give it to her if that's what it would take to stop this horrible business. "I have done you wrong in the past. I admit it. How can I make amends?"

"What wrong have you done me? I don't understand. Please explain to me why you are here."

"I threatened your life in Jerusalem. I threatened to kill you there."

"Oh that!" she exclaimed, brushing it aside. "I had almost forgotten it." She waved her hand reassuringly. "I knew you weren't serious. A Roman procurator wouldn't threaten the life of someone who was loyal to Rome, especially if that someone is a member of the royal family. Oh, surely you don't think I took you seriously. I certainly hope you don't."

"Then why have you had me come here dressed in this manner?"

"Oh, my dear Florus," Bernice said regretfully, "I must apologize for that. But, you see, to be very candid with you, you're not very popular in Rome these days, and it would not do my reputation any good if it were known that I was entertaining you. So I had you come incognito, so to speak, so that no one would know who you were."

"And why am I not popular, princess?" Florus asked indignantly. "Why does everyone shun me?"

"Why, Florus, my dear fellow, surely you know. It's because you want to become the emperor. At least that's what everyone says."

"I do not want to become the emperor!" he protested.

"Well, perhaps not," she allowed, "but everyone says that you do. They say that you'd like to kill Vespasian and then take the throne yourself."

"But that's not true, I tell you! It's not true!"

Bernice remained calm and somewhat aloof. "Well, be that as it may," she sighed, "I still have my reputation to uphold. Do you realize, for example, what people might say if they knew you had come here today?"

"What?" he asked, approaching the point where he did not care anymore.

"Well," she said, "they just might say that the two of us are in league, that you tried to get me to assassinate Titus when he comes to visit me again. Oh, I know it's foolish and that people tell such lies and spread such stories these days. But what can you do? People will talk. What's a person to do?"

Florus glowered at her. "You're the one!" he said. "You'd probably tell that lie about me if they gave you half a chance."

"I, dear Florus? How can you say that? I'm not the sort of person who would say such a thing. Even if it were true, I wouldn't repeat it to anyone."

Florus, in his weakened and unsteady state, lost his self-control. He pointed his fingers at his body. "You've done this to me!" he shouted. "Look at what you've done to me! You Jewish whore! You bitch!"

Bernice, unblinking, stared at his face. She waited no more than a second. "Guards!" she called, and two tall men came charging into the room. "This beggar, this creature, this odious worm, has a mouth that's fit for garbage. Take him out and put him where he belongs."

The guards together lifted Florus. His slave dared not interfere. They carried him outside the kitchen and dumped him into a pile of filth, in which decaying fruit rinds and putrid entrails mingled with animal excrement. The guards stood waiting to be sure he left, as the slave helped his dripping master out of the offal.

One of the guards said to the slave, "Help your master get out of here fast, or he'll find more than crap on his clothes."

Florus slinked away with the help of his slave, muttering imprecations under his breath.

When he got home, he faced a new surprise: he was told that his wife had left.

"What do you mean, she's left?" he asked.

The woman who had been his wife's attendant tried hard not to turn her face from the stench that emanated from her master's wet raiment. "I am sorry, master," she said. "She has left for good."

When she asked if she could remove Florus' sack and prepare a bath for him, he waved her away. He went directly to his bedroom and lay on his back on his bed. He lay like that throughout the night. In the morning, when the servants came to awaken him, they found him dead. Whether he died because he had willed himself so or because he had taken poison, I do not know. But later that day, when Titus visited

Bernice and told her that Florus was gone, she sat on the floor at Titus' feet and said simply, "It was too soon."

I left Rome and joined the Ebionites. What else was there for me to do? Jesus-following was a crime in Rome, as it was in the rest of the empire, and that was enough reason for me to leave. But then there was also Sharon. I could not bear to be so close to her when she was married to another man. So I left Rome and joined the Ebionites and told them all that I knew — about Paul and Peter and James, about Rabath and her father and Jacob. And they listened and wrote down the things I said, just as I record them for you now. I met Christians and tried to tell them the things that Paul had promised to tell them but could not tell them now: that the Jews had not killed Jesus but had loved and respected him. And I tried to tell them what Paul may or may not have said if he had had the chance: that Jesus had revered the Torah and had wanted us to do the same.

But very few of them listened to me, and those who did didn't believe me. Not only were Jews the enemies of God, they said, but the destruction of Israel and Jerusalem were God's way of punishing the Jews for their rejection of Jesus. If the Jewish nation was destroyed, they said, then the Jews got what they deserved. If that was true, I asked them, then what sins had Christians committed that they should suffer as they had? It was not because of sin, they said. *Their* suffering was because the Romans were misguided and had lumped them together with Jews. Jewish suffering was the will of God but Christian suffering was not.

They told me that Mary, the mother of Jesus, had given birth to Jesus while she still had been a virgin; that she had not yet slept with her husband, Joseph, and that God was Jesus' father. But why then, I asked, had Peter so meticulously traced back the lineage of Jesus, generation by generation, through the line of Joseph to King David? And why had Paul spoken in Antioch about Jesus being of David's seed? Joseph was of David's seed, and in order for Jesus to have been the same, Joseph would have had to have been his father. And how could the prophecy then be fulfilled that the king would come out of David if Joseph was *not* Jesus' father? And how could that reconcile with Paul's letter to the Romans, in which he had said, "Concerning His son, Jesus Christ our lord, which was made of the seed of David according to the flesh..."?

The Christians I meet are telling me that our synagogues are the synagogues of Satan and that whoever keeps Jewish observances and practices are doomed to the abyss of the Devil. I tell them that Paul himself allowed these things and that when we were together in a cavern in Rome, he said that it was all right for Christians who wanted to follow such practices to do so if they had learned those things from their parents. But that also fell on deaf ears. Their beliefs were now as engraved in their minds as if they had been carved in stone, just as the commandments of Moses had been carved on the tablets he had brought down from Mount Sinai. And concerning those commandments of Moses, the Christians rejected them all, except for the ten from Sinai. Everything else that Moses had said in the way of rules and diet and dress and morality was not to be accepted by followers of Jesus. I wondered if that was because there was something wrong with those rules or because the rejection of them was just another way of ensuring that Christians would not become Jews. Paul had wanted to bring Jesus to the Gentiles in a way that they could accept. Then, later, he had hoped to make Judaism evolve from its existent form into a new, enlightened awareness, which meant seeing Jesus as a savior from sin with no more need for the Torah. Then, later still, because of the entrenchment of the old way in people's minds, he had wanted to create a new and separate religion that superseded Judaism and made it obsolete. And then, after that, he had wanted to discredit Judaism, to make it appear as something inchoate *before* Jesus and bad after Jesus. For if Judaism was seen as an acceptable alternative to Christianity, then many people might choose Judaism over Christianity as their preferred pathway to God. It had to be made to appear that Judaism was not an alternative that was acceptable to God, and in order to establish that, Judaism had to be made to appear vile and evil, even illegitimate from its very inception.

And, too, the survival and persistence of Judaism in the world could be interpreted as an indication of the illegitimacy of Christianity. And even if it was not interpreted that way, every Jew who persisted in following the Torah — even those who believed in Jesus — no, especially those who believed in Jesus — was saying to Paul, in essence, that even if his way was legitimate, then the way of the Torah was too. Such a compromise might have been acceptable to Paul — indeed, he was ready to make it in a limited way when we spoke together in the cavern — except that he did not want to run the risk of seeing people desert his doctrine for the Torah and for the doctrine of Peter. So he made it all or nothing; to wit, there is only one pathway to God. That was the Christian way, of course, and no other one would do. All others were false and deficient: Nazarene, Jewish and God-fearer ways and, of course, the way of the pagan. And anyone who followed one of those other ways was a heretic and a sinner, a person who was bad, whom Christians might pity or despise, depending on their dispositions. To try to influence someone who was a Christian to consider one of these alternative ways was the highest transgression (just as Jesus had made the highest transgression an attempt to influence someone away from the Torah). But to try to influence someone of another religion to accept Christianity was considered the highest virtue (just as Jesus had made the highest virtue the attempt to teach others to accept the Torah). In this way, Paul could stop the competitive diversion which he had seen occurring with the Galatians and others.

The new religion, from its inception, had to address itself to Judaism, because it grew out of Judaism and had as its raison d'etre the negation of some part of Judaism. But those parts of Judaism that it kept, because they were moral and good, it claimed exclusivity for, denying that those parts were part of Judaism and claiming that they came into existence only when Jesus arrived on the earth and when Christianity got started. Judaism was falsely painted by them as a religion of ritual and rote, as compared to Christianity, which was the religion of spirituality and morality and actively doing good. In short, they found it necessary to denigrate Judaism in order to justify the very existence of Christianity, for if Judaism was not faulty and Christianity not corrective of those faults, then why should Christianity replace Judaism? If Judaism was not painted as faulty, then it might appear as an attractive alternative to a moral-seeking person and give Christianity too much competition. And faulty might not be enough to claim, not strong enough to keep them away. So it had to be claimed that Judaism was more than that, that it actually was evil, the work of the Devil, so that "good" people would not turn to it when they decided how to seek God. But the highest pinnacle of this distortion was the claim that the Jews killed Jesus. The world had to be made to think that the Jews were not just innocent sheep pursuing their ignorant lives but rather active doers of evil who murdered the son of God. (One might take issue with their logic, I suppose, in hating the people who, purportedly, had made their salvation possible. For if no one had killed Jesus, then how could they have been saved? Were the people who gave them salvation to be hated for having given them that very thing?) But, of course, it was the Romans, just as it always had been, and the Christians could not seem to find in their minds the ability to recognize that nor in their hearts the courage to call the real murderers evil.

This is why I finally left all that Paul had taught me. Not because some of it — or even all of it concerning the meaning of Jesus' presence

— might not be right, but because to accept all of it meant I would have to hate Jews or, at the very least, to believe a lie about what they had done. So while I never knew for certain whether Jesus was divine and whether his death, if I accepted it as such, was the only expiation for my inborn sin, I stopped being a Christian. Even if those things about divinity and salvation were right, I could not endorse them to people, because those who did endorse them taught lies about the Jews. And in answer to the egregious claim that Pilate wanted to spare Jesus' life, I submit the crucifying record of that notorious tyrant who not only wanted to spare no one but delighted in crucifying the innocent. Do Christians think to gain favor with Romans by painting Pilate as a man reluctant to kill someone he thought innocent? Of all the procurators who had ever held office, the one — the only one — who had been deposed ignominiously was Pilate. The legate who deposed him had found him so intolerable that he had not been able to wait for his exigent recommendation to reach the emperor and for the emperor's order for the removal to arrive. He had discharged Pilate on his own. What more can I say to prove to you that Pilate was the worst of them all? Yet the Christians paint him as a man who was merciful but weak. They paint Romans as good and Jews as evil, and that is why I left them.

I have said that I was a friend of Paul's in spite of our disagreements. I say that I am still his friend and will remain so all my life. I have said that I knew him better than anyone else on earth, but *that*, even if it be true, does not say much about knowing a man, because no one can really know another person and see him as God does, stripped and bared to the soul. No one can hear the inner thoughts or see the clandestine acts; no one can fathom the motives beneath an altruistic deed.

If I were asked to give an account of the complex character of Paul, I would have to say that he lived, contemporaneously, with two different sides of himself. On the one hand, he proclaimed that love was the greatest virtue; on the other, he cursed and reviled and once condemned a pitiful sinner to death.

This last incident was in Corinth, but before I relate it to you, I would ask you to remember two men who greatly influenced Paul. The first was the Stoic, Seneca, who, for all his hatred of Jews, wrote a moral code inspired by Jews that Paul took much to heart. Seneca would not contemn wrongdoers, since each of us has sinned. The other, of course, was Jesus, who saved an adulteress from death when he told the people who surrounded her that whichever of them was devoid of sin should be the one to throw the first stone. But when Paul learned of a Christian in Corinth who had married his father's wife, he told his followers to "...deliver such a one to Satan, for the destruction of the flesh, that the spirit might be saved...". Like Seneca, he could stand on a hill and utter lofty phrases. But like Seneca, too, when he descended and stood among the people, finding doubt and dissension and challenge before him, he could be aroused to passionate hatred and forget Jesus' message of love. So where Jesus would have had us spare a sinner with no more than a mild admonition, Paul would have had us destroy the life so that the spirit could be free and cleansed.

That was my friend, Paul of Tarsus: determined, bitter, driven, inspired; accommodating when he had to be, adamant when it was safe to be; part pagan, part Jew, all Christian; a man of mysterious motives, bursting passions and conflicting convictions; self-contradictory, yet convincing; in disagreement with the very man he worshipped, yet filled with a heavenly light that deified the man and made even me, his reticent friend, believe some, though not all, of his words. I know I will meet him again when my time for departure comes and that all will be made known to me then, as it now has been made known to him. Until then, I plod my way as an aging Nazarene, teaching the things I feel I must teach and hoping for Jesus' return.

CHAPTER XLIV

It seems to me now that it was a good thing that I left Cyprus as young as I did; and it's good that God has given me this long life that He has. This is what has enabled me to see much and understand much about all the followers of Jesus — and about the Romans too — in a kind of vast tableaux of history. I saw Vespasian die and Titus take his place. I saw Titus set Bernice aside once he became the emperor, and I heard that he told her it was because he now had to show a propriety that he had not had to show before. When he walked out her door for the final time, it was said, they parted with these words: "Titus, remember all that I gave you, and be kind to my people for that;" and he, "I will, Bernice," and then he kissed her and left her and never looked back. His reign, it was said, was kinder and more benevolent because of her, and maybe that was the hidden reason behind what she had done, the reason for which she thought God would forgive her for her sin. I saw Salome, who had danced for the head of John the Baptizer, marry Herod of Chalcis' son and rule as queen over Chalcis and Chalcidene. I saw Bernice return to Agrippa and then to Titus after he became emperor and then back to Agrippa again when Titus decided he could never make her empress because she was a foreigner. I saw Josephus write a history of our people and send each section to Agrippa for approval. I saw Johanan ben Zakkai, who had left Jerusalem in a coffin, develop his Pharisee school and preserve our ancient religion. I saw Mount Vesuvius erupt and splatter its fire on the unprepared Romans below. I heard Jews say that that was God's punishment for what the Romans had done to the Jews, just as I heard Christians say that the destruction of Israel was God's punishment for the Jewish rejection of Jesus. Two years after that, I saw Titus die of a fever and Domitian take his place. I grew old during the fifteen years of Domitian's sadistic reign. I saw him call himself a god; I saw him require all his governors to address their letters to him by saying, "Our Lord and our God commands." I saw him expand the Jewish tax to include not only Jews and Jewish converts but also those who followed the Jewish way of life. I saw him execute his cousin, Flavius Clemens, and banish his cousin's wife, Flavia, because they both had converted to Judaism. I saw him execute the consul, Glabrio, and kill others or confiscate their property for the very same reason. Yes, even after the destruction of Jerusalem, when they said that Judaism and the Jewish people would cease to exist, there were Gentiles — even high-placed Roman ones — who saw in Judaism God's way for man and who converted to our religion. I saw Jacob and Zechariah, the grandsons of Jesus' brother, Jude, plucked from their small farm in Galilee and interviewed by Domitian. (As descendants of David and relatives of Jesus, they could still be the focus of a revolution.) And I saw Domitian release them as harmless because they posed no political threat. Then I saw Domitian killed by a servant. And I saw Nerva take his place and last for a year and then Trajan, who is now the emperor, ascend. I saw Agrippa die and Bernice grieve his loss and then grow old without him.

Once I visited Antioch. Ignatius was bishop there at the time. When he learned who I was, he welcomed me with open arms. I was something of a celebrity, I suppose, because I had known both Peter and Paul personally. He invited me to hear him preach.

"And next week," he said, "I hope *you* will preach to us. There are so many things we want to know."

I heard him speak to his congregation. The meeting was not held on the Sabbath but on the day after that. Ignatius called it "the Lord's Day" and exulted in its superiority over the Jewish day of worship. He preached salvation through grace and attributed this doctrine to both Peter and Paul, both of whom he acknowledged as authentic leaders and authorities when it came to Jesus. Immediately, I understood that he thought that Peter and Paul had agreed.

"There will be people who will come to you and tell you to follow Judaism," he said, "while accepting Jesus as your savior. That is an absurdity! It's impossible! You cannot follow both. And what does Judaism offer you anyway? Good-for-nothing leaven, that's what! Leaven that's grown stale and sour with all its outmoded ideas. It's good for nothing and good for no one, so don't get tempted by it.

"There are two coinages in circulation, so to speak, and you must shun the one that's false and embrace the one that's true. You must avoid the people who promote the false one as if they were a pack of wild animals. They'll snap at you unawares, and their bites will not heal easily. They're nothing but unclean wretches, and they're bound for the unquenchable fire. And if any of you so much as listens to them, you're doomed; you'll burn in that fire with them. Mark my words, I have your best interests at heart: if you so much as listen to what they have to say, you'll burn in the eternal fire.

"Hear me, my brothers, I speak the truth. They have nothing useful to give you. They teach nothing but fables, and they try to deny you the gift of grace, the forgiveness of sins, that God has so generously offered.

"Even their Eucharist is false. Yes, even their Eucharist. A watered-down version of what the true Eucharist should be. They call Jesus the servant of God instead of the son of God. Can you imagine that? They don't recognize the bread as Jesus' body or the wine as Jesus' blood. That's not part of their belief, they say. Well, I'll tell you this, and hear me well: beware of them. If you value your souls, beware of them. If you fear the Lord God, beware of them. I say again as I said before: if you listen to them, you'll be consigned to burn in the eternal fire. I love you too much to allow that to happen, so keep away from them if they come."

He spoke again of the eternal fire and the errant gospel they might hear. Then he softened and told them that they must show love to all who come their way.

I waited until the sermon was over. Ignatius wiped his brow. His sermon had been exhausting, and I had the feeling that he was outdoing himself for me.

"How did you like it?" he asked me when I came to him.

"You're an effective preacher," I said. "You remind me a little of Paul. He used to preach that way."

"Really?" I could see he was genuinely flattered.

"Yes, really. You have the same energy and conviction I saw in him. I can see why you're a bishop."

"You don't know how glad it makes me, Barnabas, that you even compare me to Paul."

I took a deep breath and swallowed. "There is one thing I think I should say, however. An error in your lecture."

"Oh, please tell me," he said. "I do want to know." There was sincerity in his voice.

"You seem to think that Peter and Paul were in agreement on everything."

"They weren't?"

"No, they weren't."

"Oh, I heard they had some minor squabbles, but that's to be expected from men who are so high-strung. It's the major things that count."

"This was major, Ignatius. It was not a minor disagreement."

"Well, what was it then? This is important to us. This is what we want to know."

441

"You warned against a counterfeit coinage, a false teaching that's circulating these days."

"Yes. It was a clever analogy, don't you think?"

"Very clever. You have a flair for analogy, I can see that."

"Oh, thank you. I'm so glad you think so."

"Well, it's about this false doctrine, this belief in following Judaism while you're accepting Jesus."

"Yes?"

"The thing you said was absurd because we could not have both."

"Oh, of course it's absurd. If the Torah is the path to salvation, then Jesus' death is meaningless. You know that, I'm sure."

"Yes, yes, I know it, of course. Paul told that to me many times."

"Well, there you have it. Truth from the mouth of an apostle."

"Yes, of course. But I wanted you to know that some people are following both — as absurd as that may sound."

"Well, I know that. That's what I was warning about. But those people are being ridiculous. How can anyone follow Jesus and follow the Torah at the same time?"

"By following a different Jesus," I said.

"A different Jesus? What do you mean?"

"A Jesus who is the Messiah, a Jesus who was resurrected, but not one whose death eradicates our sins."

"Well then, they follow a false Jesus, obviously."

"Peter didn't think so."

"What do you mean?"

"He didn't believe in the sacrificial death. Paul did, and that's why they fought."

"Well, what did Peter believe?"

"That we should follow the Torah."

"What are you saying?"

"I'm saying that the false gospel that you warn us about is Peter's. *His* Jesus is different from Paul's."

Ignatius gaped in stark disbelief. He raised his hands and covered his ears, emitted a scream so terrible that I felt a sudden chasm descend between us too deep for any light to reach.

"No!" he bellowed. "Away, away! I will not listen to you anymore."

He fled from me as from the fire he feared. He would not see me again. I thought of his perceived incongruity between the Torah and Jesus as savior. I wondered if my own secret goal to merge the two was, as Ignatius had called it, absurd. Beyond that, I marvelled at how effectively Paul had made Christians believe that Peter, who had differed with him so sharply about the Torah, had rejected it for sacrificial death. It showed me again how people believe whomever reaches them first. Just as Peter had come too late for some of the Christians in Galatia, so had I come to late for Ignatius. I left Antioch in defeat.

I lived through all these things by the grace of God, and Symeon lived through them too. Somehow, in the ruin of what had been our greatest pride, he and the Nazarenes lived on, he still their leader, the bishop of Jesus in Jerusalem. He still sat in the bishop's chair, the one that James had sat on, the chair that was always to be preserved in honor and remembrance of James. I didn't know how many more years I might have to live, and I was determined to see Symeon again, perhaps for the very last time, to report to him, as it were, as a loyal soldier reports to his general.

I returned to Jerusalem after all those years to meet with him again. He and the Nazarenes there were meeting in secret, just as Paul had met his Christians in secret in Rome. He looked much older, of course, and that made me realize how much older I must have looked. He was still teaching Peter's gospel and continuing to argue its authenticity over Paul's where necessary. When I told him that the savior belief was gaining ground among the Gentiles, he fretted as James had done and asked why Peter's gospel could not do more.

"It's because we lost the war," I said. "Israel has been destroyed, and there's no longer a nation over which Jesus can rule."

"There is!" he protested. "The nation of Israel is not dead. It will never die as long as there is a God in heaven."

I sighed. "The Gentiles don't believe that. They think it's all over for the Jews, that our land is gone and that we'll die out as a people."

"They think wrong!" Symeon said. "Israel will be restored, and Jesus will come back to claim it. Already, they're talking of starting a movement to organize an army and to make me king in Jesus' place until he comes back."

I was not as optimistic as he, but where God is concerned, one never knows. The most difficult task can be accomplished with His help.

But the reality of what was going on outside Israel had to be made clear to him, so I said, "Symeon, you know that I respect you. You're Jesus' cousin, and you're a pious Jew. And you know that I love Jesus and everyone related to him. But I have to tell you, as painful as it is for you to hear, that Paul's gospel is winning. *His* gospel is bringing Jesus to the world; ours is not. It wasn't winning before the war, but it is now. *Our* Jesus is dying; Paul's is spreading. And I'll tell you why: *his* Jesus isn't dependent on Israel; ours is. The Jesus of the Gentiles isn't dependent on any nation to give meaning to his life. They're taking Jesus away from us, Symeon. They're taking him away from his Jewish ties and putting him on a throne of their own. It's not a Jewish throne; it's not the throne of Israel — unless they change the meaning of what Israel is.

"The Eucharist prayer has been changed. They don't thank God for bread and wine and for having sent His servant, Jesus, the way we Nazarenes do. They say that the bread is Jesus' body and the wine is Jesus' blood and that that is what Jesus told his disciples at the last supper he had with them and also at the synagogue in Capernaum. And the fact that Jesus' words were conveyed to Paul in a vision and that none of the men who were there with Jesus at the supper heard him say those words and that none of the disciples who were with him at Capernaum have told us anything about it makes no difference to them. They write now that this is what Jesus said."

"Where do they get their information?" he asked.

"From Paul," I said.

"Well where did Paul get it? He wasn't there at the supper in Jerusalem or at Capernaum either. Who told him about it?"

"Nobody told him about it. I told you, he got it in a vision or in a revelation of some sort. They've made a prayer out of it. You eat the bread and say it's Jesus' body; you drink the wine and say it's Jesus' blood. If I tell them that the men who were there with Jesus that night at the supper and that the men who were there with him in the synagogue in Capernaum don't recite that kind of a prayer, if I say that Nazarenes recite other kinds of words over the bread and wine but that they don't say anything about eating a body or drinking blood, they say to me that, if that's true, then the Nazarenes must be wrong. They insist that Jesus said what they claim, but they can't tell me who was a witness to it."

"Do they know how offensive the drinking of blood is to our people, how against Moses' law it is?"

"I don't know if *they* know it, but I do know that Paul knew it. I used to think that it was the pagan influence having its effect on him. But later, I wondered if it was intentional — if he did it *because* he knew how offensive it was to us, because he knew how much of an issue James had made of it, because it was just another thing to make Christianity the opposite from Judaism, just the way he made covering the head or not covering it the opposite.

"And I'll tell you something else, Symeon. Do you remember what Jesus said about Roman tax money? 'Give to Caesar the things that are

Caesar's and to God the things that are God's.' Do you remember that?"

"Yes, he was telling us not to pay tribute to the Romans."

"Well, all that's been changed, Symeon. The Christians are interpreting that to mean that he *wanted* us to pay tribute to the emperor."

"But that's impossible! Jesus never could have sanctioned such a thing. To pay tribute to the Romans is disloyal to God. Jesus *told* us that, just as Judas of Galilee did before him. When Caiaphas and his crowd brought Jesus to Pilate, don't you remember what Caiaphas said? 'We found this man perverting our nation and *forbidding us to give tribute to Caesar* and saying that he himself is Christ, a king.' One of the reasons that Caiaphas took Jesus to Pilate was because Jesus told us *not* to pay tribute to the Romans. How can the Christians now say that he told us to do the opposite? And when Jesus was having dinner with Levi, the tax collector, and some of the other tax collectors in the city, he called them sinners. Don't you remember? How could he have called them that if he thought their tax collecting was right? And when he spoke to us from that hill in Galilee, didn't he tell us that even those as bad as tax collectors love their friends and that we should go beyond that and love our enemies? How can they say he approved of taxes?"

"They say it, Symeon, because they don't want to stir up the Romans against themselves. And for that reason, they say things about Peter too. Peter, our beloved Peter: they have him saying things that we know he never could have said. They're saying that he told us to have a fear of God and — in the same breath, mind you — to honor the emperor. To fear God and to honor the emperor all in the same breath."

"Peter?"

"Peter."

Symeon began to chuckle. "That's — almost funny. It's so impossible, it's funny."

I could understand his incredulity, but I could see no humor in it.

"No, it's not funny," I said. "People say and write whatever they want. It doesn't have to be true; it only has to be believed."

He spoke haltingly then, moving his finger for emphasis, seeming to measure everything that he knew about Peter, fact by fact, against the contention of this new belief. "Peter was arrested by King Agrippa because he was threatening Agrippa's position and his appointment by Emperor Caligula. Was Peter honoring the emperor when he did that? Peter was executed in Rome because he was thought to be threatening the emperor's authority. Was he honoring the emperor then? All of us who were worthy of the name, Nazarene — whether we were Zealots or Pharisees or lower priests or Essenes or whatever else we were — all of us were against the emperor and his Jewish puppet and just waiting for the day when Jesus would return to drive those tyrants out. Could any of us — especially Peter — have declared that we should honor the emperor? It's...". And here he could find no words to express his disbelief. He simply threw up his hands to heaven and emitted a futile grunt.

"They want to be sure that Jesus will belong to them and not to us," I said, "so they're telling the story that we rejected him, that we wanted him dead and that we threatened his followers afterwards. And they're saying that Israel's destruction is our punishment for having killed him."

"But that's lie!" he said. "Our people flocked to him by the thousands — by the tens of thousands. And they revered his brother. How can they say that?"

"I know it and you know it, but when I tell it to them, they think I'm lying. They say that our people wanted Jesus to be crucified and that the Romans wouldn't have done it if we hadn't forced them into it. They're even putting words into Peter's mouth and saying that he told our people that *they* delivered Jesus to Pilate."

"But Caiaphas delivered him!"

"But they're saying that Peter told our people that *they* had done it. And they're saying that when Ananus killed James, it pleased our people."

"But our people protested it!"

"I know. But they still say what they say. Do you remember when Paul was brought before King Agrippa because of the accusations against him by the chief priests and the Sadducees?"

"Yes, I remember it."

"Well, according to the way they tell it now, it was the Jews who accused him. Meaning *all* our people, not just the high priest and the Sadducees. And do you remember how Felix let him run around Caesarea free for two years and then bound him and imprisoned him just before he presented him to Festus so it wouldn't look as if he had been lax with prisoners?"

"And to counteract the rumor that he had been taking bribes from Paul."

"Yes, do you remember that? Well now, according to the Christians, he did it to please the Jews."

"Which Jews?"

"All the Jews. Don't you understand, Symeon? All Jews must be made to look bad."

"Felix chained Paul to please the Jews? Is that what they're saying?"

"Yes, Symeon, that's what they're saying."

"That means that the Jews would have been pleased to see him chained."

"That's right."

"And, presumably, that includes the Jews in the Sanhedrin who argued to save his life."

"Yes, it means them too."

"Why would people who had argued to save his life want to see him chained?"

I could only smile in answer to his question.

He went on as if arguing in court. "In Caesarea Felix whipped the Jews and imprisoned them. Then, when they wouldn't give up the land they had won in fighting against the Gentiles, he sent in his soldiers to kill them and then plunder them. Was he interested in pleasing the Jews then? Obviously not. But right after that, when he's about to leave his position as governor, we're supposed to believe that he suddenly wants to please the Jews of Caesarea? He's just finished killing them! Why would he want to please them? What a miraculous change of heart he must have had! And the Jews themselves, even those who fought to save Paul's life, decide that the thing that will please them most is to see Paul chained? Can anyone believe that? The truth of the matter, Barnabas, is that Felix hated us because we disapproved of his marriage to Drusilla. His only interest in Jews was to hurt us. Do people really believe that Felix wanted to *please* us?"

"They do believe it, Symeon. And they believe a lot more than that. Do you know that when they tell the story about Jesus, every time our people do something good to him, they call them "the people" or "the multitudes" or "the crowds", trying to hide the fact that they were Jews; but every time the Sadducees do something bad to him, they call *them* "the Jews"? They don't want anyone to know how our people loved him. And they're saying that our people were pleased when Agrippa killed James, Zebedee's son. And they're saying that our people wanted to kill Peter or have him killed and would have done it if they could."

"But the Pharisees saved Peter's life!"

"They saved Jesus' life too, but it doesn't suit their purposes to acknowledge it. And something else: they're saying that all the differences between the Nazarenes and the Christians were resolved years ago and that we came to an agreement with each other and that Peter

447

and Paul had agreed, after Peter had had some dream about no more dietary restrictions and Paul had straightened him out about other things, and that all the Jesus-followers in Jerusalem were — and are — Christians. And they want to belittle James, because he was opposed to Paul, so they say that when Jesus was alive, James opposed him and thought he was deranged."

"But they loved each other! I'm their cousin; I know. Jesus himself appointed James to be our leader!"

"And do you know what they say of me? Do you know what words they attribute to me? Here I am, still alive, and I have to listen to words that people attribute to me that I never said — that are actually the opposite of what I would say if I were asked. They have me calling the law of Moses a work conceived by a wily demon. I, a Levite, against the Torah, against the law of Moses! They have me quoting things out of the Bible that don't even exist in the Bible.

"I'm supposed to be telling them that when we Jews see Jesus when he returns, dressed in a red woolen robe — I don't know how I'm supposed to know what he'll be wearing when he returns — we're going to say, 'Isn't this the man whom we once crucified and mocked and pierced and spat upon?' They're saying that Jerusalem and our nation was destroyed because we crucified Jesus!"

"But the Romans did those things! Pontius Pilate and his soldiers, they spit on him and crucified him and did all those other things. Are they saying that a Jew pierced him with a spear? Are they saying that we Jews crucified him? We Jews never crucified anybody! Why are they saying these things?"

"I told you, Symeon: Our existence poses a competitive threat to their way of following Jesus."

"But to claim that we Jews did things that the *Romans* actually did? To outright lie about it?"

"More than that. They have to have a knowledgeable, authoritative person saying it. So they say that *I* teach this.

"And John, our dear old baptizing John, when he sees Jesus coming to him to be baptized, they have him saying, 'Behold the lamb of God, who takes away the sins of the world!'"

"Paul's savior idea! Jesus' death takes away our sins!"

"Exactly! The idea didn't even exist back then. None of us even heard of it until Paul came along. But they have John saying it as if the idea came from him and not from Paul. They want to make it seem as if all of us who preceded Paul in following Jesus had the same ideas as Paul. They can't have it thought that all of this came from Paul.

"When the Galileans marvel at Jesus' wisdom and deeds, they have the Galileans ask, 'Isn't this the carpenter, the son of Mary and the brother of James and Joses and Judas and Simon, and aren't his sisters here with us?' But they don't say, 'Isn't this the carpenter's *son?*' or 'Isn't this the carpenter, the son of Mary *and Joseph?*' because they don't want to make it appear that the Galileans recognized Joseph as Jesus' father. They want to make it seem that the Galileans never identified Joseph as his father, which implies that they recognized *God* as his father."

"God was his spiritual father," Symeon said. "Joseph was his bodily one."

"Not according the virgin birth idea that's going around now. They're saying that Mary was still a virgin when she gave birth to Jesus and that God is the one who impregnated her."

"I know of this story," Symeon said, "but it's only come into existence recently. It didn't exist back then."

"But they don't want people to know that. They want people to think that everyone who was there in Galilee was aware that Mary was a virgin when she gave birth to Jesus. So by having the Galileans avoid mentioning Joseph as Jesus' father at the same time that they're mentioning the rest of Jesus' family, it makes it seem that the Galileans accepted the virgin birth long before Paul or the Christians ever came along and started it. And the ironic part of it is that when they tell the story about Jesus at Capernaum, they have the Jewish people *there* saying, 'Isn't this Jesus, the son of Joseph, whose father and mother we know?' So here, in contrast to one part of the Jewish people in Galilee, they have our people in Capernaum recognizing *Joseph* as his father."

"But *Jesus* recognized Joseph as his father. I'm his cousin. I know."

"They won't allow us to have that, Symeon. And it's not enough to have *other* people say that Jesus was fathered by God. They have to have Jesus saying it too."

"That Joseph wasn't his father?"

"He doesn't actually say it, but he implies it. They have Jesus arguing with some Pharisees. He asks them whose son the Messiah is. They say David's. Then Jesus says that if that is so, why does King David say in one of his Psalms, 'The Lord said to my lord'? The second lord is the Messiah, says Jesus, and since a Jew usually never calls anyone but God his lord, that means that the Messiah is divine."

"I see," Symeon said. "I see what's happening. We live isolated here, and news doesn't come to us so easily. Everything seems to be changing out there, changing from everything I've always known and believed."

I felt as if I was hurting him, as if I was being cruel by telling him the truth. Yet I couldn't stop. I had to finish pouring all this out of me, like a burden I'd been carrying around for years and finally had to unload. So I went on and said to him, "Symeon, they have Jesus denying the law. You should be aware of what they say he said about food: that it's all right to eat anything; food restrictions can be forgotten. And about his predictions: 'The Temple will be destroyed!' But we only hear about that prediction now, after the destruction has taken place. And about our people: 'Your father is the Devil... You are not of God'. He tells us that we're the sons of those who murdered the prophets, although he doesn't say which prophets our fathers murdered. He calls us serpents and a brood of vipers and asks us how we can possibly expect to escape being sentenced to hell. He tells us that we're going to crucify righteous people in the future. We, who've been the victims of crucifixion and who, as you've said, never crucified anybody, are being told by Jesus that we'll be crucifying good people that he's going to be sending us in the future!"

Symeon said to me in a tone of disbelief, "Jesus, who loved all men, called us those vile names? Jesus, who loved us as we loved him, made those false accusations against us?"

"Of course he didn't, Symeon. But these are the words they're claiming he said!"

"And if all of us who were with Jesus say that these are lies, will these people not believe us? Are eyewitnesses less to them than storytellers?" he asked.

"If all the eyewitnesses die out, then how do we tell them the truth?" I said.

"We can write it!" he exclaimed. "If we're not alive to say it, then we can have our letters and our books live after us."

"And if they take the books and letters and change them after we're dead, then what do we do? We can't come back from our graves to tell the world what they've done."

"Can't the history itself show what they've done?"

"Maybe," I said. "If anyone bothers to read history. And then, what *is* history, Symeon? What is history other than what people *say* it is? They have everybody reciting speeches they never said. Is that history? When Gamaliel speaks on Peter's behalf to the Sanhedrin, they have him mentioning the Theudas movement as something in the past. Meanwhile, the Theudas movement didn't even occur until years after Gamaliel made that speech. So what's history? What they say Gamaliel said or what actually happened?

450

"It's because of Paul. Do you understand, Symeon? It's because of Paul. My old friend! My determined, resentful, inspired and beloved old friend. He didn't want Peter's gospel to take his Christians away from him, so he discredited the Torah and then the Jews. And now his followers say whatever they want to say to make all Jews look evil. Everything has to be made to conform with Paul's conception of Jesus. Do you understand? Jesus and Peter and even I have to be made to say things that show that Paul was right and that James was wrong. That's what it's all about, Symeon! That's what it's all about! They use me and Jesus the way they used Peter. They have us saying things we never said. And when I cry out against it, it's as if I'm crying in the wilderness. I'm laughed at; I'm ignored; I'm resented.

"And...," and here I hesitated, because I knew that this last thing I had to tell him was going to be so devastating, so frightening, that even *saying* it would be an insult to God, "...they say...it's something that even Paul would not have gone so far as to say...they say...they say that Jesus *is* God. Not just the son of God, Symeon, but God."

He looked at me in absolute astonishment. In an intense whisper, he said, "What?" And then nothing more, so overwhelmed was he by what I had said.

I thought to myself, Your child, Paul, it has a life of its own now. It has surpassed you; it's gone beyond you. It breathes and lives and thinks by itself. It grows with a life of its own.

Tears suddenly came to my eyes, so overcome was I with emotion. I covered my face with my hands and blurted out, "Paul! Oh, Paul, I admired you so much! I could have followed you to the ends of the earth. Why did you do this?"

I started sobbing uncontrollably, and I remember feeling a little ashamed of myself because of it. But I couldn't help it. Too much had been pent up within me, more than I had realized, and it came out of me now in this flood, this release, of my outrage and despair, in this deluge of love and frustration.

Symeon said nothing. He sat in contemplative silence, absorbing all that I had told him and allowed me the dignity of recovering my composure without making any comment. It could not have been easy for him. He was still our leader, and the final responsibility for a common policy rested on his shoulders.

"I have a copy of James' last letter," he said. "There's a part in it I want you to hear."

He reached for a scroll on the shelf behind him. He placed it on the table and unrolled it with meticulous care. Then he scanned the pages.

"Here it is," he said. "Listen, Barnabas. Listen to what my cousin wrote shortly before he died." I wiped the tears from my eyes and listened to his raspy voice and watched his finger move beneath the words as he read.

"For every kind of beast and bird, of reptile and sea creature, can be tamed and has been tamed by humankind, but no human can tame the tongue — a restless evil, full of deadly poison. With it we bless the Lord and Father and with it we curse men who are made in the likeness of God. From the same mouth come blessing and cursing. My brethren, this ought not to be so."

"You think he wrote that because of Paul?" I asked.

"Yes. Yes, I do," he answered. "Some time after that last meeting in Jerusalem, he learned what Paul was saying in his letters."

I repeated the words: "'From the same mouth come blessing and cursing.' But you must know that Paul was against cursing. When he wrote to the Romans, he told them not to curse those who persecuted them but to bless them instead."

"Yes, I know that," Symeon said. "But I also know that when he was miffed over James' emissaries telling the Galatians that *his* gospel was wrong and that Peter's was right, he told the Galatians that he wished those emissaries would mutilate themselves. That doesn't sound like a blessing to me, Barnabas. And I know that he told the unbelieving Corinthians, 'Your blood be on your head.' Wasn't that a curse, Barnabas? And I know that he turned Hymaneus and Alexander over to Satan because they didn't agree with him. Was that a blessing or a curse? And that he told the Corinthians to turn a sinner over to Satan for the destruction of the man's flesh. What was that, Barnabas, a curse or a blessing? 'If any man doesn't love the Lord,' he said, 'let him be accursed.' To the Galatians, he said, 'If we or an angel from heaven preach a different gospel to you than the one we originally preached, let him be accursed.' He told the Thessalonians that when Jesus comes from heaven, his angels in flaming fire, are going to have vengeance on those who rejected his gospel and that they will destroy those unbelievers eternally. Alexander, the coppersmith did something against him, so God, who is always on Paul's side, is going to retaliate against the man. The people in the circumcision party, he says — and, of course, that means us Nazarenes — have to be silenced. What are all those things, Barnabas? Curses or blessings?"

I couldn't bring myself to answer him. I disagreed with Paul on some things, I agreed with him on others, but I always had this love for him that no amount of imperfection could dislodge. It hurt me to hear

452

the contrasting truth about my friend, his undeniable hatred pitted against his messages of tolerance and love. James' words kept coming back to me: "From the same mouth come blessing and cursing."

Symeon went on: "I must do something about this."

"We're old men, Symeon," I said to him. "Who knows how many more years we have to live. Maybe we're past the point of being able to do anything about it. Stories take on a life of their own, and once people believe them..."

"I may be old, but I'm not dead," he interjected. "I won't sit back and let this happen."

I patted his shoulder with a kind of despondent encouragement. Old as he was, he had the fighting spirit of a Jew within him, and nothing I would say was going to take that away from him. So I left him and wished him well and told him I would keep on trying to tell the things I knew.

I made one more trip before I left Judaea, because I didn't know if I would ever return. I traveled to the Essene community near the Dead Sea to look for the venerable Abram. There were not many people there. Only some ghostlike stragglers who told me that their settlement had been attacked by the Romans and that Abram was gone. He and many of the others had gone to Masada to fight. They had sacrificed their lives after putting up a good fight, killing themselves along with the Zealots there rather than allowing themselves to be crucified or sold as slaves. Only these few devout remnants of the Essene community remained here. But Abram, they said, had had the scribes commit their story to writing. He had had them record the history of our time onto scrolls which they put into jars. And the jars were hidden in the caves thereabout for some future generation to read. The scrolls told the story of James, Jesus' brother, whom they called The Teacher of Righteousness; and they told the story of his murderer, Ananus, whom they called The Wicked Priest; and they told of how our people killed Ananus and abused his dead body afterwards; and they told of a man they called The Spewer of Lies, who had set up his own false religious communities based on deceit. I winced when they told me this last thing. I winced and felt saddened for my friend. I felt like saying, "Can you not conceive that he said what he said sincerely? Can you not conceive that these visions he had — visions that you yourselves taught him how to have — made him feel that what he did was right?" But I did not ask them that because they went on with more about their scrolls. They spoke of the Torah, saying that it was God's eternal law, saying that it was meant for all men to follow and that Jews would preserve it for the world. Just as Paul had said that Jesus' death was God's gift to the world, so did these men say that the Torah was that very same thing.

Then, before I left Judaea, in the tenth year of Trajan's rule, I learned how serious Symeon was about doing something. Word came to me that he had intensified his efforts to organize a movement for the restoration of the nation, and that the Romans, under Trajan's governor, Atticus, had arrested him and, old as he was, had crucified him for the crime of trying to set himself up as a king. He was one-hundred and two years old and still filled with energy and spirit. Yet, in spite of his age, the Romans knew that as a living relative of the Messiah, he had the power to inspire people and start a new revolt. So they killed him, thinking that that would end the threat that he posed and make the Jews compliant again. The Christians can talk about Jesus as being completely pacific and devoid of any political aspirations or interests, but the Romans never saw it that way and neither did Symeon or the Nazarenes. To the Romans, Symeon was a political threat, just as Jesus had been, and that is why they killed him. Justus, another relative of Jesus replaced him, and I am sure there will be someone else after him. But I wonder if, in the torrent of things the way they are going, a day will come when a Christian and not a Nazarene will sit as a bishop in Jerusalem.

In that same year in which they killed Symeon, they killed Ignatius too. Like Symeon, he was considered a political threat, an enemy of Rome. They transferred him from Antioch to Rome to be devoured by wild beasts. To the Romans, all Jesus-followers were the same. Our differences about the Torah and sacrificial death were of no concern to them. All of us were enemies of Rome. All of us had to be destroyed.

I made my way to Cyprus. My uncle, God bless him, was gone now. In his great and selfless love for me, he had left me his property. So, once again, I became what I had been before I started on this quest: an owner of land in Cyprus.

When I first came back after all those years, I learned that Sharon was living there too. She was living in the house that her parents had left her after they had died. Her unmarried son was with her, I was told, but John (Mark) was not there with them. I decided to visit her.

She was older, of course, with graying hair but with eyes that were as soulful as ever. Her son was a man full of years, with graying hair himself, but still tall and strong and handsome.

"Your son is a fine-looking man," I said to her.

"He is not my son," she answered. "He is Marcus, Peter's and Rachel's son. I have no children of my own."

"Then why is he with *you* instead of Rachel?"

"You didn't know?" she asked. "Rachel died shortly after you left. She asked me to take care of him."

"And John (Mark), why is he not here with you?"

"We're divorced," she said. "We're no longer together."

"Divorced?" I blurted. "Why? What happened between you?"

"He changed, Joses, and I didn't change with him. I asked him for a divorce."

"But why? What did he do?"

"Let's walk," she said.

We went outside and skirted the puddles left by a recent rain, then onto a field where the wet grass glistened like emeralds beneath our feet.

"We both believed in Jesus, we both believed he'd return," she said. "I kept our house in accordance with the law, just as Jesus had told us to do. But John spent time with Paul — oh, how they argued! — and then he spent time with Christians. And then one day he said to me that we had to forsake the Torah, that if we tried to follow it, we wouldn't be forgiven for our sins, that God's gift of forgiveness through Jesus' death wouldn't be ours to have."

"What irony!" I said to her. "What irony! John was against Paul because of that. What made him change his mind?"

She didn't answer my question at first but told me about herself. "I couldn't forsake the Torah, Joses. I know in my heart that it's right."

"Is that why you left him?"

"No, not because of that. He was willing to tolerate my adherence to the Torah if I could tolerate his rejection of it. After all, we still had Jesus in common."

"Do you remember when I met with Paul in Rome, after Peter was killed?"

"Yes, I remember it. I was trying to console Rachel at the time."

"Well, Paul told me back then that it was all right for Christians to follow the Torah if they'd learned it from their parents."

"But John said that if the Torah still had meaning, then Jesus' death meant nothing."

"Yes, Paul said that too. He wasn't always consistent. Yet you say that's not why you left him."

"No, it was because of something else: he said that we Jews killed Jesus."

"John (Mark) said that?" I asked.

"Yes," she said. "He believed it."

"He was too young when Jesus was killed to know what was going on," I said. "But his mother must have told him what happened. And he saw how our people joined the Nazarenes. How could he have come to believe that?"

"Through Paul, through the Christians. I suppose if you say something long enough, some people will believe it. He admitted the Romans did it, but he said our people forced them into it unwillingly. I couldn't live with that, Joses. I couldn't go on with him after that."

We were climbing a grassy hill now, and we felt a breeze from the sea. The lambent sun showed every crack in her scrubbed, unpainted face, and I thought she was beautiful, as beautiful as she had been that day when I told her I loved her but could not marry her. Strange to report, I suddenly realized that this was the same hill we had climbed back then.

"Do you remember what I asked you when we climbed this hill before?" she asked.

"Yes, Sharon, I remember it. I remember it very well."

"And what you answered me?" she asked.

"That too," I said. "I remember that too."

She did not look at me, but she asked me that same question that she had asked so many years before, as if its echo had reverberated undiminshed through the hills and was returning to the place of its origin: "Do you love me, Joses?"

"Yes, Sharon, I love you," I said.

"Do you want to marry me?"

"Yes, Sharon, I want to marry you."

And she, in that halcyon way of hers, said, "Then, Joses, I shall be yours."

And so, at last, by the grace of God, through the goodness with which He imbues our lives when we wait and serve and endure, I married the woman I loved. I consider it a blessing beyond hope that He did this, that He allows me to live my remaining years with her now — this woman, this Sharon, this beacon of light. I love her and I love God for having given her to me. There is nothing more I can wish for than this — except, perhaps, that I be believed and that all that I say and contend and write be seen as the truth of what transpired.

I have spoken of irony in regard to John (Mark). But it is, perhaps, the final irony that the original symbol of the Christians in Rome — by that I mean the fish, based on Jesus having told Peter, the fisherman, that he would make him a fisher of men — that that original symbol is now being replaced by the symbol of the Zealots — the cross. Just as the Zealots never wanted their followers to forget how Judas of Galilee died, so do Christians never want to forget how Jesus, their savior, died.

Paul had once told me that he considered himself the greatest sinner of them all. He may have been thinking of his weakness for Rabath when he said that, or maybe it was because he had hunted Nazarenes. Or maybe because, in his search for the truth about himself, he had thought about what he had said of the Jews.

I have said many things about Paul and his gospel, but even at this hoary stage of life, when my bones ache and my teeth are loose and my skin is as wrinkled as the skin of a prune, I must confess what I dared not tell Symeon when we were together, what I dare not tell Sharon or my disciples, because I can hardly understand it myself: that I never knew more joy in my heart than when I was a Christian. But the kind of Christian I was, you see, was not the kind I see now. I believed in the savior, I believed in the Torah, but I could not abide the false belief that the Jews killed Jesus. If the truth be known, I am a man with one foot in each camp. Perhaps it is wrong to stuff people into one recognized category or another. It doesn't allow them to have any thoughts of their own that are different from the thoughts of the group. If someone thinks the way I think, then where does he belong? I am an incomplete Christian and an aberrant kind of Jew — no, not just an aberrant kind of Jew, an aberrant kind of Nazarene — but I'm too old to start a new religion that combines the best of them both. Perhaps someday, a younger man with many more years to give, will think the way I think and find a way to do it. And who knows, perhaps it will be Jesus. It would be worth his time.

*

CHAPTER NOTES

CHAPTER I

STEPHEN ATTACKS ROMANS: Fictional. Stephen, however, was known to be among the more militant of the Nazarenes.

GAMALIEL REJECTS SAUL: See NOTE for CHAPTER VII entitled, PAUL'S CIRCUMCISION AND FULL CONVERSION TO JUDAISM.

SADDUCEES: Matthew 3:7, 16:1, 16:11, 16:12, 22:23, 22:34; Mark 12:18; Luke 20:27; Acts 4:1, 5:17, 23:6-8; Josephus, Antiquities 13.5.9, 13.10.6, 18.1.4; Josephus, Jewish War 2.8.14; Brandon, Jesus and Zealots pp. 31, 34, 37, 38, 40, 48, 51, 52, 54, 56; Klausner, From Jesus to Paul pp. 55, 402, 443, 512; Wilson, Our Father Abraham pp. 40, 60, 64, 67, 77; Maccoby, Mythmaker pp. 8, 14, 22, 25, 26, 34-35, 51, 58, 165, 218; Schonfield, Passover Plot pp. 19-20.

GOD-FEARER LAWS: Cornfeld, Daniel to Paul p. 167. Some authors cite the seven laws of Noah (Noahide laws) as the moral code adopted by the God-fearers: no idolatry; no blasphemy; no fornication; no murder; no robbery; no eating of flesh with blood in it; and the charge to set up courts of justice. These seven laws, were first formally listed in the Fourth Century Talmud. Other, fragmented lists were seen before that time. For that reason, I have not included the full list in this First Century story. What I have attributed to God-fearers at this stage of history are the minimum number of those laws, as cited by James, Jesus' brother, in Acts 15:20: no idolatry; no fornication (unchastity); no eating of strangled animals; no shedding of blood through murder. (The interpretation of James' adjuration to "abstain from blood" as meaning the avoidance of murder, rather than the seemingly more obvious interpretation that it is a superfluous repetition of the rule against eating blood or strangled animals, is found in Maccoby, The Mythmaker p. 141, and is based on the fact that in Genesis 9, immediately after God speaks to Noah about not eating animals with the blood still in them, He speaks of not shedding the blood of one's fellow man.)

LIVELIHOODS OF SAGES: Maccoby, Mythmaker p. 24.

SAGES: Maccoby, Mythmaker p.21, points out that the term "sage" rather than the term "rabbi" was used for the Pharisee religious leaders in Jesus' time.

SANHEDRIN: Cornfeld, Daniel to Paul p. 143; Maccoby, Mythmaker pp. 10, 51, 74, 122, 164.

PHARISEES LENIENT IN PUNISHMENTS: Josephus, Antiquities 13.10.6.

PHARISEE MAJORITY IN SANHEDRIN: Maccoby, Mythmaker p. 10.

CHAPTER II

PHILO'S DESCRIPTION OF MESSIAH: Klausner, From Jesus to Paul p.179 (from De Praemiis et Poenis 95-7).

MESSIAH PROPHECIES: Isaiah 11; Daniel 7; Micah 5.

PHILO'S BIRTH: 20-15 B.C. or B.C.E.

PHILO'S DEATH: 45-50 A.D. or C.E.

DEATH OF EZEKIAS: Josephus, Antiquities 14.9.2.

SHILOH PROPHECY: Genesis 49:10; Brandon, Jesus and Zealots p. 36.

JUDAS OF GALILEE: Josephus, Antiquities 17.10.5; Josephus, Jewish War 2.4.1; Brandon, Jesus and Zealots pp. 101, 132, 167, 306, 347, 355, 356, 358; Klausner, From Jesus to Paul pp. 225, 226, 285; Maccoby, Mythmaker pp. 37, 46, 48, 52, 53, 178; Schonfield, Passover Plot p. 45.

The census to which Judas of Galilee objected had been started a few years earlier by Quirinius, the legate of Syria, under a decree from the emperor, Augustus. Many Jews had had to leave their cities of residence and travel to the cities of their origin to be counted. Joseph had had to take his pregnant wife, Mary, from Nazareth in Galilee to Bethlehem in Judaea in order to do this. With such a large migration of people, it was not surprising that Joseph had found no rooms available at the inn where he stopped and that he had had to take Mary to an adjacent stable where she could rest and give birth to Jesus (Luke 2:1-7).

ARETUS HELPS VARUS: Josephus, Antiquities 17.10.9.

DEFEAT OF JUDAS OF GALILEE: Josephus, Antiquities 17.10.4-5; Josephus, Jewish War 2.4.1,2; Brandon, Jesus and Zealots pp. 30, 33, 40, 48, 52-54, 56, 101, 355; Schonfield, Passover Plot p. 30.

THE ZEALOTS: Brandon, Jesus and Zealots pp. 10, 16, 30-34, 36-38,42-43, 45-46, 49, 54-55, 57, 61, 63-64, 67, 74, 78, 87, 114, 125-126, 129, 132, 141, 344, 355, 356; Klausner, From Jesus to Paul pp. 55, 438; Maccoby, Mythmaker pp. 48, 53, 158; Schonfield, Passover Plot p. 189; Wilson, Our Father Abraham pp. 40, 58, 59, 75-77, 82.

SADDUCEES: See NOTE for CHAPTER I entitled, SADDUCEES. I agree with Maccoby (Mythmaker) that the New Testament writers, either inadvertently or out of ignorance or even intentionally attributed characteristics and acts to the Pharisees that only could have come from the Sadducees. Pharisaic beliefs were too consistent with Jesus' teachings, and Pharisees too often demonstrated sympathy towards Jesus and the Nazarenes, to have warranted describing them as the inflexible adherents to the letter of the law that the Sadducees were and to have warranted their disapproval by Jesus. Pharisees tried to save Jesus from Herod Antipas (Luke 13:31); Pharisees saved Peter's life (Acts 5:33-39); Pharisees joined the Nazarene movement (Acts 15:5); Pharisees fought to save Paul (Acts 23:9). Jesus' purported deprecation of Pharisees could only have been the deprecation of Sadducees, with the possible exception of those Pharisees from the School of Shammai, who were more conservative than the School of Hillel, while still not being as inflexibly strict as the Sadducees. In Mark 3:6, we read in regard to Jesus, "The Pharisees went out, and immediately held counsel with the Herodians against him, how to destroy him." This is too inconsistent with the favorable attitude of the Pharisees towards the Jesus-movement found elsewhere in the New Testament. It makes more sense if they were Sadducees, the traditional allies of the Herodians. There was no love lost between Pharisees and Herodians.

Where Maccoby (Mythmaker) feels that this error was intentional — certainly a possibility — I would also consider that it may have been unintentional, an error written in ignorance by persons far removed in time and place from the seat of the events. In any case, this antagonistic relationship between the Pharisees on the one hand and Jesus and the Nazarenes on the other cannot be historically accurate. Jesus' statements and acts could only have pleased the Pharisees and disturbed the Sadducees.

In regard to the issue of Sabbath healing, there is no direct evidence for Sadducee objection to Sabbath healing, but their rigidity in following other biblical rules makes a presumption of such an objection plausible. There is, however, evidence that the Essenes opposed it (James Tabor, Personal Communication 1992). Maccoby (Mythmaker p. 33) proposes such an objection by the Sadducees. For further elucidation on this point, see Jesus the Pharisee by Rabbi Harvey Falk (New York, Paulist Press 1985).

ESSENES: Josephus, Antiquities 13.5.9, 18.1.5; Josephus, Jewish War 2.8.2-14; Brandon, Jesus and Zealots pp. 31, 34, 37, 39, 45-46, 61, 327; Klausner, From Jesus to Paul pp. 55, 114, 278, 509, 512; Wilson, Our Father Abraham pp. 40, 64, 67, 77; Maccoby, Mythmaker pp. 27, 187; Schonfield, Passover Plot pp. 200-204.

PHARISEE BELIEF AND SADDUCEE DISBELIEF IN RESURRECTION: Acts 23:8; 18:8; Klausner, From Jesus to Paul pp. 28, 264, 282, 376, 402; Maccoby, Mythmaker pp. 35, 165.

RESURRECTIONS BY JESUS: Luke 7:11-15, 8:41-56; John 11:1-44; Matthew 9:18-26; Mark 5:22-43.

SANHEDRIN: Cornfeld, Daniel to Paul pp. 269-270; Maccoby, Mythmaker pp. 10, 51, 74, 122, 164.

PHARISEE MAJORITY IN SANHEDRIN: Maccoby, Mythmaker p. 10.

While there is no written evidence that the Sanhedrin ever was convened with less than its full membership, it does not seem unreasonable that sickness or travel sometimes kept some members away. Also, in an age when civil authorities were not as accountable for minor transgressions of the law as they are today, it is conceivable that the high priest's messengers did not summon all the Pharisees to a hastily called meeting, the pretext being that they could not find everyone on such short notice. Such an explanation seems plausible for what would otherwise be a markedly inconsistent Sanhedrin that condemns Jesus, saves Peter, saves Paul and then condemns Jesus' brother, James. A learned body of men does not condemn one man and exonerate another for the very same offense.

We must also ask where Gamaliel was if the full Sanhedrin was convened in the case of Jesus. The most respected member of the Sanhedrin, who saved Peter's life because Jesus' imminent return might be true, would hardly be likely to desire the death of a man he believed might be the Messiah. Furthermore, if Gamaliel *was* present at Jesus' trial, why do the New Testament writers not mention it, as they mention, for example, his presence at Peter's trial?

One must also ask where the Jesus-supporting Joseph of Arimathea was if the full Sanhedrin was assembled.

Schonfield (Passover Plot p. 143) expresses the opinion that not all the Sanhedrin members may have been called to Jesus' interrogation. Maccoby (Mythmaker p. 36) makes the point that the Sanhedrin was not even present at Jesus' interrogation. Brandon (Jesus and Zealots pp. 116, 117[1]) makes the point that the procurator's permission was necessary for convoking the Sanhedrin. Apparently, no such permission was sought by Caiaphas prior to his having brought Jesus to Pilate.

Cornfeld, citing S. Zeitlin, subscribes to the view that "...the court before which Jesus was arraigned was the inner circle of the High Priest." Cornfeld states further, "It also explains the silence of the Pharisees...It seems reasonable to assume that whatever happened between the late evening and the following mid-day was not known to them and they had no part in the arrest, trial or condemnation of Jesus." Cornfeld also cites Paul Winter's analysis of the trial of Jesus, which states that "...many of the contradictory elements in the story may be regarded as later insertions..." (Cornfeld, Daniel to Paul p. 270).

ROMANS APPOINT HIGH PRIESTS: Finegan, Light From the Ancient Past p. 262(43); Brandon, Jesus and Zealots pp. 67-68.

JEWISH KINGS APPOINT HIGH PRIESTS: Brandon, Jesus and Zealots p. 113; Finegan, Light From the Ancient Past p. 262(43). Procurator-appointed high priesthoods ended with Vitellius appointing Theophilus, son of Annas, in 37 A.D. or C.E. After that, Agrippa I appointed Simon Kantheras to the post.

JEWISH METHOD OF EXECUTION (STONING): John 8:1-11; Acts 7:6-15; Josephus, Antiquities 20.9.1; Schonfield, Passover Plot p. 141.

PHARISEE ORIGIN: Josephus, Antiquities 17.2.4; Maccoby, Mythmaker p. 25.

LOWER PRIESTS PHARISEES (SOME ZEALOTS): Brandon, Jesus and Zealots pp. 114, 118, 121, 125, 141, 157, 189; Maccoby, Mythmaker p. 26.

JESUS AND ZEALOTS IN SYMPATHY: Josephus, Antiquities 18.1.6; Brandon, Jesus and Zealots p. 355. See NOTE about APOSTLE SIMON THE ZEALOT in this chapter.

ZEALOTS WERE PHARISAIC: Josephus, Antiquities 18.1.1, 18.1.6; Brandon, Jesus and Zealots pp. 37-38; Maccoby, Mythmaker p. 48. We should remember that Judas of Galilee, the man from whom the Zealot movement came, joined with Zaddok the Pharisee in his march on the Romans in Jerusalem.

PHARISEE SUPPORT FOR JESUS AND HIS VIEWS: Pharisees protect Jesus from Herod Antipas (Luke 13:31); Pharisees protect Peter (Acts 5:33-39); Pharisees join Nazarenes (Acts 5:15); Pharisees fight for Paul (Acts 23:9). Klausner, From Jesus to Paul p. 4; Brandon, Jesus and Zealots pp. 157, 190(2); Brandon, Fall of Jerusalem p. 28(3); Wilson, Our Father Abraham pp. 48, 297; Maccoby, Mythmaker pp. 30, 32-37, 40-44, 46, 48-49, 51, 165-166, 218. It is also highly unlikely that Pharisees (unlike Sadducees) would have desired a death penalty for anyone (except, perhaps, for the most extreme violations of religious law) as seen in Josephus' Antiquities of the Jews 13.10.6, in which Josephus reports that Pharisees were not apt to be severe in punishments.

ZACHARIAH PROPHECY: Zachariah 9:9.

JESUS' TEMPLE TAKEOVER: Mark 11:11-18.

NO MERCHANTS IN TEMPLE ON MESSIAH DAY: Zachariah 14:21.

LOWER PRIESTS BECOME NAZARENES: Acts 6:7; Brandon, Jesus and Zealots pp. 118, 121, 125, 157; Maccoby, Mythmaker p. 26.

LOWER PRIESTS BECOME ZEALOTS: Brandon, Jesus and Zealots pp. 114, 118, 121, 189.

SADDUCEES ATTRACT WEALTHY; PHARISEES ATTRACT MASSES: Josephus, Antiquities 13.10.6; Maccoby, Mythmaker p. 26.

NAZARENES ALIGNED WITH ZEALOTS: Brandon, Jesus and Zealots p. 125.

APOSTLE SIMON THE ZEALOT: Acts 1:13; Matthew 10:4; Mark 3:18; Luke 6:15; Brandon, Jesus and Zealots pp. 10, 16, 42-43, 55, 78, 200, 201, 201(4), 205, 243-245.

PHARISEE BELIEFS: Josephus, Antiquities 13.5.9, 13.10.6, 17.2.4, 18.1.3; Josephus, Jewish War 2.18.4; Schonfield, Passover Plot p. 20; Maccoby, Mythmaker pp. 19-28.

LIVELIHOODS OF SAGES: Maccoby, Mythmaker p. 24.

HIGH PRIESTS NOT LEARNED: Maccoby, Mythmaker pp 23-24, 26.

HIGH PRIESTS PRO-ROMAN: Josephus, Antiquities 20.1.1, 5.11.5; Josephus, Apion 2:23; Brandon, Jesus and Zealots p.114.

CHIEF PRIESTHOOD HEREDITARY: Josephus, Antiquities 5.11.5, 20.10.1; Josephus, Apion 2:23; Brandon, Jesus and Zealots pp. 114, 140(4); Maccoby, Mythmaker p. 23.

NAOMI: Fictional name in this story for Caiaphas' wife.

RABATH: Fictional name in this story for Caiaphas' daughter. That Caiaphas had a daughter is related by the Ebionites, according to Epiphanius, Ascension of James, Haer. 30.16.

EFFIGIES INTO JERUSALEM: Josephus, Antiquities 18.3.1; Brandon, Jesus and Zealots pp. 72-73.

GILDED SHIELDS INTO JERUSALEM: Brandon, Jesus and Zealots pp. 72-73.

PILATE'S REIGN: 26-36 A.D. or C.E. Finegan, Light From the Ancient Past p. 257; Brandon, Jesus and Zealots p. 74.

AQUEDUCT: Josephus, Antiquities 18.3.2; Josephus, Jewish War 2.9.4; Brandon, Jesus and Zealots pp. 75-76; Schonfield, Passover Plot p. 100.

PILATE AND JESUS: Mark 15; Schonfield, Passover Plot pp. 121-122, 141-142, 143-146; Brandon, Jesus and Zealots pp. 2-6, 77-78, 248, 253, 254-264, 364; Maccoby, Mythmaker p. 47. A comment seems in order concerning a particular passage in John 18:31. The chief priests are talking to Pilate: "The Jews said to him, 'It is not lawful for us to put any man to death.'" If this was true, it means that all the attempts by the Sadducees to kill Nazarenes (Stephen, Peter, Paul and James), whether successful or not, were illegal. This could hardly have been the case. Death by stoning, ordered by the Sanhedrin, was an established institution under the Romans, albeit with the procurator's permission. That Jesus was not executed in this way implies either that the full Sanhedrin would have been against it, thus forcing Caiaphas to turn to the Romans to do the job, or that the

464

transgression was not religious but rather political in nature, thus requiring a Roman penalty and not a Jewish one. In either case, the author of John is mistaken (or Caiaphas himself was, if he actually said those words) about it being unlawful for Jews to condemn anyone to death. Paul himself condemned a sinner to death for a religious transgression (First Letter to Corinthians 5:5).

FULVIA AND EXPULSION OF FOREIGN JEWS AND JESUS-FOLLOWERS FROM ROME: 19 A.D. or C.E. Josephus, Antiquities 18.3.5; Klausner, From Jesus to Paul pp. 20-21; Gager, Origins of Anti-Semitism p. 60, 75, 87.

JOHN THE BAPTIZER: Mark 1:4; 6:14-25; Matthew 3:13-15; Acts 18:24-25; Klausner, From Jesus to Paul pp. 257, 387-388, 509-510, 520; Brandon, Jesus and Zealots pp. 268, 352, 356-357; Maccoby, Mythmaker pp. 126, 177; Schonfield, Passover Plot pp. 41, 44, 65-69, 84.

FOLLOWERS OF JOHN THE BAPTIZER: Acts 19:1-7. In John 3:25, John the Baptizer makes a speech in which he says that Jesus, not he, is the Messiah and that Jesus "...gives the spirit". Yet in Acts 19:1-7, the followers of John say that they have "...never even heard that there is a Holy Spirit". In addition to this, the followers of John considered him the Messiah, and the literature preserved by the Mandaeans considers John the true Messiah and Jesus a false one (Schonfield, Passover Plot p. 68, referring to Book of John, Sidra d'Yahya, section 30, translated by G.R.S. Mead, The Gnostic Baptizer pp. 48-51).

The question then is how the followers of John could have continued to identify him as the true Messiah if John himself had said that Jesus was the true one, as reported in John 3:25. Either John's followers were ignoring their leader's pronouncement or the writer of John 3:25 was inventing the speech. The latter interpretation implies that John the Baptizer considered himself the Messiah. Is there any evidence that supports that, in contradiction to John 3:25? Schonfield (Passover Plot p. 68) reports that in the earliest version of Mark's gospel, John does not identify Jesus as the Messiah and that Jesus' spiritual experience after John's baptism of him was experienced only by Jesus himself with no one else witnessing it.

JESUS NEVER BAPTIZED; HIS DISCIPLES DID: John 4:1-2. In John 3:22, however, after the desciption of the conversation between Jesus and Nicodemus, we read, "After this Jesus and his disciples went into the land of Judea; there he remained with them and baptized." To avoid contradiction, we may interpret the person who "remained with them and baptized" to be Nicodemus.

JOHN THE BAPTIST SENDS DISCIPLES TO ASK IF JESUS IS MESSIAH: Matthew 11:2-5.

HEROD ANTIPAS: Josephus, Antiquities 18.2.1, 18.4.5, 18.5.1, 18.7.1; Josephus, Jewish War 2.9.1, 2.9.6; Brandon, Jesus and the Zealots pp. 65, 75(1), 81, 83, 268, 317, 343; Schonfield, Passover Plot pp. 69, 73, 84, 95, 101, 122, 144-145, 255-258, 268; Maccoby, Mythmaker pp. 34, 35, 41.

ARETUS OF PETRA: Josephus, Antiquities 17.10.9, 18.5.1; Klausner, From Jesus to Paul p. 332; Schonfield, Passover Plot p. 256; Maccoby, Mythmaker pp. 86-87.

SALOME: Mark 6:20-25.

JESUS IS JOHN RESURRECTED (HEROD ANTIPAS' BELIEF): Mark 6:16; Brandon, Jesus and Zealots p. 181; Schonfield, Passover Plot pp. 84-85, 101, 108, 170, 204, 212, 213.

PHARISEES WARN JESUS OF DANGER: Luke 13:31; Schonfield, Passover Plot p. 84; Maccoby, Mythmaker p. 35.

GALILEAN JEWS WANT TO FORCE JESUS TO BE KING: John 6:15.

CHIEF PRIESTS FEAR REBELLION OF PEOPLE IF THEY ANSWER JESUS OR TRY TO ARREST HIM: Matthew 21:26, 21:46, 26:5; Mark 11:18, 11:32, 12:12, 14:1-2; Luke 19:47, 20:6, 20:19, 19:26, 22:2.

JUDAS ISCARIOT BETRAYS JESUS AND DOES IT SECRETLY BECAUSE OF FEAR OF PEOPLE'S REACTION IF HE DOES IT OPENLY: Mark 14; Luke 22:3-6.

JESUS APPOINTS HIS BROTHER, JAMES, TO TAKE OVER IN HIS ABSENCE: See NOTE for CHAPTER III entitled, JESUS APPOINTED JAMES TO LEAD HIS MOVEMENT.

DATE OF JESUS' CRUCIFIXION: In this story, 30 A.D. or C.E.

ANNAS (ANANUS), SON OF SETH: John 18:13; Schonfield, Passover Plot p. 139. The author of Acts erroneously calls Annas the high priest at a time when Caiaphas held the office. But the retention of the title by those who had held the office in the past appears to have been a custom in those days, and that may be why Annas was called the high priest.

JOAZAR: Josephus, Antiquities 17.13.1, 17.8.4, 18.1.1, 18.2.1; Brandon, Jesus and Zealots pp. 30, 33, 49, 67.

ROMANS BEAT AND TORTURE JESUS: Mark 15.

MULTITUDE OF WAILING JEWS FOLLOWS JESUS TO HIS EXECUTION: Luke 23:27.

MULTITUDE OF SADDENED JEWS RETURNS HOME BEATING BREASTS AFTER WITNESSING JESUS' EXECUTION: Luke 23:48.

JOSEPH OF ARIMATHEA: Mark 15:43-46; Luke 23:50-53.

RESURRECTION OF JESUS: Mark 16; Matthew 28; Luke 24; Letter to Romans 6:9-10.

DATES OF PROCURATORS: In part from Finegan, Light From the Ancient Past pp. 256-262.

Coponius	6-8 A.D. or C.E.
Ambivius	9-12 A.D. or C.E.
Rufus	12-15 A.D. or C.E.
Gratus	15-26 A.D. or C.E.
Pilate	26-36 A.D. or C.E.
Marcellus	37 A.D. or C.E.
Capito	37-41 A.D. or C.E.
Fadus	44-46 A.D. or C.E.
Alexander	46-48 A.D. or C.E.
Felix	52-60 A.D. or C.E.
Festus	60-62 A.D. or C.E.
Albinus	62-64 A.D. or C.E.
Florus	64-66 A.D. or C.E.

CAIAPHAS' MARRIAGE: Estimated in this story at 11-14 A.D. or C.E.

DATES OF HIGH PRIESTS AND THEIR APPOINTERS: From Finegan, Light From the Ancient Past p. 262(43).

Ananus (Annas), Son of Seth	6-15 A.D. or C.E.
Appointed by Quirinius	6 A.D. or C.E.
Ishmael, son of Ananus (Annas)	15-16 A.D. or C.E
Appointed by Valerius Gratus	15-26 A.D. or C.E.
Eleazar, son of Ananus (Annas)	16-17 A.D. or C.E.
Appinted by Valerius Gratus	15-26 A.D. or C.E.
Simon, son of Ananus (Annas)	17-18 A.D. or C.E.
Appointed by Valerius Gratus	15-26 A.D. or C.E.
Caiaphas (son-in-law of Annas)	18-36 A.D. or C.E.
Appointed by Valerius Gratus	15-26 A.D. or C.E.
Jonathan, son of Ananus (Annas)	36-37 A.D. or C.E.
Appointed by Vitellius	35-39 A.D. or C.E.
Theophilus, son of Ananus (Annas)	37-40 A.D. or C.E.
Appointed by Vitellius	36-39 A.D. or C.E.
Simon Kantheras, son of Boethus	41-43 A.D. or C.E.
Appointed by Agrippa I	41-44 A.D. or C.E.
Matthias, son of Ananus (Annas)	43 A.D. or C.E.
Appointed by Agrippa I	41-44 A.D. or C.E.
Elianaios, son of Kantheras	44 A.D. or C.E.
Appointed by Agrippa I	41-44 A.D. or C.E.
Joseph, son of Camus	44-47 A.D. or C.E.
Appointed by Herod of Chalcis	44-48 A.D. or C.E.
Ananias, son of Nedabaios	47-59 A.D. or C.E.
Appointed by Herod of Chalcis	44-48 A.D. or C.E.

Ishmael	59-61 A.D. or C.E.
Appointed by Agrippa II	50-100 A.D. or C.E.
Joseph Kabi, son of Simon	61-62 A.D. or C.E.
Appointed by Agrippa II	50-100 A.D. or C.E.
Ananus, son of Ananus (Annas)	62 A.D. or C.E.
Appointed by Agrippa II	50-100 A.D. or C.E.
Jesus, son of Damnaios	62-63 A.D. or C.E.
Appointed by Agrippa II	50-100 A.D. or C.E.
Jesus, son of Gamaliel	63-65 A.D. or C.E.
Appointed by Agrippa II	50-100 A.D. or C.E.
Matthias, son of Theophilus	67-68 A.D. or C.E.

Appointed by Jewish defenders of Jerusalem in the war.

| Phannias | 68-70 A.D. or C.E. |

Chosen by lot during the war against Rome.

BEGINNING OF NAZARENES: Acts 24:5.

NAZARENE NAME (THE WAY): Acts 9:2, 18:25, 19:9, 19:23, 22:4, 24:14, 24:22.

MACHAIAH: Fictional.

BARNABAS' ORIGIN: Acts 4:36-37.

BARNABAS' UNCLE: Fictional.

CHAPTER III

DATE OF JESUS' RETURN: Thessalonians 5:1-3; Acts 1:7-8; Matthew 24:34-44; Letter of James 5:8; Klausner, From Jesus to Paul p. 540.

PETER ALSO CALLED CEPHAS AND SIMON: John 1:42.

OVERLAPPING AMONG ZEALOTS, PHARISEES AND NAZARENES: See NOTES for CHAPTER II.

NAZARENES RESEMBLE ESSENES AS WELL AS PHARISEES: Klausner, (From Jesus to Paul pp. 278, 280) speaks of the Church Fathers picturing Jesus' brother, James, as "an ascetic living a life very much like that of the Essenes" and describes him as "a Pharisee with Essenic inclinations." Black (The Dead Sea Scrolls and Christianity p. 99, as reported in Baigent and Leigh, The Dead Sea Scrolls Deception p. 173) states that Christianity is descended from an Essene type of Judaism.

PHARISEES SAVE JESUS: See NOTES for CHAPTER II.

JESUS' BROTHER JAMES ESTEEMED: Brandon, Jesus and Zealots pp. 122, 122(2), 124-125, 156, 167-168.

RECHABITE AND NAZARITE VOWS: Brandon, Jesus and Zealots p. 122; Numbers 6.

JOHN BELOVED DISCIPLE A LOWER PRIEST: Schonfield, Passover Plot p. 98.

ANNAS WARNS PETER AGAINST PREACHING: Acts 4:18.

ALL JEWISH PEOPLE (EXCEPT SADDUCEES) RESPECT THE NAZARENES: Acts 2:47.

PETER'S FIRST ARREST: Acts 4:1-22. The author of Acts states that the chief priests released Peter and his co-workers, "...finding no way to punish them, because of the people...for all men praised God for what had happened." It is significant that the author says "the people" rather than "the Jews", for, throughout the Book of Acts, whenever the Jews do something good, the author calls them "the people" or "the multitudes" or some other such nondescript appellation, whereas when they do something bad, he calls them "the Jews". For example, in Acts 5:13-14, the author writes, "...the people held them in high honor, and more than ever believers were added to the Lord, multitudes of both men and women...". All these "people" were Jews, but the author avoids saying it. In contrast, in Acts 9:23, when the people purportedly plot to kill Paul, the author calls them "the Jews": "When many days had passed, the Jews plotted to kill him." Many examples of this can be found throughout the New Testament; a listing of them can be found in the NOTES for CHAPTER XLIV.

JEWS FLOCK TO PETER FOR HEALING: Acts 5:12-16.

PETER'S SECOND ARREST AND HIS ESCAPE: Acts 5:17-23.

PETER'S THIRD ARREST: Acts 5:24-26.

PETER AND SANHEDRIN (GAMALIEL): Date of this event in the present story is 33 A.D. or C.E. Acts 5:27-42.

SANHEDRIN MEETING PLACE: Schonfield, Passover Plot p. 139.

SANHEDRIN SEATING ARRANGEMENT: Fictional.

HIGH PRIEST'S OPENING REMARKS: Fictional but convey the history of the time.

PETER'S REMARKS TO SANHEDRIN: I have not included Peter's Acts speech before the Sanhedrin, in which he says, "The god of our fathers raised Jesus whom you killed..." because of the uncertainty of the meaning of "you".

If the author wants Peter to be making that accusation to the Sadducees and means that they were responsible for getting Jesus killed by the Romans, then such words are quite possible. If, on the other hand, the author is having Peter make that accusation to the entire assembly, Pharisees as well as Sadducees, then that is so inconsistent with the historical facts about Jesus and the Pharisees — and also the Nazarenes and the Pharisees — as to make the speech suspect and to imply that it is reflective of the author's desire to denigrate Jews rather than Peter's actual words.

The other part of Peter's Book of Acts speech, in which he says, "God exalted him at his right hand as leader and savior, to give repentance to Israel and forgiveness of sins," can only be the author's insertion, for by calling Jesus a savior and by specifying that in particular as a savior from punishment for sin rather than a savior from the Romans, Peter would be declaring a concept of Jesus that did not exist at the time. The savior concept, introduced by Paul of Tarsus, was meant to be a replacement for penance through the Torah. Of the four characteristics of Jesus — messiahship, resurrection, saviorship and divinity — the Nazarenes at this time believed (and only knew of) the first two. Hence, Peter at this time, while he certainly would have called Jesus the Messiah and while he certainly would have believed in resurrection, could not have called Jesus the Torah-abrogating savior that Paul and the Christians called him later. Not only would that have been contradictory to Jesus' own words about the Torah, it also would have contradicted Peter's own Gospel of the Circumcision, which held the Torah as the path to salvation.

CAIAPHAS-PHARISEE POLEMIC: Fictional but representative of the beliefs of the time.

WHO DESIRES PETER'S DEATH? Acts 5:33 says, "When they heard this, they were enraged and wanted to kill them," the "them" being Peter and John, the son of Zebedee, and the others who were with them. Since a Pharisee leader (Gamaliel) is about to speak in their defense, whom does the author mean by "they"? If he means the Sadducees, then the statement is understandable. But if he means all — or the majority of — the members in the Sanhedrin, then this must be construed as false, for the Pharisees, saving Jesus' life as they did, supplying the philosophy that he preached and joining the ranks of the Nazarenes as they were doing, could not have been against Peter and the Nazarenes at this time.

GAMALIEL'S SPEECH: In this story, this is partly fictional and partly from Acts 5:35-39.

In the present story, I have not had Gamaliel mention the Theudas revolutionary movement, as the Book of Acts speech does, since that took place about 45 A.D. or C.E. when Cuspius Fadus was procurator (44-46 A.D. or C.E.), while Gamaliel's speech was in 33 A.D. or C.E. Gamaliel could hardly have spoken about a failed revolutionary movement when that movement had not yet occurred (Josephus, Antiquities 20.5.1; Klausner, From Jesus to Paul p. 285; Maccoby, The Mythmaker p. 53). Errors such as that make questionable how much was actually said and how much was the author's invention.

It is significant that Gamaliel precedes his appraisal of the Nazarene movement by mentioning other revolutionary movements that were similar to it. It means that he considered the Nazarene movement political.

JAMES PERMITTED INTO INNER SANCTUARY OF TEMPLE: Eusebius (Ecclesiastical History, II xxiii, 166-168) quoting Hegisippus, who lived about 180 A.D. or C.E., as reported by Klausner (From Jesus to Paul p. 279).

DISCUSSION AFTER GAMALIEL: In this story, the Sanhedrin discussion that follows Gamaliel's speech is fictional but serves to show the disparate attitudes between Pharisees and Sadducees.

PHARISEES RESERVE JUDGMENT ABOUT PAROUSIA: Acts 5:38-39; Maccoby, Mythmaker p. 166.

PHARISEES TRY TO PROTECT JESUS: Luke 13:31; Maccoby, Mythmaker p. 35.

BEATING OF PETER AND COMPANIONS: The beating of Peter, John and the other Nazarenes is puzzling insofar as the manner in which it is reported (Acts 5:40). Again, the use of the word "they" by the author is ambiguous. Gamaliel has just convinced the majority of the Sanhedrin that Peter and his companions may be doing the will of God. Presumably, a vote is taken — the usual way of deciding things in the Sanhedrin — and Peter and his companions are found innocent of wrongdoing. They are to be released. If the Pharisees were convinced that doing something against Nazarenes might be doing something against God, why would they now want the Nazarenes beaten? And why would they tell the Nazarenes to discontinue what they were doing? Surely, thinking as they did, they would have told the Nazarenes to *continue* what they were doing (speaking about Jesus), so that the possible will of God could be served. The only people who would have wanted Peter to discontinue his teaching were those who did *not* believe he was doing the will of God. That would have been the Sadducees, the losers in the voting. The high priest alone had command of the police force. He alone could give the order for release. He alone was the one who could order a beating. Forced to acquiesce to the Pharisees' decision, it was only he, along with his fellow chief priests, who could have wanted to stop Peter's preaching and only he alone who could have ordered the beating. This is why I have written this segment of the story with the Pharisees leaving and the frustrated Sadducees still trying to exert their outvoted will over the exonerated defendants.

PETER AND RACHEL CONVERSATION: Fictional.

JESUS APPOINTED JAMES TO LEAD HIS MOVEMENT: Schoeps, Jewish Christianity p. 39, referring to Ebionite tradition in Recognitions 1.43. Schoeps points out that Recognitions 1 has been attributed to the Ebionite "Acts of the Apostles", which was witnessed by Epiphanius (Pan. 30.6.9; 16.7) but which is no longer in existence. Schoeps states that the Ebionite "Acts of the Apostles" is older than the Pseudo-Clementines, which have been called the Kerygmata Petrou. It is unfortunate for historians that this original Ebionite record has been lost or destroyed and that we must obtain the information from those who witnessed the document.

CHAPTER IV

This fictional conversation probes Caiaphas' possible motives and attitudes towards Jesus and the Nazarenes.

CHAPTER V

SAUL-CAIAPHAS CONVERSATION: This is fictional, but, historically, we must conclude that some affiliation existed between Saul and Caiaphas and that Saul was acting in an official capacity when he hounded Nazarenes, since he did it openly, without the objection of the chief priests or Romans. Saul's non-Jewish origin is derived from the writings of the Ebionites, as reported in Epiphanius, Ascension of James, Haer. 30.16. In this story, I have made the date of Saul's involvement with Caiaphas 33 A.D. or C.E.

CHAPTER VI

STEPHEN'S DEATH: Acts 7:58. In this story, I have placed the date of Stephen's death at 35 A.D. or C.E.

CHARGES AGAINST STEPHEN: In this story, the charges are sedition and defiance of the high priesthood. In the Book of Acts, the charges are somewhat different. There the charges against Stephen were that he had said Jesus would destroy the Temple and that he had said Jesus would change the customs prescribed by Mosaic law (Acts 6:13-14). The author of Acts says that the persons who made those accusations were "false witnesses", meaning that they were not telling the truth (Acts 6:13). We must then conclude, on the basis of that account, that Stephen and Jesus were not against the Torah. Support for that conclusion can be seen by the fact that Stephen advocated the Torah by denouncing his captors for not keeping it (Acts 7:53) and the fact that Stephen was operating under the leadership of James and that James, who was said to be strong for the Torah, was a widely recognized follower of Mosaic law. James' attachment to that law is recorded in the Book of Acts itself (Acts 15:21) as well as in the Letter of James (James 1:22-25, 2:8, 2:12). It would be unlikely that James would have tolerated in his organization a man who was speaking against the Torah. He certainly did not tolerate Paul speaking against it at their final meeting in Jerusalem (Acts 21:20-24). Furthermore, in Stephen's pre-execution remarks, he supports the Torah and accuses his captors of violating it (Acts 7:51-53). It is well to remember that Acts was written in the last quarter of the First Century (perhaps as late as 95 A.D. or C.E.) by a Jesus-follower who was against Mosaic law.

STEPHEN'S PRE-EXECUTION REMARKS: I have not included Stephen's lengthy historical oration that the author of Acts reports (Acts 7:2-53). If Stephen did make such a speech, the council attending him was certainly indulgent, and Stephen must have had an amazing courage as well as presence of mind to have insulted the very people he might have won over or softened by less accusatory remarks. Whether these were actually Stephen's words or an attempt by the author of Acts, faced with the compatibility between Nazarenes and Judaism, to establish an anti-Torah nature of Jesus-following earlier than Paul is for the reader alone to decide. In this speech, Stephen apparently is referring to all the Jewish people when he says, "You stiff-necked people...". He accuses the Jews and their ancestors of resisting the Holy Spirit, by which, presumably, he means God; he accuses their ancestors of persecuting the prophets, although he does not specify which prophets; he accuses the ancestors of the Jews of having killed those persons who predicted the coming of the Messiah, although he does not name the people who were killed or where or when they were killed; he accuses the Jews of having betrayed and murdered Jesus; he accuses the Jews of failing to follow the Torah (Acts 7:51-53).

That last accusation carries with it the implication that following the Torah was the right thing to do. To say that the Jews did not follow it is difficult to understand. Who did follow the Torah if not the Jews? Could Stephen have been speaking only of his captors (the Sadducee priests and their minions), while the author of Acts wrote it to encompass all the Jewish people?

The other accusations, made so non-specifically, are difficult to confirm or refute. Who were the prophets whom the Jewish ancestors killed? I am not aware of any. Who were the foretellers of the Messiah whom the Jewish ancestors killed? I am not aware of any of those either. I would have thought that Jews in general would have liked a person who predicted the coming of the Messiah. That certainly seems to be what they were longing to have.

In this story, I have had the accusation that the Jews killed Jesus coming as a later development. If Stephen made that accusation at this early date (about 35 A.D. or C.E.), I wonder how the thousands of Jews who, as the Book of Acts says, were following Jesus at this time would have reacted to having themselves accused of such a murder and why James, the leader of the Nazarenes, was not making the accusation as well. Again, the objective reader should ask whether this accusation by Stephen is another attempt by the author of Acts to establish an anti-Jewish quality to early Jesus-followers in order to show them in agreement with Paul.

It is most interesting that the Roman historian, Tacitus (55-117 A.D. or C.E.), in the fifteenth book of his Annals, while mentioning that Christ "...had been put to death in the reign of Tiberius by the procurator Pontius Pilate", does not say anything about "the Jews" being responsible for that. If the Jews had been considered responsible at the time that Tacitus did his writing, it is unlikely that he would not have mentioned it. If, on the other hand, there was no such prevalent belief at the time, and if the accusation against the Jews was a later innovation by Christian writers, then Tacitus' silence about the Jews killing Jesus is understandable.

STEPHEN ADVOCATES ADHERENCE TO TORAH: Acts 7:53.

SAUL CONSENTS TO STEPHEN'S EXECUTION: Acts 7:60. What sort of voting took place in which Saul was such a decision-maker that he would have had to give his consent? The suggestion is that it took place out-of-doors and that the policemen did the voting. If Saul did have a say in this, it rules out the Sanhedrin as the voting body.

STEPHEN PURPORTEDLY ACCUSES JEWS OF KILLING JESUS: Acts 7:52. As suggested in the note, STEPHEN'S PRE-EXECUTION REMARKS, above, Stephen may have been accusing only his captors of that crime.

NAZARENE ANANIAS RESPECTED BY JEWS IN DAMASCUS: Acts 22:12.

CHAPTER VII

ATTEMPTED ASSASSINATION OF JAMES: Maccoby, Mythmaker p. 87, referring to the pseudo-Clementine Recognitions i, 70 ff.

STEPHEN'S NAZARENES FLED TO DAMASCUS: Klausner, From Jesus to Paul p. 319; Maccoby, Mythmaker pp. 86-87.

SADDUCEES PERSECUTE NAZARENES: Acts 9:1; First Letter to Corinthians 15:9; Letter to Galatians 1:13, 1:23; Letter to Philppians 3:6; Wilson, Our Father Abraham p. 64; Maccoby, Mythmaker pp. 51, 218.

PAUL'S LOVE FOR CAIAPHAS' DAUGHTER: Ebionite account, from Epiphanius, Ascension of James, Haer. 30.16. Though this report is sometimes considered apocryphal (a possible attempt to place Paul above sexual interests, his frequent references to sex and confessions of sin notwithstanding), I find it difficult to believe that the Ebionites concocted such a tale out of the blue with no basis or foundation in fact. If the Ebionites did not care about truth and wanted only to sully Paul's name, and if they were willing to do this solely out of their own imaginations, they certainly could have found a more damaging story than one of a young man falling in love with a young woman, which is certainly not a sin and which would be more likely to evoke sympathy and compassion rather than repugnance from the public. Adultery, theft, or some other such immoral act would have been a much more effective choice of lies.

PAUL'S CIRCUMCISION AND FULL CONVERSION TO JUDAISM: Ebionite account, from Epiphanius, Ascension of James, Haer. 30.16. As I have said previously, this Ebionite report is sometimes considered apocryphal. Yet there is no more reason to claim that about the Ebionite records than there is to claim it about the Gospels. To claim legitimacy for one and falsehood for the other without due cause is arbitrary. Objective historians should be free from religious obligations that force them to favor one view over another. The weight of the evidence should be the sole determinant for the seeker of truth.

In Acts 23:3 Paul tells a crowd and in Acts 23:6 he tells the Sanhedrin that he is a Pharisee (which means that his Nazarene affiliation did not cancel his Pharisaic one) and that his father was a Pharisee. In addition, he tells the crowd that he was brought up at the feet of Gamaliel. Was this the truth? If it was, then the Ebionite account of him converting to Judaism is wrong; if it was not (for such an untruth may have been something that Paul felt compelled to tell in order to gain status and credibility with his audience), then the Ebionite account may be correct. Gamaliel was a member of the Sanhedrin, and it is interesting that just after Paul says to the crowd that he was brought up at the feet of Gamaliel, he does not make that same claim to the Sanhedrin. If Gamaliel was his former teacher, would it not have been to Paul's advantage to tell that to the Sanhedrin, as he had just done to the crowd? Furthermore, there is no mention of any recognition between Gamaliel and Paul on that occasion. Aside from the doubtfulness of Gamaliel taking children as students (a point that Maccoby makes in his book, The Mythmaker), this non-recognition between teacher and pupil gives one cause to wonder. This is not a matter of looking to find fault under every rock but rather of using the available evidence to determine the authenticity of one contradictory account over another.

SAUL TAKES LETTERS TO DAMASCUS: Acts 9:2.

SAUL-RABATH CONVERSATION: Fictional.

CAIAPHAS' DAUGHTER REJECTS SAUL: Ebionite account, from Epiphanius, Ascension of James, Haer. 30.16

PHYSICAL DESCRIPTION OF PAUL: Thecla, Acts of Paul and Thecla 3, in which Paul is described as having crooked legs and a hooked nose, with eyebrows that come together without separation, sometimes with the face of an angel.

CHAPTER VIII

PAUL'S DAMASCUS ROAD VISION: Saul's experience of a radiant light on the road to Damascus is reported successively in Acts 9:3-8, 22:6-9, and 26:12-16. In trying to determine what transpired in Saul's Damascus road experience, I find the author of Acts giving somewhat different accounts in the three places in which he describes this. In Acts 9:3-8, Saul sees a radiant light, falls down and hears a voice. When he gets up, he opens his eyes and finds that he cannot see: he is blind. While his companions hear the voice, they do not see the light. This is the version I have used in the present story. One of the difficulties with it is that it does not say *when* Saul closed his eyes (in order for him then to have opened them). Furthermore, it does not tell us whether he was able to shut out the light by closing his eyes or whether the appearance of the light persisted even after he had closed them. I, therefore, have assumed that the light persisted throughout. A spiritual experience such as Saul was having should not depend on the retina, since the experience was a mental phenomenon, not dependent on photons. Saul probably saw the light while his eyes were closed just as he had seen it when they were open. His blindness also would have been a mental phenomenon — psychosomatic — which later, through the power of suggestion or the intervention of God, was cured without any damage to the retinal cells having occurred. It was not, in other words, like looking directly into the sun. Another possible explanation, of course, is that the retinal cells *were* destroyed and that they were replenished or restored through a divine miracle.

In the second version (Acts 22:6-9), Saul, as before, sees a radiant light, falls down and hears a voice. And, as before, when he gets up and opens his eyes, he cannot see. But in this version, his companions see the light, and they *apparently* do not fall down (this version doesn't say), but they do not hear the voice. Yet they are not blinded. If the light was physical, they should have been blinded by it as well. (Photons do not selectively discriminate whose cells they are destroying.) Why did the light not blind them? To avoid that difficult question, I have chosen not to use this version of the story over the first one.

In the third version of the story (Acts 26:12-16), Saul's companions do see the light but now fall to the ground with him. I did not use this version for the same reason that I did not use the second.

One could, I suppose, make a case for this experience never having occurred, that Saul created it to explain his incredible apostasy, while the real reason for his change was his desire for revenge on Caiaphas and his daughter for having rejected him. Though I concede that possibility, I prefer in this story to give Saul the benefit of the doubt and to accept his experience as real.

JUDAS' HOUSE IN DAMASCUS: Acts 9:11.

ANANIAS CURES SAUL: Acts 9:17-18, 9:22:12-13. The response of Saul's fellow policemen to his becoming a Nazarene is conjectural. But they must have been either for it or against it. Since they were anti-Nazarene when they left Jerusalem, and since no mention is made of them changing their loyalties, I would assume that they were against Saul's change of heart and resented his scuttling the enterprise.

CHAPTER IX

ANANIAS OF DAMASCUS REVERED BY JEWS: Acts 22:12.

JESUS' PHILOSOPHY TO LOVE NEIGHBORS AND ENEMIES: Matthew 5:43-48.

MOSES' PHILOSOPHY TO LOVE NEIGHBORS: Leviticus 19:18.

MOSES' PHILOSOPHY TO LOVE STRANGERS: Leviticus 19:33-34.

MOSES' PHILOSOPHY TO HELP THOSE WHO HATE US: Exodus 23:4.

MOSES' PHILOSOPHY TO LOVE OUR ENEMIES: Proverbs 25:21. This also stems from Deuteronomy 23:7, in which Moses says not to abhor the Egyptian, which Philo interprets to mean that we should love our enemies. Klausner (From Jesus to Paul p. 193) cites a paraphrased translation of Philo's understanding of Moses, which says, "In spite of all the wrongs which the Egyptians did to us, love of man must triumph in us over hate of the enemy." Klausner cites a further interpretation: "Love of man extends itself to all mankind, even to foreigners and enemies." Klausner, further, cites G.H. Gilbert, Greek Thought in the New Testament (New York 1928), pp. 30, 31.

GETHSEMANE GARDEN INCIDENT: Matthew 26:36

RESPONSE OF DAMASCUS JEWS TO SAUL'S PREACHING: In Acts 9:22, the author relates that Saul "...confounded the Jews of Damascus by proving that Jesus was the Christ." We might wonder what it was that confounded them. Certainly, they were amazed that a policeman for the high priest was now a member of the group he had been hounding (Acts 9:21), and the Nazarenes were, no doubt, as amazed as all the other Jews. But the confounding mentioned in Acts 9:22 was apparently not due to that but to the proof that Saul was able to present that Jesus was the Christ. Presumably, the Jews he confounded were not Nazarenes, since those Jews already would have been convinced that Jesus was the Messiah. But since Ananias and the other Damascus Nazarenes had been in that city for some time before Saul, it is most likely that the other Jews had heard the Nazarene doctrine from them many times before Saul arrived. They could not have been offended by it, since Ananias and his adherence to the Torah had gained the respect of all the Jews (Acts 22:12). Furthermore, the coming of the Messiah was something that all Jews (except for the Sadducees, perhaps) were anxiously awaiting. Perhaps Saul's proof was more cogent and compelling than that of the other Nazarenes and that that was the reason for the confoundment. On the other hand, one must ask if they really were confounded or if the author of Acts is simply saying so for an ulterior motive.

WHY SAUL LEFT DAMASCUS: In his Second Letter to the Corinthians 11:32-33, Paul says he left Damascus because the Damascan authorities were seeking to arrest him. This reason seems plausible in light of Saul's illegal intentions in going to Damascus. It is the reason I have used in this story. This letter, according to Brandon (Jesus and the Zealots p. 4), was written between 50 and 60 A.D. or C.E., and according to Maccoby (The Mythmaker p. 87), between 55 and 60 A.D. or C.E., as were all of Paul's major letters. But in Acts 9:23 (written about 90-100 A.D. or C.E.), the author states that Saul left Damascus because "...the Jews plotted to kill him". Here are two Christian accounts of why Saul left Damascus, each giving a markedly different reason.

477

I have not used this latter reason in this story because I cannot understand how the Jews of Damascus could have held the Nazarene Ananias in such esteem (Acts 22:12), knowing that he considered Jesus the Messiah, and then have held Saul of Tarsus in such life-threatening contempt for believing the very same thing. It should further be understood that this purported assassination plot by the Jews would have created a violation of Nabataean law. If the Jews were willing to risk doing this to Saul, why had they not done it previously to Ananias? Could the author of Acts have been referring to Saul's former police companions when he wrote of Jews plotting assassination? Such an explanation would allow for compatibility between Saul's version and the version in Acts, although the way that Acts is written sounds more like all the Damascan Jews wanted to assassinate Saul. What else could be the reason for this difference between Paul's version and the version written by the author of Acts?

WATCHERS FOR SAUL AT DAMASCUS GATE: Who was watching the gates of Damascus for Saul? In Acts 9:24, it was "the Jews", whose purpose was to kill him. In the Second Letter to the Corinthians 11:32, it was the governor under King Aretus.

CHAPTER X

SAUL IN DESERT: In Acts 9:25-26, the author says that Saul went directly to Jerusalem after he left Damascus. But in his Letter to the Galatians 1:17-18, Paul says that he went into the desert after he left Damascus, then later back to Damascus and then to Jerusalem. This covered a period of three years. It is most likely that the bulk of that time was spent in the desert. It is not likely that Saul returned to Damascus immediately after having escaped from the life-threatening danger that faced him there. It is also understandable that Saul would not have wanted to make an immediate appearance in Jerusalem, considering how Caiaphas would feel about his betrayal. If, then, Saul spent the bulk of those three years in the desert, where would he have stayed that would have supplied him with food and shelter? The most likely place would seem to have been the Essene community near the Dead Sea (this place later having been given the Arabic name, Qumran).

Also, since these Essenes were practitioners in visions, Paul's statement that he had seen the Third Heaven and Paradise is consistent with an association with such people.

In an article in the Biblical Archeology Review (Nov./Dec. 1991), Hershel Shanks cites references from Robert Eisenman's Maccabees, Zadokites, Christians and Qumran (Leiden, E.J. Brill Publishing 1983) and Eisenman's James the Just in the Habakkuk Pesher (Vatican, Tipographia Gregoriana 1985), in which Eisenman contends that Saul spent three years at the Essene community near the Dead Sea.

ESSENES LIVED IN CITIES AS WELL AS DESERT: Josephus, Jewish War 2.8.4; Baigent and Leigh, Dead Sea Scrolls Deception p. 165.

ZEALOTS IN DEAD SEA COMMUNITY: Baigent and Leigh, Dead Sea
Scrolls Deception p. 70.

RAMPART, TOWERS AND FORGE FOR WEAPONS IN DEAD SEA
COMMUNITY: Baigent and Leigh, Dead Sea Scrolls Deception pp. 154, 166.
Norman Golb (Symposium by Library of Congress and Baltimore Hebrew
University, April 21, 1993, as reported in Biblical Archeology Review,
July/August 1993, pp. 70, 72) believes that this was a military fortress but does
not accept it as an Essene ascetic community. In contrast, Magen Broshi,
curator of the Shrine of the Book in Jerusalem (same reference p. 70) does not
believe it was a fortress because the two-foot-thick walls were too thin to qualify
it as such.
    In this story, I have portrayed it as an ascetic Essene community and
a fortress, which I think is what Baigent and Leigh have done.

ESSENES REVERE MOSES SECOND ONLY TO GOD: Josephus, Jewish War
2.8.9; Baigent and Leigh, Dead Sea Scrolls Deception p. 166.

MOSES SAYS STAR WILL COME FROM JACOB: Book of Numbers 24:17;
Baigent and Leigh, Dead Sea Scrolls Deception p. 141.

NOT ALL ESSENES CELIBATE; THOSE WHO WERE MIGHT ADOPT
CHILDREN: Josephus, Jewish War 2.8.2; Baigent and Leigh, Dead Sea Scroll
Deception pp. 165, 169.

MEAL PRAYERS OF ESSENES AND NAZARENES SIMILAR: Baigent and
Leigh, Dead Sea Scrolls Deception p. 140.

SAME TYPE OF RULING STRUCTURE FOR ESSENES AND
NAZARENES: Baigent and Leigh, Dead Sea Scrolls Deception p. 140.

ESSENES GOT RE-BAPTIZED EVERY DAY: Baigent and Leigh, Dead Sea
Scrolls Deception p. 140.

ESSENES ATONED FOR SINS BY PRACTICING JUSTICE, SUFFERING
AFFLICTION AND OBEYING MOSAIC LAW: Baigent and Leigh, Dead Sea
Scrolls Deception p. 140.

ESSENE LIARS DID PENANCE FOR SIX MONTHS: Baigent and Leigh,
Dead Sea Scrolls Deception p. 140.

BLASPHEMING MOSES IS CAPITAL OFFENSE TO ESSENES: Josephus,
Jewish War 2.8.9.

ESSENE CONTEMPT FOR DANGER AND PAIN: Josephus, Jewish War
2.8.10; Baigent and Leigh, Dead Sea Scrolls Deception pp. 166-167.

JESUS WITH ESSENES: Conjectural. Jesus' cousin, John the Baptizer, lived in the Essene community near the Dead Sea. There is some indication in the Dead Sea Scrolls that the Dead Sea Essenes entertained the possibility of, or gave tentative acceptance to, Jesus being the Messiah.

JOHN THE BAPTIZER WITH ESSENES: In this story, I have made the date of John's baptizing near the Dead Sea approximately 27 A.D. or C.E. Otto Betz (Was John the Baptist an Essene? Biblical Archeology Review, December 1990) says that John lived with the Essenes.

LOCATION OF DESERT ESSENES: Their community was near the Dead Sea. It was destroyed by the Romans. The Arabic name, Qumran, was given to this place later.

ESSENE, PHARISEE AND SADDUCEE VIEWS OF FATE: Josephus, Antiquities 13.5.9.

PRACTICES OF ESSENES: Josephus, Antiquities 13.5.9, 18.1.5; Josephus, Jewish War 2.8.2-13.

PAUL SEES PARADISE: Second Letter to Corinthians 12:2.

ESSENE VIEW OF JESUS: This is uncertain. The release of all the Dead Sea Scrolls to a wide variety of scholars might have revealed an answer. Since that has not been done, the information that might have been obtained may or may not become available to us. In this story, I have had the Essene attitude be one of entertaining the possibility that Jesus could be the Messiah. We do know that their view, like that of Jesus, was strongly pro-Torah. They were also strongly anti-Roman.

TEACHER OF RIGHTEOUSNESS: In this story, he is James the Just, the brother of Jesus. I have since learned that Eisenman espouses this identification. Cornfeld, in 1962, however, stated that "...there are still doubts about the identification of the Righteous Teacher and the Wicked Preist." (Cornfeld, Daniel to Paul p. 194.)

CHAPTER XI

PILATE AND THE SAMARITANS: Josephus, Antiquities 18.4.1; Brandon, Jesus and Zealots p. 80; Schonfield, Passover Plot p. 255, 259.

LEGATE VITELLIUS EXPELS PILATE: Date 36 A.D. or C.E. Josephus, Antiquities 18.4.2.

VITELLIUS DEPOSES CAIAPHAS; APPOINTS JONATHAN HIGH PRIEST: Josephus, Antiquities 18.4.3.

NABATAEAN EXPEDITION: Date 37 A.D. or C.E. Josephus, Antiquities 18.5.3.

VITELLIUS VISITS JERUSALEM: Josephus, Antiquities 18.5.3.

VITELLIUS DEPOSES JONATHAN; APPOINTS THEOPHILUS HIGH PRIEST: Josephus, Antiquities 18.5.3.

TIBERIUS DIES: 37 A.D. or C.E. Josephus, Antiquities 18.5.3.

CALIGULA EXILES HEROD ANTIPAS: In Josephus, Jewish War 2.9.6, the exile is to Spain. In Josephus, Antiquities 18.7.2, the exile is to Lyons, a city in Gaul. In both accounts, Herodias accompanies her husband into exile. In the latter account, it should be noted that Herodias shows a high degree of nobility when she declines Caligula's offer of freedom: for when Caligula, after transferring Herod Antipas' money to Herod Agrippa, offers to allow Herodias to retain her own money and not to go into exile with her husband (favoring her because she was Agrippa's sister), she responded, "Thou, indeed, O emperor! actest after a magnificent manner, and as becomes thyself, in what thou offerest me; but the kindness which I have for my husband hinders me from partaking of the favor of thy gift; for it is not just that I who have been made a partner in his prosperity, should forsake him in his misfortunes." Caligula then angrily transfers her property to Agrippa and banishes her along with her husband.

PARTHIANS: Time-Life Books, Empires Ascendant pp. 123-125.

PARTHIANS GOLD-PLATED JEWELRY: The Parthians may have used electric batteries for gold-plating jewelry. Battery, Encyclopedia Britannica 1973, vol. 3 p. 283.

KING AGRIPPA I: 41-44 A.D. or C.E.

CALIGULA GIVES LAND TO AGRIPPA I: Josephus, Antiquities 18.6.10; 19.5.1.

CHAPTER XII

SAUL MEETS BARNABAS: Acts 9:27. In this story, I have made the date that Saul arrives in Jerusalem after his conversion about 37-38 A.D. or C.E. The Ebionite "Book of Acts", however, as reported in Schoeps, Jewish Christianity p. 46, dates Saul's conversion as seven years after Jesus' death, which would make his trip to Jerusalem three years after that — a later time than used in this story.

SAUL NEEDS BARNABAS FOR ACCEPTANCE BY JERUSALEM NAZARENES: Acts 9:26-27.

SAUL WAS MARRIED: Klausner, From Jesus to Paul p. 571(40), according to Clement of Alexandria: See Enslin op. cit., p. 138.

SAUL WAS A WIDOWER: Klausner, From Jesus to Paul p.571 (according to the opinion of A.F. Puuko-Paulus und das Judentum S.28, Amm.1, end). In disagreement with this is Stauffer Theologisches Worterbuch zum Neuen Testament, I, 650.

SAUL MEETS PETER: Letter to Galatians 1:18.

ISAIAH PROPHECY: Isaiah 11.

JESUS' LINEAGE: Matthew 1:1-16; Luke 3:23-38. There is no evidence that Peter himself ever traced this lineage. In this story, however, I have had him trace the Matthew lineage only as a means of presenting it to the reader. The fact that the early Jesus-followers repeatedly announced Jesus' descent from King David means that they must have believed in some sort of lineage that showed it. Peter, being an early Jesus-follower, must have believed in such a lineage. Hence it is not inappropriate to have him mentioning it in this story.

There is a discrepancy, however, between the lineage listed in Matthew (in which Jesus' father, Joseph, is the son of Jacob) and the lineage listed in Luke 3:23-38 (in which Jesus' father, Joseph, is the son of Heli). In explanation of this, the second lineage is sometimes said to be that of Mary, with the naming of Heli as the father of Joseph being incorrect.

If Jesus *was* descended from King David through Mary and not through Joseph, that supports the belief that Jesus' father was God and that Mary was a virgin when she conceived him. While that may be true, we are still left with the fact that the earliest followers of Jesus did *not* believe in the lineage in Luke, that they believed in the lineage in Matthew, in which Joseph *was* Jesus' father. This is important, for it means that the concept that Joseph was not Jesus' father came along later and did not exist among the Jesus-followers at this early date.

Eusebius (Ecclesiatical History, I vii), writing in the Fourth Century, explains the discrepency by reporting that there were two ways in which to record family lineages in Jesus' time, one being "by nature" (the true biological father listed) and the other "by law" (a father siring a child in the name of his brother who has died childless). Thus, according to Eusebius, the reason that Matthew says that Jacob was Joseph's father whereas Luke says that Heli was the father was that Jacob and Heli had the same mother (they were brothers) and that when Heli died childless, his brother Jacob took the widow as his wife, had a son named Joseph with her and, out of respect for his deceased brother, named the child Joseph, son of Heli (a name that he was permitted to give *by law*) instead of the name Joseph, son of Jacob (a name that some people persisted in calling him because it was *by nature*). Eusebius cites no earlier historical source for this.

To the other explanation for this discrepency (Heli was Mary's father), Eusebius translator G.A. Williamson states, "The one certainty is that the discrepency cannot be explained away by the absurd suggestion that one genealogy is that of our Lord's mother." (Eusebius, The History of the Church from Christ to Constantine, Translated with an Introduction by G.A. Williamson, Penguin Books 1965, p. 56[1].)

GREEK-SPEAKING JEWS AGAINST SAUL: Acts 9:29.

SAUL LEAVES JERUSALEM: Acts 9:30.

STEPHEN'S FOLLOWERS TO PHOENICIA, CYPRUS AND ANTIOCH: Acts 11:19; Klausner, From Jesus to Paul p. 340.

STEPHEN'S DISCIPLES FROM CYPRUS AND CYRENE PREACH TO GENTILES IN ANTIOCH: Acts 11:20.

PETER CURES ENEAS: Dated about 38-39 A.D. or C.E. in this story. Acts 9:32-35.

PETER RESURRECTS TABITHA: Acts 9:36-43.

PETER BAPTIZES CORNELIUS: Acts 10:47-48.

CORNELIUS WAS A GOD-FEARER: Acts 10:1-2.

BARNABAS SENT TO ANTIOCH: Acts 11:22.

ANTIOCH GENTILES TURN TO JESUS: Acts 11:23.

JESUS WANTS TO HEAL ONLY JEWS BUT MAKES EXCEPTION: Mark 7:25-30.

JESUS WANTED DISCIPLES TO GO ONLY TO JEWS: Matthew 10:5-6.

BARNABAS VISITS TARSUS: Acts 11:25.

EPICUREANISM STARTED: About 350 years before the period in which Barnabas is writing. Klausner, From Jesus to Paul p. 81.

EPICURUS: Klausner, From Jesus to Paul p. 82.

LUCRETIUS CARUS: Klausner From Jesus to Paul pp. 82, 88.

EPICUREAN PHILOSOPHY: Klausner, From Jesus to Paul pp. 82-94.

DEMOCRITUS AND LEUCIPPUS: Klausner, From Jesus to Paul p. 82.

POSIDONIUS' STOIC TEACHINGS: Klausner, From Jesus to Paul pp. 62-68.

SENECA AND STOIC TEACHINGS: Klausner, From Jesus to Paul pp. 68-80.

"CLEAVE TO THE STANDARDS OF THE HOLY ONE, BLESSED BE HE": Ketuboth, reported in Klausner, From Jesus to Paul p. 69.

BEN SIRA: Ben-Sira 8:5, as reported in Klausner, From Jesus to Paul p. 69.

CATO'S RESPONSE TO MALTREATMENT: On Firmness (De Constantia) XIV 3, translated by Basore (Loeb Class. Lib.), I, 91, as reported by Klausner, From Jesus to Paul pp. 69-70.

JESUS' RESPONSE TO BEING STRUCK: Matthew 5:39.

JESUS TEACHES TORAH ADHERENCE: Matthew 5:19.

JEWS THANK GOD FOR BOTH GOOD AND BAD NEWS: Babylonian Talmud, Berakhot either 35a or 60b, as reported by Wilson, Our Father Abraham p. 157.

JESUS PROTECTS ADULTERESS: John 8.3-11.

SENECA CLAIMS SOME MEN ARE GODS: Seneca, To Maria on Consolation XV 1, as reported by Klausner, From Jesus to Paul p. 110.

PAGAN RULERS CALLED DIVINE: Klausner, From Jesus to Paul pp. 108-112.

EPHESUS INSCRIPTION: Dittenberger, Syllog, 3. Aufl., no. 760, as reported in Klausner, From Jesus to Paul p. 109.

JULIUS CAESAR CALLED DIVINE: Klausner, From Jesus to Paul p. 110.

OCTAVIAN CALLED DIVINE: Klausner, From Jesus to Paul p. 110.

TIBERIUS NOT CALLED DIVINE: Klausner, From Jesus to Paul p. 110.

CALIGULA CALLED DIVINE: Josephus, Antiquities 19.1.1; Brandon, Jesus and Zealots pp. 84-86; Schonfield, Passover Plot pp. 191-192, 224.

PAGAN INGESTION OF GODS: Morton Smith, Jesus the Magician (Harper and Rowe 1978) pp. 111, 122.

PAGAN GODS: Klausner, From Jesus to Paul pp. 102-107.

CHAPTER XIII

PAGAN WRITERS ADMIRE JUDAISM: Gager, Origins of Anti-Semitism pp. 39-40, 68-87.

JEWS UBIQUITOUS: Josephus quotes Strabo, who says, "Now these Jews are already gotten into all cities; and it is hard to find a place in the habitable earth that has not admitted this tribe of men, and is not possessed by them: and it hath come to pass that Egypt and Cyrene, as having the same governors, and a great number of other nations, imitate their way of living and maintain great bodies of these Jews in a peculiar manner, and grow up to greater prosperity with them, and make use of the same laws with that nation also." Josephus, Antiquities 14.7.2; Josephus also speaks to the Jews and says, "...for there is no people upon the habitable earth which have not some portion of you among them..."; Josephus, Jewish War 2.16.4; Klausner, From Jesus to Paul pp.10-12.

MNASEAS OF PTARA: Gager, Origins of Anti-Semitism p. 40.

HECATAEUS' CASUAL NEGATIVE REMARK: Gager, Origins of Anti-Semitism p. 40.

CICERO AND APOLLONIUS MOLON ANTI-JEWISH: Gager, Origins of Anti-Semitism pp. 41, 56.

ANTIOCHUS EPIPHANES AND MACCABEAN REVOLT: Hammerton, New Illustrated World History p. 221; Learsi, Israel: A History of the Jewish People pp. 130-138; Brandon, Jesus and Zealots p. 88; Schonfield, Passover Plot pp. 18, 224; Klausner, From Jesus to Paul pp. 9-10, 137, 139, 151, 504; Gager, Origins of Anti-Semitism pp. 39, 46; Wilson, Our Father Abraham p. 120.

PAGAN WRITERS AGAINST JUDAISM: Gager, Origins of Anti-Semitism p. 40.

PAGANS DRAWN TO JUDAISM: Gager, Origins of Anti-Semitism pp. 66-88; Feldman, The Omnipresence of the God-fearers, Biblical Archeology Review 1986; Maccoby, Mythmaker p. 94.

CORNELIUS HISPANUS: Gager, Orgins of Anti-Semitism p. 59.

TIBERIUS EXPELS ROMAN JEWS: Date 19 A.D. or C.E. Josephus, Antiquities 18.3.5; Klausner, From Jesus to Paul pp. 20-21.

LAOGRAPHIA: Gager, Origins of Anti-Semitism pp. 45, 46, 49.

LYSIMACHUS: Gager, Origins of Anti-Semitism pp. 43-45.

APION: Gager, Origins of Anti-Semitism pp. 32, 36, 43, 45-47, 49, 71, 82.

ISIDORUS, LAMPO AND DIONYSIUS: Gager, Origins of Anti-Semitism pp. 49-50.

FLACCUS: Gager, Origins of Anti-Semitism pp. 47-54.

CHAPTER XIV

CAIAPHAS-JAMES DEBATE, GAMALIEL MODERATES, PEOPLE CONGREGATE NIGHT BEFORE: Schoeps, Jewish Christianity p. 42, referring to Recognitions 1.66-67; 1,43; 1.54-56; 1.66-67. The particular prophecy discussed in this debate was from Deuteronomy 18:15.

JOHN THE BAPTIZER'S FOLLOWERS ARE NUMEROUS AND SAY HE IS MESSIAH: Schoeps, Jewish Christianity p. 36, referring to Recognitions 1.60; p. 41, referring to Syriac Version of Recognitions 1.54.

JAMNIA INCIDENT: In this story, I have placed this incident at about 41 A.D. or C.E. or slightly earlier. Brandon, Jesus and Zealots p. 84.

CALIGULA'S FEVER: Hammerton, New Illustrated World History p. 270.

VITELLIUS WITH CALIGULA: Schonfield, Passover Plot p. 191, from Suetonius, Gaius xxii.

STATUES OF GODS: Josephus, Antiquities 18.8.2, 19.1.1; Schonfield, Passover Plot p. 192.

CALIGULA'S TEMPLE: Schonfield, Passover Plot p. 192, from Suetonius, Gaius xxii.

CAPITO'S REPORT: Brandon, Jesus and the Zealots p. 84.

PETRONIUS AND STATUE: Josephus, Antiquities 18.8.2.

CALIGULA AND JEWISH TEMPLE: Josephus, Antiquities 18.8.2; Brandon, Jesus and Zealots pp. 84-86.

HELICON: Gager, Origins of Anti-Semitism p. 62.

AGRIPPA APPEAL TO CALIGULA: Josephus, Antiquities 18.8.7, 18.8.8.

PETRONIUS' LETTER: Josephus, Antiquities 18.8.5, 18.8.6, 18.8.8.

FLACCUS AND CALIGULA: Gager, Origins of Anti-Semitism pp. 47-54.

DEATH OF PILATE: Eusebius reports that Pilate, in the reign of Caligula, was "...involved in such calamities that he was forced to become his own executioner and to punish himself with his own hand..." (Ecclesiastical History, II vii). The plot against the emperor is conjectural, but what else would have forced Pilate to become his own executioner? An assassination subsequently did take place, of course.

CALIGULA ASSASSINATION: Josephus, Antiquities 18.8.9.

ANTIOCHUS EPIPHANES: Josephus, Antiquities 13.8.2; Hammerton, New Illustrated World History pp. 220-223; Learsi, Israel: A History of the Jewish People p. 131.

CHAPTER XV

JEWS FIGHT EGYPTIANS AFTER CALIGULA: Josephus, Antiquities 19.5.2.

CLAUDIUS AS EMPEROR: 41-54 A.D. or C.E. Josephus, Antiquities 19.2.1, 19.3.1; Josephus, Jewish War 2.11.1.

AGRIPPA I AS KING: 41-44 A.D. or C.E. Josephus, Antiquities 18.6.10.

CLAUDIUS' LETTER TO EGYPTIANS ABOUT JEWS: Josephus, Antiquities 19.5.2-3.

APION IN ROME: Josephus, Antiquities 18.8.1.

LAMPO AND ISIDORUS EXECUTED: Gager, Origins of Anti-Semitism p. 50.

CLAUDIUS REWARDS AGRIPPA I: Josephus, Antiquities 19.5.1.

AGRIPPA I RAISED WITH HALF-BROTHERS: Josephus, Antiquities 18.5.4.

AGRIPPA I'S CHILDREN: Josephus, Antiquities 18.5.4; Jones, The Herods of Judaea p. 209.

AGRIPPA I'S HALF-BROTHER, HEROD, MARRIES WIDOWED BERNICE: Josephus, Antiquities 19.5.1.

AGRIPPA I GETS CHALCIS FOR HALF-BROTHER HEROD: Josephus, Antiquities 19.5.1, 19.8.1.

SIMON KANTHERAS HIGH PRIEST: 41-43 A.D. or C.E.

WHEN WILL JESUS RESTORE KINGDOM? Acts 1:6; Mark 11:10. The implication of the passage in Mark is that the date would be soon.

AGRIPPA I RELIGIOUS: Klausner, From Jesus to Paul pp. 346-347; Brandon, Jesus and Zealots p. 93, as reported in Bikkurim, III. 4; Sotah, VII. 8 (in Danby, The Mishnah, pp. 97, 301); cf. Schurer, G.J.V. I, 554-5; cf. Derenbourg, Essai, p. 217; Schurer, G.J.V. I, 554(23), 555(27), 560.
    The fact that Agrippa I had statues of his daughters in his house in Caesarea, however, casts doubt on how well he followed the Torah (Josephus, Antiquities 19.9.1). The same may be said for his having the images of himself and the emperor stamped on the coins of his realm (Jones, The Herods of Judaea

p. 211). And impiety was indicated too when he staged gladiatorial shows and threw men to be eaten by beasts (Jones, The Herods of Judaea p. 212).

PETER WAS MILITANT: Klausner, From Jesus to Paul p. 348; Brandon, Jesus and Zealots p. 97.

SONS OF THUNDER: Mark 3:17; Brandon, Jesus and Zealots p. 98.

AGRIPPA I EXECUTES JAMES, SON OF ZEBEDEE: In this story, about 43 A.D. or C.E. Acts 12:2.

JONATHAN DECLINES SECOND TIME AS HIGH PRIEST: 43 A.D. or C.E. Josephus, Antiquities 19.6.4.

MATTHIAS, SON OF ANNAS, APPOINTED HIGH PRIEST: 43-43 A.D. or C.E. Josephus, Antiquities 19.6.4.

AGRIPPA I ARRESTS PETER: In this story, about 43 A.D. or C.E. Acts 12:3.

AGRIPPA I DELAYS PETER'S EXECUTION: In this story, about 43 A.D. or C.E. Acts 12:4.

PETER ESCAPES: In this story, about 43 A.D. or C.E. Acts 12:6-10.

AGRIPPA I EXECUTES GUARDS: In this story, about 43 A.D. or C.E. Acts 12:19.

PETER TELLS FRIENDS OF ESCAPE: In this story, about 43 A.D. or C.E. Acts 12:12-17.

PETER'S CONVERSATION WITH SIMON THE ZEALOT: Fictional.

PETER'S CONVERSATION WITH HIS WIFE RACHEL: Fictional.

PETER TO ALEXANDRIA: In this story, about 43 A.D. or C.E. Acts 12:17. The author of Acts tells us only that Peter went to a different place; he does not specify where. In this story, Peter's flight to Alexandria is conjectural; however, Brandon (Fall of Jerusalem pp. 211-212 and Jesus and Zealots pp. 93, 164, 191, 196-198, 297-298) makes a strong case for this location.

JAMES LEADS NAZARENES WITHOUT PETER: In this story, about 43 A.D. or C.E. The pre-eminence of James as leader of the Nazarenes seems to have taken place with Peter's departure after his escape from Agrippa I, if not sooner.

ELIANAIOS HIGH PRIEST: 43-44 A.D. or C.E. Josephus, Antiquities 18.8.1.

SYCOPHANTIC JEWS CALL AGRIPPA I A GOD: Josephus, Antiquities 19.8.2; Acts 12:20-22; Klausner, From Jesus to Paul p. 226.

AGRIPPA I DIES: 44 A.D. or C.E. Josephus, Antiquities 19.9.1.

GENTILES REVEL OVER AGRIPPA I'S DEATH AND DESECRATE HIS DAUGHTERS' STATUES: Josephus, Antiquities 19.9.1.

AGRIPPA II KING WITHOUT TERRITORY: Josephus, Antiquities 19.9.2.

AGRIPPA II MARRIES OFF MARIAMNE BUT NOT DRUSILLA: Josephus, Antiquities 20.7.1.

ALL ISRAEL UNDER PROCURATOR: 44 A.D. or C.E. Josephus, Antiquities 19.9.2.

HEROD OF CHALCIS GETS PRIVILEGES FROM CLAUDIUS: Josephus, Antiquities 20.1.3.

JOSEPH HIGH PRIEST: 44-47 A.D. or C.E. From 41-43 the high priest was Simon Kantheras; from 43-43 it was Matthias, son of Annas; from 43-44 it was Elianaios, son of Kantheras. Hence, the high priest whom Joseph replaced was Elianaios, son of Kantheras. Yet Josephus, in his Antiquities of the Jews 20.1.3, says that Herod of Chalcis "...removed the last high priest called Kantheras, and bestowed that dignity upon his successor, Joseph, the son of Camus." This is confusing unless we understand that the name Kantheras, in this case, did not apply to Simon Kantheras but to his son Elianaios.

CUPIUS FADUS PROCURATOR: Josephus, Antiquities 19.9.2.

THOLOMAIS: Brandon, Jesus and Zealots p. 99.

THEUDAS: Josephus, Antiquities 20.5.1.

TIBERIUS ALEXANDER PROCURATOR: Josephus, Antiquities 20.5.2.

JACOB AND SIMON EXECUTED: Josephus, Antiquities 20.5.2.

CHAPTER XVI

AGABUS PREDICTS FAMINE: Acts 11:28 states that it occurred during the reign of Claudius (41-54 A.D. or C.E.); Klausner (From Jesus to Paul) dates it in 46 A.D. or C.E.

TIBERIUS ALEXANDER'S UNCLE IS PHILO: Klausner, From Jesus to Paul p. 26; Brandon, Jesus and Zealots p. 103.

TIBERIUS ALEXANDER LEFT JUDAISM FOR PAGANISM: Klausner, From Jesus to Paul p. 26; Brandon, Jesus and Zealots p. 103.

SAUL AND BARNABAS COLLECT MONEY: Acts 11:29-30.

SAUL BUYS ROMAN CITIZENSHIP: This view is proposed by Maccoby (Mythmaker pp. 161-162) with some cogent reasons. I have used it in this story, although at a different time than Maccoby's. Maccoby asks why this Roman citizenship was not revealed by Paul on other occasions when it could have benefited him and spared him trouble. In addition, I would think that if Paul possessed this Roman citizenship from birth, and if his parents were Jewish (as he claims before the Sanhedrin), then his parents must have been wealthy and influential. A poor Jewish family probably would not have had a Roman citizenship. A wealthy boy, on the other hand, would not have had to earn his living as a leather worker and is not likely to have sought employment doing the unpleasant work of arresting, beating and executing people.

QUEEN HELENA OF ADIABENE: Josephus, Antiquities 20.2.1, 20.2.5; Talmud, Baba Bathra 11a.

SAUL AND BARNABAS GIVE MONEY TO JERUSALEM NAZARENES: Acts 11:30.

PETER PREACHING TO GENTILES: In Acts 10, Peter preaches to the Gentile, Cornelius. In the Letter to the Galatians 2:12, it states that Peter ate with Gentiles (presumably more than once) prior to the arrival of James' emissaries; such meetings must surely have involved teaching and discussions about Jesus. Maccoby (Mythmaker pp. 146-147) states "...as the account in Acts makes clear and as can be gathered from other sources, the Jerusalem leaders by no means gave up their proselytizing activities among Gentiles, nor did they regard themselves as merely 'apostles to the Jews'. The Jerusalem Council did not hand over the whole Gentile missionary field to Paul. Nor did it ban the conversion of Gentiles to full Judaism; it merely decided that such conversion was not a necessity." Indeed, according to Acts 15:22, the apostles and the elders in Jerusalem not only sent Paul but also Barnabas, Silas and Judas (Barsabbas) to speak to the Gentiles in Antioch.

Obversely, it is evident throughout the Book of Acts that Paul's activities were not restricted to Gentiles. Repeatedly, he spoke in synagogues; repeatedly he spoke to Jews.

In the First Letter to the Corinthians 1:12, Paul speaks of some Jesus-followers considering themselves members of a Peter-following group. Many of these people were Gentiles, and it reveals that Peter must have preached to them.

Brandon, Jesus and Zealots p. 63(3). Brandon states, "...according to the evidence of Acts, which is supported, for example, by the Epistle to the Romans, Paul usually commenced his evangelization by speaking in the local synagogue. It is also evident that Peter did not confine his missionary activity to the 'circumcision'." Thus, Peter preached to Gentiles, and Paul preached to Jews. Brandon goes further and states that the author of Acts *intentionally* avoided mentioning Peter's missionary activities (Brandon, Jesus and Zealots p. 165).

Klausner, From Jesus to Paul p.228. Klausner states that Peter was one of the first who attempted to spread (what Klausner calls) Christianity among the pagans. Since in this story, I have distinguished the Torah-following Jesus-followers from the Torah-rejecting Jesus-followers by using the names "Nazarene" and "Christian" respectively for each, and since Klausner does not do this here but, instead, uses the name "Christian" for both, I maintain that Klausner here is referring to the Torah-following form of "Christianity", which reflected Peter's Gospel of the Circumcision. Elsewhere, Klausner does use the word "Nazarene", and he uses it specifically to show that Peter required all followers of Jesus to first become Jews. Klausner states, "Simon Cephas (Peter) could not agree to convert Cutheans, who were only half Jews; only genuine Jews were to be received as Nazarenes." Klausner, From Jesus to Paul p.296

Elsewhere, Klausner says "...the essential thing was to win converts to belief in Jesus from among the Gentiles; particularly since, without much thinking, Barnabas and his associates, and even Peter, had already actually attempted to do this...". Klausner, From Jesus to Paul p. 446.

JOHN (MARK) JOINS SAUL AND BARNABAS: Acts 12:25.

JOHN (MARK) IS BARNABAS' NEPHEW: Klausner, From Jesus to Paul p. 222, 351.

WELCOME PARTY FOR BARNABAS IN CYPRUS: Fictional.

SAUL, BARNABAS AND JOHN (MARK) PREACH IN SALAMIS (CYPRUS): Acts 13:5.

SAUL, BARNABAS AND JOHN (MARK) PREACH TO SERGIUS PAULUS IN PAPHOS: Acts 13:6-7.

BARNABAS AND JOHN (MARK) PREACH IN PAPHOS SYNAGOGUE: Fictional. This has been used in this story to establish why Saul saw Sergius Paulus alone the next day.

SAUL BLINDS ELYMAS: Acts 13:8-11.

SERGIUS PAULUS SERVES SAUL KOSHER FOOD: Fictional. In this story, Saul has not yet abandoned the Mosaic dietary rules for himself; he will do so later. Had he done so at this time, he undoubtedly would have incurred disapproval from Barnabas and John (Mark). Sergius Paulus, now a good host rather than a testing one, presumably accommodated his honored guest's dietary needs.

SAUL BECOMES PAUL: Acts 13:9.

PREACHING TO GENTILES IN PERGA AND PAMPHYLIA: Acts 13:13.

JOHN (MARK) LEAVES: Acts 13:13. Although Acts 13:13 does not reveal that this was a contentious departure, Paul's later refusal to travel with John (Mark) again because of this departure (Acts 15:37-38) implies that it was just that.

PAUL AND BARNABAS TO ANTIOCH: Acts 13:14.

PAUL REVEALS HE HAS VISIONS: Second Letter to the Corinthinians 12:1-4.

PAUL REVEALS JESUS' DEATH IS EXPIATION FOR SINS FOR THOSE WHO BELIEVE: Acts 13:38; Letter to Romans 3:24-26, 4:25, 8:1-2, 10:9, 11:5; Letter to Galatians 2:16, 3:10-13, 3:23-26, 5:2-4; Letter to Ephesians 1:13, 2:8; First Letter to Corinthians 15:3; Letter to Colossians 1:21-23.

PAUL REVEALS INBORN SIN CONCEPT: Letter to Romans 7:17-20.

PAUL REVEALS INADEQUACY OF TORAH AND GOOD DEEDS FOR SALVATION: Letter to Romans 3:21, 3:28, 4:6, 4:9, 6:14, 7:4-8, 8:3, 9:30, 10:4, 10:9, 11:5; Letter to Galatians 2:16, 3:10-13, 3:23-26, 5:2-4; Letter to Colossians 2:23. This should be compared with Paul's statement in Romans 2:13, in which he says, "For it is not the hearers of the law who are righteous before God, but the doers of the law who will be justified."

PAUL ADVOCATES FOLLOWING THE LAW: Letter to Romans 2:6, 2:10, 2:13, 3:31, 7:16, 7:22.

PAUL REVEALS THAT JESUS IS EXCLUSIVE SON OF GOD: Matthew 3:17, 27:54; Letter to Colossians 1:13; Letter to Galatians 1:16.

JESUS CALLS GOD THE FATHER OF US ALL: Matthew 5:9, 5:14, 5:43, 6:4, 6:6, 6:8-9, 6:14-15, 6:18, 6:26, 6:32, 7:11.

PAUL CALLS GOD THE FATHER OF US ALL: Ephesians 4:6.

PAUL CALLS ALL OF US THE SONS AND CHILDREN OF GOD: Letter to Romans 8:14, 16, 17, 19, 21; 9:4; Letter to Galatians 3:26; Acts 17:28-29.

JEWISH SAGES (INCLUDING SOLOMON) TEACH GOD IS FATHER OF ALL: Samuel 7:14; Klausner, From Jesus to Paul p. 126, 194, from Ben-Sira 4:10 (Heb.), 51:10 (Heb.) and Wisdom of Solomon 2:16, 2:18.

DEUTERONOMY CALLS JEWS CHILDREN OF GOD: Deuteronomy 14:1.

PHILO CALLS GOD THE FATHER OF ALL: Klausner, From Jesus to Paul p. 194, from De Confusione Linguarum XXVIII 145, M., I, 426; C.-W., II, 256.

PHILO CALLS RIGHTEOUS MEN "SONS OF GOD": Klausner, From Jesus to Paul p.194, from De Confusione Linguarum XXVIII 145, M., I, 426; C.-W., II, 256.

PAUL CALLS ALL EXCEPT JESUS ADOPTED SONS OF GOD: Letter to Romans 8:23; Letter to Galatians 4:5.

GOD CALLS ISRAEL HIS FIRST-BORN SON: Exodus 4:22

MESSIAH MIGHT BE ACCOMPANIED BY PROPHET: Maccoby, Mythmaker p.62.

GNOSTICS: Gager, Origins of Anti-Semitism pp. 267-173; Maccoby, Mythmaker pp. 93, 185, 220(7).

MYSTERY RELIGIONS: Schonfield, Passover Plot pp. 193, 195; Maccoby, Mythmaker pp. 16, 196, 220; Wilson, Our Father Abraham p. 8.

ATTIS: Klausner, From Jesus to Paul pp. 105, 106, 113, 166, 197-198, 204, 211-212, 267, 298-299, 356, 437-439, 477, 484, 535, 545, 563; Maccoby, Mythmaker 102, 107, 136. Klausner (From Jesus to Paul p. 107), after speaking of Attis, says, "Moreover, we have a certain amount of information that a god was sacrificed as a propitiation offering for the people and their sins; yet this god rose again — surely, therefore, he was a god."

PSALMS SPEAK OF BEGOTTEN SON OF GOD: Psalms 2:7.

NEW NAME FOR SOME JESUS-FOLLOWERS IS "CHRISTIANS": Acts 11:26. Staniforth (Early Christian Writings, Penguin Classics p. 92) states that the earliest known appearance of the noun, Christianity, in literature was in Ignatius' Letter to the Magnesians. But since this letter was written shortly before Ignatius' martyrdom in Rome in 107 A.D. or C.E. (Staniforth, Early Christian Writings p.64), and since the Book of Acts was written earlier (last quarter of the First Century), it would seem that Acts preceded Magnesians in the use of this term.

TWO DIFFERENT MEANINGS OF MESSIAH: Brandon, Jesus and Zealots pp. 110, 112-113; Klausner, From Jesus to Paul pp. 167, 445; Schonfield, Passover Plot pp. 26-28, 33, 195, 207; Maccoby, Mythmaker pp. 15, 37, 38, 62, 75.

CHRISTIANS WILD OLIVE SHOOTS OFF ISRAEL: Letter to Romans 11:17.

CHAPTER XVII

PAUL AND BARNABAS SPEAK IN ANTIOCH SYNAGOGUE: Acts 13:14-16.

PAUL MENTIONS JESUS' LINEAGE: Letter to Romans 1:3; Second Timotheus 2:8.

PAUL SAYS JERUSALEM JEWS DESIRED JESUS' DEATH: Acts 13:27-28.

JEWS WELCOMED JESUS INTO JERUSALEM: Matthew 21:8-9; Mark 11:8-10; John 12:12-13, 12:18-19.

JEWS HATED CHIEF PRIESTS: Josephus (Jewish War 7.8.1), in speaking of the Jews, says, "...for they all, vile wretches as they were, cut the throats of the high priests..."; Maccoby, Mythmaker pp. 27-28.

PAUL TEACHES THAT JESUS' DEATH EXPIATES SIN (FOR BELIEVERS): Letter to Romans 3:21, 3:22, 3:24-26, 3:27, 3:28, 5:1-2, 5:18-19, 8:3, 8:32, 10.4, 10:9; Letter to Galatians 2:16, 3:13, 3:22, 5:6; First Letter to Timotheus 2:5-6; Acts 13:38-39.

PAUL TEACHES THAT TORAH-FOLLOWING NO LONGER EXPIATES SIN: Letter to Romans 3:20, 4:6, 4:16, 6:15, 7:4, 7:6, 8:8, 9:30-32, 10.4; Letter to Galatians 2:16, 3:10, 3:11, 3:13, 3:24, 5:2-4, 5:18.

JESUS DEFENDS THE TORAH: Matthew 5:17-19.

JEWS REJECT SECOND ANTIOCH PREACHING: Acts 13:44-45.

PAUL SAYS IT WAS NECESSARY THAT HE PREACH TO JEWS FIRST AND ONLY AFTER THAT TO GENTILES: Acts 13:46.

PAUL REJECTS JEWS AND PREACHES TO GENTILES: Acts 13:46.

JEWS BESMIRCH PAUL AND BARNABAS: Acts 13:50.

PAUL AND BARNABAS EXPELLED FROM ANTIOCH: Acts 13:50.

PAUL AND BARNABAS FLEE ICONIUM: Acts 14:5-6.

PAUL CURES CRIPPLE IN LYSTRA: Acts 14:8-10.

GENTILES THINK PAUL AND BARNABAS ARE GODS: Acts 4:11-13.

ANTIOCH JEWS TURN JEWS AND GENTILES IN LYSTRA AGAINST PAUL AND BARNABAS: Acts 14:19.

JEWS AND GENTILES OF LYSTRA STONE PAUL: Acts 14:19.

PAUL AND BARNABAS TO DERBE: Acts 14:20.

PAUL AND BARNABAS RETURN TO LYSTRA, ICONIUM AND ANTIOCH: Acts 14:21.

PAUL AND BARNABAS TO PERGA, ATTALIA AND ANTIOCH: Acts 14:24-26.

ANANIAS, SON OF NEDABAIOS, HIGH PRIEST: 47-59 A.D. or C.E. Josephus, Antiquities 20.5.2.

ELEAZAR, SON OF ANANIAS: Josephus, Jewish War 2.17.2.

ELEAZAR, RABATH'S FRIEND: Fictional.

CUMANUS BECOMES PROCURATOR: 48-52 A.D. or C.E.

HEROD OF CHALCIS DIES: Approximate time in this story is 48 A.D. or C.E. Josephus, Antiquities 20.5.2.

AGRIPPA II GIVEN HEROD OF CHALCIS' TERRITORY: Approximate time in this story is 48 A.D. or C.E. Josephus, Antiquities 20.5.2; Josephus, Jewish War 2.12.1.

INTIMATE ENCOUNTER BETWEEN AGRIPPA AND BERNICE: Fictional.

INTIMATE AFFAIR BETWEEN AGRIPPA AND BERNICE: See Note for Chapter XXX entitled, AFFAIR BETWEEN AGRIPPA AND BERNICE.

TEMPLE RIOT FROM ROMAN OBSCENITY: Josephus, Jewish War 2.12.1.

BETH-HORON INCIDENT: Josephus, Jewish War 2.12.2.

CHAPTER XVIII

JAMES SENDS OUT EMISSARIES: Schoeps, Jewish Christianity p. 39, referring to the Ebionite tradition in Recognitions 1.43, says that James sent out emissaries. He does not make clear what message James' emissaries were carrying. On pp. 18-19, however, he cannot accept that the itinerant Jesus-followers who refuted Paul were carrying letters from James. He must, therefore, consider them people who were not James' emissaries. If they were, it would mean that James was against Paul, which is antithetical to the New Testament attempt to show them in agreement. Schoeps opines that the letters were

"...probably written by extremists and not by James himself." This posits the existence of a deviant group, acting without James' authorization and opposed to his agreement with Paul — a Jerusalem group that James could not control, as he later could control Paul when he ordered him to pray publicly from the Torah in the Temple. Schoeps describes this recalcitrant group as "zealous for the law" and says that its members charged Paul with apostasy several years later in Jerusalem. Interestingly, he does not classify James as belonging to this group but puts James in opposition to it.

Since Paul was against the Torah, Schoeps would have us believe that James was against it too. Yet such a belief is contradictory to other evidence: James was called "strong for the Torah"; the Nazarenes (led by James) were called the "Zealots of the Torah"; James, at his final meeting with Paul in Jerusalem, bragged about how many Jesus-followers were zealous for the Torah; the Letter of James, as Martin Luther stated several hundred years later, was a defense of the Torah and contradictory to Paul's teachings.

Schoeps' attempt to put Paul and James on the same side, showing them to be opposed to the "extremists" who were "zealous for the law," reflects the age-old attempt to obfuscate a situation in which the original form of Jesus-following was contradictory to Christianity. Paul, in his Second Letter to the Corinthians (11:4-5), reveals that there were such differences when he says of James and the apostles, "For if someone comes and preaches another Jesus than the one we preached, or if you receive a different spirit from the one you received, or if you accept a different gospel from the one you accepted, you submit to it readily enough. I think that I am not in the least inferior to these superlative apostles" (whom he refers to again in that sarcastic manner in his Second Letter to the Corinthians 12:11). The important point is that Paul recognized this other gospel as coming from "these superlative apostles"! Paul's effort to aggrandize himself, presenting himself as equal to "these superlative apostles", is carried on centuries later by Eusebius, who tells us that Paul was a witness to Jesus' resurrection, a false assertion that even Eusebius' translator finds "astonishing" (Eusebius, Ecclesiastical History, translated by G.A. Williamson, Penguin Books 1965, p. 65) and which shows how far the ancient Christian writers were willing to go to make Paul and his gospel preeminent.

The gospel writers' attempts to represent Nazarenes and Christians as one solid Torah-rejecting group creates difficulties for theologians and historians, both of whom stumble over the inconsistencies created by this contention. Historians who are concerned to substantiate the unity of James and Paul, lest cherished religious beliefs be shattered, resort to strained explanations, such as "...probably written by extremists" in place of the straightforward and obvious conclusion that an objective observer would choose.

Cornfeld concurs when he states that after 50 C.E., Paul faced opposition from the Jerusalem Church (Cornfeld, Daniel to Paul p. 312.).

JAMES' EMISSARIES DEMAND CIRCUMCISION FOR ALL JESUS-FOLLOWERS: Acts 15:1.

PAUL TELLS CHRISTIANS TO ASK HIM FOR ANSWERS TO QUESTIONS RATHER THAN TORAH: First Letter to Corinthians 4:16, 11:1;

Letter to Galatians 4:12; Letter to Philippians 3:17; Second Letter to Thessalonians 3:7, 3:9. In each instance, Paul says, "Be imitators of me," or "...become as I am," or "...join in imitating me," or "...you ought to imitate us," or "...our conduct an example to imitate."

PAUL USES TORAH TO FRAME ANSWERS TO QUESTIONS: First Letter to Corinthians 1:19, 2:9, 2:16, 3:19-20, 5:6, 5:13, 6:2, 6:9, 6:16, 9:8-9, 9:14, 14:34-35 — "...for they (women) should be subordinate, *even as the law says*", although I should mention, as an aside, that Maccoby (Mythmaker p. 201) says that the Hebrew Bible actually contradicts this claim by Paul — 15:27, 15:45, 15:54; Letter to Romans 2:21-23, 2:25-26, 3:4, 4:3, 4:6-8, 4:17-18, 7:2-3, 7:7, 9:6, 9:9-13, 9:15, 9:17:2-3, 9:25-29, 9:33, 10:5, 10:11, 10:13, 10:16, 10:18-21, 11:1-4, 11:8-10, 11:26-27, 11:34-36, 12:14-20, 13:9, 14:11, 15:3-4, 15:9-12, 15:21; Second Letter to Corinthians 4:6, 6:2, 6:16-18, 8:15, 9:9; Letter to Galatians 3:6, 3:8, 3:10-13, 3:16, 4:22-27, 4:30, 5:9; Letter to Ephesians 4:8, 5:14; First Letter to Timotheus 2:13-15, 5:18; Second Letter to Timotheus 2:11-13, 2:19; Acts 13:16-36, 13:40-41, 28:25-27. Klausner (From Jesus to Paul p. 606) states, "And Paul...in spite of his abrogation of the Torah, he leaned for support in almost every important religious question upon verses from that Torah. To be sure, this constitutes an internal contradiction in his teaching; but it is a fact which cannot be denied... In the nine Pauline letters which are considered genuine, there are 84 quotations from the Old Testament...". James Tabor concurs with this (Personal Communication 1991).

PAUL AND BARNABAS TO JERUSALEM: Acts 15:2-4.

JAMES APPOINTED SEVENTY-ONE TEACHERS TO HELP MAKE JUDGEMENTS: Schoeps, Jewish Christianity p. 39, referring to Ebionite tradition in Recognitions 1.43.

NAZARENE EUCHARIST PRAYER: Maxwell Staniforth (translator), Early Christian Writings, The Didache pp. 231-232 (Baltimore, Penguin Classics 1972).

JAMES VERY RIGHTEOUS: Klausner, From Jesus to Paul pp. 278-279, 282, 348; Brandon, Jesus and Zealots pp. 122, 167; Schonfield, Passover Plot pp. 56, 204-205; Maccoby, Mythmaker 144, 154.

PAUL LATER ADVISES ROUTINELY DRINKING SOME WINE: First Letter to Timotheus 5:23.

JERUSALEM MEETING (ON QUESTION OF GENTILE CONVERTS): Acts 15:5-21. The date in this story is approximately 49 A.D. or C.E. Klausner (From Jesus to Paul p. 365) puts it at 47 A.D. or C.E.

PETER AND CORNELIUS: Acts 10. If, as Paul states, Peter's was the Gospel of the Circumcision, one must wonder why Peter did not encourage Cornelius to become circumcised. After all, Peter would not accept the Cutheans as Nazarenes because they were not fully converted Jews and were considered only half Jews (Klausner, From Jesus to Paul p. 296). If the story of Cornelius was a spurious insertion by the author of Acts, written in an attempt to counter the claim that Peter had always encouraged his Gentile converts to become Jews, then it posits that Peter was acting in violation of the very gospel that Paul attributed to him. In other words, if Peter's gospel really was one of circumcision (a Torah-following gospel), then the Cornelius story means that not even Peter adhered to that gospel. If the Cornelius story is true, (I have assumed that it is), then a more plausible explanation — one that I have used in this story — is that Peter did adhere to his own gospel (Nazarenes should be Jews) but made Cornelius an exception because of his unusual righteousness. Exceptions such as this are not implausible when one considers that Paul circumcised Timotheus in violation of *his* gospel — the Gospel of the Uncircumcision — which said not only that circumcision was unnecessary but that it was evil and obliterative of salvation through grace.

JAMES' PRAYER TAUGHT BY JESUS: Matthew 6:9-13.

JOHN (MARK) AND BARNABAS ARGUE ABOUT PAUL: Fictional. Cornfeld does state, however, that Barnabas stood between the original followers of Jesus in Jerusalem and the teachings of Paul, which came later (Cornfeld, Daniel to Paul p. 305.).

CHAPTER XIX

PAUL AND BARNABAS TO ANTIOCH WITH JUDAS (BARNABAS) AND SILAS: Acts 15:22. In this story, approximately 51 A.D. or C.E.

JOHN (MARK) TO ANTIOCH: Acts 15:37.

PAUL ADAPTS TO DIFFERENT GROUPS: First Letter to Corinthians 9:19-23.

PAUL NOT UNDER MOSAIC LAW BUT LAW OF CHRIST: First Letter to Corinthians 9:20-21. Schoeps (Jewish Christianity p. 55) reports that Paul was considered to be against Mosiac law.

TWO GOSPELS NAMED BY PAUL: Letter to Galatians 2:7. That the other gospel came from the Jerusalem group can be seen in Second Letter to Corinthians 11:4-5, when Paul says, "For if some one comes and preaches another Jesus than the one we preached, or if you receive a different spirit from the one you received, or if you accept a different gospel from the one you accepted, you submit to it readily enough. I think that I am not in the least inferior to these superlative apostles" (whom he refers to again in that manner in the Second Letter to Corinthians 12:11).

That Paul calls Gentiles "the uncircumcision" and Jews "the circumcision" can be seen in the Letter to the Ephesians 2:11 and again in the Letter to the Galations 2:9.

Schoeps (Jewish Christianity p. 54) states that Paul's gospel diverged from the teaching of the older apostles. He further states (p. 58): "That Paul had the truth and his opponents were in error is not the case! Nor can one say that Paul understood the person, intention, and teaching of Jesus better than the Pharasaic Christians of Jerusalem."

TORAH IS HOLY, JUST AND GOOD, SAYS PAUL: Letter to Romans 7:12, 7:16.

PAUL IS PRISONER OF HIS FLESH: Letter to Romans 7:14-25.

JESUS' DEATH CANCELS SINS OF BELIEVERS: See NOTES for CHAPTER XVII.

COMMANDMENTS NOT HARD: Deuteronomy 30:11.

INCOMPLETE TORAH ADHERENCE DAMNING: Letter to Galatians 3:10; Letter of James 2:10.

PAUL ALLOWS FREEDOM IN DIET, EXCEPT WHEN DISCOMFORTING OTHERS: First Letter to Corinthians 8, 10.

PAUL DOES NOT ADHERE TO ALL OF JAMES' REQUIREMENTS FOR GENTILES: First Letter to Corinthians 6:12-13, 8:4-13, 10:23-33.

DINNER WITH GENTILES CONTROVERSY: Letter to Galatians 2:11-14. Eusebius (Ecclesiastical History I viii) refers to a story by the early Christian writer, Clement (Outlines Book V) in which the Peter who disagrees with Paul at this dinner is not the Peter who was Jesus' first disciple but another Peter, who is one of the seventy less-important disciples. Eusebius translator, G.A. Williamson, considers this an "absurd suggestion" (Eusebius, Ecclesiastical History, Penguin Books 1965, p. 64[6]). Early Christian writers, presented with embarrassing evidence that Peter and Paul disagreed, had to deal with the implications of that reality. To accept it meant the possibility that Paul's form of Jesus-following was false. The validity of Christianity was at stake. To circumvent this, they had to make it appear that Peter and Paul agreed. Hence, when presented with contrary evidence, they sought tortuous explanations, even making two men out of one, in order to have Paul unchallenged.

GOD GIVES DIETARY RESTRICTIONS TO NOAH: Genesis 9:4.

MOSAIC INJUNCTION AGAINST EATING FAT: Leviticus 7:22-24.

PAUL AND BARNABAS SEPARATE: Acts 15:38-39.

PAUL LEAVES ANTIOCH WITH SILAS: Acts 15:40.

BARNABAS AND JOHN (MARK) TO CYPRUS: Acts 15:39.

ELEAZAR'S PRAYER: Fourth Maccabees 6:26-29, as reported by Klausner, From Jesus to Paul p. 139.

PROPITIATORY DEATH IN MACCABEES: Fourth Maccabees 17:21, 22, as reported by Klausner, From Jesus to Paul p. 139.

PROPITIATORY DEATH IN ISAIAH: Isaiah 53.

HILLEL AND SHAMMAI PHILOSOPHIES: Maccoby, Mythmaker pp. 45, 54-55, 98; Wilson, Our Father Abraham pp. 78, 299.

SAMARITAN KILLING AFFAIR: Josephus, Antiquities 18.4.1-2; Brandon, Jesus and Zealots pp. 80, 106-107, 259.

FELIX BECOMES PROCURATOR: 52-60 A.D. or C.E. Josephus, Antiquities 20.7.1.

CHAPTER XX

The approximate time for the events in this chapter is 53 A.D. or C.E.

PAUL AND SILAS IN DERBE: Acts 16:1.

PAUL AND SILAS IN LYSTRA: Acts 16:1.

PAUL CIRCUMCISES TIMOTHEUS: Acts 16:1-3. In this story, Paul's reason for circumcising Timotheus is conjectural, although the author of Acts hints at the same reason.

PAUL AND DISCIPLES TO PHRYGIA AND GALATIA: Acts 16:6.

PAUL'S VISION OF JESUS FORBIDS ASIA: Acts 16:6-7.

PAUL AND DISCIPLES TO TROAS: Acts 16:8.

MACEDONIAN MAN VISION: Acts 16:9.

PAUL, SILAS AND TIMOTHEUS TO SAMOTHRACIA, NEAPOLIS AND PHILIPPI: Acts 16:11-12.

LYDIA OF THYATIRA: Acts 16:14-15.

PAUL EXORCISES DIVINING SPIRIT FROM SLAVE GIRL: Acts 16:16-18.

SLAVE GIRL'S OWNERS SEIZE PAUL AND SILAS: Acts 16:19.

MAGISTRATES BEAT AND IMPRISON PAUL AND SILAS: Acts 16:20-24.

PAUL AND SILAS DISTURB OTHER PRISONERS: Acts 16:25.

EARTHQUAKE AT PRISON: Acts 16:26.

JAILER ATTEMPTS SUICIDE: Acts 16:27.

PAUL STOPS JAILER FROM SUICIDE: Acts 16:28.

PAUL BAPTIZES JAILER AND FAMILY: Acts 16:29-33.

JAILER FEEDS PAUL AND SILAS: Acts 16:34.

PAUL DECLINES FREEDOM WITHOUT MAGISTRATES' PERSONAL APPEAL: Acts 16:35-40.

CHAPTER XXI

PAUL, SILAS AND TIMOTHEUS TO AMPHIPOLIS, APOLLONIA AND THESSALONICA: Acts 17:1.

JASON: Acts 17:5-9.

PAUL CALLS TORAH (THE LAW) GOOD: Letter to Romans 2:13, 2:25, 3:2, 7:12, 7:14, 7:16, 7:22, 13:10.

PAUL CALLS TORAH (THE LAW) IRRELEVANT OR BAD: Acts 13:38; Letter to Romans 3:21, 3:28, 3:31, 4:3, 4:5, 4:6, 4:8, 4:9, 4:14, 4:16, 4:24, 5:9, 5:20, 6:14, 7:4-8, 8:3, 9:30, 10:4, 10:9, 11:5; Letter to Galatians 2:16, 3:10-13; First Letter to Corinthians 15:56. Schoeps (Jewish Christianity p. 55) states that Paul was considered to be against Mosaic law.

PAUL DISTINGUISHES DIFFERENT LAWS: Paul mentions the law of God, the law of the mind and the law of sin in Romans 7:22-23; he mentions the law of the spirit of life and the law of death in Romans 8:2; he mentions the law of Christ in First Letter to Corinthians 9:21.

SOME THESSALONIAN JEWS BELIEVE PAUL: Acts 17:4.

SOME THESSALONIAN JEWS REJECT PAUL: Acts 17:5.

PAUL BLAMES THESSALONIAN ANIMOSITY ON JEALOUSY: Acts 17:5.

DISGRUNTLED THESSALONIANS TAKE JASON AND OTHERS TO ROMANS: Acts 17:6-7.

ROMANS RELEASE JASON AND OTHERS: Acts 17:9.

PAUL, SILAS AND TIMOTHEUS TO BEROEA: Acts 17:10.

MOSAIC LAW REQUIRES HOSPITALITY AND LOVING STRANGERS: Leviticus 19:33-34.

PAUL CALLS BEROEAN JEWS NOBLER: Acts 17:11.

HOSTILE THESSALONIANS CAUSE BEROEAN CHANGE: Acts 17:13.

PAUL LEAVES BEROEA; SILAS AND TIMOTHEUS STAY: Acts 17:14.

PAUL TO ATHENS: Acts 17:15.

ATHENIAN EPICUREANS AND STOICS: Acts 17:18-34.

PAUL SAYS WE ARE ALL THE OFFSPRING OF GOD: Acts 17:28-29.

SOME STOICS AND EPICUREANS BELIEVE IN JESUS' RESURRECTION; OTHERS DO NOT: Acts 17:32-34.

PAUL TO CORINTH: Acts 18:1.

AQUILA AND PRISCILLA MEET PAUL: In this story, the approximate date of that meeting is 53 A.D. or C.E. Acts 18:2.

EXPULSION OF FOREIGN JEWS FROM ROME: In this story, the approximate date of that event is 53 A.D. or C.E. Acts 18:2; Schonfield, Passover Plot p. 189.

AQUILA'S ACCOUNT OF JEWISH EXPULSION FROM ROME: Fictional. It should be remembered, however, that the emperor Claudius abhorred the Jesus-followers because of the disturbances they were making. Schonfield, Passover Plot p. 189; Suetonius, Claudius xxv; Dio Cassius ix, 6; Acts 18:2.

BERNICE JEALOUS OF DRUSILLA: Josephus, Antiquities 20.7.2.

CLAUDIUS GIVES AGRIPPA II LAND: In this story, this occurs about 53 A.D. or C.E. Josephus, Antiquities 20.7.1.

DRUSILLA MARRIES AZIZUS: In this story, this takes place about 53 A.D. or C.E. Josephus, Antiquities 20.7.1.

DRUSILLA LEAVES AZIZUS FOR FELIX: Josephus, Antiquities 20.7.2.

SILAS AND TIMOTHEUS IN CORINTH: Acts 18:5.

CORINTHIAN JEWS OPPOSE PAUL: Acts 18:6.

PAUL CURSES CORINTHIAN JEWS: Acts 18:6.

IN CORINTH PAUL SWEARS TO PREACH ONLY TO GENTILES (AS HE PREVIOUSLY HAD SWORN IN PISIDIA): Acts 18:6.

PAUL WRITES FIRST LETTER TO THESSALONIANS: In this story, the approximate date of this is 54 A.D. or C.E.

PAUL TELLS THESSALONIANS THE JEWS KILLED JESUS: First Letter to Thessalonians 1:14-15. Also, see STEPHEN'S PRE-EXECUTION REMARKS in NOTES for CHAPTER VI.

PAUL, SILAS, TIMOTHEUS MOVE INTO JUSTUS' HOUSE: Acts 18:7.

PAUL PREACHES TO JEWS AGAIN: Acts 18:8-11.

PAUL BAPTIZES CRISPUS AND FAMILY: Acts 18:8.

PAUL SAYS HE MIGHT VISIT ROME ON WAY TO SPAIN: Letter to Romans 15:24:28. The Scofield Bible dates the writing of the Letter to the Romans from Corinth at 60 A.D. or C.E. I did not use that date in this story. First of all, Paul was Governor Felix's prisoner for two years. Festus replaced Felix in 60 A.D. or C.E. At that time, Felix turned Paul over to Festus. Therefore, Paul must have been under detention by Felix from 58-60 A.D. or C.E. He could not, then, have been in Corinth in 60 A.D. or C.E. Also, the Letter to the Romans says that Paul intends to go to Jerusalem to minister to the saints there. This means that the letter was written before he actually did go to Jerusalem for his final meeting with James, which took place about 58 A.D. or C.E. I, therefore, wrote this story with Paul writing the Letter to the Romans from Corinth at a date earlier than 58 A.D. or C.E.

PAUL SAYS JESUS WAS DESCENDED FROM DAVID: Letter to Romans 1:3; Second Letter to Timotheus 2:8.

PAUL SAYS ONE MUST DO WHAT TORAH SAYS: Letter to Romans 1:12-29.

PAUL ADVOCATES MOSAIC LAW EVEN AFTER SALVATION THROUGH GRACE: Letter to Romans 3:31.

PAUL PROHIBITS SINNING AFTER EXPIATION THROUGH JESUS' DEATH: Letter to Romans 6:1-2; 6:15.

PAUL SAYS IF GENTILES DO GOOD DEEDS OF TORAH, CIRCUMCISION UNNECESSARY: Letter to Romans 2:26.

PAUL SAYS DUTY TO GOD FULFILLED ONLY BY ACCEPTANCE OF EXPIATING DEATH OF JESUS, NOT THROUGH GOOD DEEDS OF TORAH: Letter to Romans 10:9; also, see NOTES for CHAPTER XVI.

PAUL PRAISES MOSAIC LAW AND COMMANDMENTS: Letter to Romans 7:12, 7:16; also, see NOTE, PAUL CALLS TORAH (THE LAW) GOOD, earlier in this chapter.

JESUS AS SAVIOR ESTABLISHED LAW OF FAITH: Letter to Romans 9:30-32.

JESUS HAS ENDED MOSAIC LAW: Letter to Romans 10:4.

PAUL'S LUST: Letter to Romans 7:14-20, 7:25.

TORAH SERVES TO SHOW WHAT IS SINFUL: Letter to Romans 7:7.

INDWELLING SIN DOES BAD DEEDS, NOT PAUL HIMSELF: Letter to Romans 7:17, 7:20.

PAUL GIVES MORAL INSTRUCTIONS: Letter to Romans 12:9-21.

PAUL SAYS HE WILL VISIT JERUSALEM BEFORE ROME OR SPAIN: Letter to Romans 15:25.

VISION OF JESUS TELLS PAUL TO BE FEARLESS: Acts 18:9.

PAUL IN CORINTH ONE AND ONE-HALF YEARS: Acts 18:11.

PAUL TELLS CORINTHIANS DEATH-SACRIFICE BELIEF IS ONLY WAY TO EXPIATE INBORN SIN: Acts 18:13; also, see NOTES elsewhere in this chapter and NOTES for CHAPTER XVII.

CORINTHIAN JEWS UNDER SOSTHENES COMPLAIN ABOUT PAUL TO GALLIO: Acts 18:12.

GALLIO DISMISSES JEWISH COMPLAINT: Acts 18:14-16.

GREEKS BEAT SOSTHENES WITHOUT GALLIO'S INTERVENTION: Acts 18:17.

GALLIO IS BROTHER OF JEW-HATING SENECA: Klausner, From Jesus to Paul p. 381; Gager, Origins of Anti-Semitism p. 60, from Augustine, City of God 6.11. Also, Klausner points out, as does The Interpreters Dictionary of the

Bible, Volume I, that an inscription found near Delphi places Gallio's governorship from 51-52 A.D or C.E. In this story, I have placed it at about 53.

CHAPTER XXII

DEATH OF CLAUDIUS: 54 A.D. or C.E.

NERO EMPEROR: 54 A.D. or C.E.

PAUL BELIEVES END TIME IS SOON: First Letter to Corinthians 7:26-31; Letter to Romans 13:11-12.

NERO EXTENDS AGRIPPA II'S DOMAIN: Josephus, Jewish War 2.13.2.

PAUL SHAVES HEAD AND TAKES VOW IN CENCHREA: Acts 18:18.

PAUL PREACHES TO JEWS IN EPHESUS: In this story, about 55 A.D. or C.E. Acts 18:19.

EPHESIAN JEWS RECEPTIVE TO PAUL'S TEACHINGS: Acts 18:20.

PAUL SAYS HE MAY RETURN TO EPHESUS: Acts 18:21.

PAUL, SILAS, TIMOTHEUS TO CAESAREA, ANTIOCH, GALATIA, PHRYGIA: Acts 18:22-23.

APOLLOS IN EPHESUS: Acts 18:24. The fact that Apollos had been instructed in the way of the Lord (Jesus) and that he was well versed in the Scriptures (Torah) and that he had been baptized in the manner of John and not of Paul indicates that Apollos was a Nazarene and not a Christian. This is further supported if we accept Brandon's belief that Peter taught his gospel in Alexandria, the city in which Apollos was raised. Although Priscilla and Aquila instructed Apollos in the Christian interpretation of Jesus, we have no indication of whether or not he accepted it. His competition with Paul (as well as with Peter) for the affections of the Corinthians (First Letter to Corinthians 1:12) suggests that his teaching may not have been quite the same as Paul's.

APOLLOS IN CORINTH, RIVALS PAUL: First Letter to Corinthians 1:12; Brandon, Jesus and Zealots p. 193(2).

PAUL RETURNS TO EPHESUS: Acts 19:1.

PAUL TEACHES DISCIPLES OF JOHN THE BAPTIZER: Acts 19:1-7.

PAUL SPEAKS THREE MONTHS IN EPHESIAN SYNAGOGUE: Acts 19:8.

PAUL SAYS ALL EPHESIAN JEWS WHO DISAGREE WITH HIM SPEAK EVIL OF HIS GOSPEL: Acts 19:9.

PAUL KEEPS FOLLOWERS AWAY FROM EPHESIAN SYNAGOGUE: Acts 19:9.

PAUL TWO YEARS IN EPHESUS: Acts 19:10.

PAUL SPREADS HIS GOSPEL INTO ASIA: Acts 19:10.

HANDKERCHIEFS, APRONS TOUCH PAUL, HEAL SICK: Acts 19:11-12.

CHAPTER XXIII

SCEVA UNSUCCESSFUL AT EXORCISM: Acts 19:13-16.

PEOPLE BURN BOOKS ON MAGIC: Acts 19:19.

JESUS' SPIRIT DIRECTS SAUL TO ACHAIA, MACEDONIA, JERUSALEM: Acts 19:21.

TIMOTHEUS AND ERASTUS TO MACEDONIA; PAUL STAYS IN ASIA: Acts 19:22.

SILVERSMITHS IN EPHESUS: In this story, the date of this affair is approximately 57 A.D. or C.E. The actual date may have been earlier. Acts 19:23-41.

PAUL IS LIKE A FATHER BEGETTING CHILDREN: First Letter to Corinthians 4:15.

PAUL ON SEXUAL ABSTINENCE AND MARRIAGE: First Letter to Corinthians 7:1-11, 7:25-28, 7:32-40.

PAUL EXPECTS DAY OF RECKONING SOON: First Letter to Corinthians 7:28-31.

PAUL ON LOVE: First Letter to Corinthians 13.

PAUL ON HAIRSTYLES: First Letter to Corinthians 11:14-15.

PAUL ON WOMEN: First Letter to Corinthians 14:34-35; First Letter to Timotheus 2:11; Letter to Epesians 5:22; Letter to Colossians 3:18; Letter to Titus 2:4-5.

PAUL ON HEAD COVERING: First Letter to Corinthians 11:4-16.

PAUL'S REVELATION ABOUT JESUS' WORDS AT LAST SUPPER; FOOD AND WINE HIS BODY AND BLOOD: The first written evidence of this is in Paul's First Letter to the Corinthians 11:23-29, written between 50 and 60 A.D. or C.E., in which Paul says that he received this information in a vision. In the last quarter of the First Century, some of the gospel writers write of it, quoting Jesus as having said it but giving no source for the information. Notwithstanding apostles' names being used as the titles for some of the gospels, the actual authorship of these texts is unknown. Generally, scholars do not attribute them to the apostles themselves. Hence, we find no witness to the supper making that report about Jesus' statement. Had any of the apostles heard it or witnessed it, it would not have been necessary for Paul to have gotten the information through a vision. He would surely have heard about it from Peter and the others. Also, the Nazarenes would have been reciting a different food prayer from the one they did recite, which was a prayer that contained nothing about Jesus' body and blood. Hence, the gospel writers must have gotten this information from Paul's First Letter to the Corinthians and then reported it as something that Jesus said.

In support of this, Schoeps (Jewish Christianity p. 62), referring to the Ebionites (Torah-adherent Jesus-followers), states, "On the same basis they celebrated the Lord's Supper as a mere remembrance of table-fellowship with Jesus and replaced the cup of blood with a cup of water (according to Irenaeus and Epiphanius). The Clementines, which knew no cup, give special emphasis to the breaking of bread with the sprinkling of salt, the salt symbolizing the incorruptibility of God's covenant with Israel."

EGYPTIANS CONSUMED GODS: Morton Smith, Jesus the Magician, On the Eucharist (Harper and Rowe 1978) p. 122.

GREEKS CONSUMED GODS: Greek Magical Papyri, Morton Smith, Jesus the Magician (Harper and Rowe 1978) pp. 122-123.

PAUL ON FOOD OFFERED TO IDOLS AND IRRELEVANCY OF DIET: First Letter to Corinthians 8:4, 8:8, 16:27-29; Letter to Colossians 2:16; Letter to Romans 14:3, 14:15, 14:17, 14:20-21, 14:23; First Letter to Timotheus. This should be compared to James' instructions to Paul in Acts 15:20 concerning dietary requirements for Gentiles who follow Jesus.

PAUL AND DISCIPLES TO MACEDONIA, GREECE: Acts 20:1-2.

PAUL CANCELS SYRIA TRIP BECAUSE OF DISGRUNTLED JEWS: Acts 20:3.

PAUL AND DISCIPLES TO PHILIPPI AND TROAS: Acts 20:5.

PAUL RESTORES EUTYCHUS: Acts 20:7-12.

PAUL AND DISCIPLES TO ASSOS, MITYLENE, SAMOS, TROGYLLIUM, MILETUS: Acts 20:14-15.

PAUL WANTS TO REACH JERUSALEM BY PENTACOST: Acts 20:16.

PAUL SPEAKS TO EPHESIAN ELDERS: Acts 20:17-38.

PAUL SAYS HE SUFFERED BECAUSE OF PLOTS OF "THE JEWS": Acts 20:19.

PAUL HINTS AT DANGER IN JERUSALEM: Acts 20:22-23, 20:25.

PAUL WARNS OF DISPARAGERS: Acts 20:29-30.

PAUL SAYS HE EARNED LIVELIHOOD BY LABOR OF HANDS, NOT CONTRIBUTIONS: Acts 20:33-34.

PAUL TEACHES CONTRIBUTIONS TO POOR: Acts 20:35.

EPICURUS TAUGHT GIVING: Klausner, From Jesus to Paul p. 87.

TORAH TEACHES GIVING: Leviticus 19:33-34; Deuteronomy 15:7-11.

PAUL AND DISCIPLES TO COS, RHODES, PATARA, TYRE: Acts 21:1-3.

PHILIP'S DAUGHTERS PROPHESY: Acts 21:9.

AGABUS PREDICTION FROM JESUS THAT JERUSALEM JEWS WILL BIND PAUL AND GIVE HIM TO GENTILES: Acts 21:10-11.

PAUL REJOICES IN SUFFERING FOR HIS FOLLOWERS: Letter to Colossians 1:24.

CHAPTER XXIV

BARNABAS AND SHARON: Fictional.

ALL NAZARENE DICIPLES AND EMISSARIES REQUIRED TO SEND ANNUAL REPORT TO JAMES: Schoeps, Jewish Christianity p. 39, as reported in Recognitions 1.60.

SECOND JERUSALEM COUNCIL MEETING: Acts 21:17. The approximate date of this event in this story is 58 A.D. or C.E. The reason for using that date: Paul became Felix's prisoner a few days after this Jerusalem meeting. He remained Felix's prisoner for the next two years. Felix then turned him over to Festus. Since Felix's procuratorship ended in 60 A.D. or C.E., I have placed Paul's first encounter with Felix (which occurred just after the Jerusalem meeting) at 58 A.D. or C.E. (Klausner gives 61 A.D. or C.E. as the year in which Felix's procuratorship ended. By that timetable, the Jerusalem meeting would have been in 59 A.D. or C.E.) Klausner (From Jesus to Paul p. 398) feels that Paul, who called Peter a hypocrite, was himself being hypocritical when he agreed to pray from the Torah in obedience to James.

JAMES HAD VISION OF JESUS: First Letter to Corinthians 15:7.

JAMES SAYS FAITH WITHOUT DEEDS, AS LISTED IN THE TORAH, IS INSUFFICIENT: Letter of James 1:22-25, 1:27, 2:8, 2:10, 2:14-26, 3:13, 4:17. James says that man is justified by works (good deeds). This should be compared to Paul's statement in Romans 3:28, in which he says, "For we hold that a man is justified by faith apart from works of law." Martin Luther recognized this discrepancy and chose in favor of Paul. He called the author of James' letter the Devil and felt that the Letter of James should be expunged from Christian literature. It appears that James and his adherence to the Torah constituted a problem for early Christians. They had been taught that the Torah was obsolete and that it had been replaced by a belief in Jesus' sacrificial death (antinomian principle). Thus it became advisable to diminish James, the great Torah advocate, even to the point of suggesting that he had not been Jesus' brother. Hence Eusebius refers to James as "one of the reputed brothers of the Lord" (Ecclesiastical History I xii) instead of "one of the brothers of the Lord," by which means he is able to cast doubt on the family relationship and render James and the Torah less important. Eusebius does this again when he writes, "...James...was called Christ's brother...", the use of "was called" instead of "was" suggesting a nickname rather than a true family relationship (Ecclesiastical History VII ixx).

JAMES SAYS PAROUSIA IS IMMINENT: Letter of James 5:8; Brandon, Jesus and Zealots pp. 241-242.

JAMES' SPEECH: Some of this is to be found in Acts 21:17-25. The conversation between James and Paul, while fictional, is consistent with each man's view and is meant to elucidate James' words in the Book of Acts.

PAUL AND BARNABAS CONVERSATION: Fictional. Acts account of the meeting with James does not reveal any revelation or discussion of divinity. Therefore, the Paul-Barnabas conversation on this subject is not contradictory to Acts. Likewise, at the meeting with James, no mention is made of the accusation that the Jews killed Jesus. Hence, again, the fictional conversation between Barnabas and Paul on that subject does not contradict the account of the council meeting in Acts.

PAUL CANNOT REVEAL ALL THAT WAS REVEALED TO HIM: Second Letter to Corinthians 12:4.

PAUL CARRIES JESUS' CRUCIFIXION MARKS: Letter to Galatians 6:17.

PAUL POMMELS HIMSELF: First Letter to Corinthians 9:27.

CHAPTER XXV

NAOMI'S DEATH: Fictional.

PAUL DISTINGUISHES BETWEEN EARTHLY AND SPIRITUAL BODIES:
First Letter to Corinthians 15:44.

OSIRIS RESURRECTION: Klausner, From Jesus to Paul p. 103.

BAAL-BEL-MARDUK RESURRECTION: Klausner, From Jesus to Paul p.
103.

ATTIS RESURRECTION: Klausner, From Jesus to Paul p. 105.

SICARII: Josephus, Jewish War 2.13.3, 7.10.1; Josephus, Antiquities 20.8.5,
20.8.10; Brandon , Jesus and Zealots pp. 31, 39, 40, 57, 67, 109-111, 115, 125,
126, 144, 204, 291-294, 305-306; Gager, Origins of Anti-Semitism p. 51. Brandon
reports that Josephus dates the beginning of the Sicarii during the procuratorship
of Felix: Brandon, Jesus and Zealots p. 204(1).

ZEALOTS PILLAGE OR KILL JEWISH COLLABORATORS WITH
ROMANS: Josephus, Antiquities 20.8.10.

ZEALOT SAYING: PICK UP YOUR CROSS AND FOLLOW ME: Brandon,
Jesus and Zealots p.57.

JESUS SAYS: IF ANY MAN WOULD COME AFTER ME, LET HIM DENY
HIMSELF AND TAKE UP HIS CROSS AND FOLLOW ME: Mark 8:34.

CROSS IS SYMBOL OF ZEALOTS: Brandon, Jesus and Zealots p. 145.

PAUL ACCOSTED BY ASIATIC JEWS: Acts 21:27, 21:30-31.

LYSIAS ARRESTS PAUL; CROWD FOLLOWS: Acts 21:31-33.

LYSIAS QUESTIONS PAUL: Acts 21:38.

EGYPTIAN REVOLUTIONARY MESSIAH: Josephus, Antiquities 20.8.6.

PAUL SAYS HE IS FROM TARSUS: Acts 21:39.

LYSIAS-MARCUS CONVERSATION: Fictional.

PAUL SPEAKS TO CROWD; SAYS HE IS PHARISEE, TAUGHT FROM
CHILDHOOD BY GAMALIEL: Acts 21:40, 22:1-21.

PAUL REVEALS ROMAN CITIZENSHIP TO AVOID FLOGGING: Acts
22:25.

LYSIAS SENDS PAUL TO SANHEDRIN: 58 A.D. or C.E. in this story. Acts 22:30.

CHAPTER XXVI

ANANIAS ANNOUNCES CHARGES AGAINST PAUL; ASKS DEATH PENALTY: Fictional.

PAUL SPEAKS IN HIS DEFENSE; ANANIAS HAS GUARD STRIKE HIM; PAUL REVILES ANANIAS; APOLOGIZES WHEN HE LEARNS ANANIAS IS HIGH PRIEST: Acts 23:1-5.

ASIATIC WITNESSES: Fictional.

CAIAPHAS' SPEECH: Fictional.

PAUL'S SPEECH: Fictional, but the theme of this is in Acts 23:6.

PHARISEE POLEMICS: Fictional.

LYSIAS TAKES PAUL FROM SANHEDRIN: Acts 23:10.

ASIATIC PLOT TO KILL PAUL: Acts 23:12-15.

ANANIAS' INVOLVEMENT IN ASIATIC PLOT: Acts 23:15.

JESUS IN VISION ORDERS PAUL TO ROME: Acts 23:11.

ABRAM VISIT: Fictional. If we accept Eisenman's identification of Paul of Tarsus as the "the Liar" in the Dead Sea Scrolls (Baigent and Leigh, Dead Sea Scrolls Deception p. 149), and as we see the Essene attitude towards that individual as a traitor to their hospitality and teaching, a conversation such as this between Paul and an Essene leader is entirely plausible.

PAUL CALLED SPEWER OF LIES WHO FOUNDED COMMUNITIES BASED ON DECEIT: The Dead Sea Scrolls mention such an individual but do not name him. Robert Eisenman identifies him as Paul (Baigent and Leigh, The Dead Sea Scrolls Deception, Summit Books, New York 1991, p. 149; The Dead Sea Scrolls Document Titled "Habakkuk", Ingenza Vermes, Ed., The Dead Sea Scrolls in English).

CHAPTER XXVII

PAUL'S NEPHEW DISCOVERS ASIATIC PLOT: Acts 23:16.

LYSIAS ORDERS PAUL TO CAESAREA: Acts 23:23.

REASON FOR PAUL'S LARGE ESCORT: Conjectural.

TERTULLUS LAUDATION TO FELIX: Acts 24:2-3. Embellished in this story.

TERTULLUS' CHARGES: Acts 24:1, 24:5-9.

TERTULLUS SAYS THEY WOULD HAVE EXECUTED PAUL HAD LYSIAS NOT INTERFERED: Fictional.

PAUL LAUDS FELIX: Acts 24:10.

PAUL'S DEFENSE BEFORE FELIX: Acts 24:10-21.

PAUL FOLLOWS TORAH, HE TELLS FELIX: Acts 24:14.

SADDUCEES HOPE FOR RESURRECTION, PAUL TELLS FELIX: Acts 24:15.

ANANIAS DENIES RESURRECTION BELIEF: Fictional but consistent with the philosophy of the Sadduces and chief priests.

PAUL CRITICIZES ASIATIC JEWS FOR ABSENCE FROM HEARING: Acts 24:19.

ANANIAS EXPLAINS ASIATICS' ABSENCE FROM HEARING: Fictional but serves to give some explanation for Asiatic absence.

FELIX'S ANALYSIS OF ASIATICS' ABSENCE FROM HEARING: Fictional.

PAUL TELLS FELIX RESURRECTION IS THE ISSUE: Acts 24:21.

ANANIAS TELLS FELIX RESURRECTION IS NOT THE ISSUE: Fictional.

FELIX MAKES PAUL PRISONER WITH FREEDOM OF CAESAREA: Acts 24:23.

FELIX WANTS BRIBE FROM PAUL: This is suggested by the author of Acts in Acts 24:26

PAUL HAS TAKEN CONTRIBUTION MONEY FOR PERSONAL SURVIVAL NEEDS: First Letter to Corinthians 9:4-7; Second Letter to Corinthians; Letter to Galatians 9:12.

FELIX WANTS DRUSILLA TO HEAR PAUL: Acts 24:24.

FELIX DISCUSSES PAUL, BERNICE, AGRIPPA WITH DRUSILLA: Fictional.

CHAPTER XXVIII

This chapter is fictional; however, in it, Caiaphas gives a possible explanation for his having taken Jesus to Pilate.

CHAPTER XXIX

In this story, the events take place during the 58-60 A.D. or C.E period.

JESUS REFERS TO MOSES AS AUTHORITY WHEN GIVING INSTRUCTION: Luke 5:14; Matthew 7:12, 19:17-20, 22:36-40; Mark 12:28-31.

PETER'S LETTER TO JAMES: Hennecke-Schneemelcher, New Testament Apocrypha p. 111; Gager, Origins of Anti-Semitism p. 186. While this may or may not have been an authentic letter written by Peter (it could have been written long after his death by a group such as the Ebionites), the position that it takes is entirely consistent with Peter's Gospel of the Circumcision. Schoeps (Jewish Christianity pp. 53-54) says that Peter became Paul's most vehement adversary and that Paul's gospel diverged from the teaching of the older apostles. Schoeps quotes Recognitions 2.55 as follows: "Whoever does not learn the law from teachers but instead regards himself as a teacher and scorns the instructions of the disciples of Jesus is bound to involve himself in absurdities against God." Schoeps states that Peter attacked Paul and called him antikeimenos, the great adversary. And, further, he reports (from Recognitions 3.61) that the early followers of Jesus considered Paul the "enemy" and even the Antichrist. He states, "That Paul had the truth and his opponents were in error is not the case! Nor can one say that Paul understood the person, intention, and teaching of Jesus better than the Pharisaic Jewish Christians of Jerusalem."
    In regard to the authenticity of this letter, Schoeps (Jewish Christianity pp. 16-17) states, "Of special interest is the letter of Peter which intoduces the Clementine writings with its appended adjuration, since it seems to represent a piece of the original writing which has not been altered as much as other parts."

PETER TRACES JESUS' LINEAGE THROUGH HIS FATHER, JOSEPH, TO KING DAVID: See a discussion of this under Jesus' Lineage in the NOTES for CHAPTER XII.

SOME CHRISTIANS TRACE JESUS' LINEAGE THROUGH MARY TO KING DAVID: See a discussion of this under JESUS' LINEAGE in the NOTES for CHAPTER XII.

PAUL WRITES TO GALATIANS AS TO HIS CHILDREN: Letter to Galatians 4:19.

PAUL WARNS GALATIANS ABOUT PETER'S GOSPEL: Letter to Galatians 1:6.

PAUL SAYS THERE IS NO OTHER GOSPEL: Letter to Galatians 1:7.

PAUL NAMES PETER'S GOSPEL AND HIS GOSPEL: Letter to Galatians 2:7.

PAUL CALLS CURSE ON ANYONE WHO TEACHES OTHER GOSPEL, EVEN AN ANGEL: Letter to Galatians 1:8-9.

PAUL MENTIONS TWO GOSPELS LATER IN HIS LETTER TO GALATIANS: Letter to Galatians 2:9.

PAUL'S ENCOUNTERS WITH JESUS' SPIRIT: Acts 16:6, 18:9, 19:21, 20:23, 23:11.

JESUS' ENCOUNTER WITH MOSES' AND ELIJAH'S SPIRITS: Matthew 17:3.

PAUL SAYS JESUS IS NOT DEAD: Letter to Galatians 6:9.

PAUL MAKES JESUS FOLLOWING AND TORAH FOLLOWING MUTUALLY EXCLUSIVE: Letter to Galatians 2:16, 2:21, 3:25, 5:2; Letter to Romans 3:20-22, 3:24-25, 3:28, 4:14, 7:4, 7:6, 9:31-32, 10:4; Second Letter to Corinthians 3:15-16; Letter to Ephesians 2:8-9.

FAILURE TO FOLLOW ONE PART OF TORAH IS FAILURE TO FOLLOW IT ALL: Letter to Galatians 3:10; Letter of James 2:10; Leviticus 26:14; Deuternomy 11:26, 28:15-68, 30:1, 30:8, 30:10; Matthew 5:19.

PAUL CALLS HIS FOLLOWERS ADOPTED SONS OF GOD: Letter to Galatians 4:5.

ALL NATIONAL, SOCIAL AND SEXUAL DIFFERENCES CEASE FOR CHRISTIANS: Letter to Galatians 3:28.

JAMES' EMISSARIES WILL ANSWER TO GOD: Letter to Galatians 5:10.

PAUL WISHES JAMES' EMISSARIES WOULD MUTILATE THEMSELVES: Letter to Galatians 5:12. I think we can conclude that Paul means castration.

PAUL LISTS SINS OF FLESH: Letter to Galatians 5:19-21.

PAUL SAYS CIRCUMCISION ADVOCATES INSINCERE: Letter to Galatians 6:13.

PAUL TELLS GALATIANS TO DO GOOD DEEDS: Letter to Galatians 6:9-10.

PAUL BEARS JESUS' CRUCIFIXION MARKS: Letter to Galatians 6:17.

JESUS IN VISIONS MORE RELIABLE THAN JESUS IN FLESH, SAYS PAUL: Letter to Galatians 1:11-12.

PAUL WRITES CORINTHIANS AGAIN: Second Letter to Corinthians. This particular letter may have been written from Rome, at a later time than presented in this story. For conciseness, I have Paul writing it along with other letters from Caesarea during his confinement there.

PAUL TELLS CORINTHIANS HE AVOIDED ASKING THEM FOR MONEY: Second Letter to Corinthians 11:7-9.

PAUL TELLS EPHESIANS HE HAS NOT ASKED THEM FOR MONEY: Acts 20:34.

PAUL TELLS THESSALONIANS HE HAS NOT ASKED THEM FOR MONEY: First Letter to Thessalonians 2:9; Second Letter to Thessalonians 3:7-8.

PAUL TELLS CORINTHIANS HE TOOK MONEY FROM OTHER CHURCHES TO AVOID ASKING IT OF THEM: Second Letter to Corinthians 11:8.

PAUL CLAIMS RIGHT TO ASK MONEY FOR PREACHING: First Letter to Corinthians 9:4-6, 9:11-12, 9:14; Second Letter to Thessalonians 3:9; First Letter to Timotheus 5:17-18.

PAUL ASKS WHAT IS WRONG WITH FOLLOWERS SUPPORTING HIM IF HE BRINGS SPIRITUAL COMFORT: First Letter to Corinthians 9:11.

PAUL SAYS THE LORD ALLOWS CHURCH SUPPORT OF PREACHERS: First Letter to Corinthians 9:8-9 (in which Paul avers that Moses also supported that), 9:14.

PAUL GIVES GOSPEL FREE OF CHARGE: First Letter to Corinthians 9:18.

PAUL DECLINES HIS RIGHT TO LIVE OFF CONTRIBUTIONS: First Letter to Corinthians 9:12, 9:18.

JESUS TAUGHT NOT TO TAKE PAYMENT FOR PREACHING: Matthew 10:8.

PAUL WRITES TO TIMOTHEUS: First Letter to Timotheus. Paul wrote two letters to Timotheus, the second possibly from Rome. For the sake of conciseness in this story, I have placed some of the material from the second letter into this first letter. The material itself is general and is not something that would not have existed at the time the first letter was written. In general, and for the same reason, I have done this with other second letters that Paul wrote to certain Christian communities.

PAUL WARNS AGAINST THOSE TEACHING DIFFERENT DOCTRINE: First Letter to Timotheus 1:3, 4:7.

PAUL SAYS SOME CHRISTIANS WILL FOLLOW DOCTRINES OF DEMONS IN FUTURE: First Letter to Timotheus 4:1.

PAUL TURNS DISLOYAL DISCIPLES OVER TO DEVIL: First Letter to Timotheus 1:19-20.

PAUL CALLS PETER'S GOSPEL THE GOSPEL OF THE DEVIL: Second Letter to Corinthians 11:14-15.

PAUL SAYS PREACHERS OF PETER'S GOSPEL ARE LIARS: First Letter to Corinthians 4:2.

PAUL SAYS TO AVOID JESUS GENEALOGIES: First Letter to Timotheus 1:4.

PAUL TELLS TIMOTHEUS JESUS DESCENDED FROM KING DAVID: Second Letter to Timotheus 2:8.

JESUS CAME TO SAVE SINNERS, SAYS PAUL: First Letter to Timotheus 1:15.

INTERMEDIARY BETWEEN GOD AND MAN NOW NECESSARY: First Letter to Timotheus 2:5-6; Letter to Romans 8:26, 8:34; Letter to Hebrews 9:15, 12:24.

PAUL SAYS HE IS GREATEST SINNER: First Letter to Timotheus 1:15.

WOMEN TO DRESS PLAINLY AND BE SUBSERVIENT, SAYS PAUL: First Letter to Timotheus 2:9-11.

PAUL PERMITS NO WOMAN TO PREACH OR HAVE AUTHORITY OVER MEN: First Letter to Timotheus 2:12.

PAUL SAYS WOMEN EQUAL TO MEN: Letter to Galatians 3:28.

PAUL TELLS TITUS TO AVOID JESUS GENEALOGIES: Letter to Titus 3:9.

PAUL WARNS TITUS ABOUT PETER'S GOSPEL: Letter to Titus 1:9-16, 2:1.

TEACHERS OF CIRCUMCISION AND OF PETER'S GOSPEL ARE DECEIVERS AND TEACH FALSELY, SAYS PAUL: Letter to Titus 1:10; Letter to Romans 16:18; Second Letter to Corinthians 11:13.

TEACHERS OF PETER'S GOSPEL MUST BE SILENCED: Letter to Titus 1:11.

PETER'S GOSPEL IS A JEWISH FABLE: Letter to Titus 1:14.

PAUL SAYS MOSAIC COMMANDMENTS COME FROM ANGELS, NOT GOD: Letter to Galatians 3:19. This supports the contention that the Torah is temporary. In Acts 7:53, Stephen says that the law was delivered by angels.

PAUL SAYS DISBELIEVERS IN HIS GOSPEL ARE CORRUPT AND DETESTABLE: Letter to Titus 1:15-16.

CHAPTER XXX

ANANIAS DEPOSED AS HIGH PRIEST: Date about 59 A.D. or C.E.

ISHMAEL AS HIGH PRIEST: 59-61 A.D. OR C.E. Josephus, Antiquities 20.8.8.

SICARII ASSASSINATE JONATHAN: Josephus, Antiquities 20.8.5. Estimated date in this story 59 A.D. or C.E. Josephus calls Jonathan the high priest at the time of his assassination. If he was the high priest at that time, he must have been appointed between the time of Ananias' removal from that office and Ishmael's appointment to it. Having been the high priest once (appointed by Vitellius), Jonathan declined that position when it was offered to him a second time (Josephus, Antiquities 19.6.4). The confusion is caused by the use of the term, "high priest". In Acts 4:6, the author refers to the former high priest Annas (Ananus, son of Seth) as the "high priest" when he encounters Peter in the street. Yet Caiaphas was actually the high priest at that time. In The Antiquities of the Jews 20.9.2, Josephus refers to Ananias as high priest at a time when Jesus, son of Damnaios, held that position. In The Wars of the Jews 2.17.9, Josephus refers to Ananias as high priest at a time when Jesus, son of Gamaliel, held that position. In The Wars of the Jews 4.5.2, Josephus refers to Ananus as high priest at a time when Matthias, son of Theophilus, held that position. Finally, in The Wars of the Jews 4.5.2, Josephus reports that the Idumaeans sought out "high priests". It appears that high priests either retained their titles after leaving office or else that Josephus uses the terms, "chief priests" and "high priests" synonymously. It is, therefore, most probable that Jonathan was not the high priest at the time of his assassination and that Ishmael followed Ananias in that office. Jack Finegan, in his Light From the Ancient Past, pages 262-263(43), shows Ishmael following Ananias as high priest, which supports this view. The footnote in the William Whiston edition of Josephus', The Antiquities of the Jews (20.8.5d), in which *Jonathas* is listed as high priest between Ananias and Ishmael, is possibly a misinterpretation caused by Josephus' reference to Jonathan as high priest at the time of his assassination.

JEWISH-SYRIAN DISAGREEMENT OVER CAESAREA: Josephus, Antiquities 20.8.7; Josephus, Jewish War 2.13.7; Brandon, Jesus and Zealots p. 115.

FELIX'S PROCURATORSHIP ENDS; FESTUS' BEGINS: Estimated date in this story is 60 A.D. or C.E. Josephus, Antiquities 20.8.9; Brandon, Jesus and Zealots p. 114.

CHIEF PRIESTS ACCUSE PAUL BEFORE FESTUS: Acts 25:2. Because of conflicting statements made in the Book of Acts, there is some question about who accused Paul to Festus. In Acts 25:2, the author states, "...the chief priests and the principal men of the Jews informed against Paul;" but in Acts 25:24, the author reports Festus saying to King Agrippa II, "...this man about whom the whole Jewish people petitioned me, both at Jerusalem and here, shouting that he ought not to live any longer." The events described in the latter statement, in which "the whole Jewish people" are involved, are not found anywhere else in the narrative. Aside from the problem of explaining how *all the Jewish people* could have conveyed to Festus a common demand for Paul's death, one wonders why such mass petitionings, occurring successively in two major cities, were not described as they purportedly occurred (as the hostile crowd with Captain Claudius Lysias, for example, and the petitioning by the chief priests had been), rather than as a belated revelation in a conversation between two rulers. The author continues his theme that the Jews and not just the chief priests accused Paul when, in Acts 26:2, Paul says, "...I am to make my defense today against all the accusations of the Jews." One might also wonder why "the whole Jewish people" did not petition Felix for Paul's death during the two years that Felix had him in custody and why they were now petitioning for Paul's death in defiance of the Sanhedrin sentiment in his favor.

In this story, I have avoided the discrepancy in Acts about who the accusers were by adhering to the first alleged accusers mentioned.

CHIEF PRIESTS SAY BELIEF IN JESUS' RESURRECTION IS A CRIME: Acts 25:19. Since the chief priests were Sadducees, it is understandable that they might bring a charge against Paul involving resurrection (but why to a Roman?), especially since no Pharisees (all of whom believed in resurrection) were there to object. But, contrary to the claim of the author of Acts that "the Jews" brought that charge, it is impossible that such a charge would have been brought by all the Jewish people, first because not all Jews lived in Israel at that time, and second and more important because most of the Jewish people *believed* in resurrection and so many thousands of them had proved their belief in *Jesus'* resurrection by joining the Nazarene movement.

PAUL DENIES OFFENDING TORAH, TEMPLE, OR EMPEROR: Acts 25:8.

CHIEF PRIESTS WANT PAUL TRIED IN JERUSALEM: Acts 25:3.

FESTUS ASKS PAUL IF HE WANTS TO STAND TRIAL IN JERUSALEM: Acts 25:9. The author of Acts gives no reason why Festus *asked* Paul about the change in venue rather than ordering it. Possibly Paul was being given consideration that was not given to other prisoners because of his Roman citizenship.

PAUL'S SPEECH TO FESTUS: Acts 25:8.

PAUL DEMANDS A HEARING BEFORE EMPEROR: Acts 25:11.

AGRIPPA AND BERNICE JOIN FESTUS: Acts 25:13.

FESTUS TELLS AGRIPPA AND BERNICE ABOUT PAUL: Acts 25:14-15.

ROMANS DO NOT EXECUTE WITHOUT TRIAL, SAYS FESTUS: Acts 25:16.

EXPLANATION FOR PAUL'S FREEDOM UNDER FELIX: Acts 24:26. The author of Acts suggests extortion but does not say it definitely occurred.

EXPLANATION FOR FELIX BINDING PAUL BEFORE LEAVING OFFICE: In the Book of Acts 24:27, the author reports that the reason for this was that Felix wanted to please the Jews. This then leads to the question of why Felix did not want to please the Jews during the two preceding years of Paul's captivity. This story suggests two plausible explanations.

Also, in Caesarea, Felix whips, imprisons, kills and plunders Jews in favor of the Gentiles (Josephus, Antiquities 20.8.7; Josephus, Jewish War 2.13.7). Shortly after that, Felix must leave his governorship. But now, according the Book of Acts, in contradistinction to his previous proclivities *against* the Jews, he now wants to please them. This flies in the face of consistency.

A further strain on credulity is the Book of Acts' claim that the Jews themselves would have been pleased to see Paul chained. Pharisee leaders of the Jews in the Sanhedrin had fought to save his life (Acts 23:9). Why would they now want him chained?

BERNICE JEALOUS OF DRUSILLA: Josephus, Antiquities 20.7.2.

AGRIPPA I WAS PIOUS: Brandon, Jesus and Zealots p. 93, referring to Danby, The Mishnah pp. 97, 301 (from Sotah, vii. 8) and referring to Bikkurim, III. 4.

AGRIPPA II WAS NOT PIOUS: Josephus, Antiquities 20.8.11; Brandon, Jesus and Zealots p. 115.

ROMANS CHEERED DEATH OF TIBERIUS: Josephus, Antiquities 18.6.10.

PAUL'S SPEECH TO AGRIPPA: Acts 26:1-23. Interestingly, in Acts 26:2, the author reports Paul as saying that the accusations were brought against him by the Jews, while in Acts 25:2 the author says that it was the chief priests. This discrepancy is due either to the author's neglectfulness in completing the transfer of ill will from chief priests to all Jews or else to his attempt to show a unity between chief priests and all other Jews. If it is the latter, then the later execution of the chief priests by the Jewish people, once the people took control of the city, is by itself, without additional evidences to the contrary, an historical refutation of that canard.

Early Christians, however, had been led to believe that the entire Jewish people were against Jesus and his followers. Thus we find Eusebius speaking of the calamities that befell the Jews "...after their conspiracy against our Saviour" (Ecclesiastical History I i) and "...the intrigue destined to be levelled against Him by the Jewish people" (Ecclesiastical History I iii). These contentions encompass all the Jewish people and not just chief priests and Sadducees.

PAUL CLAIMS UPBRINGING IN JERUSALEM: Acts 26:4. In Acts 21:39, however, Paul tells Captain Claudius Lysias that he is a citizen of Tarsus, implying that his origin and upbringing were there.

PAUL TELLS AGRIPPA HE IS A PHARISEE: Acts 26:5.

WAS PAUL A SADDUCEE WHEN HE WORKED FOR THE SADDUCEE HIGH PRIEST, CAIAPHAS? It would certainly have been to Paul's advantage if he had been. It is not likely that he would have been a Pharisee holding such a position, considering the animosity between Sadducees and Pharisees. He could have been a God-fearer, however, which is what Malthus, the Arab, (the man whose ear Peter sliced off at Gethsemane) may have been when he worked for Caiaphas — unless, of course, Malthus had become a Jew and, specifically, a Sadducee one.

PAUL TELLS AGRIPPA II ABOUT DAMASCUS ROAD VISION: Acts 26:12-18. The differences in details between this version and the others in Acts have been discussed previously. (See NOTES for CHAPTER VIII.)

MOSES AND PROPHETS PREDICTED CHRIST WOULD BE FIRST TO RISE FROM DEAD, SAYS PAUL: Acts 26:22-23.

AGRIPPA'S QUESTION ABOUT FIRST RESURRECTION: Fictional but shows the need for clarification of this point.

AGRIPPA'S QUESTION ABOUT KINGDOM OF GOD: Fictional.

PAUL SAYS JESUS WILL DELIVER KINGDOM TO GOD AFTER DESTROYING EVERY AUTHORITY: First Letter to Corinthians 15:24.

AFFAIR BETWEEN BERNICE AND AGRIPPA: Josephus tells of a report that there was a "criminal conversation" between Bernice and her brother, which was the cause of her leaving his household and marrying the King of Cilicia (Josephus, Antiquities 20.7.3). The nature of this conversation is conjectural, but, considering the closeness of Bernice and Agrippa and their frequent appearances together (something that Agrippa did not do with Drusilla when she lived with him), an incestuous relationship, for the purposes of this story, is not inconceivable.

BERNICE MARRIES POLEMO, KING OF CILICIA: Josephus, Antiquities 20.7.3.

CHAPTER XXXI

AGRIPPA'S BUILDING SITE FOR DINING ROOM IN PALACE: Josephus, Antiquities 20.8.11.

EMPRESS POPPAEA: Josephus, Antiquities 20.8.11.

ISHMAEL DEPOSED FROM HIGH PRIESTHOOD: Josephus, Antiquities 20.8.11.

JOSEPH CABI, SON OF SIMON, HIGH PRIEST: 61-62 A.D. or C.E. Josephus, Antiquities 20.8.11.

BERNICE LEAVES KING POLEMO AND REJOINS AGRIPPA: Estimated date in this story is 61 A.D. or C.E. Josephus, Antiquities 20.7.3.

BERNICE AND AGRIPPA DISCUSS THEIR AFFAIR VIS-A-VIS TORAH: Fictional.

MARIAMNE LEAVES HUSBAND ARCHELAUS AND MARRIES DEMETRIUS: Estimated date in this story is 61 A.D. or C.E. Josephus, Antiquities 20.7.3.

LOWER PRIESTS BECOME ZEALOTS : Brandon, Jesus and Zealots p. 114, referring to Jeremias, Jerusalem, II, 60-87.

JAMES GIVEN HONORARY PRIESTLY STATUS: Brandon, Jesus and Zealots p. 122, referring to Eusebius, Ecclesiatical History II xxxiii, 5-6.

JAMES CALLED "JAMES THE JUST" AND "THE RAMPART OF THE PEOPLE AND OF RIGHTEOUSNESS": Klausner, From Jesus to Paul p. 278; Brandon, Jesus and Zealots p. 122 -123, referring to Eusebius, Ecclesiatical History II xxxiii, 7.

JAMES SAYS JESUS WILL RETURN SOON: Letter of James 5:8.

FESTUS DIES: The date in this story is 62 A.D. or C.E. Josephus, Antiquities 20.9.1.

ANANUS, SON OF ANNAS, HIGH PRIEST: 62 A.D. or C.E. for three months. Josephus, Antiquities 20.9.1.

ANANUS EXECUTES JAMES BY STONING: 62 A.D. or C.E. Josephus, Antiquities 20.9.1. The reason for James' execution is conjectural. If the real reason was because of the denial of incomes to the lower priests by the chief priests (a punishment for the lower priests joining the Zealot and Nazarene movements), and because of James' public declamations against this, then Ananus, understandably, would not have wanted that reason to be known and also would not have been able to bring charges against James on that basis. Another sort of charge would have had to be concocted — one that had legal legitimacy on either political or religious grounds. Both sedition and violation of the Torah satisfied that requirement. Whereas, customarily, a sedition charge would not be handled by the high priest, the absence of a procurator at that time did allow Ananus the excuse, if he wanted to use it, of having to act in the capacity of a procurator because of the immediate danger to the public order being posed by a fomenter of rebellion. Likewise, if a religious violation charge was used (instead of a sedition one), Ananus could again act without the customary procurator's permission to execute such offenders, by saying that no procurator was present and that the matter could not wait. Unfortunately, the historical literature gives us no concrete information about the actual crime for which James and his close associates were executed. Brandon (Jesus and Zealots pp. 125, 169, 189) also gives possible explanations for the execution.

NEW PROCURATOR ALBINUS ARRIVES IN JUDAEA: Josephus, Antiquities 20.9.1.

PROMINENT JEWS COMPLAIN TO ALBINUS ABOUT JAMES' EXECUTION: Josephus, Antiquities 20.9.1.

PROMINENT JEWS COMPLAIN TO AGRIPPA II ABOUT JAMES' EXECUTION: Josephus, Antiquities 20.9.1. It seems highly unlikely that these prominent Jews who complained about Ananus were Sadducees, since Ananus himself was a Sadducee. The only non-Sadducee prominent Jews would have been Pharisee members of the Sanhedrin.

ANANUS DEPOSED AS HIGH PRIEST: About 62 A.D. or C.E. in this story. Josephus, Antiquities 20.9.1.

JESUS, SON OF DAMNAIOS, APPOINTED HIGH PRIEST: 62-63 A.D. or C.E. Josephus, Antiquities 20.9.1.

ALL JESUS' BROTHERS DEAD: Brandon, Jesus and Zealots p. 166.

JESUS' COUSIN, SYMEON, SON OF CLEOPHAS, SUCCEEDS JAMES AS HEAD OF NAZARENES: Brandon, Jesus and Zealots p. 165(4), referring to Eusebius, Ecclesiatical History II xxxiii, 1.

PAUL THROUGH STORM TO MELITA (MALTA): Acts 28:1.

PAUL SURVIVES VIPER BITE: Acts 28:3-5.

MELITA PEOPLE THINK PAUL IS A GOD: Acts 28:6.

PAUL HEALS MELITA PEOPLE: Acts 28:8-9.

PAUL ARRIVES IN ROME: Acts 28:14.

PAUL IN CHAINS UNDER HOUSE ARREST WITH GUARD: Acts 28:16.

PAUL TELLS ROMAN JEWS THAT THOUGH HE HAD DONE NOTHING AGAINST JUDAISM, HE WAS DELIVERED A PRISONER FROM JERUSALEM TO THE ROMANS: Acts 28:17. This statement implies that persons who were not Romans did the delivering. Yet the author of Acts elsewhere says that the Romans delivered him (Acts 23:31-33).

PAUL TELLS ROMAN JEWS THAT FESTUS WANTED HIM FREE BUT THAT JEWISH OBJECTIONS FORCED HIS APPEAL TO CAESAR; SAYS NOTHING OF JESUS' INSTRUCTION TO GO TO ROME: Acts 28:18-19.

PAUL TELLS ROMAN JEWS ALL JEWISH PEOPLE (ISRAEL) HOPED HE BE FOUND GUILTY: Acts 28:20. Paul says nothing about the Pharisees fighting for him against the Sadducees. Also, see PAUL'S SPEECH TO AGRIPPA in NOTES for CHAPTER XXX.

ROMAN JEWISH LEADERS SAY THEY RECEIVED NO BAD REPORTS ABOUT PAUL: Acts 28:21. Obviously, what the Roman Jewish leaders were confused about was that a person whom so many Jewish people purportedly wished to harm, was not mentioned by Jewish travelers bringing news to them from Jerusalem.

PAUL PREACHES TO JEWS IN ROME: Acts 28:23.

PAUL ANGERED AT UNBELIEVING JEWS; SWEARS FUTURE PREACHING ONLY TO GENTILES: Acts 28:24-29.

PAUL PREACHES IN ROME TWO YEARS: Acts 28:30.

CHAPTER XXXII

ELEAZAR, SON OF ANANIAS, COMMANDER OF TEMPLE; HIS SCRIBE TAKEN HOSTAGE BY SICARII: Josephus, Antiquities 20.9.3.

SICARII PRISONERS EXCHANGED FOR HOSTAGES: Josephus, Antiquities 20.9.3.

JESUS, SON OF DAMNAIOS, DEPOSED FROM HIGH PRIESTHOOD: Josephus, Antiquities 20.9.4.

JESUS, SON OF GAMALIEL, APPOINTED HIGH PRIEST: Josephus, Antiquities 20.9.4. According to Finegan, Light From the Ancient Past p. 262(43), this took place in 63 A.D. or C.E.

VESTMENTS OF LEVITES: Josephus, Antiquities 20.9.6.

UNEMPLOYMENT IN JERUSALEM: Josephus, Antiquities 20.9.7.

JESUS, SON OF GAMALIEL, DEPOSED AS HIGH PRIEST: Josephus, Antiquities 20.9.7. According to Finegan, Light From the Ancient Past p. 262(43), the tenure of Jesus, son of Gamaliel, as high priest was 63-65 A.D. or C.E. Since Florus replaced Albinus as procurator in 64 A.D. or C.E., this would place the end of the high priesthood of Jesus, son of Gamaliel, one year into Florus' reign. But Josephus describes the end of that high priesthood in the chapter in which he is still discussing Albinus as procurator (Antiquities 20.10.7). Josephus does not start to describe Florus' reign until one chapter later (Antiquities 20.11.1). In this story, therefore, I have described the end of the high priesthood of Jesus, son of Gamaliel, as taking place in 64 A.D. or C.E.

ROME FIRE; NERO IN ANTIUM: 64 A.D. or C.E. Hammerton, New Illustrated World History p. 274; Time-Life Books, Empires Ascendant p. 84.

NERO CALLED "THE GOOD GOD": Klausner, From Jesus to Paul p. 111(45).

JESUS' FOLLOWERS ASK WHEN HE WILL RESTORE KINGDOM TO ISRAEL: Acts 1:6.

PAUL SAYS JESUS WILL DELIVER KINGDOM TO GOD AFTER DESTROYING EVERY AUTHORITY: First Letter to Corinthians 15:24.

CHRISTIANS PREDICT KINGDOM OF WORLD WILL BECOME KINGDOM OF LORD GOD AND HIS CHRIST: Revelations 11:15.

PAUL SAYS JESUS' KINGDOM NOT IN THIS WORLD: John 18:36. There is no direct evidence that Paul made such a statement. The reference for it here is from a document that was written in the last quarter of the First Century, well after Paul's death, with the author attributing the statement to Jesus. Disregarding the improbability of Jesus having said it, in the light of all the evidence that his kingdom was to be on the earth (Acts 1:6; First Letter to Corinthians 15:24; Revelations 11:15; his involvement with Simon, one of the Zealots, all of whom fought for an earthly kingdom of God, as is reported in Acts 1:13, Matthew 10:4, Mark 3:18 and Luke 3:15; Eusebius, Ecclesiastical History IV xi, xxxiii, 1-4, in which even Symeon, Jesus' cousin, was executed at the end of the First Century because the Romans feared him trying to set himself up as a king), the question arises as to whether Paul could have made such a statement. In his First Letter to the Corinthians 15:24, Paul says what amounts to the opposite. Yet the claim for a heavenly kingdom of Jesus as opposed to an earthly one occurred somewhere in Christian evolution. That it may have occurred after Paul's death and for the same reasons as given in this story, is certainly a possibility. In this story, however, I have had *Paul* making the change, and not necessarily because he believed it but because he wanted to deceive the Romans so that they would stop molesting the Christians. In this story, Paul maintains his belief in an earthly kingdom of Jesus (albeit in secret) while professing (for Roman consumption) a kingdom only in heaven. Whether he was or was not responsible for the heavenly-kingdom-only concept, his followers certainly promoted it into an established Christian idea.

JESUS' ATTITUDE TOWARDS ROMAN TAXES: In Luke 23:2, Jesus is accused of having been against the payment of taxes to Rome. This is consistent with the attitudes of Judas of Galilee, the Zealots and the mass of the Jewish people. In Mark 12:17, Matthew 22:21 and Luke 20:22-25, however, Jesus, upon being shown a Roman coin and asked about Roman taxes, is reported as saying, "Render to Caesar the things that are Caesar's and to God the things that are God's."

Christians, at the time when the gospels were written, were considered political rebels by the Romans. Nero's persecution of them and the accusation that they had set Rome on fire (presumably as an act of rebellion) reflected that particular Roman belief about their politics. The belief persisted even to the end of the First Century and was certainly there when the Romans arrested Jesus' aging cousin, Symeon, as a political upstart and killed him in obedience to Vespasian's original edict that all descendants of the House of David be executed. It is understandable, then, that Christians at that time would have wanted to present themselves in a non-political light for purposes of survival. Therefore, evidence to the contrary notwithstanding, Jesus was to be presented to the world as an advocate of Roman taxation. Whether Jesus actually uttered that passage about the Roman coin or whether it was an insertion by Christians themselves, the *interpretation*, in either case, was to be one of advocacy of taxation. The fact that that interpretation conflicted with Luke's account in 23:2 was not addressed.

If the passage about the coin was actually stated by Jesus, then the question becomes solely one of interpretation. A superficial interpretation shows advocacy; an underlying one shows the opposite. By an underlying interpretation, I mean that if Jesus *had* been against Roman taxation (as reported in Luke 23:2), he may have wanted to say it in such a way that the authorities could not pin him down — especially on this one occasion when he was being baited. If Jesus' real message was to give money to God and to give nothing to the Romans (which is what the Jewish people were expecting their Messiah to say), then better to obfuscate the answer through a *specious* advocacy of taxation and trust that those who know you will know what you really mean. In such a case, the contradiction between Luke 23:2 on the one hand and Mark 12:17 and Matthew 22:21 and Luke 20:22-25 on the other ceases to exist.

Brandon (Jesus and Zealots p. 348) believes this coin passage reflects that Jesus was saying *not* to give money to Rome, and he says, "...he would never have been popularly regarded as the Messiah, if he had ruled that the Jews had rightly to pay tribute to Rome" (Brandon, Jesus and Zealots p. 347).

Further support for this view as opposed to the advocacy view is seen in the Gospels (Luke 5:30-32 is representative of this), in which Jesus, when asked why he is sitting with tax collectors, says, "Those who are well have no need of a physician, but those who are sick; I have not come to call the righteous, but sinners to repentance." Obviously, Jesus considered tax collectors as unrighteous and in need of correction — not a very favorable attitude towards taxes and tax collecting. Likewise, in Matthew 6:46, Jesus imputes moral deficiency to tax collectors when he tells us to love our enemies and says, "For if you love those who love you, what reward have you? Do not even tax collectors do the same?" (In other words, even tax collectors, as evil as they are, love people who love them; you who are good must exceed that and love those who hate you.)

PAUL'S ATTITUDE TOWARDS ROMAN TAXES: In Letter to Romans 13:6-7, Paul tells Jews to pay them.

PAUL BLAMES "THE JEWS" FOR JESUS' CRUCIFIXION: Acts 13:27-28; First Letter to Thessalonians 2:14-15; Brandon, Jesus and Zealots pp. 256-258, 303. Also see STEPHEN'S PRE-EXECUTION REMARKS in NOTES for CHAPTER VI and PAUL'S SPEECH TO AGRIPPA in NOTES for CHAPTER XXX.

CHRISTIANS DESCRIBE PILATE AS MERCIFUL: Mark 15:6-15.

CHRISTIANS REMOVE POLITICAL GOALS FROM JESUS: John 18:36; Brandon, Jesus and Zealots pp. 17-18, 280-282.

JESUS FOLLOWING INCREASES IN JUDAEA AS WELL AS ROME: Finegan, Light From the Ancient Past pp. 378-379, referring to Tacitus, Annals, 15th Book, in which Tacitus says, "The deadly superstition, having been checked for awhile, began to break out again, not only throughout Judaea where this mischief first arose, but also at Rome...".

NERO BLAMES ROME FIRE ON CHRISTIANS: Hammerton, New Illustrated World History p. 274; Time-Life Books, Empires Ascendant p.84; Klausner, From Jesus to Paul p.420.

NERO THROWS CHRISTIANS TO DOGS: Finegan, Light From the Ancient Past pp. 378-379, referring to Tacitus, Annals, 15th Book.

NERO TORCHES CHRISTIANS IN GARDEN: Hammerton, New Illustrated World History p. 274; Time-Life Books, Empires Ascendant p.84; Finegan, Light From the Ancient Past pp. 378-379, referring to Tacitus, Annals, 15th Book.

PAUL TRAVELS TO SPAIN: Klausner (From Jesus to Paul pp. 246-247, 417) points out the contradictions between what we find in the Book of Acts and what we find in Paul's letters and relates that certain scholars, in order to reconcile these differences, have proposed an hypothesis of a second imprisonment of Paul. The hypothesis: the Romans released Paul from imprisonment for a time; Paul traveled to Spain to preach (as he said he wanted to do in his Letter to the Romans 15:24, 15:28); Paul returned to Rome to face imprisonment again.

Finegan (Finegan, Light From the Ancient Past p. 377), after tracing Paul to the end of the Book of Acts, in which Paul is reported to have spent two years preaching freely in Rome, says, "Whether his martyrdom followed at the close of these two years, as the further silence of Acts might seem to imply, cannot now be said with certainty. Perhaps he was set free at the expiration of that period and enabled to achieve his cherished purpose of preaching in Spain (Romans 15:24, 28), before eventually suffering death in Rome." In a reference note on that page, Finegan says, "I Clement 5, which is quoted more fully just below, gives support to this view for it speaks of Paul as 'having come to the farthest bounds of the West,' which to one writing in Rome as Clement did surely would have meant Spain." This same reference and interpretation was made by Staniforth in his translation of Clement's letter to the Corinthians (Staniforth, Maxwell: Early Christian Writings, The Apostolic Fathers, Penguin Classics pp. 25, 58), in which Clement writes of Paul having reached "...the furthest limits of the West," which Staniforth interprets as "The Pillars of Hercules (Straits of Gibraltar)," and which Staniforth takes as evidence that Paul did reach Spain. The Muratorian Fragment (middle of the 2d century A.D.) also refers to 'the departure of Paul from the city (i.e. Rome) on his journey to Spain.' (ASBACH p. 118)."

CHAPTER XXXIII

GESSIUS FLORUS BECOMES PROCURATOR: 64 A.D. or C.E. Josephus, Antiquities 20.11.1.

FLORUS EXTORTS MONEY: Josephus, Antiquities 20.11.1; Josephus, Jewish War 2.14.2.

JEWS APPEAL TO FLORUS: Josephus, Jewish War 2.14.2.

FLORUS DESIRES REBELLION: Josephus, Jewish war 2.14.3.

NERO'S CAESAREA DECISION FAVORS GREEKS OVER JEWS: Josephus, Jewish War 2.14.4.

GREEK BUILDING PROVOCATION AT JEWISH SYNAGOGUE: Josephus, Jewish War 2.14.4.

JEWS BRIBE FLORUS: Josephus, Jewish War 2.14.4.

GREEK BIRD-SACRIFICE PROVOCATION AT JEWISH SYNAGOGUE: Josephus, Jewish War 2.14.5.

JEWS FLEE TO NARBATH: Josephus, Jewish War 2.14.5.

FLORUS RESENTS BRIBE REMINDER AND IMPRISONS JEWS: Josephus, Jewish War 2.14.5.

BERNICE SEEKS GAMALIEL'S ADVICE: Fictional.

FLORUS TO JERUSALEM FOR TEMPLE TREASURE: Josephus, Jewish War 2.14.6.

CAPITO'S CAVALRY DISPERSES PEACEFUL JERUSALEM JEWS: Josephus, Jewish War 2.14.7.

FLORUS SLAUGHTERS JERUSALEM JEWS: Josephus, Jewish War 2.14.9.

FLORUS THREATENS PRINCESS BERNICE: Josephus, Jewish War 2.15.1.

FLORUS' NEW CAVALRY SCATTERS JEWISH WELCOMERS: Josephus, Jewish War 2.15.3.

JEWS FIGHT FLORUS' SOLDIERS: Josephus, Jewish War 2.15.5.

FLORUS LEAVES JERUSALEM: Josephus, Jewish War 2.15.6.

FLORUS TELLS GALLUS JERUSALEM JEWS REVOLTED: Josephus, Jewish War 2.16.1.

BERNICE WRITES GALLUS OF FLORUS' TYRANNY: Josephus, Jewish War 2.16.1.

GALLUS' ENVOY, NEAPOLITANUS, FINDS JERUSALEM JEWS INNOCENT OF REBELLION: Josephus, Jewish War 2.16.1-2.

UNEMPLOYMENT IN JERUSALEM AFTER WHITE BRICK LAID: Presumed. The more than eighteen-thousand workmen unemployed after the completion of the Temple, who were then given temporary employment paving the city, had to become unemployed again at some point in time when the paving work was completed.

BERNICE TELLS AGRIPPA AFFAIR IS OVER: Fictional.

AGRIPPA'S FIRST SPEECH ACCEPTED BY THE PEOPLE: Josephus, Jewish War 2.17.1.

AGRIPPA'S SECOND SPEECH REJECTED BY THE PEOPLE: Josephus, Jewish War 2.17.1.

CHAPTER XXXIV

MENAHEM AND ZEALOTS TAKE MASADA: 66 A.D. or C.E. Josephus, Jewish War 2.17.2; Brandon, Jesus and Zealots p. 131.

ELEAZAR, SON OF ANANIAS, STOPS TEMPLE SACRIFICES FOR ROMANS: Josephus, Jewish War 2.17.2-3.

AGRIPPA'S ANTI-REBELLION TROOPS TO JERUSALEM: Josephus, Jewish War 2.17.4.

ELEAZAR BURNS FATHER'S HOUSE AND FIGHTS AGRIPPA'S TROOPS: Josephus, Jewish War 2.17.6; Brandon, Jesus and Zealots p. 132.

MENAHEM FROM MASADA ENTERS JERUSALEM AS KING OF JEWS: Josephus, Jewish War 2.17.8.

MENAHEM TAKES REVOLUTION LEADERSHIP FROM ELEAZAR: Josephus, Jewish War 2.17.8.

MENAHEM-ANANIAS CONVERSATION: Fictional.

MENAHEM KILLS ANANIAS AND EZEKIAL: Approximately 66 A.D. or C.E. in this story. Josephus, Jewish War 2.17.9. Although Josephus refers to Ananias as high priest at this time, he actually was not the high priest; Matthias, son of Theophilus, was.

ELEAZAR, SON OF ANANIAS, VISITS RABATH: Fictional.

CAIAPHAS HIDES: Fictional.

MENAHEM A TYRANT: Josephus, Jewish War 2.17.9.

ELEAZAR, SON OF ANANIAS, DEFEATS MENAHEM: Josephus, Jewish War 2.17.9.

ELEAZAR DECEIVES AND KILLS ROMAN GARRISON, EXCEPT FOR ITS LEADER, WHO BECOMES A JEW: Josephus, Jewish War 4.17.10.

CHAPTER XXXV

ROMANS AND SYRIANS SLAUGHTER AND ENSLAVE JEWS IN CAESAREA: Josephus, Jewish War 2.18.1.

JEWISH REPRISAL KILLINGS IN OTHER CITIES: Josephus, Jewish War 2.18.2.

SCYTHOPOLIS JEWS UNDER SIMON SIDE WITH GENTILES WHO DECEPTIVELY SLAUGHTER THEM: Josephus, Jewish War 2.18.3-4.

GENTILE REPRISALS AGAINST JEWISH REPRISALS: Josephus, Jewish War 2.18.5.

ALEXANDRIAN GREEKS TRY TO BURN JEWS ALIVE: Josephus, Jewish War 2.18.7.

ALEXANDRIAN JEWS TRY TO SAVE JEWISH VICTIMS: Josephus, Jewish War 2.18.7.

TIBERIUS ALEXANDER SENDS ROMAN SOLDIERS AGAINST ALEXANDRIAN JEWS: Josephus, Jewish War 2.18.8.

ROMANS SLAUGHTER ALEXANDRIAN JEWS, INCLUDING INFANTS: Josephus, Jewish War 2.18.8.

AGRIPPA GOES TO ANTIOCH: Josephus, Jewish War 2.18.6.

NOARUS SLAUGHTERS PEACEFUL JEWS; STEALS FROM PEOPLE: Josephus, Jewish War 2.18.6.

AGRIPPA AND GALLUS LEAD ARMY TO JERUSALEM: Josephus, Jewish War 2.18.9.

DAMASCUS JEWS IMPRISONED IN GYMNASIUM: Josephus, Jewish War 2.20.2.

ZEBULON: Josephus, Jewish War 2.18.9.

SLAUGHTER OF JEWS AT JOPPA: Josephus, Jewish War 2.18.10.

SLAUGHTER OF JEWS AT NARBATENE: Josephus, Jewish War 2.18.10.

SEPPHORIS SURRENDERS: Josephus, Jewish War 2.18.11.

ANNIHILATION OF JEWISH RESISTORS AT MOUNT ASAMON: Josephus, Jewish War 2.18.11.

ANTIPATRIS AND LYDDIA: Josephus, Jewish War 2.19.1.

JEWS ATTACK AND KILL ROMANS AT GIBEON (GABAO): Josephus, Jewish War 2.19.1.

ROMANS RETREAT TO BETH-HORON: Josephus, Jewish War 2.19.2.

AGRIPPA'S MESSENGERS ATTACKED BY JEWS: Josephus, Jewish War 2.19.3.

ROMANS ADVANCE TO JERUSALEM: Josephus, Jewish War 2.19.4.

ROMANS ENTER JERUSALEM: Josephus, Jewish War 2.19.4.

ANANUS, SON OF JONATHAN, AND OTHER SURRENDER-PRONE SADDUCEES EVICTED FROM JERUSALEM BY ELEAZAR: Josephus, Jewish War 2.19.5.

ANANUS, SON OF JONATHAN, AND OTHER EVICTED SADDUCEES MEET AGRIPPA: Fictional.

AGRIPPA-GALLUS CONVERSATION: Fictional. Historical sources provide no certain reason for Gallus' withdrawal from Jerusalem when his army was on the verge of a complete victory. This conversation between Agrippa and Gallus provides a possible explanation. It is difficult to accept Josephus' explanation (Josephus, Jewish War 2.19.4) that Gallus' officers were so under Florus' influence (the reason for their surreptitious apostasy not given) and that they so colluded with Florus in his devious scheme to persecute the Jews beyond endurance (so that the Jews would have no choice but to rebel), that they dissuaded Gallus from completely suppressing the rebellion (a rebellion that Florus originally wanted in order to see the Jews destroyed) and from destroying Jerusalem with it, so that they could allow the Jews to re-group and rebel again, thus making it harder for the Romans to defeat them the next time around, but ensuring an even greater Roman destruction of Israel in the future. To the question, then: If Florus wanted the Jews and Jerusalem to be destroyed, why didn't he have his secret agents *encourage* Gallus to go ahead instead of making him stop? Josephus answers that it was in order to set the stage for an even greater destruction of the Jews in the future.

It does seem unlikely that Florus could have based his scheme on such an undependable future as that. It strains credulity to think that Gallus' officers also thought along those lines and turned an imminent victory into an ignominious defeat. This explanation by Josephus seems so unbelievable that it suggests the hiding of some other, more plausible, reason. It is interesting that later in his account, Josephus says that Gallus withdrew from the city "...without any reason in the world" (Josephus, Jewish War 2.19.7).

AGRIPPA LEAVES JERUSALEM: Conjectural. There is no historical source saying that Agrippa accompanied Gallus in his withdrawal. Furthermore, Agrippa's general, Philip, son of Jacimus, was in Jerusalem during the withdrawal and left the city *after* Gallus' defeat (Josephus, Jewish War 2.20.1). Since there is also no mention of Agrippa leaving with Philip, it is probable that Agrippa left before either of them.

GALLUS' ARMY WITHDRAWS: Josephus, Jewish War 2.19.7.

AGRIPPA'S ARMY, UNDER PHILIP, SON OF JACIMUS, REMAINS PEACEFULLY IN JERUSALEM FOR A TIME BEFORE LEAVING: Josephus, Jewish War 2.20.1.

ZEALOTS PURSUE AND DEVASTATE ROMANS: Josephus, Jewish War 2.19.7-9.

CHAPTER XXXVI

PHILIP, SON OF JACIMUS, AND TROOPS JOIN GALLUS: Josephus, Jewish War 2.20.1.

GALLUS' EXPLANATION FOR WITHDRAWAL: Partly fictional and partly from Josephus, Jewish War 2.20.1.

DAMASCUS JEWISH PRISONERS SLAUGHTERED IN GYMNASIUM: Josephus, Jewish War 2.20.2.

DEATH OF SARAH AND ANANIAS: Fictional.

JOSEPHUS CHOSEN TO LEAD JEWS IN GALILEE: Josephus, Jewish War 2.20.4.

ELEAZAR, SON OF ANANIAS, CHOSEN TO LEAD IN IDUMAEA: Josephus, Jewish War 2.20.4.

JOSEPH, SON OF GORION, AND ANANIAS, SON OF ANNAS, CHOSEN TO LEAD JEWS IN JERUSALEM: Josephus, Jewish War 2.20.3.

JOSEPHUS DENIGRATES JOHN OF GISCHALA: Josephus, Jewish War 2.21.1.

AGRIPPA'S STOLEN MONEY: Josephus, Jewish War 2.21.3.

VESPASIAN AND TITUS RAISE ARMY: Josephus, Jewish War 3.1.2-3.

AGRIPPA JOINS VESPASIAN: Josephus, Jewish War 3.2.4.

JEWS LOSE AT ASCALON AND BELZEDEK (BEZEDEL): Josephus, Jewish War 3.2.1, 3.2.3.

VESPASIAN TAKES SEPPHORIS: Josephus, Jewish War 3.2.4.

JOSEPHUS REPULSES ROMAN JOTAPATA ATTACK: Josephus, Jewish War 3.6.1.

VESPASIAN TAKES GABARA (GADARA): Josephus, Jewish War 3.7.1.

JOTAPATA JEWS RESIST: Josephus, Jewish War 3.7.3-30, 3.7.33-36.

JAPHA FALLS TO ROMANS: Josephus, Jewish War 3.7.31.

ROMANS DEFEAT SAMARITANS AT MOUNT GIRIZIM: Josephus, Jewish War 3.7.32.

ROMANS CRUCIFY CAPTURED JOTAPATA JEW: Josephus, Jewish War 3.7.33.

VESPASIAN TAKES JOTAPATA: Josephus, Jewish War 3.7.34-36.

JOSEPHUS TRICKS HIS MEN TO SAVE HIS LIFE: Josephus, Jewish War 3.8.1-7.

VESPASIAN KEEPS JOSEPHUS PRISONER: Josephus, Jewish War 3.8.8-9.

JOSEPHUS PREDICTS VESPASIAN AND TITUS WILL BE EMPERORS: Josephus, Jewish War 3.8.9.

ROMANS DESTROY JOPPA AND JEWISH PIRATES: Josephus, Jewish War 3.9.2-3.

CHAPTER XXXVII

JOSEPHUS' FAMILY: Josephus, Jewish War 5.13.1, 5.13.3.

AGRIPPA ASKS VESPASIAN'S HELP: Josephus, Jewish War 3.9.7.

ROMANS TAKE TIBERIAS: Josephus, Jewish War 3.9.7-8.

ROMANS CONQUER TARICHAEAE: Josephus, Jewish War 3.10.1.

ROMANS FIRST LOSE IN GAMALA: Josephus, Jewish War 4.1.4-5.

MOUNT TABOR DECEPTION AND KILLING: Josephus, Jewish War 4.1.8.

ROMANS CONQUER GAMALA: Josephus, Jewish War 4.1.9-10.

GISCHALA: Josephus, Jewish War 4.2.1-5.

CHAPTER XXXVIII

BARNABAS TELLS PETER OF JOHN (MARK) AND SHARON MARRIAGE: Fictional.

JERUSALEM UNDER ELEAZAR, SON OF SIMON, AND ZACHARIAH, SON OF AMPHICALLEUS: Josephus, Jewish War 4.4.1.

NEW HIGH PRIEST PHANNIAS, SON OF SAMUEL: 67-68 A.D. or C.E. Josephus, Jewish War 4.3.8.

ANANUS, SON OF ANNAS, DEFEATS ZEALOTS: Josephus, Jewish War 4.3.11-12.

JOHN OF GISCHALA SPIES FOR ZEALOTS: Josephus, Jewish War 4.3.13-14.

ANANUS, SON OF ANNAS, SECRETLY FAVORS SURRENDER: Josephus, Jewish War 4.3.14, 4.4.1.

IDUMAEANS ARE CONVERTS TO JUDAISM: Josephus, Antiquities 13.9.1.

IDUMAEANS RAISE ARMY: Josephus, Jewish War 4.4.2.

SPEECH BY PRIEST JESUS: Josephus, Jewish War 4.4.3.

COUNTERSPEECH BY IDUMAEAN LEADER: Josephus, Jewish War 4.4.4.

IDUMAEANS HELP ZEALOTS: Josephus, Jewish War 4.5.1.

PRIESTS, ANANUS AND JESUS, KILLED; THEIR CORPSES DEFILED: Josephus, Jewish War 4.5.2.

IDUMAEANS LEAVE JERUSALEM: Josephus, Jewish War 4.5.5, 4.6.1.

ROMANS TAKE GADARA: Josephus, Jewish War 4.7.3.

ROMANS TAKE BETHENNABRIS AFTER ZEALOTS HURL BODIES LIKE MISSILES: Josephus, Jewish War 4.7.4-5.

ROMANS SLAUGHTER JEWS FLEEING FOR JERICHO: Josephus, Jewish War 4.8.2.

SOME NAZARENES LEAVE JERUSALEM; MOST STAY: Schonfield, Passover Plot pp. 186-187; Brandon, Jesus and Zealots pp. 14, 208-209, 210-216, 219-220. Brandon can see only elation from the Nazarenes when Gallus withdrew his army from Jerusalem and can see in them an attitude to fight a defeatable enemy in preparation for the Messiah. He sharply criticizes the Pella flight tradition, which purports that the Nazarenes left Jerusalem en masse and crossed the Jordan River for Pella once the war with the Romans intensified.

Brandon points out that this tradition dates back to the Fourth Century, when it first appears in the Ecclesiastical History of Eusebius of Caesarea (III v, 2-3). It is repeated, says Brandon, with some variations, in the following century by Epiphanius. Brandon goes on to say that the Epiphanius statements about a Pella flight are brief and vague and are not historical facts but hearsay reference to some older belief, since if Epiphanius had had a definite historical source, he certainly would have stated it to give more authenticity to his account. Brandon goes on to say, "There are grave reasons for doubting the authority of this tradition, quite apart from its inherent improbability in the light of the evidence already noticed," this evidence being the initial success of the Jews in repelling the Romans and, therefore, the attraction for the Nazarenes to stay in Jerusalem rather than leave. I would add to this the fact that Symeon, the Nazarene leader, being present in Jerusalem up until the end of the First Century indicates that a certain number of Nazarenes must have remained with him, and also that if a large number of the many thousands of Nazarenes in Jerusalem would have left for Pella, they could not have done so unnoticed by the Romans and would not have been allowed to travel without being attacked and killed (just as had happened to the families leaving Jericho). Furthermore, as Brandon, in his Jesus and the Zealots p.209(1), points out, if the Zealots, discouraging desertion, so guarded the exits of Jerusalem that the deserting Johanan ben Zakkai had to escape by hiding in a coffin, how could the thousands of Nazarenes living in Jerusalem at that time have walked through unmolested? That there *were* thousands of Nazarenes, and that they may have exceeded the number of Gentile followers of Jesus at that time, is suggested in Acts 21:20 as well as elsewhere in that book and, as Brandon points out in his Jesus and the Zealots p. 190(2) and in his Fall of Jerusalem p. 28(3), contradicts what Brandon calls the unsubstantiated claim by Hoennicke, in his Judenchristentum im ersten and zweiten Jahrhundert, Berlin, 1908, p. 175, that Gentile converts outnumbered Jewish converts at that time.

In regard to Johanan ben Zakkai, I have used his coffin-escape in this story as a means of illustrating the difficulty any person would have had in leaving Jerusalem once the Zealot policy of preventing departures began. I have placed the exodus of Peter and Barnabas shortly after that. In the story, all this takes place shortly before the Romans appear at the walls of Jerusalem. The actual date of Johanan's escape probably was a little later, at a time when the Romans already encircled the city.

Brandon further reports his own investigation of the Pella flight story in 1951, in which he concluded that it began in the Second Century as a means for the Torah-rejecting Christians, who established a church in Aelia Capitolina (the new Roman name for Jerusalem), to give legitimacy to their claim that their Christian church was a direct descendant of the original Nazarene church in Jerusalem, the idea being that the Jerusalemites left for Pella, stayed there for a time and then returned to Jerusalem (now called Aelia Capitolina) to carry on the old, traditional church there once again. Obviously, if such a mass exodus had not taken place, one would have to conclude that the vast numbers of Nazarenes in Jerusalem remained there during the Roman siege and that the survivors of the siege carried on with the original church without dependency on the return of a Christian group from Pella. In such a case, the establishment of this new church in Aelia Capitolina would have to be considered as a separate and independent creation, unrelated to the Nazarene one and either superseding it or replacing the vacuum it left after the ill-fated Jewish revolt in 135 A.D. or C.E.

Eusebius, in his Ecclesiastical History IV v, 1-4, by giving a list of fifteen Jewish bishops of the Nazarene Church in Jerusalem after the death of Symeon, shows a continuity of this movement independent of any return of the faithful from Pella or anywhere else. In this same work (IV vi, 4), Eusebius describes a change of leadership after these fifteen Jewish bishops in Jerusalem (now Aelia Capitolina) from Jewish to Gentile, with no explanation of how this came about. Brandon, in his Jesus and the Zealots p. 213(2), states, "It seems quite evident, therefore, that there was no continuity between the original mother church of Jerusalem and the church of Aelia Capitolina", which became the present Christian Church of today.

As further evidence against this Pella tradition, Brandon, in his Fall of Jerusalem pp. 170-172, reminds us of the military situation in Pella itself from 66-70 A.D. or C.E. The Jews had attacked Pella, among other Gentile cities, in 66 A.D. or C.E. in retaliation for the massive killing of Jews in Caesarea (Josephus, Jewish War 2.18.1). The Gentiles had abandoned the city. Vespasian had then launched a punitive expedition against the Jews in the Pella area in 68 A.D. or C.E. (Josephus, Jewish War 4.7.3-6). If the mass exodus of Nazarenes from Jerusalem to Pella took place in 67 A.D. or C.E., as Schoeps proposes (H.J. Schoeps, Paulus: die Theologie des Apostels im Lichte der judischen Religionsgeschichte p. 102), then the Romans would have encountered a large group of Nazarene Jews who were new occupants of a city recently ravaged by Jews and vacated by Gentiles. It does not seem likely that these Nazarenes would have escaped being slaughtered by the Romans at a time when the purpose of the Romans was to kill Jews and, especially, the detestable variety of them that followed Jesus.

Brandon, in his Fall of Jerusalem pp. 170-172, also points out the dating difficulties incurred by this legend and complains that no scholar has attempted to answer the questions he has raised.

Schoeps (Jewish Christianity p. 23) adds his objection to the legend by stating that Eusebius' claim that Jerusalem was completely emptied of "Christians" at this time is an exaggeration.

SYMEON STAYS IN JERUSALEM: Brandon, Jesus and Zealots p. 213(2). Symeon was in Jerusalem when he was chosen to lead the Nazarenes. We hear of him again in Jerusalem shortly before his death at the end of the First Century. He either must have left the city and then returned to it or else stayed there continuously until his death. Brandon takes the latter view, as does this story. For further evidence of a continuous stay, see NOTE above, entitled, SOME NAZARENES LEAVE JERUSALEM; MOST STAY.

PETER VISITS "JEWS OF THE DISPERSION" BEFORE ARRIVING IN ROME: Eusebius (Ecclesiatical History, II xxv; III i; also cited by Finegan, Light From the Ancient Past p. 380 [14]) reports that Peter visited the "Jews of the Dispersion" in Pontus, Galatia, Bithynia, Cappadocia and Asia before his arrival in Rome. Barnabas traveling with him is fictional.

JULIUS, LEADER OF GALATIAN CHRISTIANS: Fictional.

EBIONITES: Schonfield, Passover Plot p. 200; Brandon, Jesus and Zealots pp. 217, 220; Gager, Origins of Anti-Semitism p. 187; Klausner, From Jesus to Paul pp. 279, 601; Maccoby, Mythmaker pp. 5, 14, 17, 60, 81, 96, 128, 172-183; Wilson, Our Father Abraham pp. 25, 52.

JESUS IN VISIONS MORE RELIABLE THAN JESUS IN FLESH, SAYS PAUL: Letter to Galatians 1:11-12.

RABATH AND JACOB TO ROME: Fictional.

NERO SEES CHRISTIAN INFLUENCE IN CAUSE OF JEWISH WAR: Schonfield, Passover Plot pp. 185, 190, referring to Tacitus, Annals xv. 44. Schonfield states, "The Romans were not fools, and must have had some justification for regarding Christianity as a dangerous and hostile superstition. It is significant that after the suppression of the first Jewish revolt, the Romans did not outlaw Judaism, though they tried to make it certain that non-Jews professing this faith were genuine converts; but they did outlaw Christianity", and later he asserts that Christians "...did produce a violently anti-Roman document in the Book of Revelation." Schonfield (p. 235) also reports that Pliny the Younger wrote these words about Christianity: "...this contagious superstition is not confined to the cities, but has spread through the villages and the countryside. Nevertheless it still seems possible to check and cure it"; Klausner, From Jesus to Paul pp. 21, 420-421, 562; Josephus, Jewish War 6.5.4, which says, "But now, what did most elevate them in undertaking this war, was an ambiguous oracle that was also found in their sacred writings, how about that time, one from their country should become governor of the habitable earth." To Nazarenes and Christians, this oracle meant Jesus; Brandon, Jesus and Zealots p. 362.

RABATH-PAUL CONVERSATION: Fictional. That Paul's negative attitude towards marriage was prompted at least in part by his belief that the return of

Jesus would be soon and that the burdens of marriage might be better avoided for that reason can be seen in Acts 7:25-31.

SPIRITUAL MEN AND VIRGIN MARRIAGES THAT NEVER CONSUMMATE: Klausner, From Jesus to Paul p. 571.

WOMEN TEACHERS IN JUDAISM: Maccoby, Mythmaker pp. 201-202.

CHAPTER XXXIX

TIME OF PETER'S ARRIVAL IN ROME: Staniforth (Early Christian Writings p.17) lists Peter as the first bishop of Rome from 62-67 A.D. or C.E. He gives no reference for these dates. In the present story, I have Peter arriving in Rome in 67 A.D. or C.E., the same year in which he and Paul were killed by the Romans.

We can determine Paul's time in Rome with more accuracy than Peter's. Felix's procuratorship ended in 60 A.D. or C.E. In that same year, Felix turned Paul over to the new procurator, Festus, from whom Paul requested an imperial hearing in Rome. Paul reached Rome in that year (or early the next year) and preached unhindered there for the next two years (Acts 28:30). He reportedly traveled to Spain on a temporary release from his house confinement and was probably absent from Rome in 64 A.D. or C.E. when the great conflagration occurred and the persecution of Christians intensified. He returned to Rome (possibly in 65 or 66 A.D. or C.E.) and was executed in 67 A.D. or C.E.

If Peter had arrived in Rome by 62 A.D. or C.E. (as Staniforth reports) and become bishop in that year, then he and Paul would have been together in that city for five years (except for the interregnum of Paul's trip to Spain). During that time, the rivalry and animosity between them would either have manifested itself overtly or would have ended in reconciliation. If the latter, one wonders why no Christian writer recorded it — or even created it. If the former, then why no record of the conflict? These were major personalities in the Jesus movement, not minor, inconsequential participants.

Furthermore, if Peter and Paul had lived in Rome at the same time, and if Peter was the bishop there, then Paul would have been living in subservience and obedience to Peter. This seems unlikely, considering Paul's inimical attitude towards Peter in the past and his efforts to hold himself out as equal to Peter in importance (Letter to Galatians 2:11-14; First Letter to Corinthians 1:12; Second Letter to Corinthians 11:4-5; 12:11). It is much more likely that Peter's arrival came at a much later date than Staniforth reports.

JOHN (MARK) IN ROME: Letter to Colossians 4:10-11; Klausner, From Jesus to Paul pp. 219, 222.

ROMANS HATE CHRISTIANS: See references for NERO SEES CHRISTIAN INFLUENCE IN CAUSE OF JEWISH WAR in NOTES for CHAPTER XXXVIII.

CHRISTIANS MEET IN SECRET IN ROME: Although it was necessary for Christians to meet in secret at this time, there is no direct evidence that they met in underground places. There is evidence that catacomb gatherings took place at a later period.

LETTER OF PETER TO PAUL: This a paraphrasing of words attributed to Peter in Homilies 17.14-19, as reported by Schoeps, Jewish Christianity p. 51. Schoeps states that while this speech may have been created by the author of Homilies in the beginning of the Second Century, it does correctly reflect the "Jewish Christian" view of Paul.

PETER CRUCIFIED UPSIDE-DOWN: In his Chronican (ed. Scaliger. 1606, p. 192) Eusebius dates the deaths of Peter and Paul in the fourteenth year of Nero. Finegan, in his Light From the Ancient Past p. 381(16), points out that this would be about 67-68 A.D. or C.E. (Finegan also clears up some past confusion over Eusebius' giving Nero's fourteenth year as the date of another event: Nero's Christian persecution. Since the date of that event is known to have been 64 A.D. or C.E., Finegan considers Eusebius' date for that an error.) Further support for the 67 A.D. or C.E. date for the deaths of Peter and Paul, states Finegan, is to be found in the statement by made by Jerome (the Fourth Century Christian biblical scholar) that Seneca died two years before Peter and Paul. (Reference for that is Orazio Marruchi, Pietro e Paolo a Roma. 4th ed. 1934, p. 21.) Since Seneca died in 65 A.D. or C.E., that would once again place the deaths of Peter and Paul in 67 A.D. or C.E. Yet, these two historical sources notwithstanding, Finegan feels a certain reluctance to accept a date three years after the Rome fire and persecution.

I do not share the reluctance to accept that amount of time between those two events, especially in light of the additional information Finegan gives us on page 377 of his book: Here he mentions Clement (I Clement 5) telling of Paul as "having come to the farthest bounds of the west," meaning Spain, and here he also mentions the Muratorian Fragment (middle 2d century A.D.) telling of "the departure of Paul from the city (i.e. Rome) on his journey to Spain" (ASBACH p. 118).

If we add these evidences of Paul's trip to Spain to Klausner's report (Klausner, From Jesus to Paul pp. 246-247, 417) that contradictions between what we find in Acts and what we find in Paul's letters can be reconciled by a situation in which Paul is released from prison (perhaps traveling to Spain after that) and then re-arrested a few years later, the 67 A.D. or C.E. date is not so difficult to accept.

The manner in which Peter was executed (crucified upside-down) is reported by Eusebius (Ecclesiastical History, II xxv, III i) and cited by Finegan on page 380(14) of his book, Light From the Ancient Past. Peter is said to have requested this manner of execution by the Romans after having first preached to the "Jews of the dispersion" in Pontus, Galatia, Bithynia, Cappadocia and Asia and then coming to Rome.

While no reason for Peter's execution is given, it appears to have been political and not religious. Jews in general were not being arrested and crucified in this way. As a matter of fact, after the defeat of Israel in 70 A.D. or C.E., the

Jewish religion was not outlawed, but the Christian religion (or the Christian or Nazarene sect of Judaism) was.

Unlike this story, in which Peter's wife outlives him, Eusebius quoting Clement (Miscellanies VII), says that she was executed before him (Ecclesiastical History I xxx).

BARNABAS-PAUL MEETING: Fictional.

NO TIME OR SEX DIFFERENCES IN SPIRIT WORLD, SAYS PAUL: Although Paul is saying this in this story, reference to this concept can be found in the Second Letter of Peter 3:8, in which he says, "...with the Lord, one day is as a thousand years and a thousand years as a day."

OUR DEEDS COME BACK TO US, SAYS PAUL: Second Letter to Corinthians 9:6; Letter to Galatians 6:7.

GREATEST VIRTUE IS LOVE, SAYS PAUL: Acts 13; Letter to Romans 12:9-10, 13.8, 13:10; Letter to Galatians 5:13-14, 5:22; First Letter to Corinthians 8:1, 16:14; Second Letter to Corinthians 2:8; Letter to Ephesians 4:2, 5:2, 5:25, 5:28; First Letter to Thessalonians 4:9, 5:2.

JESUS TELLS JEWS WHO BELIEVE IN HIM THEY WISH TO KILL HIM: John 8:30-31, 8:37, 8:40.

JESUS TELLS JEWS WHO BELIEVE IN HIM THEIR FATHER IS THE DEVIL: John 8:44.

JEWS WHO BELIEVE IN JESUS LOOK FOR STONES IN TEMPLE TO THROW AT HIM: John 8:59.

PAUL CALLS NAZARENES DOGS, EVIL-WORKERS, FALSE BROTHERS, FALSE APOSTLES, HYPOCRITES, DISSEMBLERS, SERVANTS OF THE DEVIL DISGUISED AS APOSTLES, MUTILATORS OF THE FLESH AND ENEMIES OF THE CROSS OF CHRIST: Second Letter to Corinthians: 11:12-15; Letter to Philippians 3:2.

PAUL RIDICULES NAZARENES BY CALLING THEM THE CIRCUMCISION PARTY: Acts 11:2; Letter to Galatians 2:12; Letter to Titus 1:10.

PAUL RIDICULES DIETARY LAWS BY SAYING THE JEWISH GOD IS IN THE BELLY: Letter to Philippians 3:19.

BARNABAS SAYS CHRISTIAN GOD IS IN THE BELLY: Fictional.

GOD'S COMMAND TO MOSES NOT TO EAT BLOOD: Leviticus 7:26, 19:26.

GOD'S COMMAND TO NOAH NOT TO EAT BLOOD: Genesis 9:4.

JAMES' ORDER TO PAUL THAT GENTILE FOLLOWERS OF JESUS NOT EAT BLOOD: Acts 15:19-20.

MEMBERS OF JEWISH MOB CALL FOR JESUS' DEATH AND THEN CALL CURSE ON THEMSELVES AND THEIR CHILDREN: Matthew 27:25. A characteristic of a civilized society is that children are not punished for the crimes of their parents. So it was disappointing to observe, in the Vatican Council of 1965, the opposition to the exoneration of present-day Jews from culpability in the death of Jesus. Even if the theme of this book (that the Jews did not kill Jesus) is deemed to be incorrect, the vicarious revenge on the descendants of the guilty seems morally inappropriate to me. While the final decision was favorable for present-day Jews, the opposition to it was disconcerting. One wonders what sort of opposition might arise if a similar attempt is made for the Jews of Jesus' time. Brandon expresses skepticism about the reliability of this story (Jesus and Zealots pp. 260-262).

PAUL ALLOWS JEWISH PRACTICES FOR CHRISTIANS WHO LEARNED THEM FROM PARENTS: Gager, Origins of Anti-Semitism pp. 188-189, referring to Augustine, Epistle 40.

DOUBT ABOUT PAROUSIA IN THEIR OWN LIFETIMES: Jesus said, "...you will not have gone through all the towns of Israel before the Son of man comes" (Matthew 10:23). He also said, "Truly, I say to you, there are some standing here who will not taste death before they see the Son of man coming in his kingdom" (Matthew 16:28) and, "Truly, I say to you, there are some standing here who will not taste death before they see the kingdom of God come with power" (Mark 9:1), and also, "Truly, I say to you, this generation will not pass away till all these things take place" (Matthew 24:34).

Thus it was that Paul expected the Parousia to be soon, as he stated in his First Letter to the Corinthians 7:29-31 and in his Letter to the Philippians 4:5. James also thought the Parousia was imminent, as in the Letter of James 5:8, and John the Baptizer said that the kingdom of God was at hand (Matthew 3:2).

CHAPTER XL

PAUL IS CONTENT WHATEVER STATE HE IS IN: Letter to Philippians 4:11.

ROMANS BEHEAD PAUL: I have used the date 67 A.D. or C.E. for this story. See the NOTE, PETER CRUCIFIED UPSIDE-DOWN for CHAPTER XXXIX.

NERO IS KILLED: 68 A.D. or C.E. Josephus, Jewish War 4.9.2; Time-Life Books, Empires Ascendant p. 86.

EMPEROR GALBA: About 69 A.D. or C.E. Josephus, Jewish War 4.9.2, 4.9.9.

EMPEROR OTHO: About 69 A.D. or C.E. Josephus, Jewish War 4.9.2, 4.9.9.

SIMON, SON OF GIORAS, RAISES ARMY IN IDUMAEA: Josephus, Jewish War 4.9.4-7.

SIMON'S WIFE CAPTURED, THEN RELEASED BY JERUSALEM ZEALOTS: Josephus, Jewish War 4.9.8.

ROMANS ENTER IDUMAEA: Josephus, Jewish War 4.9.9.

EMPEROR VITELLIUS UNPOPULAR: About 69 A.D. or C.E. Josephus, Jewish War 4.10.1.

SIMON, SON OF GIORAS, FIGHTS JOHN OF GISCHALA AND ZEALOTS IN JERUSALEM: Josephus, Jewish War 4.9.11.

VESPASIAN'S TROOPS WANT HIM EMPEROR: About 69 A.D. or C.E. Josephus, Jewish War 4.10.3-4.

TIBERIUS ALEXANDER SUPPORTS VESPASIAN'S BID FOR EMPEROR: Josephus, Jewish War 4.10.5-6.

PRIMUS: Josephus, Jewish War 4.11.2-3.

SABINUS: Josephus, Jewish War 4.11.4, 5.8.1.

MUCIANUS: Josephus, Jewish War 4.10.6, 4.11.1, 4.11.4.

DOMITIAN TEMPORARY EMPEROR: Josephus, Jewish War 4.11.4.

SPLIT IN ZEALOT FORCE (ELEAZAR AND JOHN OF GISCHALA): Josephus, Jewish War 4.4.1, 5.1.2.

SYMEON JOINS ELEAZAR BRANCH OF ZEALOTS: Fictional.

INTERNECINE JEWISH FIGHTING: Josephus, Jewish War 5.1.4.

TITUS AT JERUSALEM WALLS: Josephus, Jewish War 5.1.6, 5.2.3.

JERUSALEM JEWS FIGHT ROMANS TOGETHER: Josephus, Jewish War 5.2.2, 5.2.4.

JEWS ATTACK TITUS: Josephus, Jewish War 5.2.4.

JEWS ATTACK ROMANS ON MOUNT OF OLIVES: Josephus, Jewish War 5.2.4.

TITUS, THROUGH JOSEPHUS, OFFERS PEACE: Josephus, Jewish War 5.6.2.

EVICTED JEWS ENTRAP ROMANS: Josephus, Jewish War 5.3.3.

TEMPLE TREASURE INVENTORIED ON COPPER SCROLLS: Baigent and Leigh, Dead Sea Scrolls Deception pp. 21, 36, 51-56, 119, 138-140.

TEMPLE TREASURE IS MOVED: Baigent and Leigh, Dead Sea Scrolls Deception p. 52.

SACRED WRITINGS ARE REMOVED: Norman Golb (Symposium by Library of Congress and Baltimore Hebrew University, April 21, 1993, as reported in Biblical Archeology Review, July/August 1993, p. 72) argues that since five-hundred different scribes wrote the Dead Sea Scrolls, the works could not have been produced in their entirety by the people living in that vicinity. (Magen Broshi, curator of the Shrine of the Book in Jerusalem, speaking at that same symposium, as reported in Biblical Archeology Review, July/August 1993, p. 70, states that the settlement contained 120 to 150 people.) Also, Golb finds differences in doctrine among the different writings. This suggests origins outside the Dead Sea community, from a diverse and wider sphere of thinking, reflective of different Jewish groups of the time.

This story posits the possibility that such writings were moved from beleaguered Jerusalem along with the Temple treasures and that they were deposited in the caves of the Dead Sea area along with the writings of the people who lived there.

CHAPTER XLI

NUMBERS OF JEWS IN DIFFERENT GROUPS: Josephus, Jewish War 5.6.1.

NAZARENE BELIEF PERVADED ALL JEWISH GROUPS: Josephus, Jewish War 6.5.4.

TITUS BUILDS PLATFORMS AND USES BATTERING RAMS: Jewish War 5.6.2-4.

ROMANS CRUCIFY CAPTURED JEW IN FRONT OF JERUSALEM WALL: Josephus, Jewish War 5.6.5.

IDUMAEAN LEADER JOHN KILLED: Josephus, Jewish War 5.6.5.

SIMON NEW IDUMAEAN LEADER: Josephus, Jewish War 5.6.1, 5.7.3, 5.9.2.

ROMANS BREACH WALL, THEN DRIVEN BACK: Josephus, Jewish War 5.7.2, 5.8.1-2.

STARVATION IN JERUSALEM: Josephus, Jewish War 5.10.2-3.

TITUS PARADES ROMAN TROOPS: Josephus, Jewish War 5.9.1-2.

JEWS HAMPER ROMAN PLATFORM BUILDING: Josephus, Jewish War 5.9.2.

JOSEPHUS SPEECH FOR SURRENDER BASED ON GOD'S WILL: Josephus, Jewish War 5.9.3-4.

SOME JEWS SWALLOW GOLD AND LEAVE JERUSALEM: Josephus, Jewish War 5.10.1.

TITUS CRUCIFIES JEWS CAPTURED FORAGING: Josephus, Jewish War 5.11.1.

CRUCIFIED BODIES ENCIRCLE JERUSALEM: Josephus, Jewish War 5.11.1.

HIGH PRIESTS' THROATS CUT: Josephus, Jewish War 7.8.1.

CAIAPHAS MEETS SYMEON: Fictional.

CAIAPHAS' DEATH: Fictional.

TITUS CUTS OFF CAPTIVE'S HANDS BECAUSE TIMBER FOR CRUCIFIXES DEPLETED: Josephus, Jewish War 5.11.1-2.

YOUNG MACEDONIANS ATTACK WALL AND ARE KILLED: Josephus, Jewish War 5.11.3.

JOHN OF GISCHALA TUNNELS UNDER TWO PLATFORMS WHICH COLLAPSE: Josephus, Jewish War 5.11.4.

SIMON'S MEN BURN ROMAN PLATFORMS AND BATTERING RAM: Josephus, Jewish War 5.11.5.

JEWS ATTACK ROMAN CAMP: Josephus, Jewish War 5.11.5.

ROMANS BUILD WALL AND FORTS AROUND JERUSALEM: Josephus, Jewish War 5.12.1-2.

SIMON EXECUTES A SURRENDER GROUP: Josephus, Jewish War 5.13.2.

JEWS STONE JOSEPHUS AT HIS NEXT SPEECH: Josephus, Jewish War 5.13.3.

ROMANS FEED JEWISH DESERTERS WHOSE BELLIES BURST: Josephus, Jewish War 5.13.4.

SYRIANS SLAUGHTER JEWISH PRISONERS FOR SWALLOWED GOLD: Josephus, Jewish War 5.13.4.

GIHON SPRING: Biblical Archeology Review, May/June 1991. Though Josephus does not clearly mention this as a source of water, the existence of the spring and its underground conduit make it a possible water supply in the siege.

JEWS EAT GARBAGE AND FOOD FROM DUNGHILLS: Josephus, Jewish War 5.13.7.

WALL COLLAPSES INTO JOHN'S OLD TUNNEL: Josephus, Jewish War 6.1.3.

JOHN'S SECOND WALL: Josephus, Jewish War 6.1.4.

SINGLE SYRIAN AND ROMAN ATTACK ON JOHN'S WALL REPULSED: Josephus, Jewish War 6.1.6.

SECOND ROMAN ATTACK ON JOHN'S WALL SUCCESSFUL: Josephus, Jewish War 6.1.7.

JEWS REPEL ROMANS FROM TEMPLE: Josephus, Jewish War 6.1.7.

ROMANS FLATTEN ANTONIA: Josephus, Jewish War 6.2.1.

JOSEPHUS' SPEECH TO JEWS IN TEMPLE: Josephus, Jewish War 6.2.1.

SOME SADDUCEES ESCAPE: Josephus, Jewish War 6.2.2.

CHAPTER XLII

CEREALIUS' ASSAULT ON TEMPLE UNSUCCESSFUL: Josephus, Jewish War 6.2.5.

NEW ROMAN PLATFORMS: Josephus, Jewish War 6.2.7.

JEWISH ATTACK ON MOUNT OF OLIVES REPULSED: Josephus, Jewish War 6.2.8.

JONATHAN-PUDEN FIGHT: Josephus, Jewish War 6.2.10.

JEWS TRAP AND BURN ROMANS ON COLONNADE: Josephus, Jewish War 6.3.1.

JEWISH WOMAN ROASTS AND EATS HER CHILD; JEWISH SOLDIERS APPALLED: Josephus, Jewish War 6.3.4.

BATTERING RAMS, UNDERMINING, LADDERS INEFFECTIVE ON TEMPLE WALL: Josephus, Jewish War 6.4.1.

ROMANS BURN TEMPLE GATE: Josephus, Jewish War 6.4.1-2.

JULIANUS NEW PROCURATOR: Josephus, Jewish War 6.4.3.

CEREALIS VITELLIUS IS LEGATE OF SYRIA: Josephus, Jewish War 7.6.1.

ROMANS BURN SANCTUARY: Josephus, Jewish War 6.4.5.

ROMANS LOOT TEMPLE: Josephus, Jewish War 6.4.7, 6.5.1.

WOMEN AND CHILDREN BURNED ON LAST COLONNADE: Josephus, Jewish War 6.5.2.

GOLD INFLATION IN SYRIA: Josephus, Jewish War 6.6.1.

SIMON AND JOHN PARLEY WITH TITUS: Josephus, Jewish War 6.6.2-3.

JEWS DRIVE ROMANS OUT OF PALACE: Josephus, Jewish War 6.7.1.

TITUS DISMISSES ROMAN SOLDIER FROM ARMY BECAUSE HE WAS TEMPORARILY CAPTURED BY JEWS: Josephus, Jewish War 6.7.1.

ROMANS IN LOWER CITY; JEWS IN HIGHER: Josephus, Jewish War 6.7.2.

JOSEPHUS APPEALS FOR SURRENDER: Josephus, Jewish War 6.7.2.

JEWS IN SEWERS: Josephus, Jewish War 6.7.3, 6.8.4.

SMALL IDUMAEAN SURRENDER PLOT STOPPED: Josephus, Jewish War 6.8.2.

JEWS FIGHT FROM CITADEL AND SEWERS: Josephus, Jewish War 6.8.4.

WEST WALL COLLAPSES: Josephus, Jewish War 6.8.4.

ROMANS BURN BUILDINGS AND HOUSES: Josephus, Jewish War 6.8.5.

ROMANS TAKE LIMITED PRISONERS FOR MANUAL LABOR OR SHOWS: Josephus, Jewish War 6.9.1-2.

JOHN AND SIMON CAPTURED: Josephus, Jewish War 6.9.4.

SYMEON HIDES IN SEWER: Fictional.

WORLD IS BETTER TEMPLE THAN JERUSALEM ONE, JEWS TELL TITUS: Josephus, Jewish War 5.11.2.

JOHN IMPRISONED FOR LIFE: Josephus, Jewish War 6.9.4.

SIMON TO ROME: Josephus, Jewish War 6.9.4, 7.2.1.

TITUS DESTROYS JERUSALEM: Josephus, Jewish War 6.9.4.

TITUS FREES JOSEPHUS' FAMILY: Josephus, Life of Flavius Josephus 75.

TITUS REWARDS ARMY: Josephus, Jewish War 7.1.1.

TITUS' SHOWS: Josephus, Jewish War 6.9.2, 7.2.1, 7.3.1.

ANTIOCH GENTILES REQUEST JEWISH EXPULSION: Josephus, Jewish War 7.3.2-4, 7.5.2.

ROMANS CALL VESPASIAN BENEFACTOR AND SAVIOR: Josephus, Jewish War 7.4.1.

ROMAN VICTORY PARADE: Josephus, Jewish War 7.5.3-5.

SIMON PUBLICLY EXECUTED: Josephus, Jewish War 7.5.6.

CHAPTER XLIII

DRUSILLA BECOMES TITUS' MISTRESS: Fictional.

BASSUS NEW LEGATE OF SYRIA: Josephus, Jewish War 7.6.1.

LIBERIUS MAXIMUS PROCURATOR: Josephus, Jewish War 7.6.6.

JEWS AT HERODIUM SURRENDER: Josephus, Jewish War 7.6.1.

JEWS AT MACHAERUS SURRENDER: Josephus, Jewish War 7.6.1.

ROMANS KILL JERUSALEM SURVIVORS IN FOREST: Josephus, Jewish War 7.6.5.

ALL JEWISH LAND TO BE SOLD TO ANYONE BUT JEWS, ORDERS VESPASIAN: Josephus, Jewish War 7.6.6.

FISCUS JUDAICUS: Josephus, Jewish War 7.6.6.

ALL DESCENDANTS OF DAVID TO BE KILLED, ORDERS VESPASIAN: Eusebius, Ecclesiastical History, III xii; Schonfield, Passover Plot p. 242.

ESSENES JOIN ZEALOTS AT MASADA: This is based on the discovery of Dead Sea Scroll-like documents (Essene documents) at Masada. Baigent and Leigh, Dead Sea Scrolls Deception pp. 69, 216.

BASSUS DIES: Josephus, Jewish War 7.8.1.

NEW PROCURATOR FLAVIUS SILVA: Josephus, Jewish War 7.8.1.

SILVA BESIEGES MASADA: Josephus, Jewish War 7.8.1-5.

MASADA JEWS COMMIT MASS SUICIDE: Josephus, Jewish War 7.8.6, 7.9.1.

TWO OLD WOMEN AND SOME CHILDREN SURVIVE TO TELL OF MASADA: Josephus, Jewish War 7.9.1.

VESPASIAN ORDERS DESTRUCTION OF JEWISH TEMPLE IN EGYPT: Josephus, Jewish War 7.10.2, 7.10.4.

GENTILES KILL JEWISH MINORITIES: Josephus, Jewish War 7.10.1, 7.11.2.

SICARII BETRAYED BY ALEXANDRIAN JEWS, REFUSE UNDER TORTURE TO CALL ANYONE BUT GOD THEIR LORD: Josephus, Jewish War 7.10.1. Josephus, in spite of his denigration of the Sicarii in deference to his Roman patrons, cannot deny them the recognition of their courage when he says, "...whose courage...everybody was amazed at; for when all sorts of torments and vexations of their bodies that could be devised were made use of them, they could not get anyone of them to comply so far as to confess or seem to confess, that Caesar was their lord...as if they received these torments and the fire itself with bodies insensible of pain, and with a soul that in a manner rejoiced under them. But what was most of all astonishing to the beholders, was the courage of the children; for not one of these children was so far overcome by these torments as to name Caesar for their lord. So far does the strength of the courage [of the soul] prevail over the weakness of the body."

RABATH MARRIES JACOB: Fictional.

BERNICE SEDUCES TITUS: Fictional.

BERNICE BECOMES TITUS' MISTRESS: 67-79 A.D. or C.E. Brandon, Jesus and Zealots pp. 249, 269(6); Jones, The Herods of Judaea pp. 257-258; Suetonius, Titus 7; Gager, The Origins of Anti-Semitism p. 62.

BERNICE'S REVENGE ON FLORUS: Fictional.

PRISCUS' ACCUSATION AGAINST FLORUS: Fictional.

CHRISTIANS SAY JEWS ARE THE ENEMIES OF GOD: Letter to Romans 11:28.

CHRISTIANS SAY ISRAEL DESTROYED BECAUSE JEWS REJECTED JESUS: Eusebius, Ecclesiastical History, III v, 3 and iv, 2; Brandon, Jesus and Zealots pp. 211-212.

CHRISTIANS SAY MARY A VIRGIN AT JESUS' BIRTH; GOD JESUS' FATHER: Matthew 1:18; Luke 1:31-35, 2:7.

CHRISTIANS SAY SYNAGOGUES ARE OF SATAN: Book of Revelations 2:9.

CHRISTIANS SAY PRACTITIONERS OF JEWISH CUSTOMS DOOMED TO DEVIL'S ABYSS: Gager, Origins of Anti-Semitism p. 189, referring to Augustine, Epistle 82.

CHRISTIANS REJECT ALL MOSAIC LAW EXCEPT TEN COMMANDMENTS: Gager, Origins of Anti-Semitism p. 189, referring to Augustine, Epistle 196.

CHRISTIANITY THE ONLY PATHWAY TO GOD: John 8:24, 8:51, 10:1, 10:7-9, 11:25, 12:48-49, 14:6, 14:21; Second Letter to Corinthians 3:15-16, 10:4-5; Letter to Galatians 1:6-9, 2:16, 3:10-11, 3:23-26, 5:2, 6:15; Letter to Ephesians 1:13, 4:5; Letter to Philippians 3:2-3; Second Letter to Thessalonians 1:7-9, 2:9-12; First Letter to Timotheus 1:3; Letter to Titus 1:10-11; Matthew 7:15, 10:32, 12:30-31.

CHRISTIAN MORALITY EXCLUSIVE AND ORIGINATED WITH JESUS: Matthew 5:21-26, 5:27-30, 5:31-32, 5:33-37, 5:38-42, 5:43-48, 23:23-39. I do not wish to imply by this note that the attribution of morality to Christianity and of immorality to Judaism originated with Jesus. To begin with, Christianity did not exist during Jesus' lifetime; it came into existence after the occurrence of certain significant events, the most notable of which was Jesus' resurrection. Jesus himself gave credit to Jewish tradition for much of the morality he taught. In Matthew 6:12, when Jesus alters Hillel's famous saying, "Do not do to others what you would not have others do to you," and when he says, "So whatever you wish that men would do to you, do so to them," he attributes this concept to Judaism by adding, "...for this is the law and the prophets." And again, when a man asks Jesus, "Teacher, what good deed must I do, to have eternal life?" Jesus answers, "...keep the commandments." And when the man asks him which, he says, "You shall not kill, You shall not commit adultery, You shall not steal, You shall not bear false witness, Honor you father and mother, and, You shall love your neighbor as yourself" (Matthew 19:16-19). All of these are recitations of Jewish beliefs, and Jesus credits them as such. Again, in Matthew 22:36-40, when a lawyer asks him, "Teacher, which is the greatest commandment in the law?" Jesus answers from Jewish scripture by saying, "You shall love the Lord your God with all your heart and with all your soul, and with all your mind. This is the great and first commandment. And a second is like it, You shall love your neighbor as yourself. On these two commandments depend all the law and the prophets." In Mark 12:28-30, when one of the scribes asks Jesus, "Which commandment is the first of all?" Jesus begins his reply with the most famous prayer in all of Judaism: "The first is, 'Hear, O Israel: The Lord our God, the Lord is one, and you shall love the Lord your God with all your heart, and with all your soul, and with all your mind, and with all your strength.' The second is this, 'You shall love your neighbor as yourself.' There is no other commandment greater than these." In Matthew 5:19, Jesus, in referring to Mosaic law, says, "Whoever then relaxes one of the least of these commandments and teaches men so, shall be called least in the kingdom of heaven; but he who does them and teaches them shall be called great in the kingdom of heaven." In Luke 18:18, when a ruler asks Jesus what he should do to inherit eternal life, Jesus says, "You know the commandments." When this same story is told in Matthew 19:16, Jesus says, "Keep the commandments." In all these instances, Jesus uses Jewish teachings as the basis for his own moral teaching. Later, however, it became fashionable for Christians to attribute all such moral teachings to Jesus alone and to speak of Judaism as being devoid of them.

PAUL CONDEMNS CORINTHIAN SINNER TO DEATH: First Letter to Corinthians 5:1-5.

CHAPTER XLIV

BERNICE NO LONGER TITUS' MISTRESS: 79 A.D. or C.E. Brandon, Jesus and Zealots pp. 249, 269(6); Jones, The Herods of Judaea pp. 257-258; Suetonius, Titus 7; Gager, Origins of Anti-Semitism p. 62.

TITUS BECOMES EMPEROR: 79-81 A.D. OR C.E. Hammerton, New Illustrated World History p. 277.

VESUVIUS ERUPTION: 79 A.D. or C.E. Hammerton, New Illustrated World History p. 277.

DOMITIAN BECOMES EMPEROR: 81-96 A.D. or C.E. Hammerton, New Illustrated World History p. 277.

DOMITIAN CALLS HIMSELF A GOD: Schonfield, Passover Plot p. 192, referring to Suetonius, Domitian xiii.

DOMITIAN EXPANDS JEWISH TAX: Gager, Origins of Anti-Semitism p. 60, referring to Suetonius, Domitian 12.2.

FLAVIUS CLEMENS AND FLAVIA: 95 A.D. or C.E. Gager, Origins of Anti-Semitism p. 60, referring to Dio, History 67.14.1-3, according to the epitome of Xiphilinus.

CONSUL GLABRIO EXECUTED BY DOMITIAN: 91 A.D. or C.E. Gager, Origins of Anti-Semitism p. 60, referring to Dio, History 67.14.1-3, according to epitome of Xiphilinus.

DOMITIAN INTERVIEWS JESUS' GRANDNEPHEWS: Eusebius, Ecclesiastical History, III xx, 6, citing Hegisippus as his source; Schoeps, Jewish Christianity pp. 30, 32, referring to Philip of Side and Eusebius.

NERVA EMPEROR: 97-98 A.D. or C.E. Hammerton, New Illustrated World History p. 279; Time-Life, Empires Ascendant p. 86.

TRAJAN EMPEROR: Hammerton, New Illustrated World History pp. 279, 280; Time-Life, Empires Ascendant p. 86.

DEATH OF AGRIPPA II: Jones, The Herods of Judaea p. 259.

IGNATIUS BISHOP OF ANTIOCH: Staniforth, Early Christian Writings p. 64.

BARNABAS MEETS IGNATIUS: Fictional.

IGNATIUS' SERMON: The content of these remarks by Ignatius are found in three of his letters: The Epistle to the Ephesians (Staniforth, Early Christian Writings p. 77); The Epistle to the Magnesians (Staniforth, Early Christian Writings pp. 88-90) and The Epistle to the Philadelphians (Staniforth, Early Christian Writings pp. 111-112).

SYMEON BISHOP IN JERUSALEM: Eusebius, Ecclesiastical History, III xi, 1 and III xxii, citing Hegisippus as his source in III xxxii, 1-7; Brandon, Jesus and Zealots p. 213(3).

PRESERVATION OF JAMES' BISHOP'S CHAIR: Schoeps, Jewish Christianity p. 35. This greatest relic of the Nazarenes (Schoeps calls them Jewish Christians) had to be abandoned after the second Jewish revolt against Rome, led by Bar Kochba, in 135 A.D. or C.E. "The chair was later exhibited in Jerusalem, even at the time of the emperor Constantine," Schoeps reports.

ORIGINAL NAZARENE EUCHARIST PRAYER: Maxwell Staniforth (translator), Early Christian Writings, The Didache pp. 231-232 (Baltimore, Penguin Classics 1972).

JESUS PURPORTEDLY SPOKE OF BREAD AND WINE AS HIS BODY AND BLOOD: Matthew 26:26-28; Mark 14:22-24; Luke 22:19; John 6:41, 6:48, 6:51-59. See NOTE for CHAPTER XXIII: PAUL'S REVELATION ABOUT

JESUS' WORDS AT LAST SUPPER: FOOD AND WINE HIS BODY AND BLOOD.

JESUS' ATTITUDE TOWARDS TAXES: See NOTE for CHAPTER XXXII with this same title.

PETER PURPORTEDLY SAID TO HONOR THE EMPEROR: First Letter of Peter 2:17.

JEWS PURPORTEDLY REJECTED JESUS: John 1:11.

JEWS PURPORTEDLY WANTED TO KILL JESUS: John 5:15-18, 7:1, 8:58-59, 10:31, 10:39, 11:8, 11:53 (Caiphas).

JEWS PURPORTEDLY WANT TO KILL JESUS' FOLLOWERS: John 19:38, 20:19. The Gospel of John has more to say about this than the other gospels. In John 7:11-13, however, in regard to Jesus, it says, "The Jews were looking for him at the feast, and saying, 'Where is he?' And there was much muttering about him among the people. While some said, 'He is a good man,' others said, 'No, he is leading the people astray.' Yet for fear of the Jews, no one spoke openly of him."

      The author has made a distinction here between the Jews and those people who were afraid of the Jews? Who were those who were afraid? Were they not the Jews themselves? Since this event was taking place in Jerusalem, the frightened people must surely have been Jews. Yet the author prefers not to identify them as such. The bad people are called "the Jews" while the good people are called "the people." What possible reason could the author have had for doing this?

      This author (as well as other writers of New Testament literature) frequently refers to the chief priests and the Sadducees as "the Jews" and to the mass of the Jewish people as "the people" or "the multitudes."

      Yet, shortly thereafter, this author refers to "the Jews" and "the people" as one. "The Jews" (in John 7:15) ask a question about Jesus' learning. Jesus answers them (in John 7:19) by saying, "Why do you seek to kill me?" But now "the people" answer him (in John 7:20) by saying, "You have a demon! Who is seeking to kill you?" So Jesus asks a question of *the Jews*, but *the people* answer it. Does this mean that *the Jews* and *the people* are now the same, where previously they were different?

      That it was not the Jewish people but rather the chief priests who wanted to kill Jesus is seen in the passage in John 7:25-26, in which it says, "Some of the people of Jerusalem therefore said, 'Is not this the man whom they seek to kill? And here he is, speaking openly, and they say nothing to him! Can it be that the authorities really know that this is the Christ?'"

      This indistinctness between the Jews (chief priests and Sadducees?) and the Jewish people becomes even more difficult in the 8th chapter of John. First, the author informs us that there were Jews who believed in Jesus, when he says (in John 8:31), "Jesus then said to the Jews who had believed in him...". But then the author says that Jesus accused these same Jews of wanting to kill him, when (in John 8:37) he says, "...yet you seek to kill me...", and (in John 8:40), "...but now you seek to kill me...". Can it be that Jesus, in speaking to these Jews who believed in him, was not referring to them when he said, "You seek to kill me" but rather to the chief priests? And if that is the situation, why has the author written his account in such a way as to make it seem that all the Jewish people wanted to kill Jesus and not just the chief priests?

This speech of Jesus to the believing Jews reaches the height of vituperation when he says (in John 8:41, 8:44, 8:45 and 8:47 respectively), "...we have one father, even God...You are of your father, the Devil...But because I tell the truth, you do not believe me...you are not of God." If Jesus said this to the believing Jews, what might he have said to the non-believing ones? And how could he have told those believing Jews that they did not believe him when they actually did? An investigator, looking as objectively as possible for historical truth, is forced to ask, first, whether this speech is consistent with the teachings and character of Jesus, and second, whether it is possible that Jesus never made this speech and that it came from the mind of the author. If it did come from the author, what would have been his purpose in writing it as he did?

Also, see PAUL'S SPEECH TO AGRIPPA in NOTES for CHAPTER XXX.

JEWS FOLLOWED JESUS AVIDLY: Some examples out of many may be found in John 11:45, 12:11, 12:19, ; "...the world has gone after him." The "world" here refers only to Jews, since the world of the Gentiles had no knowledge of Jesus at this time. In general, the reader will find numerous examples of the Jews following Jesus in the NOTE (below) entitled, JEWS CALLED "THE CROWD", "THE MULTITUDE", OR "THE PEOPLE" WHEN DOING GOOD; CALLED "THE JEWS" WHEN DOING BAD.

PETER PURPORTEDLY TELLS JEWS THAT THEY DELIVERED JESUS TO PILATE: Acts 3:13.

CHRISTIANS SAY JERUSALEM DESTROYED BECAUSE JEWS CRUCIFIED JESUS: Wilson, Our Father Abraham pp. 93, 95. Origen (Brandon, Jesus and Zealots p. 119) gives a different reason for the destruction of Jerusalem: namely, the killing of Jesus' brother, James.

JEWS CALLED "THE CROWD", "THE MULTITUDE", OR "THE PEOPLE" WHEN DOING GOOD; CALLED "THE JEWS" WHEN DOING BAD: The following are selected instances of Jews being called by names other than Jews when doing good, the names being used for them being, "they; a ruler; a woman; many; the people; them; the men; the throng; they all; children; one; the young man; two blind men; the blind and the lame; the multitude; a woman; all; the whole city; every one; a leper; a great multitude; those; the Gerasenes; a man; the herdsmen; all men; a great throng; these men; a blind man; a blind beggar; the scribe; a passer-by; shepherds; a prophetess":

Matthew 4:25, 5:1, 7:28, 8:1, 8:16, 8:18-19, 8:21, 8:23, 8:27, 9:2, 9:8-9, 9:18, 9:20, 9:25, 9:31-32, 9:36, 11:7, 11:15, 12:23, 12:40, 13:2, 13:34, 13:36, 13:51,

13:54, 14:13-15, 14:19-23, 14:35, 15:10, 15:30, 15:32-33, 15:35-36, 17:14, 19:2, 20:29, 20:31, 21:8-9, 21:11, 21:15, 21:46, 23:1, 26:5, 26:7;

  Mark 1:5, 1:27, 1:32-34, 1:40, 1:45, 2:2-4, 2:12-13, 2:15, 3:7-10, 3:20, 3:32, 4:1-2, 4:10-11, 4:33-34, 4:36, 5:1, 5:14-17, 5:20-21, 5:24, 5:30, 6:2, 6:33-34, 6:39-45, 6:54-56, 7:14, 7:17, 7:32-33, 7:36-37, 8:1-4, 8:6-9, 8:22, 8:34, 9:14-16, 9:25, 10:1, 10:13, 10:17, 10:46, 11:8-9, 11:18, 11:32, 12:1, 12:12, 12:32, 12:41, 14:2-3, 14:13, 15:21; Luke 2:8, 2:15, 2:20, 2:25, 2:36-38, 3:7, 3:10, 3:15, 3:18, 3:21, 4:15, 4:31, 4:33, 4:36, 4:42, 5:3, 5:12, 5:15, 5:18-19, 5:26, 6:6, 6:17, 7:1, 7:11, 7:16, 7:24, 7:29, 7:37, 8:4, 8:19, 8:26, 8:34, 8:40, 8:45, 9:11-12, 9:37-38, 9:43, 9:45, 9:57, 10:17, 11:27, 11:29, 12:1, 12:13, 12:54, 13:10, 13:17, 14:2, 14:25, 17:12, 18:15, 18:36, 19:3, 19:37, 19:48, 20:1, 20:19, 22:2, 22:6, 23:27, 23:48;

  John 2:23, 4:28-29, 4:45, 5:3, 6:2, 6:5, 6:10, 6:14-15, 6:22, 6:24-25, 7:30, 7:32, 7:40, 7:43, 7:49, 8:30, 9:38, 10:42, 12:12, 12:42;

  Acts 2:4, 3:12, 4:1-2, 5:12-13, 13:42, 28:24.

  The following are selected instances of persons doing bad and being called, "the Jews" or "his own people":

  Matthew 10:17, 28:15;

  John 1:11, 1:19, 1:22, 5:10, 5:16, 5:18, 6:22, 6:41, 6:52, 7:1, 7:13, 7:15, 7:19, 7:35, 8:22, 8:37, 8:48, 8:57, 9:18, 9:32, 10:19, 10:31-32, 10:39, 11:8, 11:54, 18:14, 18:31, 18:38, 19:7, 19:12, 19:14-15, 19:38, 20:19;

  Acts 2:22-23, 2:36, 5:30, 7:52-53, 9:22-23, 12:11, 13:27-28, 13:45, 13:50, 14:2, 14:4, 14:19, 17:5, 17:13, 18:12, 18:19, 18:28, 20:3, 20:19, 21:27, 23:12, 24:27, 25:7, 25:24, 26:21;

  First Letter to Thessalonians 2:14-16.

JEWS PURPORTEDLY PLEASED AT DEATH OF JAMES, SON OF ZEBEDEE: Acts 12:1-3.

JEWS PURPORTEDLY ACCUSE PAUL TO FESTUS: Acts 25:7, 25:9, 25:24, 26:2, 26:21.

FELIX PURPORTEDLY IMPRISONED PAUL TO PLEASE JEWS: Acts 24:27.

JEWS PURPORTEDLY WANTED PETER KILLED: Acts 12:11.

JAMES PURPORTEDLY THOUGHT JESUS DERANGED: John 7:5.

JESUS APPOINTED JAMES TO LEAD THE NAZARENES: See NOTE for CHAPTER III entitled, JESUS APPOINTED JAMES TO LEAD HIS MOVEMENT.

BARNABAS PURPORTEDLY SAYS TORAH WRITTEN BY WILY DEMON: Maxwell Staniforth, Early Christian Writings, Epistle of Barnabas pp. 189-222. Although Clement of Alexandria thought this letter was written by Paul's companion, Barnabas, Eusebius did not. Staniforth also doubts it, wondering why Barnabas, a Levite, would have reviled the Torah. Scholars date the letter at about 130 A.D. or C.E. Barnabas probably was not alive then. Also, Staniforth states that the writer, whoever he was, had "few scruples" about altering or adding material.

JOHN THE BAPTIZER PURPORTEDLY CALLS JESUS LAMB OF GOD WHO REMOVES SINS OF WORLD: John 1:29.

GALILEANS PURPORTEDLY AVOID RECOGNITION OF JOSEPH AS JESUS' FATHER: Mark 6:2.

JEWS AT CAPERNAUM RECOGNIZE JOSEPH AS JESUS' FATHER: John 6:42.

JESUS PURPORTEDLY PROVES HIS OWN DIVINITY BY QUOTING KING DAVID: In Matthew 22:41-46, Jesus asks some Pharisees whose son Christ (the Messiah) is. They say David's. (Presumably, they mean that the Messiah is King David's descendant, not his son.) Jesus then refers them to Psalm 110, in which David says, "The Lord said to my lord...," and explains that the second lord mentioned is the Messiah. Since most Jews called no one but God their lord, this proved that the Messiah was divine. (This point is made by Hal Lindsey in his book, The Road to Holocaust p. 61.)

Aside from my previous point that contentious discussions between Jesus and the Pharisees were highly improbable and that those who wrote of them were probably describing Sadducees but mislabeling them as Pharisees, and assuming that this exchange between Jesus and some group of Jewish philosophers did take place, the Nazarenes must have been aware of it. Yet, in spite of it, they did not recognize Jesus as divine. Their Eucharist prayer, for example, calls Jesus the servant (not the son) of God. This suggests that the substance of that discussion contained material different from what has been reported.

Also, because Matthew wrote his gospel at a time when Pauline followers of Jesus were concerned to establish the supremacy of Paul's gospel over Peter's, we must entertain the possibility that this purported public discussion was a factitious insertion, designed to show Jesus claiming divinity for himself before Paul appeared on the scene. Otherwise, Jesus' divinity might appear to be Paul's invention.

By reporting this divinity passage in the same book in which he so carefully traces Jesus' lineage from King David (Matthew 1:6-16), the author creates a contradiction. If Jesus was not descended from David, as Matthew 22:42-45 purports, then why does Matthew 1:1-16 tell us he was? One possibility, as I have said, is that this son-of-God incident with the Pharisees was a later insertion by someone else, someone determined to originate the divinity belief prior to Paul and to place it with Jesus himself. Indeed, the earliest version of Matthew, known as the Evan Bohan text and considered by paleographers to have been written in the last quarter of the First Century, does not contain much of the material found in the modern version.

The Matthew lineage and the Isaiah prophecy pose a contradiction to the son-of-God belief. To reconcile this, the claim has been made that the Jesus lineage can be traced from Mary to David (Luke 3:23-38), with Joseph's lineage being irrelevant in spite of its appearance in Matthew. That may be true, but even that is negated by this Matthew incident, for in this incident Jesus rejects *any* family relationship with David, regardless of which lineage is used.

The implication of this incident is based on the common understanding that Jews used the word "lord" for God exclusively, for in Nehemiah 9:6, we find Ezra saying to God, "Thou art the Lord, thou alone." Though the Jews knew of no divine offspring, it may be presumed that if they had known of any, they would have used that appellation for those offspring as well. In the Matthew interpretation of Psalm 110, King David recognizes such an offspring, calling him "my lord" and, by recognizing his divinity, denies any family relationship to him (denying Isaiah in the process), the Pharisee answer about David being immediately corrected.

While there were two opposing factions (those for Davidic descent and those for divine descent), Paul seemed comfortable in both, for he claimed Davidic descent in his Letter to the Romans 1:3 and Second Letter to Timotheus 2:8 and divine descent in his Letter to Colossians 1:13 and Letter to Galatians 1:16. While we might reconcile these contradictions by using Mary's lineage to David (which allows for Jesus' divine birth while still tracing him to David), we cannot use that without rejecting the authenticity of Matthew 22:42-45, which makes any Davidic descent incorrect. It may well be that the Matthew lineage denying divinity came first, that the Pharisee incident allowing divinity was inserted later (to give authenticity to Paul's idea) and that the Mary lineage allowing both God and David to be related to Jesus was presented later still, thus making the Pharisee incident unnecessary but still left as an embarrassing relic of an anachronistic need. We must also consider the possibility of later insertions about divinity into the Pauline letters themselves.

The entire argument in Matthew 22:42-45 is based on the premise that Jews would not call anyone "lord" but God. While this was generally true, there were exceptions to it. We see fawning Jews around Agrippa I calling him a god (which, presumably, would have allowed them to call him their lord); we see Peter writing to James and calling him his lord; we see early Nazarenes, who knew nothing of the divine birth, calling Jesus their lord; we see Sarah calling Abraham her lord (First Letter of Peter 3:6). We must ask, then, if David's remark in Psalm 110 was referring to someone human and not someone divine. It may have been customary, for example, for some Jews to refer to the Messiah as "lord", with no divine connotation intended. That may have been David's original meaning. Meanwhile, there were other Jews who were willing to die rather than call anyone but God their lord, since to them the word *did* connote divinity. The passage in Matthew 22 seems to have taken David's non-divine meaning of the word and used it to suggest the divine connotation with which many Jews were investing it.

MOSAIC DIETARY RULES PURPORTEDLY CANCELED BY JESUS:

Mark 7:18-19. This purported statement by Jesus conflicts with his statement in Matthew 5:17-19, in which he emphasizes the need to follow Mosaic law *completely*. Such law would have had to include rules and restrictions on food. This section in Mark also conflicts with James' instructions to Paul in the Book of Acts 15:19-20, in which some of the Mosaic rules of diet are to be followed by the Gentile followers of Jesus. It also conflicts with Matthew 19:17, in which Jesus says, "...keep the commandments," and with Luke 18:20, in which Jesus says the same. Because of these contradictions, we must ask whether Jesus contradicted himself in making the statement attributed to him in Mark or whether the author of Mark invented it for the purpose of showing that Paul's violation of that part of the law was approved even by Jesus himself.

JESUS PURPORTEDLY PREDICTS DESTRUCTION OF TEMPLE: Matthew 24:1-2.

JESUS PURPORTEDLY TELLS JEWS THEIR FATHER IS DEVIL; SAYS JEWS ARE NOT OF GOD: John 8:44, 8:47.

JESUS PURPORTEDLY TELLS JEWS THEIR FATHERS MURDERED PROPHETS: Matthew 23:31.

JESUS PURPORTEDLY CALLS JEWS SERPENTS AND VIPERS AND FORECASTS THEIR GOING TO HELL: Matthew 23:33.

JESUS PURPORTEDLY PREDICTS JEWS WILL CRUCIFY GOOD MEN: Matthew 23:34.

BARNABAS PURPORTEDLY SAYS WHEN JESUS RETURNS, JEWS WILL SAY THEY MOCKED, PIERCED, SPAT UPON AND CRUCIFIED HIM: Maxwell Staniforth, Early Christian Writings, Epistle of Barnabas p. 203.

CHRISTIANS SAY JESUS IS GOD: In considering this subject, it is well to keep in mind some approximate dates when different accounts were written. Jesus did his preaching before 30 A.D. or C.E.; Paul wrote his letters between 50 and 60 A.D. or C.E.; the Jewish revolt started in 66 A.D. or C.E.; Paul died in 67 A.D. or C.E.; Jerusalem was defeated in 70 A.D. or C.E.; Masada was defeated in 73 A.D. or C.E.; the four gospels were written in the last quarter of the First Century; Acts was written about 95 A.D. or C.E.

If we proceed chronologically, we might start with a period before Jesus' time when Isaiah was written. Isaiah is sometimes used to support a Christian claim that Jews prior to Jesus' time considered God and the Messiah as one. Isaiah 9:6-7 has been translated, "For unto us a child is born, to us a son is given, and the government will be upon his shoulder and his name will be called 'Wonderful Counselor, Mighty God, Everlasting Father, Prince of Peace.'" Dr. James Tabor (Personal Communication 1992) corrects this mistranslation to read, "...and his name will be called 'Wonderful in council is the mighty God, our eternal father, Prince of Peace.'" He further states that it was common for Jews to name a child with an appellation in praise of God without implying, thereby, that the child *was* God. Hence, Elijah should not be translated as "Jehovah" but as "My strength in Jehovah." Likewise, when Immanuel is translated as "God with us", it is meant to imply God's presence in having blessed the family with a child and not that the child itself is God.

We come next to Paul's letters and the question of whether Paul equated Jesus with God or limited his concept to that of Jesus as the exclusive son of God. In his Letter to Titus 2:13, we read Paul saying, "...awaiting our blessed hope, the appearing of the glory of our great God and Savior Jesus Christ." Did Paul, then, consider Jesus and God the same? A footnote in the Revised Standard Edition of the Bible retranslates this passage to "...awaiting our blessed hope, the appearing of the glory of our great God *and* our Savior Jesus Christ," thus establishing God and Jesus as separate. In his First Letter to Timotheus 3:15-16, Paul speaks of "...the living God, the pillar and bulwark of truth." He then speaks of the mysteriousness of the Christian religion and then says, "He was manifested in the flesh." Did Paul mean that God or that Jesus was manifested in the flesh? We can answer this by examining other statements made by Paul. In his First Letter to Timotheus 5:21, 6:13 and 6:15, and in his Second Letter to Timotheus 4:1, we find Paul speaking of Jesus and God as separate entities. Consistency precludes any radical departure from this interpretation. Schonfield (Passover Plot p. 192-193) concurs with this when he says, "Even the Hellenized Paul in his mystical philosophy never went as far as speaking of Christ as God, though his doctrine of the Messiah as the pre-eminent expression of God is so delicately poised in its terminology that it could be misunderstood by those unacquainted with its peculiar esoteric Jewish background of thought connected with the Archetypal Man." Dr. James Tabor shares this view (Personal Communication 1991). In the Letter to the Colossians 1:12-20, which may or may not have been written by Paul, we find reference to "the Father" and "his beloved Son," of whom the author says, "He is the image of the invisible God...all things were created through him and for him...in him all the fullness of God was pleased to dwell..." and later in Colossians 2:9, "For in him the whole fullness of deity dwells bodily......" One Christian interpretation of this is that God chose a human body in which to live and that God, therefore, existed in human form as Jesus. A Nazarene or ancient Jewish interpretation of this, however, would be that Jesus, by acting as nobly as he did, reflected the goodness of God existing in a human being. Which interpretation did Paul use? Again, consistency with Paul's previously mentioned separation concept would indicate the latter. Arguments about this distinction, however, have persisted (even among Christians) from ancient times to the present.

We proceed next to the gospels. These were written after Paul's execution and the destruction of Israel as a nation. Although some of the gospels are titled with the names of apostles, the actual authors are unknown. Scholars seem to agree, however, that they were not written by the apostles themselves (James Tabor, Personal Communication 1992). We find in Luke 7:16 the author saying that the Jews proclaimed, "A great prophet has arisen among us" and "God has visited his people." The author may have meant that God visited his people by sending his prophet, Jesus, to them (much as God had visited Moses through the angel in the burning bush in Exodus 3:2-6), or, contrary to that, they may have meant that God in the form of Jesus was present there at the time. If the latter (an arguable interpretation), it was not based on any earlier tradition and would have represented the independent opinion of the author. In John 20:28 the author reports that the disciple, Thomas, called Jesus, "My Lord and my God." The late date of this report (last quarter of First Century), the lack of any earlier tradition telling of a disciple referring to Jesus as God, and the evidence of Jewish rejection of calling any human being a god suggests a questionable authenticity to this statement and a consideration that it was the creation of the author. In John 1:1 we read, "...the Word was God" and in John 1:14, "...the Word became flesh and dwelt among us..." A simple syllogism could then be derived to say, "God became flesh and dwelt among us." The idea of God's word being a manifestation of God developed from the Logos idea of the Stoics. How could God, the Stoics asked, being so perfect, manifest Himself in this world? To the Stoics this was done through His word, that word being the perfect representation of God. The idea of the author of the Gospel of John was that this word — this perfect representation of God — became manifest in a human being (Jesus). It does not mean, however, that God vacated heaven to dwell in the body of Jesus. It does mean that Jesus was a perfect reflection and manifestation of God but not that he *was* God. Even this gospel writer, while going beyond Paul in his identification of Jesus as divine, keeps God and Jesus separate (without ambiguity) elsewhere in his account, for in John 17:1, he says, "Father, the hour has come; glorify thy Son that the Son may glorify thee...," and in John 17:3, "...that they know thee the only true God, and Jesus Christ whom thou hast sent" (James Tabor, Personal Communication 1992). And a perfect picture of the Jesus-following Jew, who sees Jesus and God as separate, is related by the author of John (3:1-2) when he tells of the Pharisee, Nicodemus, saying to Jesus, "Rabbi, we know that you are a teacher come from God; for no one can do these signs that you do, unless God is with him. In the Gospel of Luke 9:20, we read, "And Jesus said to them, But who say you that I am? And Peter answered and said, 'The Messiah of God'." Schonfield, in his book, Those Incredible Christians, elucidates the subtle nuances of this subject.

The gospel statements just mentioned tell of people other than Jesus referring to Jesus as God. But the gospels also contain statements in which Jesus also refers to himself in that way. In John 10:38, for example, Jesus is reported as saying, "...the Father is in me." With these words, was Jesus saying that he himself was God or merely that God's inspiration was in him? As with Paul, a comparison with other statements by Jesus may help us. Throughout the gospels, we find Jesus referring to God as his father. (For some of these statements, see JESUS CALLS GOD FATHER OF US ALL in NOTES for CHAPTER XVI.) These statements show a separateness between God and Jesus. Consistent with that, in John 14:28, the author reports Jesus as saying, "...the Father is greater than I." (In fairness, however, someone taking the opposite view might think of two different states of God, one being greater than the other.) But separateness also seems implied when Jesus asks God to let the cup (of affliction and death) pass from him, and it also seems implied in Jesus' dying words from the cross, in which he prays to God as to someone other than himself and asks God why He has forsaken him. It does not seem reasonable that in praying to God, Jesus was praying to himself. We find further evidence of Jesus seeing himself as separate from God in Luke 18:18-19, when someone refers to him as "Good Teacher" and Jesus answers, "Why do you call me good? No one is good but God alone."

For further evidence of this separation, we look at the Book of Acts. Here we find the following passages showing Jesus and God as separate:

"Therefore let all the house of Israel know for certain that God hath made him both Lord and Messiah — this Jesus whom you crucified" (Acts 2:36); "The God of Abraham, Isaac, and Jacob, the God of our fathers has glorified His servant Jesus" (Acts 3:13); "Sovereign Lord, it is You who did make the heaven and the earth and the sea and all that is in them...for truly in this city there were gathered together against Your holy servant Jesus, whom Thou didst anoint, both Herod and Pontius Pilate, along with the Gentiles and the peoples of Israel" (Acts 4:24, 4:27); "You know of Jesus of Nazareth, how God anointed Him with the Holy Spirit and with power, and how he went about doing good, and healing all who were oppressed by the devil; for God was with Him" (Acts 10:38); "The God who made the world and all things in it, since He is Lord of heaven and earth...has fixed a day in which He will judge the world in righteousness through a man whom He has appointed, having furnished proof to all men by raising Him from the dead" (Acts 17:24, 17:31).

And finally, in the Revelation to St. John (11:15), we find further evidence of separation when we read, "The kingdom of our Lord and of His Messiah, and He will reign forever and ever."

While none of this excludes the possibility that Jesus was a human incarnation of God, it does seem that neither Jesus nor Paul made that identification during their own lifetimes and that at least some of the Christian writers who came after them did not make it either. In further support of this, when we consider Jesus' popularity with the Jewish people and their proscription against calling any human being a god, it is unlikely that Jesus would have called himself God and continued in the affections of his people. Since these affections existed not only during Jesus' lifetime but, as the Gospel of John itself tells us, even after his death on the cross, we may conclude that Jesus did not refer to himself as God. The equating of Jesus with God appears to have developed some years after the death of Paul in the last quarter of the First Century when the gospels were being written but even then with inconsistency as seen in the examples just given .

This argument about Jesus as God was the major point of contention at the Christian religious council in Nicaea in 325 A.D. or C.E. The followers of Athanasius (also called Bishop Alexander) of Alexandria held that Jesus was another form of God; the followers of Athanasius' presbyter, Arius of Alexandria, held that Jesus was of a lower level than God. At a synod held in Alexandria in 321 A.D. or C.E., Arius was deposed and excommunicated. Yet many still supported him, including Eusebius, Bishop of Nicodemia. The emperor Constantine, now a supporter of Christianity, was disturbed by the controversy and sent his advisor, Ossius, the Bishop of Cordova, to investigate. Ossius sided with Athanasius. To make it official, Constantine then called the Council of Nicaea, inviting two-hundred and twenty bishops to attend. The majority of these men apparently favored Arius. There was bitter wrangling and even blows, but the fear of Constantine's displeasure led many of them to vote against their own convictions, so that, in the end, two-hundred and eighteen voted for Athanasius while only two held their ground for Arius. Constantine considered the outcome divinely inspired, his own coercive influence apparently not being considered a factor by him. Yet the dissension continued, necessitating a second such meeting in 381 A.D. or C.E., this one in Constantinople, in which the Nicene Creed was reaffirmed and the doctrine of the Holy Trinity established (Rufus Learsi, Israel pp. 203-204; Victor Paul Wierwille, Jesus Christ Is Not God, The American Christian Press pp. 22-25; Encyclopedia Britannica). Yet the controversy among Christians continues to this day.

SYMEON READS PART OF JAMES' LETTER: Fictional. The content of the letter, however, is taken from the Letter of James 3:7-10.

PAUL TELLS ROMANS TO BLESS NOT CURSE PERSECUTORS: Letter to Romans 12:14.

PAUL WISHES JAMES' EMISSARIES MUTILATE THEMSELVES: Letter to Galatians 5:12.

PAUL TELLS UNBELIEVING CORINTHIANS THEIR BLOOD BE ON THEIR HEADS: Acts 18:6.

PAUL SENDS HYMANEUS AND ALEXANDER TO DEVIL: First Letter to Timotheus 1:19-20.

PAUL CONSIGNS SINNER TO DEATH: First Letter to Corinthians 5:5.

PAUL SAYS THOSE NOT LOVING LORD TO BE ACCURSED: First Letter to Corinthians 16:22.

PAUL SAYS THOSE PREACHING OTHER GOSPEL TO BE ACCURSED: Letter to Galatians 1:8-9.

PAUL SAYS UNBELIEVERS TO BE DESTROYED BY FLAMING ANGELS: First Letter to Thessalonians 1:7-10.

ALEXANDER, THE COPPERSMITH TO BE PUNISHED FOR OFFENDING PAUL: Second Letter to Timotheus 4:14-15.

PAUL SAYS CIRCUMCISION PARTY TO BE SILENCED: Letter to Titus 1:10-11.

ESSENES WRITE OF TEACHER OF RIGHTEOUSNESS; WICKED PRIEST; AND SPEWER OF LIES: These appellations are found in the Dead Sea Scrolls and the respective interpretation of them as James the Just; Ananus, son of Annas; and Paul of Tarsus has been made by Robert Eisenman (Baigent and Leigh, Dead Sea Scrolls Deception pp. 146, 149, 195-196, referring to Eisenman: Maccabees, Zadokites, Christians and Qumran p. 68, n. 120; p. 69, n. 122 and also the Habakkuk Commentary II, 2 [Vermes p. 284]). Support for the belief that Ananus is the Wicked Priest may be found in Josephus' description of the treatment of Ananus' corpse by the Idumaeans after they executed him (Josephus, Jewish War 4.5.2), which matches the account in the Dead Sea Scrolls in which the dead body of the Wicked Priest is abused by those who kill him.

Somewhat earlier, however, Cornfeld stated, "...there are still doubts about the identification of the Righteous Teacher and the Wicked Priest." (Cornfeld, Daniel to Paul p. 194.).

ROMANS EXECUTE SYMEON: Eusebius, Ecclesiastical History, III xi; Schonfield, Passover Plot p. 237; Eusebius, Ecclesiastical History, III xxxii, 1-7; Brandon, Jesus and Zealots p. 213(2); Schoeps, Jewish Christianity pp. 33-34. Schoeps gives 107 A.D. or C.E. as the date for this.

JUSTUS REPLACES SYMEON: Eusebius, Ecclesiastical History, IV v, 1-4; Brandon, Jesus and Zealots p. 213(2); Schonfield, Passover Plot p. 238.

JUSTUS IS A RELATIVE OF JESUS: This is conjectural but is based on the report by Schoeps (Jewish Christianity pp. 33-34), referring to Eusebius (Ecclesiastical History, V xii), that the last of the fifteen bishops of the circumcision who succeeded each other in Jerusalem (this series of successions ending in 135 A.D. or C.E. with the Bar Kochba revolt against Rome) was named Judas Kyriakos, whose surname implies a relationship to Jesus. If Judas Kryiakos was related to Jesus, and if Symeon was selected to succeed James because he was Jesus' cousin, then it suggests that all the bishops up to 135 A.D. or C.E. were in some way related to Jesus.

ROMANS EXECUTE IGNATIUS: Staniforth, Early Christian Writings p. 64.

JOHN (MARK) FOLLOWS PAUL'S ANTI-TORAH GOSPEL: In Paul's Second Letter to Timotheus 4:11, he asks Timotheus to bring Mark with him, saying that Mark has been very useful to him. If this Mark is the same as the John (Mark) who previously disagreed with Paul, it suggests that John (Mark) changed his mind. We have no way of knowing if it is the same person, but in this story I have made them the same.

CHRISTIANS MAKE ZEALOT SYMBOL (THE CROSS) THEIR OWN: Brandon, Jesus and Zealots pp. 57, 145.

PAUL SAYS HE IS GREATEST SINNER OF ALL: First Letter to Timotheus 1:15; Letter to Romans 7:25.

*